THE COMPLETE
SHORT STORIES OF
Ambrose Bierce

COMPILED WITH COMMENTARY BY

Ernest Jerome Hopkins

Foreword by Cathy N. Davidson

University of Nebraska Press
Lincoln and London

Library of Congress Cataloging in Publication Data
Bierce, Ambrose, 1842–1914?
    The complete short stories of Ambrose Bierce.
    I. Hopkins, Ernest Jerome, 1887–   . II. Title.
PS1097.A15 1984   813'.4   84-8575
ISBN 0-8032-6071-7 (pbk.)

Reprinted by arrangement with Doubleday & Company, Inc.

♾

Foreword

His desk held a skull and a cigar box. When asked, he ventured that the former was all that remained of an erstwhile friend while the latter contained the ashes of a rival critic. Reputedly, he did not smile when he said this. Corrupt politicians, warmongering generals, conniving businessmen, and incompetent literary figures (in which category he included W. D. Howells, Henry James, and Jack London) were all targets for his rapier wit, his devastating ability to point out chicanery, hypocrisy, ineptness, and pomposity wherever he found them. He was known by such sobriquets as "bitter Bierce," the "devils' lexicographer," the "wickedest man in San Francisco." And in 1913, at the age of seventy-one, he went off into Pancho Villa's Mexico and simply disappeared—an end made plausible only by the improbable life that it capped.

Yet of all the improbable features of Ambrose Bierce's extraordinary life and uncertain death none is more striking—and more enduring—than the ninety or so stories that he left behind. Collected together in this volume, these stories represent an almost unprecedented accomplishment in American literary history. They differ markedly from the realistic or naturalistic fiction admired in Bierce's time and from the tales of western regionalism made popular by Bret Harte and Joaquin Miller. Given the taste of his contemporaries and the dramatic difference between his own work and anything else written in America in the 1880s and 1890s, it is surprising that Bierce was published in the first place. Yet he was, and his work has survived for a century in literary anthologies and in the imagination of a continuing coterie of fans who delight in his iconoclasm; his formal and thematic ingenuity; his ability, always, to surprise.

Indeed, in all of his best work, it is improbability that spins the plot. "Nothing," he wrote, "is so improbable as what is true. It is the unexpected that occurs; but that is not saying enough; it is also the unlikely—one might almost say the impossible."[1] Bierce derided the novel of his time precisely because it groaned under the burden of a predictable, ponderous devotion to probability. He found the short story a superior form of fiction because it was limited only by the truths of the psyche rather than by a hidebound, earthbound, photographic attention to social events. Bierce claims a much larger realm for realism—improbable truths, impossible truths, truths that make the skin crawl or the heart pound or the mind freeze in fear or wonder or recognition.

His stories characteristically turn on improbable twists of tone, perspective, or plot—twists calculated to jar the reader out of a comfortable complacency. Consider, as a classic example of this technique in action, Bierce's best-known and most anthologized work, "An Occurrence at Owl Creek Bridge." The story, it will be recalled, tells of Peyton Farquhar's fate after he has been apprehended by Yankee soldiers during his failed attempt to burn a railroad bridge. Sentenced to an immediate death by hanging, Farquhar still enjoys an unexpected stay of execution as he returns, imaginatively, to his previous peaceful life. Yet Bierce breaks off Farquhar's wistful remembrance of things past with a flashback in which the Southern plantation owner is seen chafing under the indignities of civilian life and longing to be a hero. The third section of the story resumes Farquhar's stream-of-consciousness fantasy, his desperate attempt to escape back to precisely the life that, in living, he fled. He is caught, then, in the circle of his delusions—civilian and martial, living and dying—as much as he is caught in the noose that hangs him. That large circle of delusions traced out in the story's shifting narrative perspective and alternating movements between subjective and objective time also catches any reader who, much like Farquhar, prefers to dwell on the adventure of a war tale and not on the inevitable presence of death in the story. In other words, the real trap sprung in "An

1. Ambrose Bierce, "The Short Story," in *The Collected Works of Ambrose Bierce* (New York: Neale Publishing, 1911), 10: 246–47.

Occurrence at Owl Creek Bridge" is the fatal presumption that war can have a happy ending.

As "Owl Creek Bridge" amply attests, Bierce's war stories are not objective descriptions of Civil War engagements. They are, instead, arresting, often shocking accounts of the incivilities perpetrated by and on men suddenly confronting their own mortality. In much that same fashion, Bierce's tales of the supernatural are less about ghosts than about the phantasms we harbor within us. Bierce's *The Devil's Dictionary* defines ghost as the "outward and visible sign of an inward fear." His best horror stories—"The Death of Halpin Frayser" is a good example—blur any dividing lines between the ostensible cause of the protagonist's terror, the terror itself, and the consequences of that terror. Furthermore, even when a supernatural event seems (always a loaded word in Bierce) objectively real, the focus is not on the supernatural per se but on the very natural inability of characters to cope with events outside the lock-step logic of everyday life. The ghost calls the quotidian into question, not vice versa.

The present collection includes all of Bierce's war stories and horror stories. It also includes some twenty stories of still another type, those that E. J. Hopkins terms the "tall tales." Not surprisingly, these works, too, challenge generic boundaries and formal conventions. Employing the broadly exaggerated humor typical of tall tales, they create a vision of a grotesque, absurd world in a fashion that especially foreshadows the North American black humorists of the 1960s as well as the contemporary South American magic realists. These tales also illustrate most fully Bierce's suspicion that the ego is desperately committed to a refusal to recognize its own limitations and that pervasive social disorders such as prejudice, corruption, and even war are not aberrations but logical extensions of the individual's incorrigible infatuation with the self.

"Early one June morning in 1872 I murdered my father—an act which made a deep impression on me at the time." This opening sentence from "An Imperfect Conflagration" captures precisely the tone and mood of Bierce's tall tales. The Kafkaesque quality of Oedipal tragedy reduced to transient comedy of manners is even more evident in the aftermath of the less-than-disquieting murder: "That afternoon I went to the chief of police, told him what I had done and asked his advice. It would be very painful to me if the facts became publicly known. My conduct would be generally condemned; the newspapers would bring it up against me if ever I should run for office. The chief saw the force of these considerations; he was himself an assassin of wide experience." Of course. If the spokesmen of morality—police officers, judges, elected officials—are as corrupt as the criminals, why should not the two confer together over their common problems? The dark humor in these fables arises from the disjunctions between the grotesque events themselves and the matter-of-fact rendering of the events; the satire derives from the consistency between the matter-of-fact tone and the ethos of the world portrayed.

The tall tales may at first seem to be distinctly different from the stories of horror and of war. But as Professor Hopkins rightly observes, all of Bierce's fictions are satires devoted to exposing both the large and small foibles of humans and the failings of the society that humans have created in their own image. Thus the grotesque exaggerations of the tall tales emphasize the already distorted egotism of their protagonists. In the horror stories we similarly see how egotism, self-delusion, and a complacent belief in one's rationality (often in the face of ample evidence to the contrary) generally result in self-destruction, while in the war stories the same egotism and consequent misperception lead the individual and often a whole host of attendant victims to massive annihilation. Bierce, in *The Devils' Dictionary,* defines war as "a by-product of the arts of peace," while peace is, "in international affairs, a period of cheating between two periods of fighting." As this collection testifies, in Bierce's fiction the worlds of war and peace, of reality and fantasy, of the individual and society all occupy the same human space.

In the ominous year of 1984, it is hard to resist claiming Bierce as a writer particularly pertinent to our own time. Certainly his war stories (really antiwar stories) should be required reading in the nuclear age. But that present claim to relevance is only one of several, for Bierce, like any major writer, speaks differently to different audiences. In his own day he was renowned as a journalist and generally ignored as a writer of fiction. Only a few of his contemporaries (Stephen Crane, for example) appreciated Bierce's radical experiments with the short story form. But following his mysterious passing, successive generations of writers and critics have noted that he was a writer ahead of his time and have claimed him as a forerunner of theirs. In the 1920s, for example, he was seen as the iconoclastic author breaking free of his society's stultifying constraints. H. L. Mencken and others, in the thirties and forties, found Bierce to be a pioneering satirist and social critic—one of America's foremost muckrakers, so to speak. In the sixties (and for all the reasons Professor Hopkins sets forth in his 1970 Introduction) Bierce enjoyed still another avatar as a writer whose art was at last winning belated recognition, while the seventies saw an unprecedented number of articles and dissertations devoted to his continuing "rediscovery." The present republication of the complete stories will no doubt carry Bierce's name forward to still further rediscoveries.

Bierce's continuing topicality is an appropriately ironic tribute to how untopical he originally was. He was not interested in chronicling the social habits of the Gilded Age and neither did he accept that age's touching faith in rationality, wealth, and the inevitability of human progress. Supporting himself by the journalism he regarded as a minor literary form, he declined to write stories for the popular magazines of his day. As he insisted (in his own inimitable way) to the editor of *Metropolitan Magazine,* "I know how to write a story . . . for magazine readers for whom literature is too good, but I will not do so as long as stealing is more honorable and interesting."[2] He defined the novel as "a short story padded" and also passed up the profits which that form could have yielded. He staked his literary reputation on the stories contained in this volume, and, one hundred years later, it is safe to say that he was right.

In his literary career as in his life, Ambrose Bierce took risks. One of his last letters describes the septuagenarian adventurer's itinerary: "My plan, so far as I have one, is to go through Mexico to one of the Pacific ports, if I can *get* through without

2. Bertha Clark Pope, ed., *The Letters of Ambrose Bierce* (San Francisco: Book Club of California, 1922), 148.

being stood up against a wall and shot as an American. Thence I hope to sail for some port in South America. Thence go across the Andes and perhaps across the continent. . . . Naturally, it is possible—even probable—that I shall not return. These be 'strange countries,' in which things happen; that is why I am going."[3] Bierce's fiction, too, is a "strange country" in which things happen, and that, for author and reader alike, is the point of going.

Cathy N. Davidson
Michigan State University
East Lansing, Michigan

3. Bierce to Nellie Sickler, September 21, 1913, "A Collection of Bierce Letters," *University of California Chronicle* 34 (January, 1932): 48.

CONTENTS

II
War

III

Tall Tales

INTRODUCTION

Ambrose Bierce, Nonconformist

In our day, as the world knows, a new and strenuous nonconformism has arisen in American life and thought. This after a long period when conformism strongly prevailed. Individualism has always been a basic strain in the American mind and its modern emergence creates new interest in the great nonconformists of the past.

Of these, Ambrose Gwinett Bierce, master satirist of the late nineteenth century, certainly cannot be neglected, and it is this consideration that emphasized the fact that Bierce's ninety-odd short stories, containing the peak of his satiric utterances, have never been presented in complete single volume form until now.

Bierce's satire has a distinct contribution to make to the present-day welter of controversial thought. His use of laughter, in the form of pointed ridicule, as his chosen weapon of nonconformism and critical thought, in his view exceeded violence as a weapon. He was, in other words, a true satirist, this being an art akin to cartooning, and as a leading scholar in world satire points out, a special and not too common talent in a writer.[1] Dr. Feinberg agrees with others

[1] Dr. Leonard Feinberg, Professor of English at Iowa State University and author of *The Satirist: His Temperament, Motivation, and Influence*, Iowa State University Press (1964) and Citadel Press, New York (1965). See pp. 5–17 for discussion.

that "both criticism and humor have to be present in a work before it can be called satiric,"[2] but adds that the satire may at times be "too bitter to be humorous."[3] Bierce was guilty of such bitterness at times.

The short stories Bierce wrote were of three main types: satirical horror stories, emphasizing the "horror"; anti-war satires, emphasizing the brutality and human wreckage of war; and, by contrast, a crazy group of old-Western "tall tales," the exaggeration being turned to satiric purposes. All were in large part or wholly of Bierce's own invention; he wrote them in his maturity, between 1882 and 1896, when he had attained his mastery of style, and not one of them has a pretty girl, a trumped-up sub-plot, a happy ending, or the "ain't-America-cute" idea of a local setting. In short, Bierce smashed the main short-story rules and enjoyed himself with an indescribable underlying laughter as he did so.

Here, in addition, was one image-smasher who made his non-conformism support him, sufficiently at least, through a long forty years of writing life. Bierce in his old age truly said to his friend and publisher, Walter Neale:

"My independence is my wealth; it is my literature. I have written to please myself, no matter who should be hurt."[4]

This independence, undoubtedly inborn, required stimulation, training, and experience like any other dominant trait and this outer part of its development may be traced.

Of eight children, all older than himself, Ambrose Bierce was the only one who wasn't crushed by the rigid discipline and hellfire religion of his parents on a primitive Ohio farm. He was born July 24, 1842. If the child psychologists are right in tracing later malad-justments to the lack of family "closeness," then Bierce's independence dated from the cradle. He read early (his father had the Bible and a few books) but his first real human influence was his vigorous and personable uncle, "General" Lucius Verus Bierce, as he was known. An early anti-slavery fanatic, Lucius Bierce had led an abortive anti-slavery demonstration into Canada, accounting for his title. As a close friend of his fellow-fanatic, John Brown of Osawatomie, the "General" presented Brown with some of the weapons which figured in Brown's capture of the Harpers Ferry arsenal and re-

[2] Ibid. p. 6.
[3] Ibid.
[4] Walter Neale, *Life of Ambrose Bierce,* New York, Walter Neale & Co. (1929), pp. 97–98.

sultant execution in 1859, causing his "soul," as the old song said, to be "marching on."

This uncle of Ambrose Bierce, attracted by the boy's redhaired and blue-eyed charm and obviously high intelligence, watched over the youth, probably lent him books and, no doubt foreseeing the Civil War, sent him at age fifteen to the Kentucky Military Institute for a single term. Young Bierce not only enjoyed the military training, but showed a distinct talent for cartoon drawing. And a third proclivity, that for journalism, also developed early, when, instead of going home to help work the farm, he became a printer's devil on a smalltown Indiana newspaper. Thus, in his childhood and boyhood, were seen in embryo all the ruling traits of his later life.

In 1861, at eighteen, Ambrose Bierce responded to Lincoln's first call for volunteers by enlisting in the 9th Indiana Regiment. The rebellion was only going to last three months, and that was the period of his enlistment. But the Confederates had a different idea; when these volunteers were sent to Virginia two sharp battles occurred, in one of which young Bierce made a fearless rescue of a wounded comrade under fire. For this and his bit of military training, when the three months were up and he reenlisted, he was made a sergeant of volunteers. And now it was war indeed, with such battles as Shiloh, Murfreesboro, Chickamauga and Chattanooga, the capture of Atlanta, and, finally, Sherman's Georgia march. Ambrose Bierce went through three years of this action as a volunteer officer and in the process encountered the second man who was to have an influence on him, the greatest influence for nonconformism in his entire life.

This was General William Babcock Hazen, a West Pointer, known to Civil War historians as one of the toughest fighting generals, and quite the most cantankerous and independent high officer, in Lincoln's army. Having charge of half-trained volunteer troops, Hazen emphasized sound preparation for battle, and looking for a lone-wolf officer who wasn't afraid of danger and who could draw maps, he discovered Second Lieutenant Ambrose Bierce, made him a member of his staff, promoted him to first lieutenant, and assigned him to the highly dangerous work of a lone pre-battle reconnaissance scout; all this in the early spring of 1863. Bierce liked the one-man nature of the work, the map-making and report-writing, and the speed and accuracy necessary if lives were to be spared. He carried on this work through the mid-Tennessee, Chattanooga and Atlanta campaigns until, on June 23, 1864, in the Battle of Kenesaw Mountain, he stopped the bullet that all but ended his days.

It was a glancing head wound and, as Bierce said later, the bullet "crushed my skull like a broken walnut." He was fortunate to survive the field rescue and to be sent home to recover, although he remained subject to sudden blackouts and dizzy spells for months. Bierce was back in active duty, after Atlanta's capture, in Sherman's Army in Georgia, where he served until Lee's surrender in April, 1865. His had been an excellent war performance, as Army records show.

Hazen, his idol, had reported with unusual sympathy on Bierce's wound, and Lincoln at Hazen's recommendation made Bierce a brevet major before the war ended and he resigned. For a dismal postwar year Bierce was engaged in reconstruction work in the South; then the Hazen theme revived.

The Army had appointed General Hazen to the Signal Corps, with the assignment of exploring and mapping the still-wild West. The general found Ambrose Bierce in the South and invited him to be his technical assistant as before. Bierce, who had recovered sufficiently from his head wound, gladly accepted; he rejoined General Hazen at Omaha in July 1866; the two promptly headed into Sioux country. At the same time General Hazen recommended Bierce for a captaincy in the Regular Army, to end his uncertain volunteer status for good.

And that is how Bierce finally came West. The two, after various adventures and map-making side trips, reached San Francisco at the end of 1866. Here they had a shock: applying to the Presidio for dispatches, they learned that Hazen's recommended captaincy for Bierce had been reduced to a second lieutenancy, the lowest commissioned rank and one that held no prospect of promotion for an indefinite time. Bierce loved the service and still wanted to give it a chance: he tossed a coin, to decide whether to accept the inferior commission or to enter the only profession of which he had the slightest knowledge, namely journalism. The coin decreed "journalism," Bierce accepted the verdict, and forty years later he was to declare: "The coin was right."

So here he was, a twenty-four-year-old ex-GI in a strange city, knowing he would have to master a new profession quickly or starve. Army friends told him of a vacant Federal job as guardian at the Mint; he took that job, his first query being whether San Francisco had a library and where it was.

For almost two years Bierce worked at the Mint, studying day and night and, after a time, trying to write something that might be accepted by one of the small San Francisco magazines. The Mint and Sub-treasury people liked him; he was six feet tall, sorrel-headed, handsome, with officer-like blue eyes that looked people directly in the face. And they admired his energy at self-study, though wishing he wouldn't argue so strongly about religion. (Since his recovery from his wound he hadn't returned home and was never to see his overstrict parents again.)

In 1868 he finally placed a magazine item or two, and here coincidence took charge. A small financial weekly, the *San Francisco News Letter and Commercial Advertiser,* with an audience mainly of mining and land gamblers, was losing its editor, James T. Watkins, to the East; its proprietor, Fred A. Marriott, wanted someone to succeed Watkins and he also had the notion of reviving an abandoned humor page, "The Town Crier," which in the past had spoofed everything in town. The outgoing editor went hunting and found a new writing figure named Ambrose Bierce; he brought Bierce to meet Marriott, with the result that a future satirist's career began on a financial journal on the first day of December 1868.

And it was here that Bierce established the unique system by which his independence was to be his "wealth" for the next forty years. Marriott soon learned to let his hired satirist strictly alone as to his writing; the subjects, objects, content and style of his "Town Crier" column were all his own, however scathing and whomever or whatever might be assailed. Marriott might reject but never alter Bierce's copy; his suggestions to Bierce weren't "orders" but requests; Marriott would, besides, back Bierce if squawks occurred, as indeed they did. It was, in short, a mutually independent relationship; it greatly profited the *News Letter* in prestige and circulation, it supported Bierce financially so that he was able in a couple of years to marry Molly Day, a society girl. San Francisco roared at the "Town Crier's" witty and fearless independence—only one libel suit was ever filed and Bierce himself laughed that one out of court.[5] Even more than money, the partner-like independence was the principal "wealth" he sought, plus the assurance of weekly publication that went with it. Here was an employment relationship which students of that problem well might study.

This relationship worked out well from 1868 to 1872. In that period Bierce mastered the barbed epigram or "jot" and the cutting

[5] *The Ambrose Bierce Satanic Reader,* compiled and edited by Ernest J. Hopkins, Doubleday & Co., New York (1968) pp. 150–64.

satirical paragraph, wrote at least one short story which Bret Harte, editor of *Overland Monthly*, accepted,[6] and won considerable journalistic prominence in the West and elsewhere. In 1872 he and his bride went to London; the trip was a wedding present from her father, a well-to-do mining man, Captain Day. Bierce's purpose was to try his hand in the London writing market; in aid of that purpose Marriott gave him letters of introduction to his old associates. Bierce, searching for ideas that would interest the English, reprinted some of his wilder writings from "Town Crier" columns, also added the mock imitation of Aesop, "fables without morals," to his skills. He wrote three London-published books, added to his culture and experience, and returned to San Francisco in September 1875 with an increased reputation but without a job.

He had a trying time financially. Then in 1877 a conservative lawyer, Frank H. Pixley, launched a new magazine, *The Argonaut*. His purpose was to uphold the "establishment"; lacking technical skills, he hired Bierce as assistant editor, keeping policy matters to himself. Bierce got out a good publication, but he was too independent for Pixley and Pixley was too wealth-subservient for him; they parted company in 1879 and never were friendly again. That summer the satirist tried goldmine management as a means of quitting journalism, but the venture was badly financed[7] and he never again tried to go against that fatal coin.

Our not-too-employable nonconformist became, at last, master of his own destinies as editor-in-chief of *Wasp*, an old-established humor-and-politics magazine. He held that position from 1881 through 1886 under owners who, except for one secret owner who sold out under fire, honored his independence.

Bierce on *Wasp*, bursting his frustrations, hit a pinnacle of daring and brilliance; he published powerful political cartoons; wrote forceful editorials; issued by installments his wittiest work, *The Devil's Dictionary;*[8] declared and waged a fearless war of satire against the all-dominant Central Pacific "rail-rogues" and their palace-building Nob Hill "Big Four";[9] wrote barbed verse and cutting paragraphs in his column, "Prattle"; and, as a new feature, wrote and published

[6] "The Haunted Valley," see Section One.

[7] For an excellent account of this venture see Paul Fatout, *Ambrose Bierce and the Black Hills,* Norman, Oklahoma (1956).

[8] Ernest J. Hopkins, editor and compiler, *The Enlarged Devil's Dictionary by Ambrose Bierce,* New York, Doubleday & Co. (1967).

[9] Collis P. Huntington, Leland Stanford, Charles Crocker, and Mark Hopkins.

five early short stories, definitely inaugurating his future in the field of fiction at last. [10]

So it was a wonderful period. At the same time, troubles were mounting. Increased by the San Francisco fogs, Bierce's asthma, a recurrence from London, was compelling him to edit his paper from a distance and to live away from his family in the hills; this in turn involved estrangement from Molly and their three children. His employment grew uncertain as the *Wasp*'s ownership changed to more conservative hands. Finally, in 1886, Bierce's beloved editorship of the greatly expanded humor-magazine came to an end.

This time he hardly resisted the fates. Locking himself into a small rented room in Oakland, he lived on his savings, devoting himself to mastering the short story as best he could. Months passed; his savings were running out; he placed a very fine war story, "One of the Missing," in *The Wave,* a literary magazine, for a small sum. Then coincidence, always his friend, came spectacularly and finally to Bierce's rescue.

Former Senator George Hearst, a fabulous developer of gold and silver mines, had run for the California senatorship in 1886, and had been elected independently of railroad support. His aggressive son, William Randolph Hearst, aged twenty-four, had become interested in journalism at Harvard University and had coveted his father's fourth-rate political newspaper, the San Francisco *Examiner*. On March 5, 1887, in celebration of his accession to the senatorship, the elder Hearst offered his son a choice of gifts; the son said: "Give me *The Examiner*."

In those four words the history of American journalism underwent a change. Young W. R. Hearst, returning immediately to San Francisco, looked up Bierce and hired him for *The Examiner,* apparently as his first act in building a staff. It was still March when Bierce's first "Prattle" column appeared on the reborn paper's editorial page, to remain there under various titles for the next twenty years. What with all his old stipulations for independence recognized and adhered to by Hearst, his financial troubles over, and publication assured, Ambrose Bierce professionally was a happy man indeed. Hearst had even adopted Bierce's anti-railroad policy, as the first of *The Examiner*'s many crusades.

But happiness eluded Bierce. He and Molly, though still loving

[10] The five are: three "tall tales," "Mr. Swiddler's Flip-Flap," July 7, 1882; "A Cargo of Cat," January 3, 1885, and "An Imperfect Conflagration," March 27, 1886; and Bierce's first two anti-war stories, "George Thurston," September 29, 1883, and "A Tough Tussle," 1884.

each other, had separated; their oldest son, Day, had anticipated the modern pattern and left home; and a newly disconcerting phenomenon was beginning to appear. This was an apparently purposeful attempt to destroy Bierce's repute and that of Hearst, since neither man could be controlled. As an example, after Day Bierce's tragic death in a suicidal gun-battle over a girl, the magazine *Argonaut*, leading representative of the "establishment," accused Bierce of responsibility for the ruin of his own son. And thereafter, in the "kept press," everything Bierce did and much that he didn't became a pile-up of slurs and rumors calculated to destroy his character. The satirist, meanwhile, was growing in fame with the rapid growth of *The Examiner,* writing impressive and original short stories and other features, and amassing a following of admiring writers that were to make him the literary mentor of San Francisco. Unfortunately, this dichotomy in Bierce's published record was to puzzle some later biographers; fact and mythology both were perpetuated into a later day, as also in the case of Hearst. Bierce coined the fatalistic phrase, "Nothing matters," as his response to the situation, but the evils that he didn't do lived after him no less than those he did.

As a minor instance, Bierce has been said to have submitted his short stories to Eastern magazines, only to have them rejected. No instance of such rejection is of record. Bierce cared nothing for the Eastern market; his publication record remained, all his life, virtually a hundred percent of what he himself wanted to print—a thing unique in writing annals and one that accounted for the fact that he published, first and last, an estimated four million words.

His problem was not that of initial publication but of reprints—a complicated picture from the start. In September 1891 Bierce's first volume of short-story reprints appeared: this was his now-famous *Tales of Soldiers and Civilians,* a valued collector's item today. The *Tales* were published in San Francisco by Bierce's friend, E. L. G. Steele, a businessman; the book contained ten "Soldier" and nine "Civilian" short stories; what was reprinted was almost his earliest work, but of a force and brilliance not seen before. "Sales moderate, praise intense" might describe the *Tales'* acceptance, and, not long afterward, an ironic sequence of events occurred.

This was the publication in England, by the firm of Chatto and Windus, of a virtual duplicate of the Steele book. It bore an attractive English-style title, *In the Midst of Life,* and such became its American acceptance that Bierce himself, years later, adopted both the title and the abridged contents in his *Collected Works*.[11] The irony has lain in the fact that the success of this early one-fourth of Bierce's short stories had the effect of dwarfing the other three-fourths; these were preserved "for the record" in various volumes and half-hidden sections of the *Collected Works*, but so subordinated and lost-sight-of as to be overlooked as far as modern reprints are concerned. As in Bierce's *Devil's Dictionary* and other writings, the fame of a part was achieved at the expense of a whole, with the unintentional effect of giving him only a fractional inclusion in our literature.

In 1896 Bierce's story-writing ended. Hearst, by now astonishing New York with his *Journal,* imported his prize satirist to Washington to do battle, successfully, against the head robber-baron of the Central Pacific Railroad on an issue affecting the national treasury.[12] Bierce's remarkable victory pinnacled his San Francisco fame, but Hearst thereafter wanted him in Washington, D.C., as a national columnist. The war with Spain was coming on; Bierce, contra-suggestible about that war, all but satirized Hearst's policy; but Hearst had other strong writers by this time and loyally kept his original feature-man on, as an independent columnist, contributor of wit, and, finally, literary critic of *Cosmopolitan* magazine. So the years passed.

The satirist's last phase was that of compiling and editing his own *Collected Works,* in partnership with a friendly publisher, Walter Neale. At the end of 1908, now aged sixty-six, Bierce resigned from Hearst's employ, receiving as a farewell gift the right to reprint anything he had written for the Hearst newspapers since 1887. *The Collected Works of Ambrose Bierce* was a colossal and beautifully printed million-word job, requiring four years, 1909–12 inclusive, to compile and publish. Too expensive for the general reader, too museum-like and chaotically organized for the Eastern reviewers to accept, still it was a permanent record and valuable monument to a great satirist's writings and is so accepted today.[13] Its publication was completed in 1912, and in 1913 Bierce made his

[11] The reference is to *The Collected Works of Ambrose Bierce*, published in 12 volumes by Walter Neale & Co. (1909–12) and reprinted in modern duplicate in 1966 by the Gordian Press, Inc., N.Y.

[12] *The Ambrose Bierce Satanic Reader,* op. cit., pp. 194–222.

[13] This amazing twelve-volume work was reprinted in exact duplicate by Gordian Press, Inc., New York, in 1966. Its aid in the compilation of this book is appreciatively acknowledged.

final visit to the scenes of his great battles in the Civil War, then vanished into revolution-wracked Mexico, never to return.

And then the storm broke. Forgetting that the vanished man had written anything at all except in name, the sensation-hungry journalists, the equally sensational psychologists of the day, and all who had envied Ambrose Bierce or winced under his satiric lash, seized on the "mysterious disappearance case" and overplayed it to the full. They concocted fantastic theories, always with Bierce at fault; branded him a brutal egoist and an offensive neurotic; picked to pieces every known or rumored item about him and destroyed the pieces. This went on for years; defenders too emerged and were ridden down; Bierce's standard biographer, Carey McWilliams, writing six years after the "mysterious disappearance," listed under the heading of "The Bierce Myth" some of the names he had been called:

"Great, bitter, idealistic, cynical, morose, frustrated, cheerful, bad, sadistic, obscure, perverted, famous, brutal, kind, a fiend, a God, a misanthrope, a poet, a realist who wrote romances, a fine satirist and something of a charlatan."[14]

He afterward added "a death-man" and a "denier of life" to the epithets. There was also the presumably neutral academic critic who openly stated that his purpose was "to trace the causes of Bierce's achievement and failure as a writer." Perhaps the deadliest of the damnings was the much quoted statement that Bierce was "more interesting as a man than as a writer," as though the two could be compared. In short, Bierce's critics used him as a mirror for their own personal reactions, whatever they might be—a thing that would have delighted Bierce, with his contempt for human judgment.

There has been, in recent years especially, another side. Dr. Leonard Feinberg, an outstanding scholar in satire ancient and modern, has regarded Bierce so highly as to include him in the honored group of world satirists in his book, *The Satirist.*[15] Some of Professor Feinberg's comments are as follows:

"Bierce defined a cynic as 'A blackguard whose faulty vision sees things as they are, not as they ought to be.' . . . It is difficult to find much evidence of love or sympathy in the satire of Juvenal, Pope, Swift, W. S. Gilbert, Bierce, and Saki . . . Many satirists, like Fielding and Sterne and Thackeray, were sentimentalists, but many, like

---

[14] Carey McWilliams, *Ambrose Bierce, A Biography,* New York, Albert and Charles Boni (1929); reprint Archon Books (1967), pp. 3–4.

[15] Dr. Leonard Feinberg, op. cit.

Rochester and Bierce and Mencken, hated sentimentality. . . . Next to that of Ambrose Bierce, Mencken's satire is the most vituperative in American literature. . . . Certainly there is tremendous vehemence in the satire of Pope and Byron and Juvenal and Bierce and Twain and Swift and Voltaire and Mencken and Victor Hugo. . . . Bolitho called Ring Lardner 'the greatest and sincerest pessimist America has produced.' To achieve that distinction, Lardner would have had to be more pessimistic than Ambrose Bierce, not an easy feat to accomplish."

The verdict of "pessimism" of course depends upon the point of view. Bierce himself would have denied it, stating that to scourge stupidity and hypocrisy was not pessimism but the reverse. In an age when all values are being questioned, Bierce's definition of "white" as "black" is very near the essence of modern thought.

His short stories, nonconformist as they are, in general embody that view. As stated at the beginning of this introduction, they fall into three groups: the horror stories, half their total number; the war (or rather anti-war) stories, a fourth of the total and his greatest; and the "tall tales," where ridicule runs wild, the final fourth. The reader will find the plots to be single-episode developments, climaxing at the end; the writing style precise, concise, and calmer than the content; and will discern, in the most disturbing passages, the underlying laughter with which each story is written. Robert Louis Stevenson, in his essays on writing, points out that regardless of plot, characterizations or setting, the thing that lingers longest in a reader's mind is the personality or "feel" of the writer, and this may well be true of *The Complete Short Stories of Ambrose Bierce*.

ERNEST JEROME HOPKINS

Arizona State University
Tempe, Arizona
1970

I

THE WORLD OF
Horror

FOREWORD

"Haïta the Shepherd" is not a horror story. It is placed at the beginning of this collection because there is no other place to put it. Alone among Bierce's tales it is a personal revelation, a pessimistic fable of the inability of mankind to win and keep happiness. Its date follows soon after that of his son's suicide and his own separation from his wife, and there is undoubtedly a connection.

Ambrose Bierce's forty-four horror stories, while never tending to belittle the "horror," are of several different degrees of the shuddering quality. The largest number are psychological horror stories, including studies of fear and of the occult. Almost as many deal with haunted houses; ghost stories rank third; and there are lesser numbers of voices from the dead, inexplicable disappearances, particularly outlandish deaths, and science-fiction horror stories anticipating the modern vein. Some of the stories are so original as to defy classification.

Virtually all of Bierce's horror stories, as will be seen, involve a death. For this, psychologists have accused the satirist of being ridden by the fear of death; in view of his heroic war record and demonstrated personal courage, few things seem more absurd. A careful reading shows that his satire in most cases attacks the superstitions, ceremonies, and customs surrounding death, rather than death itself; his purpose, as in his other writings, was to ridicule falsity and hypocrisy as a form of social satire. In this satire, often enough, he included the reader, at least by implication; the reader, in his view, creates his own horror by having a stereotyped reaction to certain purely objective facts.

As to style, as a master of brief, pungent, and accurate diction, Bierce can hardly be excelled. He followed his own advice in his manual for copyreaders, *Write It Right,* making each word do the work of four by selecting precisely the right one. The result was that, of his forty-four horror stories, thirty-three are less than three thousand words in length, and seven are even less than a thousand words —"short short stories" indeed. One of these, "John Mortonson's Funeral," in less than seven hundred words attains the maximum of horror in a few commonplace factual words near the end.

In several of his horror stories, however, he allows himself the luxury of building fine "atmosphere." Of these, "The Stranger" and "An Inhabitant of Carcosa" are among the best examples.

Bierce once met a friend in the dark and asked him why he was out so late. "I'm reading a book of horror stories," the friend explained, "and don't want to go inside where it's light enough to read." Bierce may have had this anecdote in mind in writing these tales.

—E. J. H.

HAÏTA THE SHEPHERD

In the heart of Haïta the illusions of youth had not been supplanted by those of age and experience. His thoughts were pure and pleasant, for his life was simple and his soul devoid of ambition. He rose with the sun and went forth to pray at the shrine of Hastur, the god of shepherds, who heard and was pleased. After performance of this pious rite Haïta unbarred the gate of the fold and with a cheerful mind drove his flock afield, eating his morning meal of curds and oat cake as he went, occasionally pausing to add a few berries, cold with dew, or to drink of the waters that came away from the hills to join the stream in the middle of the valley and be borne along with it, he knew not whither.

During the long summer day, as his sheep cropped the good grass which the gods had made to grow for them, or lay with their fore-legs doubled under their breasts and chewed the cud, Haïta, reclining in the shadow of a tree, or sitting upon a rock, played so sweet music upon his reed pipe that sometimes from the corner of his eye he got accidental glimpses of the minor sylvan deities, leaning forward out of the copse to hear; but if he looked at them directly they vanished. From this—for he must be thinking if he would not turn into one of his own sheep—he drew the solemn inference that happiness may come if not sought, but if looked for will never be seen; for next to the favor of Hastur, who never disclosed himself, Haïta most valued the friendly interest of his neighbors, the shy immortals of the wood and stream. At nightfall he drove his flock back to the fold, saw that the gate was secure and retired to his cave for refreshment and for dreams.

So passed his life, one day like another, save when the storms uttered the wrath of an offended god. Then Haïta cowered in his cave, his face hidden in his hands, and prayed that he alone might be punished for his sins and the world saved from destruction. Sometimes when there was a great rain, and the stream came out of its banks, compelling him to urge his terrified flock to the uplands, he interceded for the people in the cities which he had been told lay in the plain beyond the two blue hills forming the gateway of his valley.

"It is kind of thee, O Hastur," so he prayed, "to give me mountains so near to my dwelling and my fold that I and my sheep can escape the angry torrents; but the rest of the world thou must thyself deliver in some way that I know not of, or I will no longer worship thee."

And Hastur, knowing that Haïta was a youth who kept his word, spared the cities and turned the waters into the sea.

So he had lived since he could remember. He could not rightly conceive any other mode of existence. The holy hermit who dwelt at the head of the valley, a full hour's journey away, from whom he had heard the tale of the great cities where dwelt people—poor souls!— who had no sheep, gave him no knowledge of that early time, when, so he reasoned, he must have been small and helpless like a lamb.

It was through thinking on these mysteries and marvels, and on that horrible change to silence and decay which he felt sure must some time come to him, as he had seen it come to so many of his flock —as it came to all living things except the birds—that Haïta first became conscious how miserable and hopeless was his lot.

"It is necessary," he said, "that I know whence and how I came; for how can one perform his duties unless able to judge what they are by the way in which he was intrusted with them? And what contentment can I have when I know not how long it is going to last? Perhaps before another sun I may be changed, and then what will become of the sheep? What, indeed, will have become of me?"

Pondering these things Haïta became melancholy and morose. He no longer spoke cheerfully to his flock, nor ran with alacrity to the shrine of Hastur. In every breeze he heard whispers of malign deities whose existence he now first observed. Every cloud was a portent signifying disaster, and the darkness was full of terrors. His reed pipe when applied to his lips gave out no melody, but a dismal wail; the sylvan and riparian intelligences no longer thronged the thicketside to listen, but fled from the sound, as he knew by the stirred leaves and bent flowers. He relaxed his vigilance and many of his sheep strayed away into the hills and were lost. Those that remained became lean and ill for lack of good pasturage, for he would not seek it for them, but conducted them day after day to the same spot, through mere abstraction, while puzzling about life and death—of immortality he knew not.

One day while indulging in the gloomiest reflections he suddenly sprang from the rock upon which he sat, and with a determined gesture of the right hand exclaimed: "I will no longer be a suppliant for knowledge which the gods withhold. Let them look to it that they do me no wrong. I will do my duty as best I can and if I err upon their own heads be it!"

Suddenly, as he spoke, a great brightness fell about him, causing him to look upward, thinking the sun had burst through a rift in the clouds; but there were no clouds. No more than an arm's length away stood a beautiful maiden. So beautiful she was that the flowers about her feet folded their petals in despair and bent their heads in token of submission; so sweet her look that the humming birds thronged her eyes, thrusting their thirsty bills almost into them, and the wild bees were about her lips. And such was her brightness that the shadows of all objects lay divergent from her feet, turning as she moved.

Haïta was entranced. Rising, he knelt before her in adoration, and she laid her hand upon his head.

"Come," she said in a voice that had the music of all the bells of his flock—"come, thou art not to worship me, who am no goddess, but if thou art truthful and dutiful I will abide with thee."

Haïta seized her hand, and stammering his joy and gratitude arose, and hand in hand they stood and smiled into each other's eyes. He gazed on her with reverence and rapture. He said: "I pray thee, lovely maid, tell me thy name and whence and why thou comest."

At this she laid a warning finger on her lip and began to withdraw. Her beauty underwent a visible alteration that made him shudder, he knew not why, for still she was beautiful. The landscape was darkened by a giant shadow sweeping across the valley with the speed of a vulture. In the obscurity the maiden's figure grew dim and indistinct and her voice seemed to come from a distance, as she said, in a tone of sorrowful reproach: "Presumptuous and ungrateful youth! must I then so soon leave thee? Would nothing do but thou must at once break the eternal compact?"

Inexpressibly grieved, Haïta fell upon his knees and implored her to remain—rose and sought her in the deepening darkness—ran in circles, calling to her aloud, but all in vain. She was no longer visible, but out of the gloom he heard her voice saying: "Nay, thou shalt not have me by seeking. Go to thy duty, faithless shepherd, or we shall never meet again."

Night had fallen; the wolves were howling in the hills and the terrified sheep crowding about Haïta's feet. In the demands of the hour he forgot his disappointment, drove his sheep to the fold and repairing to the place of worship poured out his heart in gratitude to Hastur for permitting him to save his flock, then retired to his cave and slept.

When Haïta awoke the sun was high and shone in at the cave, illuminating it with a great glory. And there, beside him, sat the maiden. She smiled upon him with a smile that seemed the visible music of his pipe of reeds. He dared not speak, fearing to offend her as before, for he knew not what he could venture to say.

"Because," she said, "thou didst thy duty by the flock, and didst not forget to thank Hastur for staying the wolves of the night, I am come to thee again. Wilt thou have me for a companion?"

"Who would not have thee forever?" replied Haïta. "Oh! never again leave me until—until I—change and become silent and motionless."

Haïta had no word for death.

"I wish, indeed," he continued, "that thou wert of my own sex, that we might wrestle and run races and so never tire of being together."

At these words the maiden arose and passed out of the cave, and Haïta, springing from his couch of fragrant boughs to overtake and detain her, observed to his astonishment that the rain was falling and the stream in the middle of the valley had come out of its banks. The sheep were bleating in terror, for the rising waters had invaded their fold. And there was danger for the unknown cities of the distant plain.

It was many days before Haïta saw the maiden again. One day he was returning from the head of the valley, where he had gone with ewe's milk and oat cake and berries for the holy hermit, who was too old and feeble to provide himself with food.

"Poor old man!" he said aloud, as he trudged along homeward. "I will return to-morrow and bear him on my back to my own dwelling, where I can care for him. Doubtless it is for this that Hastur has reared me all these many years, and gives me health and strength."

As he spoke, the maiden, clad in glittering garments, met him in the path with a smile that took away his breath.

"I am come again," she said, "to dwell with thee if thou wilt now have me, for none else will. Thou mayest have learned wisdom, and art willing to take me as I am, nor care to know."

Haïta threw himself at her feet. "Beautiful being," he cried, "if thou wilt but deign to accept all the devotion of my heart and soul —after Hastur be served—it is thine forever. But, alas! thou art capricious and wayward. Before to-morrow's sun I may lose thee again. Promise, I beseech thee, that however in my ignorance I may offend, thou wilt forgive and remain always with me."

Scarcely had he finished speaking when a troop of bears came out of the hills, racing toward him with crimson mouths and fiery eyes. The maiden again vanished, and he turned and fled for his life. Nor did he stop until he was in the cot of the holy hermit, whence he had set out. Hastily barring the door against the bears he cast himself upon the ground and wept.

"My son," said the hermit from his couch of straw, freshly gathered that morning by Haïta's hands, "it is not like thee to weep for bears—tell me what sorrow hath befallen thee, that age may minister to the hurts of youth with such balms as it hath of its wisdom."

Haïta told him all: how thrice he had met the radiant maid, and thrice she had left him forlorn. He related minutely all that had passed between them, omitting no word of what had been said.

When he had ended, the holy hermit was a moment silent, then said: "My son, I have attended to thy story, and I know the maiden. I have myself seen her, as have many. Know, then, that her name, which she would not even permit thee to inquire, is Happiness. Thou saidst the truth to her, that she is capricious for she imposeth conditions that man can not fulfill, and delinquency is punished by desertion. She cometh only when unsought, and will not be questioned. One manifestation of curiosity, one sign of doubt, one expression of misgiving, and she is away! How long didst thou have her at any time before she fled?"

"Only a single instant," answered Haïta, blushing with shame at the confession. "Each time I drove her away in one moment."

"Unfortunate youth!" said the holy hermit, "but for thine indiscretion thou mightst have had her for two."

❋　　❋　　❋

THE SECRET OF
MACARGER'S GULCH

Northwestwardly from Indian Hill, about nine miles as the crow flies, is Macarger's Gulch. It is not much of a gulch—a mere depression between two wooded ridges of inconsiderable height. From its mouth up to its head—for gulches, like rivers, have an anatomy of their own—the distance does not exceed two miles, and the width at bottom is at only one place more than a dozen yards; for most of the distance on either side of the little brook which drains it in winter, and goes dry in the early spring, there is no level ground at all; the steep slopes of the hills, covered with an almost impenetrable growth of manzanita and chemisal, are parted by nothing but the width of the water course. No one but an occasional enterprising hunter of the vicinity ever goes into Macarger's Gulch, and five miles away it is unknown, even by name. Within that distance in any direction are far more conspicuous topographical features without names, and one might try in vain to ascertain by local inquiry the origin of the name of this one.

About midway between the head and the mouth of Macarger's Gulch, the hill on the right as you ascend is cloven by another gulch, a short dry one, and at the junction of the two is a level space of two or three acres, and there a few years ago stood an old board house containing one small room. How the component parts of the house, few and simple as they were, had been assembled at that almost inaccessible point is a problem in the solution of which there would be greater satisfaction than advantage. Possibly the creek bed is a reformed road. It is certain that the gulch was at one time pretty thoroughly prospected by miners, who must have had some means of getting in with at least pack animals carrying tools and supplies; their profits, apparently, were not such as would have justified any considerable outlay to connect Macarger's Gulch with any center of civilization enjoying the distinction of a sawmill. The house, however, was there, most of it. It lacked a door and a window frame, and the chimney of mud and stones had fallen into an unlovely heap, overgrown with rank weeds. Such humble furniture as there may once have been and much of the lower weatherboarding, had served as fuel in the camp fires of hunters; as had also, probably, the curbing of an old well, which at the time I write of existed in the form of a rather wide but not very deep depression near by.

One afternoon in the summer of 1874, I passed up Macarger's Gulch from the narrow valley into which it opens, by following the dry bed of the brook. I was quail-shooting and had made a bag of about a dozen birds by the time I had reached the house described, of whose existence I was until then unaware. After rather carelessly inspecting the ruin I resumed my sport, and having fairly good success prolonged it until near sunset, when it occurred to me that I was a long way from any human habitation—too far to reach one by nightfall. But in my game bag was food, and the old house would afford shelter, if shelter were needed on a warm and dewless night in the foothills of the Sierra Nevada, where one may sleep in comfort on the pine needles, without covering. I am fond of solitude and love the night, so my resolution to "camp out" was soon taken, and by the time that it was dark I had made my bed of boughs and grasses in a corner of the room and was roasting a quail at a fire that I had kindled on the hearth. The smoke escaped out of the ruined chimney, the light illuminated the room with a kindly glow, and as I ate my simple meal of plain bird and drank the remains of a bottle of red wine which had served me all the afternoon in place of the water, which the region did not supply, I experienced a sense of comfort which better fare and accommodations do not always give.

Nevertheless, there was something lacking. I had a sense of comfort, but not of security. I detected myself staring more frequently at the open doorway and blank window than I could find warrant for doing. Outside these apertures all was black, and I was unable to repress a certain feeling of apprehension as my fancy pictured the outer world and filled it with unfriendly entities, natural and supernatural—chief among which, in their respective classes, were the grizzly bear, which I knew was occasionally still seen in that region, and the ghost, which I had reason to think was not. Unfortunately, our feelings do not always respect the law of probabilities, and to me that evening, the possible and the impossible were equally disquieting.

Everyone who has had experience in the matter must have observed that one confronts the actual and imaginary perils of the night with far less apprehension in the open air than in a house with an open doorway. I felt this now as I lay on my leafy couch in a corner of the room next to the chimney and permitted my fire to die out. So strong became my sense of the presence of something malign and menacing in the place, that I found myself almost unable to withdraw my eyes from the opening, as in the deepening darkness it became more and more indistinct. And when the last little flame flickered and went out I grasped the shotgun which I had laid at my side and actually turned the muzzle in the direction of the now invisible entrance, my thumb on one of the hammers, ready to cock the piece, my breath suspended, my muscles rigid and tense. But later I laid down the weapon with a sense of shame and mortification. What did I fear, and why?—I, to whom the night had been

> a more familiar face
> Than that of man—

I, in whom that element of hereditary superstition from which none of us is altogether free had given to solitude and darkness and silence only a more alluring interest and charm! I was unable to comprehend my folly, and losing in the conjecture the thing conjectured of, I fell asleep. And then I dreamed.

I was in a great city in a foreign land—a city whose people were of my own race, with minor differences of speech and costume; yet precisely what these were I could not say; my sense of them was indistinct. The city was dominated by a great castle upon an overlooking height whose name I knew, but could not speak. I walked through many streets, some broad and straight with high, modern buildings, some narrow, gloomy, and tortuous, between the gables of quaint old houses whose overhanging stories, elaborately ornamented with carvings in wood and stone, almost met above my head.

I sought someone whom I had never seen, yet knew that I should recognize when found. My quest was not aimless and fortuitous; it had a definite method. I turned from one street into another without hesitation and threaded a maze of intricate passages, devoid of the fear of losing my way.

Presently I stopped before a low door in a plain stone house which might have been the dwelling of an artisan of the better sort, and without announcing myself, entered. The room, rather sparely furnished, and lighted by a single window with small diamond-shaped panes, had but two occupants; a man and a woman. They took no notice of my intrusion, a circumstance which, in the manner of dreams, appeared entirely natural. They were not conversing; they sat apart, unoccupied and sullen.

The woman was young and rather stout, with fine large eyes and a certain grave beauty; my memory of her expression is exceedingly vivid, but in dreams one does not observe the details of faces. About her shoulders was a plaid shawl. The man was older, dark, with an evil face made more forbidding by a long scar extending from near the left temple diagonally downward into the black mustache; though in my dreams it seemed rather to haunt the face as a thing apart—I can express it no otherwise—than to belong to it. The moment that I found the man and woman I knew them to be husband and wife.

What followed, I remember indistinctly; all was confused and inconsistent—made so, I think, by gleams of consciousness. It was as if two pictures, the scene of my dream, and my actual surroundings, had been blended, one overlying the other, until the former, gradually fading, disappeared, and I was broad awake in the deserted cabin, entirely and tranquilly conscious of my situation.

My foolish fear was gone, and opening my eyes I saw that my fire, not altogether burned out, had revived by the falling of a stick and was again lighting the room. I had probably slept only a few minutes, but my commonplace dream had somehow so strongly impressed me that I was no longer drowsy; and after a little while I rose, pushed the embers of my fire together, and lighting my pipe proceeded in a rather ludicrously methodical way to meditate upon my vision.

It would have puzzled me then to say in what respect it was worth attention. In the first moment of serious thought that I gave to the matter I recognized the city of my dream as Edinburgh, where I had never been; so if the dream was a memory it was a memory of pictures and description. The recognition somehow deeply impressed me; it was as if something in my mind insisted rebelliously against will and reason on the importance of all this. And that faculty, whatever it was, asserted also a control of my speech. "Surely," I said aloud, quite involuntarily, "the MacGregors must have come here from Edinburgh."

At the moment, neither the substance of this remark nor the fact of my making it, surprised me in the least; it semed entirely natural that I should know the name of my dreamfolk and something of their history. But the absurdity of it all soon dawned upon me: I laughed aloud, knocked the ashes from my pipe and again stretched myself upon my bed of boughs and grass, where I lay staring absently into my failing fire, with no further thought of either my dream or my surroundings. Suddenly the single remaining flame crouched for a moment, then, springing upward, lifted itself clear of its embers and expired in air. The darkness was absolute.

At that instant—almost, it seemed, before the gleam of the blaze had faded from my eyes—there was a dull, dead sound, as of some heavy body falling upon the floor, which shook beneath me as I lay. I sprang to a sitting posture and groped at my side for my gun; my notion was that some wild beast had leaped in through the open window. While the flimsy structure was still shaking from the impact I heard the sound of blows, the scuffling of feet upon the floor, and then—it seemed to come from almost within reach of my hand, the sharp shrieking of a woman in mortal agony. So horrible a cry I had never heard nor conceived; it utterly unnerved me; I was conscious for a moment of nothing but my own terror! Fortunately my hand now found the weapon of which it was in search, and the familiar touch somewhat restored me. I leaped to my feet, straining my eyes to pierce the darkness. The violent sounds had ceased, but more terrible than these, I heard, at what seemed long intervals, the faint intermittent gasping of some living, dying thing!

As my eyes grew accustomed to the dim light of the coals in the fireplace, I saw first the shapes of the door and window, looking blacker than the black of the walls. Next, the distinction between wall and floor became discernible, and at last I was sensible to the form and full expanse of the floor from end to end and side to side. Nothing was visible and the silence was unbroken.

With a hand that shook a little, the other still grasping my gun, I restored my fire and made a critical examination of the place. There was nowhere any sign that the cabin had been entered. My own tracks were visible in the dust covering the floor, but there were no others. I relit my pipe, provided fresh fuel by ripping a thin board or two from the inside of the house—I did not care to go into the darkness out of doors—and passed the rest of the night smoking and thinking, and feeding my fire; not for added years of life would I have permitted that little flame to expire again.

Some years afterward I met in Sacramento a man named Morgan, to whom I had a note of introduction from a friend in San Francisco. Dining with him one evening at his home I observed various "trophies" upon the wall, indicating that he was fond of shooting. It turned out that he was, and in relating some of his feats he mentioned having been in the region of my adventure.

"Mr. Morgan," I asked abruptly, "do you know a place up there called Macarger's Gulch?"

"I have good reason to," he replied; "it was I who gave to the newspapers, last year, the accounts of the finding of the skeleton there."

I had not heard of it; the accounts had been published, it appeared, while I was absent in the East.

"By the way," said Morgan, "the name of the gulch is a corruption; it should have been called 'MacGregor's.' My dear," he added, speaking to his wife, "Mr. Elderson has upset his wine."

That was hardly accurate—I had simply dropped it, glass and all.

"There was an old shanty once in the gulch," Morgan resumed when the ruin wrought by my awkwardness had been repaired, "but just previously to my visit it had been blown down, or rather blown away, for its *débris* was scattered all about, the very floor being parted, plank from plank. Between two of the sleepers still in position I and my companion observed the remnant of a plaid shawl, and examining it found that it was wrapped about the shoulders of the body of a woman, of which but little remained besides the bones, partly covered with fragments of clothing, and brown dry skin. But we will spare Mrs. Morgan," he added with a smile. The lady had indeed exhibited signs of disgust rather than sympathy.

"It is necessary to say, however," he went on, "that the skull was fractured in several places, as by blows of some blunt instrument; and that instrument itself—a pick-handle, still stained with blood—lay under the boards near by."

Mr. Morgan turned to his wife. "Pardon me, my dear," he said with affected solemnity, "for mentioning these disagreeable particulars, the natural though regrettable incidents of a conjugal quarrel—resulting, doubtless, from the luckless wife's insubordination."

"I ought to be able to overlook it," the lady replied with composure; "you have so many times asked me to in those very words."

I thought he seemed rather glad to go on with his story.

"From these and other circumstances," he said, "the coroner's jury found that the deceased, Janet MacGregor, came to her death from blows inflicted by some person to the jury unknown; but it was added that the evidence pointed strongly to her husband, Thomas MacGregor, as the guilty person. But Thomas MacGregor has never been found nor heard of. It was learned that the couple came from Edinburgh, but not—my dear, do you not observe that Mr. Elderson's boneplate has water in it?"

I had deposited a chicken bone in my finger bowl.

"In a little cupboard I found a photograph of MacGregor, but it did not lead to his capture."

"Will you let me see it?" I said.

The picture showed a dark man with an evil face made more forbidding by a long scar extending from near the temple diagonally downward into the black mustache.

"By the way, Mr. Elderson," said my affable host, "may I know why you asked about 'Macarger's Gulch'?"

"I lost a mule near there once," I replied, "and the mischance has —has quite—upset me."

"My dear," said Mr. Morgan, with the mechanical intonation of an interpreter translating, "the loss of Mr. Elderson's mule has peppered his coffee."

❊　　　❊　　　❊

THE EYES OF THE PANTHER

I

ONE DOES NOT ALWAYS MARRY WHEN INSANE

A man and a woman—nature had done the grouping—sat on a rustic seat, in the late afternoon. The man was middle-aged, slender, swarthy, with the expression of a poet and the complexion of a pirate—a man at whom one would look again. The woman was young, blonde, graceful, with something in her figure and movements suggesting the word "lithe." She was habited in a gray gown with odd brown markings in the texture. She may have been beautiful; one could not readily say, for her eyes denied attention to all else. They were gray-green, long and narrow, with an expression defying analysis. One could only know that they were disquieting. Cleopatra may have had such eyes.

The man and the woman talked.

"Yes," said the woman, "I love you, God knows! But marry you, no. I cannot, will not."

"Irene, you have said that many times, yet always have denied me a reason. I've a right to know, to understand, to feel and prove my fortitude if I have it. Give me a reason."

"For loving you?"

The woman was smiling through her tears and her pallor. That did not stir any sense of humor in the man.

"No; there is no reason for that. A reason for not marrying me. I've a right to know. I must know. I will know!"

He had risen and was standing before her with clenched hands, on his face a frown—it might have been called a scowl. He looked as if he might attempt to learn by strangling her. She smiled no more —merely sat looking up into his face with a fixed, set regard that was utterly without emotion or sentiment. Yet it had something in it that tamed his resentment and made him shiver.

"You are determined to have my reason?" she asked in a tone that was entirely mechanical—a tone that might have been her look made audible.

"If you please—if I'm not asking too much."

Apparently this lord of creation was yielding some part of his dominion over his co-creature.

"Very well, you shall know: I am insane."

The man started, then looked incredulous and was conscious that he ought to be amused. But, again, the sense of humor failed him in his need and despite his disbelief he was profoundly disturbed by that which he did not believe. Between our convictions and our feelings there is no good understanding.

"That is what the physicians would say," the woman continued—"if they knew. I might myself prefer to call it a case of 'possession.' Sit down and hear what I have to say."

The man silently resumed his seat beside her on the rustic bench by the wayside. Over-against them on the eastern side of the valley the hills were already sunset-flushed and the stillness all about was of that peculiar quality that foretells the twilight. Something of its mysterious and significant solemnity had imparted itself to the man's mood. In the spiritual, as in the material world, are signs and presages of night. Rarely meeting her look, and whenever he did so conscious of the indefinable dread with which, despite their feline beauty, her eyes always affected him, Jenner Brading listened in silence to the story told by Irene Marlowe. In deference to the reader's possible prejudice against the artless method of an unpractised historian the author ventures to substitute his own version for hers.

II

A ROOM MAY BE TOO NARROW FOR THREE, THOUGH ONE IS OUTSIDE

In a little log house containing a single room sparely and rudely furnished, crouching on the floor against one of the walls, was a woman, clasping to her breast a child. Outside, a dense unbroken forest extended for many miles in every direction. This was at night and the room was black dark: no human eye could have discerned the woman and the child. Yet they were observed, narrowly, vigilantly, with never even a momentary slackening of attention; and that is the pivotal fact upon which this narrative turns.

Charles Marlowe was of the class, now extinct in this country, of woodmen pioneers—men who found their most acceptable surroundings in sylvan solitudes that stretched along the eastern slope of the Mississippi Valley, from the Great Lakes to the Gulf of Mexico. For more than a hundred years these men pushed ever westward, generation after generation, with rifle and ax, reclaiming from Nature and her savage children here and there an isolated acreage for the plow, no sooner reclaimed than surrendered to their less venturesome but more thrifty successors. At last they burst through the edge of the forest into the open country and vanished as if they had fallen over a cliff. The woodman pioneer is no more; the pioneer of the plains—he whose easy task it was to subdue for occupancy two-thirds of the country in a single generation—is another and inferior creation. With Charles Marlowe in the wilderness, sharing the dangers, hardships and privations of that strange, unprofitable life, were his wife and child, to whom, in the manner of his class, in which the domestic virtues were a religion, he was passionately attached. The woman was still young enough to be comely, new enough to the awful isolation of her lot to be cheerful. By withholding the large capacity for happiness which the simple satisfactions of the forest life could not have filled, Heaven had dealt honorably with her. In her light household tasks, her child, her husband and her few foolish books, she found abundant provision for her needs.

One morning in midsummer Marlowe took down his rifle from the wooden hooks on the wall and signified his intention of getting game.

"We've meat enough," said the wife; "please don't go out to-day. I dreamed last night, O, such a dreadful thing! I cannot recollect it, but I'm almost sure that it will come to pass if you go out."

It is painful to confess that Marlowe received this solemn statement with less of gravity than was due to the mysterious nature of the calamity foreshadowed. In truth, he laughed.

"Try to remember," he said. "Maybe you dreamed that Baby had lost the power of speech."

The conjecture was obviously suggested by the fact that Baby, clinging to the fringe of his hunting-coat with all her ten pudgy thumbs was at that moment uttering her sense of the situation in a series of exultant goo-goos inspired by sight of her father's raccoon-skin cap.

The woman yielded: lacking the gift of humor she could not hold out against his kindly badinage. So, with a kiss for the mother and a kiss for the child, he left the house and closed the door upon his happiness forever.

At nightfall he had not returned. The woman prepared supper and waited. Then she put Baby to bed and sang softly to her until she slept. By this time the fire on the hearth, at which she had cooked supper, had burned out and the room was lighted by a single candle. This she afterward placed in the open window as a sign and welcome to the hunter if he should approach from that side. She had thoughtfully closed and barred the door against such wild animals as might prefer it to an open window—of the habits of beasts of prey in entering a house uninvited she was not advised, though with true female prevision she may have considered the possibility of their entrance by way of the chimney. As the night wore on she became not less anxious, but more drowsy, and at last rested her arms upon the bed by the child and her head upon the arms. The candle in the window burned down to the socket, sputtered and flared a moment and went out unobserved; for the woman slept and dreamed.

In her dreams she sat beside the cradle of a second child. The first one was dead. The father was dead. The home in the forest was lost and the dwelling in which she lived was unfamiliar. There were heavy oaken doors, always closed, and outside the windows, fastened into the thick stone walls, were iron bars, obviously (so she thought) a provision against Indians. All this she noted with an infinite self-pity, but without surprise—an emotion unknown in dreams. The child in the cradle was invisible under its coverlet which something impelled her to remove. She did so, disclosing the face of a wild animal! In the shock of this dreadful revelation the dreamer awoke, trembling in the darkness of her cabin in the wood.

As a sense of her actual surroundings came slowly back to her she felt for the child that was not a dream, and assured herself by its breathing that all was well with it; nor could she forbear to pass a hand lightly across its face. Then, moved by some impulse for which she probably could not have accounted, she rose and took the sleeping babe in her arms, holding it close against her breast. The head of the child's cot was against the wall to which the woman now turned her back as she stood. Lifting her eyes she saw two bright objects starring the darkness with a reddish-green glow. She took them to be two coals on the hearth, but with her returning sense of direction came the disquieting consciousness that they were not in that quarter of the room, moreover were too high, being nearly at the level of the eyes—of her own eyes. For these were the eyes of a panther.

The beast was at the open window directly opposite and not five paces away. Nothing but those terrible eyes was visible, but in the dreadful tumult of her feelings as the situation disclosed itself to her understanding she somehow knew that the animal was standing on its hinder feet, supporting itself with its paws on the window-ledge. That signified a malign interest—not the mere gratification of an indolent curiosity. The consciousness of the attitude was an added horror, accentuating the menace of those awful eyes, in whose steadfast fire her strength and courage were alike consumed. Under their silent questioning she shuddered and turned sick. Her knees failed her, and by degrees, instinctively striving to avoid a sudden movement that might bring the beast upon her, she sank to the floor, crouched against the wall and tried to shield the babe with her trembling body without withdrawing her gaze from the luminous orbs that were killing her. No thought of her husband came to her in her agony—no hope nor suggestion of rescue or escape. Her capacity for thought and feeling had narrowed to the dimensions of a single emotion—fear of the animal's spring, of the impact of its body, the buffeting of its great arms, the feel of its teeth in her throat, the mangling of her babe. Motionless now and in absolute silence, she awaited her doom, the moments growing to hours, to years, to ages; and still those devilish eyes maintained their watch.

Returning to his cabin late at night with a deer on his shoulders Charles Marlowe tried the door. It did not yield. He knocked; there was no answer. He laid down his deer and went round to the window. As he turned the angle of the building he fancied he heard a sound as of stealthy footfalls and a rustling in the undergrowth of the forest, but they were too slight for certainty, even to his practised ear. Approaching the window, and to his surprise finding it open, he threw his leg over the sill and entered. All was darkness and silence. He groped his way to the fire-place, struck a match and lit a candle. Then he looked about. Cowering on the floor against a wall was his wife, clasping his child. As he sprang toward her she rose and broke into laughter, long, loud, and mechanical, devoid of gladness and devoid of sense—the laughter that is not out of keeping with the clanking of a chain. Hardly knowing what he did he extended his arms. She laid the babe in them. It was dead—pressed to death in its mother's embrace.

III
THE THEORY OF THE DEFENSE

That is what occurred during a night in a forest, but not all of it did Irene Marlowe relate to Jenner Brading; not all of it was known to her. When she had concluded the sun was below the horizon and the long summer twilight had begun to deepen in the hollows of the land. For some moments Brading was silent, expecting the narrative to be carried forward to some definite connection with the conversation introducing it; but the narrator was as silent as he, her face averted, her hands clasping and unclasping themselves as they lay in her lap, with a singular suggestion of an activity independent of her will.

"It is a sad, a terrible story," said Brading at last, "but I do not understand. You call Charles Marlowe father; that I know. That he is old before his time, broken by some great sorrow, I have seen, or thought I saw. But, pardon me, you said that you—that you——"

"That I am insane," said the girl, without a movement of head or body.

"But, Irene, you say—please, dear, do not look away from me— you say that the child was dead, not demented."

"Yes, that one—I am the second. I was born three months after that night, my mother being mercifully permitted to lay down her life in giving me mine."

Brading was again silent; he was a trifle dazed and could not at once think of the right thing to say. Her face was still turned away. In his embarrassment he reached impulsively toward the hands that lay closing and unclosing in her lap, but something—he could not have said what—restrained him. He then remembered, vaguely, that he had never altogether cared to take her hand.

"Is it likely," she resumed, "that a person born under such circumstances is like others—is what you call sane?"

Brading did not reply; he was preoccupied with a new thought that was taking shape in his mind—what a scientist would have called an hypothesis; a detective, a theory. It might throw an added light, albeit a lurid one, upon such doubt of her sanity as her own assertion had not dispelled.

The country was still new and, outside the villages, sparsely populated. The professional hunter was still a familiar figure, and among his trophies were heads and pelts of the larger kinds of game. Tales variously credible of nocturnal meetings with savage animals in lonely roads were sometimes current, passed through the customary stages of growth and decay, and were forgotten. A recent addition to these popular apocrypha, originating, apparently, by spontaneous generation in several households, was of a panther which had frightened some of their members by looking in at windows by night. The yarn had caused its little ripple of excitement—had even attained to the distinction of a place in the local newspaper; but

Brading had given it no attention. Its likeness to the story to which he had just listened now impressed him as perhaps more than accidental. Was it not possible that one story had suggested the other—that finding congenial conditions in a morbid mind and a fertile fancy, it had grown to the tragic tale that he had heard?

Brading recalled certain circumstances of the girl's history and disposition, of which, with love's incuriosity, he had hitherto been heedless—such as her solitary life with her father, at whose house no one, apparently, was an acceptable visitor and her strange fear of the night, by which those who knew her best accounted for her never being seen after dark. Surely in such a mind imagination once kindled might burn with a lawless flame, penetrating and enveloping the entire structure. That she was mad, though the conviction gave him the acutest pain, he could no longer doubt; she had only mistaken an effect of her mental disorder for its cause, bringing into imaginary relation with her own personality the vagaries of the local myth-makers. With some vague intention of testing his new "theory," and no very definite notion of how to set about it he said, gravely, but with hesitation:

"Irene, dear, tell me—I beg you will not take offence, but tell me—"

"I have told you," she interrupted, speaking with a passionate earnestness that he had not known her to show—"I have already told you that we cannot marry; is anything else worth saying?"

Before he could stop her she had sprung from her seat and without another word or look was gliding away among the trees toward her father's house. Brading had risen to detain her; he stood watching her in silence until she had vanished in the gloom. Suddenly he started as if he had been shot; his face took on an expression of amazement and alarm: in one of the black shadows into which she had disappeared he had caught a quick, brief glimpse of shining eyes! For an instant he was dazed and irresolute; then he dashed into the wood after her, shouting: "Irene, Irene, look out! The panther! The panther!"

In a moment he had passed through the fringe of forest into open ground and saw the girl's gray skirt vanishing into her father's door. No panther was visible.

AN APPEAL TO THE CONSCIENCE OF GOD

Jenner Brading, attorney-at-law, lived in a cottage at the edge of the town. Directly behind the dwelling was the forest. Being a bachelor, and therefore, by the Draconian moral code of the time and place denied the services of the only species of domestic servant known thereabout, the "hired girl," he boarded at the village hotel, where also was his office. The woodside cottage was merely a lodging maintained—at no great cost, to be sure—as an evidence of prosperity and respectability. It would hardly do for one to whom the local newspaper had pointed with pride as "the foremost jurist of his time" to be "homeless," albeit he may sometimes have suspected that the words "home" and "house" were not strictly synonymous. Indeed, his consciousness of the disparity and his will to harmonize it were matters of logical inference, for it was generally reported that soon after the cottage was built its owner had made a futile venture in the direction of marriage—had, in truth, gone so far as to be rejected by the beautiful but eccentric daughter of Old Man Marlowe, the recluse. This was publicly believed because he had told it himself and she had not—a reversal of the usual order of things which could hardly fail to carry conviction.

Brading's bedroom was at the rear of the house, with a single window facing the forest. One night he was awakened by a noise at that window; he could hardly have said what it was like. With a little thrill of the nerves he sat up in bed and laid hold of the revolver which, with a forethought most commendable in one addicted to the habit of sleeping on the ground floor with an open window, he had put under his pillow. The room was in absolute darkness, but being unterrified he knew where to direct his eyes, and there he held them, awaiting in silence what further might occur. He could now dimly discern the aperture—a square of lighter black. Presently there appeared at its lower edge two gleaming eyes that burned with a malignant lustre inexpressibly terrible! Brading's heart gave a great jump, then seemed to stand still. A chill passed along his spine and through his hair; he felt the blood forsake his cheeks. He could not have cried out—not to save his life; but being a man of courage he would not, to save his life, have done so if he had been able. Some trepidation his coward body might feel, but his spirit was of sterner stuff. Slowly the shining eyes rose with a steady motion that seemed an approach, and slowly rose Brading's right hand, holding the pistol. He fired!

Blinded by the flash and stunned by the report, Brading nevertheless heard, or fancied that he heard, the wild, high scream of the panther, so human in sound, so devilish in suggestion. Leaping from the bed he hastily clothed himself and, pistol in hand, sprang from the door, meeting two or three men who came running up from the road. A brief explanation was followed by a cautious search of the house. The grass was wet with dew; beneath the window it had been trodden and partly leveled for a wide space, from which a devious trail, visible in the light of a lantern, led away into the bushes. One of the men stumbled and fell upon his hands, which as he rose and rubbed them together were slippery. On examination they were seen to be red with blood.

An encounter, unarmed, with a wounded panther was not agreeable to their taste; all but Brading turned back. He, with lantern and pistol, pushed courageously forward into the wood. Passing through a difficult undergrowth he came into a small opening, and there his courage had its reward, for there he found the body of his victim. But it was no panther. What it was is told, even to this day, upon a weather-worn headstone in the village churchyard, and for many years was attested daily at the graveside by the bent figure and sorrow-seamed face of Old Man Marlowe, to whose soul, and to the soul of his strange, unhappy child, peace. Peace and reparation.

❊   ❊   ❊

THE STRANGER

A man stepped out of the darkness into the little illuminated circle about our failing campfire and seated himself upon a rock.

"You are not the first to explore this region," he said, gravely.

Nobody controverted his statement; he was himself proof of its truth, for he was not of our party and must have been somewhere near when we camped. Moreover, he must have companions not far away; it was not a place where one would be living or traveling alone. For more than a week we had seen, besides ourselves and our animals, only such living things as rattlesnakes and horned toads. In an Arizona desert one does not long coexist with only such creatures as these: one must have pack animals, supplies, arms—"an outfit." And all these imply comrades. It was perhaps a doubt as to what manner of men this unceremonious stranger's comrades might be, together with something in his words interpretable as a challenge, that caused every man of our half-dozen "gentlemen adventurers" to rise to a sitting posture and lay his hand upon a weapon —an act signifying, in that time and place, a policy of expectation. The stranger gave the matter no attention and began again to speak in the same deliberate, uninflected monotone in which he had delivered his first sentence:

"Thirty years ago Ramon Gallegos, William Shaw, George W. Kent and Berry Davis, all of Tucson, crossed the Santa Catalina mountains and traveled due west, as nearly as the configuration of the country permitted. We were prospecting and it was our intention, if we found nothing, to push through to the Gila river at some point near Big Bend, where we understood there was a settlement. We had a good outfit but no guide—just Ramon Gallegos, William Shaw, George W. Kent and Berry Davis."

The man repeated the names slowly and distinctly, as if to fix them in the memories of his audience, every member of which was now attentively observing him, but with a slackened apprehension regarding his possible companions somewhere in the darkness that seemed to enclose us like a black wall; in the manner of this volunteer historian was no suggestion of an unfriendly purpose. His act was rather that of a harmless lunatic than an enemy. We were not so new to the country as not to know that the solitary life of many a plainsman had a tendency to develop eccentricities of conduct and character not always easily distinguishable from mental aberration. A man is like a tree: in a forest of his fellows he will grow as straight as his generic and individual nature permits; alone in the open, he yields to the deforming stresses and tortions that environ him. Some such thoughts were in my mind as I watched the man from the shadow of my hat, pulled low to shut out the firelight. A witless fellow, no doubt, but what could he be doing there in the heart of a desert?

Having undertaken to tell this story, I wish that I could describe the man's appearance; that would be a natural thing to do. Unfortunately, and somewhat strangely, I find myself unable to do so with any degree of confidence, for afterward no two of us agreed as to what he wore and how he looked; and when I try to set down my own impressions they elude me. Anyone can tell some kind of story; narration is one of the elemental powers of the race. But the talent for description is a gift.

Nobody having broken silence the visitor went on to say:

"This country was not then what it is now. There was not a ranch between the Gila and the Gulf. There was a little game here and there in the mountains, and near the infrequent water-holes grass enough to keep our animals from starvation. If we should be so fortunate as to encounter no Indians we might get through. But within a week the purpose of the expedition had altered from discovery of wealth to preservation of life. We had gone too far to go back, for what was ahead could be no worse than what was behind; so we pushed on, riding by night to avoid Indians and the intolerable heat, and concealing ourselves by day as best we could. Sometimes, having exhausted our supply of wild meat and emptied our casks, we were days without food or drink; then a water-hole or a shallow pool in the bottom of an *arroyo* so restored our strength and sanity that we were able to shoot some of the wild animals that sought it also. Sometimes it was a bear, sometimes an antelope, a coyote, a cougar—that was as God pleased; all were food.

"One morning as we skirted a mountain range, seeking a practicable pass, we were attacked by a band of Apaches who had followed our trail up a gulch—it is not far from here. Knowing that they outnumbered us ten to one, they took none of their usual cowardly precautions, but dashed upon us at a gallop, firing and yelling. Fighting was out of the question: we urged our feeble animals up the gulch as far as there was footing for a hoof, then threw ourselves out of our saddles and took to the *chaparral* on one of the slopes, abandoning our entire outfit to the enemy. But we retained our rifles, every man—Ramon Gallegos, William Shaw, George W. Kent and Berry Davis."

"Same old crowd," said the humorist of our party. He was an Eastern man, unfamiliar with the decent observances of social intercourse. A gesture of disapproval from our leader silenced him and the stranger proceeded with his tale:

"The savages dismounted also, and some of them ran up the gulch beyond the point at which we had left it, cutting off further retreat in that direction and forcing us on up the side. Unfortunately the *chaparral* extended only a short distance up the slope, and as we came into the open ground above we took the fire of a dozen rifles; but Apaches shoot badly when in a hurry, and God so willed it that none of us fell. Twenty yards up the slope, beyond the edge of the brush, were vertical cliffs, in which, directly in front of us, was a narrow opening. Into that we ran, finding ourselves in a cavern about as large as an ordinary room in a house. Here for a time we were safe: a single man with a repeating rifle could defend the entrance against all the Apaches in the land. But against hunger and thirst we had no defense. Courage we still had, but hope was a memory.

"Not one of those Indians did we afterward see, but by the smoke and glare of their fires in the gulch we knew that by day and by night they watched with ready rifles in the edge of the bush—knew that if we made a sortie not a man of us would live to take three steps into the open. For three days, watching in turn, we held out before our suffering became insupportable. Then—it was the morning of the fourth day—Ramon Gallegos said:

" 'Senores, I know not well of the good God and what please him. I have live without religion, and I am not acquaint with that of you. Pardon, senores, if I shock you, but for me the time is come to beat the game of the Apache.'

"He knelt upon the rock floor of the cave and pressed his pistol against his temple. 'Madre de Dios,' he said, 'comes now the soul of Ramon Gallegos.'

"And so he left us—William Shaw, George W. Kent and Berry Davis.

"I was the leader: it was for me to speak.

" 'He was a brave man,' I said—'he knew when to die, and how. It is foolish to go mad from thirst and fall by Apache bullets, or be skinned alive—it is in bad taste. Let us join Ramon Gallegos.'

" 'That is right,' said William Shaw.

" 'That is right,' said George W. Kent.

"I straightened the limbs of Ramon Gallegos and put a handkerchief over his face. Then William Shaw said: 'I should like to look like that—a little while.'

"And George W. Kent said that he felt that way, too.

" 'It shall be so,' I said: 'the red devils will wait a week. William Shaw and George W. Kent, draw and kneel.'

"They did so and I stood before them.

" 'Almighty God, our Father,' said I.

" 'Almighty God, our Father,' said William Shaw.

" 'Almighty God, our Father,' said George W. Kent.

" 'Forgive us our sins,' said I.

" 'Forgive us our sins,' said they.

" 'And receive our souls.'

" 'And receive our souls.'

" 'Amen!'

" 'Amen!'

"I laid them beside Ramon Gallegos and covered their faces."

There was a quick commotion on the opposite side of the camp-fire: one of our party had sprung to his feet, pistol in hand.

"And you!" he shouted—"*you* dared to escape?—you dare to be alive? You cowardly hound, I'll send you to join them if I hang for it!"

But with the leap of a panther the captain was upon him, grasping his wrist. "Hold it in, Sam Yountsey, hold it in!"

We were now all upon our feet—except the stranger, who sat motionless and apparently inattentive. Some one seized Yountsey's other arm.

"Captain," I said, "there is something wrong here. This fellow is either a lunatic or merely a liar—just a plain, every-day liar whom Yountsey has no call to kill. If this man was of that party it had five members, one of whom—probably himself—he has not named."

"Yes," said the captain, releasing the insurgent, who sat down, "there is something—unusual. Years ago four dead bodies of white men, scalped and shamefully mutilated, were found about the mouth of that cave. They are buried there; I have seen the graves —we shall all see them to-morrow."

The stranger rose, standing tall in the light of the expiring fire, which in our breathless attention to his story we had neglected to keep going.

"There were four," he said—"Ramon Gallegos, William Shaw, George W. Kent and Berry Davis."

With this reiterated roll-call of the dead he walked into the darkness and we saw him no more.

At that moment one of our party, who had been on guard, strode in among us, rifle in hand and somewhat excited.

"Captain," he said, "for the last half-hour three men have been standing out there on the *mesa*." He pointed in the direction taken by the stranger. "I could see them distinctly, for the moon is up, but as they had no guns and I had them covered with mine I thought it was their move. They have made none, but, damn it! they have got on to my nerves."

"Go back to your post, and stay till you see them again," said the captain. "The rest of you lie down again, or I'll kick you all into the fire."

The sentinel obediently withdrew, swearing, and did not return.

As we were arranging our blankets the fiery Yountsey said: "I beg your pardon, Captain, but who the devil do you take them to be?"

"Ramon Gallegos, William Shaw and George W. Kent."

"But how about Berry Davis? I ought to have shot him."

"Quite needless; you couldn't have made him any deader. Go to sleep."

❊ ❊ ❊

AN INHABITANT OF CARCOSA

For there be divers sorts of death—some wherein the body remaineth; and in some it vanisheth quite away with the spirit. This commonly occurreth only in solitude (such is God's will) and, none seeing the end, we say the man is lost, or gone on a long journey—which indeed he hath; but sometimes it hath happened in sight of many, as abundant testimony showeth. In one kind of death the spirit also dieth, and this it hath been known to do while yet the body was in vigor for many years. Sometimes, as is veritably attested, it dieth with the body, but after a season is raised up again in that place where the body did decay.

Pondering these words of Hali (whom God rest) and questioning their full meaning, as one who, having an intimation, yet doubts if there be not something behind, other than that which he has discerned, I noted not whither I had strayed until a sudden chill wind striking my face revived in me a sense of my surroundings. I observed with astonishment that everything seemed unfamiliar. On every side of me stretched a bleak and desolate expanse of plain, covered with a tall overgrowth of sere grass, which rustled and whistled in the autumn wind with heaven knows what mysterious and disquieting suggestion. Protruded at long intervals above it, stood strangely shaped and somber-colored rocks, which seemed to have an understanding with one another and to exchange looks of uncomfortable significance, as if they had reared their heads to watch the issue of some foreseen event. A few blasted trees here and there appeared as leaders in this malevolent conspiracy of silent expectation.

The day, I thought, must be far advanced, though the sun was invisible; and although sensible that the air was raw and chill my consciousness of that fact was rather mental than physical—I had no feeling of discomfort. Over all the dismal landscape a canopy of low, lead-colored clouds hung like a visible curse. In all this there were a menace and a portent—a hint of evil, an intimation of doom. Bird, beast, or insect there was none. The wind sighed in the bare branches of the dead trees and the gray grass bent to whisper its dread secret to the earth; but no other sound nor motion broke the awful repose of that dismal place.

I observed in the herbage a number of weather-worn stones, evidently shaped with tools. They were broken, covered with moss and half sunken in the earth. Some lay prostrate, some leaned at various angles, none was vertical. They were obviously headstones of graves, though the graves themselves no longer existed as either mounds or depressions; the years had leveled all. Scattered here and there, more massive blocks showed where some pompous tomb or ambitious monument had once flung its feeble defiance at oblivion. So old seemed these relics, these vestiges of vanity and memorials of affection and piety, so battered and worn and stained—so neglected, deserted, forgotten the place, that I could not help thinking myself the discoverer of the burial-ground of a prehistoric race of men whose very name was long extinct.

Filled with these reflections, I was for some time heedless of the sequence of my own experiences, but soon I thought, "How came I hither?" A moment's reflection seemed to make this all clear and explain at the same time, though in a disquieting way, the singular character with which my fancy had invested all that I saw or heard. I was ill. I remembered now that I had been prostrated by a sudden fever, and that my family had told me that in my periods of delirium I had constantly cried out for liberty and air, and had been held in bed to prevent my escape out-of-doors. Now I had eluded the vigilance of my attendants and had wandered hither to—to where? I could not conjecture. Clearly I was at a considerable distance from the city where I dwelt—the ancient and famous city of Carcosa.

No signs of human life were anywhere visible nor audible; no rising smoke, no watchdog's bark, no lowing of cattle, no shouts of children at play—nothing but that dismal burial-place, with its air of mystery and dread, due to my own disordered brain. Was I not becoming again delirious, there beyond human aid? Was it not indeed *all* an illusion of my madness? I called aloud the names of my wives and sons, reached out my hands in search of theirs, even as I walked among the crumbling stones and in the withered grass.

A noise behind me caused me to turn about. A wild animal—a lynx—was approaching. The thought came to me: If I break down here in the desert—if the fever return and I fail, this beast will be at my throat. I sprang toward it, shouting. It trotted tranquilly by within a hand's breadth of me and disappeared behind a rock.

A moment later a man's head appeared to rise out of the ground a short distance away. He was ascending the farther slope of a low hill whose crest was hardly to be distinguished from the general level. His whole figure soon came into view against the background of gray cloud. He was half naked, half clad in skins. His hair was unkempt, his beard long and ragged. In one hand he carried a bow and arrow; the other held a blazing torch with a long trail of black smoke. He walked slowly and with caution, as if he feared falling into some open grave concealed by the tall grass. This strange apparition surprised but did not alarm, and taking such a course as to intercept him I met him almost face to face, accosting him with the familiar salutation, "God keep you."

He gave no heed, nor did he arrest his pace.

"Good stranger," I continued, "I am ill and lost. Direct me, I beseech you, to Carcosa."

The man broke into a barbarous chant in an unknown tongue, passing on and away.

An owl on the branch of a decayed tree hooted dismally and was answered by another in the distance. Looking upward, I saw through a sudden rift in the clouds Aldebaran and the Hyades! In all this there was a hint of night—the lynx, the man with the torch, the owl. Yet I saw—I saw even the stars in absence of the darkness. I saw, but was apparently not seen nor heard. Under what awful spell did I exist?

I seated myself at the root of a great tree, seriously to consider what it were best to do. That I was mad I could no longer doubt, yet recognized a ground of doubt in the conviction. Of fever I had no trace. I had, withal, a sense of exhilaration and vigor altogether unknown to me—a feeling of mental and physical exaltation. My senses seemed all alert; I could feel the air as a ponderous substance; I could hear the silence.

A great root of the giant tree against whose trunk I leaned as I sat held inclosed in its grasp a slab of stone, a part of which protruded into a recess formed by another root. The stone was thus partly protected from the weather, though greatly decomposed. Its edges were worn round, its corners eaten away, its surface deeply furrowed and scaled. Glittering particles of mica were visible in the earth about it—vestiges of its decomposition. This stone had apparently marked the grave out of which the tree had sprung ages ago. The tree's exacting roots had robbed the grave and made the stone a prisoner.

A sudden wind pushed some dry leaves and twigs from the uppermost face of the stone; I saw the low-relief letters of an inscription and bent to read it. God in Heaven! *my* name in full!—the date of *my* birth!—the date of *my* death!

A level shaft of light illuminated the whole side of the tree as I sprang to my feet in terror. The sun was rising in the rosy east. I stood between the tree and his broad red disk—no shadow darkened the trunk!

A chorus of howling wolves saluted the dawn. I saw them sitting on their haunches, singly and in groups, on the summits of irregular mounds and tumuli filling a half of my desert prospect and extending to the horizon. And then I knew that these were ruins of the ancient and famous city of Carcosa.

———————

Such are the facts imparted to the medium Bayrolles by the spirit Hoseib Alar Robardin.

❋   ❋   ❋

THE APPLICANT

Pushing his adventurous shins through the deep snow that had fallen overnight, and encouraged by the glee of his little sister, following in the open way that he made, a sturdy small boy, the son of Grayville's most distinguished citizen, struck his foot against something of which there was no visible sign on the surface of the snow. It is the purpose of this narrative to explain how it came to be there.

No one who has had the advantage of passing through Grayville by day can have failed to observe the large stone building crowning the low hill to the north of the railway station—that is to say, to the right in going toward Great Mowbray. It is a somewhat dull-looking edifice, of the Early Comatose order, and appears to have been designed by an architect who shrank from publicity, and although unable to conceal his work—even compelled, in this instance, to set it on an eminence in the sight of men—did what he honestly could to insure it against a second look. So far as concerns its outer and visible aspect, the Abersush Home for Old Men is unquestionably inhospitable to human attention. But it is a building of great magnitude, and cost its benevolent founder the profit of many a cargo of the teas and silks and spices that his ships brought up from the under-world when he was in trade in Boston; though the main expense was its endowment. Altogether, this reckless person had robbed his heirs-at-law of no less a sum than half a million dollars and flung it away in riotous giving. Possibly it was with a view to get out of sight of the silent big witness to his extravagance that he shortly afterward disposed of all his Grayville property that remained to him, turned his back upon the scene of his prodigality and went off across the sea in one of his own ships. But the gossips who got their inspiration most directly from Heaven declared that he went in search of a wife—a theory not easily reconciled with that of the village humorist, who solemnly averred that the bachelor philanthropist had departed this life (left Grayville, to wit) because the marriageable maidens had made it too hot to hold him. However this may have been, he had not returned, and although at long intervals there had come to Grayville, in a desultory way, vague rumors of his wanderings in strange lands, no one seemed certainly to know about him, and to the new generation he was no more than a name. But from above the portal of the Home for Old Men the name shouted in stone.

Despite its unpromising exterior, the Home is a fairly commodious place of retreat from the ills that its inmates have incurred by being poor and old and men. At the time embraced in this brief chronicle they were in number about a score, but in acerbity, querulousness, and general ingratitude they could hardly be reckoned at fewer than a hundred; at least that was the estimate of the superintendent, Mr. Silas Tilbody. It was Mr. Tilbody's steadfast conviction that always, in admitting new old men to replace those who had gone to another and a better Home, the trustees had distinctly in will the infraction of his peace, and the trial of his patience. In truth, the longer the institution was connected with him, the stronger was his feeling that the founder's scheme of benevolence was sadly impaired by providing any inmates at all. He had not much imagination, but with what he had he was addicted to the reconstruction of the Home for Old Men into a kind of "castle in Spain," with himself as castellan, hospitably entertaining about a score of sleek and prosperous middle-aged gentlemen, consummately good-humored and civilly willing to pay for their board and lodging. In this revised

project of philanthropy the trustees, to whom he was indebted for
his office and responsible for his conduct, had not the happiness to
appear. As to them, it was held by the village humorist aforemen-
tioned that in their management of the great charity Providence
had thoughtfully supplied an incentive to thrift. With the inference
which he expected to be drawn from that view we have nothing to
do; it had neither support nor denial from the inmates, who certainly were most concerned. They lived out their little remnant of
life, crept into graves neatly numbered, and were succeeded by other
old men as like them as could be desired by the Adversary of Peace.
If the Home was a place of punishment for the sin of unthrift the
veteran offenders sought justice with a persistence that attested the
sincerity of their penitence. It is to one of these that the reader's
attention is now invited.

In the matter of attire this person was not altogether engaging.
But for this season, which was midwinter, a careless observer might
have looked upon him as a clever device of the husbandman indisposed to share the fruits of his toil with the crows that toil not,
neither spin—an error that might not have been dispelled without
longer and closer observation than he seemed to court; for his progress up Abersush Street, toward the Home in the gloom of the
winter evening, was not visibly faster than what might have been
expected of a scarecrow blessed with youth, health, and discontent.
The man was indisputably ill-clad, yet not without a certain fitness
and good taste, withal; for he was obviously an applicant for admittance to the Home, where poverty was a qualification. In the
army of indigence the uniform is rags; they serve to distinguish the
rank and file from the recruiting officers.

As the old man, entering the gate of the grounds, shuffled up the
broad walk, already white with the fast-falling snow, which from
time to time he feebly shook from its various coigns of vantage on
his person, he came under inspection of the large globe lamp that
burned always by night over the great door of the building. As if
unwilling to incur its revealing beams, he turned to the left and,
passing a considerable distance along the face of the building, rang
at a smaller door emitting a dimmer ray that came from within,
through the fanlight, and expended itself incuriously overhead. The
door was opened by no less a personage than the great Mr. Tilbody
himself. Observing his visitor, who at once uncovered, and somewhat shortened the radius of the permanent curvature of his back,
the great man gave visible token of neither surprise nor displeasure.
Mr. Tilbody was, indeed, in an uncommonly good humor, a phenom-

enon ascribable doubtless to the cheerful influence of the season; for this was Christmas Eve, and the morrow would be that blessed 365th part of the year that all Christian souls set apart for mighty feats of goodness and joy. Mr. Tilbody was so full of the spirit of the season that his fat face and pale blue eyes, whose ineffectual fire served to distinguish it from an untimely summer squash, effused so genial a glow that it seemed a pity that he could not have lain down in it, basking in the consciousness of his own identity. He was hatted, booted, overcoated, and umbrellaed, as became a person who was about to expose himself to the night and the storm on an errand of charity; for Mr. Tilbody had just parted from his wife and children to go "down town" and purchase the wherewithal to confirm the annual falsehood about the hunch-bellied saint who frequents the chimneys to reward little boys and girls who are good, and especially truthful. So he did not invite the old man in, but saluted him cheerily:

"Hello! just in time; a moment later and you would have missed me. Come, I have no time to waste; we'll walk a little way together."

"Thank you," said the old man, upon whose thin and white but not ignoble face the light from the open door showed an expression that was perhaps disappointment; "but if the trustees—if my application——"

"The trustees," Mr. Tilbody said, closing more doors than one, and cutting off two kinds of light, "have agreed that your application disagrees with them."

Certain sentiments are inappropriate to Christmastide, but Humor, like Death, has all seasons for his own.

"Oh, my God!" cried the old man, in so thin and husky a tone that the invocation was anything but impressive, and to at least one of his two auditors sounded, indeed, somewhat ludicrous. To the Other —but that is a matter which laymen are devoid of the light to expound.

"Yes," continued Mr. Tilbody, accommodating his gait to that of his companion, who was mechanically, and not very successfully, retracing the track that he had made through the snow; "they have decided that, under the circumstances—under the very peculiar circumstances, you understand—it would be inexpedient to admit you. As superintendent and *ex officio* secretary of the honorable board"— as Mr. Tilbody "read his title clear" the magnitude of the big building, seen through its veil of falling snow, appeared to suffer somewhat in comparison—"it is my duty to inform you that, in the words of Deacon Byram, the chairman, your presence in the Home would

—under the circumstances—be peculiarly embarrassing. I felt it my duty to submit to the honorable board the statement that you made to me yesterday of your needs, your physical condition, and the trials which it has pleased Providence to send upon you in your very proper effort to present your claims in person; but, after careful, and I may say prayerful, consideration of your case—with something too, I trust, of the large charitableness appropriate to the season—it was decided that we would not be justified in doing anything likely to impair the usefulness of the institution intrusted (under Providence) to our care."

They had now passed out of the grounds; the street lamp opposite the gate was dimly visible through the snow. Already the old man's former track was obliterated, and he seemed uncertain as to which way he should go. Mr. Tilbody had drawn a little away from him, but paused and turned half toward him, apparently reluctant to forego the continuing opportunity.

"Under the circumstances," he resumed, "the decision——"

But the old man was inaccessible to the suasion of his verbosity; he had crossed the street into a vacant lot and was going forward, rather deviously toward nowhere in particular—which, he having nowhere in particular to go to, was not so reasonless a proceeding as it looked.

And that is how it happened that the next morning, when the church bells of all Grayville were ringing with an added unction appropriate to the day, the sturdy little son of Deacon Byram, breaking a way through the snow to the place of worship, struck his foot against the body of Amasa Abersush, philanthropist.

❅   ❅   ❅

THE DEATH OF HALPIN FRAYSER

I

For by death is wrought greater change than hath been shown. Whereas in general the spirit that removed cometh back upon occasion, and is sometimes seen of those in flesh (appearing in the form of the body it bore) yet it hath happened that the veritable body without the spirit hath walked. And it is attested of those encountering who have lived to speak thereon that a lich so raised up hath no natural affection, nor remembrance thereof, but only hate. Also, it is known that some spirits which in life were benign become by death evil altogether.—*Hali.*

One dark night in midsummer a man waking from a dreamless sleep in a forest lifted his head from the earth, and staring a few moments into the blackness, said: "Catherine Larue." He said nothing more; no reason was known to him why he should have said so much.

The man was Halpin Frayser. He lived in St. Helena, but where he lives now is uncertain, for he is dead. One who practices sleeping in the woods with nothing under him but the dry leaves and the damp earth, and nothing over him but the branches from which the leaves have fallen and the sky from which the earth has fallen, cannot hope for great longevity, and Frayser had already attained the age of thirty-two. There are persons in this world, millions of persons, and far and away the best persons, who regard that as a very advanced age. They are the children. To those who view the voyage of life from the port of departure the bark that has accomplished any considerable distance appears already in close approach to the farther shore. However, it is not certain that Halpin Frayser came to his death by exposure.

He had been all day in the hills west of the Napa Valley, looking for doves and such small game as was in season. Late in the afternoon it had come on to be cloudy, and he had lost his bearings; and although he had only to go always downhill—everywhere the way to safety when one is lost—the absence of trails had so impeded him that he was overtaken by night while still in the forest. Unable in the darkness to penetrate the thickets of manzanita and other undergrowth, utterly bewildered and overcome with fatigue, he had lain down near the root of a large madroño and fallen into a dreamless sleep. It was hours later, in the very middle of the night, that one of God's mysterious messengers, gliding ahead of the incalculable host of his companions sweeping westward with the dawn line, pronounced the awakening word in the ear of the sleeper, who sat upright and spoke, he knew not why, a name, he knew not whose.

Halpin Frayser was not much of a philosopher, nor a scientist. The circumstance that, waking from a deep sleep at night in the midst of a forest, he had spoken aloud a name that he had not in memory and hardly had in mind did not arouse an enlightened curiosity to investigate the phenomenon. He thought it odd, and with a little perfunctory shiver, as if in deference to a seasonal presumption that the night was chill, he lay down again and went to sleep. But his sleep was no longer dreamless.

He thought he was walking along a dusty road that showed white in the gathering darkness of a summer night. Whence and whither it led, and why he traveled it, he did not know, though all seemed simple and natural, as is the way in dreams; for in the Land Beyond the Bed surprises cease from troubling and the judgment is at rest. Soon he came to a parting of the ways; leading from the highway was a road less traveled, having the appearance, indeed, of having been long abandoned, because, he thought, it led to something evil; yet he turned into it without hesitation, impelled by some imperious necessity.

As he pressed forward he became conscious that his way was haunted by invisible existences whom he could not definitely figure to his mind. From among the trees on either side he caught broken and incoherent whispers in a strange tongue which yet he partly understood. They seemed to him fragmentary utterances of a monstrous conspiracy against his body and soul.

It was now long after nightfall, yet the interminable forest through which he journeyed was lit with a wan glimmer having no point of diffusion, for in its mysterious lumination nothing cast a shadow. A shallow pool in the guttered depression of an old wheel rut, as from a recent rain, met his eye with a crimson gleam. He stooped and plunged his hand into it. It stained his fingers; it was blood! Blood, he then observed, was about him everywhere. The weeds growing rankly by the roadside showed it in blots and splashes on their big, broad leaves. Patches of dry dust between the wheelways were pitted and spattered as with a red rain. Defiling the trunks of the trees were broad maculations of crimson, and blood dripped like dew from their foliage.

All this he observed with a terror which seemed not incompatible with the fulfillment of a natural expectation. It seemed to him that it was all in expiation of some crime which, though conscious of his guilt, he could not rightly remember. To the menaces and mysteries of his surroundings the consciousness was an added horror. Vainly he sought by tracing life backward in memory, to reproduce the moment of his sin; scenes and incidents came crowding tumultuously into his mind, one picture effacing another, or commingling with it in confusion and obscurity, but nowhere could he catch a glimpse of what he sought. The failure augmented his terror; he felt as one who has murdered in the dark, not knowing whom nor why. So frightful was the situation—the mysterious light burned with so silent and awful a menace; the noxious plants, the trees that by common consent are invested with a melancholy or baleful character, so openly in his sight conspired against his peace; from overhead and all about came so audible and startling whispers and the sighs of creatures so obviously not of earth—that he could endure it no longer, and with a great effort to break some malign spell that bound his faculties to silence and inaction, he shouted with the full strength of his lungs! His voice broken, it seemed, into an infinite multitude of unfamiliar sounds, went babbling and stammering away into the distant reaches of the forest, died into silence, and all was as before. But he had made a beginning at resistance and was encouraged. He said:

"I will not submit unheard. There may be powers that are not malignant traveling this accursed road. I shall leave them a record and an appeal. I shall relate my wrongs, the persecutions that I endure—I, a helpless mortal, a penitent, an unoffending poet!" Halpin Frayser was a poet only as he was a penitent: in his dream.

Taking from his clothing a small red-leather pocketbook, one-half of which was leaved for memoranda, he discovered that he was without a pencil. He broke a twig from a bush, dipped it into a pool of blood and wrote rapidly. He had hardly touched the paper with the point of his twig when a low, wild peal of laughter broke out at a measureless distance away, and growing ever louder, seemed approaching ever nearer; a soulless, heartless, and unjoyous laugh, like that of the loon, solitary by the lakeside at midnight; a laugh which culminated in an unearthly shout close at hand, then died away by slow gradations, as if the accursed being that uttered it had withdrawn over the verge of the world whence it had come. But the man felt that this was not so—that it was near by and had not moved.

A strange sensation began slowly to take possession of his body and his mind. He could not have said which, if any, of his senses was affected; he felt it rather as a consciousness—a mysterious mental assurance of some overpowering presence—some supernatural malevolence different in kind from the invisible existences that swarmed about him, and superior to them in power. He knew that it had uttered that hideous laugh. And now it seemed to be approaching him; from what direction he did not know—dared not conjecture. All his former fears were forgotten or merged in the gigantic terror that now held him in thrall. Apart from that, he had but one thought: to complete his written appeal to the benign powers who, traversing the haunted wood, might some time rescue him if he should be denied the blessing of annihilation. He wrote with terrible rapidity, the

twig in his fingers rilling blood without renewal; but in the middle of
a sentence his hands denied their service to his will, his arms fell to
his sides, the book to the earth; and powerless to move or cry out, he
found himself staring into the sharply drawn face and blank, dead
eyes of his own mother, standing white and silent in the garments of
the grave!

II

In his youth Halpin Frayser had lived with his parents in Nashville, Tennessee. The Fraysers were well-to-do, having a good position in such society as had survived the wreck wrought by civil war.
Their children had the social and educational opportunities of their
time and place, and had responded to good associations and instruction with agreeable manners and cultivated minds. Halpin being
the youngest and not over robust was perhaps a trifle "spoiled." He
had the double disadvantage of a mother's assiduity and a father's
neglect. Frayser *père* was what no Southern man of means is not—a
politician. His country, or rather his section and State, made demands
upon his time and attention so exacting that to those of his family
he was compelled to turn an ear partly deafened by the thunder of
the political captains and the shouting, his own included.

Young Halpin was of a dreamy, indolent and rather romantic
turn, somewhat more addicted to literature than law, the profession
to which he was bred. Among those of his relations who professed
the modern faith of heredity it was well understood that in him the
character of the late Myron Bayne, a maternal great-grandfather,
had revisited the glimpses of the moon—by which orb Bayne had in
his lifetime been sufficiently affected to be a poet of no small Colonial
distinction. If not specially observed, it was observable that while a
Frayser who was not the proud possessor of a sumptuous copy of the
ancestral "poetical works" (printed at the family expense, and long
ago withdrawn from an inhospitable market) was a rare Frayser indeed, there was an illogical indisposition to honor the great deceased
in the person of his spiritual successor. Halpin was pretty generally
deprecated as an intellectual black sheep who was likely at any moment to disgrace the flock by bleating in meter. The Tennessee
Fraysers were a practical folk—not practical in the popular sense of
devotion to sordid pursuits, but having a robust contempt for any
qualities unfitting a man for the wholesome vocation of politics.

In justice to young Halpin it should be said that while in him were

pretty faithfully reproduced most of the mental and moral characteristics ascribed by history and family tradition to the famous Colonial
bard, his succession to the gift and faculty divine was purely in-
ferential. Not only had he never been known to court the muse, but
in truth he could not have written correctly a line of verse to save
himself from the Killer of the Wise. Still, there was no knowing
when the dormant faculty might wake and smite the lyre.

In the meantime the young man was rather a loose fish, anyhow.
Between him and his mother was the most perfect sympathy, for
secretly the lady was herself a devout disciple of the late and great
Myron Bayne, though with the tact so generally and justly admired
in her sex (despite the hardy calumniators who insist that it is es-
sentially the same thing as cunning) she had always taken care to
conceal her weakness from all eyes but those of him who shared it.
Their common guilt in respect of that was an added tie between
them. If in Halpin's youth his mother had "spoiled" him, he had
assuredly done his part toward being spoiled. As he grew to such
manhood as is attainable by a Southerner who does not care which
way elections go the attachment between him and his beautiful
mother—whom from early childhood he had called Katy—became
yearly stronger and more tender. In these two romantic natures was
manifest in a signal way that neglected phenomenon, the dominance
of the sexual element in all the relations of life, strengthening,
softening, and beautifying even those of consanguinity. The two
were nearly inseparable, and by strangers observing their manner
were not infrequently mistaken for lovers.

Entering his mother's boudoir one day Halpin Frayser kissed her
upon the forehead, toyed for a moment with a lock of her dark hair
which had escaped from its confining pins, and said, with an obvious
effort at calmness:

"Would you greatly mind, Katy, if I were called away to California
for a few weeks?"

It was hardly needful for Katy to answer with her lips a question
to which her telltale cheeks had made instant reply. Evidently she
would greatly mind; and the tears, too, sprang into her large brown
eyes as corroborative testimony.

"Ah, my son," she said, looking up into his face with infinite tenderness, "I should have known that this was coming. Did I not lie
awake a half of the night weeping because, during the other half,
Grandfather Bayne had come to me in a dream, and standing by his
portrait—young, too, and handsome as that—pointed to yours on the
same wall? And when I looked it seemed that I could not see the

features; you had been painted with a face cloth, such as we put upon the dead. Your father has laughed at me, but you and I, dear, know that such things are not for nothing. And I saw below the edge of the cloth the marks of hands on your throat—forgive me, but we have not been used to keep such things from each other. Perhaps you have another interpretation. Perhaps it does not mean that you will go to California. Or maybe you will take me with you?"

It must be confessed that this ingenious interpretation of the dream in the light of newly discovered evidence did not wholly commend itself to the son's more logical mind; he had, for the moment at least, a conviction that it foreshadowed a more simple and immediate, if less tragic, disaster than a visit to the Pacific Coast. It was Halpin Frayser's impression that he was to be garroted on his native heath.

"Are there not medicinal springs in California?" Mrs. Frayser resumed before he had time to give her the true reading of the dream —"places where one recovers from rheumatism and neuralgia? Look —my fingers feel so stiff; and I am almost sure they have been giving me great pain while I slept."

She held out her hands for his inspection. What diagnosis of her case the young man may have thought it best to conceal with a smile the historian is unable to state, but for himself he feels bound to say that fingers looking less stiff, and showing fewer evidences of even insensible pain, have seldom been submitted for medical inspection by even the fairest patient desiring a prescription of unfamiliar scenes.

The outcome of it was that of these two odd persons having equally odd notions of duty, the one went to California, as the interest of his client required, and the other remained at home in compliance with a wish that her husband was scarcely conscious of entertaining.

While in San Francisco Halpin Frayser was walking one dark night along the water front of the city, when, with a suddenness that surprised and disconcerted him, he became a sailor. He was in fact "shanghaied" aboard a gallant, gallant ship, and sailed for a far countree. Nor did his misfortunes end with the voyage; for the ship was cast ashore on an island of the South Pacific, and it was six years afterward when the survivors were taken off by a venturesome trading schooner and brought back to San Francisco.

Though poor in purse, Frayser was no less proud in spirit than he had been in the years that seemed ages and ages ago. He would accept no assistance from strangers, and it was while living with a fellow survivor near the town of St. Helena, awaiting news and remittances from home, that he had gone gunning and dreaming.

III

The apparition confronting the dreamer in the haunted wood—the thing so like, yet so unlike his mother—was horrible! It stirred no love nor longing in his heart; it came unattended with pleasant memories of a golden past—inspired no sentiment of any kind; all the finer emotions were swallowed up in fear. He tried to turn and run from before it, but his legs were as lead; he was unable to lift his feet from the ground. His arms hung helpless at his sides; of his eyes only he retained control, and these he dared not remove from the lusterless orbs of the apparition, which he knew was not a soul without a body, but that most dreadful of all existences infesting that haunted wood —a body without a soul! In its blank stare was neither love, nor pity, nor intelligence—nothing to which to address an appeal for mercy. "An appeal will not lie," he thought, with an absurd reversion to professional slang, making the situation more horrible, as the fire of a cigar might light up a tomb.

For a time, which seemed so long that the world grew gray with age and sin, and the haunted forest, having fulfilled its purpose in this monstrous culmination of its terrors, vanished out of his consciousness with all its sights and sounds, the apparition stood within a pace, regarding him with the mindless malevolence of a wild brute; then thrust its hands forward and sprang upon him with appalling ferocity! The act released his physical energies without unfettering his will; his mind was still spellbound, but his powerful body and agile limbs, endowed with a blind, insensate life of their own, resisted stoutly and well. For an instant he seemed to see this unnatural contest between a dead intelligence and a breathing mechanism only as a spectator—such fancies are in dreams; then he regained his identity almost as if by a leap forward into his body, and the straining automaton had a directing will as alert and fierce as that of its hideous antagonist.

But what mortal can cope with a creature of his dream? The imagination creating the enemy is already vanquished; the combat's result is the combat's cause. Despite his struggles—despite his strength and activity, which seemed wasted in a void, he felt the cold fingers close upon his throat. Borne backward to the earth, he saw above him the dead and drawn face within a hand's breadth of his own, and then all was black. A sound as of the beating of distant drums—a murmur of swarming voices, a sharp, far cry signing all to silence, and Halpin Frayser dreamed that he was dead.

IV

A warm, clear night had been followed by a morning of drenching fog. At about the middle of the afternoon of the preceding day a little whiff of light vapor—a mere thickening of the atmosphere, the ghost of a cloud—had been observed clinging to the western side of Mount St. Helena, away up along the barren altitudes near the summit. It was so thin, so diaphanous, so like a fancy made visible, that one would have said: "Look quickly! in a moment it will be gone."

In a moment it was visibly larger and denser. While with one edge it clung to the mountain, with the other it reached farther and farther out into the air above the lower slopes. At the same time it extended itself to north and south, joining small patches of mist that appeared to come out of the mountainside on exactly the same level, with an intelligent design to be absorbed. And so it grew and grew until the summit was shut out of view from the valley, and over the valley itself was an ever-extending canopy, opaque and gray. At Calistoga, which lies near the head of the valley and the foot of the mountain, there were a starless night and a sunless morning. The fog, sinking into the valley, had reached southward, swallowing up ranch after ranch, until it had blotted out the town of St. Helena, nine miles away. The dust in the road was laid; trees were adrip with moisture; birds sat silent in their coverts; the morning light was wan and ghastly, with neither color nor fire.

Two men left the town of St. Helena at the first glimmer of dawn, and walked along the road northward up the valley toward Calistoga. They carried guns on their shoulders, yet no one having knowledge of such matters could have mistaken them for hunters of bird or beast. They were a deputy sheriff from Napa and a detective from San Francisco—Holker and Jaralson, respectively. Their business was man-hunting.

"How far is it?" inquired Holker, as they strode along, their feet stirring white the dust beneath the damp surface of the road.

"The White Church? Only a half mile farther," the other answered. "By the way," he added, "it is neither white nor a church; it is an abandoned schoolhouse, gray with age and neglect. Religious services were once held in it—when it was white, and there is a graveyard that would delight a poet. Can you guess why I sent for you, and told you to come heeled?"

"Oh, I never have bothered you about things of that kind. I've always found you communicative when the time came. But if I may hazard a guess, you want me to help you arrest one of the corpses in the graveyard."

"You remember Branscom?" said Jaralson, treating his companion's wit with the inattention that it deserved.

"The chap who cut his wife's throat? I ought; I wasted a week's work on him and had my expenses for my trouble. There is a reward of five hundred dollars, but none of us ever got a sight of him. You don't mean to say——"

"Yes, I do. He has been under the noses of you fellows all the time. He comes by night to the old graveyard at the White Church."

"The devil! That's where they buried his wife."

"Well, you fellows might have had sense enough to suspect that he would return to her grave some time."

"The very last place that anyone would have expected him to return to."

"But you had exhausted all the other places. Learning your failure at them, I 'laid for him' there."

"And you found him?"

"Damn it! he found *me*. The rascal got the drop on me—regularly held me up and made me travel. It's God's mercy that he didn't go through me. Oh, he's a good one, and I fancy the half of that reward is enough for me if you're needy."

Holker laughed good humoredly, and explained that his creditors were never more importunate.

"I wanted merely to show you the ground, and arrange a plan with you," the detective explained. "I thought it as well for us to be heeled, even in daylight."

"The man must be insane," said the deputy sheriff. "The reward is for his capture and conviction. If he's mad he won't be convicted."

Mr. Holker was so profoundly affected by that possible failure of justice that he involuntarily stopped in the middle of the road, then resumed his walk with abated zeal.

"Well, he looks it," assented Jaralson. "I'm bound to admit that a more unshaven, unshorn, unkempt, and uneverything wretch I never saw outside the ancient and honorable order of tramps. But I've gone in for him, and can't make up my mind to let go. There's glory in it for us, anyhow. Not another soul knows that he is this side of the Mountains of the Moon."

"All right," Holker said; "we will go and view the ground," and he added, in the words of a once favorite inscription for tombstones: "'where you must shortly lie'—I mean, if old Branscom ever gets tired of you and your impertinent intrusion. By the way, I heard the other day that 'Branscom' was not his real name."

"What is?"

"I can't recall it. I had lost all interest in the wretch, and it did not fix itself in my memory—something like Pardee. The woman whose throat he had the bad taste to cut was a widow when he met her. She had come to California to look up some relatives—there are persons who will do that sometimes. But you know all that."

"Naturally."

"But not knowing the right name, by what happy inspiration did you find the right grave? The man who told me what the name was said it had been cut on the headboard."

"I don't know the right grave." Jaralson was apparently a trifle reluctant to admit his ignorance of so important a point of his plan. "I have been watching about the place generally. A part of our work this morning will be to identify that grave. Here is the White Church."

For a long distance the road had been bordered by fields on both sides, but now on the left there was a forest of oaks, madroños, and gigantic spruces whose lower parts only could be seen, dim and ghostly in the fog. The undergrowth was, in places, thick, but nowhere impenetrable. For some moments Holker saw nothing of the building, but as they turned into the woods it revealed itself in faint gray outline through the fog, looking huge and far away. A few steps more, and it was within an arm's length, distinct, dark with moisture, and insignificant in size. It had the usual country-schoolhouse form—belonged to the packing-box order of architecture; had an underpinning of stones, a moss-grown roof, and blank window spaces, whence both glass and sash had long departed. It was ruined, but not a ruin—a typical Californian substitute for what are known to guide-bookers abroad as "monuments of the past." With scarcely a glance at this uninteresting structure Jaralson moved on into the dripping undergrowth beyond.

"I will show you where he held me up," he said. "This is the graveyard."

Here and there among the bushes were small inclosures containing graves, sometimes no more than one. They were recognized as graves by the discolored stones or rotting boards at head and foot, leaning at all angles, some prostrate; by the ruined picket fences surrounding them; or, infrequently, by the mound itself showing its gravel through the fallen leaves. In many instances nothing marked the spot where lay the vestiges of some poor mortal—who, leaving "a large circle of sorrowing friends," had been left by them in turn—except a depression in the earth, more lasting than that in the spirits of the mourners. The paths, if any paths had been, were long obliterated; trees of a considerable size had been permitted to grow up from the graves and thrust aside with root or branch the inclosing fences. Over all was that air of abandonment and decay which seems nowhere so fit and significant as in a village of the forgotten dead.

As the two men, Jaralson leading, pushed their way through the growth of young trees, that enterprising man suddenly stopped and brought up his shotgun to the height of his breast, uttered a low note of warning, and stood motionless, his eyes fixed upon something ahead. As well as he could, obstructed by brush, his companion, though seeing nothing, imitated the posture and so stood, prepared for what might ensue. A moment later Jaralson moved cautiously forward, the other following.

Under the branches of an enormous spruce lay the dead body of a man. Standing silent above it they noted such particulars as first strike the attention—the face, the attitude, the clothing; whatever most promptly and plainly answers the unspoken question of a sympathetic curiosity.

The body lay upon its back, the legs wide apart. One arm was thrust upward, the other outward; but the latter was bent acutely, and the hand was near the throat. Both hands were tightly clenched. The whole attitude was that of desperate but ineffectual resistance to —what?

Near by lay a shotgun and a game bag through the meshes of which was seen the plumage of shot birds. All about were evidences of a furious struggle; small sprouts of poison-oak were bent and denuded of leaf and bark; dead and rotting leaves had been pushed into heaps and ridges on both sides of the legs by the action of other feet than theirs; alongside the hips were unmistakable impressions of human knees.

The nature of the struggle was made clear by a glance at the dead man's throat and face. While breast and hands were white, those were purple—almost black. The shoulders lay upon a low mound, and the head was turned back at an angle otherwise impossible, the expanded eyes staring blankly backward in a direction opposite to that of the feet. From the froth filling the open mouth the tongue protruded, black and swollen. The throat showed horrible contusions; not mere finger-marks, but bruises and lacerations wrought by two strong hands that must have buried themselves in the yielding flesh, maintaining their terrible grasp until long after death. Breast, throat, face, were wet; the clothing was saturated; drops of water, condensed from the fog, studded the hair and mustache.

All this the two men observed without speaking—almost at a glance. Then Holker said:

"Poor devil! he had a rough deal."

Jaralson was making a vigilant circumspection of the forest, his shotgun held in both hands and at full cock, his finger upon the trigger.

"The work of a maniac," he said, without withdrawing his eyes from the inclosing wood. "It was done by Branscom—Pardee."

Something half hidden by the disturbed leaves on the earth caught Holker's attention. It was a red-leather pocketbook. He picked it up and opened it. It contained leaves of white paper for memoranda, and upon the first leaf was the name "Halpin Frayser." Written in red on several succeeding leaves—scrawled as if in haste and barely legible—were the following lines, which Holker read aloud, while his companion continued scanning the dim gray confines of their narrow world and hearing matter of apprehension in the drip of water from every burdened branch:

> "Enthralled by some mysterious spell, I stood
> In the lit gloom of an enchanted wood.
>   The cypress there and myrtle twined their boughs,
> Significant, in baleful brotherhood.
>
> "The brooding willow whispered to the yew;
> Beneath, the deadly nightshade and the rue,
>   With immortelles self-woven into strange
> Funereal shapes, and horrid nettles grew.
>
> "No song of bird nor any drone of bees,
> Nor light leaf lifted by the wholesome breeze:
>   The air was stagnant all, and Silence was
> A living thing that breathed among the trees.
>
> "Conspiring spirits whispered in the gloom,
> Half-heard, the stilly secrets of the tomb.
>   With blood the trees were all adrip; the leaves
> Shone in the witch-light with a ruddy bloom.

"I cried aloud!—the spell, unbroken still,
Rested upon my spirit and my will.
   Unsouled, unhearted, hopeless and forlorn,
I strove with monstrous presages of ill!

"At last the viewless——"

Holker ceased reading; there was no more to read. The manuscript broke off in the middle of a line.

"That sounds like Bayne," said Jaralson, who was something of a scholar in his way. He had abated his vigilance and stood looking down at the body.

"Who's Bayne?" Holker asked rather incuriously.

"Myron Bayne, a chap who flourished in the early years of the nation—more than a century ago. Wrote mighty dismal stuff; I have his collected works. That poem is not among them, but it must have been omitted by mistake."

"It is cold," said Holker; "let us leave here; we must have up the coroner from Napa."

Jaralson said nothing, but made a movement in compliance. Passing the end of the slight elevation of earth upon which the dead man's head and shoulders lay, his foot struck some hard substance under the rotting forest leaves, and he took the trouble to kick it into view. It was a fallen headboard, and painted on it were the hardly decipherable words, "Catherine Larue."

"Larue, Larue!" exclaimed Holker, with sudden animation. "Why, that is the real name of Branscom—not Pardee. And—bless my soul! how it all comes to me—the murdered woman's name had been Frayser!"

"There is some rascally mystery here," said Detective Jaralson. "I hate anything of that kind."

There came to them out of the fog—seemingly from a great distance—the sound of a laugh, a low, deliberate, soulless laugh, which had no more of joy than that of a hyena night-prowling in the desert; a laugh that rose by slow gradation, louder and louder, clearer, more distinct and terrible, until it seemed barely outside the narrow circle of their vision; a laugh so unnatural, so unhuman, so devilish, that it filled those hardy man-hunters with a sense of dread unspeakable! They did not move their weapons nor think of them; the menace of that horrible sound was not of the kind to be met with arms. As it had grown out of silence, so now it died away; from a culminating shout which had seemed almost in their ears, it drew itself away into the distance, until its failing notes, joyless and mechanical to the last, sank to silence at a measureless remove.

❊   ❊   ❊

A WATCHER BY THE DEAD

I

In an upper room of an unoccupied dwelling in the part of San Francisco known as North Beach lay the body of a man, under a sheet. The hour was near nine in the evening; the room was dimly lighted by a single candle. Although the weather was warm, the two windows, contrary to the custom which gives the dead plenty of air, were closed and the blinds drawn down. The furniture of the room consisted of but three pieces—an arm-chair, a small reading-stand supporting the candle, and a long kitchen table, supporting the body of the man. All these, as also the corpse, seemed to have been recently brought in, for an observer, had there been one, would have seen that all were free from dust, whereas everything else in the room was pretty thickly coated with it, and there were cobwebs in the angles of the walls.

Under the sheet the outlines of the body could be traced, even the features, these having that unnaturally sharp definition which seems to belong to faces of the dead, but is really characteristic of those only that have been wasted by disease. From the silence of the room one would rightly have inferred that it was not in the front of the house, facing a street. It really faced nothing but a high breast of rock, the rear of the building being set into a hill.

As a neighboring church clock was striking nine with an indolence which seemed to imply such an indifference to the flight of time that one could hardly help wondering why it took the trouble to strike at all, the single door of the room was opened and a man entered, advancing toward the body. As he did so the door closed, apparently of its own volition; there was a grating, as of a key turned with difficulty, and the snap of the lock bolt as it shot into its socket. A sound of retiring footsteps in the passage outside ensued, and the man was to all appearance a prisoner. Advancing to the table, he

stood a moment looking down at the body; then with a slight shrug
of the shoulders walked over to one of the windows and hoisted the
blind. The darkness outside was absolute, the panes were covered
with dust, but by wiping this away he could see that the window
was fortified with strong iron bars crossing it within a few inches
of the glass and imbedded in the masonry on each side. He examined
the other window. It was the same. He manifested no great curiosity in the matter, did not even so much as raise the sash. If he was
a prisoner he was apparently a tractable one. Having completed his
examination of the room, he seated himself in the arm-chair, took a
book from his pocket, drew the stand with its candle alongside and
began to read.

The man was young—not more than thirty—dark in complexion,
smooth-shaven, with brown hair. His face was thin and high-nosed,
with a broad forehead and a "firmness" of the chin and jaw which
is said by those having it to denote resolution. The eyes were gray
and steadfast, not moving except with definitive purpose. They were
now for the greater part of the time fixed upon his book, but he occasionally withdrew them and turned them to the body on the table,
not, apparently, from any dismal fascination which under such circumstances it might be supposed to exercise upon even a courageous
person, nor with a conscious rebellion against the contrary influence
which might dominate a timid one. He looked at it as if in his reading he had come upon something recalling him to a sense of his
surroundings. Clearly this watcher by the dead was discharging his
trust with intelligence and composure, as became him.

After reading for perhaps a half-hour he seemed to come to the
end of a chapter and quietly laid away the book. He then rose and
taking the reading-stand from the floor carried it into a corner of
the room near one of the windows, lifted the candle from it and returned to the empty fireplace before which he had been sitting.

A moment later he walked over to the body on the table, lifted
the sheet and turned it back from the head, exposing a mass of dark
hair and a thin face-cloth, beneath which the features showed with
even sharper definition than before. Shading his eyes by interpos-
ing his free hand between them and the candle, he stood looking at
his motionless companion with a serious and tranquil regard. Satisfied with his inspection, he pulled the sheet over the face again
and returning to the chair, took some matches off the candlestick,
put them in the side pocket of his sack-coat and sat down. He then
lifted the candle from its socket and looked at it critically, as if cal-

culating how long it would last. It was barely two inches long; in another hour he would be in darkness. He replaced it in the candlestick and blew it out.

II

In a physician's office in Kearny Street three men sat about a table, drinking punch and smoking. It was late in the evening, almost midnight, indeed, and there had been no lack of punch. The gravest of the three, Dr. Helberson, was the host—it was in his rooms they sat. He was about thirty years of age; the others were even younger; all were physicians.

"The superstitious awe with which the living regard the dead," said Dr. Helberson, "is hereditary and incurable. One needs no more be ashamed of it than of the fact that he inherits, for example, an incapacity for mathematics, or a tendency to lie."

The others laughed. "Oughtn't a man to be ashamed to lie?" asked the youngest of the three, who was in fact a medical student not yet graduated.

"My dear Harper, I said nothing about that. The tendency to lie is one thing; lying is another."

"But do you think," said the third man, "that this superstitious feeling, this fear of the dead, reasonless as we know it to be, is universal? I am myself not conscious of it."

"Oh, but it is 'in your system' for all that," replied Helberson; "it needs only the right conditions—what Shakespeare calls the 'confederate season'—to manifest itself in some very disagreeable way that will open your eyes. Physicians and soldiers are of course more nearly free from it than others."

"Physicians and soldiers!—why don't you add hangmen and headsmen? Let us have in all the assassin classes."

"No, my dear Mancher; the juries will not let the public executioners acquire sufficient familiarity with death to be altogether unmoved by it."

Young Harper, who had been helping himself to a fresh cigar at the sideboard, resumed his seat. "What would you consider conditions under which any man of woman born would become insupportably conscious of his share of our common weakness in this regard?" he asked, rather verbosely.

"Well, I should say that if a man were locked up all night with a corpse—alone—in a dark room—of a vacant house—with no bed covers to pull over his head—and lived through it without going altogether mad, he might justly boast himself not of woman born, nor yet, like Macduff, a product of Cæsarean section."

"I thought you never would finish piling up conditions," said Harper, "but I know a man who is neither a physician nor a soldier who will accept them all, for any stake you like to name."

"Who is he?"

"His name is Jarette—a stranger here; comes from my town in New York. I have no money to back him, but he will back himself with loads of it."

"How do you know that?"

"He would rather bet than eat. As for fear—I dare say he thinks it some cutaneous disorder, or possibly a particular kind of religious heresy."

"What does he look like?" Helberson was evidently becoming interested.

"Like Mancher, here—might be his twin brother."

"I accept the challenge," said Helberson, promptly.

"Awfully obliged to you for the compliment, I'm sure," drawled Mancher, who was growing sleepy. "Can't I get into this?"

"Not against me," Helberson said. "I don't want *your* money."

"All right," said Mancher; "I'll be the corpse."

The others laughed.

The outcome of this crazy conversation we have seen.

III

In extinguishing his meagre allowance of candle Mr. Jarette's object was to preserve it against some unforeseen need. He may have thought, too, or half thought, that the darkness would be no worse at one time than another, and if the situation became insupportable it would be better to have a means of relief, or even release. At any rate it was wise to have a little reserve of light, even if only to enable him to look at his watch.

No sooner had he blown out the candle and set it on the floor at his side than he settled himself comfortably in the arm-chair, leaned back and closed his eyes, hoping and expecting to sleep. In this he was disappointed; he had never in his life felt less sleepy, and in a few minutes he gave up the attempt. But what could he do? He could not go groping about in absolute darkness at the risk of bruising himself—at the risk, too, of blundering against the table and rudely disturbing the dead. We all recognize their right to lie at rest, with immunity from all that is harsh and violent. Jarette almost succeeded in making himself believe that considerations of this kind restrained him from risking the collision and fixed him to the chair.

While thinking of this matter he fancied that he heard a faint sound in the direction of the table—what kind of sound he could hardly have explained. He did not turn his head. Why should he— in the darkness? But he listened—why should he not? And listening he grew giddy and grasped the arms of the chair for support. There was a strange ringing in his ears; his head seemed bursting; his chest was oppressed by the constriction of his clothing. He wondered why it was so, and whether these were symptoms of fear. Then, with a long and strong expiration, his chest appeared to collapse, and with the great gasp with which he refilled his exhausted lungs the vertigo left him and he knew that so intently had he listened that he had held his breath almost to suffocation. The revelation was vexatious; he arose, pushed away the chair with his foot and strode to the centre of the room. But one does not stride far in darkness; he began to grope, and finding the wall followed it to an angle, turned, followed it past the two windows and there in another corner came into violent contact with the reading-stand, overturning it. It made a clatter that startled him. He was annoyed. "How the devil could I have forgotten where it was?" he muttered, and groped his way along the third wall to the fireplace. "I must put things to rights," said he, feeling the floor for the candle.

Having recovered that, he lighted it and instantly turned his eyes to the table, where, naturally, nothing had undergone any change. The reading-stand lay unobserved upon the floor: he had forgotten to "put it to rights." He looked all about the room, dispersing the deeper shadows by movements of the candle in his hand, and crossing over to the door tested it by turning and pulling the knob with all his strength. It did not yield and this seemed to afford him a certain satisfaction; indeed, he secured it more firmly by a bolt which he had not before observed. Returning to his chair, he looked at his watch; it was half-past nine. With a start of surprise he held the watch at his ear. It had not stopped. The candle was now visibly shorter. He again extinguished it, placing it on the floor at his side as before.

Mr. Jarette was not at his ease; he was distinctly dissatisfied with his surroundings, and with himself for being so. "What have I to fear?" he thought. "This is ridiculous and disgraceful; I will not be so great a fool." But courage does not come of saying, "I will be courageous," nor of recognizing its appropriateness to the occasion. The more Jarette condemned himself, the more reason he gave himself for condemnation; the greater the number of variations which he played upon the simple theme of the harmlessness of the dead, the more insupportable grew the discord of his emotions. "What!" he cried aloud in the anguish of his spirit, "what! shall I, who have not a shade of superstition in my nature—I, who have no belief in immortality—I, who know (and never more clearly than now) that the after-life is the dream of a desire—shall I lose at once my bet, my honor and my self-respect, perhaps my reason, because certain savage ancestors dwelling in caves and burrows conceived the monstrous notion that the dead walk by night?—that——" Distinctly, unmistakably, Mr. Jarette heard behind him a light, soft sound of footfalls, deliberate, regular, successively nearer!

IV

Just before daybreak the next morning Dr. Helberson and his young friend Harper were driving slowly through the streets of North Beach in the doctor's coupé.

"Have you still the confidence of youth in the courage or stolidity of your friend?" said the elder man. "Do you believe that I have lost this wager?"

"I *know* you have," replied the other, with enfeebling emphasis. "Well, upon my soul, I hope so."

It was spoken earnestly, almost solemnly. There was a silence for a few moments.

"Harper," the doctor resumed, looking very serious in the shifting half-lights that entered the carriage as they passed the street lamps, "I don't feel altogether comfortable about this business. If your friend had not irritated me by the contemptuous manner in which he treated my doubt of his endurance—a purely physical quality—and by the cool incivility of his suggestion that the corpse be that of a physician, I should not have gone on with it. If anything should happen we are ruined, as I fear we deserve to be."

"What can happen? Even if the matter should be taking a serious turn, of which I am not at all afraid, Mancher has only to 'resurrect' himself and explain matters. With a genuine 'subject' from the dissecting-room, or one of your late patients, it might be different."

Dr. Mancher, then, had been as good as his promise; he was the "corpse."

Dr. Helberson was silent for a long time, as the carriage, at a snail's pace, crept along the same street it had traveled two or three times already. Presently he spoke: "Well, let us hope that Mancher, if he has had to rise from the dead, has been discreet about it. A mistake in that might make matters worse instead of better."

"Yes," said Harper, "Jarette would kill him. But, Doctor"—looking at his watch as the carriage passed a gas lamp—"it is nearly four o'clock at last."

A moment later the two had quitted the vehicle and were walking briskly toward the long-unoccupied house belonging to the doctor in which they had immured Mr. Jarette in accordance with the terms of the mad wager. As they neared it they met a man running. "Can you tell me," he cried, suddenly checking his speed, "where I can find a doctor?"

"What's the matter?" Helberson asked, non-committal.

"Go and see for yourself," said the man, resuming his running.

They hastened on. Arrived at the house, they saw several persons entering in haste and excitement. In some of the dwellings near by and across the way the chamber windows were thrown up, showing a protrusion of heads. All heads were asking questions, none heeding the questions of the others. A few of the windows with closed blinds were illuminated; the inmates of those rooms were dressing to come down. Exactly opposite the door of the house that they sought a street lamp threw a yellow, insufficient light upon the scene, seeming to say that it could disclose a good deal more if it wished. Harper paused at the door and laid a hand upon his companion's arm. "It is all up with us, Doctor," he said in extreme agitation, which contrasted strangely with his free-and-easy words; "the game has gone against us all. Let's not go in there; I'm for lying low."

"I'm a physician," said Dr. Helberson, calmly; "there may be need of one."

They mounted the doorsteps and were about to enter. The door was open; the street lamp opposite lighted the passage into which it opened. It was full of men. Some had ascended the stairs at the farther end, and, denied admittance above, waited for better fortune. All were talking, none listening. Suddenly, on the upper landing there was a great commotion; a man had sprung out of a door and was breaking away from those endeavoring to detain him. Down through the mass of affrighted idlers he came, pushing them aside, flattening them against the wall on one side, or compelling them to cling to the rail on the other, clutching them by the throat, striking them savagely, thrusting them back down the stairs and walking over the fallen. His clothing was in disorder, he was without a hat.

His eyes, wild and restless, had in them something more terrifying than his apparently superhuman strength. His face, smooth-shaven, was bloodless, his hair frost-white.

As the crowd at the foot of the stairs, having more freedom, fell away to let him pass Harper sprang forward. "Jarette! Jarette!" he cried. Dr. Helberson seized Harper by the collar and dragged him back. The man looked into their faces without seeming to see them and sprang through the door, down the steps, into the street, and away. A stout policeman, who had had inferior success in conquering his way down the stairway, followed a moment later and started in pursuit, all the heads in the windows—those of women and children now—screaming in guidance.

The stairway being now partly cleared, most of the crowd having rushed down to the street to observe the flight and pursuit, Dr. Helberson mounted to the landing, followed by Harper. At a door in the upper passage an officer denied them admittance. "We are physicians," said the doctor, and they passed in. The room was full of men, dimly seen, crowded about a table. The newcomers edged their way forward and looked over the shoulders of those in the front rank. Upon the table, the lower limbs covered with a sheet, lay the body of a man, brilliantly illuminated by the beam of a bull's-eye lantern held by a policeman standing at the feet. The others, excepting those near the head—the officer himself—all were in darkness. The face of the body showed yellow, repulsive, horrible! The eyes were partly open and upturned and the jaw fallen; traces of froth defiled the lips, the chin, the cheeks. A tall man, evidently a doctor, bent over the body with his hand thrust under the shirt front. He withdrew it and placed two fingers in the open mouth. "This man has been about six hours dead," said he. "It is a case for the coroner."

He drew a card from his pocket, handed it to the officer and made his way toward the door.

"Clear the room—out, all!" said the officer, sharply, and the body disappeared as if it had been snatched away, as shifting the lantern he flashed its beam of light here and there against the faces of the crowd. The effect was amazing! The men, blinded, confused, almost terrified, made a tumultuous rush for the door, pushing, crowding, and tumbling over one another as they fled, like the hosts of Night before the shafts of Apollo. Upon the struggling, trampling mass the officer poured his light without pity and without cessation. Caught in the current, Helberson and Harper were swept out of the room and cascaded down the stairs into the street.

"Good God, Doctor! did I not tell you that Jarette would kill him?" said Harper, as soon as they were clear of the crowd.

"I believe you did," replied the other, without apparent emotion.

They walked on in silence, block after block. Against the graying east the dwellings of the hill tribes showed in silhouette. The familiar milk wagon was already astir in the streets; the baker's man would soon come upon the scene; the newspaper carrier was abroad in the land.

"It strikes me, youngster," said Helberson, "that you and I have been having too much of the morning air lately. It is unwholesome; we need a change. What do you say to a tour in Europe?"

"When?"

"I'm not particular. I should suppose that four o'clock this afternoon would be early enough."

"I'll meet you at the boat," said Harper.

v

Seven years afterward these two men sat upon a bench in Madison Square, New York, in familiar conversation. Another man, who had been observing them for some time, himself unobserved, approached and, courteously lifting his hat from locks as white as frost, said: "I beg your pardon, gentlemen, but when you have killed a man by coming to life, it is best to change clothes with him, and at the first opportunity make a break for liberty."

Helberson and Harper exchanged significant glances. They were obviously amused. The former then looked the stranger kindly in the eye and replied:

"That has always been my plan. I entirely agree with you as to its advant——"

He stopped suddenly, rose and went white. He stared at the man, open-mouthed; he trembled visibly.

"Ah!" said the stranger, "I see that you are indisposed, Doctor. If you cannot treat yourself Dr. Harper can do something for you, I am sure."

"Who the devil are you?" said Harper, bluntly.

The stranger came nearer and, bending toward them, said in a whisper: "I call myself Jarette sometimes, but I don't mind telling you, for old friendship, that I am Dr. William Mancher."

The revelation brought Harper to his feet. "Mancher!" he cried; and Helberson added: "It is true, by God!"

"Yes," said the stranger, smiling vaguely, "it is true enough, no doubt."

He hesitated and seemed to be trying to recall something, then began humming a popular air. He had apparently forgotten their presence.

"Look here, Mancher," said the elder of the two, "tell us just what occurred that night—to Jarette, you know."

"Oh, yes, about Jarette," said the other. "It's odd I should have neglected to tell you—I tell it so often. You see I knew, by overhearing him talking to himself, that he was pretty badly frightened. So I couldn't resist the temptation to come to life and have a bit of fun out of him—I couldn't really. That was all right, though certainly I did not think he would take it so seriously; I did not, truly. And afterward—well, it was a tough job changing places with him, and then—damn you! you didn't let me out!"

Nothing could exceed the ferocity with which these last words were delivered. Both men stepped back in alarm.

"We?—why—why," Helberson stammered, losing his self-possession utterly, "we had nothing to do with it."

"Didn't I say you were Drs. Hell-born and Sharper?" inquired the man, laughing.

"My name is Helberson, yes; and this gentleman is Mr. Harper," replied the former, reassured by the laugh. "But we are not physicians now; we are—well, hang it, old man, we are gamblers."

And that was the truth.

"A very good profession—very good, indeed; and, by the way, I hope Sharper here paid over Jarette's money like an honest stakeholder. A very good and honorable profession," he repeated, thoughtfully, moving carelessly away; "but I stick to the old one. I am High Supreme Medical Officer of the Bloomingdale Asylum; it is my duty to cure the superintendent."

❅   ❅   ❅

THE MAN AND THE SNAKE

It is of veritabyll report, and attested of so many that there be nowe of wyse and learned none to gaynsaye it, that yᵉ serpente hys eye hath a magnetick propertie that whosoe falleth into its svasion is drawn forwards in despyte of his wille, and perisheth miserabyll by yᵉ creature hys byte.

Stretched at ease upon a sofa, in gown and slippers, Harker Brayton smiled as he read the foregoing sentence in old Morryster's *Marvells of Science.* "The only marvel in the matter," he said to himself, "is that the wise and learned in Morryster's day should have believed such nonsense as is rejected by most of even the ignorant in ours."

A train of reflection followed—for Brayton was a man of thought —and he unconsciously lowered his book without altering the direction of his eyes. As soon as the volume had gone below the line of sight, something in an obscure corner of the room recalled his attention to his surroundings. What he saw, in the shadow under his bed, was two small points of light, apparently about an inch apart. They might have been reflections of the gas jet above him, in metal nail heads; he gave them but little thought and resumed his reading. A moment later something—some impulse which it did not occur to him to analyze—impelled him to lower the book again and seek for what he saw before. The points of light were still there. They seemed to have become brighter than before, shining with a greenish lustre that he had not at first observed. He thought, too, that they might have moved a trifle—were somewhat nearer. They were still too much in shadow, however, to reveal their nature and origin to an indolent attention, and again he resumed his reading. Suddenly something in the text suggested a thought that made him start and drop the book for the third time to the side of the sofa, whence, escaping from his hand, it fell sprawling to the floor, back upward. Brayton, half-risen, was staring intently into the obscurity beneath the bed, where the points of light shone with, it seemed to him, an added fire. His attention was now fully aroused, his gaze eager and imperative. It disclosed, almost directly under the foot-rail of the bed, the coils of a large serpent—the points of light were its eyes! Its horrible head, thrust flatly forth from the innermost coil and resting upon the outermost, was directed straight toward him, the definition of the wide, brutal jaw and the idiot-like forehead serving to show the direction of its malevolent gaze. The eyes were no longer merely luminous points; they looked into his own with a meaning, a malign significance.

II

A snake in a bedroom of a modern city dwelling of the better sort is, happily, not so common a phenomenon as to make explanation altogether needless. Harker Brayton, a bachelor of thirty-five, a scholar, idler and something of an athlete, rich, popular and of sound health, had returned to San Francisco from all manner of remote and unfamiliar countries. His tastes, always a trifle luxurious, had taken on an added exuberance from long privation; and the resources of even the Castle Hotel being inadequate to their perfect gratification, he had gladly accepted the hospitality of his friend, Dr. Druring, the distinguished scientist. Dr. Druring's house, a large, old-fashioned one in what is now an obscure quarter of the city, had an outer and visible aspect of proud reserve. It plainly would not associate with the contiguous elements of its altered environment, and appeared to have developed some of the eccentricities which come of isolation. One of these was a "wing," conspicuously irrelevant in point of architecture, and no less rebellious in matter of purpose; for it was a combination of laboratory, menagerie and museum. It was here that the doctor indulged the scientific side of his nature in the study of such forms of animal life as engaged his interest and comforted his taste—which, it must be confessed, ran rather to the lower types. For one of the higher nimbly and sweetly to recommend itself unto his gentle senses it had at least to retain certain rudimentary characteristics allying it to such "dragons of the prime" as toads and snakes. His scientific sympathies were distinctly reptilian; he loved nature's vulgarians and described himself as the Zola of zoölogy. His wife and daughters not having the advantage to share his enlightened curiosity regarding the works and ways of our ill-starred fellow-creatures, were with needless austerity excluded from what he called the Snakery and doomed to companionship with their own kind, though to soften the rigors of their lot he had permitted them out of his great wealth to outdo the reptiles in the gorgeousness of their surroundings and to shine with a superior splendor.

Architecturally and in point of "furnishing" the Snakery had a severe simplicity befitting the humble circumstances of its occupants, many of whom, indeed, could not safely have been intrusted with the liberty that is necessary to the full enjoyment of luxury, for they have the troublesome peculiarity of being alive. In their own apartments, however, they were under as little personal restraint as was compatible with their protection from the baneful habit of swallowing one another; and, as Brayton had thoughtfully been apprised, it was more than a tradition that some of them had at divers times been found in parts of the premises where it would have embarrassed them to explain their presence. Despite the Snakery and its uncanny associations—to which, indeed, he gave little attention—Brayton found life at the Druring mansion very much to his mind.

III

Beyond a smart shock of surprise and a shudder of mere loathing Mr. Brayton was not greatly affected. His first thought was to ring the call bell and bring a servant; but although the bell cord dangled within easy reach he made no movement toward it; it had occurred to his mind that the act might subject him to the suspicion of fear, which he certainly did not feel. He was more keenly conscious of the incongruous nature of the situation than affected by its perils; it was revolting, but absurd.

The reptile was of a species with which Brayton was unfamiliar. Its length he could only conjecture; the body at the largest visible part seemed about as thick as his forearm. In what way was it dangerous, if in any way? Was it venomous? Was it a constrictor? His knowledge of nature's danger signals did not enable him to say; he had never deciphered the code.

If not dangerous the creature was at least offensive. It was *de trop* —"matter out of place"—an impertinence. The gem was unworthy of the setting. Even the barbarous taste of our time and country, which had loaded the walls of the room with pictures, the floor with furniture and the furniture with bric-a-brac, had not quite fitted the place for this bit of the savage life of the jungle. Besides—insupportable thought!—the exhalations of its breath mingled with the atmosphere which he himself was breathing.

These thoughts shaped themselves with greater or less definition in Brayton's mind and begot action. The process is what we call consideration and decision. It is thus that we are wise and unwise. It is thus that the withered leaf in an autumn breeze shows greater or less intelligence than its fellows, falling upon the land or upon the lake. The secret of human action is an open one: something contracts our muscles. Does it matter if we give to the preparatory molecular changes the name of will?

Brayton rose to his feet and prepared to back softly away from the snake, without disturbing it if possible, and through the door.

Men retire so from the presence of the great, for greatness is power and power is a menace. He knew that he could walk backward without error. Should the monster follow, the taste which had plastered the walls with paintings had consistently supplied a rack of murderous Oriental weapons from which he could snatch one to suit the occasion. In the mean time the snake's eyes burned with a more pitiless malevolence than before.

Brayton lifted his right foot free of the floor to step backward. That moment he felt a strong aversion to doing so.

"I am accounted brave," he thought; "is bravery, then, no more than pride? Because there are none to witness the shame shall I retreat?"

He was steadying himself with his right hand upon the back of a chair, his foot suspended.

"Nonsense!" he said aloud; "I am not so great a coward as to fear to seem to myself afraid."

He lifted the foot a little higher by slightly bending the knee and thrust it sharply to the floor—an inch in front of the other! He could not think how that occurred. A trial with the left foot had the same result; it was again in advance of the right. The hand upon the chair back was grasping it; the arm was straight, reaching somewhat backward. One might have said that he was reluctant to lose his hold. The snake's malignant head was still thrust forth from the inner coil as before, the neck level. It had not moved, but its eyes were now electric sparks, radiating an infinity of luminous needles.

The man had an ashy pallor. Again he took a step forward, and another, partly dragging the chair, which when finally released fell upon the floor with a crash. The man groaned; the snake made neither sound nor motion, but its eyes were two dazzling suns. The reptile itself was wholly concealed by them. They gave off enlarging rings of rich and vivid colors, which at their greatest expansion successively vanished like soap-bubbles; they seemed to approach his very face, and anon were an immeasurable distance away. He heard, somewhere, the continuous throbbing of a great drum, with desultory bursts of far music, inconceivably sweet, like the tones of an æolian harp. He knew it for the sunrise melody of Memnon's statue, and thought he stood in the Nileside reeds hearing with exalted sense that immortal anthem through the silence of the centuries.

The music ceased; rather, it became by insensible degrees the distant roll of a retreating thunder-storm. A landscape, glittering with sun and rain, stretched before him, arched with a vivid rainbow framing in its giant curve a hundred visible cities. In the middle distance a vast serpent, wearing a crown, reared its head out of its voluminous convolutions and looked at him with his dead mother's eyes. Suddenly this enchanting landscape seemed to rise swiftly upward like the drop scene at a theatre, and vanished in a blank. Something struck him a hard blow upon the face and breast. He had fallen to the floor; the blood ran from his broken nose and his bruised lips. For a time he was dazed and stunned, and lay with closed eyes, his face against the floor. In a few moments he had recovered, and then knew that this fall, by withdrawing his eyes, had broken the spell that held him. He felt that now, by keeping his gaze averted, he would be able to retreat. But the thought of the serpent within a few feet of his head, yet unseen—perhaps in the very act of springing upon him and throwing its coils about his throat—was too horrible! He lifted his head, stared again into those baleful eyes and was again in bondage.

The snake had not moved and appeared somewhat to have lost its power upon the imagination; the gorgeous illusions of a few moments before were not repeated. Beneath that flat and brainless brow its black, beady eyes simply glittered as at first with an expression unspeakably malignant. It was as if the creature, assured of its triumph, had determined to practise no more alluring wiles.

Now ensued a fearful scene. The man, prone upon the floor, within a yard of his enemy, raised the upper part of his body upon his elbows, his head thrown back, his legs extended to their full length. His face was white between its stains of blood; his eyes were strained open to their uttermost expansion. There was froth upon his lips; it dropped off in flakes. Strong convulsions ran through his body, making almost serpentile undulations. He bent himself at the waist, shifting his legs from side to side. And every movement left him a little nearer to the snake. He thrust his hands forward to brace himself back, yet constantly advanced upon his elbows.

IV

Dr. Druring and his wife sat in the library. The scientist was in rare good humor.

"I have just obtained by exchange with another collector," he said, "a splendid specimen of the *ophiophagus*."

"And what may that be?" the lady inquired with a somewhat languid interest.

"Why, bless my soul, what profound ignorance! My dear, a man who ascertains after marriage that his wife does not know Greek is entitled to a divorce. The *ophiophagus* is a snake that eats other snakes."

"I hope it will eat all yours," she said, absently shifting the lamp. "But how does it get the other snakes? By charming them, I suppose."

"That is just like you, dear," said the doctor, with an affectation of petulance. "You know how irritating to me is any allusion to that vulgar superstition about a snake's power of fascination."

The conversation was interrupted by a mighty cry, which rang through the silent house like the voice of a demon shouting in a tomb! Again and yet again it sounded, with terrible distinctness. They sprang to their feet, the man confused, the lady pale and speechless with fright. Almost before the echoes of the last cry had died away the doctor was out of the room, springing up the stairs two steps at a time. In the corridor in front of Brayton's chamber he met some servants who had come from the upper floor. Together they rushed at the door without knocking. It was unfastened and gave way. Brayton lay upon his stomach on the floor, dead. His head and arms were partly concealed under the foot rail of the bed. They pulled the body away, turning it upon the back. The face was daubed with blood and froth, the eyes were wide open, staring—a dreadful sight!

"Died in a fit," said the scientist, bending his knee and placing his hand upon the heart. While in that position, he chanced to look under the bed. "Good God!" he added, "how did this thing get in here?"

He reached under the bed, pulled out the snake and flung it, still coiled, to the center of the room, whence with a harsh, shuffling sound it slid across the polished floor till stopped by the wall, where it lay without motion. It was a stuffed snake; its eyes were two shoe buttons.

❋   ❋   ❋

JOHN MORTONSON'S FUNERAL*

* Rough notes of this tale were found among the papers of the late Leigh Bierce. It is printed here with such revision only as the author might himself have made in transcription. (Note by Bierce.)

John Mortonson was dead: his lines in "the tragedy 'Man'" had all been spoken and he had left the stage.

The body rested in a fine mahogany coffin fitted with a plate of glass. All arrangements for the funeral had been so well attended to that had the deceased known he would doubtless have approved. The face, as it showed under the glass, was not disagreeable to look upon: it bore a faint smile, and as the death had been painless, had not been distorted beyond the repairing power of the undertaker. At two o'clock of the afternoon the friends were to assemble to pay their last tribute of respect to one who had no further need of friends and respect. The surviving members of the family came severally every few minutes to the casket and wept above the placid features beneath the glass. This did them no good; it did no good to John Mortonson; but in the presence of death reason and philosophy are silent.

As the hour of two approached the friends began to arrive and after offering such consolation to the stricken relatives as the proprieties of the occasion required, solemnly seated themselves about the room with an augmented consciousness of their importance in the scheme funereal. Then the minister came, and in that overshadowing presence the lesser lights went into eclipse. His entrance was followed by that of the widow, whose lamentations filled the room. She approached the casket and after leaning her face against the cold glass for a moment was gently led to a seat near her daughter. Mournfully and low the man of God began his eulogy of the dead, and his doleful voice, mingled with the sobbing which it was its purpose to stimulate and sustain, rose and fell, seemed to come and go, like the sound of a sullen sea. The gloomy day grew darker as he spoke; a curtain of cloud underspread the sky and a few drops of rain fell audibly. It seemed as if all nature were weeping for John Mortonson.

When the minister had finished his eulogy with prayer a hymn was sung and the pallbearers took their places beside the bier. As the last notes of the hymn died away the widow ran to the coffin, cast herself upon it and sobbed hysterically. Gradually, however, she yielded to dissuasion, becoming more composed; and as the minister was in the act of leading her away her eyes sought the face of the dead beneath the glass. She threw up her arms and with a shriek fell backward insensible.

The mourners sprang forward to the coffin, the friends followed, and as the clock on the mantel solemnly struck three all were staring down upon the face of John Mortonson, deceased.

They turned away, sick and faint. One man, trying in his terror to escape the awful sight, stumbled against the coffin so heavily as to knock away one of its frail supports. The coffin fell to the floor, the glass was shattered to bits by the concussion.

From the opening crawled John Mortonson's cat, which lazily leapt to the floor, sat up, tranquilly wiped its crimson muzzle with a forepaw, then walked with dignity from the room.

❋   ❋   ❋

MOXON'S MASTER

"Are you serious?—do you really believe that a machine thinks?"

I got no immediate reply; Moxon was apparently intent upon the coals in the grate, touching them deftly here and there with the fire-poker till they signified a sense of his attention by a brighter glow. For several weeks I had been observing in him a growing habit of delay in answering even the most trivial of commonplace questions. His air, however, was that of preoccupation rather than deliberation: one might have said that he had "something on his mind."

Presently he said:

"What is a 'machine'? The word has been variously defined. Here is one definition from a popular dictionary: 'Any instrument or organization by which power is applied and made effective, or a desired effect produced.' Well, then, is not a man a machine? And you will admit that he thinks—or thinks he thinks."

"If you do not wish to answer my question," I said, rather testily, "why not say so?—all that you say is mere evasion. You know well enough that when I say (machine) I do not mean a man, but something that man has made and controls."

"When it does not control him," he said, rising abruptly and looking out of a window, whence nothing was visible in the blackness of a stormy night. A moment later he turned about and with a smile said: "I beg your pardon; I had no thought of evasion. I considered the dictionary man's unconscious testimony suggestive and worth something in the discussion. I can give your question a direct answer easily enough; I do believe that a machine thinks about the work that it is doing."

That was direct enough, certainly. It was not altogether pleasing, for it tended to confirm a sad suspicion that Moxon's devotion to study and work in his machine-shop had not been good for him. I knew, for one thing, that he suffered from insomnia, and that is no light affliction. Had it affected his mind? His reply to my question seemed to me then evidence that it had; perhaps I should think differently about it now. I was younger then, and among the blessings that are not denied to youth is ignorance. Incited by that great stimulant to controversy, I said:

"And what, pray, does it think with—in the absence of a brain?"

The reply, coming with less than his customary delay, took his favorite form of counter-interrogation:

"With what does a plant think—in the absence of a brain?"

"Ah, plants also belong to the philosopher class! I should be pleased to know some of their conclusions; you may omit the premises."

"Perhaps," he replied, apparently unaffected by my foolish irony, "you may be able to infer their convictions from their acts. I will spare you the familiar examples of the sensitive mimosa, the several insectivorous flowers and those whose stamens bend down and shake their pollen upon the entering bee in order that he may fertilize their distant mates. But observe this. In an open spot in my garden I planted a climbing vine. When it was barely above the surface I set a stake into the soil a yard away. The vine at once made for it, but as it was about to reach it after several days I removed it a few feet. The vine at once altered its course, making an acute angle, and again made for the stake. This manœuvre was repeated several times, but finally, as if discouraged, the vine abandoned the pursuit and ignoring further attempts to divert it traveled to a small tree, further away, which it climbed.

"Roots of the eucalyptus will prolong themselves incredibly in search of moisture. A well-known horticulturist relates that one entered an old drain pipe and followed it until it came to a break, where a section of the pipe had been removed to make way for a stone wall that had been built across its course. The root left the drain and followed the wall until it found an opening where a stone had fallen out. It crept through and following the other side of the wall back to the drain, entered the unexplored part and resumed its journey."

"And all this?"

"Can you miss the significance of it? It shows the consciousness of plants. It proves that they think."

"Even if it did—what then? We were speaking, not of plants, but of machines. They may be composed partly of wood—wood that has no longer vitality—or wholly of metal. Is thought an attribute also of the mineral kingdom?"

"How else do you explain the phenomena, for example, of crystallization?"

"I do not explain them."

"Because you cannot without affirming what you wish to deny, namely, intelligent cooperation among the constituent elements of the crystals. When soldiers form lines, or hollow squares, you call it reason. When wild geese in flight take the form of a letter V you say instinct. When the homogeneous atoms of a mineral, moving freely in solution, arrange themselves into shapes mathematically perfect, or particles of frozen moisture into the symmetrical and beautiful forms of snowflakes, you have nothing to say. You have not even invented a name to conceal your heroic unreason."

Moxon was speaking with unusual animation and earnestness. As he paused I heard in an adjoining room known to me as his "machine-shop," which no one but himself was permitted to enter, a singular thumping sound, as of some one pounding upon a table with an open hand. Moxon heard it at the same moment and, visibly agitated, rose and hurriedly passed into the room whence it came. I thought it odd that any one else should be in there, and my interest in my friend—with doubtless a touch of unwarrantable curiosity—led me to listen intently, though, I am happy to say, not at the key-hole. There were confused sounds, as of a struggle or scuffle; the floor shook. I distinctly heard hard breathing and a hoarse whisper which said "Damn you!" Then all was silent, and presently Moxon reappeared and said, with a rather sorry smile:

"Pardon me for leaving you so abruptly. I have a machine in there that lost its temper and cut up rough."

Fixing my eyes steadily upon his left cheek, which was traversed by four parallel excoriations showing blood, I said:

"How would it do to trim its nails?"

I could have spared myself the jest; he gave it no attention, but seated himself in the chair that he had left and resumed the interrupted monologue as if nothing had occurred:

"Doubtless you do not hold with those (I need not name them to a man of your reading) who have taught that all matter is sentient, that every atom is a living, feeling, conscious being. *I* do. There is no such thing as dead, inert matter; it is all alive; all instinct with force, actual and potential; all sensitive to the same forces in its environment and susceptible to the contagion of higher and subtler ones residing in such superior organisms as it may be brought into relation with, as those of man when he is fashioning it into an instrument of his will. It absorbs something of his intelligence and purpose —more of them in proportion to the complexity of the resulting machine and that of its work.

"Do you happen to recall Herbert Spencer's definition of 'Life'? I read it thirty years ago. He may have altered it afterward, for anything I know, but in all that time I have been unable to think of a single word that could profitably be changed or added or removed. It seems to me not only the best definition, but the only possible one.

"'Life,' he says, 'is a definite combination of heterogeneous changes, both simultaneous and successive, in correspondence with external coexistences and sequences.'"

"That defines the phenomenon," I said, "but gives no hint of its cause."

"That," he replied, "is all that any definition can do. As Mill points out, we know nothing of cause except as an antecedent—nothing of effect except as a consequent. Of certain phenomena, one never occurs without another, which is dissimilar: the first in point of time we call cause, the second, effect. One who had many times seen a rabbit pursued by a dog, and had never seen rabbits and dogs otherwise, would think the rabbit the cause of the dog.

"But I fear," he added, laughing naturally enough, "that my rabbit is leading me a long way from the track of my legitimate quarry: I'm indulging in the pleasure of the chase for its own sake. What I want you to observe is that in Herbert Spencer's definition of 'life' the activity of a machine is included—there is nothing in the definition that is not applicable to it. According to this sharpest of observers and deepest of thinkers, if a man during his period of activity is alive, so is a machine when in operation. As an inventor and constructor of machines I know that to be true."

Moxon was silent for a long time, gazing absently into the fire. It was growing late and I thought it time to be going, but somehow I did not like the notion of leaving him in that isolated house, all alone except for the presence of some person of whose nature my conjectures could go no further than that it was unfriendly, perhaps malign. Leaning toward him and looking earnestly into his eyes while making a motion with my hand through the door of his workshop, I said:

"Moxon, whom have you in there?"

Somewhat to my surprise he laughed lightly and answered without hesitation:

"Nobody; the incident that you have in mind was caused by my folly in leaving a machine in action with nothing to act upon, while I undertook the interminable task of enlightening your understanding. Do you happen to know that Consciousness is the creature of Rhythm?"

"O bother them both!" I replied, rising and laying hold of my overcoat. "I'm going to wish you good night; and I'll add the hope that the machine which you inadvertently left in action will have her gloves on the next time you think it needful to stop her."

Without waiting to observe the effect of my shot I left the house.

Rain was falling, and the darkness was intense. In the sky beyond the crest of a hill toward which I groped my way along precarious plank sidewalks and across miry, unpaved streets I could see the faint glow of the city's lights, but behind me nothing was visible but a single window of Moxon's house. It glowed with what seemed to me a mysterious and fateful meaning. I knew it was an uncurtained aperture in my friend's "machine-shop," and I had little doubt that he had resumed the studies interrupted by his duties as my instructor in mechanical consciousness and the fatherhood of Rhythm. Odd, and in some degree humorous, as his convictions seemed to me at that time, I could not wholly divest myself of the feeling that they had some tragic relation to his life and character—perhaps to his destiny—although I no longer entertained the notion that they were the vagaries of a disordered mind. Whatever might be thought of his views, his exposition of them was too logical for that. Over and over, his last words came back to me: "Consciousness is the creature of Rhythm." Bald and terse as the statement was, I now found it infinitely alluring. At each recurrence it broadened in meaning and deepened in suggestion. Why, here, (I thought) is something upon which to found a philosophy. If consciousness is the product of rhythm all things *are* conscious, for all have motion, and all motion is rhythmic. I wondered if Moxon knew the significance and breadth of his thought—the scope of this momentous generalization; or had he arrived at his philosophic faith by the tortuous and uncertain road of observation?

That faith was then new to me, and all Moxon's expounding had failed to make me a convert; but now it seemed as if a great light shone about me, like that which fell upon Saul of Tarsus; and out there in the storm and darkness and solitude I experienced what Lewes calls "The endless variety and excitement of philosophic thought." I exulted in a new sense of knowledge, a new pride of reason. My feet seemed hardly to touch the earth; it was as if I were uplifted and borne through the air by invisible wings.

Yielding to an impulse to seek further light from him whom I now recognized as my master and guide, I had unconsciously turned about, and almost before I was aware of having done so found myself again at Moxon's door. I was drenched with rain, but felt no discomfort. Unable in my excitement to find the doorbell I instinctively tried the knob. It turned and, entering, I mounted the stairs to the room that I had so recently left. All was dark and silent; Moxon, as I had supposed, was in the adjoining room—the "machine-shop." Groping along the wall until I found the communicating door I knocked loudly several times, but got no response, which I attributed to the uproar outside, for the wind was blowing a gale and dashing the rain against the thin walls in sheets. The drumming upon the shingle roof spanning the unceiled room was loud and incessant.

I had never been invited into the machine-shop—had, indeed, been denied admittance, as had all others, with one exception, a skilled metal worker, of whom no one knew anything except that his name was Haley and his habit silence. But in my spiritual exaltation, discretion and civility were forgotten and I opened the door. What I saw took all philosophical speculation out of me in short order.

Moxon sat facing me at the farther side of a small table upon which a single candle made all the light that was in the room. Opposite him, his back toward me, sat another person. On the table between the two was a chessboard; the men were playing. I knew little of chess, but as only a few pieces were on the board it was obvious that the game was near its close. Moxon was intensely interested—not so much, it seemed to me, in the game as in his antagonist, upon whom he had fixed so intent a look that, standing though I did directly in the line of his vision, I was altogether unobserved. His face was ghastly white, and his eyes glittered like diamonds. Of his antagonist I had only a back view, but that was sufficient; I should not have cared to see his face.

He was apparently not more than five feet in height, with proportions suggesting those of a gorilla—a tremendous breadth of shoulders, thick, short neck and broad, squat head, which had a tangled growth of black hair and was topped with a crimson fez. A tunic of the same color, belted tightly to the waist, reached the seat —apparently a box—upon which he sat; his legs and feet were not seen. His left forearm appeared to rest in his lap; he moved his pieces with his right hand, which seemed disproportionately long.

I had shrunk back and now stood a little to one side of the doorway and in shadow. If Moxon had looked farther than the face of his opponent he could have observed nothing now, except that the door was open. Something forbade me either to enter or to retire, a feeling —I know not how it came—that I was in the presence of an imminent tragedy and might serve my friend by remaining. With a scarcely conscious rebellion against the indelicacy of the act I remained.

The play was rapid. Moxon hardly glanced at the board before making his moves, and to my unskilled eye seemed to move the piece most convenient to his hand, his motions in doing so being quick, nervous and lacking in precision. The response of his antagonist, while equally prompt in the inception, was made with a slow, uniform, mechanical and, I thought, somewhat theatrical movement of the arm, that was a sore trial to my patience. There was something unearthly about it all, and I caught myself shuddering. But I was wet and cold.

Two or three times after moving a piece the stranger slightly inclined his head, and each time I observed that Moxon shifted his king. All at once the thought came to me that the man was dumb. And then that he was a machine—an automaton chessplayer! Then I remembered that Moxon had once spoken to me of having invented such a piece of mechanism, though I did not understand that it had actually been constructed. Was all his talk about the consciousness and intelligence of machines merely a prelude to eventual exhibition of this device—only a trick to intensify the effect of its mechanical action upon me in my ignorance of its secret?

A fine end, this, of all my intellectual transports—my "endless variety and excitement of philosophic thought!" I was about to retire in disgust when something occurred to hold my curiosity. I observed a shrug of the thing's great shoulders, as if it were irritated: and so natural was this—so entirely human—that in my new view of the matter it startled me. Nor was that all, for a moment later it struck the table sharply with its clenched hand. At that gesture Moxon seemed even more startled than I: he pushed his chair a little backward, as in alarm.

Presently Moxon, whose play it was, raised his hand high above the board, pounced upon one of his pieces like a sparrow-hawk and with the exclamation "checkmate!" rose quickly to his feet and stepped behind his chair. The automaton sat motionless.

The wind had now gone down, but I heard, at lessening intervals and progressively louder, the rumble and roll of thunder. In the pauses between I now became conscious of a low humming or buzzing which, like the thunder, grew momentarily louder and more distinct. It seemed to come from the body of the automaton, and was unmistakably a whirring of wheels. It gave me the impression of a disordered mechanism which had escaped the repressive and regulating action of some controlling part—an effect such as might be expected if a pawl should be jostled from the teeth of a ratchet-wheel. But before I had time for much conjecture as to its nature my attention was taken by the strange motions of the automaton itself. A slight but continuous convulsion appeared to have possession of it. In body and head it shook like a man with palsy or an ague chill, and the motion augmented every moment until the entire figure was in violent agitation. Suddenly it sprang to its feet and with a movement almost too quick for the eye to follow shot forward across table and chair, with both arms thrust forth to their full length—the posture and lunge of a diver. Moxon tried to throw himself backward out of reach, but he was too late: I saw the horrible thing's hands close upon his throat, his own clutch its wrists. Then the table was overturned, the candle thrown to the floor and extinguished, and all was black dark. But the noise of the struggle was dreadfully distinct, and most terrible of all were the raucous, squawking sounds made by the strangled man's efforts to breathe. Guided by the infernal hubbub, I sprang to the rescue of my friend, but had hardly taken a stride in the darkness when the whole room blazed with a blinding white light that burned into my brain and heart and memory a vivid picture of the combatants on the floor, Moxon underneath, his throat still in the clutch of those iron hands, his head forced backward, his eyes protruding, his mouth wide open and his tongue thrust out; and—horrible contrast!—upon the painted face of his assassin an expression of tranquil and profound thought, as in the solution of a problem in chess! This I observed, then all was blackness and silence.

Three days later I recovered consciousness in a hospital. As the memory of that tragic night slowly evolved in my ailing brain I recognized in my attendant Moxon's confidential workman, Haley. Responding to a look he approached, smiling.

"Tell me about it," I managed to say, faintly—"all about it."

"Certainly," he said; "you were carried unconscious from a burning house—Moxon's. Nobody knows how you came to be there. You may have to do a little explaining. The origin of the fire is a bit mysterious, too. My own notion is that the house was struck by lightning."

"And Moxon?"

"Buried yesterday—what was left of him."

Apparently this reticent person could unfold himself on occasion. When imparting shocking intelligence to the sick he was affable enough. After some moments of the keenest mental suffering I ventured to ask another question:

"Who rescued me?"

"Well, if that interests you—I did."

"Thank you, Mr. Haley, and may God bless you for it. Did you rescue, also, that charming product of your skill, the automaton chess-player that murdered its inventor?"

The man was silent a long time, looking away from me. Presently he turned and gravely said:

"Do you know that?"

"I do," I replied; "I saw it done."

That was many years ago. If asked to-day I should answer less confidently.

※　　　※　　　※

THE DAMNED THING

I

ONE DOES NOT ALWAYS EAT WHAT IS ON THE TABLE

By the light of a tallow candle which had been placed on one end of a rough table a man was reading something written in a book. It was an old account book, greatly worn; and the writing was not, apparently, very legible, for the man sometimes held the page close to the flame of the candle to get a stronger light on it. The shadow of the book would then throw into obscurity a half of the room, darkening a number of faces and figures; for besides the reader, eight other men were present. Seven of them sat against the rough log walls, silent, motionless, and the room being small, not very far from the table. By extending an arm any one of them could have touched the eighth man, who lay on the table, face upward, partly covered by a sheet, his arms at his sides. He was dead.

The man with the book was not reading aloud, and no one spoke; all seemed to be waiting for something to occur; the dead man only was without expectation. From the blank darkness outside came in, through the aperture that served for a window, all the ever unfamiliar noises of night in the wilderness—the long nameless note of a distant coyote; the stilly pulsing thrill of tireless insects in trees; strange cries of night birds, so different from those of the birds of day; the drone of great blundering beetles, and all that mysterious chorus of small sounds that seem always to have been but half heard when they have suddenly ceased, as if conscious of an indiscretion. But nothing of all this was noted in that company; its members were not overmuch addicted to idle interest in matters of no practical importance; that was obvious in every line of their rugged faces—obvious even in the dim light of the single candle. They were evidently men of the vicinity—farmers and woodsmen.

The person reading was a trifle different; one would have said of him that he was of the world, worldly, albeit there was that in his attire which attested a certain fellowship with the organisms of his environment. His coat would hardly have passed muster in San Francisco; his foot-gear was not of urban origin, and the hat that lay by him on the floor (he was the only one uncovered) was such that if one had considered it as an article of mere personal adornment he would have missed its meaning. In countenance the man was rather prepossessing, with just a hint of sternness; though that he may have assumed or cultivated, as appropriate to one in authority. For he was a coroner. It was by virtue of his office that he had possession of the book in which he was reading; it had been found among the dead man's effects—in his cabin, where the inquest was now taking place.

When the coroner had finished reading he put the book into his breast pocket. At that moment the door was pushed open and a young man entered. He, clearly, was not of mountain birth and breeding: he was clad as those who dwell in cities. His clothing was dusty, however, as from travel. He had, in fact, been riding hard to attend the inquest.

The coroner nodded; no one else greeted him.

"We have waited for you," said the coroner. "It is necessary to have done with this business to-night."

The young man smiled. "I am sorry to have kept you," he said. "I went away, not to evade your summons, but to post to my newspaper an account of what I suppose I am called back to relate."

The coroner smiled.

"The account that you posted to your newspaper," he said, "differs, probably, from that which you will give here under oath."

"That," replied the other, rather hotly and with a visible flush, "is as you please. I used manifold paper and have a copy of what I sent. It was not written as news, for it is incredible, but as fiction. It may go as a part of my testimony under oath."

"But you say it is incredible."

"That is nothing to you, sir, if I also swear that it is true."

The coroner was silent for a time, his eyes upon the floor. The men about the sides of the cabin talked in whispers, but seldom withdrew their gaze from the face of the corpse. Presently the coroner lifted his eyes and said: "We will resume the inquest."

The men removed their hats. The witness was sworn.

"What is your name?" the coroner asked.

"William Harker."

"Age?"

"Twenty-seven."

"You knew the deceased, Hugh Morgan?"

"Yes."

"You were with him when he died?"

"Near him."

"How did that happen—your presence, I mean?"

"I was visiting him at this place to shoot and fish. A part of my purpose, however, was to study him and his odd, solitary way of life. He seemed a good model for a character in fiction. I sometimes write stories."

"I sometimes read them."

"Thank you."

"Stories in general—not yours."

Some of the jurors laughed. Against a sombre background humor shows high lights. Soldiers in the intervals of battle laugh easily, and a jest in the death chamber conquers by surprise.

"Relate the circumstances of this man's death," said the coroner. "You may use any notes or memoranda that you please."

The witness understood. Pulling a manuscript from his breast pocket he held it near the candle and turning the leaves until he found the passage that he wanted began to read.

II

WHAT MAY HAPPEN IN A FIELD OF WILD OATS

". . . The sun had hardly risen when we left the house. We were looking for quail, each with a shotgun, but we had only one dog. Morgan said that our best ground was beyond a certain ridge that he pointed out, and we crossed it by a trail through the *chaparral*. On the other side was comparatively level ground, thickly covered with wild oats. As we emerged from the *chaparral* Morgan was but a few yards in advance. Suddenly we heard, at a little distance to our right and partly in front, a noise as of some animal thrashing about in the bushes, which we could see were violently agitated.

" 'We've started a deer,' I said. 'I wish we had brought a rifle.'

"Morgan, who had stopped and was intently watching the agitated *chaparral,* said nothing, but had cocked both barrels of his gun and was holding it in readiness to aim. I thought him a trifle excited, which surprised me, for he had a reputation for exceptional coolness, even in moments of sudden and imminent peril.

" 'O, come,' I said. 'You are not going to fill up a deer with quail-shot, are you?'

"Still he did not reply; but catching a sight of his face as he turned it slightly toward me I was struck by the intensity of his look. Then I understood that we had serious business in hand and my first conjecture was that we had 'jumped' a grizzly. I advanced to Morgan's side, cocking my piece as I moved.

"The bushes were now quiet and the sounds had ceased, but Morgan was as attentive to the place as before.

" 'What is it? What the devil is it?' I asked.

" 'That Damned Thing!' he replied, without turning his head. His voice was husky and unnatural. He trembled visibly.

"I was about to speak further, when I observed the wild oats near the place of the disturbance moving in the most inexplicable way. I can hardly describe it. It seemed as if stirred by a streak of wind, which not only bent it, but pressed it down—crushed it so that it did not rise; and this movement was slowly prolonging itself directly toward us.

"Nothing that I had ever seen had affected me so strangely as this unfamiliar and unaccountable phenomenon, yet I am unable to recall any sense of fear. I remember—and tell it here because, singularly enough, I recollected it then—that once in looking carelessly out of an open window I momentarily mistook a small tree close at hand for one of a group of larger trees at a little distance away. It looked the same size as the others, but being more distinctly and sharply defined in mass and detail seemed out of harmony with them. It was a mere falsification of the law of aërial perspective, but it startled, almost terrified me. We so rely upon the orderly operation of familiar natural laws that any seeming suspension of them is noted as a menace to our safety, a warning of unthinkable calamity. So now the apparently causeless movement of the herbage and the slow, undeviating approach of the line of disturbance were distinctly disquieting. My companion appeared actually frightened, and I could hardly credit my senses when I saw him suddenly throw his gun to his shoulder and fire both barrels at the agitated grain! Before the smoke of the discharge had cleared away I heard a loud savage cry—a scream like that of a wild animal—and flinging his gun upon the ground Morgan sprang away and ran swiftly from the spot. At the same instant I was thrown violently to the ground by the impact of something unseen in the smoke—some soft, heavy substance that seemed thrown against me with great force.

"Before I could get upon my feet and recover my gun, which seemed to have been struck from my hands, I heard Morgan crying out as if in mortal agony, and mingling with his cries were such hoarse, savage sounds as one hears from fighting dogs. Inexpressibly terrified, I struggled to my feet and looked in the direction of Morgan's retreat; and may Heaven in mercy spare me from another sight like that! At a distance of less than thirty yards was my friend, down upon one knee, his head thrown back at a frightful angle, hatless, his long hair in disorder and his whole body in violent movement from side to side, backward and forward. His right arm was lifted and seemed to lack the hand—at least, I could see none. The other arm was invisible. At times, as my memory now reports this extraordinary scene, I could discern but a part of his body; it was as if he had been partly blotted out—I cannot otherwise express it— then a shifting of his position would bring it all into view again.

"All this must have occurred within a few seconds, yet in that time Morgan assumed all the postures of a determined wrestler vanquished by superior weight and strength. I saw nothing but him, and him not always distinctly. During the entire incident his shouts and curses were heard, as if through an enveloping uproar of such sounds of rage and fury as I had never heard from the throat of man or brute!

"For a moment only I stood irresolute, then throwing down my gun I ran forward to my friend's assistance. I had a vague belief that he was suffering from a fit, or some form of convulsion. Before I could reach his side he was down and quiet. All sounds had ceased, but with a feeling of such terror as even these awful events had not inspired I now saw again the mysterious movement of the wild oats, prolonging itself from the trampled area about the prostrate man toward the edge of a wood. It was only when it had reached the wood that I was able to withdraw my eyes and look at my companion. He was dead."

III
A MAN THOUGH NAKED MAY BE IN RAGS

The coroner rose from his seat and stood beside the dead man. Lifting an edge of the sheet he pulled it away, exposing the entire body, altogether naked and showing in the candle-light a claylike yellow. It had, however, broad maculations of bluish black, obviously caused by extravasated blood from contusions. The chest and sides looked as if they had been beaten with a bludgeon. There were dreadful lacerations; the skin was torn in strips and shreds.

The coroner moved round to the end of the table and undid a silk handkerchief which had been passed under the chin and knotted on the top of the head. When the handkerchief was drawn away it exposed what had been the throat. Some of the jurors who had risen to get a better view repented their curiosity and turned away their faces. Witness Harker went to the open window and leaned out across the sill, faint and sick. Dropping the handkerchief upon the dead man's neck the coroner stepped to an angle of the room and from a pile of clothing produced one garment after another, each of which he held up a moment for inspection. All were torn, and stiff with blood. The jurors did not make a closer inspection. They seemed rather uninterested. They had, in truth, seen all this before; the only thing that was new to them being Harker's testimony.

"Gentlemen," the coroner said, "we have no more evidence, I think. Your duty has been already explained to you; if there is nothing you wish to ask you may go outside and consider your verdict."

The foreman rose—a tall, bearded man of sixty, coarsely clad.

"I should like to ask one question, Mr. Coroner," he said. "What asylum did this yer last witness escape from?"

"Mr. Harker," said the coroner, gravely and tranquilly, "from what asylum did you last escape?"

Harker flushed crimson again, but said nothing, and the seven jurors rose and solemnly filed out of the cabin.

"If you have done insulting me, sir," said Harker, as soon as he and the officer were left alone with the dead man, "I suppose I am at liberty to go?"

"Yes."

Harker started to leave, but paused, with his hand on the door latch. The habit of his profession was strong in him—stronger than his sense of personal dignity. He turned about and said:

"The book that you have there—I recognize it as Morgan's diary. You seemed greatly interested in it; you read in it while I was testifying. May I see it? The public would like——"

"The book will cut no figure in this matter," replied the official, slipping it into his coat pocket; "all the entries in it were made before the writer's death."

As Harker passed out of the house the jury reëntered and stood about the table, on which the now covered corpse showed under the sheet with sharp definition. The foreman seated himself near the candle, produced from his breast pocket a pencil and scrap of paper and wrote rather laboriously the following verdict, which with various degrees of effort all signed:

"We, the jury, do find that the remains come to their death at the hands of a mountain lion, but some of us thinks, all the same, they had fits."

IV

AN EXPLANATION FROM THE TOMB

In the diary of the late Hugh Morgan are certain interesting entries having, possibly, a scientific value as suggestions. At the inquest upon his body the book was not put in evidence; possibly the coroner thought it not worth while to confuse the jury. The date of the first of the entries mentioned cannot be ascertained; the upper part of the leaf is torn away; the part of the entry remaining follows:

". . . would run in a half-circle, keeping his head turned always toward the centre, and again he would stand still, barking furiously. At last he ran away into the brush as fast as he could go. I thought at first that he had gone mad, but on returning to the house found no other alteration in his manner than what was obviously due to fear of punishment.

"Can a dog see with his nose? Do odors impress some cerebral centre with images of the thing that emitted them? . . .

"Sept. 2.—Looking at the stars last night as they rose above the crest of the ridge east of the house, I observed them successively disappear—from left to right. Each was eclipsed but an instant, and only a few at the same time, but along the entire length of the ridge all that were within a degree or two of the crest were blotted out. It was as if something had passed along between me and them; but I could not see it, and the stars were not thick enough to define its outline. Ugh! I don't like this.". . .

Several weeks' entries are missing, three leaves being torn from the book.

"Sept. 27.—It has been about here again—I find evidences of its presence every day. I watched again all last night in the same cover, gun in hand, double-charged with buckshot. In the morning the fresh footprints were there, as before. Yet I would have sworn that I did not sleep—indeed, I hardly sleep at all. It is terrible, insupportable! If these amazing experiences are real I shall go mad; if they are fanciful I am mad already.

"Oct. 3.—I shall not go—it shall not drive me away. No, this is *my* house, *my* land. God hates a coward. . . .

"Oct. 5.—I can stand it no longer; I have invited Harker to pass a few weeks with me—he has a level head. I can judge from his manner if he thinks me mad.

"Oct. 7.—I have the solution of the mystery; it came to me last night—suddenly, as by revelation. How simple—how terribly simple!

"There are sounds that we cannot hear. At either end of the scale are notes that stir no chord of that imperfect instrument, the human ear. They are too high or too grave. I have observed a flock of blackbirds occupying an entire tree-top—the tops of several trees—and all in full song. Suddenly—in a moment—at absolutely the same instant —all spring into the air and fly away. How? They could not all see one another—whole tree-tops intervened. At no point could a leader have been visible to all. There must have been a signal of warning or command, high and shrill above the din, but by me unheard. I have observed, too, the same simultaneous flight when all were silent, among not only blackbirds, but other birds—quail, for example, widely separated by bushes—even on opposite sides of a hill.

"It is known to seamen that a school of whales basking or sporting on the surface of the ocean, miles apart, with the convexity of the earth between, will sometimes dive at the same instant—all gone out of sight in a moment. The signal has been sounded—too grave for the ear of the sailor at the masthead and his comrades on the deck—who nevertheless feel its vibrations in the ship as the stones of a cathedral are stirred by the bass of the organ.

"As with sounds, so with colors. At each end of the solar spectrum the chemist can detect the presence of what are known as 'actinic' rays. They represent colors—integral colors in the composition of light—which we are unable to discern. The human eye is an imperfect instrument; its range is but a few octaves of the real 'chromatic scale.' I am not mad; there are colors that we cannot see.

"And, God help me! the Damned Thing is of such a color!"

❅   ❅   ❅

THE REALM OF THE UNREAL

I

For a part of the distance between Auburn and Newcastle the road —first on one side of a creek and then on the other—occupies the whole bottom of the ravine, being partly cut out of the steep hillside, and partly built up with bowlders removed from the creek-bed by the miners. The hills are wooded, the course of the ravine is sinuous. In a dark night careful driving is required in order not to go off into the water. The night that I have in memory was dark, the creek a torrent, swollen by a recent storm. I had driven up from Newcastle and was within about a mile of Auburn in the darkest and narrowest part of the ravine, looking intently ahead of my horse for the roadway. Suddenly I saw a man almost under the animal's nose, and reined in with a jerk that came near setting the creature upon its haunches.

"I beg your pardon," I said; "I did not see you, sir."

"You could hardly be expected to see me," the man replied, civilly, approaching the side of the vehicle; "and the noise of the creek prevented my hearing you."

I at once recognized the voice, although five years had passed since I had heard it. I was not particularly well pleased to hear it now.

"You are Dr. Dorrimore, I think," said I.

"Yes; and you are my good friend Mr. Manrich. I am more than glad to see you—the excess," he added, with a light laugh, "being due to the fact that I am going your way, and naturally expect an invitation to ride with you."

"Which I extend with all my heart."

That was not altogether true.

Dr. Dorrimore thanked me as he seated himself beside me, and I drove cautiously forward, as before. Doubtless it is fancy, but it seems to me now that the remaining distance was made in a chill fog; that I was uncomfortably cold; that the way was longer than ever before, and the town, when we reached it, cheerless, forbidding, and desolate. It must have been early in the evening, yet I do not recollect a light in any of the houses nor a living thing in the streets. Dorrimore explained at some length how he happened to be there, and where he had been during the years that had elapsed since I had seen him. I recall the fact of the narrative, but none of the facts narrated. He had been in foreign countries and had returned— this is all that my memory retains, and this I already knew. As to myself I cannot remember that I spoke a word, though doubtless I did. Of one thing I am distinctly conscious: the man's presence at my side was strangely distasteful and disquieting—so much so that when I at last pulled up under the lights of the Putnam House I experienced a sense of having escaped some spiritual peril of a nature peculiarly forbidding. This sense of relief was somewhat modified by the discovery that Dr. Dorrimore was living at the same hotel.

II

In partial explanation of my feelings regarding Dr. Dorrimore I will relate briefly the circumstances under which I had met him some years before. One evening a half-dozen men of whom I was one were sitting in the library of the Bohemian Club in San Francisco. The conversation had turned to the subject of sleight-of-hand and the feats of the *prestidigitateurs,* one of whom was then exhibiting at a local theatre.

"These fellows are pretenders in a double sense," said one of the party; "they can do nothing which it is worth one's while to be made a dupe by. The humblest wayside juggler in India could mystify them to the verge of lunacy."

"For example, how?" asked another, lighting a cigar.

"For example, by all their common and familiar performances— throwing large objects into the air which never come down; causing plants to sprout, grow visibly and blossom, in bare ground chosen by spectators; putting a man into a wicker basket, piercing him through and through with a sword while he shrieks and bleeds, and then—the basket being opened nothing is there; tossing the free end of a silken ladder into the air, mounting it and disappearing."

"Nonsense!" I said, rather uncivilly, I fear. "You surely do not believe such things?"

"Certainly not: I have seen them too often."

"But I do," said a journalist of considerable local fame as a picturesque reporter. "I have so frequently related them that nothing but observation could shake my conviction. Why, gentlemen, I have my own word for it."

Nobody laughed—all were looking at something behind me. Turning in my seat I saw a man in evening dress who had just entered the room. He was exceedingly dark, almost swarthy, with a thin face, black-bearded to the lips, an abundance of coarse black hair in some disorder, a high nose and eyes that glittered with as soulless an expression as those of a cobra. One of the group rose and introduced him as Dr. Dorrimore, of Calcutta. As each of us was presented in turn he acknowledged the fact with a profound bow in the Oriental manner, but with nothing of Oriental gravity. His smile impressed me as cynical and a trifle contemptuous. His whole demeanor I can describe only as disagreeably engaging.

His presence led the conversation into other channels. He said little—I do not recall anything of what he did say. I thought his voice singularly rich and melodious, but it affected me in the same way as his eyes and smile. In a few minutes I rose to go. He also rose and put on his overcoat.

"Mr. Manrich," he said, "I am going your way."

"The devil you are!" I thought. "How do you know which way I am going?" Then I said, "I shall be pleased to have your company."

We left the building together. No cabs were in sight, the street cars had gone to bed, there was a full moon and the cool night air was delightful; we walked up the California street hill. I took that direction thinking he would naturally wish to take another, toward one of the hotels.

"You do not believe what is told of the Hindu jugglers," he said abruptly.

"How do you know that?" I asked.

Without replying he laid his hand lightly upon my arm and with the other pointed to the stone sidewalk directly in front. There, almost at our feet, lay the dead body of a man, the face upturned and white in the moonlight! A sword whose hilt sparkled with gems stood fixed and upright in the breast; a pool of blood had collected on the stones of the sidewalk.

I was startled and terrified—not only by what I saw, but by the circumstances under which I saw it. Repeatedly during our ascent of the hill my eyes, I thought, had traversed the whole reach of that sidewalk, from street to street. How could they have been insensible to this dreadful object now so conspicuous in the white moonlight?

As my dazed faculties cleared I observed that the body was in evening dress; the overcoat thrown wide open revealed the dress-coat, the white tie, the broad expanse of shirt front pierced by the sword. And—horrible revelation!—the face, except for its pallor, was that of my companion! It was to the minutest detail of dress and feature Dr. Dorrimore himself. Bewildered and horrified, I turned to look for the living man. He was nowhere visible, and with an added terror I retired from the place, down the hill in the direction whence I had come. I had taken but a few strides when a strong grasp upon my shoulder arrested me. I came near crying out with terror: the dead man, the sword still fixed in his breast, stood beside me! Pulling out the sword with his disengaged hand, he flung it from him, the moonlight glinting upon the jewels of its hilt and the unsullied steel of its blade. It fell with a clang upon the sidewalk ahead and —vanished! The man, swarthy as before, relaxed his grasp upon my shoulder and looked at me with the same cynical regard that I had observed on first meeting him. The dead have not that look—it partly restored me, and turning my head backward, I saw the smooth white expanse of sidewalk, unbroken from street to street.

"What is all this nonsense, you devil?" I demanded, fiercely enough, though weak and trembling in every limb.

"It is what some are pleased to call jugglery," he answered, with a light, hard laugh.

He turned down Dupont street and I saw him no more until we met in the Auburn ravine.

III

On the day after my second meeting with Dr. Dorrimore I did not see him: the clerk in the Putnam House explained that a slight illness confined him to his rooms. That afternoon at the railway station I was surprised and made happy by the unexpected arrival of Miss Margaret Corray and her mother, from Oakland.

This is not a love story. I am no storyteller, and love as it is cannot be portrayed in a literature dominated and enthralled by the debasing tyranny which "sentences letters" in the name of the Young Girl. Under the Young Girl's blighting reign—or rather under the rule of those false Ministers of the Censure who have appointed themselves to the custody of her welfare—love

> veils her sacred fires,
> And, unaware, Morality expires,

famished upon the sifted meal and distilled water of a prudish purveyance.

Let it suffice that Miss Corray and I were engaged in marriage. She and her mother went to the hotel at which I lived, and for two weeks I saw her daily. That I was happy needs hardly be said; the only bar to my perfect enjoyment of those golden days was the presence of Dr. Dorrimore, whom I had felt compelled to introduce to the ladies.

By them he was evidently held in favor. What could I say? I knew absolutely nothing to his discredit. His manners were those of a cultivated and considerate gentleman; and to women a man's manner is the man. On one or two occasions when I saw Miss Corray walking with him I was furious, and once had the indiscretion to protest. Asked for reasons, I had none to give and fancied I saw in her expression a shade of contempt for the vagaries of a jealous mind. In time I grew morose and consciously disagreeable, and resolved in my madness to return to San Francisco the next day. Of this, however, I said nothing.

IV

There was at Auburn an old, abandoned cemetery. It was nearly in the heart of the town, yet by night it was as gruesome a place as the most dismal of human moods could crave. The railings about the plats were prostrate, decayed, or altogether gone. Many of the graves were sunken, from others grew sturdy pines, whose roots had committed unspeakable sin. The headstones were fallen and broken across; brambles overran the ground; the fence was mostly gone, and cows and pigs wandered there at will; the place was a dishonor to the living, a calumny on the dead, a blasphemy against God.

The evening of the day on which I had taken my madman's resolution to depart in anger from all that was dear to me found me in that congenial spot. The light of the half moon fell ghostly through the foliage of trees in spots and patches, revealing much that was unsightly, and the black shadows seemed conspiracies with-holding to the proper time revelations of darker import. Passing along what had been a gravel path, I saw emerging from shadow the figure of Dr. Dorrimore. I was myself in shadow, and stood still with clenched hands and set teeth, trying to control the impulse to leap upon and strangle him. A moment later a second figure joined him and clung to his arm. It was Margaret Corray!

I cannot rightly relate what occurred. I know that I sprang forward, bent upon murder; I know that I was found in the gray of the morning, bruised and bloody, with finger marks upon my throat. I was taken to the Putnam House, where for days I lay in a delirium. All this I know, for I have been told. And of my own knowledge I know that when consciousness returned with convalescence I sent for the clerk of the hotel.

"Are Mrs. Corray and her daughter still here?" I asked.

"What name did you say?"

"Corray."

"Nobody of that name has been here."

"I beg you will not trifle with me," I said petulantly. "You see that I am all right now; tell me the truth."

"I give you my word," he replied with evident sincerity, "we have had no guests of that name."

His words stupefied me. I lay for a few moments in silence; then I asked: "Where is Dr. Dorrimore?"

"He left on the morning of your fight and has not been heard of since. It was a rough deal he gave you."

V

Such are the facts of this case. Margaret Corray is now my wife. She has never seen Auburn, and during the weeks whose history as it shaped itself in my brain I have endeavored to relate, was living at her home in Oakland, wondering where her lover was and why he did not write. The other day I saw in the Baltimore *Sun* the following paragraph:

"Professor Valentine Dorrimore, the hypnotist, had a large audience last night. The lecturer, who has lived most of his life in India, gave some marvelous exhibitions of his power, hypnotizing anyone who chose to submit himself to the experiment, by merely looking at him. In fact, he twice hypnotized the entire audience (reporters alone exempted), making all entertain the most extraordinary illusions. The most valuable feature of the lecture was the disclosure of the methods of the Hindu jugglers in their famous performances, familiar in the mouths of travelers. The professor declares that these thaumaturgists have acquired such skill in the art which he learned at their feet that they perform their miracles by simply throwing the 'spectators' into a state of hypnosis and telling them what to see and hear. His assertion that a peculiarly susceptible subject may be kept in the realm of the unreal for weeks, months, and even years, dominated by whatever delusions and hallucinations the operator may from time to time suggest, is a trifle disquieting."

❋   ❋   ❋

A FRUITLESS ASSIGNMENT

Henry Saylor, who was killed in Covington, in a quarrel with Antonio Finch, was a reporter on the Cincinnati *Commercial*. In the year 1859 a vacant dwelling in Vine street, in Cincinnati, became the center of a local excitement because of the strange sights and sounds said to be observed in it nightly. According to the testimony of many reputable residents of the vicinity these were inconsistent with any other hypothesis than that the house was haunted. Figures with something singularly unfamiliar about them were seen by crowds on the sidewalk to pass in and out. No one could say just where they appeared upon the open lawn on their way to the front door by which they entered, nor at exactly what point they vanished as they came out; or, rather, while each spectator was positive enough about these matters, no two agreed. They were all similarly at variance in their descriptions of the figures themselves. Some of the bolder of the curious throng ventured on several evenings to stand upon the doorsteps to intercept them, or failing in this, get a nearer look at them. These courageous men, it was said, were unable to force the door by their united strength, and always were hurled from the steps by some invisible agency and severely injured; the door immediately afterward opening, apparently of its own volition, to admit or free some ghostly guest. The dwelling was known as the Roscoe house, a family of that name having lived there for some years, and then, one by one, disappeared, the last to leave being

an old woman. Stories of foul play and successive murders had always been rife, but never were authenticated.

One day during the prevalence of the excitement Saylor presented
himself at the office of the *Commercial* for orders. He received a note
from the city editor which read as follows: "Go and pass the night
alone in the haunted house in Vine street and if anything occurs
worth while make two columns." Saylor obeyed his superior; he could
not afford to lose his position on the paper.

Apprising the police of his intention, he effected an entrance
through a rear window before dark, walked through the deserted
rooms, bare of furniture, dusty and desolate, and seating himself at
last in the parlor on an old sofa which he had dragged in from
another room watched the deepening of the gloom as night came on.
Before it was altogether dark the curious crowd had collected in
the street, silent, as a rule, and expectant, with here and there a
scoffer uttering his incredulity and courage with scornful remarks
or ribald cries. None knew of the anxious watcher inside. He feared
to make a light; the uncurtained windows would have betrayed his
presence, subjecting him to insult, possibly to injury. Moreover, he
was too conscientious to do anything to enfeeble his impressions and
unwilling to alter any of the customary conditions under which the
manifestations were said to occur.

It was now dark outside, but light from the street faintly illuminated the part of the room that he was in. He had set open every
door in the whole interior, above and below, but all the outer ones
were locked and bolted. Sudden exclamations from the crowd caused
him to spring to the window and look out. He saw the figure of a
man moving rapidly across the lawn toward the building—saw it
ascend the steps; then a projection of the wall concealed it. There
was a noise as of the opening and closing of the hall door; he heard
quick, heavy footsteps along the passage—heard them ascend the
stairs—heard them on the uncarpeted floor of the chamber immediately overhead.

Saylor promptly drew his pistol, and groping his way up the stairs
entered the chamber, dimly lighted from the street. No one was there.
He heard footsteps in an adjoining room and entered that. It was
dark and silent. He struck his foot against some object on the floor,
knelt by it, passed his hand over it. It was a human head—that of a
woman. Lifting it by the hair this iron-nerved man returned to the
half-lighted room below, carried it near the window and attentively
examined it. While so engaged he was half conscious of the rapid
opening and closing of the outer door, of footfalls sounding all about

him. He raised his eyes from the ghastly object of his attention and saw himself the center of a crowd of men and women dimly seen; the room was thronged with them. He thought the people had broken in.

"Ladies and gentlemen," he said, coolly, "you see me under suspicious circumstances, but——" his voice was drowned in peals of laughter—such laughter as is heard in asylums for the insane. The persons about him pointed at the object in his hand and their merriment increased as he dropped it and it went rolling among their feet. They danced about it with gestures grotesque and attitudes obscene and indescribable. They struck it with their feet, urging it about the room from wall to wall; pushed and overthrew one another in their struggles to kick it; cursed and screamed and sang snatches of ribald songs as the battered head bounded about the room as if in terror and trying to escape. At last it shot out of the door into the hall, followed by all, with tumultuous haste. That moment the door closed with a sharp concussion. Saylor was alone, in dead silence.

Carefully putting away his pistol, which all the time he had held in his hand, he went to a window and looked out. The street was deserted and silent; the lamps were extinguished; the roofs and chimneys of the houses were sharply outlined against the dawnlight in the east. He left the house, the door yielding easily to his hand, and walked to the *Commercial* office. The city editor was still in his office—asleep. Saylor waked him and said: "I have been at the haunted house."

The editor stared blankly as if not wholly awake. "Good God!" he cried, "are you Saylor?"

"Yes—why not?"

The editor made no answer, but continued staring.

"I passed the night there—it seems," said Saylor.

"They say that things were uncommonly quiet out there," the editor said, trifling with a paper-weight upon which he had dropped his eyes, "did anything occur?"

"Nothing whatever."

A VINE ON A HOUSE

About three miles from the little town of Norton, in Missouri, on the road leading to Maysville, stands an old house that was last occupied by a family named Harding. Since 1886 no one has lived in it, nor is anyone likely to live in it again. Time and the disfavor of persons dwelling thereabout are converting it into a rather picturesque ruin. An observer unacquainted with its history would hardly put it into the category of "haunted houses," yet in all the region round such is its evil reputation. Its windows are without glass, its doorways without doors; there are wide breaches in the shingle roof, and for lack of paint the weatherboarding is a dun gray. But these unfailing signs of the supernatural are partly concealed and greatly softened by the abundant foliage of a large vine overrunning the entire structure. This vine—of a species which no botanist has ever been able to name—has an important part in the story of the house.

The Harding family consisted of Robert Harding, his wife Matilda, Miss Julia Went, who was her sister, and two young children. Robert Harding was a silent, cold-mannered man who made no friends in the neighborhood and apparently cared to make none. He was about forty years old, frugal and industrious, and made a living from the little farm which is now overgrown with brush and brambles. He and his sister-in-law were rather tabooed by their neighbors, who seemed to think that they were seen too frequently together—not entirely their fault, for at these times they evidently did not challenge observation. The moral code of rural Missouri is stern and exacting.

Mrs. Harding was a gentle, sad-eyed woman, lacking a left foot.

At some time in 1884 it became known that she had gone to visit her mother in Iowa. That was what her husband said in reply to inquiries, and his manner of saying it did not encourage further questioning. She never came back, and two years later, without selling his farm or anything that was his, or appointing an agent to look after his interests, or removing his household goods, Harding, with the rest of the family, left the country. Nobody knew whither he went; nobody at that time cared. Naturally, whatever was movable about the place soon disappeared and the deserted house became "haunted" in the manner of its kind.

One summer evening, four or five years later, the Rev. J. Gruber, of Norton, and a Maysville attorney named Hyatt met on horseback in front of the Harding place. Having business matters to discuss, they hitched their animals and going to the house sat on the porch to talk. Some humorous reference to the somber reputation of the place was made and forgotten as soon as uttered, and they talked of their business affairs until it grew almost dark. The evening was oppressively warm, the air stagnant.

Presently both men started from their seats in surprise: a long vine that covered half the front of the house and dangled its branches from the edge of the porch above them was visibly and audibly agitated, shaking violently in every stem and leaf.

"We shall have a storm," Hyatt exclaimed.

Gruber said nothing, but silently directed the other's attention to the foliage of adjacent trees, which showed no movement; even the delicate tips of the boughs silhouetted against the clear sky were motionless. They hastily passed down the steps to what had been a lawn and looked upward at the vine, whose entire length was now visible. It continued in violent agitation, yet they could discern no disturbing cause.

"Let us leave," said the minister.

And leave they did. Forgetting that they had been traveling in opposite directions, they rode away together. They went to Norton, where they related their strange experience to several discreet friends. The next evening, at about the same hour, accompanied by two others whose names are not recalled, they were again on the porch of the Harding house, and again the mysterious phenomenon occurred: the vine was violently agitated while under the closest scrutiny from root to tip, nor did their combined strength applied to the trunk serve to still it. After an hour's observation they retreated, no less wise, it is thought, than when they had come.

No great time was required for these singular facts to rouse the curiosity of the entire neighborhood. By day and by night crowds of persons assembled at the Harding house "seeking a sign." It does not appear that any found it, yet so credible were the witnesses mentioned that none doubted the reality of the "manifestations" to which they testified.

By either a happy inspiration or some destructive design, it was one day proposed—nobody appeared to know from whom the suggestion came—to dig up the vine, and after a good deal of debate this was done. Nothing was found but the root, yet nothing could have been more strange!

For five or six feet from the trunk, which had at the surface of the ground a diameter of several inches, it ran downward, single and straight, into a loose, friable earth; then it divided and sub-divided into rootlets, fibers and filaments, most curiously interwoven. When carefully freed from soil they showed a singular formation. In their ramifications and doublings back upon themselves they made a compact network, having in size and shape an amazing resemblance to the human figure. Head, trunk and limbs were there; even the fingers and toes were distinctly defined; and many professed to see in the distribution and arrangement of the fibers in the globular mass representing the head a grotesque suggestion of a face. The figure was horizontal; the smaller roots had begun to unite at the breast.

In point of resemblance to the human form this image was imperfect. At about ten inches from one of the knees, the *cilia* forming that leg had abruptly doubled backward and inward upon their course of growth. The figure lacked the left foot.

There was but one inference—the obvious one; but in the ensuing excitement as many courses of action were proposed as there were incapable counselors. The matter was settled by the sheriff of the county, who as the lawful custodian of the abandoned estate ordered the root replaced and the excavation filled with the earth that had been removed.

Later inquiry brought out only one fact of relevancy and significance: Mrs. Harding had never visited her relatives in Iowa, nor did they know that she was supposed to have done so.

Of Robert Harding and the rest of his family nothing is known. The house retains its evil reputation, but the replanted vine is as orderly and well-behaved a vegetable as a nervous person could wish to sit under of a pleasant night, when the katydids grate out their immemorial revelation and the distant whippoorwill signifies his notion of what ought to be done about it.

THE HAUNTED VALLEY[1]

I

HOW TREES ARE FELLED IN CHINA

A half-mile north from Jo. Dunfer's, on the road from Hutton's to Mexican Hill, the highway dips into a sunless ravine which opens out on either hand in a half-confidential manner, as if it had a secret to impart at some more convenient season. I never used to ride through it without looking first to the one side and then to the other, to see if the time had arrived for the revelation. If I saw nothing—and I never did see anything—there was no feeling of disappointment, for I knew the disclosure was merely withheld temporarily for some good reason which I had no right to question. That I should one day be taken into full confidence I no more doubted than I doubted the existence of Jo. Dunfer himself, through whose premises the ravine ran.

It was said that Jo. had once undertaken to erect a cabin in some remote part of it, but for some reason had abandoned the enterprise and constructed his present hermaphrodite habitation, half residence and half groggery, at the roadside, upon an extreme corner of his estate; as far away as possible, as if on purpose to show how radically he had changed his mind.

This Jo. Dunfer—or, as he was familiarly known in the neighborhood, Whisky Jo.—was a very important personage in those parts. He was apparently about forty years of age, a long, shock-headed fellow, with a corded face, a gnarled arm and a knotty hand like a bunch of prison-keys. He was a hairy man, with a stoop in his walk, like that of one who is about to spring upon something and rend it.

Next to the peculiarity to which he owed his local appellation, Mr. Dunfer's most obvious characteristic was a deep-seated antipathy to the Chinese. I saw him once in a towering rage because one of his herdsmen had permitted a travel-heated Asian to slake his thirst at the horse-trough in front of the saloon end of Jo.'s establishment.

[1] Ambrose Bierce's first short story, published in *Overland Monthly* in 1871. This was very early in Bierce's professional life, while he was columnist on *The News Letter*, a magazine edited by Bret Harte.

I ventured faintly to remonstrate with Jo. for his unchristian spirit, but he merely explained that there was nothing about Chinamen in the New Testament, and strode away to wreak his displeasure upon his dog, which also, I suppose, the inspired scribes had overlooked.

Some days afterward, finding him sitting alone in his barroom, I cautiously approached the subject, when, greatly to my relief, the habitual austerity of his expression visibly softened into something that I took for condescension.

"You young Easterners," he said, "are a mile-and-a-half too good for this country, and you don't catch on to our play. People who don't know a Chileño from a Kanaka can afford to hang out liberal ideas about Chinese immigration, but a fellow that has to fight for his bone with a lot of mongrel coolies hasn't any time for foolishness."

This long consumer, who had probably never done an honest day's-work in his life, sprung the lid of a Chinese tobacco-box and with thumb and forefinger forked out a wad like a small haycock. Holding this reinforcement within supporting distance he fired away with renewed confidence.

"They're a flight of devouring locusts, and they're going for everything green in this God blest land, if you want to know."

Here he pushed his reserve into the breach and when his gabble-gear was again disengaged resumed his uplifting discourse.

"I had one of them on this ranch five years ago, and I'll tell you about it, so that you can see the nub of this whole question. I didn't pan out particularly well those days—drank more whisky than was prescribed for me and didn't seem to care for my duty as a patriotic American citizen; so I took that pagan in, as a kind of cook. But when I got religion over at the Hill and they talked of running me for the Legislature it was given to me to see the light. But what was I to do? If I gave him the go somebody else would take him, and mightn't treat him white. *What* was I to do? What would any good Christian do, especially one new to the trade and full to the neck with the brotherhood of Man and the fatherhood of God?"

Jo. paused for a reply, with an expression of unstable satisfaction, as of one who has solved a problem by a distrusted method. Presently he rose and swallowed a glass of whisky from a full bottle on the counter, then resumed his story.

"Besides, he didn't count for much—didn't know anything and gave himself airs. They all do that. I said him nay, but he muled it through on that line while he lasted; but after turning the other cheek seventy and seven times I doctored the dice so that he didn't last forever. And I'm almighty glad I had the sand to do it."

Jo.'s gladness, which somehow did not impress me, was duly and ostentatiously celebrated at the bottle.

"About five years ago I started in to stick up a shack. That was before this one was built, and I put it in another place. I set Ah Wee and a little cuss named Gopher to cutting the timber. Of course I didn't expect Ah Wee to help much, for he had a face like a day in June and big black eyes—I guess maybe they were the damn'dest eyes in this neck o' woods."

While delivering this trenchant thrust at common sense Mr. Dunfer absently regarded a knot-hole in the thin board partition separating the bar from the living-room, as if that were one of the eyes whose size and color had incapacitated his servant for good service.

"Now you Eastern galoots won't believe anything against the yellow devils," he suddenly flamed out with an appearance of earnestness not altogether convincing, "but I tell you that Chink was the perversest scoundrel outside San Francisco. The miserable pig-tail Mongolian went to hewing away at the saplings all round the stems, like a worm o' the dust gnawing a radish. I pointed out his error as patiently as I knew how, and showed him how to cut them on two sides, so as to make them fall right; but no sooner would I turn my back on him, like this"—and he turned it on me, amplifying the illustration by taking some more liquor—"than he was at it again. It was just this way: while I looked at him, *so*"—regarding me rather unsteadily and with evident complexity of vision—"he was all right; but when I looked away, *so*"—taking a long pull at the bottle —"he defied me. Then I'd gaze at him reproachfully, *so*, and butter wouldn't have melted in his mouth."

Doubtless Mr. Dunfer honestly intended the look that he fixed upon me to be merely reproachful, but it was singularly fit to arouse the gravest apprehension in any unarmed person incurring it; and as I had lost all interest in his pointless and interminable narrative, I rose to go. Before I had fairly risen, he had again turned to the counter, and with a barely audible "so," had emptied the bottle at a gulp.

Heavens! what a yell! It was like a Titan in his last, strong agony. Jo. staggered back after emitting it, as a cannon recoils from its own thunder, and then dropped into his chair, as if he had been "knocked in the head" like a beef—his eyes drawn sidewise toward the wall, with a stare of terror. Looking in the same direction, I saw that the knot-hole in the wall had indeed become a human eye—a full, black eye, that glared into my own with an entire lack of expression more awful than the most devilish glitter. I think I must have covered my face with my hands to shut out the horrible illusion, if such it was, and Jo.'s little white man-of-all-work coming into the room broke the spell, and I walked out of the house with a sort of dazed fear that *delirium tremens* might be infectious. My horse was hitched at the watering-trough, and untying him I mounted and gave him his head, too much troubled in mind to note whither he took me.

I did not know what to think of all this, and like every one who does not know what to think I thought a great deal, and to little purpose. The only reflection that seemed at all satisfactory, was, that on the morrow I should be some miles away, with a strong probability of never returning.

A sudden coolness brought me out of my abstraction, and looking up I found myself entering the deep shadows of the ravine. The day was stifling; and this transition from the pitiless, visible heat of the parched fields to the cool gloom, heavy with pungency of cedars and vocal with twittering of the birds that had been driven to its leafy asylum, was exquisitely refreshing. I looked for my mystery, as usual, but not finding the ravine in a communicative mood, dismounted, led my sweating animal into the undergrowth, tied him securely to a tree and sat down upon a rock to meditate.

I began bravely by analyzing my pet superstition about the place. Having resolved it into its constituent elements I arranged them in convenient troops and squadrons, and collecting all the forces of my logic bore down upon them from impregnable premises with the thunder of irresistible conclusions and a great noise of chariots and general intellectual shouting. Then, when my big mental guns had overturned all opposition, and were growling almost inaudibly away on the horizon of pure speculation, the routed enemy straggled in upon their rear, massed silently into a solid phalanx, and captured me, bag and baggage. An indefinable dread came upon me. I rose to shake it off, and began threading the narrow dell by an old, grass-grown cow-path that seemed to flow along the bottom, as a substitute for the brook that Nature had neglected to provide.

The trees among which the path straggled were ordinary, well-behaved plants, a trifle perverted as to trunk and eccentric as to bough, but with nothing unearthly in their general aspect. A few loose bowlders, which had detached themselves from the sides of the depression to set up an independent existence at the bottom, had dammed up the pathway, here and there, but their stony repose had nothing in it of the stillness of death. There was a kind of death-chamber hush in the valley, it is true, and a mysterious whisper above: the wind was just fingering the tops of the trees—that was all.

I had not thought of connecting Jo. Dunfer's drunken narrative with what I now sought, and only when I came into a clear space and stumbled over the level trunks of some small trees did I have the revelation. This was the site of the abandoned "shack." The discovery was verified by noting that some of the rotting stumps were hacked all round, in a most unwoodmanlike way, while others were cut straight across, and the butt ends of the corresponding trunks had the blunt wedge-form given by the axe of a master.

The opening among the trees was not more than thirty paces across. At one side was a little knoll—a natural hillock, bare of shrubbery but covered with wild grass, and on this, standing out of the grass, the headstone of a grave!

I do not remember that I felt anything like surprise at this discovery. I viewed that lonely grave with something of the feeling that Columbus must have had when he saw the hills and headlands of the new world. Before approaching it I leisurely completed my survey of the surroundings. I was even guilty of the affectation of winding my watch at that unusual hour, and with needless care and deliberation. Then I approached my mystery.

The grave—a rather short one—was in somewhat better repair than was consistent with its obvious age and isolation, and my eyes, I dare say, widened a trifle at a clump of unmistakable garden flowers showing evidence of recent watering. The stone had clearly enough done duty once as a doorstep. In its front was carved, or rather dug, an inscription. It read thus:

AH WEE—CHINAMAN.
Age unknown. Worked for Jo. Dunfer.
This monument is erected by him to keep the Chink's
memory green. Likewise as a warning to Celestials
not to take on airs. Devil take 'em!
She Was a Good Egg.

I cannot adequately relate my astonishment at this uncommon inscription! The meagre but sufficient identification of the deceased; the impudent candor of confession; the brutal anathema; the ludicrous change of sex and sentiment—all marked this record as the work of one who must have been at least as much demented as bereaved. I felt that any further disclosure would be a paltry anticlimax, and with an unconscious regard for dramatic effect turned squarely about and walked away. Nor did I return to that part of the county for four years.

II

WHO DRIVES SANE OXEN SHOULD HIMSELF
BE SANE

"Gee-up, there, old Fuddy-Duddy!"

This unique adjuration came from the lips of a queer little man perched upon a wagonful of firewood, behind a brace of oxen that were hauling it easily along with a simulation of mighty effort which had evidently not imposed on their lord and master. As that gentleman happened at the moment to be staring me squarely in the face as I stood by the roadside it was not altogether clear whether he was addressing me or his beasts; nor could I say if they were named Fuddy and Duddy and were both subjects of the imperative verb "to gee-up." Anyhow the command produced no effect on us, and the queer little man removed his eyes from mine long enough to spear Fuddy and Duddy alternately with a long pole, remarking, quietly but with feeling: "Dern your skin," as if they enjoyed that integument in common. Observing that my request for a ride took no attention, and finding myself falling slowly astern, I placed one foot upon the inner circumference of a hind wheel and was slowly elevated to the level of the hub, whence I boarded the concern, *sans cérémonie,* and scrambling forward seated myself beside the driver— who took no notice of me until he had administered another indiscriminate castigation to his cattle, accompanied with the advice to "buckle down, you derned Incapable!" Then, the master of the outfit (or rather the former master, for I could not suppress a whimsical feeling that the entire establishment was my lawful prize) trained his big, black eyes upon me with an expression strangely, and somewhat unpleasantly, familiar, laid down his rod—which neither blossomed nor turned into a serpent, as I half expected—folded his arms, and gravely demanded, "W'at did you do to W'isky?"

My natural reply would have been that I drank it, but there was something about the query that suggested a hidden significance, and something about the man that did not invite a shallow jest. And so, having no other answer ready, I merely held my tongue, but felt as if I were resting under an imputation of guilt, and that my silence was being construed into a confession.

Just then a cold shadow fell upon my cheek, and caused me to look up. We were descending into my ravine! I can not describe the sensation that came upon me: I had not seen it since it unbosomed itself four years before, and now I felt like one to whom a friend has made some sorrowing confession of crime long past, and who has basely deserted him in consequence. The old memories of Jo. Dunfer, his fragmentary revelation, and the unsatisfying explanatory note by the headstone, came back with singular distinctness. I wondered what had become of Jo., and—I turned sharply round and asked my prisoner. He was intently watching his cattle, and without withdrawing his eyes replied:

"Gee-up, old Terrapin! He lies aside of Ah Wee up the gulch. Like to see it? They always come back to the spot—I've been expectin' you. H-woa!"

At the enunciation of the aspirate, Fuddy-Duddy, the incapable terrapin, came to a dead halt, and before the vowel had died away up the ravine had folded up all his eight legs and lain down in the dusty road, regardless of the effect upon his derned skin. The queer little man slid off his seat to the ground and started up the dell without deigning to look back to see if I was following. But I was.

It was about the same season of the year, and at near the same hour of the day, of my last visit. The jays clamored loudly, and the trees whispered darkly, as before; and I somehow traced in the two sounds a fanciful analogy to the open boastfulness of Mr. Jo. Dunfer's mouth and the mysterious reticence of his manner, and to the mingled hardihood and tenderness of his sole literary production— the epitaph. All things in the valley seemed unchanged, excepting the cow-path, which was almost wholly overgrown with weeds. When we came out into the "clearing," however, there was change enough. Among the stumps and trunks of the fallen saplings, those that had been hacked "China fashion" were no longer distinguishable from those that were cut " 'Melican way." It was as if the Old-World barbarism and the New-World civilization had reconciled their differences by the arbitration of an impartial decay—as is the way of civilizations. The knoll was there, but the Hunnish brambles had overrun and all but obliterated its effete grasses; and the patrician garden-violet had capitulated to his plebeian brother—perhaps had merely reverted to his original type. Another grave—a long, robust mound—had been made beside the first, which seemed to shrink from the comparison; and in the shadow of a new headstone the old one lay prostrate, with its marvelous inscription illegible by accumulation of leaves and soil. In point of literary merit the new was inferior to the old—was even repulsive in its terse and savage jocularity:

JO. DUNFER. DONE FOR.

I turned from it with indifference, and brushing away the leaves from the tablet of the dead pagan restored to light the mocking words which, fresh from their long neglect, seemed to have a certain pathos. My guide, too, appeared to take on an added seriousness as he read it, and I fancied that I could detect beneath his whimsical manner something of manliness, almost of dignity. But while I looked at him his former aspect, so subtly unhuman, so tantalizingly familiar, crept back into his big eyes, repellant and attractive. I resolved to make an end of the mystery if possible.

"My friend," I said, pointing to the smaller grave, "did Jo. Dunfer murder that Chinaman?"

He was leaning against a tree and looking across the open space into the top of another, or into the blue sky beyond. He neither withdrew his eyes, nor altered his posture as he slowly replied:

"No, sir; he justifiably homicided him."

"Then he really did kill him."

"Kill 'im? I should say he did, rather. Doesn't everybody know that? Didn't he stan' up before the coroner's jury and confess it? And didn't they find a verdict of 'Came to 'is death by a wholesome Christian sentiment workin' in the Caucasian breast'? An' didn't the church at the Hill turn W'isky down for it? And didn't the sovereign people elect him Justice of the Peace to get even on the gospelers? I don't know where you were brought up."

"But did Jo. do that because the Chinaman did not, or would not, learn to cut down trees like a white man?"

"Sure!—it stan's so on the record, which makes it true an' legal. My knowin' better doesn't make any difference with legal truth; it wasn't my funeral and I wasn't invited to deliver an oration. But the fact is, W'isky was jealous o' *me*"—and the little wretch actually swelled out like a turkeycock and made a pretense of adjusting an imaginary neck-tie, noting the effect in the palm of his hand, held up before him to represent a mirror.

"Jealous of *you!*" I repeated with ill-mannered astonishment.

"That's what I said. Why not?—don't I look all right?"

He assumed a mocking attitude of studied grace, and twitched the wrinkles out of his threadbare waistcoat. Then, suddenly dropping his voice to a low pitch of singular sweetness, he continued:

"W'isky thought a lot o' that Chink; nobody but me knew how 'e doted on 'im. Couldn't bear 'im out of 'is sight, the derned protoplasm! And w'en 'e came down to this clearin' one day an' found him an' me neglectin' our work—him asleep an' me grapplin a tarantula out of 'is sleeve—W'isky laid hold of my axe and let us have it, good an' hard! I dodged just then, for the spider bit me, but Ah Wee got it bad in the side an' tumbled about like anything. W'isky was just weighin' me out one w'en 'e saw the spider fastened on my finger; then 'e knew he'd made a jack ass of 'imself. He threw away the axe and got down on 'is knees alongside of Ah Wee, who gave a last little kick and opened 'is eyes—he had eyes like mine—an' puttin' up 'is hands drew down W'isky's ugly head and held it there w'ile 'e stayed. That wasn't long, for a tremblin' ran through 'im and 'e gave a bit of a moan an' beat the game."

During the progress of the story the narrator had become transfigured. The comic, or rather, the sardonic element was all out of him, and as he painted that strange scene it was with difficulty that I kept my composure. And this consummate actor had somehow so managed me that the sympathy due to his *dramatis personæ* was given to himself. I stepped forward to grasp his hand, when suddenly a broad grin danced across his face and with a light, mocking laugh he continued:

"W'en W'isky got 'is nut out o' that 'e was a sight to see! All his fine clothes—he dressed mighty blindin' those days—were spoiled everlastin'! 'Is hair was towsled and his face—what I could see of it— was whiter than the ace of lilies. 'E stared once at me, and looked away as if I didn't count; an' then there were shootin' pains chasin' one another from my bitten finger into my head, and it was Gopher to the dark. That's why I wasn't at the inquest."

"But why did you hold your tongue afterward?" I asked.

"It's that kind of tongue," he replied, and not another word would he say about it.

"After that W'isky took to drinkin' harder an' harder, and was rabider an' rabider anti-coolie, but I don't think 'e was ever particularly glad that 'e dispelled Ah Wee. He didn't put on so much dog about it w'en we were alone as w'en he had the ear of a derned Spectacular Extravaganza like you. 'E put up that headstone and gouged the inscription accordin' to his varyin' moods. It took 'im three weeks, workin' between drinks. I gouged his in one day."

"When did Jo. die?" I asked rather absently. The answer took my breath:

"Pretty soon after I looked at him through that knot-hole, w'en you had put something in his w'isky, you derned Borgia!"

Recovering somewhat from my surprise at this astounding charge, I was half-minded to throttle the audacious accuser, but was restrained by a sudden conviction that came to me in the light of a revelation. I fixed a grave look upon him and asked, as calmly as I could: "And when did you go luny?"

"Nine years ago!" he shrieked, throwing out his clenched hands—"nine years ago, w'en that big brute killed the woman who loved him better than she did me!—me who had followed 'er from San Francisco, where 'e won 'er at draw poker!—me who had watched over 'er for years w'en the scoundrel she belonged to was ashamed to acknowledge 'er and treat 'er white!—me who for her sake kept 'is cussed secret till it ate 'im up!—me who w'en you poisoned the beast fulfilled 'is last request to lay 'im alongside 'er and give 'im a stone to the head of 'im! And I've never since seen 'er grave till now, for I didn't want to meet 'im here."

"Meet him? Why, Gopher, my poor fellow, he is dead!"

"That's why I'm afraid of 'im."

I followed the little wretch back to his wagon and wrung his hand at parting. It was now nightfall, and as I stood there at the roadside in the deepening gloom, watching the blank outlines of the receding wagon, a sound was borne to me on the evening wind—a sound as of a series of vigorous thumps—and a voice came out of the night:

"Gee-up, there, you derned old Geranium."

❀   ❀   ❀

ONE OF TWINS

A LETTER FOUND AMONG THE PAPERS OF THE
LATE MORTIMER BARR

You ask me if in my experience as one of a pair of twins I ever observed anything unaccountable by the natural laws with which we have acquaintance. As to that you shall judge; perhaps we have not all acquaintance with the same natural laws. You may know some that I do not, and what is to me unaccountable may be very clear to you.

You knew my brother John—that is, you knew him when you knew that I was not present; but neither you nor, I believe, any human being could distinguish between him and me if we chose to seem alike. Our parents could not; ours is the only instance of which I have any knowledge of so close resemblance as that. I speak of my brother John, but I am not at all sure that his name was not Henry and mine John. We were regularly christened, but afterward, in the very act of tattooing us with small distinguishing marks, the operator lost his reckoning; and although I bear upon my forearm a small "H" and he bore a "J," it is by no means certain that the letters ought not to have been transposed. During our boyhood our parents tried to distinguish us more obviously by our clothing and other simple devices, but we would so frequently exchange suits and otherwise circumvent the enemy that they abandoned all such ineffectual attempts, and during all the years that we lived together at home everybody recognized the difficulty of the situation and made the best of it by calling us both "Jehnry." I have often wondered at my father's forbearance in not branding us conspicuously upon our unworthy brows, but as we were tolerably good boys and used our power of embarrassment and annoyance with commendable moderation, we escaped the iron. My father was, in fact, a singularly good-natured man, and I think quietly enjoyed nature's practical joke.

Soon after we had come to California, and settled at San Jose (where the only good fortune that awaited us was our meeting with so kind a friend as you) the family, as you know, was broken up by the death of both my parents in the same week. My father died insolvent and the homestead was sacrificed to pay his debts. My sisters returned to relatives in the East, but owing to your kindness John and I, then twenty-two years of age, obtained employment in San Francisco, in different quarters of the town. Circumstances did not permit us to live together, and we saw each other infrequently, sometimes not oftener than once a week. As we had few acquaintances in common, the fact of our extraordinary likeness was little known. I come now to the matter of your inquiry.

One day soon after we had come to this city I was walking down Market street late in the afternoon, when I was accosted by a well-dressed man of middle age, who after greeting me cordially said: "Stevens, I know, of course, that you do not go out much, but I have told my wife about you, and she would be glad to see you at the house. I have a notion, too, that my girls are worth knowing. Suppose you come out to-morrow at six and dine with us, *en famille;* and then if the ladies can't amuse you afterward I'll stand in with a few games of billiards."

This was said with so bright a smile and so engaging a manner that I had not the heart to refuse, and although I had never seen the man in my life I promptly replied: "You are very good, sir, and it will give me great pleasure to accept the invitation. Please present my compliments to Mrs. Margovan and ask her to expect me."

With a shake of the hand and a pleasant parting word the man passed on. That he had mistaken me for my brother was plain enough. That was an error to which I was accustomed and which it was not my habit to rectify unless the matter seemed important. But how had I known that this man's name was Margovan? It certainly is not a name that one would apply to a man at random, with a probability that it would be right. In point of fact, the name was as strange to me as the man.

The next morning I hastened to where my brother was employed and met him coming out of the office with a number of bills that he was to collect. I told him how I had "committed" him and added that if he didn't care to keep the engagement I should be delighted to continue the impersonation.

"That's queer," he said thoughtfully. "Margovan is the only man in the office here whom I know well and like. When he came in this morning and we had passed the usual greetings some singular impulse prompted me to say: 'Oh, I beg your pardon, Mr. Margovan, but I neglected to ask your address.' I got the address, but what under the sun I was to do with it, I did not know until now. It's good of you to offer to take the consequence of your impudence, but I'll eat that dinner myself, if you please."

He ate a number of dinners at the same place—more than were good for him, I may add without disparaging their quality; for he fell in love with Miss Margovan, proposed marriage to her and was heartlessly accepted.

Several weeks after I had been informed of the engagement, but before it had been convenient for me to make the acquaintance of the young woman and her family, I met one day on Kearny street a handsome but somewhat dissipated-looking man whom something prompted me to follow and watch, which I did without any scruple whatever. He turned up Geary street and followed it until he came to Union square. There he looked at his watch, then entered the square. He loitered about the paths for some time, evidently waiting for someone. Presently he was joined by a fashionably dressed and beautiful young woman and the two walked away up Stockton street, I following. I now felt the necessity of extreme caution, for although the girl was a stranger it seemed to me that she would recognize me at a glance. They made several turns from one street to another and finally, after both had taken a hasty look all about—which I narrowly evaded by stepping into a doorway—they entered a house of which I do not care to state the location. Its location was better than its character.

I protest that my action in playing the spy upon these two strangers was without assignable motive. It was one of which I might or might not be ashamed, according to my estimate of the character of the person finding it out. As an essential part of a narrative educed by your question it is related here without hesitancy or shame.

A week later John took me to the house of his prospective father-in-law, and in Miss Margovan, as you have already surmised, but to my profound astonishment, I recognized the heroine of that discreditable adventure. A gloriously beautiful heroine of a discreditable adventure I must in justice admit that she was; but that fact has only this importance: her beauty was such a surprise to me that it cast a doubt upon her identity with the young woman I had seen before; how could the marvelous fascination of her face have failed to strike me at that time? But no—there was no possibility of error; the difference was due to costume, light and general surroundings.

John and I passed the evening at the house, enduring, with the fortitude of long experience, such delicate enough banter as our likeness naturally suggested. When the young lady and I were left alone for a few minutes I looked her squarely in the face and said with sudden gravity:

"You, too, Miss Margovan, have a double: I saw her last Tuesday afternoon in Union square."

She trained her great gray eyes upon me for a moment, but her glance was a trifle less steady than my own and she withdrew it, fixing it on the tip of her shoe.

"Was she very like me?" she asked, with an indifference which I thought a little overdone.

"So like," said I, "that I greatly admired her, and being unwilling to lose sight of her I confess that I followed her until—Miss Margovan, are you sure that you understand?"

She was now pale, but entirely calm. She again raised her eyes to mine, with a look that did not falter.

"What do you wish me to do?" she asked. "You need not fear to name your terms. I accept them."

It was plain, even in the brief time given me for reflection, that in dealing with this girl ordinary methods would not do, and ordinary exactions were needless.

"Miss Margovan," I said, doubtless with something of the compassion in my voice that I had in my heart, "it is impossible not to think you the victim of some horrible compulsion. Rather than impose new embarrassments upon you I would prefer to aid you to regain your freedom."

She shook her head, sadly and hopelessly, and I continued, with agitation:

"Your beauty unnerves me. I am disarmed by your frankness and your distress. If you are free to act upon conscience you will, I believe, do what you conceive to be best; if you are not—well, Heaven help us all! You have nothing to fear from me but such opposition to this marriage as I can try to justify on—on other grounds."

These were not my exact words, but that was the sense of them, as nearly as my sudden and conflicting emotions permitted me to express it. I rose and left her without another look at her, met the others as they re-entered the room and said, as calmly as I could: "I have been bidding Miss Margovan good evening; it is later than I thought."

John decided to go with me. In the street he asked if I had observed anything singular in Julia's manner.

"I thought her ill," I replied; "that is why I left." Nothing more was said.

The next evening I came late to my lodgings. The events of the previous evening had made me nervous and ill; I had tried to cure myself and attain to clear thinking by walking in the open air, but I was oppressed with a horrible presentiment of evil—a presentiment which I could not formulate. It was a chill, foggy night; my clothing and hair were damp and I shook with cold. In my dressing-gown and slippers before a blazing grate of coals I was even more uncomfortable. I no longer shivered but shuddered—there is a difference. The dread of some impending calamity was so strong and dispiriting that I tried to drive it away by inviting a real sorrow—tried to dispel the conception of a terrible future by substituting the memory of a painful past. I recalled the death of my parents and endeavored to fix my mind upon the last sad scenes at their bedsides and their graves. It all seemed vague and unreal, as having occurred ages ago and to another person. Suddenly, striking through my thought and parting it as a tense cord is parted by the stroke of steel—I can think of no other comparison—I heard a sharp cry as of one in mortal agony! The voice was that of my brother and seemed to come from the street outside my window. I sprang to the window and threw it open. A street lamp directly opposite threw a wan and ghastly light upon the wet pavement and the fronts of the houses. A single police-man, with upturned collar, was leaning against a gatepost, quietly smoking a cigar. No one else was in sight. I closed the window and pulled down the shade, seated myself before the fire and tried to fix my mind upon my surroundings. By way of assisting, by performance of some familiar act, I looked at my watch; it marked half-past eleven. Again I heard that awful cry! It seemed in the room—at my side. I was frightened and for some moments had not the power to move. A few minutes later—I have no recollection of the intermediate time —I found myself hurrying along an unfamiliar street as fast as I could walk. I did not know where I was, nor whither I was going, but presently sprang up the steps of a house before which were two or three carriages and in which were moving lights and a subdued con-fusion of voices. It was the house of Mr. Margovan.

You know, good friend, what had occurred there. In one chamber lay Julia Margovan, hours dead by poison; in another John Stevens, bleeding from a pistol wound in the chest, inflicted by his own hand. As I burst into the room, pushed aside the physicians and laid my hand upon his forehead he unclosed his eyes, stared blankly, closed them slowly and died without a sign.

I knew no more until six weeks afterward, when I had been nursed back to life by your own saintly wife in your own beautiful home. All of that you know, but what you do not know is this— which, however, has no bearing upon the subject of your psychologi-cal researches—at least not upon that branch of them in which, with a delicacy and consideration all your own, you have asked for less as-sistance than I think I have given you:

One moonlight night several years afterward I was passing through Union square. The hour was late and the square deserted. Certain memories of the past naturally came into my mind as I came to the spot where I had once witnessed that fateful assignation, and with that unaccountable perversity which prompts us to dwell upon thoughts of the most painful character I seated myself upon one of the benches to indulge them. A man entered the square and came along the walk toward me. His hands were clasped behind him, his head was bowed; he seemed to observe nothing. As he approached the shadow in which I sat I recognized him as the man whom I had seen meet Julia Margovan years before at that spot. But he was ter-ribly altered—gray, worn and haggard. Dissipation and vice were in evidence in every look; illness was no less apparent. His clothing was in disorder, his hair fell across his forehead in a derangement which was at once uncanny and picturesque. He looked fitter for restraint than liberty—the restraint of a hospital.

With no defined purpose I rose and confronted him. He raised his head and looked me full in the face. I have no words to describe the ghastly change that came over his own; it was a look of unspeakable terror—he thought himself eye to eye with a ghost. But he was a courageous man. "Damn you, John Stevens!" he cried, and lifting his trembling arm he dashed his fist feebly at my face and fell headlong upon the gravel as I walked away.

Somebody found him there, stone-dead. Nothing more is known of him, not even his name. To know of a man that he is dead should be enough.

❊   ❊   ❊

PRESENT AT A HANGING

An old man named Daniel Baker, living near Lebanon, Iowa, was suspected by his neighbors of having murdered a peddler who had obtained permission to pass the night at his house. This was in 1853, when peddling was more common in the Western country than it is now, and was attended with considerable danger. The peddler with his pack traversed the country by all manner of lonely roads, and was compelled to rely upon the country people for hospitality. This brought him into relation with queer characters, some of whom were not altogether scrupulous in their methods of making a living, murder being an acceptable means to that end. It occasionally occurred that a peddler with diminished pack and swollen purse would be traced to the lonely dwelling of some rough character and never could be traced beyond. This was so in the case of "old man Baker," as he was always called. (Such names are given in the Western "settlements" only to elderly persons who are not esteemed; to the general disrepute of social unworth is affixed the special reproach of age.) A peddler came to his house and none went away—that is all that anybody knew.

Seven years later the Rev. Mr. Cummings, a Baptist minister well known in that part of the country, was driving by Baker's farm one night. It was not very dark: there was a bit of moon somewhere above the light veil of mist that lay along the earth. Mr. Cummings, who was at all times a cheerful person, was whistling a tune, which he would occasionally interrupt to speak a word of friendly encouragement to his horse. As he came to a little bridge across a dry ravine he saw the figure of a man standing upon it, clearly outlined against the gray background of a misty forest. The man had something strapped on his back and carried a heavy stick—obviously an itinerant peddler. His attitude had in it a suggestion of abstraction, like that of a sleep-walker. Mr. Cummings reined in his horse when he arrived in front of him, gave him a pleasant salutation and invited him to a seat in the vehicle—"if you are going my way," he added. The man raised his head, looked him full in the face, but neither answered nor made any further movement. The minister, with good-natured persistence, repeated his invitation. At this the man threw his right hand forward from his side and pointed downward as he stood on the extreme edge of the bridge. Mr. Cummings looked past him, over into the ravine, saw nothing unusual and withdrew his eyes to address the man again. He had disappeared. The horse, which all this time had been uncommonly restless, gave at the same moment a snort of terror and started to run away. Before he had regained control of the animal the minister was at the crest of the hill a hundred yards along. He looked back and saw the figure again, at the same place and in the same attitude as when he had first observed it. Then for the first time he was conscious of a sense of the supernatural and drove home as rapidly as his willing horse would go.

On arriving at home he related his adventure to his family, and early the next morning, accompanied by two neighbors, John White Corwell and Abner Raiser, returned to the spot. They found the body of old man Baker hanging by the neck from one of the beams of the bridge, immediately beneath the spot where the apparition had stood. A thick coating of dust, slightly dampened by the mist, covered the floor of the bridge, but the only footprints were those of Mr. Cummings' horse.

In taking down the body the men disturbed the loose, friable earth of the slope below it, disclosing human bones already nearly uncovered by the action of water and frost. They were identified as those of the lost peddler. At the double inquest the coroner's jury found that Daniel Baker died by his own hand while suffering from temporary insanity, and that Samuel Morritz was murdered by some person or persons to the jury unknown.

※　　※　　※

A WIRELESS MESSAGE

In the summer of 1896 Mr. William Holt, a wealthy manufacturer of Chicago, was living temporarily in a little town of central New York, the name of which the writer's memory has not retained. Mr. Holt had had "trouble with his wife," from whom he had parted a year before. Whether the trouble was anything more serious than "incompatibility of temper," he is probably the only living person that knows: he is not addicted to the vice of confidences. Yet he has related the incident herein set down to at least one person without exacting a pledge of secrecy. He is now living in Europe.

One evening he had left the house of a brother whom he was visiting, for a stroll in the country. It may be assumed—whatever the value of the assumption in connection with what is said to have occurred—that his mind was occupied with reflections on his domestic infelicities and the distressing changes that they had wrought in his life. Whatever may have been his thoughts, they so possessed him that he observed neither the lapse of time nor whither his feet were carrying him; he knew only that he had passed far beyond the town limits and was traversing a lonely region by a road that bore no resemblance to the one by which he had left the village. In brief, he was "lost."

Realizing his mischance, he smiled; central New York is not a region of perils, nor does one long remain lost in it. He turned about and went back the way that he had come. Before he had gone far he observed that the landscape was growing more distinct—was brightening. Everything was suffused with a soft, red glow in which he saw his shadow projected in the road before him. "The moon is rising," he said to himself. Then he remembered that it was about the time of the new moon, and if that tricksy orb was in one of its stages of visibility it had set long before. He stopped and faced about, seeking the source of the rapidly broadening light. As he did so, his shadow turned and lay along the road in front of him as before. The light still came from behind him. That was surprising; he could not understand. Again he turned, and again, facing successively to every point of the horizon. Always the shadow was before—always the light behind, "a still and awful red."

Holt was astonished—"dumfounded" is the word that he used in telling it—yet seems to have retained a certain intelligent curiosity. To test the intensity of the light whose nature and cause he could not determine, he took out his watch to see if he could make out the figures on the dial. They were plainly visible, and the hands indicated the hour of eleven o'clock and twenty-five minutes. At that moment the mysterious illumination suddenly flared to an intense, an almost blinding splendor, flushing the entire sky, extinguishing the stars and throwing the monstrous shadow of himself athwart the landscape. In that unearthly illumination he saw near him, but apparently in the air at a considerable elevation, the figure of his wife, clad in her night-clothing and holding to her breast the figure of his child. Her eyes were fixed upon his with an expression which he afterward professed himself unable to name or describe, further than that it was "not of this life."

The flare was momentary, followed by black darkness, in which, however, the apparition still showed white and motionless; then by insensible degrees it faded and vanished, like a bright image on the retina after the closing of the eyes. A peculiarity of the apparition, hardly noted at the time, but afterward recalled, was that it showed only the upper half of the woman's figure: nothing was seen below the waist.

The sudden darkness was comparative, not absolute, for gradually all objects of his environment became again visible.

In the dawn of the morning Holt found himself entering the village at a point opposite to that at which he had left it. He soon arrived at the house of his brother, who hardly knew him. He was wild-eyed, haggard, and gray as a rat. Almost incoherently, he related his night's experience.

"Go to bed, my poor fellow," said his brother, "and—wait. We shall hear more of this."

An hour later came the predestined telegram. Holt's dwelling in one of the suburbs of Chicago had been destroyed by fire. Her escape cut off by the flames, his wife had appeared at an upper window, her child in her arms. There she had stood, motionless, apparently dazed. Just as the firemen had arrived with a ladder, the floor had given way, and she was seen no more.

The moment of this culminating horror was eleven o'clock and twenty-five minutes, standard time.

THE MOONLIT ROAD

I

STATEMENT OF JOEL HETMAN, JR.

I am the most unfortunate of men. Rich, respected, fairly well educated and of sound health—with many other advantages usually valued by those having them and coveted by those who have them not —I sometimes think that I should be less unhappy if they had been denied me, for then the contrast between my outer and my inner life would not be continually demanding a painful attention. In the stress of privation and the need of effort I might sometimes forget the somber secret ever baffling the conjecture that it compels.

I am the only child of Joel and Julia Hetman. The one was a well-to-do country gentleman, the other a beautiful and accomplished woman to whom he was passionately attached with what I now know to have been a jealous and exacting devotion. The family home was a few miles from Nashville, Tennessee, a large, irregularly built dwelling of no particular order of architecture, a little way off the road, in a park of trees and shrubbery.

At the time of which I write I was nineteen years old, a student at Yale. One day I received a telegram from my father of such urgency that in compliance with its unexplained demand I left at once for home. At the railway station in Nashville a distant relative awaited me to apprise me of the reason for my recall: my mother had been barbarously murdered—why and by whom none could conjecture, but the circumstances were these:

My father had gone to Nashville, intending to return the next afternoon. Something prevented his accomplishing the business in hand, so he returned on the same night, arriving just before the dawn. In his testimony before the coroner he explained that having no latchkey and not caring to disturb the sleeping servants, he had, with no clearly defined intention, gone round to the rear of the house. As he turned an angle of the building, he heard a sound as of a door gently closed, and saw in the darkness, indistinctly, the figure of a man, which instantly disappeared among the trees of the lawn. A hasty pursuit and brief search of the grounds in the belief that the trespasser was some one secretly visiting a servant proving fruitless, he entered at the unlocked door and mounted the stairs to my mother's chamber. Its door was open, and stepping into black darkness he fell headlong over some heavy object on the floor. I may spare myself the details; it was my poor mother, dead of strangulation by human hands!

Nothing had been taken from the house, the servants had heard no sound, and excepting those terrible finger-marks upon the dead woman's throat—dear God! that I might forget them!—no trace of the assassin was ever found.

I gave up my studies and remained with my father, who, naturally, was greatly changed. Always of a sedate, taciturn disposition, he now fell into so deep a dejection that nothing could hold his attention, yet anything—a footfall, the sudden closing of a door—aroused in him a fitful interest; one might have called it an apprehension. At any small surprise of the senses he would start visibly and sometimes turn pale, then relapse into a melancholy apathy deeper than before. I suppose he was what is called a "nervous wreck." As to me, I was younger then than now—there is much in that. Youth is Gilead, in which is balm for every wound. Ah, that I might again dwell in that enchanted land! Unacquainted with grief, I knew not how to appraise my bereavement; I could not rightly estimate the strength of the stroke.

One night, a few months after the dreadful event, my father and I walked home from the city. The full moon was about three hours above the eastern horizon; the entire countryside had the solemn stillness of a summer night; our footfalls and the ceaseless song of the katydids were the only sound aloof. Black shadows of bordering trees lay athwart the road, which, in the short reaches between, gleamed a ghostly white. As we approached the gate to our dwelling, whose front was in shadow, and in which no light shone, my father suddenly stopped and clutched my arm, saying, hardly above his breath:

"God! God! what is that?"

"I hear nothing," I replied.

"But see—see!" he said, pointing along the road, directly ahead.

I said: "Nothing is there. Come, father, let us go in—you are ill."

He had released my arm and was standing rigid and motionless in the center of the illuminated roadway, staring like one bereft of sense. His face in the moonlight showed a pallor and fixity inexpressibly distressing. I pulled gently at his sleeve, but he had forgotten my existence. Presently he began to retire backward, step by step, never for an instant removing his eyes from what he saw, or thought he saw. I turned half round to follow, but stood irresolute. I do not recall any feeling of fear, unless a sudden chill was its physical manifestation. It seemed as if an icy wind had touched my face and enfolded my body from head to foot; I could feel the stir of it in my hair.

At that moment my attention was drawn to a light that suddenly streamed from an upper window of the house: one of the servants, awakened by what mysterious premonition of evil who can say, and in obedience to an impulse that she was never able to name, had lit a lamp. When I turned to look for my father he was gone, and in all the years that have passed no whisper of his fate has come across the borderland of conjecture from the realm of the unknown.

II
STATEMENT OF CASPAR GRATTAN

To-day I am said to live; to-morrow, here in this room, will lie a senseless shape of clay that all too long was I. If anyone lift the cloth from the face of that unpleasant thing it will be in gratification of a mere morbid curiosity. Some, doubtless, will go further and inquire, "Who was he?" In this writing I supply the only answer that I am able to make—Caspar Grattan. Surely, that should be enough. The name has served my small need for more than twenty years of a life of unknown length. True, I gave it to myself, but lacking another I had the right. In this world one must have a name; it prevents confusion, even when it does not establish identity. Some, though, are known by numbers, which also seem inadequate distinctions.

One day, for illustration, I was passing along a street of a city, far from here, when I met two men in uniform, one of whom, half pausing and looking curiously into my face, said to his companion, "That man looks like 767." Something in the number seemed familiar and horrible. Moved by an uncontrollable impulse, I sprang into a side street and ran until I fell exhausted in a country lane.

I have never forgotten that number, and always it comes to memory attended by gibbering obscenity, peals of joyless laughter, the clang of iron doors. So I say a name, even if self-bestowed, is better than a number. In the register of the potter's field I shall soon have both. What wealth!

Of him who shall find this paper I must beg a little consideration. It is not the history of my life; the knowledge to write that is denied me. This is only a record of broken and apparently unrelated memories, some of them as distinct and sequent as brilliant beads upon a thread, others remote and strange, having the character of crimson dreams with interspaces blank and black—witch-fires glowing still and red in a great desolation.

Standing upon the shore of eternity, I turn for a last look landward over the course by which I came. There are twenty years of footprints fairly distinct, the impressions of bleeding feet. They lead through poverty and pain, devious and unsure, as of one staggering beneath a burden—

Remote, unfriended, melancholy, slow.

Ah, the poet's prophecy of Me—how admirable, how dreadfully admirable!

Backward beyond the beginning of this *via dolorosa*—this epic of suffering with episodes of sin—I see nothing clearly; it comes out of a cloud. I know that it spans only twenty years, yet I am an old man.

One does not remember one's birth—one has to be told. But with me it was different; life came to me full-handed and dowered me with all my faculties and powers. Of a previous existence I know no more than others, for all have stammering intimations that may be memories and may be dreams. I know only that my first consciousness was of maturity in body and mind—a consciousness accepted without surprise or conjecture. I merely found myself walking in a forest, half-clad, footsore, unutterably weary and hungry. Seeing a farmhouse, I approached and asked for food, which was given me by one who inquired my name. I did not know, yet knew that all had names. Greatly embarrassed, I retreated, and night coming on, lay down in the forest and slept.

The next day I entered a large town which I shall not name. Nor shall I recount further incidents of the life that is now to end—a life of wandering, always and everywhere haunted by an overmastering sense of crime in punishment of wrong and of terror in punishment of crime. Let me see if I can reduce it to narrative.

I seem once to have lived near a great city, a prosperous planter, married to a woman whom I loved and distrusted. We had, it sometimes seems, one child, a youth of brilliant parts and promise. He is at all times a vague figure, never clearly drawn, frequently altogether out of the picture.

One luckless evening it occurred to me to test my wife's fidelity in a vulgar, commonplace way familiar to everyone who has acquaintance with the literature of fact and fiction. I went to the city, telling my wife that I should be absent until the following afternoon. But I returned before daybreak and went to the rear of the house, purposing to enter by a door with which I had secretly so tampered that it would seem to lock, yet not actually fasten. As I approached it, I heard it gently open and close, and saw a man steal away into the darkness. With murder in my heart, I sprang after him, but he had vanished without even the bad luck of identification. Sometimes now I cannot even persuade myself that it was a human being.

Crazed with jealousy and rage, blind and bestial with all the elemental passions of insulted manhood, I entered the house and sprang up the stairs to the door of my wife's chamber. It was closed, but having tampered with its lock also, I easily entered and despite the black darkness soon stood by the side of her bed. My groping hands told me that although disarranged it was unoccupied.

"She is below," I thought, "and terrified by my entrance has evaded me in the darkness of the hall."

With the purpose of seeking her I turned to leave the room, but took a wrong direction—the right one! My foot struck her, cowering in a corner of the room. Instantly my hands were at her throat, stifling a shriek, my knees were upon her struggling body; and there in the darkness, without a word of accusation or reproach, I strangled her till she died!

There ends the dream. I have related it in the past tense, but the present would be the fitter form, for again and again the somber tragedy reenacts itself in my consciousness—over and over I lay the plan, I suffer the confirmation, I redress the wrong. Then all is blank; and afterward the rains beat against the grimy window-panes, or the snows fall upon my scant attire, the wheels rattle in the squalid streets where my life lies in poverty and mean employment. If there is ever sunshine I do not recall it; if there are birds they do not sing.

There is another dream, another vision of the night. I stand among the shadows in a moonlit road. I am aware of another presence, but whose I cannot rightly determine. In the shadow of a great dwelling I catch the gleam of white garments; then the figure of a woman confronts me in the road—my murdered wife! There is death in the face; there are marks upon the throat. The eyes are fixed on mine with an infinite gravity which is not reproach, nor hate, nor menace, nor anything less terrible than recognition. Before this awful apparition I retreat in terror—a terror that is upon

me as I write. I can no longer rightly shape the words. See! they—
Now I am calm, but truly there is no more to tell: the incident
ends where it began—in darkness and in doubt.

Yes, I am again in control of myself: "the captain of my soul."
But that is not respite; it is another stage and phase of expiation.
My penance, constant in degree, is mutable in kind: one of its
variants is tranquillity. After all, it is only a life-sentence. "To Hell
for life"—that is a foolish penalty: the culprit chooses the duration
of his punishment. To-day my term expires.

To each and all, the peace that was not mine.

III

STATEMENT OF THE LATE JULIA HETMAN,
THROUGH THE MEDIUM BAYROLLES

I had retired early and fallen almost immediately into a peaceful
sleep, from which I awoke with that indefinable sense of peril which
is, I think, a common experience in that other, earlier life. Of its
unmeaning character, too, I was entirely persuaded, yet that did not
banish it. My husband, Joel Hetman, was away from home; the
servants slept in another part of the house. But these were familiar
conditions; they had never before distressed me. Nevertheless, the
strange terror grew so insupportable that conquering my reluctance
to move I sat up and lit the lamp at my bedside. Contrary to my expectation this gave me no relief; the light seemed rather an added
danger, for I reflected that it would shine out under the door, disclosing my presence to whatever evil thing might lurk outside. You
that are still in the flesh, subject to horrors of the imagination, think
what a monstrous fear that must be which seeks in darkness security
from malevolent existences of the night. That is to spring to close
quarters with an unseen enemy—the strategy of despair!

Extinguishing the lamp I pulled the bedclothing about my head
and lay trembling and silent, unable to shriek, forgetful to pray. In
this pitiable state I must have lain for what you call hours—with us
there are no hours, there is no time.

At last it came—a soft, irregular sound of footfalls on the stairs!
They were slow, hesitant, uncertain, as of something that did not
see its way; to my disordered reason all the more terrifying for that,
as the approach of some blind and mindless malevolence to which
is no appeal. I even thought that I must have left the hall lamp burning and the groping of this creature proved it a monster of the night.

This was foolish and inconsistent with my previous dread of the light, but what would you have? Fear has no brains; it is an idiot. The dismal witness that it bears and the cowardly counsel that it whispers are unrelated. We know this well, we who have passed into the Realm of Terror, who skulk in eternal dusk among the scenes of our former lives, invisible even to ourselves and one another, yet hiding forlorn in lonely places; yearning for speech with our loved ones, yet dumb, and as fearful of them as they of us. Sometimes the disability is removed, the law suspended: by the deathless power of love or hate we break the spell—we are seen by those whom we would warn, console, or punish. What form we seem to them to bear we know not; we know only that we terrify even those whom we most wish to comfort, and from whom we most crave tenderness and sympathy.

Forgive, I pray you, this inconsequent digression by what was once a woman. You who consult us in this imperfect way—you do not understand. You ask foolish questions about things unknown and things forbidden. Much that we know and could impart in our speech is meaningless in yours. We must communicate with you through a stammering intelligence in that small fraction of our language that you yourselves can speak. You think that we are of another world. No, we have knowledge of no world but yours, though for us it holds no sunlight, no warmth, no music, no laughter, no song of birds, nor any companionship. O God! what a thing it is to be a ghost, cowering and shivering in an altered world, a prey to apprehension and despair!

No, I did not die of fright: the Thing turned and went away. I heard it go down the stairs, hurriedly, I thought, as if itself in sudden fear. Then I rose to call for help. Hardly had my shaking hand found the doorknob when—merciful heaven!—I heard it returning. Its footfalls as it remounted the stairs were rapid, heavy and loud; they shook the house. I fled to an angle of the wall and crouched upon the floor. I tried to pray. I tried to call the name of my dear husband. Then I heard the door thrown open. There was an interval of unconsciousness, and when I revived I felt a strangling clutch upon my throat—felt my arms feebly beating against something that bore me backward—felt my tongue thrusting itself from between my teeth! And then I passed into this life.

No, I have no knowledge of what it was. The sum of what we knew at death is the measure of what we know afterward of all that went before. Of this existence we know many things, but no new light falls upon any page of that; in memory is written all of it that we can read. Here are no heights of truth overlooking the confused landscape of that dubitable domain. We still dwell in the Valley of the Shadow, lurk in its desolate places, peering from brambles and thickets at its mad, malign inhabitants. How should we have new knowledge of that fading past?

What I am about to relate happened on a night. We know when it is night, for then you retire to your houses and we can venture from our places of concealment to move unafraid about our old homes, to look in at the windows, even to enter and gaze upon your faces as you sleep. I had lingered long near the dwelling where I had been so cruelly changed to what I am, as we do while any that we love or hate remain. Vainly I had sought some method of manifestation, some way to make my continued existence and my great love and poignant pity understood by my husband and son. Always if they slept they would wake, or if in my desperation I dared approach them when they were awake, would turn toward me the terrible eyes of the living, frightening me by the glances that I sought from the purpose that I held.

On this night I had searched for them without success, fearing to find them; they were nowhere in the house, nor about the moonlit lawn. For, although the sun is lost to us forever, the moon, full-orbed or slender, remains to us. Sometimes it shines by night, sometimes by day, but always it rises and sets, as in that other life.

I left the lawn and moved in the white light and silence along the road, aimless and sorrowing. Suddenly I heard the voice of my poor husband in exclamations of astonishment, with that of my son in reassurance and dissuasion; and there by the shadow of a group of trees they stood—near, so near! Their faces were toward me, the eyes of the elder man fixed upon mine. He saw me—at last, at last, he saw me! In the consciousness of that, my terror fled as a cruel dream. The death-spell was broken: Love had conquered Law! Mad with exultation I shouted—I *must* have shouted, "He sees, he sees: he will understand!" Then, controlling myself, I moved forward, smiling and consciously beautiful, to offer myself to his arms, to comfort him with endearments, and, with my son's hand in mine, to speak words that should restore the broken bonds between the living and the dead.

Alas! alas! his face went white with fear, his eyes were as those of a hunted animal. He backed away from me, as I advanced, and at last turned and fled into the wood—whither, it is not given to me to know.

To my poor boy, left doubly desolate, I have never been able to impart a sense of my presence. Soon he, too, must pass to this Life Invisible and be lost to me forever.

❋   ❋   ❋

AN ARREST

Having murdered his brother-in-law, Orrin Brower of Kentucky was a fugitive from justice. From the county jail where he had been confined to await his trial he had escaped by knocking down his jailer with an iron bar, robbing him of his keys and, opening the outer door, walking out into the night. The jailer being unarmed, Brower got no weapon with which to defend his recovered liberty. As soon as he was out of the town he had the folly to enter a forest; this was many years ago, when that region was wilder than it is now.

The night was pretty dark, with neither moon nor stars visible, and as Brower had never dwelt thereabout, and knew nothing of the lay of the land, he was, naturally, not long in losing himself. He could not have said if he were getting farther away from the town or going back to it—a most important matter to Orrin Brower. He knew that in either case a posse of citizens with a pack of bloodhounds would soon be on his track and his chance of escape was very slender; but he did not wish to assist in his own pursuit. Even an added hour of freedom was worth having.

Suddenly he emerged from the forest into an old road, and there before him saw, indistinctly, the figure of a man, motionless in the gloom. It was too late to retreat: the fugitive felt that at the first movement back toward the wood he would be, as he afterward explained, "filled with buckshot." So the two stood there like trees, Brower nearly suffocated by the activity of his own heart; the other —the emotions of the other are not recorded.

A moment later—it may have been an hour—the moon sailed into a patch of unclouded sky and the hunted man saw that visible embodiment of Law lift an arm and point significantly toward and beyond him. He understood. Turning his back to his captor, he walked submissively away in the direction indicated, looking to neither the right nor the left; hardly daring to breathe, his head and back actually aching with a prophecy of buckshot.

Brower was as courageous a criminal as ever lived to be hanged; that was shown by the conditions of awful personal peril in which he had coolly killed his brother-in-law. It is needless to relate them here; they came out at his trial, and the revelation of his calmness in confronting them came near to saving his neck. But what would you have?—when a brave man is beaten, he submits.

So they pursued their journey jailward along the old road through the woods. Only once did Brower venture a turn of the head: just once, when he was in deep shadow and he knew that the other was in moonlight, he looked backward. His captor was Burton Duff, the jailer, as white as death and bearing upon his brow the livid mark of the iron bar. Orrin Brower had no further curiosity.

Eventually they entered the town, which was all alight, but deserted; only the women and children remained, and they were off the streets. Straight toward the jail the criminal held his way. Straight up to the main entrance he walked, laid his hand upon the knob of the heavy iron door, pushed it open without command, entered and found himself in the presence of a half-dozen armed men. Then he turned. Nobody else entered.

On a table in the corridor lay the dead body of Burton Duff.

❋   ❋   ❋

A JUG OF SIRUP

This narrative begins with the death of its hero. Silas Deemer died on the 16th day of July, 1863, and two days later his remains were buried. As he had been personally known to every man, woman and well-grown child in the village, the funeral, as the local newspaper phrased it, "was largely attended." In accordance with a custom of the time and place, the coffin was opened at the graveside and the entire assembly of friends and neighbors filed past, taking a last look at the face of the dead. And then, before the eyes of all, Silas Deemer was put into the ground. Some of the eyes were a trifle dim, but in a general way it may be said that at that interment there was lack of neither observance nor observation; Silas was indubitably dead, and none could have pointed out any ritual delinquency that would have justified him in coming back from the grave. Yet if human testimony is good for anything (and certainly it once put an end to witchcraft in and about Salem) he came back.

I forgot to state that the death and burial of Silas Deemer occurred in the little village of Hillbrook, where he had lived for thirty-one years. He had been what is known in some parts of the Union (which is admittedly a free country) as a "merchant"; that is to say, he kept a retail shop for the sale of such things as are commonly sold in shops of that character. His honesty had never been questioned, so far as is known, and he was held in high esteem by all. The only thing that could be urged against him by the most censorious was a too close attention to business. It was not urged against him, though many another, who manifested it in no greater degree, was less leniently judged. The business to which Silas was devoted was mostly his own—that, possibly, may have made a difference.

At the time of Deemer's death nobody could recollect a single day, Sundays excepted, that he had not passed in his "store," since he had opened it more than a quarter-century before. His health having been perfect during all that time, he had been unable to discern any validity in whatever may or might have been urged to lure him astray from his counter; and it is related that once when he was summoned to the county seat as a witness in an important law case and did not attend, the lawyer who had the hardihood to move that he be "admonished" was solemnly informed that the Court regarded the proposal with "surprise." Judicial surprise being an emotion that attorneys are not commonly ambitious to arouse, the motion was hastily withdrawn and an agreement with the other side effected as to what Mr. Deemer would have said if he had been there—the other side pushing its advantage to the extreme and making the supposititious testimony distinctly damaging to the interests of its proponents. In brief, it was the general feeling in all that region that Silas Deemer was the one immobile verity of Hillbrook, and that his translation in space would precipitate some dismal public ill or strenuous calamity.

Mrs. Deemer and two grown daughters occupied the upper rooms of the building, but Silas had never been known to sleep elsewhere than on a cot behind the counter of the store. And there, quite by accident, he was found one night, dying, and passed away just before the time for taking down the shutters. Though speechless, he appeared conscious, and it was thought by those who knew him best that if the end had unfortunately been delayed beyond the usual hour for opening the store the effect upon him would have been deplorable.

Such had been Silas Deemer—such the fixity and invariety of his life and habit, that the village humorist (who had once attended college) was moved to bestow upon him the sobriquet of "Old Ibidem," and, in the first issue of the local newspaper after the death, to explain without offence that Silas had taken "a day off." It was more than a day, but from the record it appears that well within a month Mr. Deemer made it plain that he had not the leisure to be dead.

One of Hillbrook's most respected citizens was Alvan Creede, a banker. He lived in the finest house in town, kept a carriage and was a most estimable man variously. He knew something of the advantages of travel, too, having been frequently in Boston, and once, it was thought, in New York, though he modestly disclaimed that glittering dist·iction. The matter is mentioned here merely as a contribution to ¹ understanding of Mr. Creede's worth, for either way it is cred able to him—to his intelligence if he had put himself, even temporai ly, into contact with metropolitan culture; to his candor if he had ı ɔt.

One pleasai t summer evening at about the hour of ten Mr. Creede, enteri g at his garden gate, passed up the gravel walk, which looked ⅴ ʒry white in the moonlight, mounted the stone steps of his fine hou: ʒ and pausing a moment inserted his latchkey in the door. As he pu: ʰed this open he met his wife, who was crossing the passage from tɦ ʒ parlor to the library. She greeted him pleasantly and pulling the door further back held it for him to enter. Instead he turned and, ooking about his feet in front of the threshold, uttered an exclama ion of surprise.

"Why!—what t ɪe devil," he said, "has become of that jug?"

"What jug, A van?" his wife inquired, not very sympathetically.

"A jug of maᵣ le sirup—I brought it along from the store and set it down here to oɉ en the door. What the——"

"There, there, Alvan, please don't swear again," said the lady, interrupting. Hil brook, by the way, is not the only place in Christendom where a vestigial polytheism forbids the taking in vain of the Evil One's n me.

The jug of maple sirup which the easy ways of village life had permitted Hillbrook's foremost citizen to carry home from the store was not there.

"Are you quite sure, Alvan?"

"My dear, do you suppose a man does not know when he is carrying a jug? I bought that sirup at Deemer's as I was passing. Deemer himself drew it and lent me the jug, and I——"

The sentence remains to this day unfinished. Mr. Creede staggered into the house, entered the parlor and dropped into an armchair, trembling in every limb. He had suddenly remembered that Silas Deemer was three weeks dead.

Mrs. Creede stood by her husband, regarding him with surprise and anxiety.

"For Heaven's sake," she said, "what ails you?"

Mr. Creede's ailment having no obvious relation to the interests of the better land he did not apparently deem it necessary to expound it on that demand; he said nothing—merely stared. There were long moments of silence broken by nothing but the measured ticking of the clock, which seemed somewhat slower than usual, as if it were civilly granting them an extension of time in which to recover their wits.

"Jane, I have gone mad—that is it." He spoke thickly and hurriedly. "You should have told me; you must have observed my symptoms before they became so pronounced that I have observed them myself. I thought I was passing Deemer's store; it was open and lit up—that is what I thought; of course it is never open now. Silas Deemer stood at his desk behind the counter. My God, Jane, I saw him as distinctly as I see you. Remembering that you had said you wanted some maple sirup, I went in and bought some—that is all—I bought two quarts of maple sirup from Silas Deemer, who is dead and underground, but nevertheless drew that sirup from a cask and handed it to me in a jug. He talked with me, too, rather gravely, I remember, even more so than was his way, but not a word of what he said can I now recall. But I saw him—good Lord, I saw and talked with him—and he is dead! So I thought, but I'm mad, Jane, I'm as crazy as a beetle; and you have kept it from me."

This monologue gave the woman time to collect what faculties she had.

"Alvan," she said, "you have given no evidence of insanity, believe me. This was undoubtedly an illusion—how should it be anything else? That would be too terrible! But there is no insanity; you are working too hard at the bank. You should not have attended the meeting of directors this evening; any one could see that you were ill; I knew something would occur."

It may have seemed to him that the prophecy had lagged a bit, awaiting the event, but he said nothing of that, being concerned

with his own condition. He was calm now, and could think co-
herently.

"Doubtless the phenomenon was subjective," he said, with a somewhat ludicrous transition to the slang of science. "Granting the
possibility of spiritual apparition and even materialization, yet the
apparition and materialization of a half-gallon brown clay jug—a
piece of coarse, heavy pottery evolved from nothing—that is hardly
thinkable."

As he finished speaking, a child ran into the room—his little
daughter. She was clad in a bedgown. Hastening to her father she
threw her arms about his neck, saying: "You naughty papa, you forgot to come in and kiss me. We heard you open the gate and got up
and looked out. And, papa dear, Eddy says mayn't he have the little
jug when it is empty?"

As the full import of that revelation imparted itself to Alvan
Creede's understanding he visibly shuddered. For the child could
not have heard a word of the conversation.

The estate of Silas Deemer being in the hands of an administrator who had thought it best to dispose of the "business" the store
had been closed ever since the owner's death, the goods having been
removed by another "merchant" who had purchased them *en bloc.*
The rooms above were vacant as well, for the widow and the daughters had gone to another town.

On the evening immediately after Alvan Creede's adventure
(which had somehow "got out") a crowd of men, women and children thronged the sidewalk opposite the store. That the place was
haunted by the spirit of the late Silas Deemer was now well known
to every resident of Hillbrook, though many affected disbelief. Of
these the hardiest, and in a general way the youngest, threw stones
against the front of the building, the only part accessible, but carefully missed the unshuttered windows. Incredulity had not grown
to malice. A few venturesome souls crossed the street and rattled
the door in its frame; struck matches and held them near the window; attempted to view the black interior. Some of the spectators
invited attention to their wit by shouting and groaning and challenging the ghost to a footrace.

After a considerable time had elapsed without any manifestation,
and many of the crowd had gone away, all those remaining began
to observe that the interior of the store was suffused with a dim,
yellow light. At this all demonstrations ceased; the intrepid souls
about the door and windows fell back to the opposite side of the
street and were merged in the crowd; the small boys ceased throw-

ing stones. Nobody spoke above his breath; all whispered excitedly and pointed to the now steadily growing light. How long a time had passed since the first faint glow had been observed none could have guessed, but eventually the illumination was bright enough to reveal the whole interior of the store; and there, standing at his desk behind the counter, Silas Deemer was distinctly visible!

The effect upon the crowd was marvelous. It began rapidly to melt away at both flanks, as the timid left the place. Many ran as fast as their legs would let them; others moved off with greater dignity, turning occasionally to look backward over the shoulder. At last a score or more, mostly men, remained where they were, speechless, staring, excited. The apparition inside gave them no attention; it was apparently occupied with a book of accounts.

Presently three men left the crowd on the sidewalk as if by a common impulse and crossed the street. One of them, a heavy man, was about to set his shoulder against the door when it opened, apparently without human agency, and the courageous investigators passed in. No sooner had they crossed the threshold than they were seen by the awed observers outside to be acting in the most unaccountable way. They thrust out their hands before them, pursued devious courses, came into violent collision with the counter, with boxes and barrels on the floor, and with one another. They turned awkwardly hither and thither and seemed trying to escape, but unable to retrace their steps. Their voices were heard in exclamations and curses. But in no way did the apparition of Silas Deemer manifest an interest in what was going on.

By what impulse the crowd was moved none ever recollected, but the entire mass—men, women, children, dogs—made a simultaneous and tumultous rush for the entrance. They congested the doorway, pushing for precedence—resolving themselves at length into a line and moving up step by step. By some subtle spiritual or physical alchemy observation had been transmuted into action—the sightseers had become participants in the spectacle—the audience had usurped the stage.

To the only spectator remaining on the other side of the street— Alvan Creede, the banker—the interior of the store with its inpouring crowd continued in full illumination; all the strange things going on there were clearly visible. To those inside all was black darkness. It was as if each person as he was thrust in at the door had been stricken blind, and was maddened by the mischance. They groped with aimless imprecision, tried to force their way out against the current, pushed and elbowed, struck at random, fell and were trampled, rose and trampled in their turn. They seized one another by the garments, the hair, the beard—fought like animals, cursed, shouted, called one another opprobrious and obscene names. When, finally, Alvan Creede had seen the last person of the line pass into that awful tumult the light that had illuminated it was suddenly quenched and all was as black to him as to those within. He turned away and left the place.

In the early morning a curious crowd had gathered about "Deemer's." It was composed partly of those who had run away the night before, but now had the courage of sunshine, partly of honest folk going to their daily toil. The door of the store stood open; the place was vacant, but on the walls, the floor, the furniture, were shreds of clothing and tangles of hair. Hillbrook militant had managed somehow to pull itself out and had gone home to medicine its hurts and swear that it had been all night in bed. On the dusty desk, behind the counter, was the salesbook. The entries in it, in Deemer's handwriting, had ceased on the 16th day of July, the last of his life. There was no record of a later sale to Alvan Creede.

That is the entire story—except that men's passions having subsided and reason having resumed its immemorial sway, it was confessed in Hillbrook that, considering the harmless and honorable character of his first commercial transaction under the new conditions, Silas Deemer, deceased, might properly have been suffered to resume business at the old stand without mobbing. In that judgment the local historian from whose unpublished work these facts are compiled had the thoughtfulness to signify his concurrence.

❅   ❅   ❅

THE ISLE OF PINES

For many years there lived near the town of Gallipolis, Ohio, an old man named Herman Deluse. Very little was known of his history, for he would neither speak of it himself nor suffer others. It was a common belief among his neighbors that he had been a pirate—if upon any better evidence than his collection of boarding pikes, cutlasses, and ancient flintlock pistols, no one knew. He lived entirely alone in a small house of four rooms, falling rapidly into decay and never repaired further than was required by the weather. It

stood on a slight elevation in the midst of a large, stony field overgrown with brambles, and cultivated in patches and only in the
most primitive way. It was his only visible property, but could hardly
have yielded him a living, simple and few as were his wants. He
seemed always to have ready money, and paid cash for all his pur-
chases at the village stores roundabout, seldom buying more than
two or three times at the same place until after the lapse of a considerable time. He got no commendation, however, for this equitable distribution of his patronage; people were disposed to regard it
as an ineffectual attempt to conceal his possession of so much money.
That he had great hoards of ill-gotten gold buried somewhere about
his tumble-down dwelling was not reasonably to be doubted by any
honest soul conversant with the facts of local tradition and gifted
with a sense of the fitness of things.

On the 9th of November, 1867, the old man died; at least his
dead body was discovered on the 10th, and physicians testified that
death had occurred about twenty-four hours previously—precisely
how, they were unable to say; for the *post-mortem* examination
showed every organ to be absolutely healthy, with no indication of
disorder or violence. According to them, death must have taken
place about noonday, yet the body was found in bed. The verdict of
the coroner's jury was that he "came to his death by a visitation of
God." The body was buried and the public administrator took charge
of the estate.

A rigorous search disclosed nothing more than was already known
about the dead man, and much patient excavation here and there
about the premises by thoughtful and thrifty neighbors went unre-
warded. The administrator locked up the house against the time
when the property, real and personal, should be sold by law with a
view to defraying, partly, the expenses of the sale.

The night of November 20 was boisterous. A furious gale stormed
across the country, scourging it with desolating drifts of sleet. Great
trees were torn from the earth and hurled across the roads. So wild
a night had never been known in all that region, but toward morning the storm had blown itself out of breath and day dawned bright
and clear. At about eight o'clock that morning the Rev. Henry
Galbraith, a well-known and highly esteemed Lutheran minister,
arrived on foot at his house, a mile and a half from the Deluse place.
Mr. Galbraith had been for a month in Cincinnati. He had come
up the river in a steamboat, and landing at Gallipolis the previous
evening had immediately obtained a horse and buggy and set out
for home. The violence of the storm had delayed him over night,

and in the morning the fallen trees had compelled him to abandon his conveyance and continue his journey afoot.

"But where did you pass the night?" inquired his wife, after he had briefly related his adventure.

"With old Deluse at the 'Isle of Pines,' "[1] was the laughing reply; "and a glum enough time I had of it. He made no objection to my remaining, but not a word could I get out of him."

Fortunately for the interests of truth there was present at this conversation Mr. Robert Mosely Maren, a lawyer and *littérateur* of Columbus, the same who wrote the delightful "Mellowcraft Papers." Noting, but apparently not sharing, the astonishment caused by Mr. Galbraith's answer this ready-witted person checked by a gesture the exclamations that would naturally have followed, and tranquilly inquired: "How came you to go in there?"

This is Mr. Maren's version of Mr. Galbraith's reply:

"I saw a light moving about the house, and being nearly blinded by the sleet, and half frozen besides, drove in at the gate and put up my horse in the old rail stable, where it is now. I then rapped at the door, and getting no invitation went in without one. The room was dark, but having matches I found a candle and lit it. I tried to enter the adjoining room, but the door was fast, and although I heard the old man's heavy footsteps in there he made no response to my calls. There was no fire on the hearth, so I made one and laying [sic] down before it with my overcoat under my head, prepared myself for sleep. Pretty soon the door that I had tried silently opened and the old man came in, carrying a candle. I spoke to him pleasantly, apologizing for my intrusion, but he took no notice of me. He seemed to be searching for something, though his eyes were unmoved in their sockets. I wonder if he ever walks in his sleep. He took a circuit a part of the way round the room, and went out the same way he had come in. Twice more before I slept he came back into the room, acting precisely the same way, and departing as at first. In the intervals I heard him tramping all over the house, his footsteps distinctly audible in the pauses of the storm. When I woke in the morning he had already gone out."

Mr. Maren attempted some further questioning, but was unable longer to restrain the family's tongues; the story of Deluse's death and burial came out, greatly to the good minister's astonishment.

"The explanation of your adventure is very simple," said Mr.

[1] The Isle of Pines was once a famous rendezvous of pirates.

Maren. "I don't believe old Deluse walks in his sleep—not in his present one; but you evidently dream in yours."

And to this view of the matter Mr. Galbraith was compelled reluctantly to assent.

Nevertheless, a late hour of the next night found these two gentlemen, accompanied by a son of the minister, in the road in front of the old Deluse house. There was a light inside; it appeared now at one window and now at another. The three men advanced to the door. Just as they reached it there came from the interior a confusion of the most appalling sounds—the clash of weapons, steel against steel, sharp explosions as of firearms, shrieks of women, groans and the curses of men in combat! The investigators stood a moment, irresolute, frightened. Then Mr. Galbraith tried the door. It was fast. But the minister was a man of courage, a man, moreover, of Herculean strength. He retired a pace or two and rushed against the door, striking it with his right shoulder and bursting it from the frame with a loud crash. In a moment the three were inside. Darkness and silence! The only sound was the beating of their hearts.

Mr. Maren had provided himself with matches and a candle. With some difficulty, begotten of his excitement, he made a light, and they proceeded to explore the place, passing from room to room. Everything was in orderly arrangement, as it had been left by the sheriff; nothing had been disturbed. A light coating of dust was everywhere. A back door was partly open, as if by neglect, and their first thought was that the authors of the awful revelry might have escaped. The door was opened, and the light of the candle shone through upon the ground. The expiring effort of the previous night's storm had been a light fall of snow; there were no footprints; the white surface was unbroken. They closed the door and entered the last room of the four that the house contained—that farthest from the road, in an angle of the building. Here the candle in Mr. Maren's hand was suddenly extinguished as by a draught of air. Almost immediately followed the sound of a heavy fall. When the candle had been hastily relighted young Mr. Galbraith was seen prostrate on the floor at a little distance from the others. He was dead. In one hand the body grasped a heavy sack of coins, which later examination showed to be all of old Spanish mintage. Directly over the body as it lay, a board had been torn from its fastenings in the wall, and from the cavity so disclosed it was evident that the bag had been taken.

Another inquest was held: another *post-mortem* examination

failed to reveal a probable cause of death. Another verdict of "the visitation of God" left all at liberty to form their own conclusions. Mr. Maren contended that the young man died of excitement.

※　　※　　※

AT OLD MAN ECKERT'S

Philip Eckert lived for many years in an old, weather-stained wooden house about three miles from the little town of Marion, in Vermont. There must be quite a number of persons living who remember him, not unkindly, I trust, and know something of the story that I am about to tell.

"Old Man Eckert," as he was always called, was not of a sociable disposition and lived alone. As he was never known to speak of his own affairs nobody thereabout knew anything of his past, nor of his relatives if he had any. Without being particularly ungracious or repellent in manner or speech, he managed somehow to be immune to impertinent curiosity, yet exempt from the evil repute with which it commonly revenges itself when baffled; so far as I know, Mr. Eckert's renown as a reformed assassin or a retired pirate of the Spanish Main had not reached any ear in Marion. He got his living cultivating a small and not very fertile farm.

One day he disappeared and a prolonged search by his neighbors failed to turn him up or throw any light upon his whereabouts or whyabouts. Nothing indicated preparation to leave: all was as he might have left it to go to the spring for a bucket of water. For a few weeks little else was talked of in that region; then "old man Eckert" became a village tale for the ear of the stranger. I do not know what was done regarding his property—the correct legal thing, doubtless. The house was standing, still vacant and conspicuously unfit, when I last heard of it, some twenty years afterward.

Of course it came to be considered "haunted," and the customary tales were told of moving lights, dolorous sounds and startling apparitions. At one time, about five years after the disappearance, these stories of the supernatural became so rife, or through some attesting circumstances seemed so important, that some of Marion's most serious citizens deemed it well to investigate, and to that end arranged for a night session on the premises. The parties to this undertaking were John Holcomb, an apothecary; Wilson Merle, a lawyer, and Andrus C. Palmer, the teacher of the public school, all men of consequence and repute. They were to meet at Holcomb's house at eight o'clock in the evening of the appointed day and go together to the scene of their vigil, where certain arrangements for their comfort, a provision of fuel and the like, for the season was winter, had been already made.

Palmer did not keep the engagement, and after waiting a half-hour for him the others went to the Eckert house without him. They established themselves in the principal room, before a glowing fire, and without other light than it gave, awaited events. It had been agreed to speak as little as possible: they did not even renew the exchange of views regarding the defection of Palmer, which had occupied their minds on the way.

Probably an hour had passed without incident when they heard (not without emotion, doubtless) the sound of an opening door in the rear of the house followed by footfalls in the room adjoining that in which they sat. The watchers rose to their feet, but stood firm, prepared for whatever might ensue. A long silence followed—how long neither would afterward undertake to say. Then the door between the two rooms opened and a man entered.

It was Palmer. He was pale, as if from excitement—as pale as the others felt themselves to be. His manner, too, was singularly distrait: he neither responded to their salutations nor so much as looked at them, but walked slowly across the room in the light of the failing fire and opening the front door passed out into the darkness.

It seems to have been the first thought of both men that Palmer was suffering from fright—that something seen, heard or imagined in the back room had deprived him of his senses. Acting on the same friendly impulse both ran after him through the open door. But neither they nor anyone ever again saw or heard of Andrus Palmer!

This much was ascertained the next morning. During the session of Messrs. Holcomb and Merle at the "haunted house" a new snow had fallen to a depth of several inches upon the old. In this snow Palmer's trail from his lodging in the village to the back door of the Eckert house was conspicuous. But there it ended: from the front door nothing led away but the tracks of the two men who swore that he preceded them. Palmer's disappearance was as complete as that of "old man Eckert" himself—whom, indeed, the editor of the local paper somewhat graphically accused of having "reached out and pulled him in."

THE SPOOK HOUSE

On the road leading north from Manchester, in eastern Kentucky, to Booneville, twenty miles away, stood, in 1862, a wooden plantation house of a somewhat better quality than most of the dwellings in that region. The house was destroyed by fire in the year following—probably by some stragglers from the retreating column of General George W. Morgan, when he was driven from Cumberland Gap to the Ohio river by General Kirby Smith. At the time of its destruction, it had for four or five years been vacant. The fields about it were overgrown with brambles, the fences gone, even the few negro quarters, and out-houses generally, fallen partly into ruin by neglect and pillage; for the negroes and poor whites of the vicinity found in the building and fences an abundant supply of fuel, of which they availed themselves without hesitation, openly and by daylight. By daylight alone; after nightfall no human being except passing strangers ever went near the place.

It was known as the "Spook House." That it was tenanted by evil spirits, visible, audible and active, no one in all that region doubted any more than he doubted what he was told of Sundays by the traveling preacher. Its owner's opinion of the matter was unknown; he and his family had disappeared one night and no trace of them had ever been found. They left everything—household goods, clothing, provisions, the horses in the stable, the cows in the field, the negroes in the quarters—all as it stood; nothing was missing—except a man, a woman, three girls, a boy and a babe! It was not altogether surprising that a plantation where seven human beings could be simultaneously effaced and nobody the wiser should be under some suspicion.

One night in June, 1859, two citizens of Frankfort, Col. J. C. McArdle, a lawyer, and Judge Myron Veigh, of the State Militia, were driving from Booneville to Manchester. Their business was so important that they decided to push on, despite the darkness and the mutterings of an approaching storm, which eventually broke upon them just as they arrived opposite the "Spook House." The lightning was so incessant that they easily found their way through the gateway and into a shed, where they hitched and unharnessed their team. They then went to the house, through the rain, and knocked at all the doors without getting any response. Attributing this to the continuous uproar of the thunder they pushed at one of the doors, which yielded. They entered without further ceremony and closed the door. That instant they were in darkness and silence. Not a gleam of the lightning's unceasing blaze penetrated the windows or crevices; not a whisper of the awful tumult without reached them there. It was as if they had suddenly been stricken blind and deaf, and McArdle afterward said that for a moment he believed himself to have been killed by a stroke of lightning as he crossed the threshold. The rest of this adventure can as well be related in his own words, from the Frankfort *Advocate* of August 6, 1876:

"When I had somewhat recovered from the dazing effect of the transition from uproar to silence, my first impulse was to reopen the door which I had closed, and from the knob of which I was not conscious of having removed my hand; I felt it distinctly, still in the clasp of my fingers. My notion was to ascertain by stepping again into the storm whether I had been deprived of sight and hearing. I turned the door-knob and pulled open the door. It led into another room!

"This apartment was suffused with a faint greenish light, the source of which I could not determine, making everything distinctly visible, though nothing was sharply defined. Everything, I say, but in truth the only objects within the blank stone walls of that room were human corpses. In number they were perhaps eight or ten—it may well be understood that I did not truly count them. They were of different ages, or rather sizes, from infancy up, and of both sexes. All were prostrate on the floor, excepting one, apparently a young woman, who sat up, her back supported by an angle of the wall. A babe was clasped in the arms of another and older woman. A half-grown lad lay face downward across the legs of a full-bearded man. One or two were nearly naked, and the hand of a young girl held the fragment of a gown which she had torn open at the breast. The bodies were in various stages of decay, all greatly shrunken in face and figure. Some were but little more than skeletons.

"While I stood stupefied with horror by this ghastly spectacle and still holding open the door, by some unaccountable perversity my attention was diverted from the shocking scene and concerned itself with trifles and details. Perhaps my mind, with an instinct of self-preservation, sought relief in matters which would relax its dangerous tension. Among other things, I observed that the door that I was holding open was of heavy iron plates, riveted. Equidistant from one another and from the top and bottom, three strong bolts protruded from the beveled edge. I turned the knob and they were retracted flush with the edge; released it, and they shot out. It was a spring lock. On the inside there was no knob, nor any kind of projection—a smooth surface of iron.

"While noting these things with an interest and attention which it now astonishes me to recall I felt myself thrust aside, and Judge Veigh, whom in the intensity and vicissitudes of my feelings I had altogether forgotten, pushed by me into the room. 'For God's sake,' I cried, 'do not go in there! Let us get out of this dreadful place!'

"He gave no heed to my entreaties, but (as fearless a gentleman as lived in all the South) walked quickly to the center of the room, knelt beside one of the bodies for a closer examination and tenderly raised its blackened and shriveled head in his hands. A strong disagreeable odor came through the doorway, completely overpowering me. My senses reeled; I felt myself falling, and in clutching at the edge of the door for support pushed it shut with a sharp click!

"I remember no more: six weeks later I recovered my reason in a hotel at Manchester, whither I had been taken by strangers the next day. For all these weeks I had suffered from a nervous fever, attended with constant delirium. I had been found lying in the road several miles away from the house; but how I had escaped from it to get there I never knew. On recovery, or as soon as my physicians permitted me to talk, I inquired the fate of Judge Veigh, whom (to quiet me, as I now know) they represented as well and at home.

"No one believed a word of my story, and who can wonder? And who can imagine my grief when, arriving at my home in Frankfort two months later, I learned that Judge Veigh had never been heard of since that night? I then regretted bitterly the pride which since the first few days after the recovery of my reason had forbidden me to repeat my discredited story and insist upon its truth.

"With all that afterward occurred—the examination of the house; the failure to find any room corresponding to that which I have described; the attempt to have me adjudged insane, and my triumph over my accusers—the readers of the *Advocate* are familiar. After all these years I am still confident that excavations which I have neither the legal right to undertake nor the wealth to make would disclose the secret of the disappearance of my unhappy friend, and possibly of the former occupants and owners of the deserted and now destroyed house. I do not despair of yet bringing about such a search, and it is a source of deep grief to me that it has been delayed by the undeserved hostility and unwise incredulity of the family and friends of the late Judge Veigh."

Colonel McArdle died in Frankfort on the thirteenth day of December, in the year 1879.

※   ※   ※

THE MIDDLE TOE OF THE RIGHT FOOT

I

It is well known that the old Manton house is haunted. In all the rural district near about, and even in the town of Marshall, a mile away, not one person of unbiased mind entertains a doubt of it; incredulity is confined to those opinionated persons who will be called "cranks" as soon as the useful word shall have penetrated the intellectual demesne of the Marshall *Advance*. The evidence that the house is haunted is of two kinds: the testimony of disinterested witnesses who have had ocular proof, and that of the house itself. The former may be disregarded and ruled out on any of the various grounds of objection which may be urged against it by the ingenious; but facts within the observation of all are material and controlling.

In the first place, the Manton house has been unoccupied by mortals for more than ten years, and with its outbuildings is slowly falling into decay—a circumstance which in itself the judicious will hardly venture to ignore. It stands a little way off the loneliest reach of the Marshall and Harriston road, in an opening which was once a farm and is still disfigured with strips of rotting fence and half covered with brambles overrunning a stony and sterile soil long unacquainted with the plow. The house itself is in tolerably good condition, though badly weather-stained and in dire need of attention from the glazier, the smaller male population of the region having attested in the manner of its kind its disapproval of dwelling without dwellers. It is two stories in height, nearly square, its front pierced by a single doorway flanked on each side by a window boarded up to the very top. Corresponding windows above, not protected, serve to admit light and rain to the rooms of the upper floor. Grass and weeds grow pretty rankly all about, and a few shade trees, somewhat the worse for wind, and leaning all in one direction, seem to be making a concerted effort to run away. In short, as the Marshall town humorist explained in the columns of the *Advance,* "the proposition that the Manton house is badly haunted is the only logical conclusion from the premises." The fact that in this dwelling Mr. Manton thought it expedient one night some ten years ago to rise and cut the throats of his wife and two small children, removing at once to another part of the country, has no doubt done its share in directing public attention to the fitness of the place for supernatural phenomena.

To this house, one summer evening, came four men in a wagon. Three of them promptly alighted, and the one who had been driving hitched the team to the only remaining post of what had been a fence. The fourth remained seated in the wagon. "Come," said one of his companions, approaching him, while the others moved away in the direction of the dwelling—"this is the place."

The man addressed did not move. "By God!" he said harshly, "this is a trick, and it looks to me as if you were in it."

"Perhaps I am," the other said, looking him straight in the face and speaking in a tone which had something of contempt in it. "You will remember, however, that the choice of place was with your own assent left to the other side. Of course if you are afraid of spooks——"

"I am afraid of nothing," the man interrupted with another oath, and sprang to the ground. The two then joined the others at the door, which one of them had already opened with some difficulty, caused by rust of lock and hinge. All entered. Inside it was dark, but the man who had unlocked the door produced a candle and matches and made a light. He then unlocked a door on their right as they stood in the passage. This gave them entrance to a large, square room that the candle but dimly lighted. The floor had a thick carpeting of dust, which partly muffled their footfalls. Cobwebs were in the angles of the walls and depended from the ceiling like strips of rotting lace, making undulatory movements in the disturbed air. The room had two windows in adjoining sides, but from neither could anything be seen except the rough inner surfaces of boards a few inches from the glass. There was no fireplace, no furniture; there was nothing: besides the cobwebs and the dust, the four men were the only objects there which were not a part of the structure.

Strange enough they looked in the yellow light of the candle. The one who had so reluctantly alighted was especially spectacular—he might have been called sensational. He was of middle age, heavily built, deep chested and broad shouldered. Looking at his figure, one would have said that he had a giant's strength; at his features, that he would use it like a giant. He was clean shaven, his hair rather closely cropped and gray. His low forehead was seamed with wrinkles above the eyes, and over the nose these became vertical. The heavy black brows followed the same law, saved from meeting only by an upward turn at what would otherwise have been the point of contact. Deeply sunken beneath these, glowed in the obscure light a pair of eyes of uncertain color, but obviously enough too small. There was something forbidding in their expression, which was not bettered by the cruel mouth and wide jaw. The nose was well enough, as noses go; one does not expect much of noses. All that was sinister in the man's face seemed accentuated by an unnatural pallor—he appeared altogether bloodless.

The appearance of the other men was sufficiently commonplace: they were such persons as one meets and forgets that he met. All were younger than the man described, between whom and the eldest of the others, who stood apart, there was apparently no kindly feeling. They avoided looking at each other.

"Gentlemen," said the man holding the candle and keys, "I believe everything is right. Are you ready, Mr. Rosser?"

The man standing apart from the group bowed and smiled.

"And you, Mr. Grossmith?"

The heavy man bowed and scowled.

"You will be pleased to remove your outer clothing."

Their hats, coats, waistcoats and neckwear were soon removed and thrown outside the door, in the passage. The man with the candle now nodded, and the fourth man—he who had urged Grossmith to leave the wagon—produced from the pocket of his overcoat two long, murderous-looking bowie-knives, which he drew now from their leather scabbards.

"They are exactly alike," he said, presenting one to each of the two principals—for by this time the dullest observer would have understood the nature of this meeting. It was to be a duel to the death.

Each combatant took a knife, examined it critically near the candle and tested the strength of blade and handle across his lifted knee. Their persons were then searched in turn, each by the second of the other.

"If it is agreeable to you, Mr. Grossmith," said the man holding the light, "you will place yourself in that corner."

He indicated the angle of the room farthest from the door, whither Grossmith retired, his second parting from him with a grasp of the hand which had nothing of cordiality in it. In the angle nearest the door Mr. Rosser stationed himself, and after a whispered consultation his second left him, joining the other near the door. At that moment the candle was suddenly extinguished, leaving all in profound darkness. This may have been done by a draught from the opened door; whatever the cause, the effect was startling.

"Gentlemen," said a voice which sounded strangely unfamiliar in the altered condition affecting the relations of the senses—"gentlemen, you will not move until you hear the closing of the outer door."

A sound of trampling ensued, then the closing of the inner door; and finally the outer one closed with a concussion which shook the entire building.

A few minutes afterward a belated farmer's boy met a light wagon which was being driven furiously toward the town of Marshall. He declared that behind the two figures on the front seat stood a third, with its hands upon the bowed shoulders of the others, who appeared to struggle vainly to free themselves from its grasp. This figure, unlike the others, was clad in white, and had undoubtedly boarded the wagon as it passed the haunted house. As the lad could boast a considerable former experience with the supernatural thereabouts his word had the weight justly due in the testimony of an expert. The story (in connection with the next day's events) eventually appeared in the *Advance*, with some slight literary embellishments and a concluding intimation that the gentlemen referred to would be allowed the use of the paper's columns for their version of the night's adventure. But the privilege remained without a claimant.

II

The events that led up to this "duel in the dark" were simple enough. One evening three young men of the town of Marshall were sitting in a quiet corner of the porch of the village hotel, smoking and discussing such matters as three educated young men of a Southern village would naturally find interesting. Their names were King, Sancher and Rosser. At a little distance, within easy hearing, but taking no part in the conversation, sat a fourth. He was a stranger to the others. They merely knew that on his arrival by the stage-coach that afternoon he had written in the hotel register the name Robert Grossmith. He had not been observed to speak to anyone except the hotel clerk. He seemed, indeed, singularly fond of his own company—or, as the *personnel* of the *Advance* expressed it, "grossly addicted to evil associations." But then it should be said in justice to the stranger that the *personnel* was himself of a too convivial disposition fairly to judge one differently gifted, and had, moreover, experienced a slight rebuff in an effort at an "interview."

"I hate any kind of deformity in a woman," said King, "whether natural or—acquired. I have a theory that any physical defect has its correlative mental and moral defect."

"I infer, then," said Rosser, gravely, "that a lady lacking the moral advantage of a nose would find the struggle to become Mrs. King an arduous enterprise."

"Of course you may put it that way," was the reply; "but, seriously, I once threw over a most charming girl on learning quite accidentally that she had suffered amputation of a toe. My conduct was brutal if you like, but if I had married that girl I should have been miserable for life and should have made her so."

"Whereas," said Sancher, with a light laugh, "by marrying a gentleman of more liberal views she escaped with a parted throat."

"Ah, you know to whom I refer. Yes, she married Manton, but I don't know about his liberality; I'm not sure but he cut her throat because he discovered that she lacked that excellent thing in woman, the middle toe of the right foot."

"Look at that chap!" said Rosser in a low voice, his eyes fixed upon the stranger.

That chap was obviously listening intently to the conversation.

"Damn his impudence!" muttered King—"what ought we to do?"

"That's an easy one," Rosser replied, rising. "Sir," he continued, addressing the stranger, "I think it would be better if you would remove your chair to the other end of the veranda. The presence of gentlemen is evidently an unfamiliar situation to you."

The man sprang to his feet and strode forward with clenched hands, his face white with rage. All were now standing. Sancher stepped between the belligerents.

"You are hasty and unjust," he said to Rosser; "this gentleman has done nothing to deserve such language."

But Rosser would not withdraw a word. By the custom of the country and the time there could be but one outcome to the quarrel.

"I demand the satisfaction due to a gentleman," said the stranger, who had become more calm. "I have not an acquaintance in this region. Perhaps you, sir," bowing to Sancher, "will be kind enough to represent me in this matter."

Sancher accepted the trust—somewhat reluctantly it must be confessed, for the man's appearance and manner were not at all to his liking. King, who during the colloquy had hardly removed his eyes from the stranger's face and had not spoken a word, consented with a nod to act for Rosser, and the upshot of it was that, the principals having retired, a meeting was arranged for the next evening. The nature of the arrangements has been already disclosed. The duel with knives in a dark room was once a commoner feature of Southwestern life than it is likely to be again. How thin a veneering of "chivalry" covered the essential brutality of the code under which such encounters were possible we shall see.

III

In the blaze of a midsummer noonday the old Manton house was hardly true to its traditions. It was of the earth, earthy. The sunshine caressed it warmly and affectionately, with evident disregard of its bad reputation. The grass greening all the expanse in its front seemed to grow, not rankly, but with a natural and joyous exuberance, and the weeds blossomed quite like plants. Full of charming lights and shadows and populous with pleasant-voiced birds, the neglected shade trees no longer struggled to run away, but bent reverently beneath their burdens of sun and song. Even in the glassless upper windows was an expression of peace and contentment, due to the light within. Over the stony fields the visible heat danced with a lively tremor incompatible with the gravity which is an attribute of the supernatural.

Such was the aspect under which the place presented itself to Sheriff Adams and two other men who had come out from Marshall to look at it. One of these men was Mr. King, the sheriff's deputy; the other, whose name was Brewer, was a brother of the late Mrs. Manton. Under a beneficent law of the State relating to property which has been for a certain period abandoned by an owner whose residence cannot be ascertained, the sheriff was legal custodian of the Manton farm and appurtenances thereunto belonging. His present visit was in mere perfunctory compliance with some order of a court in which Mr. Brewer had an action to get possession of the property as heir to his deceased sister. By a mere coincidence, the visit was made on the day after the night that Deputy King had unlocked the house for another and very different purpose. His presence now was not of his own choosing: he had been ordered to accompany his superior and at the moment could think of nothing more prudent than simulated alacrity in obedience to the command.

Carelessly opening the front door, which to his surprise was not locked, the sheriff was amazed to see, lying on the floor of the passage into which it opened, a confused heap of men's apparel. Examination showed it to consist of two hats, and the same number of coats, waistcoats and scarves, all in a remarkably good state of preservation, albeit somewhat defiled by the dust in which they lay. Mr. Brewer was equally astonished, but Mr. King's emotion is not of record. With a new and lively interest in his own actions the sheriff now unlatched and pushed open a door on the right, and the three entered. The room was apparently vacant—no; as their eyes became accustomed to the dimmer light something was visible in the farthest angle of the wall. It was a human figure—that of a man crouching close in the corner. Something in the attitude made the intruders halt when they had barely passed the threshold. The figure more and more clearly defined itself. The man was upon one knee, his back in the angle of the wall, his shoulders elevated to the level of his ears, his hands before his face, palms outward, the fingers spread and crooked like claws; the white face turned upward on the retracted neck had an expression of unutterable fright, the mouth half open, the eyes incredibly expanded. He was stone dead. Yet, with the exception of a bowie-knife, which had evidently fallen from his own hand, not another object was in the room.

In thick dust that covered the floor were some confused footprints near the door and along the wall through which it opened. Along one of the adjoining walls, too, past the boarded-up windows, was the trail made by the man himself in reaching his corner. Instinctively in approaching the body the three men followed that trail. The sheriff grasped one of the outthrown arms; it was as rigid as iron, and the application of a gentle force rocked the entire body without altering the relation of its parts. Brewer, pale with excitement, gazed intently into the distorted face. "God of mercy!" he suddenly cried, "it is Manton!"

"You are right," said King, with an evident attempt at calmness: "I knew Manton. He then wore a full beard and his hair long, but this is he."

He might have added: "I recognized him when he challenged Rosser. I told Rosser and Sancher who he was before we played him this horrible trick. When Rosser left this dark room at our heels, forgetting his outer clothing in the excitement, and driving away with us in his shirt sleeves—all through the discreditable proceedings we knew whom we were dealing with, murderer and coward that he was!"

But nothing of this did Mr. King say. With his better light he was trying to penetrate the mystery of the man's death. That he had not once moved from the corner where he had been stationed; that his posture was that of neither attack nor defense; that he had dropped his weapon; that he had obviously perished of sheer horror of something that he *saw*—these were circumstances which Mr. King's disturbed intelligence could not rightly comprehend.

Groping in intellectual darkness for a clew to his maze of doubt, his gaze, directed mechanically downward in the way of one who ponders momentous matters, fell upon something which, there, in the light of day and in the presence of living companions, affected him with terror. In the dust of years that lay thick upon the floor—leading from the door by which they had entered, straight across the room to within a yard of Manton's crouching corpse—were three parallel lines of footprints—light but definite impressions of bare feet, the outer ones those of small children, the inner a woman's. From the point at which they ended they did not return; they pointed all one way. Brewer, who had observed them at the same moment, was leaning forward in an attitude of rapt attention, horribly pale.

"Look at that!" he cried, pointing with both hands at the nearest print of the woman's right foot, where she had apparently stopped and stood. "The middle toe is missing—it was Gertrude!"

Gertrude was the late Mrs. Manton, sister to Mr. Brewer.

❊   ❊   ❊

THE THING AT NOLAN

To the south of where the road between Leesville and Hardy, in the State of Missouri, crosses the east fork of May Creek stands an abandoned house. Nobody has lived in it since the summer of 1879, and it is fast going to pieces. For some three years before the date mentioned above, it was occupied by the family of Charles May, from one of whose ancestors the creek near which it stands took its name. Mr. May's family consisted of a wife, an adult son and two young girls. The son's name was John—the names of the daughters are unknown to the writer of this sketch.

John May was of a morose and surly disposition, not easily moved to anger, but having an uncommon gift of sullen, implacable hate. His father was quite otherwise; of a sunny, jovial disposition, but with a quick temper like a sudden flame kindled in a wisp of straw, which consumes it in a flash and is no more. He cherished no resentments, and his anger gone, was quick to make overtures for reconciliation. He had a brother living near by who was unlike him in respect of all this, and it was a current witticism in the neighborhood that John had inherited his disposition from his uncle.

One day a misunderstanding arose between father and son, harsh words ensued, and the father struck the son full in the face with his fist. John quietly wiped away the blood that followed the blow, fixed his eyes upon the already penitent offender and said with cold composure, "You will die for that."

The words were overheard by two brothers named Jackson, who were approaching the men at the moment; but seeing them engaged in a quarrel they retired, apparently unobserved. Charles May afterward related the unfortunate occurrence to his wife and explained that he had apologized to the son for the hasty blow, but without avail; the young man not only rejected his overtures, but refused to withdraw his terrible threat. Nevertheless, there was no open rupture of relations: John continued living with the family, and things went on very much as before.

One Sunday morning in June, 1879, about two weeks after what has been related, May senior left the house immediately after breakfast, taking a spade. He said he was going to make an excavation at a certain spring in a wood about a mile away, so that the cattle could obtain water. John remained in the house for some hours, variously occupied in shaving himself, writing letters and reading a newspaper. His manner was very nearly what it usually was; perhaps he was a trifle more sullen and surly.

At two o'clock he left the house. At five, he returned. For some reason not connected with any interest in his movements, and which is not now recalled, the time of his departure and that of his return were noted by his mother and sisters, as was attested at his trial for murder. It was observed that his clothing was wet in spots, as if (so the prosecution afterward pointed out) he had been removing bloodstains from it. His manner was strange, his look wild. He complained of illness, and going to his room took to his bed.

May senior did not return. Later that evening the nearest neighbors were aroused, and during that night and the following day a search was prosecuted through the wood where the spring was. It resulted in little but the discovery of both men's footprints in the clay about the spring. John May in the meantime had grown rapidly worse with what the local physician called brain fever, and in his delirium raved of murder, but did not say whom he conceived to have been murdered, nor whom he imagined to have done the deed. But his threat was recalled by the brothers Jackson and he was arrested on suspicion and a deputy sheriff put in charge of him at his home. Public opinion ran strongly against him and but for his illness he would probably have been hanged by a mob. As it was, a meeting of the neighbors was held on Tuesday and a committee appointed to watch the case and take such action at any time as circumstances might seem to warrant.

On Wednesday all was changed. From the town of Nolan, eight miles away, came a story which put a quite different light on the matter. Nolan consisted of a school house, a blacksmith's shop, a "store" and a half-dozen dwellings. The store was kept by one Henry Odell, a cousin of the elder May. On the afternoon of the Sunday of May's disappearance Mr. Odell and four of his neighbors, men of credibility, were sitting in the store smoking and talking. It was a warm day; and both the front and the back door were open. At about three o'clock Charles May, who was well known to three of them, entered at the front door and passed out at the rear. He was without hat or coat. He did not look at them, nor return their greeting, a circumstance which did not surprise, for he was evidently seriously hurt. Above the left eyebrow was a wound—a deep gash from which the blood flowed, covering the whole left side of the face and neck and saturating his light-gray shirt. Oddly enough, the thought uppermost in the minds of all was that he had been fighting and was going to the brook directly at the back of the store, to wash himself.

Perhaps there was a feeling of delicacy—a backwoods etiquette which restrained them from following him to offer assistance; the court records, from which, mainly, this narrative is drawn, are silent as to anything but the fact. They waited for him to return, but he did not return.

Bordering the brook behind the store is a forest extending for six miles back to the Medicine Lodge Hills. As soon as it became known in the neighborhood of the missing man's dwelling that he had been seen in Nolan there was a marked alteration in public sentiment and feeling. The vigilance committee went out of existence without the formality of a resolution. Search along the wooded bottom lands of May Creek was stopped and nearly the entire male population of the region took to beating the bush about Nolan and in the Medicine Lodge Hills. But of the missing man no trace was found.

One of the strangest circumstances of this strange case is the formal indictment and trial of a man for murder of one whose body no human being professed to have seen—one not known to be dead. We are all more or less familiar with the vagaries and eccentricities of frontier law, but this instance, it is thought, is unique. However that may be, it is of record that on recovering from his illness John May was indicted for the murder of his missing father. Counsel for the defense appears not to have demurred and the case was tried on its merits. The prosecution was spiritless and perfunctory; the defense easily established—with regard to the deceased—an *alibi*. If during the time in which John May must have killed Charles May, if he killed him at all, Charles May was miles away from where John May must have been, it is plain that the deceased must have come to his death at the hands of someone else.

John May was acquitted, immediately left the country, and has never been heard of from that day. Shortly afterward his mother and sisters removed to St. Louis. The farm having passed into the possession of a man who owns the land adjoining, and has a dwelling of his own, the May house has ever since been vacant, and has the somber reputation of being haunted.

One day after the May family had left the country, some boys, playing in the woods along May Creek, found concealed under a mass of dead leaves, but partly exposed by the rooting of hogs, a spade, nearly new and bright, except for a spot on one edge, which was rusted and stained with blood. The implement had the initials C. M. cut into the handle.

This discovery renewed, in some degree, the public excitement of a few months before. The earth near the spot where the spade was found was carefully examined, and the result was the finding of the dead body of a man. It had been buried under two or three feet of soil and the spot covered with a layer of dead leaves and twigs. There was but little decomposition, a fact attributed to some preservative property in the mineral-bearing soil.

Above the left eyebrow was a wound—a deep gash from which blood had flowed, covering the whole left side of the face and neck and saturating the light-gray shirt. The skull had been cut through by the blow. The body was that of Charles May.

But what was it that passed through Mr. Odell's store at Nolan?

THE DIFFICULTY OF CROSSING
A FIELD

One morning in July, 1854, a planter named Williamson, living six miles from Selma, Alabama, was sitting with his wife and a child on the veranda of his dwelling. Immediately in front of the house was a lawn, perhaps fifty yards in extent between the house and public road, or, as it was called, the "pike." Beyond this road lay a close-cropped pasture of some ten acres, level and without a tree, rock, or any natural or artificial object on its surface. At the time there was not even a domestic animal in the field. In another field, beyond the pasture, a dozen slaves were at work under an overseer.

Throwing away the stump of a cigar, the planter rose, saying: "I forgot to tell Andrew about those horses." Andrew was the overseer.

Williamson strolled leisurely down the gravel walk, plucking a flower as he went, passed across the road and into the pasture, pausing a moment as he closed the gate leading into it, to greet a passing neighbor, Armour Wren, who lived on an adjoining plantation. Mr. Wren was in an open carriage with his son James, a lad of thirteen. When he had driven some two hundred yards from the point of meeting, Mr. Wren said to his son: "I forgot to tell Mr. Williamson about those horses."

Mr. Wren had sold to Mr. Williamson some horses, which were to have been sent for that day, but for some reason not now remembered it would be inconvenient to deliver them until the morrow. The coachman was directed to drive back, and as the vehicle turned Williamson was seen by all three, walking leisurely across the pasture. At that moment one of the coach horses stumbled and came near falling. It had no more than fairly recovered itself when James Wren cried: "Why, father, what has become of Mr. Williamson?"

It is not the purpose of this narrative to answer that question.

Mr. Wren's strange account of the matter, given under oath in the course of legal proceedings relating to the Williamson estate, here follows:

"My son's exclamation caused me to look toward the spot where I had seen the deceased [sic] an instant before, but he was not there, nor was he anywhere visible. I cannot say that at the moment

I was greatly startled, or realized the gravity of the occurrence, though I thought it singular. My son, however, was greatly astonished and kept repeating his question in different forms until we arrived at the gate. My black boy Sam was similarly affected, even in a greater degree, but I reckon more by my son's manner than by anything he had himself observed. [This sentence in the testimony was stricken out.] As we got out of the carriage at the gate of the field, and while Sam was hanging [sic] the team to the fence, Mrs. Williamson, with her child in her arms and followed by several servants, came running down the walk in great excitement, crying: 'He is gone, he is gone! O God! what an awful thing!' and many other such exclamations, which I do not distinctly recollect. I got from them the impression that they related to something more than the mere disappearance of her husband, even if that had occurred before her eyes. Her manner was wild, but not more so, I think, than was natural under the circumstances. I have no reason to think she had at that time lost her mind. I have never since seen nor heard of Mr. Williamson."

This testimony, as might have been expected, was corroborated in almost every particular by the only other eye-witness (if that is a proper term)—the lad James. Mrs. Williamson had lost her reason and the servants were, of course, not competent to testify. The boy James Wren had declared at first that he *saw* the disappearance, but there is nothing of this in his testimony given in court. None of the field hands working in the field to which Williamson was going had seen him at all, and the most rigorous search of the entire plantation and adjoining country failed to supply a clew. The most monstrous and grotesque fictions, originating with the blacks, were current in that part of the State for many years, and probably are to this day; but what has been here related is all that is certainly known of the matter. The courts decided that Williamson was dead, and his estate was distributed according to law.

❊   ❊   ❊

AN UNFINISHED RACE

James Burne Worson was a shoemaker who lived in Leamington, Warwickshire, England. He had a little shop in one of the by-ways leading off the road to Warwick. In his humble sphere he was esteemed an honest man, although like many of his class in English towns he was somewhat addicted to drink. When in liquor he would make foolish wagers. On one of these too frequent occasions he was boasting of his prowess as a pedestrian and athlete, and the outcome was a match against nature. For a stake of one sovereign he undertook to run all the way to Coventry and back, a distance of something more than forty miles. This was on the 3d day of September in 1873. He set out at once, the man with whom he had made the bet—whose name is not remembered—accompanied by Barham Wise, a linen draper, and Hamerson Burns, a photographer, I think, following in a light cart or wagon.

For several miles Worson went on very well, at an easy gait, without apparent fatigue, for he had really great powers of endurance and was not sufficiently intoxicated to enfeeble them. The three men in the wagon kept a short distance in the rear, giving him occasional friendly "chaff" or encouragement, as the spirit moved them. Suddenly—in the very middle of the roadway, not a dozen yards from them, and with their eyes full upon him—the man seemed to stumble, pitched headlong forward, uttered a terrible cry and vanished! He did not fall to the earth—he vanished before touching it. No trace of him was ever discovered.

After remaining at and about the spot for some time, with aimless irresolution, the three men returned to Leamington, told their astonishing story and were afterward taken into custody. But they were of good standing, had always been considered truthful, were sober at the time of the occurrence, and nothing ever transpired to discredit their sworn account of their extraordinary adventure, concerning the truth of which, nevertheless, public opinion was divided, throughout the United Kingdom. If they had something to conceal, their choice of means is certainly one of the most amazing ever made by sane human beings.

❊　　❊　　❊

CHARLES ASHMORE'S TRAIL

The family of Christian Ashmore consisted of his wife, his mother, two grown daughters, and a son of sixteen years. They lived in Troy, New York, were well-to-do, respectable persons, and had many friends, some of whom, reading these lines, will doubtless learn for the first time the extraordinary fate of the young man. From Troy the Ashmores moved in 1871 or 1872 to Richmond, Indiana, and a year or two later to the vicinity of Quincy, Illinois, where Mr. Ashmore bought a farm and lived on it. At some little distance from the farmhouse was a spring with a constant flow of clear, cold water, whence the family derived its supply for domestic use at all seasons.

On the evening of the 9th of November in 1878, at about nine o'clock, young Charles Ashmore left the family circle about the hearth, took a tin bucket and started toward the spring. As he did not return, the family became uneasy, and going to the door by which he had left the house, his father called without receiving an answer. He then lighted a lantern and with the eldest daughter, Martha, who insisted on accompanying him, went in search. A light snow had fallen, obliterating the path, but making the young man's trail conspicuous; each footprint was plainly defined. After going a little more than half-way—perhaps seventy-five yards—the father, who was in advance, halted, and elevating his lantern stood peering intently into the darkness ahead.

"What is the matter, father?" the girl asked.

This was the matter: the trail of the young man had abruptly ended, and all beyond was smooth, unbroken snow. The last footprints were as conspicuous as any in the line; the very nail-marks were distinctly visible. Mr. Ashmore looked upward, shading his eyes with his hat held between them and the lantern. The stars were shining; there was not a cloud in the sky; he was denied the explanation which had suggested itself, doubtful as it would have been—a new snowfall with a limit so plainly defined. Taking a wide circuit round the ultimate tracks, so as to leave them undisturbed for further examination, the man proceeded to the spring, the girl following, weak and terrified. Neither had spoken a word of what both had observed. The spring was covered with ice, hours old.

Returning to the house they noted the appearance of the snow on both sides of the trail its entire length. No tracks led away from it.

The morning light showed nothing more. Smooth, spotless, unbroken, the shallow snow lay everywhere.

Four days later the grief-stricken mother herself went to the spring for water. She came back and related that in passing the spot where the footprints had ended she had heard the voice of her son and had been eagerly calling to him, wandering about the place, as she had fancied the voice to be now in one direction, now in another, until she was exhausted with fatigue and emotion. Questioned as to what the voice had said, she was unable to tell, yet averred that the words were perfectly distinct. In a moment the entire family was at the place, but nothing was heard, and the voice was believed to be an hallucination caused by the mother's great anxiety and her disordered nerves. But for months afterward, at irregular intervals of a few days, the voice was heard by the several members of the family, and by others. All declared it unmistakably the voice of Charles Ashmore; all agreed that it seemed to come from a great distance, faintly, yet with entire distinctness of articulation; yet none could determine its direction, nor repeat its words. The intervals of silence grew longer and longer, the voice fainter and farther, and by midsummer it was heard no more.

If anybody knows the fate of Charles Ashmore it is probably his mother. She is dead.

❊   ❊   ❊

STALEY FLEMING'S HALLUCINATION

Of two men who were talking one was a physician.

"I sent for you, Doctor," said the other, "but I don't think you can do me any good. May be you can recommend a specialist in psychopathy. I fancy I'm a bit loony."

"You look all right," the physician said.

"You shall judge—I have hallucinations. I wake every night and see in my room, intently watching me, a big black Newfoundland dog with a white forefoot."

"You say you wake; are you sure about that? 'Hallucinations' are sometimes only dreams."

"Oh, I wake, all right. Sometimes I lie still a long time, looking at the dog as earnestly as the dog looks at me—I always leave the light going. When I can't endure it any longer I sit up in bed—and nothing is there!"

"' 'M, 'm—what is the beast's expression?"

"It seems to me sinister. Of course I know that, except in art, an animal's face in repose has always the same expression. But this is not a real animal. Newfoundland dogs are pretty mild looking, you know; what's the matter with this one?"

"Really, my diagnosis would have no value: I am not going to treat the dog."

The physician laughed at his own pleasantry, but narrowly watched his patient from the corner of his eye. Presently he said: "Fleming, your description of the beast fits the dog of the late Atwell Barton."

Fleming half-rose from his chair, sat again and made a visible attempt at indifference. "I remember Barton," he said; "I believe he was—it was reported that—wasn't there something suspicious in his death?"

Looking squarely now into the eyes of his patient, the physician said: "Three years ago the body of your old enemy, Atwell Barton, was found in the woods near his house and yours. He had been stabbed to death. There have been no arrests; there was no clew. Some of us had 'theories.' I had one. Have you?"

"I? Why, bless your soul, what could I know about it? You remember that I left for Europe almost immediately afterward—a considerable time afterward. In the few weeks since my return you could not expect me to construct a 'theory.' In fact, I have not given the matter a thought. What about his dog?"

"It was first to find the body. It died of starvation on his grave."

We do not know the inexorable law underlying coincidences. Staley Fleming did not, or he would perhaps not have sprung to his feet as the night wind brought in through the open window the long wailing howl of a distant dog. He strode several times across the room in the steadfast gaze of the physician; then, abruptly confronting him, almost shouted: "What has all this to do with my trouble, Dr. Halderman? You forget why you were sent for."

Rising, the physician laid his hand upon his patient's arm and said, gently: "Pardon me. I cannot diagnose your disorder offhand —to-morrow, perhaps. Please go to bed, leaving your door unlocked; I will pass the night here with your books. Can you call me without rising?"

"Yes, there is an electric bell."

"Good. If anything disturbs you push the button without sitting up. Good night."

Comfortably installed in an armchair the man of medicine stared into the glowing coals and thought deeply and long, but apparently to little purpose, for he frequently rose and opening a door leading to the staircase, listened intently; then resumed his seat. Presently, however, he fell asleep, and when he woke it was past midnight. He stirred the failing fire, lifted a book from the table at his side and looked at the title. It was Denneker's "Meditations." He opened it at random and began to read:

"Forasmuch as it is ordained of God that all flesh hath spirit and thereby taketh on spiritual powers, so, also, the spirit hath powers of the flesh, even when it is gone out of the flesh and liveth as a thing apart, as many a violence performed by wraith and lemure sheweth. And there be who say that man is not single in this, but the beasts have the like evil inducement, and——"

The reading was interrupted by a shaking of the house, as by the fall of a heavy object. The reader flung down the book, rushed from the room and mounted the stairs to Fleming's bed-chamber. He tried the door, but contrary to his instructions it was locked. He set his shoulder against it with such force that it gave way. On the floor near the disordered bed, in his night clothes, lay Fleming gasping away his life.

The physician raised the dying man's head from the floor and observed a wound in the throat. "I should have thought of this," he said, believing it suicide.

When the man was dead an examination disclosed the unmistakable marks of an animal's fangs deeply sunken into the jugular vein.

But there was no animal.

❊   ❊   ❊

THE NIGHT-DOINGS AT
"DEADMAN'S"

A STORY THAT IS UNTRUE

It was a singularly sharp night, and clear as the heart of a diamond. Clear nights have a trick of being keen. In darkness you may be cold and not know it; when you see, you suffer. This night was bright enough to bite like a serpent. The moon was moving mysteriously along behind the giant pines crowning the South Mountain, striking a cold sparkle from the crusted snow, and bringing out against the black west the ghostly outlines of the Coast Range, beyond which lay the invisible Pacific. The snow had piled itself, in the open spaces along the bottom of the gulch, into long ridges that seemed to heave, and into hills that appeared to toss and scatter spray. The spray was sunlight, twice reflected: dashed once from the moon, once from the snow.

In this snow many of the shanties of the abandoned mining camp were obliterated, (a sailor might have said they had gone down) and at irregular intervals it had overtopped the tall trestles which had once supported a river called a flume; for, of course, "flume" is *flumen*. Among the advantages of which the mountains cannot deprive the gold-hunter is the privilege of speaking Latin. He says of his dead neighbor, "He has gone up the flume." This is not a bad way to say, "His life has returned to the Fountain of Life."

While putting on its armor against the assaults of the wind, this snow had neglected no coign of vantage. Snow pursued by the wind is not wholly unlike a retreating army. In the open field it ranges itself in ranks and battalions; where it can get a foothold it makes a stand; where it can take cover it does so. You may see whole platoons of snow cowering behind a bit of broken wall. The devious old road, hewn out of the mountain-side, was full of it. Squadron upon squadron had struggled to escape by this line, when suddenly pursuit had ceased. A more desolate and dreary spot than Deadman's Gulch in a winter midnight it is impossible to imagine. Yet Mr. Hiram Beeson elected to live there, the sole inhabitant.

Away up the side of the North Mountain his little pine-log shanty projected from its single pane of glass a long, thin beam of light, and looked not altogether unlike a black beetle fastened to the hill-side with a bright new pin. Within it sat Mr. Beeson himself, before a roaring fire, staring into its hot heart as if he had never before seen such a thing in all his life. He was not a comely man. He was gray; he was ragged and slovenly in his attire; his face was wan and haggard; his eyes were too bright. As to his age, if one had attempted to guess it, one might have said forty-seven, then corrected himself and said seventy-four. He was really twenty-eight. Emaciated he was; as much, perhaps, as he dared be, with a needy undertaker at Bentley's Flat and a new and enterprising coroner at Sonora. Poverty and zeal are an upper and a nether millstone. It is dangerous to make a third in that kind of sandwich.

As Mr. Beeson sat there, with his ragged elbows on his ragged knees, his lean jaws buried in his lean hands, and with no apparent intention of going to bed, he looked as if the slightest movement would tumble him to pieces. Yet during the last hour he had winked no fewer than three times.

There was a sharp rapping at the door. A rap at that time of night and in that weather might have surprised an ordinary mortal who had dwelt two years in the gulch without seeing a human face, and could not fail to know that the country was impassable; but Mr. Beeson did not so much as pull his eyes out of the coals. And even when the door was pushed open he only shrugged a little more closely into himself, as one does who is expecting something that he would rather not see. You may observe this movement in women when, in a mortuary chapel, the coffin is borne up the aisle behind them.

But when a long old man in a blanket overcoat, his head tied up in a handkerchief and nearly his entire face in a muffler, wearing green goggles and with a complexion of glittering whiteness where it could be seen, strode silently into the room, laying a hard, gloved hand on Mr. Beeson's shoulder, the latter so far forgot himself as to look up with an appearance of no small astonishment; whomever he may have been expecting, he had evidently not counted on meeting anyone like this. Nevertheless, the sight of this unexpected guest produced in Mr. Beeson the following sequence: a feeling of astonishment; a sense of gratification; a sentiment of profound good will. Rising from his seat, he took the knotty hand from his shoulder, and shook it up and down with a fervor quite unaccountable; for in the old man's aspect was nothing to attract, much to repel. However, attraction is too general a property for repulsion to be without it. The most attractive object in the world is the face we instinctively cover with a cloth. When it becomes still more attractive—fascinating —we put seven feet of earth above it.

"Sir," said Mr. Beeson, releasing the old man's hand, which fell passively against his thigh with a quiet clack, "it is an extremely disagreeable night. Pray be seated; I am very glad to see you."

Mr. Beeson spoke with an easy good breeding that one would hardly have expected, considering all things. Indeed, the contrast between his appearance and his manner was sufficiently surprising to be one of the commonest of social phenomena in the mines. The old man advanced a step toward the fire, glowing cavernously in the green goggles. Mr. Beeson resumed:

"You bet your life I am!"

Mr. Beeson's elegance was not too refined; it had made reasonable concessions to local taste. He paused a moment, letting his eyes drop from the muffled head of his guest, down along the row of moldy buttons confining the blanket overcoat, to the greenish cowhide boots powdered with snow, which had begun to melt and run along the floor in little rills. He took an inventory of his guest, and appeared satisfied. Who would not have been? Then he continued:

"The cheer I can offer you is, unfortunately, in keeping with my surroundings; but I shall esteem myself highly favored if it is your pleasure to partake of it, rather than seek better at Bentley's Flat."

With a singular refinement of hospitable humility Mr. Beeson spoke as if a sojourn in his warm cabin on such a night, as compared with walking fourteen miles up to the throat in snow with a cutting crust, would be an intolerable hardship. By way of reply, his guest unbuttoned the blanket overcoat. The host laid fresh fuel on the fire, swept the hearth with the tail of a wolf, and added:

"But I think you'd better skedaddle."

The old man took a seat by the fire, spreading his broad soles to the heat without removing his hat. In the mines the hat is seldom removed except when the boots are. Without further remark Mr. Beeson also seated himself in a chair which had been a barrel, and which, retaining much of its original character, seemed to have been designed with a view to preserving his dust if it should please him to crumble. For a moment there was silence; then, from somewhere among the pines, came the snarling yelp of a coyote; and simultaneously the door rattled in its frame. There was no other connection between the two incidents than that the coyote has an aversion to storms, and the wind was rising; yet there seemed somehow a kind of supernatural conspiracy between the two, and Mr. Beeson shuddered with a vague sense of terror. He recovered himself in a moment and again addressed his guest.

"There are strange doings here. I will tell you everything, and then if you decide to go I shall hope to accompany you over the worst of the way; as far as where Baldy Peterson shot Ben Hike—I dare say you know the place."

The old man nodded emphatically, as intimating not merely that he did, but that he did indeed.

"Two years ago," began Mr. Beeson, "I, with two companions, occupied this house; but when the rush to the Flat occurred we left, along with the rest. In ten hours the Gulch was deserted. That evening, however, I discovered I had left behind me a valuable pistol (that is it) and returned for it, passing the night here alone, as I have passed every night since. I must explain that a few days before we left, our Chinese domestic had the misfortune to die while the ground was frozen so hard that it was impossible to dig a grave in the usual way. So, on the day of our hasty departure, we cut through the floor there, and gave him such burial as we could. But before putting him down I had the extremely bad taste to cut off his pigtail and spike it to that beam above his grave, where you may see it at this moment, or, preferably, when warmth has given you leisure for observation.

"I stated, did I not, that the Chinaman came to his death from natural causes? I had, of course, nothing to do with that, and returned through no irresistible attraction, or morbid fascination, but only because I had forgotten a pistol. This is clear to you, is it not, sir?"

The visitor nodded gravely. He appeared to be a man of few words, if any. Mr. Beeson continued:

"According to the Chinese faith, a man is like a kite: he cannot go to heaven without a tail. Well, to shorten this tedious story—which, however, I thought it my duty to relate—on that night, while I was here alone and thinking of anything but him, that Chinaman came back for his pigtail.

"He did not get it."

At this point Mr. Beeson relapsed into blank silence. Perhaps he was fatigued by the unwonted exercise of speaking; perhaps he had conjured up a memory that demanded his undivided attention. The wind was now fairly abroad, and the pines along the mountain-side sang with singular distinctness. The narrator continued:

"You say you do not see much in that, and I must confess I do not myself.

"But he keeps coming!"

There was another long silence, during which both stared into the fire without the movement of a limb. Then Mr. Beeson broke out, almost fiercely, fixing his eyes on what he could see of the impassive face of his auditor:

"Give it him? Sir, in this matter I have no intention of troubling anyone for advice. You will pardon me, I am sure"—here he became singularly persuasive—"but I have ventured to nail that pigtail fast, and have assumed the somewhat onerous obligation of guarding it. So it is quite impossible to act on your considerate suggestion.

"Do you play me for a Modoc?"

Nothing could exceed the sudden ferocity with which he thrust this indignant remonstrance into the ear of his guest. It was as if he had struck him on the side of the head with a steel gauntlet. It was a protest, but it was a challenge. To be mistaken for a coward—to be played for a Modoc: these two expressions are one. Sometimes it is a Chinaman. Do you play me for a Chinaman? is a question frequently addressed to the ear of the suddenly dead.

Mr. Beeson's buffet produced no effect, and after a moment's pause, during which the wind thundered in the chimney like the sound of clods upon a coffin, he resumed:

"But, as you say, it is wearing me out. I feel that the life of the last two years has been a mistake—a mistake that corrects itself; you see how. The grave! No; there is no one to dig it. The ground is frozen, too. But you are very welcome. You may say at Bentley's—but that is not important. It was very tough to cut: they braid silk into their pigtails. Kwaagh."

Mr. Beeson was speaking with his eyes shut, and he wandered. His last word was a snore. A moment later he drew a long breath, opened his eyes with an effort, made a single remark, and fell into a deep sleep. What he said was this:

"They are swiping my dust!"

Then the aged stranger, who had not uttered one word since his arrival, arose from his seat and deliberately laid off his outer clothing, looking as angular in his flannels as the late Signorina Festorazzi, an Irish woman, six feet in height, and weighting fifty-six pounds, who used to exhibit herself in her chemise to the people of San Francisco. He then crept into one of the "bunks," having first placed a revolver in easy reach, according to the custom of the country. This revolver he took from a shelf, and it was the one which Mr. Beeson had mentioned as that for which he had returned to the Gulch two years before.

In a few moments Mr. Beeson awoke, and seeing that his guest had retired he did likewise. But before doing so he approached the long, plaited wisp of pagan hair and gave it a powerful tug, to assure himself that it was fast and firm. The two beds—mere shelves covered with blankets not overclean—faced each other from opposite sides of the room, the little square trapdoor that had given access to the Chinaman's grave being midway between. This, by the way, was crossed by a double row of spike-heads. In his resistance of the supernatural, Mr. Beeson had not disdained the use of material precautions.

The fire was now low, the flames burning bluely and petulantly, with occasional flashes, projecting spectral shadows on the walls— shadows that moved mysteriously about, now dividing, now uniting. The shadow of the pendent queue, however, kept moodily apart, near the roof at the further end of the room, looking like a note of admiration. The song of the pines outside had now risen to the dignity of a triumphal hymn. In the pauses the silence was dreadful.

It was during one of these intervals that the trap in the floor began to lift. Slowly and steadily it rose, and slowly and steadily rose the swaddled head of the old man in the bunk to observe it. Then, with a clap that shook the house to its foundation, it was thrown clean back, where it lay with its unsightly spikes pointing threateningly upward. Mr. Beeson awoke, and without rising, pressed his fingers into his eyes. He shuddered; his teeth chattered. His guest was now reclining on one elbow, watching the proceedings with the goggles that glowed like lamps.

Suddenly a howling gust of wind swooped down the chimney, scattering ashes and smoke in all directions, for a moment obscuring everything. When the firelight again illuminated the room there was seen, sitting gingerly on the edge of a stool by the hearthside, a swarthy little man of prepossessing appearance and dressed with faultless taste, nodding to the old man with a friendly and engaging smile. "From San Francisco, evidently," thought Mr. Beeson, who having somewhat recovered from his fright was groping his way to a solution of the evening's events.

But now another actor appeared upon the scene. Out of the square black hole in the middle of the floor protruded the head of the departed Chinaman, his glassy eyes turned upward in their angular slits and fastened on the dangling queue above with a look of yearning unspeakable. Mr. Beeson groaned, and again spread his hands upon his face. A mild odor of opium pervaded the place. The phantom, clad only in a short blue tunic quilted and silken but covered with grave-mold, rose slowly, as if pushed by a weak spiral spring. Its knees were at the level of the floor, when with a quick upward impulse like the silent leaping of a flame it grasped the queue with both hands, drew up its body and took the tip in its horrible yellow teeth. To this it clung in a seeming frenzy, grimacing ghastly, surging and plunging from side to side in its efforts to disengage its property from the beam, but uttering no sound. It was like a corpse artificially convulsed by means of a galvanic battery. The contrast between its superhuman activity and its silence was no less than hideous!

Mr. Beeson cowered in his bed. The swarthy little gentleman uncrossed his legs, beat an impatient tattoo with the toe of his boot and consulted a heavy gold watch. The old man sat erect and quietly laid hold of the revolver.

Bang!

Like a body cut from the gallows the Chinaman plumped into the black hole below, carrying his tail in his teeth. The trapdoor turned over, shutting down with a snap. The swarthy little gentleman from San Francisco sprang nimbly from his perch, caught something in the air with his hat, as a boy catches a butterfly, and vanished into the chimney as if drawn up by suction.

From away somewhere in the outer darkness floated in through the open door a faint, far cry—a long, sobbing wail, as of a child death-strangled in the desert, or a lost soul borne away by the Adversary. It may have been the coyote.

In the early days of the following spring a party of miners on their way to new diggings passed along the Gulch, and straying through the deserted shanties found in one of them the body of Hiram Beeson, stretched upon a bunk, with a bullet hole through the heart. The ball had evidently been fired from the opposite side of the room, for in one of the oaken beams overhead was a shallow blue dint, where it had struck a knot and been deflected downward to the breast of its victim. Strongly attached to the same beam was what appeared to be an end of a rope of braided horsehair, which had been cut by the bullet in its passage to the knot. Nothing else of interest was noted, excepting a suit of moldy and incongruous clothing, several articles of which were afterward identified by respectable witnesses as those in which certain deceased citizens of Deadman's had been buried years before. But it is not easy to understand how that could be, unless, indeed, the garments had been worn as a disguise by Death himself—which is hardly credible.

❀   ❀   ❀

A BABY TRAMP

If you had seen little Jo standing at the street corner in the rain, you would hardly have admired him. It was apparently an ordinary autumn rainstorm, but the water which fell upon Jo (who was hardly old enough to be either just or unjust, and so perhaps did not come under the law of impartial distribution) appeared to have some property peculiar to itself: one would have said it was dark and adhesive—sticky. But that could hardly be so, even in Blackburg, where things certainly did occur that were a good deal out of the common.

For example, ten or twelve years before, a shower of small frogs had fallen, as is credibly attested by a contemporaneous chronicle, the record concluding with a somewhat obscure statement to the effect that the chronicler considered it good growing-weather for Frenchmen.

Some years later Blackburg had a fall of crimson snow; it is cold in Blackburg when winter is on, and the snows are frequent and deep. There can be no doubt of it—the snow in this instance was of the color of blood and melted into water of the same hue, if water it was, not blood. The phenomenon had attracted wide attention, and science had as many explanations as there were scientists who knew nothing about it. But the men of Blackburg—men who for many years had lived right there where the red snow fell, and might be supposed to know a good deal about the matter—shook their heads and said something would come of it.

And something did, for the next summer was made memorable by the prevalence of a mysterious disease—epidemic, endemic, or the Lord knows what, though the physicians didn't—which carried away a full half of the population. Most of the other half carried themselves away and were slow to return, but finally came back, and were now increasing and multiplying as before, but Blackburg had not since been altogether the same.

Of quite another kind, though equally "out of the common," was the incident of Hetty Parlow's ghost. Hetty Parlow's maiden name had been Brownon, and in Blackburg that meant more than one would think.

The Brownons had from time immemorial—from the very earliest of the old colonial days—been the leading family of the town. It was the richest and it was the best, and Blackburg would have shed the last drop of its plebeian blood in defense of the Brownon fair fame. As few of the family's members had ever been known to live permanently away from Blackburg, although most of them were educated elsewhere and nearly all had traveled, there was quite a number of them. The men held most of the public offices, and the woman were foremost in all good works. Of these latter, Hetty was most beloved by reason of the sweetness of her disposition, the purity of her character and her singular personal beauty. She married in Boston a young scapegrace named Parlow, and like a good Brownon brought him to Blackburg forthwith and made a man and a town councilman of him. They had a child which they named Joseph and dearly loved, as was then the fashion among parents in all that region. Then they died of the mysterious disorder already mentioned, and at the age of one whole year Joseph set up as an orphan.

Unfortunately for Joseph the disease which had cut off his parents did not stop at that; it went on and extirpated nearly the whole

Brownon contingent and its allies by marriage; and those who fled did not return. The tradition was broken, the Brownon estates passed into alien hands and the only Brownons remaining in that place were underground in Oak Hill Cemetery, where, indeed, was a colony of them powerful enough to resist the encroachment of surrounding tribes and hold the best part of the grounds. But about the ghost:

One night, about three years after the death of Hetty Parlow, a number of the young people of Blackburg were passing Oak Hill Cemetery in a wagon—if you have been there you will remember that the road to Greenton runs alongside it on the south. They had been attending a May Day festival at Greenton; and that serves to fix the date. Altogether there may have been a dozen, and a jolly party they were, considering the legacy of gloom left by the town's recent somber experiences. As they passed the cemetery the man driving suddenly reined in his team with an exclamation of surprise. It was sufficiently surprising, no doubt, for just ahead, and almost at the roadside, though inside the cemetery, stood the ghost of Hetty Parlow. There could be no doubt of it, for she had been personally known to every youth and maiden in the party. That established the thing's identity; its character as ghost was signified by all the customary signs—the shroud, the long, undone hair, the "far-away look"—everything. This disquieting apparition was stretching out its arms toward the west, as if in supplication for the evening star, which, certainly, was an alluring object, though obviously out of reach. As they all sat silent (so the story goes) every member of that party of merrymakers—they had merrymade on coffee and lemonade only—distinctly heard that ghost call the name "Joey, Joey!" A moment later nothing was there. Of course one does not have to believe all that.

Now, at that moment, as was afterward ascertained, Joey was wandering about in the sagebrush on the opposite side of the continent, near Winnemucca, in the State of Nevada. He had been taken to that town by some good persons distantly related to his dead father, and by them adopted and tenderly cared for. But on that evening the poor child had strayed from home and was lost in the desert.

His after history is involved in obscurity and has gaps which conjecture alone can fill. It is known that he was found by a family of Piute Indians, who kept the little wretch with them for a time and then sold him—actually sold him for money to a woman on one of the east-bound trains, at a station a long way from Winnemucca. The woman professed to have made all manner of inquiries, but all in vain: so, being childless and a widow, she adopted him herself. At this point of his career Jo seemed to be getting a long way from the condition of orphanage; the interposition of a multitude of parents between himself and that woeful state promised him a long immunity from its disadvantages.

Mrs. Darnell, his newest mother, lived in Cleveland, Ohio. But her adopted son did not long remain with her. He was seen one afternoon by a policeman, new to that beat, deliberately toddling away from her house, and being questioned answered that he was "a doin' home." He must have traveled by rail, somehow, for three days later he was in the town of Whiteville, which, as you know, is a long way from Blackburg. His clothing was in pretty fair condition, but he was sinfully dirty. Unable to give any account of himself he was arrested as a vagrant and sentenced to imprisonment in the Infants' Sheltering Home—where he was washed.

Jo ran away from the Infants' Sheltering Home at Whiteville—just took to the woods one day, and the Home knew him no more forever.

We find him next, or rather get back to him, standing forlorn in the cold autumn rain at a suburban street corner in Blackburg; and it seems right to explain now that the raindrops falling upon him there were really not dark and gummy; they only failed to make his face and hands less so. Jo was indeed fearfully and wonderfully besmirched, as by the hand of an artist. And the forlorn little tramp had no shoes; his feet were bare, red, and swollen, and when he walked he limped with both legs. As to clothing—ah, you would hardly have had the skill to name any single garment that he wore, or say by what magic he kept it upon him. That he was cold all over and all through did not admit of a doubt; he knew it himself. Anyone would have been cold there that evening; but, for that reason, no one else was there. How Jo came to be there himself, he could not for the flickering little life of him have told, even if gifted with a vocabulary exceeding a hundred words. From the way he stared about him one could have seen that he had not the faintest notion of where (nor why) he was.

Yet he was not altogether a fool in his day and generation; being cold and hungry, and still able to walk a little by bending his knees very much indeed and putting his feet down toes first, he decided to enter one of the houses which flanked the street at long intervals and looked so bright and warm. But when he attempted to act upon that very sensible decision a burly dog came bowsing out and disputed his right. Inexpressibly frightened and believing, no doubt (with some reason, too) that brutes without meant brutality within, he hobbled away from all the houses, and with gray, wet fields to right of him and gray, wet fields to left of him—with the rain half blinding him and the night coming in mist and darkness, held his way along the road that leads to Greenton. That is to say, the road leads those to Greenton who succeed in passing the Oak Hill Cemetery. A considerable number every year do not.

Jo did not.

They found him there the next morning, very wet, very cold, but no longer hungry. He had apparently entered the cemetery gate—hoping, perhaps, that it led to a house where there was no dog—and gone blundering about in the darkness, falling over many a grave, no doubt, until he had tired of it all and given up. The little body lay upon one side, with one soiled cheek upon one soiled hand, the other hand tucked away among the rags to make it warm, the other cheek washed clean and white at last, as for a kiss from one of God's great angels. It was observed—though nothing was thought of it at the time, the body being as yet unidentified—that the little fellow was lying upon the grave of Hetty Parlow. The grave, however, had not opened to receive him. That is a circumstance which, without actual irreverence, one may wish had been ordered otherwise.

❋   ❋   ❋

A PSYCHOLOGICAL SHIPWRECK

In the summer of 1874 I was in Liverpool, whither I had gone on business for the mercantile house of Bronson & Jarrett, New York. I am William Jarrett; my partner was Zenas Bronson. The firm failed last year, and unable to endure the fall from affluence to poverty he died.

Having finished my business, and feeling the lassitude and exhaustion incident to its dispatch, I felt that a protracted sea voyage would be both agreeable and beneficial, so instead of embarking for my return on one of the many fine passenger steamers I booked for New York on the sailing vessel *Morrow*, upon which I had shipped a large and valuable invoice of the goods I had bought. The *Morrow* was an English ship with, of course, but little accommodation for passengers, of whom there were only myself, a young woman and her servant, who was a middle-aged negress. I thought it singular that a traveling English girl should be so attended, but she afterward explained to me that the woman had been left with her family by a man and his wife from South Carolina, both of whom had died on the same day at the house of the young lady's father in Devonshire—a circumstance in itself sufficiently uncommon to remain rather distinctly in my memory, even had it not afterward transpired in conversation with the young lady that the name of the man was William Jarrett, the same as my own. I knew that a branch of my family had settled in South Carolina, but of them and their history I was ignorant.

The *Morrow* sailed from the mouth of the Mersey on the 15th of June and for several weeks we had fair breezes and unclouded skies. The skipper, an admirable seaman but nothing more, favored us with very little of his society, except at his table; and the young woman, Miss Janette Harford, and I became very well acquainted. We were, in truth, nearly always together, and being of an introspective turn of mind I often endeavored to analyze and define the novel feeling with which she inspired me—a secret, subtle, but powerful attraction which constantly impelled me to seek her; but the attempt was hopeless. I could only be sure that at least it was not love. Having assured myself of this and being certain that she was quite as whole-hearted, I ventured one evening (I remember it was on the 3d of July) as we sat on deck to ask her, laughingly, if she could assist me to resolve my psychological doubt.

For a moment she was silent, with averted face, and I began to fear I had been extremely rude and indelicate; then she fixed her eyes gravely on my own. In an instant my mind was dominated by as strange a fancy as ever entered human consciousness. It seemed as if she were looking at me, not *with,* but *through,* those eyes—from an immeasurable distance behind them—and that a number of other persons, men, women and children, upon whose faces I caught strangely familiar evanescent expressions, clustered about her, struggling with gentle eagerness to look at me through the same orbs. Ship, ocean, sky—all had vanished. I was conscious of nothing but the figures in this extraordinary and fantastic scene. Then all at once darkness fell upon me, and anon from out of it, as to one who grows accustomed by degrees to a dimmer light, my former surroundings of deck and mast and cordage slowly resolved themselves. Miss Harford had closed her eyes and was leaning back in her chair, apparently asleep, the book she had been reading open in her lap. Impelled by surely I cannot say what motive, I glanced at the top of the page;

it was a copy of that rare and curious work, "Denneker's Meditations," and the lady's index finger rested on this passage:

"To sundry it is given to be drawn away, and to be apart from the body for a season; for, as concerning rills which would flow across each other the weaker is borne along by the stronger, so there be certain of kin whose paths intersecting, their souls do bear company, the while their bodies go fore-appointed ways, unknowing."

Miss Harford arose, shuddering; the sun had sunk below the horizon, but it was not cold. There was not a breath of wind; there were no clouds in the sky, yet not a star was visible. A hurried tramping sounded on the deck; the captain, summoned from below, joined the first officer, who stood looking at the barometer. "Good God!" I heard him exclaim.

An hour later the form of Janette Harford, invisible in the darkness and spray, was torn from my grasp by the cruel vortex of the sinking ship, and I fainted in the cordage of the floating mast to which I had lashed myself.

It was by lamplight that I awoke. I lay in a berth amid the familiar surroundings of the stateroom of a steamer. On a couch opposite sat a man, half undressed for bed, reading a book. I recognized the face of my friend Gordon Doyle, whom I had met in Liverpool on the day of my embarkation, when he was himself about to sail on the steamer *City of Prague,* on which he had urged me to accompany him.

After some moments I now spoke his name. He simply said, "Well," and turned a leaf in his book without removing his eyes from the page.

"Doyle," I repeated, "did they save *her?*"

He now deigned to look at me and smiled as if amused. He evidently thought me but half awake.

"Her? Whom do you mean?"

"Janette Harford."

His amusement turned to amazement; he stared at me fixedly, saying nothing.

"You will tell me after a while," I continued; "I suppose you will tell me after a while."

A moment later I asked: "What ship is this?"

Doyle stared again. "The steamer *City of Prague,* bound from Liverpool to New York, three weeks out with a broken shaft. Principal passenger, Mr. Gordon Doyle; ditto lunatic, Mr. William Jarrett. These two distinguished travelers embarked together, but they are about to part, it being the resolute intention of the former to pitch the latter overboard."

I sat bolt upright. "Do you mean to say that I have been for three weeks a passenger on this steamer?"

"Yes, pretty nearly; this is the 3d of July."

"Have I been ill?"

"Right as a trivet all the time, and punctual at your meals."

"My God! Doyle, there is some mystery here; do have the goodness to be serious. Was I not rescued from the wreck of the ship *Morrow?*"

Doyle changed color, and approaching me, laid his fingers on my wrist. A moment later, "What do you know of Janette Harford?" he asked very calmly.

"First tell me what *you* know of her?"

Mr. Doyle gazed at me for some moments as if thinking what to do, then seating himself again on the couch, said:

"Why should I not? I am engaged to marry Janette Harford, whom I met a year ago in London. Her family, one of the wealthiest in Devonshire, cut up rough about it, and we eloped—are eloping rather, for on the day that you and I walked to the landing stage to go aboard this steamer she and her faithful servant, a negress, passed us, driving to the ship *Morrow*. She would not consent to go in the same vessel with me, and it had been deemed best that she take a sailing vessel in order to avoid observation and lessen the risk of detection. I am now alarmed lest this cursed breaking of our machinery may detain us so long that the *Morrow* will get to New York before us, and the poor girl will not know where to go."

I lay still in my berth—so still I hardly breathed. But the subject was evidently not displeasing to Doyle, and after a short pause he resumed:

"By the way, she is only an adopted daughter of the Harfords. Her mother was killed at their place by being thrown from a horse while hunting, and her father, mad with grief, made away with himself the same day. No one ever claimed the child, and after a reasonable time they adopted her. She has grown up in the belief that she is their daughter."

"Doyle, what book are you reading?"

"Oh, it's called 'Denneker's Meditations.' It's a rum lot, Janette gave it to me; she happened to have two copies. Want to see it?"

He tossed me the volume, which opened as it fell. On one of the exposed pages was a marked passage:

"To sundry it is given to be drawn away, and to be apart from the body for a season; for, as concerning rills which would flow across each other the weaker is borne along by the stronger, so there be certain of kin whose paths intersecting, their souls do bear company, the while their bodies go fore-appointed ways, unknowing."

"She had—she has—a singular taste in reading," I managed to say, mastering my agitation.

"Yes. And now perhaps you will have the kindness to explain how you knew her name and that of the ship she sailed in."

"You talked of her in your sleep," I said.

A week later we were towed into the port of New York. But the *Morrow* was never heard from.

❊   ❊   ❊

A COLD GREETING

This is a story told by the late Benson Foley of San Francisco:

"In the summer of 1881 I met a man named James H. Conway, a resident of Franklin, Tennessee. He was visiting San Francisco for his health, deluded man, and brought me a note of introduction from Mr. Lawrence Barting. I had known Barting as a captain in the Federal army during the civil war. At its close he had settled in Franklin, and in time became, I had reason to think, somewhat prominent as a lawyer. Barting had always seemed to me an honorable and truthful man, and the warm friendship which he expressed in his note for Mr. Conway was to me sufficient evidence that the latter was in every way worthy of my confidence and esteem. At dinner one day Conway told me that it had been solemnly agreed between him and Barting that the one who died first should, if possible, communicate with the other from beyond the grave, in some unmistakable way—just how, they had left (wisely, it seemed to me) to be decided by the deceased, according to the opportunities that his altered circumstances might present.

"A few weeks after the conversation in which Mr. Conway spoke of this agreement, I met him one day, walking slowly down Montgomery street, apparently, from his abstracted air, in deep thought. He greeted me coldly with merely a movement of the head and passed on, leaving me standing on the walk, with half-proffered hand, surprised and naturally somewhat piqued. The next day I met him again in the office of the Palace Hotel, and seeing him about to repeat the disagreeable performance of the day before, intercepted him in a doorway, with a friendly salutation, and bluntly requested an explanation of his altered manner. He hesitated a moment; then, looking me frankly in the eyes, said:

"'I do not think, Mr. Foley, that I have any longer a claim to your friendship, since Mr. Barting appears to have withdrawn his own from me—for what reason, I protest I do not know. If he has not already informed you he probably will do so.'

"'But,' I replied, 'I have not heard from Mr. Barting.'

"'Heard from him!' he repeated, with apparent surprise. 'Why, he is here. I met him yesterday ten minutes before meeting you. I gave you exactly the same greeting that he gave me. I met him again not a quarter of an hour ago, and his manner was precisely the same: he merely bowed and passed on. I shall not soon forget your civility to me. Good morning, or—as it may please you—farewell.'

"All this seemed to me singularly considerate and delicate behavior on the part of Mr. Conway.

"As dramatic situations and literary effects are foreign to my purpose I will explain at once that Mr. Barting was dead. He had died in Nashville four days before this conversation. Calling on Mr. Conway, I apprised him of our friend's death, showing him the letters announcing it. He was visibly affected in a way that forbade me to entertain a doubt of his sincerity.

"'It seems incredible,' he said, after a period of reflection. 'I suppose I must have mistaken another man for Barting, and that man's cold greeting was merely a stranger's civil acknowledgment of my own. I remember, indeed, that he lacked Barting's mustache.'

"'Doubtless it was another man,' I assented; and the subject was never afterward mentioned between us. But I had in my pocket a photograph of Barting, which had been inclosed in the letter from his widow. It had been taken a week before his death, and was without a mustache."

❉   ❉   ❉

BEYOND THE WALL

Many years ago, on my way from Hongkong to New York, I passed a week in San Francisco. A long time had gone by since I had been in that city, during which my ventures in the Orient had prospered beyond my hope; I was rich and could afford to revisit my own country to renew my friendship with such of the companions of my youth as still lived and remembered me with the old affection. Chief of these, I hoped, was Mohun Dampier, an old schoolmate with whom I had held a desultory correspondence which had long ceased, as is the way of correspondence between men. You may have observed that the indisposition to write a merely social letter is in the ratio of the square of the distance between you and your correspondent. It is a law.

I remembered Dampier as a handsome, strong young fellow of scholarly tastes, with an aversion to work and a marked indifference to many of the things that the world cares for, including wealth, of which, however, he had inherited enough to put him beyond the reach of want. In his family, one of the oldest and most aristocratic in the country, it was, I think, a matter of pride that no member of it had ever been in trade nor politics, nor suffered any kind of distinction. Mohun was a trifle sentimental, and had in him a singular element of superstition, which led him to the study of all manner of occult subjects, although his sane mental health safeguarded him against fantastic and perilous faiths. He made daring incursions into the realm of the unreal without renouncing his residence in the partly surveyed and charted region of what we are pleased to call certitude.

The night of my visit to him was stormy. The Californian winter was on, and the incessant rain plashed in the deserted streets, or, lifted by irregular gusts of wind, was hurled against the houses with incredible fury. With no small difficulty my cabman found the right place, away out toward the ocean beach, in a sparsely populated suburb. The dwelling, a rather ugly one, apparently, stood in the center of its grounds, which as nearly as I could make out in the gloom were destitute of either flowers or grass. Three or four trees, writhing and moaning in the torment of the tempest, appeared to be trying to escape from their dismal environment and take the chance of finding a better one out at sea. The house was a two-story brick structure with a tower, a story higher, at one corner. In a window of that was the only visible light. Something in the appearance of the place made me shudder, a performance that may have been assisted by a rill of rain-water down my back as I scuttled to cover in the doorway.

In answer to my note apprising him of my wish to call, Dampier had written, "Don't ring—open the door and come up." I did so. The staircase was dimly lighted by a single gas-jet at the top of the second flight. I managed to reach the landing without disaster and entered by an open door into the lighted square room of the tower. Dampier came forward in gown and slippers to receive me, giving me the greeting that I wished, and if I had held a thought that it might more fitly have been accorded me at the front door the first look at him dispelled any sense of his inhospitality.

He was not the same. Hardly past middle age, he had gone gray and had acquired a pronounced stoop. His figure was thin and angular, his face deeply lined, his complexion dead-white, without a touch of color. His eyes, unnaturally large, glowed with a fire that was almost uncanny.

He seated me, proffered a cigar, and with grave and obvious sincerity assured me of the pleasure that it gave him to meet me. Some unimportant conversation followed, but all the while I was dominated by a melancholy sense of the great change in him. This he must have perceived, for he suddenly said with a bright enough smile, "You are disappointed in me—*non sum qualis eram.*"

I hardly knew what to reply, but managed to say: "Why, really, I don't know: your Latin is about the same."

He brightened again. "No," he said, "being a dead language, it grows in appropriateness. But please have the patience to wait: where I am going there is perhaps a better tongue. Will you care to have a message in it?"

The smile faded as he spoke, and as he concluded he was looking into my eyes with a gravity that distressed me. Yet I would not surrender myself to his mood, nor permit him to see how deeply his prescience of death affected me.

"I fancy that it will be long," I said, "before human speech will cease to serve our need; and then the need, with its possibilities of service, will have passed."

He made no reply, and I too was silent, for the talk had taken a dispiriting turn, yet I knew not how to give it a more agreeable character. Suddenly, in a pause of the storm, when the dead silence was almost startling by contrast with the previous uproar, I heard a gentle tapping, which appeared to come from the wall behind my chair. The sound was such as might have been made by a human hand, not as upon a door by one asking admittance, but rather, I thought, as an agreed signal, an assurance of someone's presence in an adjoining room; most of us, I fancy, have had more experience of such communications than we should care to relate. I glanced at Dampier. If possibly there was something of amusement in the look he did not observe it. He appeared to have forgotten my presence, and was star-

ing at the wall behind me with an expression in his eyes that I am
unable to name, although my memory of it is as vivid to-day as was
my sense of it then. The situation was embarrassing; I rose to take
my leave. At this he seemed to recover himself.

"Please be seated," he said; "it is nothing—no one is there."

But the tapping was repeated, and with the same gentle, slow insistence as before.

"Pardon me," I said, "it is late. May I call to-morrow?"

He smiled—a little mechanically, I thought. "It is very delicate of
you," said he, "but quite needless. Really, this is the only room in the
tower, and no one is there. At least——" He left the sentence incom-
plete, rose, and threw up a window, the only opening in the wall
from which the sound seemed to come. "See."

Not clearly knowing what else to do I followed him to the window and looked out. A street-lamp some little distance away gave
enough light through the murk of the rain that was again falling in
torrents to make it entirely plain that "no one was there." In truth
there was nothing but the sheer blank wall of the tower.

Dampier closed the window and signing me to my seat resumed
his own.

The incident was not in itself particularly mysterious; any one of
a dozen explanations was possible (though none has occurred to me),
yet it impressed me strangely, the more, perhaps, from my friend's
effort to reassure me, which seemed to dignify it with a certain
significance and importance. He had proved that no one was there,
but in that fact lay all the interest; and he proffered no explanation.
His silence was irritating and made me resentful.

"My good friend," I said, somewhat ironically, I fear, "I am not
disposed to question your right to harbor as many spooks as you find
agreeable to your taste and consistent with your notions of companionship; that is no business of mine. But being just a plain man
of affairs, mostly of this world, I find spooks needless to my peace
and comfort. I am going to my hotel, where my fellow-guests are still
in the flesh."

It was not a very civil speech, but he manifested no feeling about
it. "Kindly remain," he said. "I am grateful for your presence here.
What you have heard to-night I believe myself to have heard twice
before. Now I *know* it was no illusion. That is much to me—more
than you know. Have a fresh cigar and a good stock of patience
while I tell you the story."

The rain was now falling more steadily, with a low, monotonous
susurration, interrupted at long intervals by the sudden slashing of

the boughs of the trees as the wind rose and failed. The night was well advanced, but both sympathy and curiosity held me a willing listener to my friend's monologue, which I did not interrupt by a single word from beginning to end.

"Ten years ago," he said, "I occupied a ground-floor apartment in one of a row of houses, all alike, away at the other end of the town, on what we call Rincon Hill. This had been the best quarter of San Francisco, but had fallen into neglect and decay, partly because the primitive character of its domestic architecture no longer suited the maturing tastes of our wealthy citizens, partly because certain public improvements had made a wreck of it. The row of dwellings in one of which I lived stood a little way back from the street, each having a miniature garden, separated from its neighbors by low iron fences and bisected with mathematical precision by a box-bordered gravel walk from gate to door.

"One morning as I was leaving my lodging I observed a young girl entering the adjoining garden on the left. It was a warm day in June, and she was lightly gowned in white. From her shoulders hung a broad straw hat profusely decorated with flowers and wonderfully beribboned in the fashion of the time. My attention was not long held by the exquisite simplicity of her costume, for no one could look at her face and think of anything earthly. Do not fear; I shall 'not profane it by description; it was beautiful exceedingly. All that I had ever seen or dreamed of loveliness was in that matchless living picture by the hand of the Divine Artist. So deeply did it move me that, without a thought of the impropriety of the act, I unconsciously bared my head, as a devout Catholic or well-bred Protestant uncovers before an image of the Blessed Virgin. The maiden showed no displeasure; she merely turned her glorious dark eyes upon me with a look that made me catch my breath, and without other recognition of my act passed into the house. For a moment I stood motionless, hat in hand, painfully conscious of my rudeness, yet so dominated by the emotion inspired by that vision of incomparable beauty that my penitence was less poignant than it should have been. Then I went my way, leaving my heart behind. In the natural course of things I should probably have remained away until nightfall, but by the middle of the afternoon I was back in the little garden, affecting an interest in the few foolish flowers that I had never before observed. My hope was vain; she did not appear.

"To a night of unrest succeeded a day of expectation and disappointment, but on the day after, as I wandered aimlessly about the neighborhood, I met her. Of course I did not repeat my folly of uncovering, nor venture by even so much as too long a look to manifest an interest in her; yet my heart was beating audibly. I trembled and consciously colored as she turned her big black eyes upon me with a look of obvious recognition entirely devoid of boldness or coquetry.

"I will not weary you with particulars; many times afterward I met the maiden, yet never either addressed her or sought to fix her attention. Nor did I take any action toward making her acquaintance. Perhaps my forbearance, requiring so supreme an effort of self-denial, will not be entirely clear to you. That I was heels over head in love is true, but who can overcome his habit of thought, or reconstruct his character?

"I was what some foolish persons are pleased to call, and others, more foolish, are pleased to be called—an aristocrat; and despite her beauty, her charms and graces, the girl was not of my class. I had learned her name—which it is needless to speak—and something of her family. She was an orphan, a dependent niece of the impossible elderly fat woman in whose lodging-house she lived. My income was small and I lacked the talent for marrying; it is perhaps a gift. An alliance with that family would condemn me to its manner of life, part me from my books and studies, and in a social sense reduce me to the ranks. It is easy to deprecate such considerations as these and I have not retained myself for the defense. Let judgment be entered against me, but in strict justice all my ancestors for generations should be made co-defendants and I be permitted to plead in mitigation of punishment the imperious mandate of heredity. To a mésalliance of that kind every globule of my ancestral blood spoke in opposition. In brief, my tastes, habits, instinct, with whatever of reason my love had left me—all fought against it. Moreover, I was an irreclaimable sentimentalist, and found a subtle charm in an impersonal and spiritual relation which acquaintance might vulgarize and marriage would certainly dispel. No woman, I argued, is what this lovely creature seems. Love is a delicious dream; why should I bring about my own awakening?

"The course dictated by all this sense and sentiment was obvious. Honor, pride, prudence, preservation of my ideals—all commanded me to go away, but for that I was too weak. The utmost that I could do by a mighty effort of will was to cease meeting the girl, and that I did. I even avoided the chance encounters of the garden, leaving my lodging only when I knew that she had gone to her music lessons, and returning after nightfall. Yet all the while I was as one in a trance, indulging the most fascinating fancies and ordering my entire intellectual life in accordance with my dream. Ah, my friend, as one whose actions have a traceable relation to reason, you cannot know the fool's paradise in which I lived.

"One evening the devil put it into my head to be an unspeakable idiot. By apparently careless and purposeless questioning I learned from my gossipy landlady that the young woman's bedroom adjoined my own, a party-wall between. Yielding to a sudden and coarse impulse I gently rapped on the wall. There was no response, naturally, but I was in no mood to accept a rebuke. A madness was upon me and I repeated the folly, the offense, but again ineffectually, and I had the decency to desist.

"An hour later, while absorbed in some of my infernal studies, I heard, or thought I heard, my signal answered. Flinging down my books I sprang to the wall and as steadily as my beating heart would permit gave three slow taps upon it. This time the response was distinct, unmistakable: one, two, three—an exact repetition of my signal. That was all I could elicit, but it was enough—too much.

"The next evening, and for many evenings afterward, that folly went on, I always having 'the last word.' During the whole period I was deliriously happy, but with the perversity of my nature I persevered in my resolution not to see her. Then, as I should have expected, I got no further answers. 'She is disgusted,' I said to myself, 'with what she thinks my timidity in making no more definite advances'; and I resolved to seek her and make her acquaintance and —what? I did not know, nor do I now know, what might have come of it. I know only that I passed days and days trying to meet her, and all in vain; she was invisible as well as inaudible. I haunted the streets where we had met, but she did not come. From my window I watched the garden in front of her house, but she passed neither in nor out. I fell into the deepest dejection, believing that she had gone away, yet took no steps to resolve my doubt by inquiry of my landlady, to whom, indeed, I had taken an unconquerable aversion from her having once spoken of the girl with less of reverence than I thought befitting.

"There came a fateful night. Worn out with emotion, irresolution and despondency, I had retired early and fallen into such sleep as was still possible to me. In the middle of the night something—some malign power bent upon the wrecking of my peace forever—caused me to open my eyes and sit up, wide awake and listening intently for I knew not what. Then I thought I heard a faint tapping on the wall—the mere ghost of the familiar signal. In a few moments it was repeated: one, two, three—no louder than before, but addressing a sense alert and strained to receive it. I was about to re-ply when the Adversary of Peace again intervened in my affairs with a rascally suggestion of retaliation. She had long and cruelly ignored me; now I would ignore her. Incredible fatuity—may God forgive it! All the rest of the night I lay awake, fortifying my ob-stinacy with shameless justifications and—listening.

"Late the next morning, as I was leaving the house, I met my landlady, entering.

"'Good morning, Mr. Dampier,' she said. 'Have you heard the news?'

"I replied in words that I had heard no news; in manner, that I did not care to hear any. The manner escaped her observation.

"'About the sick young lady next door,' she babbled on. 'What! you did not know? Why, she has been ill for weeks. And now——'

"I almost sprang upon her. 'And now,' I cried, 'now what?'

"'She is dead.'

"That is not the whole story. In the middle of the night, as I learned later, the patient, awakening from a long stupor after a week of delirium, had asked—it was her last utterance—that her bed be moved to the opposite side of the room. Those in attendance had thought the request a vagary of her delirium, but had complied. And there the poor passing soul had exerted its failing will to re-store a broken connection—a golden thread of sentiment between its innocence and a monstrous baseness owning a blind, brutal al-legiance to the Law of Self.

"What reparation could I make? Are there masses that can be said for the repose of souls that are abroad such nights as this—spirits 'blown about by the viewless winds'—coming in the storm and dark-ness with signs and portents, hints of memory and presages of doom?

"This is the third visitation. On the first occasion I was too skepti-cal to do more than verify by natural methods the character of the incident; on the second, I responded to the signal after it had been several times repeated, but without result. To-night's recurrence completes the 'fatal triad' expounded by Parapelius Necromantius. There is no more to tell."

When Dampier had finished his story I could think of nothing relevant that I cared to say, and to question him would have been a hideous impertinence. I rose and bade him good night in a way to convey to him a sense of my sympathy, which he silently acknowl-edged by a pressure of the hand. That night, alone with his sorrow and remorse, he passed into the Unknown.

JOHN BARTINE'S WATCH

A STORY BY A PHYSICIAN

"The exact time? Good God! my friend, why do you insist? One would think—but what does it matter; it is easily bedtime—isn't that near enough? But, here, if you must set your watch, take mine and see for yourself."

With that he detached his watch—a tremendously heavy, old-fashioned one—from the chain, and handed it to me; then turned away, and walking across the room to a shelf of books, began an examination of their backs. His agitation and evident distress surprised me; they appeared reasonless. Having set my watch by his, I stepped over to where he stood and said, "Thank you."

As he took his timepiece and reattached it to the guard I observed that his hands were unsteady. With a tact upon which I greatly prided myself, I sauntered carelessly to the sideboard and took some brandy and water; then, begging his pardon for my thoughtlessness, asked him to have some and went back to my seat by the fire, leaving him to help himself, as was our custom. He did so and presently joined me at the hearth, as tranquil as ever.

This odd little incident occurred in my apartment, where John Bartine was passing an evening. We had dined together at the club, had come home in a cab and—in short, everything had been done in the most prosaic way; and why John Bartine should break in upon the natural and established order of things to make himself spectacular with a display of emotion, apparently for his own entertainment, I could nowise understand. The more I thought of it, while his brilliant conversational gifts were commending themselves to my inattention, the more curious I grew, and of course had no difficulty in persuading myself that my curiosity was friendly solicitude. That is the disguise that curiosity usually assumes to evade resentment. So I ruined one of the finest sentences of his disregarded monologue by cutting it short without ceremony.

"John Bartine," I said, "you must try to forgive me if I am wrong, but with the light that I have at present I cannot concede your right to go all to pieces when asked the time o' night. I cannot admit that it is proper to experience a mysterious reluctance to look your own watch in the face and to cherish in my presence, without explanation, painful emotions which are denied to me, and which are none of my business."

To this ridiculous speech Bartine made no immediate reply, but sat looking gravely into the fire. Fearing that I had offended I was about to apologize and beg him to think no more about the matter, when looking me calmly in the eyes he said:

"My dear fellow, the levity of your manner does not at all disguise the hideous impudence of your demand; but happily I had already decided to tell you what you wish to know, and no manifestation of your unworthiness to hear it shall alter my decision. Be good enough to give me your attention and you shall hear all about the matter.

"This watch," he said, "had been in my family for three generations before it fell to me. Its original owner, for whom it was made, was my great-grandfather, Bramwell Olcott Bartine, a wealthy planter of Colonial Virginia, and as stanch a Tory as ever lay awake nights contriving new kinds of maledictions for the head of Mr. Washington, and new methods of aiding and abetting good King George. One day this worthy gentleman had the deep misfortune to perform for his cause a service of capital importance which was not recognized as legitimate by those who suffered its disadvantages. It does not matter what it was, but among its minor consequences was my excellent ancestor's arrest one night in his own house by a party of Mr. Washington's rebels. He was permitted to say farewell to his weeping family, and was then marched away into the darkness which swallowed him up forever. Not the slenderest clew to his fate was ever found. After the war the most diligent inquiry and the offer of large rewards failed to turn up any of his captors or any fact concerning his disappearance. He had disappeared, and that was all."

Something in Bartine's manner that was not in his words—I hardly knew what it was—prompted me to ask:

"What is your view of the matter—of the justice of it?"

"My view of it," he flamed out, bringing his clenched hand down upon the table as if he had been in a public house dicing with blackguards—"my view of it is that it was a characteristically dastardly assassination by that damned traitor, Washington, and his ragamuffin rebels!"

For some minutes nothing was said: Bartine was recovering his temper, and I waited. Then I said:

"Was that all?"

"No—there was something else. A few weeks after my great-grandfather's arrest his watch was found lying on the porch at the front door of his dwelling. It was wrapped in a sheet of letter paper bearing the name of Rupert Bartine, his only son, my grandfather. I am wearing that watch."

Bartine paused. His usually restless black eyes were staring fixedly into the grate, a point of red light in each, reflected from the glowing coals. He seemed to have forgotten me. A sudden threshing of the branches of a tree outside one of the windows, and almost at the same instant a rattle of rain against the glass, recalled him to a sense of his surroundings. A storm had risen, heralded by a single gust of wind, and in a few moments the steady plash of the water on the pavement was distinctly heard. I hardly know why I relate this incident; it seemed somehow to have a certain significance and relevancy which I am unable now to discern. It at least added an element of seriousness, almost solemnity. Bartine resumed:

"I have a singular feeling toward this watch—a kind of affection for it; I like to have it about me, though partly from its weight, and partly for a reason I shall now explain, I seldom carry it. The reason is this: Every evening when I have it with me I feel an unaccountable desire to open and consult it, even if I can think of no reason for wishing to know the time. But if I yield to it, the moment my eyes rest upon the dial I am filled with a mysterious apprehension—a sense of imminent calamity. And this is the more insupportable the nearer it is to eleven o'clock—by this watch, no matter what the actual hour may be. After the hands have registered eleven the desire to look is gone; I am entirely indifferent. Then I can consult the thing as often as I like, with no more emotion than you feel in looking at your own. Naturally I have trained myself not to look at that watch in the evening before eleven; nothing could induce me. Your insistence this evening upset me a trifle. I felt very much as I suppose an opium-eater might feel if his yearning for his special and particular kind of hell were re-enforced by opportunity and advice.

"Now that is my story, and I have told it in the interest of your trumpery science; but if on any evening hereafter you observe me wearing this damnable watch, and you have the thoughtfulness to ask me the hour, I shall beg leave to put you to the inconvenience of being knocked down."

His humor did not amuse me. I could see that in relating his delusion he was again somewhat disturbed. His concluding smile was positively ghastly, and his eyes had resumed something more than their old restlessness; they shifted hither and thither about the room with apparent aimlessness and I fancied had taken on a wild expression, such as is sometimes observed in cases of dementia. Perhaps this was my own imagination, but at any rate I was now persuaded that my friend was afflicted with a most singular and interesting monomania. Without, I trust, any abatement of my affectionate solicitude for him as a friend, I began to regard him as a patient, rich in possibilities of profitable study. Why not? Had he not described his delusion in the interest of science? Ah, poor fellow, he was doing more for science than he knew: not only his story but himself was in evidence. I should cure him if I could, of course, but first I should make a little experiment in psychology—nay, the experiment itself might be a step in his restoration.

"That is very frank and friendly of you, Bartine," I said cordially, "and I'm rather proud of your confidence. It is all very odd, certainly. Do you mind showing me the watch?"

He detached it from his waistcoat, chain and all, and passed it to me without a word. The case was of gold, very thick and strong, and singularly engraved. After closely examining the dial and observing that it was nearly twelve o'clock, I opened it at the back and was interested to observe an inner case of ivory, upon which was painted a miniature portrait in that exquisite and delicate manner which was in vogue during the eighteenth century.

"Why, bless my soul!" I exclaimed, feeling a sharp artistic delight—"how under the sun did you get that done? I thought miniature painting on ivory was a lost art."

"That," he replied, gravely smiling, "is not I; it is my excellent great-grandfather, the late Bramwell Olcott Bartine, Esquire, of Virginia. He was younger then than later—about my age, in fact. It is said to resemble me; do you think so?"

"Resemble you? I should say so! Barring the costume, which I supposed you to have assumed out of compliment to the art—or for *vraisemblance,* so to say—and the no mustache, that portrait is you in every feature, line, and expression."

No more was said at that time. Bartine took a book from the table and began reading. I heard outside the incessant plash of the rain in the street. There were occasional hurried footfalls on the sidewalks; and once a slower, heavier tread seemed to cease at my door—a policeman, I thought, seeking shelter in the doorway. The boughs of the trees tapped significantly on the window panes, as if asking for admittance. I remember it all through these years and years of a wiser, graver life.

Seeing myself unobserved, I took the old-fashioned key that dangled from the chain and quickly turned back the hands of the watch a full hour; then, closing the case, I handed Bartine his property and saw him replace it on his person.

"I think you said," I began, with assumed carelessness, "that after eleven the sight of the dial no longer affects you. As it is now nearly twelve"—looking at my own timepiece—"perhaps, if you don't resent my pursuit of proof, you will look at it now."

He smiled good-humoredly, pulled out the watch again, opened it, and instantly sprang to his feet with a cry that Heaven has not had the mercy to permit me to forget! His eyes, their blackness strikingly intensified by the pallor of his face, were fixed upon the watch, which he clutched in both hands. For some time he remained in that attitude without uttering another sound; then, in a voice that I should not have recognized as his, he said:

"Damn you! it is two minutes to eleven!"

I was not unprepared for some such outbreak, and without rising replied, calmly enough:

"I beg your pardon; I must have misread your watch in setting my own by it."

He shut the case with a sharp snap and put the watch in his pocket. He looked at me and made an attempt to smile, but his lower lip quivered and he seemed unable to close his mouth. His hands, also, were shaking, and he thrust them, clenched, into the pockets of his sack-coat. The courageous spirit was manifestly endeavoring to subdue the coward body. The effort was too great; he began to sway from side to side, as from vertigo, and before I could spring from my chair to support him his knees gave way and he pitched awkwardly forward and fell upon his face. I sprang to assist him to rise; but when John Bartine rises we shall all rise.

The *post-mortem* examination disclosed nothing; every organ was normal and sound. But when the body had been prepared for burial a faint dark circle was seen to have developed around the neck; at least I was so assured by several persons who said they saw it, but of my own knowledge I cannot say if that was true.

Nor can I set limitations to the law of heredity. I do not know that in the spiritual world a sentiment or emotion may not survive the heart that held it, and seek expression in a kindred life, ages removed. Surely, if I were to guess at the fate of Bramwell Olcott Bartine, I should guess that he was hanged at eleven o'clock in the evening, and that he had been allowed several hours in which to prepare for the change.

As to John Bartine, my friend, my patient for five minutes, and—

Heaven forgive me!—my victim for eternity, there is no more to say. He is buried, and his watch with him—I saw to that. May God rest his soul in Paradise, and the soul of his Virginian ancestor, if, indeed, they are two souls.

❈   ❈   ❈

THE MAN OUT OF THE NOSE

At the intersection of two certain streets in that part of San Francisco known by the rather loosely applied name of North Beach, is a vacant lot, which is rather more nearly level than is usually the case with lots, vacant or otherwise, in that region. Immediately at the back of it, to the south, however, the ground slopes steeply upward, the acclivity broken by three terraces cut into the soft rock. It is a place for goats and poor persons, several families of each class having occupied it jointly and amicably "from the foundation of the city." One of the humble habitations of the lowest terrace is noticeable for its rude resemblance to the human face, or rather to such a simulacrum of it as a boy might cut out of a hollowed pumpkin, meaning no offense to his race. The eyes are two circular windows, the nose is a door, the mouth an aperture caused by removal of a board below. There are no doorsteps. As a face, this house is too large; as a dwelling, too small. The blank, unmeaning stare of its lidless and browless eyes is uncanny.

Sometimes a man steps out of the nose, turns, passes the place where the right ear should be and making his way through the throng of children and goats obstructing the narrow walk between his neighbors' doors and the edge of the terrace gains the street by descending a flight of rickety stairs. Here he pauses to consult his watch and the stranger who happens to pass wonders why such a man as that can care what is the hour. Longer observations would show that the time of day is an important element in the man's movements, for it is at precisely two o'clock in the afternoon that he comes forth 365 times in every year.

Having satisfied himself that he has made no mistake in the hour he replaces the watch and walks rapidly southward up the street two squares, turns to the right and as he approaches the next corner fixes his eyes on an upper window in a three-story building across the way. This is a somewhat dingy structure, originally of red brick and now gray. It shows the touch of age and dust. Built for a dwelling, it is now a factory. I do not know what is made there; the things that are commonly made in a factory, I suppose. I only know that at two o'clock in the afternoon of every day but Sunday it is full of activity and clatter; pulsations of some great engine shake it and there are recurrent screams of wood tormented by the saw. At the window on which the man fixes an intensely expectant gaze nothing ever appears; the glass, in truth, has such a coating of dust that it has long ceased to be transparent. The man looks at it without stopping; he merely keeps turning his head more and more backward as he leaves the building behind. Passing along to the next corner, he turns to the left, goes round the block, and comes back till he reaches the point diagonally across the street from the factory—a point on his former course, which he then retraces, looking frequently backward over his right shoulder at the window while it is in sight. For many years he has not been known to vary his route nor to introduce a single innovation into his action. In a quarter of an hour he is again at the mouth of his dwelling, and a woman, who has for some time been standing in the nose, assists him to enter. He is seen no more until two o'clock the next day.

The woman is his wife. She supports herself and him by washing for the poor people among whom they live, at rates which destroy Chinese and domestic competition.

This man is about fifty-seven years of age, though he looks greatly older. His hair is dead white. He wears no beard, and is always newly shaven. His hands are clean, his nails well kept. In the matter of dress he is distinctly superior to his position, as indicated by his surroundings and the business of his wife. He is, indeed, very neatly, if not quite fashionably, clad. His silk hat has a date no earlier than the year before the last, and his boots, scrupulously polished, are innocent of patches. I am told that the suit which he wears during his daily excursions of fifteen minutes is not the one that he wears at home. Like everything else that he has, this is provided and kept in repair by the wife, and is renewed as frequently as her scanty means permit.

Thirty years ago John Hardshaw and his wife lived on Rincon Hill in one of the finest residences of that once aristocratic quarter. He had once been a physician, but having inherited a considerable estate from his father concerned himself no more about the ailments of his fellow-creatures and found as much work as he cared for in managing his own affairs. Both he and his wife were highly cultivated persons, and their house was frequented by a small set of such men and women as persons of their tastes would think worth knowing. So far as these knew, Mr. and Mrs. Hardshaw lived happily together; certainly the wife was devoted to her handsome and accomplished husband and exceedingly proud of him.

Among their acquaintances were the Barwells—man, wife and two young children—of Sacramento. Mr. Barwell was a civil and mining engineer, whose duties took him much from home and frequently to San Francisco. On these occasions his wife commonly accompanied him and passed much of her time at the house of her friend, Mrs. Hardshaw, always with her two children, of whom Mrs. Hardshaw, childless herself, grew fond. Unluckily, her husband grew equally fond of their mother—a good deal fonder. Still more unluckily, that attractive lady was less wise than weak.

At about three o'clock one autumn morning Officer No. 13 of the Sacramento police saw a man stealthily leaving the rear entrance of a gentleman's residence and promptly arrested him. The man—who wore a slouch hat and shaggy overcoat—offered the policeman one hundred, then five hundred, then one thousand dollars to be released. As he had less than the first mentioned sum on his person the officer treated his proposal with virtuous contempt. Before reaching the station the prisoner agreed to give him a check for ten thousand dollars and remain ironed in the willows along the river bank until it should be paid. As this only provoked new derision he would say no more, merely giving an obviously fictitious name. When he was searched at the station nothing of value was found on him but a miniature portrait of Mrs. Barwell—the lady of the house at which he was caught. The case was set with costly diamonds; and something in the quality of the man's linen sent a pang of unavailing regret through the severely incorruptible bosom of Officer No. 13. There was nothing about the prisoner's clothing nor person to identify him and he was booked for burglary under the name that he had given, the honorable name of John K. Smith. The K. was an inspiration upon which, doubtless, he greatly prided himself.

In the mean time the mysterious disappearance of John Hardshaw was agitating the gossips of Rincon Hill in San Francisco, and was even mentioned in one of the newspapers. It did not occur to the lady whom that journal considerately described as his "widow," to look for him in the city prison at Sacramento—a town which he was not known ever to have visited. As John K. Smith he was arraigned and, waiving examination, committed for trial.

About two weeks before the trial, Mrs. Hardshaw, accidentally learning that her husband was held in Sacramento under an assumed name on a charge of burglary, hastened to that city without daring to mention the matter to any one and presented herself at the prison, asking for an interview with her husband, John K. Smith. Haggard and ill with anxiety, wearing a plain traveling wrap which covered her from neck to foot, and in which she had passed the night on the steamboat, too anxious to sleep, she hardly showed for what she was, but her manner pleaded for her more strongly than anything that she chose to say in evidence of her right to admittance. She was permitted to see him alone.

What occurred during that distressing interview has never transpired; but later events prove that Hardshaw had found means to subdue her will to his own. She left the prison, a broken-hearted woman, refusing to answer a single question, and returning to her desolate home renewed, in a half-hearted way, her inquiries for her missing husband. A week later she was herself missing: she had "gone back to the States"—nobody knew any more than that.

On his trial the prisoner pleaded guilty—"by advice of his counsel," so his counsel said. Nevertheless, the judge, in whose mind several unusual circumstances had created a doubt, insisted on the district attorney placing Officer No. 13 on the stand, and the deposition of Mrs. Barwell, who was too ill to attend, was read to the jury. It was very brief: she knew nothing of the matter except that the likeness of herself was her property, and had, she thought, been left on the parlor table when she had retired on the night of the arrest. She had intended it as a present to her husband, then and still absent in Europe on business for a mining company.

This witness's manner when making the deposition at her residence was afterward described by the district attorney as most extraordinary. Twice she had refused to testify, and once, when the deposition lacked nothing but her signature, she had caught it from the clerk's hands and torn it in pieces. She had called her children to the bedside and embraced them with streaming eyes, then suddenly sending them from the room, she verified her statement by oath and signature, and fainted—"slick away," said the district attorney. It was at that time that her physician, arriving upon the scene, took in the situation at a glance and grasping the representative of the law by the collar chucked him into the street and kicked his assistant after him. The insulted majesty of the law was not vindicated; the victim of the indignity did not even mention anything of all this in court. He was ambitious to win his case, and the circumstances of the taking of that deposition were not such as would give it weight if related; and after all, the man on trial had committed an offense against the law's majesty only less heinous than that of the irascible physician.

By suggestion of the judge the jury rendered a verdict of guilty; there was nothing else to do, and the prisoner was sentenced to the penitentiary for three years. His counsel, who had objected to nothing and had made no plea for lenity—had, in fact, hardly said a word—wrung his client's hand and left the room. It was obvious to the whole bar that he had been engaged only to prevent the court from appointing counsel who might possibly insist on making a defense.

John Hardshaw served out his term at San Quentin, and when discharged was met at the prison gates by his wife, who had returned from "the States" to receive him. It is thought they went straight to Europe; anyhow, a general power-of-attorney to a lawyer still living among us—from whom I have many of the facts of this simple history—was executed in Paris. This lawyer in a short time sold everything that Hardshaw owned in California, and for years nothing was heard of the unfortunate couple; though many to whose ears had come vague and inaccurate intimations of their strange story, and who had known them, recalled their personality with tenderness and their misfortunes with compassion.

Some years later they returned, both broken in fortune and spirits and he in health. The purpose of their return I have not been able to ascertain. For some time they lived, under the name of Johnson, in a respectable enough quarter south of Market Street, pretty well out, and were never seen away from the vicinity of their dwelling. They must have had a little money left, for it is not known that the man had any occupation, the state of his health probably not permitting. The woman's devotion to her invalid husband was matter of remark among their neighbors; she seemed never absent from his side and always supporting and cheering him. They would sit for hours on one of the benches in a little public park, she reading to him, his hand in hers, her light touch occasionally visiting his pale brow, her still beautiful eyes frequently lifted from the book to look into his as she made some comment on the text, or closed the volume to beguile his mood with talk of—what? Nobody ever overheard a conversation between these two. The reader who has had the patience to follow their history to this point may possibly find a pleasure in conjecture: there was probably something to be avoided. The bearing of the man was one of profound dejection; indeed, the unsympathetic youth of the neighborhood, with that keen sense for visible characteristics which ever distinguishes the young male of our species, sometimes mentioned him among themselves by the name of Spoony Glum.

It occurred one day that John Hardshaw was possessed by the spirit of unrest. God knows what led him whither he went, but he crossed Market Street and held his way northward over the hills, and downward into the region known as North Beach. Turning aimlessly to the left he followed his toes along an unfamiliar street until he was opposite what for that period was a rather grand dwelling, and for this is a rather shabby factory. Casting his eyes casually upward he saw at an open window what it had been better that he had not seen—the face and figure of Elvira Barwell. Their eyes met. With a sharp exclamation, like the cry of a startled bird, the lady sprang to her feet and thrust her body half out of the window, clutching the casing on each side. Arrested by the cry, the people in the street below looked up. Hardshaw stood motionless, speechless, his eyes two flames. "Take care!" shouted some one in the crowd, as the woman strained further and further forward, defying the silent, implacable law of gravitation, as once she had defied that other law which God thundered from Sinai. The suddenness of her movements had tumbled a torrent of dark hair down her shoulders, and now it was blown about her cheeks, almost concealing her face. A moment so, and then—! A fearful cry rang through the street, as, losing her balance, she pitched headlong from the window, a confused and whirling mass of skirts, limbs, hair, and white face, and struck the pavement with a horrible sound and a force of impact that was felt a hundred feet away. For a moment all eyes refused their office and turned from the sickening spectacle on the sidewalk. Drawn again to that horror, they saw it strangely augmented. A man, hatless, seated flat upon the paving stones, held the broken, bleeding body against his breast, kissing the mangled cheeks and streaming mouth through tangles of wet hair, his own features indistinguishably crimson with the blood that half-strangled him and ran in rills from his soaken beard.

The reporter's task is nearly finished. The Barwells had that very morning returned from a two years' absence in Peru. A week later the widower, now doubly desolate, since there could be no missing the significance of Hardshaw's horrible demonstration, had sailed for I know not what distant port; he has never come back to stay. Hardshaw—as Johnson no longer—passed a year in the Stockton asylum for the insane, where also, through the influence of pitying friends, his wife was admitted to care for him. When he was discharged, not cured but harmless, they returned to the city; it would seem ever to have had some dreadful fascination for them. For a time they lived near the Mission Dolores, in poverty only less abject than that which is their present lot; but it was too far away from the objective point of the man's daily pilgrimage. They could not afford car fare. So that poor devil of an angel from Heaven—wife to this convict and lunatic—obtained, at a fair enough rental, the blank-faced shanty on the lower terrace of Goat Hill. Thence to the structure that was a dwelling and is a factory the distance is not so great; it is, in fact, an agreeable walk, judging from the man's eager and cheerful look as he takes it. The return journey appears to be a trifle wearisome.

❋   ❋   ❋

AN ADVENTURE AT BROWNVILLE[1]

I taught a little country school near Brownville, which, as every one knows who has had the good luck to live there, is the capital of a considerable expanse of the finest scenery in California. The town is somewhat frequented in summer by a class of persons whom it is the habit of the local journal to call "pleasure seekers," but who by a juster classification would be known as "the sick and those in adversity." Brownville itself might rightly enough be described, indeed, as a summer place of last resort. It is fairly well endowed with boarding-houses, at the least pernicious of which I performed twice a day (lunching at the schoolhouse) the humble rite of cementing the alliance between soul and body. From this "hostelry" (as the local journal preferred to call it when it did not call it a "caravanserai") to the schoolhouse the distance by the wagon road was about a mile and a half; but there was a trail, very little used, which led over an intervening range of low, heavily wooded hills, considerably shortening the distance. By this trail I was returning one evening later than usual. It was the last day of the term and I had been detained at the schoolhouse until almost dark, preparing an account of my stewardship for the trustees—two of whom, I proudly reflected, would be able to read it, and the third (an instance of the dominion

---

[1] This story was written in collaboration with Miss Ina Lillian Peterson, to whom is rightly due the credit for whatever merit it may have.

of mind over matter) would be overruled in his customary antagonism to the schoolmaster of his own creation.

I had gone not more than a quarter of the way when, finding an interest in the antics of a family of lizards which dwelt thereabout and seemed full of reptilian joy for their immunity from the ills incident to life at the Brownville House, I sat upon a fallen tree to observe them. As I leaned wearily against a branch of the gnarled old trunk the twilight deepened in the somber woods and the faint new moon began casting visible shadows and gilding the leaves of the trees with a tender but ghostly light.

I heard the sound of voices—a woman's, angry, impetuous, rising against deep masculine tones, rich and musical. I strained my eyes, peering through the dusky shadows of the wood, hoping to get a view of the intruders on my solitude, but could see no one. For some yards in each direction I had an uninterrupted view of the trail, and knowing of no other within a half mile thought the persons heard must be approaching from the wood at one side. There was no sound but that of the voices, which were now so distinct that I could catch the words. That of the man gave me an impression of anger, abundantly confirmed by the matter spoken.

"I will have no threats; you are powerless, as you very well know. Let things remain as they are or, by God! you shall both suffer for it."

"What do you mean?"—this was the voice of the woman, a cultivated voice, the voice of a lady. "You would not—murder us."

There was no reply, at least none that was audible to me. During the silence I peered into the wood in hope to get a glimpse of the speakers, for I felt sure that this was an affair of gravity in which ordinary scruples ought not to count. It seemed to me that the woman was in peril; at any rate the man had not disavowed a willingness to murder. When a man is enacting the rôle of potential assassin he has not the right to choose his audience.

After some little time I saw them, indistinct in the moonlight among the trees. The man, tall and slender, seemed clothed in black; the woman wore, as nearly as I could make out, a gown of gray stuff. Evidently they were still unaware of my presence in the shadow, though for some reason when they renewed their conversation they spoke in lower tones and I could no longer understand. As I looked the woman seemed to sink to the ground and raise her hands in supplication, as is frequently done on the stage and never, so far as I knew, anywhere else, and I am now not altogether sure that it was done in this instance. The man fixed his eyes upon her;

they seemed to glitter bleakly in the moonlight with an expression that made me apprehensive that he would turn them upon me. I do not know by what impulse I was moved, but I sprang to my feet out of the shadow. At that instant the figures vanished. I peered in vain through the spaces among the trees and clumps of undergrowth. The night wind rustled the leaves; the lizards had retired early, reptiles of exemplary habits. The little moon was already slipping behind a black hill in the west.

I went home, somewhat disturbed in mind, half doubting that I had heard or seen any living thing excepting the lizards. It all seemed a trifle odd and uncanny. It was as if among the several phenomena, objective and subjective, that made the sum total of the incident there had been an uncertain element which had diffused its dubious character over all—had leavened the whole mass with unreality. I did not like it.

At the breakfast table the next morning there was a new face; opposite me sat a young woman at whom I merely glanced as I took my seat. In speaking to the high and mighty female personage who condescended to seem to wait upon us, this girl soon invited my attention by the sound of her voice, which was like, yet not altogether like, the one still murmuring in my memory of the previous evening's adventure. A moment later another girl, a few years older, entered the room and sat at the left of the other, speaking to her a gentle "good morning." By *her* voice I was startled: it was without doubt the one of which the first girl's had reminded me. Here was the lady of the sylvan incident sitting bodily before me, "in her habit as she lived."

Evidently enough the two were sisters. With a nebulous kind of apprehension that I might be recognized as the mute inglorious hero of an adventure which had in my consciousness and conscience something of the character of eavesdropping, I allowed myself only a hasty cup of the lukewarm coffee thoughtfully provided by the prescient waitress for the emergency, and left the table. As I passed out of the house into the grounds I heard a rich, strong male voice singing an aria from "Rigoletto." I am bound to say that it was exquisitely sung, too, but there was something in the performance that displeased me, I could say neither what nor why, and I walked rapidly away.

Returning later in the day I saw the elder of the two young women standing on the porch and near her a tall man in black clothing—the man whom I had expected to see. All day the desire to know something of these persons had been uppermost in my mind and I now resolved to learn what I could of them in any way that was neither dishonorable nor low.

The man was talking easily and affably to his companion, but at the sound of my footsteps on the gravel walk he ceased, and turning about looked me full in the face. He was apparently of middle age, dark and uncommonly handsome. His attire was faultless, his bearing easy and graceful, the look which he turned upon me open, free, and devoid of any suggestion of rudeness. Nevertheless it affected me with a distinct emotion which on subsequent analysis in memory appeared to be compounded of hatred and dread—I am unwilling to call it fear. A second later the man and woman had disappeared. They seemed to have a trick of disappearing. On entering the house, however, I saw them through the open doorway of the parlor as I passed; they had merely stepped through a window which opened down to the floor.

Cautiously "approached" on the subject of her new guests my landlady proved not ungracious. Restated with, I hope, some small reverence for English grammar the facts were these: the two girls were Pauline and Eva Maynard of San Francisco; the elder was Pauline. The man was Richard Benning, their guardian, who had been the most intimate friend of their father, now deceased. Mr. Benning had brought them to Brownville in the hope that the mountain climate might benefit Eva, who was thought to be in danger of consumption.

Upon these short and simple annals the landlady wrought an embroidery of eulogium which abundantly attested her faith in Mr. Benning's will and ability to pay for the best that her house afforded. That he had a good heart was evident to her from his devotion to his two beautiful wards and his really touching solicitude for their comfort. The evidence impressed me as insufficient and I silently found the Scotch verdict, "Not proven."

Certainly Mr. Benning was most attentive to his wards. In my strolls about the country I frequently encountered them—sometimes in company with other guests of the hotel—exploring the gulches, fishing, rifle shooting, and otherwise wiling away the monotony of country life; and although I watched them as closely as good manners would permit I saw nothing that would in any way explain the strange words that I had overheard in the wood. I had grown tolerably well acquainted with the young ladies and could exchange looks and even greetings with their guardian without actual repugnance.

A month went by and I had almost ceased to interest myself in their affairs when one night our entire little community was thrown into excitement by an event which vividly recalled my experience in the forest.

This was the death of the elder girl, Pauline.

The sisters had occupied the same bedroom on the third floor of the house. Waking in the gray of the morning Eva had found Pauline dead beside her. Later, when the poor girl was weeping beside the body amid a throng of sympathetic if not very considerate persons, Mr. Benning entered the room and appeared to be about to take her hand. She drew away from the side of the dead and moved slowly toward the door.

"It is you," she said—"you who have done this. You—you—you!"

"She is raving," he said in a low voice. He followed her, step by step, as she retreated, his eyes fixed upon hers with a steady gaze in which there was nothing of tenderness nor of compassion. She stopped; the hand that she had raised in accusation fell to her side, her dilated eyes contracted visibly, the lids slowly dropped over them, veiling their strange wild beauty, and she stood motionless and almost as white as the dead girl lying near. The man took her hand and put his arm gently about her shoulders, as if to support her. Suddenly she burst into a passion of tears and clung to him as a child to its mother. He smiled with a smile that affected me most disagreeably—perhaps any kind of smile would have done so—and led her silently out of the room.

There was an inquest—and the customary verdict: the deceased, it appeared, came to her death through "heart disease." It was before the invention of heart *failure,* though the heart of poor Pauline had indubitably failed. The body was embalmed and taken to San Francisco by some one summoned thence for the purpose, neither Eva nor Benning accompanying it. Some of the hotel gossips ventured to think that very strange, and a few hardy spirits went so far as to think it very strange indeed; but the good landlady generously threw herself into the breach, saying it was owing to the precarious nature of the girl's health. It is not of record that either of the two persons most affected and apparently least concerned made any explanation.

One evening about a week after the death I went out upon the veranda of the hotel to get a book that I had left there. Under some vines shutting out the moonlight from a part of the space I saw Richard Benning, for whose apparition I was prepared by having previously heard the low, sweet voice of Eva Maynard, whom also I now discerned, standing before him with one hand raised to his shoulder and her eyes, as nearly as I could judge, gazing upward into his. He held her disengaged hand and his head was bent with a

singular dignity and grace. Their attitude was that of lovers, and as
I stood in deep shadow to observe I felt even guiltier than on that
memorable night in the wood. I was about to retire, when the girl
spoke, and the contrast between her words and her attitude was so
surprising that I remained, because I had merely forgotten to go
away.

"You will take my life," she said, "as you did Pauline's. I know your
intention as well as I know your power, and I ask nothing, only that
you finish your work without needless delay and let me be at peace."

He made no reply—merely let go the hand that he was holding,
removed the other from his shoulder, and turning away descended
the steps leading to the garden and disappeared in the shrubbery. But
a moment later I heard, seemingly from a great distance, his fine
clear voice in a barbaric chant, which as I listened brought before
some inner spiritual sense a consciousness of some far, strange land
peopled with beings having forbidden powers. The song held me in
a kind of spell, but when it had died away I recovered and instantly
perceived what I thought an opportunity. I walked out of my shadow
to where the girl stood. She turned and stared at me with something
of the look, it seemed to me, of a hunted hare. Possibly my intrusion
had frightened her.

"Miss Maynard," I said, "I beg you to tell me who that man is and
the nature of his power over you. Perhaps this is rude in me, but it
is not a matter for idle civilities. When a woman is in danger any
man has a right to act."

She listened without visible emotion—almost I thought without
interest, and when I had finished she closed her big blue eyes as if
unspeakably weary.

"You can do nothing," she said.

I took hold of her arm, gently shaking her as one shakes a person
falling into a dangerous sleep.

"You must rouse yourself," I said; "something must be done and
you must give me leave to act. You have said that that man killed
your sister, and I believe it—that he will kill you, and I believe that."

She merely raised her eyes to mine.

"Will you not tell me all?" I added.

"There is nothing to be done, I tell you—nothing. And if I could
do anything I would not. It does not matter in the least. We shall be
here only two days more; we go away then, oh, so far! If you have
observed anything, I beg you to be silent."

"But this is madness, girl." I was trying by rough speech to break
the deadly repose of her manner. "You have accused him of murder.

Unless you explain these things to me I shall lay the matter before the authorities."

This roused her, but in a way that I did not like. She lifted her head proudly and said: "Do not meddle, sir, in what does not concern you. This is my affair, Mr. Moran, not yours."

"It concerns every person in the country—in the world," I answered, with equal coldness. "If you had no love for your sister I, at least, am concerned for you."

"Listen," she interrupted, leaning toward me. "I loved her, yes, God knows! But more than that—beyond all, beyond expression, I love *him*. You have overheard a secret, but you shall not make use of it to harm him. I shall deny all. Your word against mine—it will be that. Do you think your 'authorities' will believe you?"

She was now smiling like an angel and, God help me! I was heels over head in love with her! Did she, by some of the many methods of divination known to her sex, read my feelings? Her whole manner had altered.

"Come," she said, almost coaxingly, "promise that you will not be impolite again." She took my arm in the most friendly way. "Come, I will walk with you. He will not know—he will remain away all night."

Up and down the veranda we paced in the moonlight, she seemingly forgetting her recent bereavement, cooing and murmuring girl-wise of every kind of nothing in all Brownville; I silent, consciously awkward and with something of the feeling of being concerned in an intrigue. It was a revelation—this most charming and apparently blameless creature coolly and confessedly deceiving the man for whom a moment before she had acknowledged and shown the supreme love which finds even death an acceptable endearment.

"Truly," I thought in my inexperience, "here is something new under the moon."

And the moon must have smiled.

Before we parted I had exacted a promise that she would walk with me the next afternoon—before going away forever—to the Old Mill, one of Brownville's revered antiquities, erected in 1860.

"If he is not about," she added gravely, as I let go the hand she had given me at parting, and of which, may the good saints forgive me, I strove vainly to repossess myself when she had said it—so charming, as the wise Frenchman has pointed out, do we find woman's infidelity when we are its objects, not its victims. In apportioning his benefactions that night the Angel of Sleep overlooked me.

The Brownville House dined early, and after dinner the next day

Miss Maynard, who had not been at table, came to me on the veranda, attired in the demurest of walking costumes, saying not a word. "He" was evidently "not about." We went slowly up the road that led to the Old Mill. She was apparently not strong and at times took my arm, relinquishing it and taking it again rather capriciously, I thought. Her mood, or rather her succession of moods, was as mutable as skylight in a rippling sea. She jested as if she had never heard of such a thing as death, and laughed on the lightest incitement, and directly afterward would sing a few bars of some grave melody with such tenderness of expression that I had to turn away my eyes lest she should see the evidence of her success in art, if art it was, not artlessness, as then I was compelled to think it. And she said the oddest things in the most unconventional way, skirting sometimes unfathomable abysms of thought, where I had hardly the courage to set foot. In short, she was fascinating in a thousand and fifty different ways, and at every step I executed a new and profounder emotional folly, a hardier spiritual indiscretion, incurring fresh liability to arrest by the constabulary of conscience for infractions of my own peace.

Arriving at the mill, she made no pretense of stopping, but turned into a trail leading through a field of stubble toward a creek. Crossing by a rustic bridge we continued on the trail, which now led uphill to one of the most picturesque spots in the country. The Eagle's Nest, it was called—the summit of a cliff that rose sheer into the air to a height of hundreds of feet above the forest at its base. From this elevated point we had a noble view of another valley and of the opposite hills flushed with the last rays of the setting sun. As we watched the light escaping to higher and higher planes from the encroaching flood of shadow filling the valley we heard footsteps, and in another moment were joined by Richard Benning.

"I saw you from the road," he said carelessly; "so I came up."

Being a fool, I neglected to take him by the throat and pitch him into the treetops below, but muttered some polite lie instead. On the girl the effect of his coming was immediate and unmistakable. Her face was suffused with the glory of love's transfiguration: the red light of the sunset had not been more obvious in her eyes than was now the lovelight that replaced it.

"I am so glad you came!" she said, giving him both her hands; and, God help me! it was manifestly true.

Seating himself upon the ground he began a lively dissertation upon the wild flowers of the region, a number of which he had with him. In the middle of a facetious sentence he suddenly ceased speaking and fixed his eyes upon Eva, who leaned against the stump of a tree, absently plaiting grasses. She lifted her eyes in a startled way to his, as if she had *felt* his look. She then rose, cast away her grasses, and moved slowly away from him. He also rose, continuing to look at her. He had still in his hand the bunch of flowers. The girl turned, as if to speak, but said nothing. I recall clearly now something of which I was but half-conscious then—the dreadful contrast between the smile upon her lips and the terrified expression in her eyes as she met his steady and imperative gaze. I know nothing of how it happened, nor how it was that I did not sooner understand; I only know that with the smile of an angel upon her lips and that look of terror in her beautiful eyes Eva Maynard sprang from the cliff and shot crashing into the tops of the pines below!

How and how long afterward I reached the place I cannot say, but Richard Benning was already there, kneeling beside the dreadful thing that had been a woman.

"She is dead—quite dead," he said coldly. "I will go to town for assistance. Please do me the favor to remain."

He rose to his feet and moved away, but in a moment had stopped and turned about.

"You have doubtless observed, my friend," he said, "that this was entirely her own act. I did not rise in time to prevent it, and you, not knowing her mental condition—you could not, of course, have suspected."

His manner maddened me.

"You are as much her assassin," I said, "as if your damnable hands had cut her throat."

He shrugged his shoulders without reply and, turning, walked away. A moment later I heard, through the deepening shadows of the wood into which he had disappeared, a rich, strong, baritone voice singing *"La donna e mobile,"* from "Rigoletto."

❊   ❊   ❊

THE SUITABLE SURROUNDINGS

THE NIGHT

One midsummer night a farmer's boy living about ten miles from the city of Cincinnati was following a bridle path through a dense and dark forest. He had lost himself while searching for some missing cows, and near midnight was a long way from home, in a part of the country with which he was unfamiliar. But he was a stout-hearted lad, and knowing his general direction from his home, he plunged into the forest without hesitation, guided by the stars. Coming into the bridle path, and observing that it ran in the right direction, he followed it.

The night was clear, but in the woods it was exceedingly dark. It was more by the sense of touch than by that of sight that the lad kept the path. He could not, indeed, very easily go astray; the under-growth on both sides was so thick as to be almost impenetrable. He had gone into the forest a mile or more when he was surprised to see a feeble gleam of light shining through the foliage skirting the path on his left. The sight of it startled him and set his heart beating audibly.

"The old Breede house is somewhere about here," he said to himself. "This must be the other end of the path which we reach it by from our side. Ugh! what should a light be doing there?"

Nevertheless, he pushed on. A moment later he had emerged from the forest into a small, open space, mostly upgrown to brambles. There were remnants of a rotting fence. A few yards from the trail, in the middle of the "clearing," was the house from which the light came, through an unglazed window. The window had once contained glass, but that and its supporting frame had long ago yielded to missiles flung by hands of venturesome boys to attest alike their courage and their hostility to the supernatural; for the Breede house bore the evil reputation of being haunted. Possibly it was not, but even the hardiest sceptic could not deny that it was deserted—which in rural regions is much the same thing.

Looking at the mysterious dim light shining from the ruined window the boy remembered with apprehension that his own hand had assisted at the destruction. His penitence was of course poignant in proportion to its tardiness and inefficacy. He half expected to be set upon by all the unworldly and bodiless malevolences whom he had outraged by assisting to break alike their windows and their peace. Yet this stubborn lad, shaking in every limb, would not retreat. The blood in his veins was strong and rich with the iron of the frontiers-man. He was but two removes from the generation that had sub-dued the Indian. He started to pass the house.

As he was going by he looked in at the blank window space and saw a strange and terrifying sight,—the figure of a man seated in the centre of the room, at a table upon which lay some loose sheets of paper. The elbows rested on the table, the hands supporting the head, which was uncovered. On each side the fingers were pushed into the hair. The face showed dead-yellow in the light of a single candle a little to one side. The flame illuminated that side of the face, the other was in deep shadow. The man's eyes were fixed upon the blank window space with a stare in which an older and cooler observer might have discerned something of apprehension, but which seemed to the lad altogether soulless. He believed the man to be dead.

The situation was horrible, but not without its fascination. The boy stopped to note it all. He was weak, faint and trembling; he could feel the blood forsaking his face. Nevertheless, he set his teeth and resolutely advanced to the house. He had no conscious intention —it was the mere courage of terror. He thrust his white face forward into the illuminated opening. At that instant a strange, harsh cry, a shriek, broke upon the silence of the night—the note of a screech-owl. The man sprang to his feet, overturning the table and extinguishing the candle. The boy took to his heels.

THE DAY BEFORE

"Good-morning, Colston. I am in luck, it seems. You have often said that my commendation of your literary work was mere civility, and here you find me absorbed—actually merged—in your latest story in the *Messenger*. Nothing less shocking than your touch upon my shoulder would have roused me to consciousness."

"The proof is stronger than you seem to know," replied the man addressed: "so keen is your eagerness to read my story that you are willing to renounce selfish considerations and forego all the pleasure that you could get from it."

"I don't understand you," said the other, folding the newspaper that he held and putting it into his pocket. "You writers are a queer lot, anyhow. Come, tell me what I have done or omitted in this matter. In what way does the pleasure that I get, or might get, from your work depend on me?"

"In many ways. Let me ask you how you would enjoy your breakfast if you took it in this street car. Suppose the phonograph so perfected as to be able to give you an entire opera,—singing, orchestration, and all; do you think you would get much pleasure out of it if you turned it on at your office during business hours? Do you really care for a serenade by Schubert when you hear it fiddled by an untimely Italian on a morning ferryboat? Are you always cocked and primed for enjoyment? Do you keep every mood on tap, ready to any demand? Let me remind you, sir, that the story which you have done me the honor to begin as a means of becoming oblivious to the discomfort of this car is a ghost story!"

"Well?"

"Well! Has the reader no duties corresponding to his privileges? You have paid five cents for that newspaper. It is yours. You have the right to read it when and where you will. Much of what is in it is neither helped nor harmed by time and place and mood; some of it actually requires to be read at once—while it is fizzing. But my story is not of that character. It is not 'the very latest advices' from Ghostland. You are not expected to keep yourself *au courant* with what is going on in the realm of spooks. The stuff will keep until you have leisure to put yourself into the frame of mind appropriate to the sentiment of the piece—which I respectfully submit that you cannot do in a street car, even if you are the only passenger. The solitude is not of the right sort. An author has rights which the reader is bound to respect."

"For specific example?"

"The right to the reader's undivided attention. To deny him this is immoral. To make him share your attention with the rattle of a street car, the moving panorama of the crowds on the sidewalks, and the buildings beyond—with any of the thousands of distractions which make our customary environment—is to treat him with gross injustice. By God, it is infamous!"

The speaker had risen to his feet and was steadying himself by one of the straps hanging from the roof of the car. The other man looked up at him in sudden astonishment, wondering how so trivial a grievance could seem to justify so strong language. He saw that his friend's face was uncommonly pale and that his eyes glowed like living coals.

"You know what I mean," continued the writer, impetuously crowding his words—"you know what I mean, Marsh. My stuff in this morning's *Messenger* is plainly subheaded 'A Ghost Story.' That is ample notice to all. Every honorable reader will understand it as prescribing by implication the conditions under which the work is to be read."

The man addressed as Marsh winced a trifle, then asked with a smile: "What conditions? You know that I am only a plain business man who cannot be supposed to understand such things. How, when, where should I read your ghost story?"

"In solitude—at night—by the light of a candle. There are certain emotions which a writer can easily enough excite—such as compassion or merriment. I can move you to tears or laughter under almost any circumstances. But for my ghost story to be effective you must be made to feel fear—at least a strong sense of the supernatural—and that is a difficult matter. I have a right to expect that if you read me at all you will give me a chance; that you will make yourself accessible to the emotion that I try to inspire."

The car had now arrived at its terminus and stopped. The trip just completed was its first for the day and the conversation of the two early passengers had not been interrupted. The streets were yet silent and desolate; the house tops were just touched by the rising sun. As they stepped from the car and walked away together Marsh narrowly eyed his companion, who was reported, like most men of uncommon literary ability, to be addicted to various destructive vices. That is the revenge which dull minds take upon bright ones in resentment of their superiority. Mr. Colston was known as a man of genius. There are honest souls who believe that genius is a mode of excess. It was known that Colston did not drink liquor, but many said that he ate opium. Something in his appearance that morning—a certain wildness of the eyes, an unusual pallor, a thickness and rapidity of speech—were taken by Mr. Marsh to confirm the report. Nevertheless, he had not the self-denial to abandon a subject which he found interesting, however it might excite his friend.

"Do you mean to say," he began, "that if I take the trouble to observe your directions—place myself in the conditions that you demand: solitude, night and a tallow candle—you can with your ghostly work give me an uncomfortable sense of the supernatural, as you call it? Can you accelerate my pulse, make me start at sudden noises, send a nervous chill along my spine and cause my hair to rise?"

Colston turned suddenly and looked him squarely in the eyes as they walked. "You would not dare—you have not the courage," he said. He emphasized the words with a contemptuous gesture. "You are brave enough to read me in a street car, but—in a deserted house —alone—in the forest—at night! Bah! I have a manuscript in my pocket that would kill you."

Marsh was angry. He knew himself courageous, and the words stung him. "If you know such a place," he said, "take me there tonight and leave me your story and a candle. Call for me when I've had time enough to read it and I'll tell you the entire plot and—kick you out of the place."

That is how it occurred that the farmer's boy, looking in at an unglazed window of the Breede house, saw a man sitting in the light of a candle.

THE DAY AFTER

Late in the afternoon of the next day three men and a boy approached the Breede house from that point of the compass toward which the boy had fled the preceding night. The men were in high spirits; they talked very loudly and laughed. They made facetious and good-humored ironical remarks to the boy about his adventure, which evidently they did not believe in. The boy accepted their raillery with seriousness, making no reply. He had a sense of the fitness of things and knew that one who professes to have seen a dead man rise from his seat and blow out a candle is not a credible witness.

Arriving at the house and finding the door unlocked, the party of investigators entered without ceremony. Leading out of the passage into which this door opened was another on the right and one on the left. They entered the room on the left—the one which had the blank front window. Here was the dead body of a man.

It lay partly on one side, with the forearm beneath it, the cheek on the floor. The eyes were wide open; the stare was not an agreeable thing to encounter. The lower jaw had fallen; a little pool of saliva had collected beneath the mouth. An overthrown table, a partly burned candle, a chair and some paper with writing on it were all else that the room contained. The men looked at the body, touching the face in turn. The boy gravely stood at the head, assuming a look of ownership. It was the proudest moment of his life. One of the men said to him, "You're a good 'un"—a remark which was received by the two others with nods of acquiescence. It was Scepticism apologizing to Truth. Then one of the men took from the floor the sheet of manuscript and stepped to the window, for already the evening shadows were glooming the forest. The song of the whip-poor-will was heard in the distance and a monstrous beetle sped by the window on roaring wings and thundered away out of hearing. The man read:

THE MANUSCRIPT

"Before committing the act which, rightly or wrongly, I have resolved on and appearing before my Maker for judgment, I, James R. Colston, deem it my duty as a journalist to make a statement to the public. My name is, I believe, tolerably well known to the people as a writer of tragic tales, but the somberest imagination never conceived anything so tragic as my own life and history. Not in incident: my life has been destitute of adventure and action. But my mental career has been lurid with experiences such as kill and damn. I shall not recount them here—some of them are written and ready for publication elsewhere. The object of these lines is to explain to whomsoever may be interested that my death is voluntary—my own act. I shall die at twelve o'clock on the night of the 15th of July—a significant anniversary to me, for it was on that day, and at that hour, that my friend in time and eternity, Charles Breede, performed his vow to me by the same act which his fidelity to our pledge now entails upon me. He took his life in his little house in the Copeton woods. There was the customary verdict of 'temporary insanity.' Had I testified at that inquest—had I told all I knew, they would have called *me* mad!"

Here followed an evidently long passage which the man reading read to himself only. The rest he read aloud.

"I have still a week of life in which to arrange my worldly affairs and prepare for the great change. It is enough, for I have but few affairs and it is now four years since death became an imperative obligation.

"I shall bear this writing on my body; the finder will please hand it to the coroner.

"JAMES R. COLSTON.

"P.S.—Willard Marsh, on this the fatal fifteenth day of July I hand you this manuscript, to be opened and read under the conditions agreed upon, and at the place which I designated. I forego my intention to keep it on my body to explain the manner of my death, which is not important. It will serve to explain the manner of yours. I am to call for you during the night to receive assurance that you have read the manuscript. You know me well enough to expect me. But, my friend, it *will be after twelve o'clock.* May God have mercy on our souls!

"J. R. C."

Before the man who was reading this manuscript had finished, the candle had been picked up and lighted. When the reader had done, he quietly thrust the paper against the flame and despite the protestations of the others held it until it was burnt to ashes. The man who did this, and who afterward placidly endured a severe reprimand from the coroner, was a son-in-law of the late Charles Breede. At the inquest nothing could elicit an intelligent account of what the paper had contained.

FROM "THE TIMES"

"Yesterday the Commissioners of Lunacy committed to the asylum Mr. James R. Colston, a writer of some local reputation, connected with the *Messenger.* It will be remembered that on the evening of the 15th inst. Mr. Colston was given into custody by one of his fellow-lodgers in the Baine House, who had observed him acting very suspiciously, baring his throat and whetting a razor—occasionally trying its edge by actually cutting through the skin of his arm, etc. On being handed over to the police, the unfortunate man made a desperate resistance, and has ever since been so violent that it has been necessary to keep him in a strait-jacket. Most of our esteemed contemporary's other writers are still at large."

❋ ❋ ❋

THE BOARDED WINDOW

In 1830, only a few miles away from what is now the great city of Cincinnati, lay an immense and almost unbroken forest. The whole region was sparsely settled by people of the frontier—restless souls who no sooner had hewn fairly habitable homes out of the wilderness and attained to that degree of prosperity which to-day we should call indigence than impelled by some mysterious impulse of their nature they abandoned all and pushed farther westward, to encounter new perils and privations in the effort to regain the meagre comforts which they had voluntarily renounced. Many of them had already forsaken that region for the remoter settlements, but among those remaining was one who had been of those first arriving. He lived alone in a house of logs surrounded on all sides by the great forest, of whose gloom and silence he seemed a part, for no one had ever known him to smile nor speak a needless word. His simple wants were supplied by the sale or barter of skins of wild animals in the river town, for not a thing did he grow upon the land which, if needful, he might have claimed by right of undisturbed possession. There were evidences of "improvement"—a few acres of ground immediately about the house had once been cleared of its trees, the decayed stumps of which were half concealed by the new growth that had been suffered to repair the ravage wrought by the ax. Apparently the man's zeal for agriculture had burned with a failing flame, expiring in penitential ashes.

The little log house, with its chimney of sticks, its roof of warping clapboards weighted with traversing poles and its "chinking" of clay, had a single door and, directly opposite, a window. The latter, however, was boarded up—nobody could remember a time when it was not. And none knew why it was so closed; certainly not because of the occupant's dislike of light and air, for on those rare occasions when a hunter had passed that lonely spot the recluse had commonly been seen sunning himself on his doorstep if heaven had provided sunshine for his need. I fancy there are few persons living to-day who ever knew the secret of that window, but I am one, as you shall see.

The man's name was said to be Murlock. He was apparently seventy years old, actually about fifty. Something besides years had had a hand in his aging. His hair and long, full beard were white, his gray, lustreless eyes sunken, his face singularly seamed with wrinkles which appeared to belong to two intersecting systems. In figure he was tall and spare, with a stoop of the shoulders—a burden bearer. I never saw him; these particulars I learned from my grandfather, from whom also I got the man's story when I was a lad. He had known him when living near by in that early day.

One day Murlock was found in his cabin, dead. It was not a time and place for coroners and newspapers, and I suppose it was agreed that he had died from natural causes or I should have been told, and should remember. I know only that with what was probably a sense of the fitness of things the body was buried near the cabin, alongside the grave of his wife, who had preceded him by so many years that local tradition had retained hardly a hint of her existence. That closes the final chapter of this true story—excepting, indeed, the circumstance that many years afterward, in company with an equally intrepid spirit, I penetrated to the place and ventured near enough to the ruined cabin to throw a stone against it, and ran away to avoid the ghost which every well-informed boy thereabout knew haunted the spot. But there is an earlier chapter—that supplied by my grandfather.

When Murlock built his cabin and began laying sturdily about with his ax to hew out a farm—the rifle, meanwhile, his means of support—he was young, strong and full of hope. In that eastern country whence he came he had married, as was the fashion, a young woman in all ways worthy of his honest devotion, who shared the dangers and privations of his lot with a willing spirit and light heart.

There is no known record of her name; of her charms of mind and person tradition is silent and the doubter is at liberty to entertain his doubt; but God forbid that I should share it! Of their affection and happiness there is abundant assurance in every added day of the man's widowed life; for what but the magnetism of a blessed memory could have chained that venturesome spirit to a lot like that?

One day Murlock returned from gunning in a distant part of the forest to find his wife prostrate with fever, and delirious. There was no physician within miles, no neighbor; nor was she in a condition to be left, to summon help. So he set about the task of nursing her back to health, but at the end of the third day she fell into unconsciousness and so passed away, apparently, with never a gleam of returning reason.

From what we know of a nature like his we may venture to sketch in some of the details of the outline picture drawn by my grandfather. When convinced that she was dead, Murlock had sense enough to remember that the dead must be prepared for burial. In performance of this sacred duty he blundered now and again, did certain things incorrectly, and others which he did correctly were done over and over. His occasional failures to accomplish some simple and ordinary act filled him with astonishment, like that of a drunken man who wonders at the suspension of familiar natural laws. He was surprised, too, that he did not weep—surprised and a little ashamed; surely it is unkind not to weep for the dead. "Tomorrow," he said aloud, "I shall have to make the coffin and dig the grave; and then I shall miss her, when she is no longer in sight; but now—she is dead, of course, but it is all right—it *must* be all right, somehow. Things cannot be so bad as they seem."

He stood over the body in the fading light, adjusting the hair and putting the finishing touches to the simple toilet, doing all mechanically, with soulless care. And still through his consciousness ran an undersense of conviction that all was right—that he should have her again as before, and everything explained. He had had no experience in grief; his capacity had not been enlarged by use. His heart could not contain it all, nor his imagination rightly conceive it. He did not know he was so hard struck; *that* knowledge would come later, and never go. Grief is an artist of powers as various as the instruments upon which he plays his dirges for the dead, evoking from some the sharpest, shrillest notes, from others the low, grave chords that throb recurrent like the slow beating of a distant drum. Some natures it startles; some it stupefies. To one it comes like the stroke of an arrow, stinging all the sensibilities to a keener life; to another as

the blow of a bludgeon, which in crushing benumbs. We may conceive Murlock to have been that way affected, for (and here we are
upon surer ground than that of conjecture) no sooner had he finished his pious work than, sinking into a chair by the side of the
table upon which the body lay, and noting how white the profile
showed in the deepening gloom, he laid his arms upon the table's
edge, and dropped his face into them, tearless yet and unutterably
weary. At that moment came in through the open window a long,
wailing sound like the cry of a lost child in the far deeps of the darkening wood! But the man did not move. Again, and nearer than before, sounded that unearthly cry upon his failing sense. Perhaps it
was a wild beast; perhaps it was a dream. For Murlock was asleep.

Some hours later, as it afterward appeared, this unfaithful
watcher awoke and lifting his head from his arms intently listened
—he knew not why. There in the black darkness by the side of the
dead, recalling all without a shock, he strained his eyes to see—he
knew not what. His senses were all alert, his breath was suspended,
his blood had stilled its tides as if to assist the silence. Who—what
had waked him, and where was it?

Suddenly the table shook beneath his arms, and at the same moment he heard, or fancied that he heard, a light, soft step—another
—sounds as of bare feet upon the floor!

He was terrified beyond the power to cry out or move. Perforce he
waited—waited there in the darkness through seeming centuries of
such dread as one may know, yet live to tell. He tried vainly to speak
the dead woman's name, vainly to stretch forth his hand across the
table to learn if she were there. His throat was powerless, his arms
and hands were like lead. Then occurred something most frightful. Some heavy body seemed hurled against the table with an impetus that pushed it against his breast so sharply as nearly to overthrow him, and at the same instant he heard and felt the fall of
something upon the floor with so violent a thump that the whole
house was shaken by the impact. A scuffling ensued, and a confusion
of sounds impossible to describe. Murlock had risen to his feet. Fear
had by excess forfeited control of his faculties. He flung his hands
upon the table. Nothing was there!

There is a point at which terror may turn to madness; and madness incites to action. With no definite intent, from no motive but
the wayward impulse of a madman, Murlock sprang to the wall,
with a little groping seized his loaded rifle, and without aim discharged it. By the flash which lit up the room with a vivid illumination, he saw an enormous panther dragging the dead woman

toward the window, its teeth fixed in her throat! Then there were darkness blacker than before, and silence; and when he returned to consciousness the sun was high and the wood vocal with songs of birds.

The body lay near the window, where the beast had left it when frightened away by the flash and report of the rifle. The clothing was deranged, the long hair in disorder, the limbs lay anyhow. From the throat, dreadfully lacerated, had issued a pool of blood not yet entirely coagulated. The ribbon with which he had bound the wrists was broken; the hands were tightly clenched. Between the teeth was a fragment of the animal's ear.

❊   ❊   ❊

A LADY FROM REDHORSE

CORONADO, JUNE 20.

I find myself more and more interested in him. It is not, I am sure, his—do you know any good noun corresponding to the adjective "handsome"? One does not like to say "beauty" when speaking of a man. He is beautiful enough, Heaven knows; I should not even care to trust you with him—faithfulest of all possible wives that you are—when he looks his best, as he always does. Nor do I think the fascination of his manner has much to do with it. You recollect that the charm of art inheres in that which is undefinable, and to you and me, my dear Irene, I fancy there is rather less of that in the branch of art under consideration than to girls in their first season. I fancy I know how my fine gentleman produces many of his effects and could perhaps give him a pointer on heightening them. Nevertheless, his manner is something truly delightful. I suppose what interests me chiefly is the man's brains. His conversation is the best I have ever heard and altogether unlike any one else's. He seems to know everything, as indeed he ought, for he has been everywhere, read everything, seen all there is to see—sometimes I think rather more than is good for him—and had acquaintance with the *queerest* people. And then his voice—Irene, when I hear it I actually feel as if I ought to have paid at the door, though of course it is my own door.

JULY 3.

I fear my remarks about Dr. Barritz must have been, being thoughtless, very silly, or you would not have written of him with such levity, not to say disrespect. Believe me, dearest, he has more dignity and seriousness (of the kind, I mean, which is not inconsistent with a manner sometimes playful and always charming) than any of the men that you and I ever met. And young Raynor—you knew Raynor at Monterey—tells me that the men all like him and that he is treated with something like deference everywhere. There is a mystery, too—something about his connection with the Blavatsky people in Northern India. Raynor either would not or could not tell me the particulars. I infer that Dr. Barritz is thought—don't you dare to laugh!—a magician. Could anything be finer than that? An ordinary mystery is not, of course, so good as a scandal, but when it relates to dark and dreadful practices—to exercise of unearthly powers—could anything be more piquant? It explains, too, the singular influence the man has upon me. It is the undefinable in his art—black art. Seriously, dear, I quite tremble when he looks me full in the eyes with those unfathomable orbs of his, which I have already vainly attempted to describe to you. How dreadful if he has the power to make one fall in love! Do you know if the Blavatsky crowd have that power—outside of Sepoy?

JULY 16.

The strangest thing! Last evening while Auntie was attending one of the hotel hops (I hate them) Dr. Barritz called. It was scandalously late—I actually believe that he had talked with Auntie in the ballroom and learned from her that I was alone. I had been all the evening contriving how to worm out of him the truth about his connection with the Thugs in Sepoy, and all of that black business, but the moment he fixed his eyes on me (for I admitted him, I'm ashamed to say) I was helpless. I trembled, I blushed, I—O Irene, Irene, I love the man beyond expression and you know how it is yourself.

Fancy! I, an ugly duckling from Redhorse—daughter (they say) of old Calamity Jim—certainly his heiress, with no living relation but an absurd old aunt who spoils me a thousand and fifty ways—absolutely destitute of everything but a million dollars and a hope in Paris,—I daring to love a god like him! My dear, if I had you here I could tear your hair out with mortification.

I am convinced that he is aware of my feeling, for he stayed but a few moments, said nothing but what another man might have said half as well, and pretending that he had an engagement went away. I learned to-day (a little bird told me—the bell-bird) that he went straight to bed. How does that strike you as evidence of exemplary habits?

July 17.

That little wretch, Raynor, called yesterday and his babble set me almost wild. He never runs down—that is to say, when he exterminates a score of reputations, more or less, he does not pause between one reputation and the next. (By the way, he inquired about you, and his manifestations of interest in you had, I confess, a good deal of *vraisemblance.*) Mr. Raynor observes no game laws; like Death (which he would inflict if slander were fatal) he has all seasons for his own. But I like him, for we knew each other at Redhorse when we were young. He was known in those days as "Giggles," and I—O Irene, can you ever forgive me?—I was called "Gunny." God knows why; perhaps in allusion to the material of my pinafores; perhaps because the name is in alliteration with "Giggles," for Gig and I were inseparable playmates, and the miners may have thought it a delicate civility to recognize some kind of relationship between us.

Later, we took in a third—another of Adversity's brood, who, like Garrick between Tragedy and Comedy, had a chronic inability to adjudicate the rival claims of Frost and Famine. Between him and misery there was seldom anything more than a single suspender and the hope of a meal which would at the same time support life and make it insupportable. He literally picked up a precarious living for himself and an aged mother by "chloriding the dumps," that is to say, the miners permitted him to search the heaps of waste rock for such pieces of "pay ore" as had been overlooked; and these he sacked up and sold at the Syndicate Mill. He became a member of our firm—"Gunny, Giggles, and Dumps" thenceforth—through my favor; for I could not then, nor can I now, be indifferent to his courage and prowess in defending against Giggles the immemorial right of his sex to insult a strange and unprotected female—myself. After old Jim struck it in the Calamity and I began to wear shoes and go to school, and in emulation Giggles took to washing his face and became Jack Raynor, of Wells, Fargo & Co., and old Mrs. Barts was herself chlorided to her fathers, Dumps drifted over to San Juan Smith and turned stage driver, and was killed by road agents, and so forth.

Why do I tell you all this, dear? Because it is heavy on my heart. Because I walk the Valley of Humility. Because I am subduing myself to permanent consciousness of my unworthiness to unloose the latchet of Dr. Barritz's shoe. Because, oh dear, oh dear, there's a cousin of Dumps at this hotel! I haven't spoken to him. I never had much acquaintance with him,—but do you suppose he has recognized me? Do, please give me in your next your candid, sure-enough opinion about it, and say you don't think so. Do you suppose He knows about me already, and that that is why He left me last evening when He saw that I blushed and trembled like a fool under His eyes? You know I can't bribe *all* the newspapers, and I can't go back on anybody who was civil to Gunny at Redhorse—not if I'm pitched out of society into the sea. So the skeleton sometimes rattles behind the door. I never cared much before, as you know, but now—*now* it is not the same. Jack Raynor I am sure of—he will not tell Him. He seems, indeed, to hold Him in such respect as hardly to dare speak to Him at all, and I'm a good deal that way myself. Dear, dear! I wish I had something besides a million dollars! If Jack were three inches taller I'd marry him alive and go back to Redhorse and wear sackcloth again to the end of my miserable days.

JULY 25.

We had a perfectly splendid sunset last evening and I must tell you all about it. I ran away from Auntie and everybody and was walking alone on the beach. I expect you to believe, you infidel! that I had not looked out of my window on the seaward side of the hotel and seen Him walking alone on the beach. If you are not lost to every feeling of womanly delicacy you will accept my statement without question. I soon established myself under my sunshade and had for some time been gazing out dreamily over the sea, when he approached, walking close to the edge of the water—it was ebb tide. I assure you the wet sand actually brightened about his feet! As he approached me he lifted his hat, saying, "Miss Dement, may I sit with you?—or will you walk with me?"

The possibility that neither might be agreeable seems not to have occurred to him. Did you ever know such assurance? Assurance? My dear, it was gall, downright *gall!* Well, I didn't find it wormwood, and replied, with my untutored Redhorse heart in my throat, "I—I shall be pleased to do *anything.*" Could words have been more stupid? There are depths of fatuity in me, friend o' my soul, that are simply bottomless!

He extended his hand, smiling, and I delivered mine into it without a moment's hesitation, and when his fingers closed about it to assist me to my feet the consciousness that it trembled made me blush worse than the red west. I got up, however, and after a while, observing that he had not let go my hand I pulled on it a little, but unsuccessfully. He simply held on, saying nothing, but looking down into my face with some kind of smile—I didn't know—how could I? —whether it was affectionate, derisive, or what, for I did not look at him. How beautiful he was!—with the red fires of the sunset burning in the depths of his eyes. Do you know, dear, if the Thugs and Experts of the Blavatsky region have any special kind of eyes? Ah, you should have seen his superb attitude, the god-like inclination of his head as he stood over me after I had got upon my feet! It was a noble picture, but I soon destroyed it, for I began at once to sink again to the earth. There was only one thing for him to do, and he did it; he supported me with an arm about my waist.

"Miss Dement, are you ill?" he said.

It was not an exclamation; there was neither alarm nor solicitude in it. If he had added: "I suppose that is about what I am expected to say," he would hardly have expressed his sense of the situation more clearly. His manner filled me with shame and indignation, for I was suffering acutely. I wrenched my hand out of his, grasped the arm supporting me and pushing myself free, fell plump into the sand and sat helpless. My hat had fallen off in the struggle and my hair tumbled about my face and shoulders in the most mortifying way.

"Go away from me," I cried, half choking. "O *please* go away, you—you Thug! How dare you think *that* when my leg is asleep?"

I actually said those identical words! And then I broke down and sobbed. Irene, I *blubbered!*

His manner altered in an instant—I could see that much through my fingers and hair. He dropped on one knee beside me, parted the tangle of hair and said in the tenderest way: "My poor girl, God knows I have not intended to pain you. How should I?—I who love you—I who have loved you for—for years and years!"

He had pulled my wet hands away from my face and was covering them with kisses. My cheeks were like two coals, my whole face was flaming and, I think, steaming. What could I do? I hid it on his shoulder—there was no other place. And, O my dear friend, how my leg tingled and thrilled, and how I wanted to kick!

We sat so for a long time. He had released one of my hands to pass his arm about me again and I possessed myself of my handkerchief and was drying my eyes and my nose. I would not look up until that was done; he tried in vain to push me a little away and gaze into my face. Presently, when all was right, and it had grown a bit dark, I lifted my head, looked him straight in the eyes and smiled my best—my level best, dear.

"What do you mean," I said, "by 'years and years'?"

"Dearest," he replied, very gravely, very earnestly, "in the absence of the sunken cheeks, the hollow eyes, the lank hair, the slouching gait, the rags, dirt, and youth, can you not—will you not understand? Gunny, I'm Dumps!"

In a moment I was upon my feet and he upon his. I seized him by the lapels of his coat and peered into his handsome face in the deepening darkness. I was breathless with excitement.

"And you are not dead?" I asked, hardly knowing what I said.

"Only dead in love, dear. I recovered from the road agent's bullet, but this, I fear, is fatal."

"But about Jack—Mr. Raynor? Don't you know——"

"I am ashamed to say, darling, that it was through that unworthy person's suggestion that I came here from Vienna."

Irene, they have roped in your affectionate friend,

MARY JANE DEMENT.

P. S.—The worst of it is that there is no mystery; that was the invention of Jack Raynor, to arouse my curiosity. James is not a Thug. He solemnly assures me that in all his wanderings he has never set foot in Sepoy.

❅   ❅   ❅

THE FAMOUS GILSON BEQUEST

It was rough on Gilson. Such was the terse, cold, but not altogether unsympathetic judgment of the better public opinion at Mammon Hill—the dictum of respectability. The verdict of the opposite, or rather the opposing, element—the element that lurked red-eyed and restless about Moll Gurney's "deadfall," while respectability took it with sugar at Mr. Jo. Bentley's gorgeous "saloon"—was to pretty much the same general effect, though somewhat more ornately expressed by the use of picturesque expletives, which it is needless to quote. Virtually, Mammon Hill was a unit on the Gilson question. And it must be confessed that in a merely temporal sense all was not well with Mr. Gilson. He had that morning been led into town by Mr. Brentshaw and publicly charged with horse stealing; the sheriff meantime busying himself about The Tree with a new manila rope and Carpenter Pete being actively employed between drinks upon a pine box about the length and breadth of Mr. Gilson. Society having rendered its verdict, there remained between Gilson and eternity only the decent formality of a trial.

These are the short and simple annals of the prisoner: He had recently been a resident of New Jerusalem, on the north fork of the Little Stony, but had come to the newly discovered placers of Mammon Hill immediately before the "rush" by which the former place was depopulated. The discovery of the new diggings had occurred opportunely for Mr. Gilson, for it had only just before been intimated to him by a New Jerusalem vigilance committee that it would better his prospects in, and for, life to go somewhere; and the list of places to which he could safely go did not include any of the older camps; so he naturally established himself at Mammon Hill. Being eventually followed thither by all his judges, he ordered his conduct with considerable circumspection, but as he had never been known to do an honest day's work at any industry sanctioned by the stern local code of morality except draw poker he was still an object of suspicion. Indeed, it was conjectured that he was the author of the many daring depredations that had recently been committed with pan and brush on the sluice boxes.

Prominent among those in whom this suspicion had ripened into a steadfast conviction was Mr. Brentshaw. At all seasonable and unseasonable times Mr. Brentshaw avowed his belief in Mr. Gilson's connection with these unholy midnight enterprises, and his own willingness to prepare a way for the solar beams through the body of any one who might think it expedient to utter a different opinion—which, in his presence, no one was more careful not to do than the peace-loving person most concerned. Whatever may have been the truth of the matter, it is certain that Gilson frequently lost more "clean dust" at Jo. Bentley's faro table than it was recorded in local history that he had ever honestly earned at draw poker in all the days of the camp's existence. But at last Mr. Bentley—fearing, it may be, to lose the more profitable patronage of Mr. Brentshaw—peremptorily refused to let Gilson copper the queen, intimating at the same time, in his frank, forthright way, that the privilege of losing money at "this bank" was a blessing appertaining to, proceeding logically from, and coterminous with, a condition of notorious commercial righteousness and social good repute.

The Hill thought it high time to look after a person whom its most honored citizen had felt it his duty to rebuke at a considerable personal sacrifice. The New Jerusalem contingent, particularly, began to abate something of the toleration begotten of amusement at their own blunder in exiling an objectionable neighbor from the place which they had left to the place whither they had come. Mammon Hill was at last of one mind. Not much was said, but that Gilson must hang was "in the air." But at this critical juncture in his affairs he showed signs of an altered life if not a changed heart. Perhaps it was only that "the bank" being closed against him he had no further use for gold dust. Anyhow the sluice boxes were molested no more forever. But it was impossible to repress the abounding energies of such a nature as his, and he continued, possibly from habit, the tortuous courses which he had pursued for profit of Mr. Bentley. After a few tentative and resultless undertakings in the way of highway robbery—if one may venture to designate road-agency by so harsh a name—he made one or two modest essays in horse-herding, and it was in the midst of a promising enterprise of this character, and just as he had taken the tide in his affairs at its flood, that he made shipwreck. For on a misty, moonlight night Mr. Brentshaw rode up alongside a person who was evidently leaving that part of the country, laid a hand upon the halter connecting Mr. Gilson's wrist with Mr. Harper's bay mare, tapped him familiarly on the cheek with the barrel of a navy revolver and requested the pleasure of his company in a direction opposite to that in which he was traveling.

It was indeed rough on Gilson.

On the morning after his arrest he was tried, convicted, and sentenced. It only remains, so far as concerns his earthly career, to hang him, reserving for more particular mention his last will and testament, which, with great labor, he contrived in prison, and in which, probably from some confused and imperfect notion of the rights of captors, he bequeathed everything he owned to his "lawfle execketer," Mr. Brentshaw. The bequest, however, was made conditional on the legatee taking the testator's body from The Tree and "planting it white."

So Mr. Gilson was—I was about to say "swung off," but I fear there has been already something too much of slang in this straight-forward statement of facts; besides, the manner in which the law took its course is more accurately described in the terms employed by the judge in passing sentence: Mr. Gilson was "strung up."

In due season Mr. Brentshaw, somewhat touched, it may well be, by the empty compliment of the bequest, repaired to The Tree to pluck the fruit thereof. When taken down the body was found to have in its waistcoat pocket a duly attested codicil to the will already noted. The nature of its provisions accounted for the manner in which it had been withheld, for had Mr. Brentshaw previously been made aware of the conditions under which he was to succeed to the Gilson estate he would indubitably have declined the responsibility. Briefly stated, the purport of the codicil was as follows:

Whereas, at divers times and in sundry places, certain persons had asserted that during his life the testator had robbed their sluice boxes; therefore, if during the five years next succeeding the date of this instrument any one should make proof of such assertion before a court of law, such person was to receive as reparation the entire personal and real estate of which the testator died seized and possessed, minus the expenses of court and a stated compensation to the executor, Henry Clay Brentshaw; provided, that if more than one person made such proof the estate was to be equally divided between or among them. But in case none should succeed in so establishing the testator's guilt, then the whole property, minus court expenses, as aforesaid, should go to the said Henry Clay Brentshaw for his own use, as stated in the will.

The syntax of this remarkable document was perhaps open to critical objection, but that was clearly enough the meaning of it. The orthography conformed to no recognized system, but being mainly phonetic it was not ambiguous. As the probate judge remarked, it would take five aces to beat it. Mr. Brentshaw smiled good-humoredly, and after performing the last sad rites with amusing ostentation, had himself duly sworn as executor and conditional legatee under the provisions of a law hastily passed (at the instance of the member from the Mammon Hill district) by a facetious legislature; which law was afterward discovered to have created also three or four lucrative offices and authorized the expenditure of a considerable sum of public money for the construction of a certain railway bridge that with greater advantage might perhaps have been erected on the line of some actual railway.

Of course Mr. Brentshaw expected neither profit from the will nor litigation in consequence of its unusual provisions; Gilson, although frequently "flush," had been a man whom assessors and tax collectors were well satisfied to lose no money by. But a careless and merely formal search among his papers revealed title deeds to valuable estates in the East and certificates of deposit for incredible sums in banks less severely scrupulous than that of Mr. Jo. Bentley.

The astounding news got abroad directly, throwing the Hill into a fever of excitement. The Mammon Hill *Patriot,* whose editor had been a leading spirit in the proceedings that resulted in Gilson's departure from New Jerusalem, published a most complimentary obituary notice of the deceased, and was good enough to call attention to the fact that his degraded contemporary, the Squaw Gulch *Clarion,* was bringing virtue into contempt by beslavering with flattery the memory of one who in life had spurned the vile sheet as a nuisance from his door. Undeterred by the press, however, claimants under the will were not slow in presenting themselves with their evidence; and great as was the Gilson estate it appeared conspicuously paltry considering the vast number of sluice boxes from which it was averred to have been obtained. The country rose as one man!

Mr. Brentshaw was equal to the emergency. With a shrewd application of humble auxiliary devices, he at once erected above the bones of his benefactor a costly monument, overtopping every rough headboard in the cemetery, and on this he judiciously caused to be inscribed an epitaph of his own composing, eulogizing the honesty, public spirit and cognate virtues of him who slept beneath, "a victim to the unjust aspersions of Slander's viper brood."

Moreover, he employed the best legal talent in the Territory to defend the memory of his departed friend, and for five long years the Territorial courts were occupied with litigation growing out of the Gilson bequest. To fine forensic abilities Mr. Brentshaw opposed abilities more finely forensic; in bidding for purchasable favors he offered prices which utterly deranged the market; the judges found at his hospitable board entertainment for man and beast, the like of which had never been spread in the Territory; with mendacious witnesses he confronted witnesses of superior mendacity.

Nor was the battle confined to the temple of the blind goddess—it invaded the press, the pulpit, the drawing-room. It raged in the mart, the exchange, the school; in the gulches, and on the street corners. And upon the last day of the memorable period to which legal action under the Gilson will was limited, the sun went down upon a region in which the moral sense was dead, the social conscience callous, the intellectual capacity dwarfed, enfeebled, and confused! But Mr. Brentshaw was victorious all along the line.

On that night it so happened that the cemetery in one corner of which lay the now honored ashes of the late Milton Gilson, Esq., was partly under water. Swollen by incessant rains, Cat Creek had spilled over its banks an angry flood which, after scooping out unsightly hollows wherever the soil had been disturbed, had partly subsided, as if ashamed of the sacrilege, leaving exposed much that had been piously concealed. Even the famous Gilson monument, the pride and glory of Mammon Hill, was no longer a standing rebuke to the "viper brood"; succumbing to the sapping current it had toppled prone to earth. The ghoulish flood had exhumed the poor, decayed pine coffin, which now lay half-exposed, in pitiful contrast to the pompous monolith which, like a giant note of admiration, emphasized the disclosure.

To this depressing spot, drawn by some subtle influence he had sought neither to resist nor analyze, came Mr. Brentshaw. An altered man was Mr. Brentshaw. Five years of toil, anxiety, and wakefulness had dashed his black locks with streaks and patches of gray, bowed his fine figure, drawn sharp and angular his face, and debased his walk to a doddering shuffle. Nor had this lustrum of fierce contention wrought less upon his heart and intellect. The careless good humor that had prompted him to accept the trust of the dead man had given place to a fixed habit of melancholy. The firm, vigorous intellect had overripened into the mental mellowness of second childhood. His broad understanding had narrowed to the accommodation of a single idea; and in place of the quiet, cynical incredulity of former days, there was in him a haunting faith in the supernatural, that flitted and fluttered about his soul, shadowy, batlike, ominous of insanity. Unsettled in all else, his understanding clung to one conviction with the tenacity of a wrecked intellect. That was an unshaken belief in the entire blamelessness of the dead Gilson. He had so often sworn to this in court and asserted it in private conversation—had so frequently and so triumphantly established it by testimony that had come expensive to him (for that very day he had paid the last dollar of the Gilson estate to Mr. Jo. Bentley, the last witness to the Gilson good character)—that it had become to him a sort of religious faith. It seemed to him the one great central and basic truth of life—the sole serene verity in a world of lies.

On that night, as he seated himself pensively upon the prostrate monument, trying by the uncertain moonlight to spell out the epitaph which five years before he had composed with a chuckle that memory had not recorded, tears of remorse came into his eyes as he remembered that he had been mainly instrumental in compassing by a false accusation this good man's death; for during some of the legal proceedings, Mr. Harper, for a consideration (forgotten) had come forward and sworn that in the little transaction with his bay mare the deceased had acted in strict accordance with the Harperian wishes, confidentially communicated to the deceased and by him faithfully concealed at the cost of his life. All that Mr. Brentshaw had since done for the dead man's memory seemed pitifully inadequate—most mean, paltry, and debased with selfishness!

As he sat there, torturing himself with futile regrets, a faint shadow fell across his eyes. Looking toward the moon, hanging low in the west, he saw what seemed a vague, watery cloud obscuring her; but as it moved so that her beams lit up one side of it he perceived the clear, sharp outline of a human figure. The apparition became momentarily more distinct, and grew, visibly; it was drawing near. Dazed as were his senses, half locked up with terror and confounded with dreadful imaginings, Mr. Brentshaw yet could but perceive, or think he perceived, in this unearthly shape a strange similitude to the mortal part of the late Milton Gilson, as that person had looked when taken from The Tree five years before. The likeness was indeed complete, even to the full, stony eyes, and a certain shadowy circle about the neck. It was without coat or hat, precisely as Gilson had been when laid in his poor, cheap casket by the not ungentle hands of Carpenter Pete—for whom some one had long since performed the same neighborly office. The spectre, if such it was, seemed to bear something in its hands which Mr. Brentshaw could not clearly make out. It drew nearer, and paused at last beside the coffin containing the ashes of the late Mr. Gilson, the lid of which was awry, half disclosing the uncertain interior. Bending over this, the phantom seemed to shake into it from a basin some dark substance of dubious consistency, then glided stealthily back to the lowest part of the cemetery. Here the retiring flood had stranded a number of open coffins, about and among which it gurgled with low sobbings and stilly whispers. Stooping over one of these, the apparition carefully brushed its contents into the basin, then returning to its own casket, emptied the vessel into that, as before. This mysterious operation was repeated at every exposed coffin, the ghost sometimes dipping its laden basin into the running water, and gently agitating it to free it of the baser clay, always hoarding the residuum in its own private box. In short, the immortal part of the late Milton Gilson was cleaning up the dust of its neighbors and providently adding the same to its own.

Perhaps it was a phantasm of a disordered mind in a fevered body. Perhaps it was a solemn farce enacted by pranking existences that throng the shadows lying along the border of another world. God knows; to us is permitted only the knowledge that when the sun of another day touched with a grace of gold the ruined cemetery of Mammon Hill his kindliest beam fell upon the white, still face of Henry Brentshaw, dead among the dead.

✳   ✳   ✳

A HOLY TERROR

I

There was an entire lack of interest in the latest arrival at Hurdy-Gurdy. He was not even christened with the picturesquely descriptive nick-name which is so frequently a mining camp's word of welcome to the newcomer. In almost any other camp thereabout this circumstance would of itself have secured him some such appellation as "The White-headed Conundrum," or "No Sarvey"—an expression naively supposed to suggest to quick intelligences the Spanish *quien sabe.* He came without provoking a ripple of concern upon the social surface of Hurdy-Gurdy—a place which to the general Californian contempt of men's personal history superadded a local indifference of its own. The time was long past when it was of any importance who came there, or if anybody came. No one was living at Hurdy-Gurdy.

Two years before, the camp had boasted a stirring population of two or three thousand males and not fewer than a dozen females. A majority of the former had done a few weeks' earnest work in demonstrating, to the disgust of the latter, the singularly mendacious character of the person whose ingenious tales of rich gold deposits had lured them thither—work, by the way, in which there was as little mental satisfaction as pecuniary profit; for a bullet from the pistol of a public-spirited citizen had put that imaginative gentleman beyond the reach of aspersion on the third day of the camp's existence. Still, his fiction had a certain foundation in fact, and many had lingered a considerable time in and about Hurdy-Gurdy, though now all had been long gone.

But they had left ample evidence of their sojourn. From the point where Injun Creek falls into the Rio San Juan Smith, up along both banks of the former into the cañon whence it emerges, extended a double row of forlorn shanties that seemed about to fall upon one another's neck to bewail their desolation; while about an equal number appeared to have straggled up the slope on either hand

and perched themselves upon commanding eminences, whence they craned forward to get a good view of the affecting scene. Most of these habitations were emaciated as by famine to the condition of mere skeletons, about which clung unlovely tatters of what might have been skin, but was really canvas. The little valley itself, torn and gashed by pick and shovel, was unhandsome with long, bending lines of decaying flume resting here and there upon the summits of sharp ridges, and stilting awkwardly across the intervals upon un-hewn poles. The whole place presented that raw and forbidding aspect of arrested development which is a new country's substitute for the solemn grace of ruin wrought by time. Wherever there re-mained a patch of the original soil a rank overgrowth of weeds and brambles had spread upon the scene, and from its dank, unwhole-some shades the visitor curious in such matters might have obtained numberless souvenirs of the camp's former glory—fellowless boots mantled with green mould and plethoric of rotting leaves; an oc-casional old felt hat; desultory remnants of a flannel shirt; sardine boxes inhumanly mutilated and a surprising profusion of black bottles distributed with a truly catholic impartiality, everywhere.

II

The man who had now rediscovered Hurdy-Gurdy was evidently not curious as to its archæology. Nor, as he looked about him upon the dismal evidences of wasted work and broken hopes, their dis-piriting significance accentuated by the ironical pomp of a cheap gilding by the rising sun, did he supplement his sigh of weariness by of sensibility. He simply removed from the back of his tired burro a miner's outfit a trifle larger than the animal itself, picketed that creature and selecting a hatchet from his kit moved off at once across the dry bed of Injun Creek to the top of a low, gravelly hill beyond.

Stepping across a prostrate fence of brush and boards he picked up one of the latter, split it into five parts and sharpened them at one end. He then began a kind of search, occasionally stooping to ex-amine something with close attention. At last his patient scrutiny appeared to be rewarded with success, for he suddenly erected his figure to its full height, made a gesture of satisfaction, pronounced the word "Scarry" and at once strode away with long, equal steps, which he counted. Then he stopped and drove one of his stakes into the earth. He then looked carefully about him, measured off a number of paces over a singularly uneven ground and hammered in another. Pacing off twice the distance at a right angle to his former course he drove down a third, and repeating the process sank home the fourth, and then a fifth. This he split at the top and in the cleft inserted an old letter envelope covered with an intricate system of pencil tracks. In short, he staked off a hill claim in strict accordance with the local mining laws of Hurdy-Gurdy and put up the customary notice.

It is necessary to explain that one of the adjuncts to Hurdy-Gurdy —one to which that metropolis became afterward itself an adjunct— was a cemetery. In the first week of the camp's existence this had been thoughtfully laid out by a committee of citizens. The day after had been signalized by a debate between two members of the committee, with reference to a more eligible site, and on the third day the necropolis was inaugurated by a double funeral. As the camp had waned the cemetery had waxed; and long before the ultimate inhabitant, victorious alike over the insidious malaria and the forthright revolver, had turned the tail of his pack-ass upon Injun Creek the outlying settlement had become a populous if not popular suburb. And now, when the town was fallen into the sere and yellow leaf of an unlovely senility, the graveyard—though somewhat marred by time and circumstance, and not altogether exempt from innovations in grammar and experiments in orthography, to say nothing of the devastating coyote—answered the humble needs of its denizens with reasonable completeness. It comprised a generous two acres of ground, which with commendable thrift but needless care had been selected for its mineral unworth, contained two or three skeleton trees (one of which had a stout lateral branch from which a weather-wasted rope still significantly dangled), half a hundred gravelly mounds, a score of rude headboards displaying the literary peculiarities above mentioned and a struggling colony of prickly pears. Altogether, God's Location, as with characteristic reverence it had been called, could justly boast of an indubitably superior quality of desolation. It was in the most thickly settled part of this interesting demesne that Mr. Jefferson Doman staked off his claim. If in the prosecution of his design he should deem it expedient to remove any of the dead they would have the right to be suitably reinterred.

III

This Mr. Jefferson Doman was from Elizabethtown, New Jersey, where six years before he had left his heart in the keeping of a golden-haired, demure-mannered young woman named Mary Matthews, as collateral security for his return to claim her hand.

"I just *know* you'll never get back alive—you never do succeed in anything," was the remark which illustrated Miss Matthews's notion of what constituted success and, inferentially, her view of the nature of encouragement. She added: "If you don't I'll go to California too. I can put the coins in little bags as you dig them out."

This characteristically feminine theory of auriferous deposits did not commend itself to the masculine intelligence: it was Mr. Doman's belief that gold was found in a liquid state. He deprecated her intent with considerable enthusiasm, suppressed her sobs with a light hand upon her mouth, laughed in her eyes as he kissed away her tears, and with a cheerful "Ta-ta" went to California to labor for her through the long, loveless years, with a strong heart, an alert hope and a steadfast fidelity that never for a moment forgot what it was about. In the mean time, Miss Matthews had granted a monopoly of her humble talent for sacking up coins to Mr. Jo. Seeman, of New York, gambler, by whom it was better appreciated than her commanding genius for unsacking and bestowing them upon his local rivals. Of this latter aptitude, indeed, he manifested his disapproval by an act which secured him the position of clerk of the laundry in the State prison, and for her the *sobriquet* of "Split-faced Moll." At about this time she wrote to Mr. Doman a touching letter of renunciation, inclosing her photograph to prove that she had no longer a right to indulge the dream of becoming Mrs. Doman, and recounting so graphically her fall from a horse that the staid "plug" upon which Mr. Doman had ridden into Red Dog to get the letter made vicarious atonement under the spur all the way back to camp. The letter failed in a signal way to accomplish its object; the fidelity which had before been to Mr. Doman a matter of love and duty was thenceforth a matter of honor also; and the photograph, showing the once pretty face sadly disfigured as by the slash of a knife, was duly instated in his affections and its more comely predecessor treated with contumelious neglect. On being informed of this, Miss Matthews, it is only fair to say, appeared less surprised than from the apparently low estimate of Mr. Doman's generosity which the tone of her former letter attested one would naturally have expected her to be. Soon after, however, her letters grew infrequent, and then ceased altogether.

But Mr. Doman had another correspondent, Mr. Barney Bree, of Hurdy-Gurdy, formerly of Red Dog. This gentleman, although a notable figure among miners, was not a miner. His knowledge of mining consisted mainly in a marvelous command of its slang, to which he made copious contributions, enriching its vocabulary with a wealth of uncommon phrases more remarkable for their aptness than their refinement, and which impressed the unlearned "tenderfoot" with a lively sense of the profundity of their inventor's acquirements. When not entertaining a circle of admiring auditors from San Francisco or the East he could commonly be found pursuing the comparatively obscure industry of sweeping out the various dance houses and purifying the cuspidors.

Barney had apparently but two passions in life—love of Jefferson Doman, who had once been of some service to him, and love of whisky, which certainly had not. He had been among the first in the rush to Hurdy-Gurdy, but had not prospered, and had sunk by degrees to the position of grave digger. This was not a vocation, but Barney in a desultory way turned his trembling hand to it whenever some local misunderstanding at the card table and his own partial recovery from a prolonged debauch occurred coincidently in point of time. One day Mr. Doman received, at Red Dog, a letter with the simple postmark, "Hurdy, Cal.," and being occupied with another matter, carelessly thrust it into a chink of his cabin for future perusal. Some two years later it was accidentally dislodged and he read it. It ran as follows:—

> Hurdy, June 6.
>
> Friend Jeff: I've hit her hard in the boneyard. She's blind and lousy. I'm on the divvy—that's me, and mum's my lay till you toot.   Yours,
>
> Barney.
>
> P. S.—I've clayed her with Scarry.

With some knowledge of the general mining camp *argot* and of Mr. Bree's private system for the communication of ideas Mr. Doman had no difficulty in understanding by this uncommon epistle that Barney while performing his duty as grave digger had uncovered a quartz ledge with no outcroppings; that it was visibly rich in free gold; that, moved by considerations of friendship, he was willing to accept Mr. Doman as a partner and awaiting that gentleman's declaration of his will in the matter would discreetly keep the discovery a secret. From the postscript it was plainly inferable that in order to conceal the treasure he had buried above it the mortal part of a person named Scarry.

From subsequent events, as related to Mr. Doman at Red Dog, it would appear that before taking this precaution Mr. Bree must have had the thrift to remove a modest competency of the gold; at any rate, it was at about that time that he entered upon that memorable series of potations and treatings which is still one of the cherished traditions of the San Juan Smith country, and is spoken of with respect as far away as Ghost Rock and Lone Hand. At its conclusion some former citizens of Hurdy-Gurdy, for whom he had performed the last kindly office at the cemetery, made room for him among them, and he rested well.

IV

Having finished staking off his claim Mr. Doman walked back to the centre of it and stood again at the spot where his search among the graves had expired in the exclamation, "Scarry." He bent again over the headboard that bore that name and as if to reinforce the senses of sight and hearing ran his forefinger along the rudely carved letters. Re-erecting himself he appended orally to the simple inscription the shockingly forthright epitaph, "She was a holy terror!"

Had Mr. Doman been required to make these words good with proof—as, considering their somewhat censorious character, he doubtless should have been—he would have found himself embarrassed by the absence of reputable witnesses, and hearsay evidence would have been the best he could command. At the time when Scarry had been prevalent in the mining camps thereabout—when, as the editor of the *Hurdy Herald* would have phrased it, she was "in the plenitude of her power"—Mr. Doman's fortunes had been at a low ebb, and he had led the vagrantly laborious life of a prospector. His time had been mostly spent in the mountains, now with one companion, now with another. It was from the admiring recitals of these casual partners, fresh from the various camps, that his judgment of Scarry had been made up; he himself had never had the doubtful advantage of her acquaintance and the precarious distinction of her favor. And when, finally, on the termination of her perverse career at Hurdy-Gurdy he had read in a chance copy of the *Herald* her column-long obituary (written by the local humorist of that lively sheet in the highest style of his art) Doman had paid to her memory and to her historiographer's genius the tribute of a smile and chivalrously forgotten her.

Standing now at the grave-side of this mountain Messalina he recalled the leading events of her turbulent career, as he had heard them celebrated at his several campfires, and perhaps with an unconscious attempt at self-justification repeated that she was a holy terror, and sank his pick into her grave up to the handle. At that moment a raven, which had silently settled upon a branch of the blasted tree above his head, solemnly snapped its beak and uttered its mind about the matter with an approving croak.

Pursuing his discovery of free gold with great zeal, which he probably credited to his conscience as a grave digger, Mr. Barney Bree had made an unusually deep sepulcher, and it was near sunset before Mr. Doman, laboring with the leisurely deliberation of one who has "a dead sure thing" and no fear of an adverse claimant's enforcement of a prior right, reached the coffin and uncovered it. When he had done so he was confronted by a difficulty for which he had made no provision; the coffin—a mere flat shell of not very well-preserved redwood boards, apparently—had no handles, and it filled the entire bottom of the excavation. The best he could do without violating the decent sanctities of the situation was to make the excavation sufficiently longer to enable him to stand at the head of the casket and getting his powerful hands underneath erect it upon its narrower end; and this he proceeded to do. The approach of night quickened his efforts. He had no thought of abandoning his task at this stage to resume it on the morrow under more advantageous conditions. The feverish stimulation of cupidity and the fascination of terror held him to his dismal work with an iron authority. He no longer idled, but wrought with a terrible zeal. His head uncovered, his outer garments discarded, his shirt opened at the neck and thrown back from his breast, down which ran sinuous rills of perspiration, this hardy and impenitent gold-getter and grave-robber toiled with a giant energy that almost dignified the character of his horrible purpose; and when the sun fringes had burned themselves out along the crest line of the western hills, and the full moon had climbed out of the shadows that lay along the purple plain, he had erected the coffin upon its foot, where it stood propped against the end of the open grave. Then, standing up to his neck in the earth at the opposite extreme of the excavation, as he looked at the coffin upon which the moonlight now fell with a full illumination he was thrilled with a sudden terror to observe upon it the startling apparition of a dark human head—the shadow of his own. For a moment this simple and natural circumstance unnerved him. The noise of his labored breathing frightened him, and he tried to still it, but his bursting lungs would not be denied. Then, laughing half-audibly and wholly without spirit, he began making movements of his head from side to side, in order to compel the apparition to repeat them. He found a comforting reassurance in asserting his command over his own shadow. He was temporizing, making, with unconscious prudence, a dilatory opposition to an impending catastrophe. He felt that invisible forces of evil were closing in upon him, and he parleyed for time with the Inevitable.

He now observed in succession several unusual circumstances. The surface of the coffin upon which his eyes were fastened was not flat; it presented two distinct ridges, one longitudinal and the other transverse. Where these intersected at the widest part there was a corroded metallic plate that reflected the moonlight with a dismal lustre. Along the outer edges of the coffin, at long intervals, were rust-eaten heads of nails. This frail product of the carpenter's art had been put into the grave the wrong side up!

Perhaps it was one of the humors of the camp—a practical manifestation of the facetious spirit that had found literary expression in the topsy-turvy obituary notice from the pen of Hurdy-Gurdy's great humorist. Perhaps it had some occult personal signification impenetrable to understandings uninstructed in local traditions. A more charitable hypothesis is that it was owing to a misadventure on the part of Mr. Barney Bree, who, making the interment unassisted (either by choice for the conservation of his golden secret, or through public apathy), had committed a blunder which he was afterward unable or unconcerned to rectify. However it had come about, poor Scarry had indubitably been put into the earth face downward.

When terror and absurdity make alliance, the effect is frightful. This strong-hearted and daring man, this hardy night worker among the dead, this defiant antagonist of darkness and desolation, succumbed to a ridiculous surprise. He was smitten with a thrilling chill —shivered, and shook his massive shoulders as if to throw off an icy hand. He no longer breathed, and the blood in his veins, unable to abate its impetus, surged hotly beneath his cold skin. Unleavened with oxygen, it mounted to his head and congested his brain. His physical functions had gone over to the enemy; his very heart was arrayed against him. He did not move; he could not have cried out. He needed but a coffin to be dead—as dead as the death that confronted him with only the length of an open grave and the thickness of a rotting plank between.

Then, one by one, his senses returned; the tide of terror that had overwhelmed his faculties began to recede. But with the return of his senses he became singularly unconscious of the object of his fear. He saw the moonlight gilding the coffin, but no longer the coffin that it gilded. Raising his eyes and turning his head, he noted, curiously and with surprise, the black branches of the dead tree, and tried to estimate the length of the weather-worn rope that dangled from its ghostly hand. The monotonous barking of distant coyotes affected him as something he had heard years ago in a dream. An owl flapped awkwardly above him on noiseless wings, and he tried to forecast the direction of its flight when it should encounter the cliff that reared its illuminated front a mile away. His hearing took account of a gopher's stealthy tread in the shadow of the cactus. He was intensely observant; his senses were all alert; but he saw not the coffin. As one can gaze at the sun until it looks black and then vanishes, so his mind, having exhausted its capacities of dread, was no longer conscious of the separate existence of anything dreadful. The Assassin was cloaking the sword.

It was during this lull in the battle that he became sensible of a faint, sickening odor. At first he thought it was that of a rattlesnake, and involuntarily tried to look about his feet. They were nearly invisible in the gloom of the grave. A hoarse, gurgling sound, like the death-rattle in a human throat, seemed to come out of the sky, and a moment later a great, black, angular shadow, like the same sound made visible, dropped curving from the topmost branch of the spectral tree, fluttered for an instant before his face and sailed fiercely away into the mist along the creek. It was the raven. The incident recalled him to a sense of the situation, and again his eyes sought the upright coffin, now illuminated by the moon for half its length. He saw the gleam of the metallic plate and tried without moving to decipher the inscription. Then he fell to speculating upon what was behind it. His creative imagination presented him a vivid picture. The planks no longer seemed an obstacle to his vision and he saw the livid corpse of the dead woman, standing in graveclothes, and staring vacantly at him, with lidless, shrunken eyes. The lower jaw was fallen, the upper lip drawn away from the uncovered teeth. He could make out a mottled pattern on the hollow cheeks—the maculations of decay. By some mysterious process his mind reverted for the first time that day to the photograph of Mary Matthews. He contrasted its blonde beauty with the forbidding aspect of this dead face—the most beloved object that he knew with the most hideous that he could conceive.

The Assassin now advanced and displaying the blade laid it against the victim's throat. That is to say, the man became at first dimly, then definitely, aware of an impressive coincidence—a relation—a parallel between the face on the card and the name on the headboard. The one was disfigured, the other described a disfiguration. The thought took hold of him and shook him. It transformed the face that his imagination had created behind the coffin lid; the contrast became a resemblance; the resemblance grew to identity. Remembering the many descriptions of Scarry's personal appearance that he had heard from the gossips of his camp-fire he tried with imperfect success to recall the exact nature of the disfiguration that had given the woman her ugly name; and what was lacking in his memory fancy supplied, stamping it with the validity of conviction. In the maddening attempt to recall such scraps of the woman's history as he had heard, the muscles of his arms and hands were strained to a painful tension, as by an effort to lift a great weight. His body writhed and twisted with the exertion. The tendons of his neck stood out as tense as whip-cords, and his breath came in short, sharp gasps. The catastrophe could not be much longer delayed, or the agony of anticipation would leave nothing to be done by the *coup de grâce* of verification. The scarred face behind the lid would slay him through the wood.

A movement of the coffin diverted his thought. It came forward to within a foot of his face, growing visibly larger as it approached. The rusted metallic plate, with an inscription illegible in the moonlight, looked him steadily in the eye. Determined not to shrink, he tried to brace his shoulders more firmly against the end of the excavation, and nearly fell backward in the attempt. There was nothing to support him; he had unconsciously moved upon his enemy, clutching the heavy knife that he had drawn from his belt. The coffin had not advanced and he smiled to think it could not retreat. Lifting his knife he struck the heavy hilt against the metal plate with all his power. There was a sharp, ringing percussion, and with a dull clatter the whole decayed coffin lid broke in pieces and came away, falling about his feet. The quick and the dead were face to face—the frenzied, shrieking man—the woman standing tranquil in her silences. She was a holy terror!

V

Some months later a party of men and women belonging to the highest social circles of San Francisco passed through Hurdy-Gurdy on their way to the Yosemite Valley by a new trail. They halted for dinner and during its preparation explored the desolate camp. One of the party had been at Hurdy-Gurdy in the days of its glory. He had, indeed, been one of its prominent citizens; and it used to be said that more money passed over his faro table in any one night than over those of all his competitors in a week; but being now a millionaire engaged in greater enterprises, he did not deem these early successes of sufficient importance to merit the distinction of remark. His invalid wife, a lady famous in San Francisco for the costly nature of her entertainments and her exacting rigor with regard to the social position and "antecedents" of those who attended them, accompanied the expedition. During a stroll among the shanties of the abandoned camp Mr. Porfer directed the attention of his wife and friends to a dead tree on a low hill beyond Injun Creek.

"As I told you," he said, "I passed through this camp in 1852, and was told that no fewer than five men had been hanged here by vigilantes at different times, and all on that tree. If I am not mistaken, a rope is dangling from it yet. Let us go over and see the place."

Mr. Porfer did not add that the rope in question was perhaps the very one from whose fatal embrace his own neck had once had an escape so narrow that an hour's delay in taking himself out of that region would have spanned it.

Proceeding leisurely down the creek to a convenient crossing, the party came upon the cleanly picked skeleton of an animal which Mr. Porfer after due examination pronounced to be that of an ass. The distinguishing ears were gone, but much of the inedible head had been spared by the beasts and birds, and the stout bridle of horsehair was intact, as was the riata, of similar material, connecting it with a picket pin still firmly sunken in the earth. The wooden and metallic elements of a miner's kit lay near by. The customary remarks were made, cynical on the part of the men, sentimental and refined by the lady. A little later they stood by the tree in the cemetery and Mr. Porfer sufficiently unbent from his dignity to place himself beneath the rotten rope and confidently lay a coil of it about his neck, somewhat, it appeared, to his own satisfaction, but greatly to the horror of his wife, to whose sensibilities the performance gave a smart shock.

An exclamation from one of the party gathered them all about an open grave, at the bottom of which they saw a confused mass of human bones and the broken remnants of a coffin. Coyotes and buzzards had performed the last sad rites for pretty much all else. Two skulls were visible and in order to investigate this somewhat unusual redundancy one of the younger men had the hardihood to spring into the grave and hand them up to another before Mrs. Porfer could indicate her marked disapproval of so shocking an act, which, nevertheless, she did with considerable feeling and in very choice words. Pursuing his search among the dismal débris at the bottom of the grave the young man next handed up a rusted coffin plate, with a rudely cut inscription, which with difficulty Mr. Porfer deciphered and read aloud with an earnest and not altogether unsuccessful attempt at the dramatic effect which he deemed befitting to the occasion and his rhetorical abilities:

> MANUELITA MURPHY.
> Born at the Mission San Pedro—Died in
> Hurdy-Gurdy,
> Aged 47.
> Hell's full of such.

In deference to the piety of the reader and the nerves of Mrs. Porfer's fastidious sisterhood of both sexes let us not touch upon the painful impression produced by this uncommon inscription, further than to say that the elocutionary powers of Mr. Porfer had never before met with so spontaneous and overwhelming recognition.

The next morsel that rewarded the ghoul in the grave was a long tangle of black hair defiled with clay: but this was such an anticlimax that it received little attention. Suddenly, with a short exclamation and a gesture of excitement, the young man unearthed a fragment of grayish rock, and after a hurried inspection handed it up to Mr. Porfer. As the sunlight fell upon it it glittered with a yellow luster—it was thickly studded with gleaming points. Mr. Porfer snatched it, bent his head over it a moment and threw it lightly away with the simple remark:

"Iron pyrites—fool's gold."

The young man in the discovery shaft was a trifle disconcerted, apparently.

Meanwhile, Mrs. Porfer, unable longer to endure the disagreeable business, had walked back to the tree and seated herself at its root. While rearranging a tress of golden hair which had slipped from its confinement she was attracted by what appeared to be and really was the fragment of an old coat. Looking about to assure herself that so unladylike an act was not observed, she thrust her jeweled hand into the exposed breast pocket and drew out a mouldy pocket-book. Its contents were as follows:

One bundle of letters, postmarked "Elizabethtown, New Jersey."
One circle of blonde hair tied with a ribbon.
One photograph of a beautiful girl.
One ditto of same, singularly disfigured.
One name on back of photograph—"Jefferson Doman."

A few moments later a group of anxious gentlemen surrounded Mrs. Porfer as she sat motionless at the foot of the tree, her head dropped forward, her fingers clutching a crushed photograph. Her husband raised her head, exposing a face ghastly white, except the long, deforming cicatrice, familiar to all her friends, which no art could ever hide, and which now traversed the pallor of her countenance like a visible curse.

Mary Matthews Porfer had the bad luck to be dead.

❆   ❆   ❆

A DIAGNOSIS OF DEATH

"I am not so superstitious as some of your physicians—men of science, as you are pleased to be called," said Hawver, replying to an accusation that had not been made. "Some of you—only a few, I confess—believe in the immortality of the soul, and in apparitions which you have not the honesty to call ghosts. I go no further than a conviction that the living are sometimes seen where they are not, but have been—where they have lived so long, perhaps so intensely, as to have left their impress on everything about them. I know, indeed, that one's environment may be so affected by one's personality as to yield, long afterward, an image of one's self to the eyes of another. Doubtless the impressing personality has to be the right kind of personality as the perceiving eyes have to be the right kind of eyes—mine, for example."

"Yes, the right kind of eyes, conveying sensations to the wrong kind of brain," said Dr. Frayley, smiling.

"Thank you; one likes to have an expectation gratified; that is about the reply that I supposed you would have the civility to make."

"Pardon me. But you say that you know. That is a good deal to say, don't you think? Perhaps you will not mind the trouble of saying how you learned."

"You will call it an hallucination," Hawver said, "but that does not matter." And he told the story.

"Last summer I went, as you know, to pass the hot weather term in the town of Meridian. The relative at whose house I had intended to stay was ill, so I sought other quarters. After some difficulty I succeeded in renting a vacant dwelling that had been occupied by an eccentric doctor of the name of Mannering, who had gone away years before, no one knew where, not even his agent. He had built the house himself and had lived in it with an old servant for about ten years. His practice, never very extensive, had after a few years been given up entirely. Not only so, but he had withdrawn himself almost altogether from social life and become a recluse. I was told by the village doctor, about the only person with whom he held any relations, that during his retirement he had devoted himself to a single line of study, the result of which he had expounded in a book that did not commend itself to the approval of his professional brethren, who, indeed, considered him not entirely sane. I have not seen the book and cannot now recall the title of it, but I am told that it expounded a rather startling theory. He held that it was possible in the case of many a person in good health to forecast his death with precision, several months in advance of the event. The limit, I think, was eighteen months. There were local tales of his having exerted his powers of prognosis, or perhaps you would say diagnosis; and it was said that in every instance the person whose friends he had warned had died suddenly at the appointed time, and from no assignable cause. All this, however, has nothing to do with what I have to tell; I thought it might amuse a physician.

"The house was furnished, just as he had lived in it. It was a rather gloomy dwelling for one who was neither a recluse nor a student, and I think it gave something of its character to me—perhaps some of its former occupant's character; for always I felt in it a certain melancholy that was not in my natural disposition, nor, I think, due to loneliness. I had no servants that slept in the house, but I have always been, as you know, rather fond of my own society, being much addicted to reading, though little to study. Whatever was the cause, the effect was dejection and a sense of impending evil; this was especially so in Dr. Mannering's study, although that room was the lightest and most airy in the house. The doctor's life-size portrait in oil hung in that room, and seemed completely to dominate it. There was nothing unusual in the picture; the man was evidently rather good looking, about fifty years old, with iron-gray hair, a smooth-shaven face and dark, serious eyes. Something in the picture always drew and held my attention. The man's appearance became familiar to me, and rather 'haunted' me.

"One evening I was passing through this room to my bedroom, with a lamp—there is no gas in Meridian. I stopped as usual before the portrait, which seemed in the lamplight to have a new expression, not easily named, but distinctly uncanny. It interested but did not disturb me. I moved the lamp from one side to the other and observed the effects of the altered light. While so engaged I felt an impulse to turn round. As I did so I saw a man moving across the room directly toward me! As soon as he came near enough for the lamplight to illuminate the face I saw that it was Dr. Mannering himself; it was as if the portrait were walking!

" 'I beg your pardon,' I said, somewhat coldly, 'but if you knocked I did not hear.'

"He passed me, within an arm's length, lifted his right forefinger, as in warning, and without a word went on out of the room, though I observed his exit no more than I had observed his entrance.

"Of course, I need not tell you that this was what you will call an hallucination and I call an apparition. That room had only two doors, of which one was locked; the other led into a bedroom, from which there was no exit. My feeling on realizing this is not an important part of the incident.

"Doubtless this seems to you a very commonplace 'ghost story'— one constructed on the regular lines laid down by the old masters of the art. If that were so I should not have related it, even if it were true. The man was not dead; I met him to-day in Union street. He passed me in a crowd."

Hawver had finished his story and both men were silent. Dr. Frayley absently drummed on the table with his fingers.

"Did he say anything to-day?" he asked—"anything from which you inferred that he was not dead?"

Hawver stared and did not reply.

"Perhaps," continued Frayley, "he made a sign, a gesture—lifted a finger, as in warning. It's a trick he had—a habit when saying something serious—announcing the result of a diagnosis, for example."

"Yes, he did—just as his apparition had done. But, good God! did you ever know him?"

Hawver was apparently growing nervous.

"I knew him. I have read his book, as will every physician some day. It is one of the most striking and important of the century's contributions to medical science. Yes, I knew him; I attended him in an illness three years ago. He died."

Hawver sprang from his chair, manifestly disturbed. He strode forward and back across the room; then approached his friend, and in a voice not altogether steady, said: "Doctor, have you anything to say to me—as a physician?"

"No, Hawver; you are the healthiest man I ever knew. As a friend I advise you to go to your room. You play the violin like an angel. Play it; play something light and lively. Get this cursed bad business off your mind."

The next day Hawver was found dead in his room, the violin at his neck, the bow upon the strings, his music open before him at Chopin's funeral march.

II

THE WORLD OF
War

FOREWORD

Ambrose Bierce knew and felt war as he knew and felt nothing else. His five years in America's greatest war gave to his "Tales of Soldiers" a deeper insight and intensity of conviction than he gave to his writing in any other field. Not more than fifteen of his Civil War stories are familiar to most readers; they actually number twenty-five, an additional ten not having been included in "In the Midst of Life," but left scattered and half-concealed in Volumes III, VIII, and XI of *The Collected Works.*

American critics, reluctant to apply the word "great" to any American short stories save those of Poe, have hesitated to apply it to those of Bierce; the English view is warmer, as was expressed in 1968 by Naomi Lewis, literary critic of *The London Observer:*

"Ambrose Bierce (1842–1914?) has sifted through to the mildly literate English reader of today as the author of a handfull of 'great' (or great, why not?) short stories about the Civil War, and some others harshly disturbing, in the vein of the supernatural-macabre."[1]

For "Civil War" one may read any war, or war today, or war as an institution; Bierce's treatment of the Civil War had, and was meant to have, a universal application. Whether intentional or not, this Civil War major's depiction of war in these tales, if regarded as the twenty-five chapters of a novel, would constitute the greatest anti-war document in American literature. To quote Carey McWilliams:

[1] Quoted from a review of the English Edition of *The Enlarged Devil's Dictionary* in the *London Observer,* (February 1, 1968) p. 27.

"It would be difficult to compute the number of times that it has been suggested that Bierce's war stories are so 'grimly realistic' that they should be compared with Tolstoy's *War and Peace*."[2]

It may be suggested that readers try reading them as a whole. Bierce had little use for the novel, defining it as "a short story padded," but if each chapter were written as a short story the criticism would not apply.

That Bierce's attitude was deeply anti-war not only can be inferred from his tales, but more directly from his striking ten-line verse, "Arma Virumque":

> "Ours is a Christian army"; so he said
> A regiment of bangomen who led.
> "And ours a Christian navy," added he
> Who sailed a thunder-junk upon the sea.
> Better they know than men unwarlike do
> What is an army, and a navy too.
> Pray God there may be sent them by-and-by
> The knowledge what a Christian is, and why.
> For somewhat lamely the conception runs
> Of a brass-buttoned Jesus firing guns."[3]

From the technical point of view these twenty-five stories are so many parables, the action-narratives being more vivid and highly developed than the parables of old, and the inferences equally inescapable. As a satirist, Bierce adhered to his ruling principle of "white is black," dramatizing in various stories the unfriendliness of fate—the purposeful malignancy of coincidence—the uselessness of glory—the hopelessness of hope—the cowardice of bravery—the grief of love and brotherhood—the failure of philosophy—the deceptiveness of human ideals—the perversion of honor—the cruelty of loyal obedience—all as intrinsic laws or aspects of the baneful World of War.

Not that Bierce had any anti-war movement or abolitionist purpose in mind; Bierce was no reformer and belonged to nothing organized. He defined "War" in his *Devil's Dictionary* as "A by-product of the arts of peace," and adds that "The soil of peace is thickly sown with seeds of war."

It is impossible that Bierce could have written his anti-war stories without having had General Hazen in mind. In one of his war

[2] Carey McWilliams, *Ambrose Bierce, A Biography*, op. cit., p. 226.
[3] The Collected Works of Ambrose Bierce, op. cit., Vol. IV, p. 57.

reminiscences he wrote of Hazen as "my commander and my friend, my master in the art of war," and added: "He was aggressive, arrogant, tyrannical, honorable, truthful, courageous, a skillful soldier, a faithful friend, and one of the most exasperating of men. 'Hazen,' said a brother brigadier, 'is a synonym of insubordination.'"

This sounds very like Bierce himself, in his point of view toward these stories, with their unsparing depiction of the World of War.

—E. J. H.

ONE OF THE MISSING

Jerome Searing, a private soldier of General Sherman's army, then confronting the enemy at and about Kennesaw Mountain, Georgia, turned his back upon a small group of officers with whom he had been talking in low tones, stepped across a light line of earthworks, and disappeared in a forest. None of the men in line behind the works had said a word to him, nor had he so much as nodded to them in passing, but all who saw understood that this brave man had been intrusted with some perilous duty. Jerome Searing, though a private, did not serve in the ranks; he was detailed for service at division headquarters, being borne upon the rolls as an orderly. "Orderly" is a word covering a multitude of duties. An orderly may be a messenger, a clerk, an officer's servant—anything. He may perform services for which no provision is made in orders and army regulations. Their nature may depend upon his aptitude, upon favor, upon accident. Private Searing, an incomparable marksman, young, hardy, intelligent and insensible to fear, was a scout. The general commanding his division was not content to obey orders blindly without knowing what was in his front, even when his command was not on detached service, but formed a fraction of the line of the army; nor was he satisfied to receive his knowledge of his *vis-à-vis* through the customary channels; he wanted to know more than he was apprised of by the corps commander and the collisions of pickets and skirmishers. Hence Jerome Searing, with his extraordinary daring, his woodcraft, his sharp eyes, and truthful tongue. On this occasion his instructions were simple: to get as near the enemy's lines as possible and learn all that he could.

In a few moments he had arrived at the picket-line, the men on duty there lying in groups of two and four behind little banks of earth scooped out of the slight depression in which they lay, their rifles protruding from the green boughs with which they had masked their small defenses. The forest extended without a break toward the front, so solemn and silent that only by an effort of the imagination could it be conceived as populous with armed men, alert and vigilant —a forest formidable with possibilities of battle. Pausing a moment in one of these rifle-pits to apprise the men of his intention Searing crept stealthily forward on his hands and knees and was soon lost to view in a dense thicket of underbrush.

"That is the last of him," said one of the men; "I wish I had his rifle; those fellows will hurt some of us with it."

Searing crept on, taking advantage of every accident of ground and growth to give himself better cover. His eyes penetrated everywhere, his ears took note of every sound. He stilled his breathing, and at the cracking of a twig beneath his knee stopped his progress and hugged the earth. It was slow work, but not tedious; the danger made it exciting, but by no physical signs was the excitement manifest. His pulse was as regular, his nerves were as steady as if he were trying to trap a sparrow.

"It seems a long time," he thought, "but I cannot have come very far; I am still alive."

He smiled at his own method of estimating distance, and crept forward. A moment later he suddenly flattened himself upon the earth and lay motionless, minute after minute. Through a narrow opening in the bushes he had caught sight of a small mound of yellow clay— one of the enemy's rifle-pits. After some little time he cautiously raised his head, inch by inch, then his body upon his hands, spread out on each side of him, all the while intently regarding the hillock of clay. In another moment he was upon his feet, rifle in hand, striding rapidly forward with little attempt at concealment. He had rightly interpreted the signs, whatever they were; the enemy was gone.

To assure himself beyond a doubt before going back to report upon so important a matter, Searing pushed forward across the line of abandoned pits, running from cover to cover in the more open forest, his eyes vigilant to discover possible stragglers. He came to the edge of a plantation—one of those forlorn, deserted homesteads of the last years of the war, upgrown with brambles, ugly with broken fences and desolate with vacant buildings having blank apertures in place of doors and windows. After a keen reconnoissance from the safe seclusion of a clump of young pines Searing ran lightly across a field and through an orchard to a small structure which stood apart from the other farm buildings, on a slight elevation. This he thought would enable him to overlook a large scope of country in the direction that he supposed the enemy to have taken in withdrawing. This building, which had originally consisted of a single room elevated upon four posts about ten feet high, was now little more than a roof; the floor had fallen away, the joists and planks loosely piled on the ground below or resting on end at various angles, not wholly torn from their fastenings above. The supporting posts were themselves no longer vertical. It looked as if the whole edifice would go down at the touch of a finger.

Concealing himself in the débris of joists and flooring Searing looked across the open ground between his point of view and a spur of Kennesaw Mountain, a half-mile away. A road leading up and across this spur was crowded with troops—the rear-guard of the retiring enemy, their gun-barrels gleaming in the morning sunlight.

Searing had now learned all that he could hope to know. It was his duty to return to his own command with all possible speed and report his discovery. But the gray column of Confederates toiling up the mountain road was singularly tempting. His rifle—an ordinary "Springfield," but fitted with a globe sight and hair-trigger—would easily send its ounce and a quarter of lead hissing into their midst. That would probably not affect the duration and result of the war, but it is the business of a soldier to kill. It is also his habit if he is a good soldier. Searing cocked his rifle and "set" the trigger.

But it was decreed from the beginning of time that Private Searing was not to murder anybody that bright summer morning, nor was the Confederate retreat to be announced by him. For countless ages events had been so matching themselves together in that wondrous mosaic to some parts of which, dimly discernible, we give the name of history, that the acts which he had in will would have marred the harmony of the pattern. Some twenty-five years previously the Power charged with the execution of the work according to the design had provided against that mischance by causing the birth of a certain male child in a little village at the foot of the Carpathian Mountains, had carefully reared it, supervised its education, directed its desires into a military channel, and in due time made it an officer of artillery. By the concurrence of an infinite number of favoring influences and their preponderance over an infinite number of opposing ones, this officer of artillery had been made to commit a breach of discipline and flee from his native country to avoid punishment. He had been directed to New Orleans (instead of New York), where a recruiting officer awaited him on the wharf. He was enlisted and promoted, and things were so ordered that he now commanded a Confederate battery some two miles along the line from where Jerome Searing, the Federal scout, stood cocking his rifle. Nothing had been neglected—at every step in the progress of both these men's lives, and in the lives of their contemporaries and ancestors, and in the lives of the contemporaries of their ancestors, the right thing had been done to bring about the desired result. Had anything in all this vast concatenation been overlooked Private Searing might have fired on the retreating Confederates that morning, and would perhaps have missed. As it fell out, a Confederate captain of artillery, having nothing better to do while awaiting his turn to pull out and be off, amused himself by sighting a field-piece obliquely to his right at what he mistook for some Federal officers on the crest of a hill, and discharged it. The shot flew high of its mark.

As Jerome Searing drew back the hammer of his rifle and with his eyes upon the distant Confederates considered where he could plant his shot with the best hope of making a widow or an orphan or a childless mother,—perhaps all three, for Private Searing, although he had repeatedly refused promotion, was not without a certain kind of ambition,—he heard a rushing sound in the air, like that made by the wings of a great bird swooping down upon its prey. More quickly than he could apprehend the gradation, it increased to a hoarse and horrible roar, as the missile that made it sprang at him out of the sky, striking with a deafening impact one of the posts supporting the confusion of timbers above him, smashing it into matchwood, and bringing down the crazy edifice with a loud clatter, in clouds of blinding dust!

When Jerome Searing recovered consciousness he did not at once understand what had occurred. It was, indeed, some time before he opened his eyes. For a while he believed that he had died and been buried, and he tried to recall some portions of the burial service. He thought that his wife was kneeling upon his grave, adding her weight to that of the earth upon his breast. The two of them, widow and earth, had crushed his coffin. Unless the children should persuade her to go home he would not much longer be able to breathe. He felt a sense of wrong. "I cannot speak to her," he thought; "the dead have no voice; and if I open my eyes I shall get them full of earth."

He opened his eyes. A great expanse of blue sky, rising from a fringe of the tops of trees. In the foreground, shutting out some of the trees, a high, dun mound, angular in outline and crossed by an intricate, patternless system of straight lines; the whole an immeasurable distance away—a distance so inconceivably great that it fatigued him, and he closed his eyes. The moment that he did so he was conscious of an insufferable light. A sound was in his ears like the low, rhythmic thunder of a distant sea breaking in successive waves upon the beach, and out of this noise, seeming a part of it, or possibly coming from beyond it, and intermingled with its ceaseless undertone, came the articulate words: "Jerome Searing, you are caught like a rat in a trap—in a trap, trap, trap."

Suddenly there fell a great silence, a black darkness, an infinite tranquillity, and Jerome Searing, perfectly conscious of his rathood, and well assured of the trap that he was in, remembering all and nowise alarmed, again opened his eyes to reconnoitre, to note the strength of his enemy, to plan his defense.

He was caught in a reclining posture, his back firmly supported by a solid beam. Another lay across his breast, but he had been able to shrink a little away from it so that it no longer oppressed him, though it was immovable. A brace joining it at an angle had wedged him against a pile of boards on his left, fastening the arm on that side. His legs, slightly parted and straight along the ground, were covered upward to the knees with a mass of débris which towered above his narrow horizon. His head was as rigidly fixed as in a vise; he could move his eyes, his chin—no more. Only his right arm was partly free. "You must help us out of this," he said to it. But he could not get it from under the heavy timber athwart his chest, nor move it outward more than six inches at the elbow.

Searing was not seriously injured, nor did he suffer pain. A smart rap on the head from a flying fragment of the splintered post, incurred simultaneously with the frightfully sudden shock to the nervous system, had momentarily dazed him. His term of unconsciousness, including the period of recovery, during which he had had the strange fancies, had probably not exceeded a few seconds, for the dust of the wreck had not wholly cleared away as he began an intelligent survey of the situation.

With his partly free right hand he now tried to get hold of the beam that lay across, but not quite against, his breast. In no way could he do so. He was unable to depress the shoulder so as to push the elbow beyond that edge of the timber which was nearest his knees; failing in that, he could not raise the forearm and hand to grasp the beam. The brace that made an angle with it downward and backward prevented him from doing anything in that direction, and between it and his body the space was not half so wide as the length of his forearm. Obviously he could not get his hand under the beam nor over it; the hand could not, in fact, touch it at all. Having demonstrated his inability, he desisted, and began to think whether he could reach any of the débris piled upon his legs.

In surveying the mass with a view to determining that point, his attention was arrested by what seemed to be a ring of shining metal immediately in front of his eyes. It appeared to him at first to surround some perfectly black substance, and it was somewhat more than a half-inch in diameter. It suddenly occurred to his mind that the blackness was simply shadow and that the ring was in fact the muzzle of his rifle protruding from the pile of débris. He was not long in satisfying himself that this was so—if it was a satisfaction. By closing either eye he could look a little way along the barrel—to the point where it was hidden by the rubbish that held it. He could see the one side, with the corresponding eye, at apparently the same angle as the other side with the other eye. Looking with the right eye, the weapon seemed to be directed at a point to the left of his head, and *vice versa.* He was unable to see the upper surface of the barrel, but could see the under surface of the stock at a slight angle. The piece was, in fact, aimed at the exact centre of his forehead.

In the perception of this circumstance, in the recollection that just previously to the mischance of which this uncomfortable situation was the result he had cocked the rifle and set the trigger so that a touch would discharge it, Private Searing was affected with a feeling of uneasiness. But that was as far as possible from fear; he was a brave man, somewhat familiar with the aspect of rifles from that point of view, and of cannon too. And now he recalled, with something like amusement, an incident of his experience at the storming of Missionary Ridge, where, walking up to one of the enemy's embrasures from which he had seen a heavy gun throw charge after charge of grape among the assailants he had thought for a moment that the piece had been withdrawn; he could see nothing in the opening but a brazen circle. What that was he had understood just in time to step aside as it pitched another peck of iron down that swarming slope. To face firearms is one of the commonest incidents in a soldier's life—firearms, too, with malevolent eyes blazing behind them. That is what a soldier is for. Still, Private Searing did not altogether relish the situation, and turned away his eyes.

After groping, aimless, with his right hand for a time he made an ineffectual attempt to release his left. Then he tried to disengage his head, the fixity of which was the more annoying from his ignorance of what held it. Next he tried to free his feet, but while exerting the powerful muscles of his legs for that purpose it occurred to him that a disturbance of the rubbish which held them might discharge the rifle; how it could have endured what had already befallen it he could not understand, although memory assisted him with several instances in point. One in particular he recalled, in which in a moment of mental abstraction he had clubbed his rifle and beaten out another gentleman's brains, observing afterward that the weapon which he had been diligently swinging by the muzzle was loaded, capped, and at full cock—knowledge of which circumstance would doubtless have cheered his antagonist to longer endurance. He had always smiled in recalling that blunder of his "green and salad days" as a soldier, but now he did not smile. He turned his eyes again to the muzzle of the rifle and for a moment fancied that it had moved; it seemed somewhat nearer.

Again he looked away. The tops of the distant trees beyond the bounds of the plantation interested him: he had not before observed how light and feathery they were, nor how darkly blue the sky was, even among their branches, where they somewhat paled it with their green; above him it appeared almost black. "It will be uncomfortably hot here," he thought, "as the day advances. I wonder which way I am looking."

Judging by such shadows as he could see, he decided that his face was due north; he would at least not have the sun in his eyes, and north—well, that was toward his wife and children.

"Bah!" he exclaimed aloud, "what have they to do with it?"

He closed his eyes. "As I can't get out I may as well go to sleep. The rebels are gone and some of our fellows are sure to stray out here foraging. They'll find me."

But he did not sleep. Gradually he became sensible of a pain in his forehead—a dull ache, hardly perceptible at first, but growing more and more uncomfortable. He opened his eyes and it was gone —closed them and it returned. "The devil!" he said, irrelevantly, and stared again at the sky. He heard the singing of birds, the strange metallic note of the meadow lark, suggesting the clash of vibrant blades. He fell into pleasant memories of his childhood, played again with his brother and sister, raced across the fields, shouting to alarm the sedentary larks, entered the sombre forest beyond and with timid steps followed the faint path to Ghost Rock, standing at last with audible heart-throbs before the Dead Man's Cave and seeking to penetrate its awful mystery. For the first time he observed that the opening of the haunted cavern was encircled by a ring of metal. Then all else vanished and left him gazing into the barrel of his rifle as before. But whereas before it had seemed nearer, it now seemed an inconceivable distance away, and all the more sinister for that. He cried out and, startled by something in his own voice—the note of fear—lied to himself in denial: "If I don't sing out I may stay here till I die."

He now made no further attempt to evade the menacing stare of the gun barrel. If he turned away his eyes an instant it was to look for assistance (although he could not see the ground on either side the ruin), and he permitted them to return, obedient to the imperative fascination. If he closed them it was from weariness, and instantly the poignant pain in his forehead—the prophecy and menace of the bullet—forced him to reopen them.

The tension of nerve and brain was too severe; nature came to his relief with intervals of unconsciousness. Reviving from one of these he became sensible of a sharp, smarting pain in his right hand, and when he worked his fingers together, or rubbed his palm with them, he could feel that they were wet and slippery. He could not see the hand, but he knew the sensation; it was running blood. In his delirium he had beaten it against the jagged fragments of the wreck, had clutched it full of splinters. He resolved that he would meet his fate more manly. He was a plain, common soldier, had no religion and not much philosophy; he could not die like a hero, with great and wise last words, even if there had been some one to hear them, but he could die "game," and he would. But if he could only know when to expect the shot!

Some rats which had probably inhabited the shed came sneaking and scampering about. One of them mounted the pile of débris that held the rifle; another followed and another. Searing regarded them at first with indifference, then with friendly interest; then, as the thought flashed into his bewildered mind that they might touch the trigger of his rifle, he cursed them and ordered them to go away. "It is no business of yours," he cried.

The creatures went away; they would return later, attack his face, gnaw away his nose, cut his throat—he knew that, but he hoped by that time to be dead.

Nothing could now unfix his gaze from the little ring of metal with its black interior. The pain in his forehead was fierce and incessant. He felt it gradually penetrating the brain more and more deeply, until at last its progress was arrested by the wood at the back of his head. It grew momentarily more insufferable: he began wantonly beating his lacerated hand against the splinters again to counteract that horrible ache. It seemed to throb with a slow, regular recurrence, each pulsation sharper than the preceding, and sometimes he cried out, thinking he felt the fatal bullet. No thoughts of home, of wife and children, of country, of glory. The whole record of memory was effaced. The world had passed away—not a vestige remained. Here in this confusion of timbers and boards is the sole universe. Here is immortality in time—each pain an everlasting life. The throbs tick off eternities.

Jerome Searing, the man of courage, the formidable enemy, the strong, resolute warrior, was as pale as a ghost. His jaw was fallen; his eyes protruded; he trembled in every fibre; a cold sweat bathed his entire body; he screamed with fear. He was not insane—he was terrified.

In groping about with his torn and bleeding hand he seized at last a strip of board, and, pulling, felt it give away. It lay parallel with his body, and by bending his elbow as much as the contracted space would permit, he could draw it a few inches at a time. Finally it was altogether loosened from the wreckage covering his legs; he could lift it clear of the ground its whole length. A great hope came into his mind: perhaps he could work it upward, that is to say backward, far enough to lift the end and push aside the rifle; or, if that were too tightly wedged, so place the strip of board as to deflect the bullet. With this object he passed it backward inch by inch, hardly daring to breathe lest that act somehow defeat his intent, and more than ever unable to remove his eyes from the rifle, which might perhaps now hasten to improve its waning opportunity. Something at least had been gained: in the occupation of his mind in this attempt at self-defense he was less sensible of the pain in his head and had ceased to wince. But he was still dreadfully frightened and his teeth rattled like castanets.

The strip of board ceased to move to the suasion of his hand. He tugged at it with all his strength, changed the direction of its length all he could, but it had met some extended obstruction behind him and the end in front was still too far away to clear the pile of débris and reach the muzzle of the gun. It extended, indeed, nearly as far as the trigger guard, which, uncovered by the rubbish, he could imperfectly see with his right eye. He tried to break the strip with his hand, but had no leverage. In his defeat, all his terror returned, augmented tenfold. The black aperture of the rifle appeared to threaten a sharper and more imminent death in punishment of his rebellion. The track of the bullet through his head ached with an intenser anguish. He began to tremble again.

Suddenly he became composed. His tremor subsided. He clenched his teeth and drew down his eyebrows. He had not exhausted his means of defense; a new design had shaped itself in his mind—another plan of battle. Raising the front end of the strip of board, he carefully pushed it forward through the wreckage at the side of the rifle until it pressed against the trigger guard. Then he moved the end slowly outward until he could feel that it had cleared it, then, closing his eyes, thrust it against the trigger with all his strength! There was no explosion; the rifle had been discharged as it dropped from his hand when the building fell. But it did its work.

Lieutenant Adrian Searing, in command of the picket-guard on that part of the line through which his brother Jerome had passed on his mission, sat with attentive ears in his breastwork behind the line. Not the faintest sound escaped him; the cry of a bird, the barking of a squirrel, the noise of the wind among the pines—all were anxiously noted by his overstrained sense. Suddenly, directly in front of his line, he heard a faint, confused rumble, like the clatter of a falling building translated by distance. The lieutenant mechanically looked at his watch. Six o'clock and eighteen minutes. At the same moment an officer approached him on foot from the rear and saluted.

"Lieutenant," said the officer, "the colonel directs you to move forward your line and feel the enemy if you find him. If not, continue the advance until directed to halt. There is reason to think that the enemy has retreated."

The lieutenant nodded and said nothing; the other officer retired. In a moment the men, apprised of their duty by the non-commissioned officers in low tones, had deployed from their rifle-pits and were moving forward in skirmishing order, with set teeth and beating hearts.

This line of skirmishers sweeps across the plantation toward the mountain. They pass on both sides of the wrecked building, observing nothing. At a short distance in their rear their commander comes. He casts his eyes curiously upon the ruin and sees a dead body half buried in boards and timbers. It is so covered with dust that its clothing is Confederate gray. Its face is yellowish white; the cheeks are fallen in, the temples sunken, too, with sharp ridges about them, making the forehead forbiddingly narrow; the upper lip, slightly lifted, shows the white teeth, rigidly clenched. The hair is heavy with moisture, the face as wet as the dewy grass all about. From his point of view the officer does not observe the rifle; the man was apparently killed by the fall of the building.

"Dead a week," said the officer curtly, moving on and absently pulling out his watch as if to verify his estimate of time. Six o'clock and forty minutes.

❊   ❊   ❊

A BAFFLED AMBUSCADE

Connecting Readyville and Woodbury was a good, hard turnpike nine or ten miles long. Readyville was an outpost of the Federal army at Murfreesboro; Woodbury had the same relation to the Confederate army at Tullahoma. For months after the big battle at Stone River these outposts were in constant quarrel, most of the trouble occurring, naturally, on the turnpike mentioned, between detachments of cavalry. Sometimes the infantry and artillery took a hand in the game by way of showing their good-will.

One night a squadron of Federal horse commanded by Major Seidel, a gallant and skillful officer, moved out from Readyville on an uncommonly hazardous enterprise requiring secrecy, caution and silence.

Passing the infantry pickets, the detachment soon afterward approached two cavalry videttes staring hard into the darkness ahead. There should have been three.

"Where is your other man?" said the major. "I ordered Dunning to be here tonight."

"He rode forward, sir," the man replied. "There was a little firing afterward, but it was a long way to the front."

"It was against orders and against sense for Dunning to do that," said the officer, obviously vexed. "Why did he ride forward?"

"Don't know, sir; he seemed mighty restless. Guess he was skeered."

When this remarkable reasoner and his companion had been absorbed into the expeditionary force, it resumed its advance. Conversation was forbidden; arms and accouterments were denied the right to rattle. The horses' tramping was all that could be heard and the movement was slow in order to have as little as possible of that. It was after midnight and pretty dark, although there was a bit of moon somewhere behind the masses of cloud.

Two or three miles along, the head of the column approached a dense forest of cedars bordering the road on both sides. The major commanded a halt by merely halting, and, evidently himself a bit "skeered," rode on alone to reconnoiter. He was followed, however, by his adjutant and three troopers, who remained a little distance behind and, unseen by him, saw all that occurred.

After riding about a hundred yards toward the forest, the major suddenly and sharply reined in his horse and sat motionless in the saddle. Near the side of the road, in a little open space and hardly ten paces away, stood the figure of a man, dimly visible and as motionless as he. The major's first feeling was that of satisfaction in having left his cavalcade behind; if this were an enemy and should escape he would have little to report. The expedition was as yet undetected.

Some dark object was dimly discernible at the man's feet; the officer could not make it out. With the instinct of the true cavalryman and a particular indisposition to the discharge of firearms, he drew his saber. The man on foot made no movement in answer to the challenge. The situation was tense and a bit dramatic. Suddenly the moon burst through a rift in the clouds and, himself in the shadow of a group of great oaks, the horseman saw the footman clearly, in a patch of white light. It was Trooper Dunning, unarmed and bareheaded. The object at his feet resolved itself into a dead horse, and at a right angle across the animal's neck lay a dead man, face upward in the moonlight.

"Dunning has had the fight of his life," thought the major, and was about to ride forward. Dunning raised his hand, motioning him back with a gesture of warning; then, lowering the arm, he pointed to the place where the road lost itself in the blackness of the cedar forest.

The major understood, and turning his horse rode back to the little group that had followed him and was already moving to the rear in fear of his displeasure, and so returned to the head of his command.

"Dunning is just ahead there," he said to the captain of his leading company. "He has killed his man and will have something to report."

Right patiently they waited, sabers drawn, but Dunning did not come. In an hour the day broke and the whole force moved cautiously forward, its commander not altogether satisfied with his faith in Private Dunning. The expedition had failed, but something remained to be done.

In the little open space off the road they found the fallen horse. At a right angle across the animal's neck face upward, a bullet in the brain, lay the body of Trooper Dunning, stiff as a statue, hours dead.

Examination disclosed abundant evidence that within a half-hour the cedar forest had been occupied by a strong force of Confederate infantry—an ambuscade.

❊   ❊   ❊

THE AFFAIR AT COULTER'S NOTCH

"Do you think, Colonel, that your brave Coulter would like to put one of his guns in here?" the general asked.

He was apparently not altogether serious; it certainly did not seem a place where any artillerist, however brave, would like to put a gun. The colonel thought that possibly his division commander meant good-humoredly to intimate that in a recent conversation between them Captain Coulter's courage had been too highly extolled.

"General," he replied warmly, "Coulter would like to put a gun anywhere within reach of those people," with a motion of his hand in the direction of the enemy.

"It is the only place," said the general. He was serious, then.

The place was a depression, a "notch," in the sharp crest of a hill. It was a pass, and through it ran a turnpike, which reaching this highest point in its course by a sinuous ascent through a thin forest made a similar, though less steep, descent toward the enemy. For a mile to the left and a mile to the right, the ridge, though occupied by Federal infantry lying close behind the sharp crest and appearing as if held in place by atmospheric pressure, was inaccessible to artillery. There was no place but the bottom of the notch, and that was barely wide enough for the roadbed. From the Confederate side this point was commanded by two batteries posted on a slightly lower elevation beyond a creek, and a half-mile away. All the guns but one were masked by the trees of an orchard; that one—it seemed a bit of impudence—was on an open lawn directly in front of a rather grandiose building, the planter's dwelling. The gun was safe enough in its exposure—but only because the Federal infantry had been forbidden to fire. Coulter's Notch—it came to be called so—was not, that pleasant summer afternoon, a place where one would "like to put a gun."

Three or four dead horses lay there sprawling in the road, three or four dead men in a trim row at one side of it, and a little back, down the hill. All but one were cavalrymen belonging to the Federal advance. One was a quartermaster. The general commanding the division and the colonel commanding the brigade, with their staffs and escorts, had ridden into the notch to have a look at the enemy's guns—which had straightway obscured themselves in towering clouds of smoke. It was hardly profitable to be curious about guns which had the trick of the cuttlefish, and the season of observation had been brief. At its conclusion—a short remove backward from where it began—occurred the conversation already partly reported. "It is the only place," the general repeated thoughtfully, "to get at them."

The colonel looked at him gravely. "There is room for only one gun, General—one against twelve."

"That is true—for only one at a time," said the commander with something like, yet not altogether like, a smile. "But then, your brave Coulter—a whole battery in himself."

The tone of irony was now unmistakable. It angered the colonel, but he did not know what to say. The spirit of military subordination is not favorable to retort, nor even to deprecation.

At this moment a young officer of artillery came riding slowly up the road attended by his bugler. It was Captain Coulter. He could not have been more than twenty-three years of age. He was of medium height, but very slender and lithe, and sat his horse with something of the air of a civilian. In face he was of a type singularly unlike the men about him; thin, high-nosed, gray-eyed, with a slight blond mustache, and long, rather straggling hair of the same color. There was an apparent negligence in his attire. His cap was worn with the visor a trifle askew; his coat was buttoned only at the sword-belt, showing a considerable expanse of white shirt, tolerably clean for that stage of the campaign. But the negligence was all in his dress and bearing; in his face was a look of intense interest in his surroundings. His gray eyes, which seemed occasionally to strike right and left across the landscape, like search-lights, were for the most part fixed upon the sky beyond the Notch; until he should arrive at the summit of the road there was nothing else in that direction to see. As he came opposite his division and brigade commanders at the roadside he saluted mechanically and was about to pass on. The colonel signed to him to halt.

"Captain Coulter," he said, "the enemy has twelve pieces over there on the next ridge. If I rightly understand the general, he directs that you bring up a gun and engage them."

There was a blank silence; the general looked stolidly at a distant regiment swarming slowly up the hill through rough undergrowth, like a torn and draggled cloud of blue smoke; the captain appeared not to have observed him. Presently the captain spoke, slowly and with apparent effort:

"On the next ridge, did you say, sir? Are the guns near the house?"

"Ah, you have been over this road before. Directly at the house."

"And it is—necessary—to engage them? The order is imperative?"

His voice was husky and broken. He was visibly paler. The colonel was astonished and mortified. He stole a glance at the commander. In that set, immobile face was no sign; it was as hard as bronze. A moment later the general rode away, followed by his staff and escort. The colonel, humiliated and indignant, was about to order Captain Coulter in arrest, when the latter spoke a few words in a low tone to his bugler, saluted, and rode straight forward into the Notch, where, presently, at the summit of the road, his fieldglass at his eyes, he showed against the sky, he and his horse, sharply defined and statuesque. The bugler had dashed down the speed and disappeared behind a wood. Presently his bugle was heard singing in the cedars, and in an incredibly short time a single gun with its caisson, each drawn by six horses and manned by its full complement of gunners, came bounding and banging up the grade in a storm of dust, unlimbered under cover, and was run forward by hand to the fatal crest among the dead horses. A gesture of the captain's arm, some strangely agile movements of the men in loading, and almost before the troops along the way had ceased to hear the rattle of the wheels, a great white cloud sprang forward down the slope, and with a deafening report the affair at Coulter's Notch had begun.

It is not intended to relate in detail the progress and incidents of that ghastly contest—a contest without vicissitudes, its alternations only different degrees of despair. Almost at the instant when Captain Coulter's gun blew its challenging cloud twelve answering clouds rolled upward from among the trees about the plantation house, a deep multiple report roared back like a broken echo, and thenceforth to the end the Federal cannoneers fought their hopeless battle in an atmosphere of living iron whose thoughts were lightnings and whose deeds were death.

Unwilling to see the efforts which he could not aid and the slaughter which he could not stay, the colonel ascended the ridge at a point a quarter of a mile to the left, whence the Notch, itself invisible, but pushing up successive masses of smoke, seemed the crater of a volcano in thundering eruption. With his glass he watched the enemy's guns, noting as he could the effects of Coulter's fire—if Coulter still lived to direct it. He saw that the Federal gunners, ignoring those of the enemy's pieces whose positions could be determined by their smoke only, gave their whole attention to the one that maintained its place in the open—the lawn in front of the house. Over and about that hardy piece the shells exploded at intervals of a few seconds. Some exploded in the house, as could be seen by thin ascensions of smoke from the breached roof. Figures of prostrate men and horses were plainly visible.

"If our fellows are doing so good work with a single gun," said the colonel to an aide who happened to be nearest, "they must be suffering like the devil from twelve. Go down and present the commander of that piece with my congratulations on the accuracy of his fire."

Turning to his adjutant-general he said, "Did you observe Coulter's damned reluctance to obey orders?"

"Yes, sir, I did."

"Well, say nothing about it, please. I don't think the general will care to make any accusations. He will probably have enough to do in explaining his own connection with this uncommon way of amusing the rear-guard of a retreating enemy."

A young officer approached from below, climbing breathless up the acclivity. Almost before he had saluted, he gasped out:

"Colonel, I am directed by Colonel Harmon to say that the enemy's guns are within easy reach of our rifles, and most of them visible from several points along the ridge."

The brigade commander looked at him without a trace of interest in his expression. "I know it," he said quietly.

The young adjutant was visibly embarrassed. "Colonel Harmon would like to have permission to silence those guns," he stammered.

"So should I," the colonel said in the same tone. "Present my compliments to Colonel Harmon and say to him that the general's orders for the infantry not to fire are still in force."

The adjutant saluted and retired. The colonel ground his heel into the earth and turned to look again at the enemy's guns.

"Colonel," said the adjutant-general, "I don't know that I ought to say anything, but there is something wrong in all this. Do you happen to know that Captain Coulter is from the South?"

"No; *was* he, indeed?"

"I heard that last summer the division which the general then commanded was in the vicinity of Coulter's home—camped there for weeks, and——"

"Listen!" said the colonel, interrupting with an upward gesture. "Do you hear *that?*"

"That" was the silence of the Federal gun. The staff, the orderlies, the lines of infantry behind the crest—all had "heard," and were looking curiously in the direction of the crater, whence no smoke now ascended except desultory cloudlets from the enemy's shells. Then came the blare of a bugle, a faint rattle of wheels; a minute later the sharp reports recommenced with double activity. The demolished gun had been replaced with a sound one.

"Yes," said the adjutant-general, resuming his narrative, "the general made the acquaintance of Coulter's family. There was trouble —I don't know the exact nature of it—something about Coulter's wife. She is a red-hot Secessionist, as they all are, except Coulter himself, but she is a good wife and high-bred lady. There was a complaint to army headquarters. The general was transferred to this division. It is odd that Coulter's battery should afterward have been assigned to it."

The colonel had risen from the rock upon which they had been sitting. His eyes were blazing with a generous indignation.

"See here, Morrison," said he, looking his gossiping staff officer straight in the face, "did you get that story from a gentleman or a liar?"

"I don't want to say how I got it, Colonel, unless it is necessary" —he was blushing a trifle—"but I'll stake my life upon its truth in the main."

The colonel turned toward a small knot of officers some distance away. "Lieutenant Williams!" he shouted.

One of the officers detached himself from the group and coming forward saluted, saying: "Pardon me, Colonel, I thought you had been informed. Williams is dead down there by the gun. What can I do, sir?"

Lieutenant Williams was the aide who had had the pleasure of conveying to the officer in charge of the gun his brigade commander's congratulations.

"Go," said the colonel, "and direct the withdrawal of that gun instantly. No—I'll go myself."

He strode down the declivity toward the rear of the Notch at a break-neck pace, over rocks and through brambles, followed by his little retinue in tumultuous disorder. At the foot of the declivity they mounted their waiting animals and took to the road at a lively trot, round a bend and into the Notch. The spectacle which they encountered there was appalling!

Within that defile, barely broad enough for a single gun, were piled the wrecks of no fewer than four. They had noted the silencing of only the last one disabled—there had been a lack of men to replace it quickly with another. The débris lay on both sides of the road; the men had managed to keep an open way between, through which the fifth piece was now firing. The men?—they looked like demons of the pit! All were hatless, all stripped to the waist, their reeking skins black with blotches of powder and spattered with gouts of blood. They worked like madmen, with rammer and cartridge, lever and lanyard. They set their swollen shoulders and bleeding hands against the wheels at each recoil and heaved the heavy gun back to its place. There were no commands; in that awful environment of whooping shot, exploding shells, shrieking fragments of iron, and flying splinters of wood, none could have been heard. Officers, if officers there were, were indistinguishable; all worked together—each while he lasted—governed by the eye. When the gun was sponged, it was loaded; when loaded, aimed and fired. The colonel observed something new to his military experience—something horrible and unnatural: the gun was bleeding at the mouth! In temporary default of water, the man sponging had dipped his sponge into a pool of comrade's blood. In all this work there was no clashing; the duty of the instant was obvious. When one fell, another, looking a trifle cleaner, seemed to rise from the earth in the dead man's tracks, to fall in his turn.

With the ruined guns lay the ruined men—alongside the wreckage, under it and atop of it; and back down the road—a ghastly procession!—crept on hands and knees such of the wounded as were able to move. The colonel—he had compassionately sent his cavalcade to the right about—had to ride over those who were entirely dead in order not to crush those who were partly alive. Into that hell he tranquilly held his way, rode up alongside the gun, and, in the obscurity of the last discharge, tapped upon the cheek the man holding the rammer—who straightway fell, thinking himself killed. A fiend seven times damned sprang out of the smoke to take his place, but paused and gazed up at the mounted officer with an unearthly regard, his teeth flashing between his black lips, his eyes fierce and

expanded, burning like coals beneath his bloody brow. The colonel
made an authoritative gesture and pointed to the rear. The fiend
bowed in token of obedience. It was Captain Coulter.

Simultaneously with the colonel's arresting sign, silence fell upon
the whole field of action. The procession of missiles no longer
streamed into that defile of death, for the enemy also had ceased
firing. His army had been gone for hours, and the commander of his
rear-guard, who had held his position perilously long in hope to silence the Federal fire, at that strange moment had silenced his own.
"I was not aware of the breadth of my authority," said the colonel
to anybody, riding forward to the crest to see what had really happened.

An hour later his brigade was in bivouac on the enemy's ground,
and its idlers were examining, with something of awe, as the faithful
inspect a saint's relics, a score of straddling dead horses and three
disabled guns, all spiked. The fallen men had been carried away;
their torn and broken bodies would have given too great satisfaction.

Naturally, the colonel established himself and his military family
in the plantation house. It was somewhat shattered, but it was better
than the open air. The furniture was greatly deranged and broken.
Walls and ceilings were knocked away here and there, and a linger-
ing odor of powder smoke was everywhere. The beds, the closets of
women's clothing, the cupboards were not greatly damaged. The
new tenants for a night made themselves comfortable, and the virtual
effacement of Coulter's battery supplied them with an interesting
topic.

During supper an orderly of the escort showed himself into the
dining-room and asked permission to speak to the colonel.

"What is it, Barbour?" said that officer pleasantly, having overheard the request.

"Colonel, there is something wrong in the cellar; I don't know
what—somebody there. I was down there rummaging about."

"I will go down and see," said a staff officer, rising.

"So will I," the colonel said; "let the others remain. Lead on,
orderly."

They took a candle from the table and descended the cellar stairs,
the orderly in visible trepidation. The candle made but a feeble light,
but presently, as they advanced, its narrow circle of illumination
revealed a human figure seated on the ground against the black
stone wall which they were skirting, its knees elevated, its head
bowed sharply forward. The face, which should have been seen in
profile, was invisible, for the man was bent so far forward that his

long hair concealed it; and, strange to relate, the beard, of a much darker hue, fell in a great tangled mass and lay along the ground at his side. They involuntarily paused; then the colonel, taking the candle from the orderly's shaking hand, approached the man and attentively considered him. The long dark beard was the hair of a woman—dead. The dead woman clasped in her arms a dead babe. Both were clasped in the arms of the man, pressed against his breast, against his lips. There was blood in the hair of the woman; there was blood in the hair of the man. A yard away, near an irregular depression in the beaten earth which formed the cellar's floor—a fresh excavation with a convex bit of iron, having jagged edges, visible in one of the sides—lay an infant's foot. The colonel held the light as high as he could. The floor of the room above was broken through, the splinters pointing at all angles downward. "This casemate is not bomb-proof," said the colonel gravely. It did not occur to him that his summing up of the matter had any levity in it.

They stood about the group awhile in silence; the staff officer was thinking of his unfinished supper, the orderly of what might possibly be in one of the casks on the other side of the cellar. Suddenly the man whom they had thought dead raised his head and gazed tranquilly into their faces. His complexion was coal black; the cheeks were apparently tattooed in irregular sinuous lines from the eyes downward. The lips, too, were white, like those of a stage negro. There was blood upon his forehead.

The staff officer drew back a pace, the orderly two paces.

"What are you doing here, my man?" said the colonel unmoved.

"This house belongs to me, sir," was the reply, civilly delivered.

"To you? Ah, I see! And these?"

"My wife and child. I am Captain Coulter."

❉　　❉　　❉

A SON OF THE GODS

A STUDY IN THE PRESENT TENSE

A breezy day and a sunny landscape. An open country to right and left and forward; behind, a wood. In the edge of this wood, facing the open but not venturing into it, long lines of troops, halted. The wood is alive with them, and full of confused noises—the occasional rattle of wheels as a battery of artillery goes into position to cover the advance; the hum and murmur of the soldiers talking; a sound of innumerable feet in the dry leaves that strew the interspaces among the trees; hoarse commands of officers. Detached groups of horsemen are well in front—not altogether exposed—many of them intently regarding the crest of a hill a mile away in the direction of the interrupted advance. For this powerful army, moving in battle order through a forest, has met with a formidable obstacle—the open country. The crest of that gentle hill a mile away has a sinister look; it says, Beware! Along it runs a stone wall extending to left and right a great distance. Behind the wall is a hedge; behind the hedge are seen the tops of trees in rather straggling order. Among the trees—what? It is necessary to know.

Yesterday, and for many days and nights previously, we were fighting somewhere; always there was cannonading, with occasional keen rattlings of musketry, mingled with cheers, our own or the enemy's, we seldom knew, attesting some temporary advantage. This morning at daybreak the enemy was gone. We have moved forward across his earthworks, across which we have so often vainly attempted to move before, through the débris of his abandoned camps, among the graves of his fallen, into the woods beyond.

How curiously we had regarded everything! how odd it all had seemed! Nothing had appeared quite familiar; the most commonplace objects—an old saddle, a splintered wheel, a forgotten canteen —everything had related something of the mysterious personality of those strange men who had been killing us. The soldier never becomes wholly familiar with the conception of his foes as men like himself; he cannot divest himself of the feeling that they are another order of beings, differently conditioned, in an environment not altogether of the earth. The smallest vestiges of them rivet his attention and engage his interest. He thinks of them as inaccessible; and, catching an unexpected glimpse of them, they appear farther away, and therefore larger, than they really are—like objects in a fog. He is somewhat in awe of them.

From the edge of the wood leading up the acclivity are the tracks of horses and wheels—the wheels of cannon. The yellow grass is beaten down by the feet of infantry. Clearly they have passed this way in thousands; they have not withdrawn by the country roads. This is significant—it is the difference between retiring and retreating.

That group of horsemen is our commander, his staff and escort. He is facing the distant crest, holding his field-glass against his eyes with both hands, his elbows needlessly elevated. It is a fashion; it seems to dignify the act; we are all addicted to it. Suddenly he lowers the glass and says a few words to those about him. Two or three aides detach themselves from the group and canter away into the woods, along the lines in each direction. We did not hear his words, but we know them: "Tell General X. to send forward the skirmish line." Those of us who have been out of place resume our positions; the men resting at ease straighten themselves and the ranks are re-formed without a command. Some of us staff officers dismount and look at our saddle girths; those already on the ground remount.

Galloping rapidly along in the edge of the open ground comes a young officer on a snow-white horse. His saddle blanket is scarlet. What a fool! No one who has ever been in action but remembers how naturally every rifle turns toward the man on a white horse; no one but has observed how a bit of red enrages the bull of battle. That such colors are fashionable in military life must be accepted as the most astonishing of all the phenomena of human vanity. They would seem to have been devised to increase the death-rate.

This young officer is in full uniform, as if on parade. He is all agleam with bullion—a blue-and-gold edition of the Poetry of War. A wave of derisive laughter runs abreast of him all along the line. But how handsome he is!—with what careless grace he sits his horse!

He reins up within a respectful distance of the corps commander and salutes. The old soldier nods familiarly; he evidently knows him. A brief colloquy between them is going on; the young man seems to be preferring some request which the elder one is indisposed to grant. Let us ride a little nearer. Ah! too late—it is ended. The young officer salutes again, wheels his horse, and rides straight toward the crest of the hill!

A thin line of skirmishers, the men deployed at six paces or so apart, now pushes from the wood into the open. The commander speaks to his bugler, who claps his instrument to his lips. *Tra-la-la! Tra-la-la!* The skirmishers halt in their tracks.

Meantime the young horseman has advanced a hundred yards. He is riding at a walk, straight up the long slope, with never a turn of the head. How glorious! Gods! what would we not give to be in his place—with his soul! He does not draw his sabre; his right hand hangs easily at his side. The breeze catches the plume in his hat and flutters it smartly. The sunshine rests upon his shoulder-straps, lovingly, like a visible benediction. Straight on he rides. Ten thousand pairs of eyes are fixed upon him with an intensity that he can hardly fail to feel; ten thousand hearts keep quick time to the inaudible hoof-beats of his snowy steed. He is not alone—he draws all souls after him. But we remember that we laughed! On and on, straight for the hedge-lined wall, he rides. Not a look backward. O, if he would but turn—if he could but see the love, the adoration, the atonement!

Not a word is spoken; the populous depths of the forest still murmur with their unseen and unseeing swarm, but all along the fringe is silence. The burly commander is an equestrian statue of himself. The mounted staff officers, their field-glasses up, are motionless all. The line of battle in the edge of the wood stands at a new kind of "attention," each man in the attitude in which he was caught by the consciousness of what is going on. All these hardened and impenitent man-killers, to whom death in its awfulest forms is a fact familiar to their every-day observation; who sleep on hills trembling with the thunder of great guns, dine in the midst of streaming missiles, and play at cards among the dead faces of their dearest friends—all are watching with suspended breath and beating hearts the outcome of an act involving the life of one man. Such is the magnetism of courage and devotion.

If now you should turn your head you would see a simultaneous movement among the spectators—a start, as if they had received an electric shock—and looking forward again to the now distant horseman you would see that he has in that instant altered his direction and is riding at an angle to his former course. The spectators suppose the sudden deflection to be caused by a shot, perhaps a wound; but take this field-glass and you will observe that he is riding toward a break in the wall and hedge. He means, if not killed, to ride through and overlook the country beyond.

You are not to forget the nature of this man's act; it is not permitted to you to think of it as an instance of bravado, nor, on the other hand, a needless sacrifice of self. If the enemy has not retreated he is in force on that ridge. The investigator will encounter nothing less than a line-of-battle; there is no need of pickets, videttes, skirmishers, to give warning of our approach; our attacking lines will be visible, conspicuous, exposed to an artillery fire that will shave the ground the moment they break from cover, and for half the distance to a sheet of rifle bullets in which nothing can live. In short, if the enemy is there, it would be madness to attack him in front; he must be manœuvred out by the immemorial plan of threatening his line of communication, as necessary to his existence as to the diver at the bottom of the sea his air tube. But how ascertain if the enemy is there? There is but one way,—somebody must go and see. The natural and customary thing to do is to send forward a line of skirmishers. But in this case they will answer in the affirmative with all their lives; the enemy, crouching in double ranks behind the stone wall and in cover of the hedge, will wait until it is possible to count each assailant's teeth. At the first volley a half of the questioning line will fall, the other half before it can accomplish the predestined retreat. What a price to pay for gratified curiosity! At what a dear rate an army must sometimes purchase knowledge! "Let me pay all," says this gallant man—this military Christ!

There is no hope except the hope against hope that the crest is clear. True, he might prefer capture to death. So long as he advances, the line will not fire—why should it? He can safely ride into the hostile ranks and become a prisoner of war. But this would defeat his object. It would not answer our question; it is necessary either that he return unharmed or be shot to death before our eyes. Only so shall we know how to act. If captured—why, that might have been done by a half-dozen stragglers.

Now begins an extraordinary contest of intellect between a man and an army. Our horseman, now within a quarter of a mile of the crest, suddenly wheels to the left and gallops in a direction parallel to it. He has caught sight of his antagonist; he knows all. Some slight advantage of ground has enabled him to overlook a part of the line. If he were here he could tell us in words. But that is now hopeless; he must make the best use of the few minutes of life remaining to him, by compelling the enemy himself to tell us as much and as plainly as possible—which, naturally, that discreet power is reluctant to do. Not a rifleman in those crouching ranks, not a cannoneer at those masked and shotted guns, but knows the needs of the situation, the imperative duty of forbearance. Besides, there has been time enough to forbid them all to fire. True, a single rifle-shot might drop him and be no great disclosure. But firing is infectious—and see how rapidly he moves, with never a pause except as he whirls his horse about to take a new direction, never directly backward toward us, never directly forward toward his executioners. All this is visible through the glass; it seems occurring within pistol-shot; we see all but the enemy, whose presence, whose thoughts, whose motives we infer. To the unaided eye there is nothing but a black figure on a white horse, tracing slow zigzags against the slope of a distant hill—so slowly they seem almost to creep.

Now—the glass again—he has tired of his failure, or sees his error, or has gone mad; he is dashing directly forward at the wall, as if to take it at a leap, hedge and all! One moment only and he wheels right about and is speeding like the wind straight down the slope— toward his friends, toward his death! Instantly the wall is topped with a fierce roll of smoke for a distance of hundreds of yards to right and left. This is as instantly dissipated by the wind, and before the rattle of the rifles reaches us he is down. No, he recovers his seat; he has but pulled his horse upon its haunches. They are up and away! A tremendous cheer bursts from our ranks, relieving the insupportable tension of our feelings. And the horse and its rider? Yes, they are up and away. Away, indeed—they are making directly to our left, parallel to the now steadily blazing and smoking wall. The rattle of the musketry is continuous, and every bullet's target is that courageous heart.

Suddenly a great bank of white smoke pushes upward from behind the wall. Another and another—a dozen roll up before the thunder of the explosions and the humming of the missiles reach our ears and the missiles themselves come bounding through clouds of dust into our covert, knocking over here and there a man and causing a temporary distraction, a passing thought of self.

The dust drifts away. Incredible!—that enchanted horse and rider have passed a ravine and are climbing another slope to unveil another conspiracy of silence, to thwart the will of another armed host. Another moment and that crest too is in eruption. The horse rears and strikes the air with its forefeet. They are down at last. But look again—the man has detached himself from the dead animal. He stands erect, motionless, holding his sabre in his right hand straight above his head. His face is toward us. Now he lowers his hand to a level with his face and moves it outward, the blade of the sabre describing a downward curve. It is a sign to us, to the world, to posterity. It is a hero's salute to death and history.

Again the spell is broken; our men attempt to cheer; they are choking with emotion; they utter hoarse, discordant cries; they clutch their weapons and press tumultuously forward into the open. The skirmishers, without orders, against orders, are going forward at a keen run, like hounds unleashed. Our cannon speak and the enemy's now open in full chorus; to right and left as far as we can see, the distant crest, seeming now so near, erects its towers of cloud and the great shot pitch roaring down among our moving masses. Flag after flag of ours emerges from the wood, line after line sweeps forth, catching the sunlight on its burnished arms. The rear battalions alone are in obedience; they preserve their proper distance from the insurgent front.

The commander has not moved. He now removes his field-glass from his eyes and glances to the right and left. He sees the human current flowing on either side of him and his huddled escort, like tide waves parted by a rock. Not a sign of feeling in his face; he is thinking. Again he directs his eyes forward; they slowly traverse that malign and awful crest. He addresses a calm word to his bugler. *Tra-la-la! Tra-la-la!* The injunction has an imperiousness which enforces it. It is repeated by all the bugles of all the subordinate commanders; the sharp metallic notes assert themselves above the hum of the advance and penetrate the sound of the cannon. To halt is to withdraw. The colors move slowly back; the lines face about and sullenly follow, bearing their wounded; the skirmishers return, gathering up the dead.

Ah, those many, many needless dead! That great soul whose beautiful body is lying over yonder, so conspicuous against the sere hillside—could it not have been spared the bitter consciousness of a vain devotion? Would one exception have marred too much the pitiless perfection of the divine, eternal plan?

❊   ❊   ❊

ONE KIND OF OFFICER

I

OF THE USES OF CIVILITY

"Captain Ransome, it is not permitted to you to know *anything*. It is sufficient that you obey my order—which permit me to repeat. If you perceive any movement of troops in your front you are to open fire, and if attacked hold this position as long as you can. Do I make myself understood, sir?"

"Nothing could be plainer. Lieutenant Price,"—this to an officer of his own battery, who had ridden up in time to hear the order—"the general's meaning is clear, is it not?"

"Perfectly."

The lieutenant passed on to his post. For a moment General Cameron and the commander of the battery sat in their saddles, looking at each other in silence. There was no more to say; apparently too much had already been said. Then the superior officer nodded coldly and turned his horse to ride away. The artillerist saluted slowly, gravely, and with extreme formality. One acquainted with the niceties of military etiquette would have said that by his manner he attested a sense of the rebuke that he had incurred. It is one of the important uses of civility to signify resentment.

When the general had joined his staff and escort, awaiting him at a little distance, the whole cavalcade moved off toward the right of the guns and vanished in the fog. Captain Ransome was alone, silent, motionless as an equestrian statue. The gray fog, thickening every moment, closed in about him like a visible doom.

II

UNDER WHAT CIRCUMSTANCES MEN DO NOT
WISH TO BE SHOT

The fighting of the day before had been desultory and indecisive. At the points of collision the smoke of battle had hung in blue sheets among the branches of the trees till beaten into nothing by the falling rain. In the softened earth the wheels of cannon and ammunition wagons cut deep, ragged furrows, and movements of infantry seemed impeded by the mud that clung to the soldiers' feet as, with soaken garments and rifles imperfectly protected by capes of overcoats they went dragging in sinuous lines hither and thither through dripping forest and flooded field. Mounted officers, their heads protruding from rubber ponchos that glittered like black armor, picked their way, singly and in loose groups, among the men, coming and going with apparent aimlessness and commanding attention from nobody but one another. Here and there a dead man, his clothing defiled with earth, his face covered with a blanket or showing yellow and claylike in the rain, added his dispiriting influence to that of the other dismal features of the scene and augmented the general discomfort with a particular dejection. Very repulsive these wrecks looked—not at all heroic, and nobody was accessible to the infection of their patriotic example. Dead upon the field of honor, yes; but the field of honor was so very wet! It makes a difference.

The general engagement that all expected did not occur, none of the small advantages accruing, now to this side and now to that, in isolated and accidental collisions being followed up. Half-hearted attacks provoked a sullen resistance which was satisfied with mere repulse. Orders were obeyed with mechanical fidelity; no one did any more than his duty.

"The army is cowardly to-day," said General Cameron, the commander of a Federal brigade, to his adjutant-general.

"The army is cold," replied the officer addressed, "and—yes, it doesn't wish to be like that."

He pointed to one of the dead bodies, lying in a thin pool of yellow water, its face and clothing bespattered with mud from hoof and wheel.

The army's weapons seemed to share its military delinquency. The rattle of rifles sounded flat and contemptible. It had no meaning and scarcely roused to attention and expectancy the unengaged parts of the line-of-battle and the waiting reserves. Heard at a little distance, the reports of cannon were feeble in volume and *timbre:* they lacked sting and resonance. The guns seemed to be fired with light charges, unshotted. And so the futile day wore on to its dreary close, and then to a night of discomfort succeeded a day of apprehension.

An army has a personality. Beneath the individual thoughts and emotions of its component parts it thinks and feels as a unit. And in this large, inclusive sense of things lies a wiser wisdom than the mere sum of all that it knows. On that dismal morning this great brute force, groping at the bottom of a white ocean of fog among trees that seemed as sea weeds, had a dumb consciousness that all was not well; that a day's manœuvring had resulted in a faulty disposition of its parts, a blind diffusion of its strength. The men felt insecure and talked among themselves of such tactical errors as with their meager military vocabulary they were able to name. Field and line officers gathered in groups and spoke more learnedly of what they apprehended with no greater clearness. Commanders of brigades and divisions looked anxiously to their connections on the right and on the left, sent staff officers on errands of inquiry and pushed skirmish lines silently and cautiously forward into the dubious region between the known and the unknown. At some points on the line the troops, apparently of their own volition, constructed such defenses as they could without the silent spade and the noisy ax.

One of these points was held by Captain Ransome's battery of six guns. Provided always with intrenching tools, his men had labored with diligence during the night, and now his guns thrust their black muzzles through the embrasures of a really formidable earthwork. It crowned a slight acclivity devoid of undergrowth and providing an unobstructed fire that would sweep the ground for an unknown distance in front. The position could hardly have been better chosen. It had this peculiarity, which Captain Ransome, who was greatly addicted to the use of the compass, had not failed to observe: it faced northward, whereas he knew that the general line of the army must face eastward. In fact, that part of the line was "refused"—that is to say, bent backward, away from the enemy. This implied that Captain Ransome's battery was somewhere near the left flank of the army; for an army in line of battle retires its flanks if the nature of the ground will permit, they being its vulnerable points. Actually, Captain Ransome appeared to hold the extreme left of the line, no troops being visible in that direction beyond his own. Immediately in rear of his guns occurred that conversation between him and his brigade commander, the concluding and more picturesque part of which is reported above.

III

HOW TO PLAY THE CANNON WITHOUT NOTES

Captain Ransome sat motionless and silent on horseback. A few yards away his men were standing at their guns. Somewhere—everywhere within a few miles—were a hundred thousand men, friends and enemies. Yet he was alone. The mist had isolated him as completely as if he had been in the heart of a desert. His world was a few square yards of wet and trampled earth about the feet of his horse. His comrades in that ghostly domain were invisible and inaudible. These were conditions favorable to thought, and he was thinking. Of the nature of his thoughts his clear-cut handsome features yielded no attesting sign. His face was as inscrutable as that of the sphinx. Why should it have made a record which there was none to observe? At the sound of a footstep he merely turned his eyes in the direction whence it came; one of his sergeants, looking a giant in stature in the false perspective of the fog, approached, and when clearly defined and reduced to his true dimensions by propinquity, saluted and stood at attention.

"Well, Morris," said the officer, returning his subordinate's salute.

"Lieutenant Price directed me to tell you, sir, that most of the infantry has been withdrawn. We have not sufficient support."

"Yes, I know."

"I am to say that some of our men have been out over the works a hundred yards and report that our front is not picketed."

"Yes."

"They were so far forward that they heard the enemy."

"Yes."

"They heard the rattle of the wheels of artillery and the commands of officers."

"Yes."

"The enemy is moving toward our works."

Captain Ransome, who had been facing to the rear of his line—toward the point where the brigade commander and his cavalcade had been swallowed up by the fog—reined his horse about and faced the other way. Then he sat motionless as before.

"Who are the men who made that statement?" he inquired, without looking at the sergeant; his eyes were directed straight into the fog over the head of his horse.

"Corporal Hassman and Gunner Manning."

Captain Ransome was a moment silent. A slight pallor came into his face, a slight compression affected the lines of his lips, but it would have required a closer observer than Sergeant Morris to note the change. There was none in the voice.

"Sergeant, present my compliments to Lieutenant Price and direct him to open fire with all the guns. Grape."

The sergeant saluted and vanished in the fog.

IV

TO INTRODUCE GENERAL MASTERSON

Searching for his division commander, General Cameron and his escort had followed the line of battle for nearly a mile to the right of Ransome's battery, and there learned that the division commander had gone in search of the corps commander. It seemed that everybody was looking for his immediate superior—an ominous circumstance. It meant that nobody was quite at ease. So General Cameron rode on for another half-mile, where by good luck he met General Masterson, the division commander, returning.

"Ah, Cameron," said the higher officer, reining up, and throwing his right leg across the pommel of his saddle in a most unmilitary way—"anything up? Found a good position for your battery, I hope—if one place is better than another in a fog."

"Yes, general," said the other, with the greater dignity appropriate to his less exalted rank, "my battery is very well placed. I wish I could say that it is as well commanded."

"Eh, what's that? Ransome? I think him a fine fellow. In the army we should be proud of him."

It was customary for officers of the regular army to speak of it as "the army." As the greatest cities are most provincial, so the self-complacency of aristocracies is most frankly plebeian.

"He is too fond of his opinion. By the way, in order to occupy the hill that he holds I had to extend my line dangerously. The hill is on my left—that is to say the left flank of the army."

"Oh, no, Hart's brigade is beyond. It was ordered up from Drytown during the night and directed to hook on to you. Better go and——"

The sentence was unfinished: a lively cannonade had broken out on the left, and both officers, followed by their retinues of aides and orderlies making a great jingle and clank, rode rapidly toward the spot. But they were soon impeded, for they were compelled by the fog to keep within sight of the line-of-battle, behind which were swarms of men, all in motion across their way. Everywhere the line was assuming a sharper and harder definition, as the men sprang to arms and the officers, with drawn swords, "dressed" the ranks. Color-bearers unfurled the flags, buglers blew the "assembly," hospital attendants appeared with stretchers. Field officers mounted and sent their impedimenta to the rear in care of negro servants. Back in the ghostly spaces of the forest could be heard the rustle and murmur of the reserves, pulling themselves together.

Nor was all this preparation vain, for scarcely five minutes had passed since Captain Ransome's guns had broken the truce of doubt before the whole region was aroar: the enemy had attacked nearly everywhere.

V

HOW SOUNDS CAN FIGHT SHADOWS

Captain Ransome walked up and down behind his guns, which were firing rapidly but with steadiness. The gunners worked alertly, but without haste or apparent excitement. There was really no reason for excitement; it is not much to point a cannon into a fog and fire it. Anybody can do as much as that.

The men smiled at their noisy work, performing it with a lessening alacrity. They cast curious regards upon their captain, who had now mounted the banquette of the fortification and was looking across the parapet as if observing the effect of his fire. But the only visible effect was the substitution of wide, low-lying sheets of smoke for their bulk of fog. Suddenly out of the obscurity burst a great sound of cheering, which filled the intervals between the reports of the guns with startling distinctness! To the few with leisure and opportunity to observe, the sound was inexpressibly strange—so loud, so near, so menacing, yet nothing seen! The men who had smiled at their work smiled no more, but performed it with a serious and feverish activity.

From his station at the parapet Captain Ransome now saw a great multitude of dim gray figures taking shape in the mist below him and swarming up the slope. But the work of the guns was now fast and furious. They swept the populous declivity with gusts of grape and canister, the whirring of which could be heard through the thunder of the explosions. In this awful tempest of iron the assailants struggled forward foot by foot across their dead, firing into the embrasures, reloading, firing again, and at last falling in their turn, a little in advance of those who had fallen before. Soon the smoke was dense enough to cover all. It settled down upon the attack and, drifting back, involved the defense. The gunners could hardly see to serve their pieces, and when occasional figures of the enemy appeared upon the parapet—having had the good luck to get near enough to it, between two embrasures, to be protected from the guns—they looked so unsubstantial that it seemed hardly worth while for the few infantrymen to go to work upon them with the bayonet and tumble them back into the ditch.

As the commander of a battery in action can find something better to do than cracking individual skulls, Captain Ransome had retired from the parapet to his proper post in rear of his guns, where he stood with folded arms, his bugler beside him. Here, during the hottest of the fight, he was approached by Lieutenant Price, who had just sabred a daring assailant inside the work. A spirited colloquy ensued between the two officers—spirited, at least, on the part of the lieutenant, who gesticulated with energy and shouted again and again into his commander's ear in the attempt to make himself heard above the infernal din of the guns. His gestures, if coolly noted by an actor, would have been pronounced to be those of protestation: one would have said that he was opposed to the proceedings. Did he wish to surrender?

Captain Ransome listened without a change of countenance or attitude, and when the other man had finished his harangue, looked him coldly in the eyes and during a seasonable abatement of the uproar said:

"Lieutenant Price, it is not permitted to you to know *anything*. It is sufficient that you obey my orders."

The lieutenant went to his post, and the parapet being now apparently clear Captain Ransome returned to it to have a look over. As he mounted the banquette a man sprang upon the crest, waving a great brilliant flag. The captain drew a pistol from his belt and shot him dead. The body, pitching forward, hung over the inner edge of the embankment, the arms straight downward, both hands still grasping the flag. The man's few followers turned and fled down the slope. Looking over the parapet, the captain saw no living thing. He observed also that no bullets were coming into the work.

He made a sign to the bugler, who sounded the command to cease firing. At all other points the action had already ended with a repulse of the Confederate attack; with the cessation of this cannonade the silence was absolute.

VI

WHY, BEING AFFRONTED BY A, IT IS NOT BEST TO AFFRONT B

General Masterson rode into the redoubt. The men, gathered in groups, were talking loudly and gesticulating. They pointed at the dead, running from one body to another. They neglected their foul and heated guns and forgot to resume their outer clothing. They ran to the parapet and looked over, some of them leaping down into the ditch. A score were gathered about a flag rigidly held by a dead man.

"Well, my men," said the general cheerily, "you have had a pretty fight of it."

They stared; nobody replied; the presence of the great man seemed to embarrass and alarm.

Getting no response to his pleasant condescension, the easy-mannered officer whistled a bar or two of a popular air, and riding forward to the parapet, looked over at the dead. In an instant he had whirled his horse about and was spurring along in rear of the guns, his eyes everywhere at once. An officer sat on the trail of one of the guns, smoking a cigar. As the general dashed up he rose and tranquilly saluted.

"Captain Ransome!"—the words fell sharp and harsh, like the clash of steel blades—"you have been fighting our own men—our own men, sir; do you hear? Hart's brigade!"

"General, I know that."

"You know it—you know that, and you sit here smoking? Oh, damn it, Hamilton, I'm losing my temper,"—this to his provost-marshal. "Sir—Captain Ransome, be good enough to say—to say why you fought our own men."

"That I am unable to say. In my orders that information was withheld."

Apparently the general did not comprehend.

"Who was the aggressor in this affair, you or General Hart?" he asked.

"I was."

"And could you not have known—could you not see, sir, that you were attacking our own men?"

The reply was astounding!

"I knew that, general. It appeared to be none of my business."

Then, breaking the dead silence that followed his answer, he said: "I must refer you to General Cameron."

"General Cameron is dead, sir—as dead as he can be—as dead as any man in this army. He lies back yonder under a tree. Do you mean to say that he had anything to do with this horrible business?"

Captain Ransome did not reply. Observing the altercation his men had gathered about to watch the outcome. They were greatly excited. The fog, which had been partly dissipated by the firing, had again closed in so darkly about them that they drew more closely together till the judge on horseback and the accused standing calmly before him had but a narrow space free from intrusion. It was the most informal of courts-martial, but all felt that the formal one to follow would but affirm its judgment. It had no jurisdiction, but it had the significance of prophecy.

"Captain Ransome," the general cried impetuously, but with something in his voice that was almost entreaty, "if you can say anything to put a better light upon your incomprehensible conduct I beg you will do so."

Having recovered his temper this generous soldier sought for something to justify his naturally sympathetic attitude toward a brave man in the imminence of a dishonorable death.

"Where is Lieutenant Price?" the captain said.

That officer stood forward, his dark saturnine face looking somewhat forbidding under a bloody handkerchief bound about his brow. He understood the summons and needed no invitation to speak. He did not look at the captain, but addressed the general:

"During the engagement I discovered the state of affairs, and apprised the commander of the battery. I ventured to urge that the firing cease. I was insulted and ordered to my post."

"Do you know anything of the orders under which I was acting?" asked the captain.

"Of any orders under which the commander of the battery was

acting," the lieutenant continued, still addressing the general, "I know nothing."

Captain Ransome felt his world sink away from his feet. In those cruel words he heard the murmur of the centuries breaking upon the shore of eternity. He heard the voice of doom; it said, in cold, mechanical, and measured tones: "Ready, aim, fire!" and he felt the bullets tear his heart to shreds. He heard the sound of the earth upon his coffin and (if the good God was so merciful) the song of a bird above his forgotten grave. Quietly detaching his sabre from its supports, he handed it up to the provost-marshal.

❊   ❊   ❊

A TOUGH TUSSLE

One night in the autumn of 1861 a man sat alone in the heart of a forest in western Virginia. The region was one of the wildest on the continent—the Cheat Mountain country. There was no lack of people close at hand, however; within a mile of where the man sat was the now silent camp of a whole Federal brigade. Somewhere about— it might be still nearer—was a force of the enemy, the numbers unknown. It was this uncertainty as to its numbers and position that accounted for the man's presence in that lonely spot; he was a young officer of a Federal infantry regiment and his business there was to guard his sleeping comrades in the camp against a surprise. He was in command of a detachment of men constituting a picket-guard. These men he had stationed just at nightfall in an irregular line, determined by the nature of the ground, several hundred yards in front of where he now sat. The line ran through the forest, among the rocks and laurel thickets, the men fifteen or twenty paces apart, all in concealment and under injunction of strict silence and unremitting vigilance. In four hours, if nothing occurred, they would be relieved by a fresh detachment from the reserve now resting in care of its captain some distance away to the left and rear. Before stationing his men the young officer of whom we are writing had pointed out to his two sergeants the spot at which he would be found if it should be necessary to consult him, or if his presence at the front line should be required.

It was a quiet enough spot—the fork of an old wood-road, on the two branches of which, prolonging themselves deviously forward in the dim moonlight, the sergeants were themselves stationed, a few paces in rear of the line. If driven sharply back by a sudden onset of the enemy—and pickets are not expected to make a stand after firing—the men would come into the converging roads and naturally following them to their point of intersection could be rallied and "formed." In his small way the author of these dispositions was something of a strategist; if Napoleon had planned as intelligently at Waterloo he would have won that memorable battle and been overthrown later.

Second-Lieutenant Brainerd Byring was a brave and efficient officer, young and comparatively inexperienced as he was in the business of killing his fellow-men. He had enlisted in the very first days of the war as a private, with no military knowledge whatever, had been made first-sergeant of his company on account of his education and engaging manner, and had been lucky enough to lose his captain by a Confederate bullet; in the resulting promotions he had gained a commission. He had been in several engagements, such as they were—at Philippi, Rich Mountain, Carrick's Ford and Greenbrier—and had borne himself with such gallantry as not to attract the attention of his superior officers. The exhilaration of battle was agreeable to him, but the sight of the dead, with their clay faces, blank eyes and stiff bodies, which when not unnaturally shrunken were unnaturally swollen, had always intolerably affected him. He felt toward them a kind of reasonless antipathy that was something more than the physical and spiritual repugnance common to us all. Doubtless this feeling was due to his unusually acute sensibilities—his keen sense of the beautiful, which these hideous things outraged. Whatever may have been the cause, he could not look upon a dead body without a loathing which had in it an element of resentment. What others have respected as the dignity of death had to him no existence —was altogether unthinkable. Death was a thing to be hated. It was not picturesque, it had no tender and solemn side—a dismal thing, hideous in all its manifestations and suggestions. Lieutenant Byring was a braver man than anybody knew, for nobody knew his horror of that which he was ever ready to incur.

Having posted his men, instructed his sergeants and retired to his station, he seated himself on a log, and with senses all alert began his vigil. For greater ease he loosened his sword-belt and taking his heavy revolver from his holster laid it on the log beside him. He felt very comfortable, though he hardly gave the fact a thought, so intently did he listen for any sound from the front which might have a menacing significance—a shout, a shot, or the footfall of one of his sergeants coming to apprise him of something worth knowing. From the vast, invisible ocean of moonlight overhead fell, here and there, a slender, broken stream that seemed to plash against the intercepting branches and trickle to earth, forming small white pools among the clumps of laurel. But these leaks were few and served only to accentuate the blackness of his environment, which his imagination found it easy to people with all manner of unfamiliar shapes, menacing, uncanny, or merely grotesque.

He to whom the portentous conspiracy of night and solitude and silence in the heart of a great forest is not an unknown experience needs not to be told what another world it all is—how even the most commonplace and familiar objects take on another character. The trees group themselves differently; they draw closer together, as if in fear. The very silence has another quality than the silence of the day. And it is full of half-heard whispers—whispers that startle—ghosts of sounds long dead. There are living sounds, too, such as are never heard under other conditions: notes of strange night-birds, the cries of small animals in sudden encounters with stealthy foes or in their dreams, a rustling in the dead leaves—it may be the leap of a wood-rat, it may be the footfall of a panther. What caused the breaking of that twig?—what the low, alarmed twittering in that bushful of birds? There are sounds without a name, forms without substance, translations in space of objects which have not been seen to move, movements wherein nothing is observed to change its place. Ah, children of the sunlight and the gaslight, how little you know of the world in which you live!

Surrounded at a little distance by armed and watchful friends, Byring felt utterly alone. Yielding himself to the solemn and mysterious spirit of the time and place, he had forgotten the nature of his connection with the visible and audible aspects and phases of the night. The forest was boundless; men and the habitations of men did not exist. The universe was one primeval mystery of darkness, without form and void, himself the sole, dumb questioner of its eternal secret. Absorbed in thoughts born of this mood, he suffered the time to slip away unnoted. Meantime the infrequent patches of white light lying amongst the tree-trunks had undergone changes of size, form and place. In one of them near by, just at the roadside, his eye fell upon an object that he had not previously observed. It was almost before his face as he sat; he could have sworn that it had not before been there. It was partly covered in shadow, but he could see that it was a human figure. Instinctively he adjusted the clasp of his sword-belt and laid hold of his pistol—again he was in a world of war, by occupation an assassin.

The figure did not move. Rising, pistol in hand, he approached. The figure lay upon its back, its upper part in shadow, but standing above it and looking down upon the face, he saw that it was a dead body. He shuddered and turned from it with a feeling of sickness and disgust, resumed his seat upon the log, and forgetting military prudence struck a match and lit a cigar. In the sudden blackness that followed the extinction of the flame he felt a sense of relief; he could no longer see the object of his aversion. Nevertheless, he kept his eyes set in that direction until it appeared again with growing distinctness. It seemed to have moved a trifle nearer.

"Damn the thing!" he muttered. "What does it want?"

It did not appear to be in need of anything but a soul.

Byring turned away his eyes and began humming a tune, but he broke off in the middle of a bar and looked at the dead body. Its presence annoyed him, though he could hardly have had a quieter neighbor. He was conscious, too, of a vague, indefinable feeling that was new to him. It was not fear, but rather a sense of the supernatural—in which he did not at all believe.

"I have inherited it," he said to himself. "I suppose it will require a thousand ages—perhaps ten thousand—for humanity to outgrow this feeling. Where and when did it originate? Away back, probably, in what is called the cradle of the human race—the plains of Central Asia. What we inherit as a superstition our barbarous ancestors must have held as a reasonable conviction. Doubtless they believed themselves justified by facts whose nature we cannot even conjecture in thinking a dead body a malign thing endowed with some strange power of mischief, with perhaps a will and a purpose to exert it. Possibly they had some awful form of religion of which that was one of the chief doctrines, sedulously taught by their priesthood, as ours teach the immortality of the soul. As the Aryans moved slowly on, to and through the Caucasus passes, and spread over Europe, new conditions of life must have resulted in the formulation of new religions. The old belief in the malevolence of the dead body was lost from the creeds and even perished from tradition, but it left its heritage of terror, which is transmitted from generation to generation—is as much a part of us as are our blood and bones."

In following out his thought he had forgotten that which suggested it; but now his eye fell again upon the corpse. The shadow had now altogether uncovered it. He saw the sharp profile, the chin in the air, the whole face, ghastly white in the moonlight. The clothing was gray, the uniform of a Confederate soldier. The coat and waistcoat, unbuttoned, had fallen away on each side, exposing the white shirt. The chest seemed unnaturally prominent, but the abdomen had sunk in, leaving a sharp projection at the line of the lower ribs. The arms were extended, the left knee was thrust upward. The whole posture impressed Byring as having been studied with a view to the horrible.

"Bah!" he exclaimed; "he was an actor—he knows how to be dead."

He drew away his eyes, directing them resolutely along one of the roads leading to the front, and resumed his philosophizing where he had left off.

"It may be that our Central Asian ancestors had not the custom of burial. In that case it is easy to understand their fear of the dead, who really were a menace and an evil. They bred pestilences. Children were taught to avoid the places where they lay, and to run away if by inadvertence they came near a corpse. I think, indeed, I'd better go away from this chap."

He half rose to do so, then remembered that he had told his men in front and the officer in the rear who was to relieve him that he could at any time be found at that spot. It was a matter of pride, too. If he abandoned his post he feared they would think he feared the corpse. He was no coward and he was unwilling to incur anybody's ridicule. So he again seated himself, and to prove his courage looked boldly at the body. The right arm—the one farthest from him—was now in shadow. He could barely see the hand which, he had before observed, lay at the root of a clump of laurel. There had been no change, a fact which gave him a certain comfort, he could not have said why. He did not at once remove his eyes; that which we do not wish to see has a strange fascination, sometimes irresistible. Of the woman who covers her eyes with her hands and looks between the fingers let it be said that the wits have dealt with her not altogether justly.

Byring suddenly became conscious of a pain in his right hand. He withdrew his eyes from his enemy and looked at it. He was grasping the hilt of his drawn sword so tightly that it hurt him. He observed, too, that he was leaning forward in a strained attitude—crouching like a gladiator ready to spring at the throat of an antagonist. His teeth were clenched and he was breathing hard. This matter was soon set right, and as his muscles relaxed and he drew a long breath he felt keenly enough the ludicrousness of the incident. It affected him to laughter. Heavens! what sound was that? what mindless devil was uttering an unholy glee in mockery of human merriment? He sprang to his feet and looked about him, not recognizing his own laugh.

He could no longer conceal from himself the horrible fact of his cowardice; he was thoroughly frightened! He would have run from the spot, but his legs refused their office; they gave way beneath him and he sat again upon the log, violently trembling. His face was wet, his whole body bathed in a chill perspiration. He could not even cry out. Distinctly he heard behind him a stealthy tread, as of some wild animal, and dared not look over his shoulder. Had the soulless living joined forces with the soulless dead?—was it an animal? Ah, if he could but be assured of that! But by no effort of will could he now unfix his gaze from the face of the dead man.

I repeat that Lieutenant Byring was a brave and intelligent man. But what would you have? Shall a man cope, single-handed, with so monstrous an alliance as that of night and solitude and silence and the dead,—while an incalculable host of his own ancestors shriek into the ear of his spirit their coward counsel, sing their doleful death-songs in his heart, and disarm his very blood of all its iron? The odds are too great—courage was not made for so rough use as that.

One sole conviction now had the man in possession: that the body had moved. It lay nearer to the edge of its plot of light—there could be no doubt of it. It had also moved its arms, for, look, they are both in the shadow! A breath of cold air struck Byring full in the face; the boughs of trees above him stirred and moaned. A strongly defined shadow passed across the face of the dead, left it luminous, passed back upon it and left it half obscured. The horrible thing was visibly moving! At that moment a single shot rang out upon the picket-line—a lonelier and louder, though more distant, shot than ever had been heard by mortal ear! It broke the spell of that enchanted man; it slew the silence and the solitude, dispersed the hindering host from Central Asia and released his modern manhood. With a cry like that of some great bird pouncing upon its prey he sprang forward, hot-hearted for action!

Shot after shot now came from the front. There were shoutings and confusion, hoof-beats and desultory cheers. Away to the rear, in the sleeping camp, were a singing of bugles and grumble of drums. Pushing through the thickets on either side the roads came the Federal pickets, in full retreat, firing backward at random as they ran. A straggling group that had followed back one of the roads, as instructed, suddenly sprang away into the bushes as half a hundred horsemen thundered by them, striking wildly with their sabres as they passed. At headlong speed these mounted madmen shot past the spot where Byring had sat, and vanished round an angle of the road, shouting and firing their pistols. A moment later there was a roar of musketry, followed by dropping shots—they had encountered the reserve-guard in line; and back they came in dire confusion, with here and there an empty saddle and many a maddened horse, bullet-stung, snorting and plunging with pain. It was all over—"an affair of out-posts."

The line was reëstablished with fresh men, the roll called, the stragglers were re-formed. The Federal commander with a part of his staff, imperfectly clad, appeared upon the scene, asked a few questions, looked exceedingly wise and retired. After standing at arms for an hour the brigade in camp "swore a prayer or two" and went to bed.

Early the next morning a fatigue-party, commanded by a captain and accompanied by a surgeon, searched the ground for dead and wounded. At the fork of the road, a little to one side, they found two bodies lying close together—that of a Federal officer and that of a Confederate private. The officer had died of a sword-thrust through the heart, but not, apparently, until he had inflicted upon his enemy no fewer than five dreadful wounds. The dead officer lay on his face in a pool of blood, the weapon still in his breast. They turned him on his back and the surgeon removed it.

"Gad!" said the captain—"It is Byring!"—adding, with a glance at the other, "They had a tough tussle."

The surgeon was examining the sword. It was that of a line officer of Federal infantry—exactly like the one worn by the captain. It was, in fact, Byring's own. The only other weapon discovered was an undischarged revolver in the dead officer's belt.

The surgeon laid down the sword and approached the other body. It was frightfully gashed and stabbed, but there was no blood. He took hold of the left foot and tried to straighten the leg. In the effort the body was displaced. The dead do not wish to be moved—it protested with a faint, sickening odor. Where it had lain were a few maggots, manifesting an imbecile activity.

The surgeon looked at the captain. The captain looked at the surgeon.

AN OCCURRENCE AT OWL CREEK
BRIDGE

I

A man stood upon a railroad bridge in northern Alabama, looking down into the swift water twenty feet below. The man's hands were behind his back, the wrists bound with a cord. A rope closely encircled his neck. It was attached to a stout cross-timber above his head and the slack fell to the level of his knees. Some loose boards laid upon the sleepers supporting the metals of the railway supplied a footing for him and his executioners—two private soldiers of the Federal army, directed by a sergeant who in civil life may have been a deputy sheriff. At a short remove upon the same temporary platform was an officer in the uniform of his rank, armed. He was a captain. A sentinel at each end of the bridge stood with his rifle in the position known as "support," that is to say, vertical in front of the left shoulder, the hammer resting on the forearm thrown straight across the chest—a formal and unnatural position, enforcing an erect carriage of the body. It did not appear to be the duty of these two men to know what was occurring at the centre of the bridge; they merely blockaded the two ends of the foot planking that traversed it.

Beyond one of the sentinels nobody was in sight; the railroad ran straight away into a forest for a hundred yards, then, curving, was lost to view. Doubtless there was an outpost farther along. The other bank of the stream was open ground—a gentle acclivity topped with a stockade of vertical tree trunks, loopholed for rifles, with a single embrasure through which protruded the muzzle of a brass cannon commanding the bridge. Midway of the slope between bridge and fort were the spectators—a single company of infantry in line, at "parade rest," the butts of the rifles on the ground, the barrels inclining slightly backward against the right shoulder, the hands crossed upon the stock. A lieutenant stood at the right of the line, the point of his sword upon the ground, his left hand resting upon his right. Excepting the group of four at the centre of the bridge, not a man moved. The company faced the bridge, staring stonily, motionless. The sentinels, facing the banks of the stream, might have been statues to adorn the bridge. The captain stood with folded arms, silent, observing the work of his subordinates, but making no sign. Death is a dignitary who when he comes announced is to be received with formal manifestations of respect, even by those most familiar with him. In the code of military etiquette silence and fixity are forms of deference.

The man who was engaged in being hanged was apparently about thirty-five years of age. He was a civilian, if one might judge from his habit, which was that of a planter. His features were good—a straight nose, firm mouth, broad forehead, from which his long, dark hair was combed straight back, falling behind his ears to the collar of his well-fitting frock-coat. He wore a mustache and pointed beard, but no whiskers; his eyes were large and dark gray, and had a kindly expression which one would hardly have expected in one whose neck was in the hemp. Evidently this was no vulgar assassin. The liberal military code makes provision for hanging many kinds of persons, and gentlemen are not excluded.

The preparations being complete, the two private soldiers stepped aside and each drew away the plank upon which he had been standing. The sergeant turned to the captain, saluted and placed himself immediately behind that officer, who in turn moved apart one pace. These movements left the condemned man and the sergeant standing on the two ends of the same plank, which spanned three of the cross-ties of the bridge. The end upon which the civilian stood almost, but not quite, reached a fourth. This plank had been held in place by the weight of the captain; it was now held by that of the sergeant. At a signal from the former the latter would step aside, the plank would tilt and the condemned man go down between two ties. The arrangement commended itself to his judgment as simple and effective. His face had not been covered nor his eyes bandaged. He looked a moment at his "unsteadfast footing," then let his gaze wander to the swirling water of the stream racing madly beneath his feet. A piece of dancing driftwood caught his attention and his eyes followed it down the current. How slowly it appeared to move! What a sluggish stream!

He closed his eyes in order to fix his last thoughts upon his wife and children. The water, touched to gold by the early sun, the brooding mists under the banks at some distance down the stream, the fort, the soldiers, the piece of drift—all had distracted him. And now he became conscious of a new disturbance. Striking through the thought of his dear ones was a sound which he could neither ignore nor understand, a sharp, distinct, metallic percussion like the stroke of a blacksmith's hammer upon the anvil; it had the same ringing quality. He wondered what it was, and whether immeasurably distant or near by—it seemed both. Its recurrence was regular, but as slow as the tolling of a death knell. He awaited each stroke with impatience and—he knew not why—apprehension. The intervals of silence grew progressively longer; the delays became maddening. With their greater infrequency the sounds increased in strength and sharpness. They hurt his ear like the thrust of a knife; he feared he would shriek. What he heard was the ticking of his watch.

He unclosed his eyes and saw again the water below him. "If I could free my hands," he thought, "I might throw off the noose and spring into the stream. By diving I could evade the bullets and, swimming vigorously, reach the bank, take to the woods and get away home. My home, thank God, is as yet outside their lines; my wife and little ones are still beyond the invader's farthest advance."

As these thoughts, which have here to be set down in words, were flashed into the doomed man's brain rather than evolved from it the captain nodded to the sergeant. The sergeant stepped aside.

II

Peyton Farquhar was a well-to-do planter, of an old and highly respected Alabama family. Being a slave owner and like other slave owners a politician he was naturally an original secessionist and ardently devoted to the Southern cause. Circumstances of an imperious nature, which it is unnecessary to relate here, had prevented him from taking service with the gallant army that had fought the disastrous campaigns ending with the fall of Corinth, and he chafed under the inglorious restraint, longing for the release of his energies, the larger life of the soldier, the opportunity for distinction. That opportunity, he felt, would come, as it comes to all in war time. Meanwhile he did what he could. No service was too humble for him to perform in aid of the South, no adventure too perilous for him to undertake if consistent with the character of a civilian who was at heart a soldier, and who in good faith and without too much qualification assented to at least a part of the frankly villainous dictum that all is fair in love and war.

One evening while Farquhar and his wife were sitting on a rustic bench near the entrance to his grounds, a gray-clad soldier rode up to the gate and asked for a drink of water. Mrs. Farquhar was only too happy to serve him with her own white hands. While she was fetching the water her husband approached the dusty horseman and inquired eagerly for news from the front.

"The Yanks are repairing the railroads," said the man, "and are getting ready for another advance. They have reached the Owl Creek bridge, put it in order and built a stockade on the north bank. The commandant has issued an order, which is posted everywhere, declaring that any civilian caught interfering with the railroad, its bridges, tunnels or trains will be summarily hanged. I saw the order."

"How far is it to the Owl Creek bridge?" Farquhar asked.

"About thirty miles."

"Is there no force on this side the creek?"

"Only a picket post half a mile out, on the railroad, and a single sentinel at this end of the bridge."

"Suppose a man—a civilian and student of hanging—should elude the picket post and perhaps get the better of the sentinel," said Farquhar, smiling, "what could he accomplish?"

The soldier reflected. "I was there a month ago," he replied. "I observed that the flood of last winter had lodged a great quantity of driftwood against the wooden pier at this end of the bridge. It is now dry and would burn like tow."

The lady had now brought the water, which the soldier drank. He thanked her ceremoniously, bowed to her husband and rode away. An hour later, after nightfall, he repassed the plantation, going northward in the direction from which he had come. He was a Federal scout.

III

As Peyton Farquhar fell straight downward through the bridge he lost consciousness and was as one already dead. From this state he was awakened—ages later, it seemed to him—by the pain of a sharp pressure upon his throat, followed by a sense of suffocation. Keen, poignant agonies seemed to shoot from his neck downward through every fibre of his body and limbs. These pains appeared to flash along well-defined lines of ramification and to beat with an inconceivably rapid periodicity. They seemed like streams of pulsating fire heating him to an intolerable temperature. As to his head, he was conscious of nothing but a feeling of fulness—of congestion. These sensations were unaccompanied by thought. The intellectual part of his nature was already effaced; he had power only to feel, and feeling was torment. He was conscious of motion. Encompassed in a luminous cloud, of which he was now merely the fiery heart, without material substance, he swung through unthinkable arcs of oscillation, like a vast pendulum. Then all at once, with terrible suddenness, the light about him shot upward with the noise of a loud plash; a frightful roaring was in his ears, and all was cold and dark. The power of thought was restored; he knew that the rope had broken and he had fallen into the stream. There was no additional strangulation; the noose about his neck was already suffocating him and kept the water from his lungs. To die of hanging at the bottom of a river!—the idea seemed to him ludicrous. He opened his eyes in the darkness and saw above him a gleam of light, but how distant, how inaccessible! He was still sinking, for the light became fainter and fainter until it was a mere glimmer. Then it began to grow and brighten, and he knew that he was rising toward the surface—knew it with reluctance, for he was now very comfortable. "To be hanged and drowned," he thought, "that is not so bad; but I do not wish to be shot. No; I will not be shot; that is not fair."

He was not conscious of an effort, but a sharp pain in his wrist apprised him that he was trying to free his hands. He gave the struggle his attention, as an idler might observe the feat of a juggler, without interest in the outcome. What splendid effort!—what magnificent, what superhuman strength! Ah, that was a fine endeavor! Bravo! The cord fell away; his arms parted and floated upward, the hands dimly seen on each side in the growing light. He watched them with a new interest as first one and then the other pounced upon the noose at his neck. They tore it away and thrust it fiercely aside, its undulations resembling those of a water-snake. "Put it back, put it back!" He thought he shouted these words to his hands, for the undoing of the noose had been succeeded by the direst pang that he had yet experienced. His neck ached horribly; his brain was on fire; his heart, which had been fluttering faintly, gave a great leap, trying to force itself out at his mouth. His whole body was racked and wrenched with an insupportable anguish! But his disobedient hands gave no heed to the command. They beat the water vigorously with quick, downward strokes, forcing him to the surface. He felt his head emerge; his eyes were blinded by the sunlight; his chest expanded convulsively, and with a supreme and crowning agony his lungs engulfed a great draught of air, which instantly he expelled in a shriek!

He was now in full possession of his physical senses. They were, indeed, preternaturally keen and alert. Something in the awful disturbance of his organic system had so exalted and refined them that they made record of things never before perceived. He felt the ripples upon his face and heard their separate sounds as they struck.

He looked at the forest on the bank of the stream, saw the individual trees, the leaves and the veining of each leaf—saw the very insects upon them: the locusts, the brilliant-bodied flies, the gray spiders stretching their webs from twig to twig. He noted the prismatic colors in all the dewdrops upon a million blades of grass. The humming of the gnats that danced above the eddies of the stream, the beating of the dragon-flies' wings, the strokes of the water-spiders' legs, like oars which had lifted their boat—all these made audible music. A fish slid along beneath his eyes and he heard the rush of its body parting the water.

He had come to the surface facing down the stream; in a moment the visible world seemed to wheel slowly round, himself the pivotal point, and he saw the bridge, the fort, the soldiers upon the bridge, the captain, the sergeant, the two privates, his executioners. They were in silhouette against the blue sky. They shouted and gesticulated, pointing at him. The captain had drawn his pistol, but did not fire; the others were unarmed. Their movements were grotesque and horrible, their forms gigantic.

Suddenly he heard a sharp report and something struck the water smartly within a few inches of his head, spattering his face with spray. He heard a second report, and saw one of the sentinels with his rifle at his shoulder, a light cloud of blue smoke rising from the muzzle. The man in the water saw the eye of the man on the bridge gazing into his own through the sights of the rifle. He observed that it was a gray eye and remembered having read that gray eyes were keenest, and that all famous marksmen had them. Nevertheless, this one had missed.

A counter-swirl had caught Farquhar and turned him half round; he was again looking into the forest on the bank opposite the fort. The sound of a clear, high voice in a monotonous singsong now rang out behind him and came across the water with a distinctness that pierced and subdued all other sounds, even the beating of the ripples in his ears. Although no soldier, he had frequented camps enough to know the dread significance of that deliberate, drawling, aspirated chant; the lieutenant on shore was taking a part in the morning's work. How coldly and pitilessly—with what an even, calm intonation, presaging, and enforcing tranquillity in the men—with what accurately measured intervals fell those cruel words:

"Attention, company! . . . Shoulder arms! . . . Ready! . . . Aim! . . . Fire!"

Farquhar dived—dived as deeply as he could. The water roared in his ears like the voice of Niagara, yet he heard the dulled thunder of the volley and, rising again toward the surface, met shining bits of metal, singularly flattened, oscillating slowly downward. Some of them touched him on the face and hands, then fell away, continuing their descent. One lodged between his collar and neck; it was uncomfortably warm and he snatched it out.

As he rose to the surface, gasping for breath, he saw that he had been a long time under water; he was perceptibly farther down stream—nearer to safety. The soldiers had almost finished reloading; the metal ramrods flashed all at once in the sunshine as they were drawn from the barrels, turned in the air, and thrust into their sockets. The two sentinels fired again, independently and ineffectually.

The hunted man saw all this over his shoulder; he was now swimming vigorously with the current. His brain was as energetic as his arms and legs; he thought with the rapidity of lightning.

"The officer," he reasoned, "will not make that martinet's error a second time. It is as easy to dodge a volley as a single shot. He has probably already given the command to fire at will. God help me, I cannot dodge them all!"

An appalling plash within two yards of him was followed by a loud, rushing sound, *diminuendo,* which seemed to travel back through the air to the fort and died in an explosion which stirred the very river to its deeps! A rising sheet of water curved over him, fell down upon him, blinded him, strangled him! The cannon had taken a hand in the game. As he shook his head free from the commotion of the smitten water he heard the deflected shot humming through the air ahead, and in an instant it was cracking and and smashing the branches in the forest beyond.

"They will not do that again," he thought; "the next time they will use a charge of grape. I must keep my eye upon the gun; the smoke will apprise me—the report arrives too late; it lags behind the missile. That is a good gun."

Suddenly he felt himself whirled round and round—spinning like a top. The water, the banks, the forests, the now distant bridge, fort and men—all were commingled and blurred. Objects were represented by their colors only; circular horizontal streaks of color—that was all he saw. He had been caught in a vortex and was being whirled on with a velocity of advance and gyration that made him giddy and sick. In a few moments he was flung upon the gravel at the foot of the left bank of the stream—the southern bank—and behind a projecting point which concealed him from his enemies. The sudden arrest of his motion, the abrasion of one of his hands on the gravel, restored him, and he wept with delight. He dug his fingers into the sand, threw it over himself in handfuls and audibly blessed it. It looked like diamonds, rubies, emeralds; he could think of nothing beautiful which it did not resemble. The trees upon the bank were giant garden plants; he noted a definite order in their arrangement, inhaled the fragrance of their blooms. A strange, roseate light shone through the spaces among their trunks and the wind made in their branches the music of æolian harps. He had no wish to perfect his escape—was content to remain in that enchanting spot until retaken.

A whiz and rattle of grapeshot among the branches high above his head roused him from his dream. The baffled cannoneer had fired him a random farewell. He sprang to his feet, rushed up the sloping bank, and plunged into the forest.

All that day he traveled, laying his course by the rounding sun. The forest seemed interminable; nowhere did he discover a break in it, not even a woodman's road. He had not known that he lived in so wild a region. There was something uncanny in the revelation.

By night fall he was fatigued, footsore, famishing. The thought of his wife and children urged him on. At last he found a road which led him in what he knew to be the right direction. It was as wide and straight as a city street, yet it seemed untraveled. No fields bordered it, no dwelling anywhere. Not so much as the barking of a dog suggested human habitation. The black bodies of the trees formed a straight wall on both sides, terminating on the horizon in a point, like a diagram in a lesson in perspective. Overhead, as he looked up through this rift in the wood, shone great golden stars looking unfamiliar and grouped in strange constellations. He was sure they were arranged in some order which had a secret and malign significance. The wood on either side was full of singular noises, among which—once, twice, and again, he distinctly heard whispers in an unknown tongue.

His neck was in pain and lifting his hand to it he found it horribly swollen. He knew that it had a circle of black where the rope had bruised it. His eyes felt congested; he could no longer close them. His tongue was swollen with thirst; he relieved its fever by thrusting it forward from between his teeth into the cold air. How softly the turf had carpeted the untraveled avenue—he could no longer feel the roadway beneath his feet!

Doubtless, despite his suffering, he had fallen asleep while walking, for now he sees another scene—perhaps he has merely recovered from a delirium. He stands at the gate of his own home. All is as he left it, and all bright and beautiful in the morning sunshine. He must have traveled the entire night. As he pushes open the gate and passes up the wide white walk, he sees a flutter of female garments; his wife, looking fresh and cool and sweet, steps down from the veranda to meet him. At the bottom of the steps she stands waiting, with a smile of ineffable joy, an attitude of matchless grace and dignity. Ah, how beautiful she is! He springs forward with extended arms. As he is about to clasp her he feels a stunning blow upon the back of the neck; a blinding white light blazes all about him with a sound like the shock of a cannon—then all is darkness and silence!

Peyton Farquhar was dead; his body, with a broken neck, swung gently from side to side beneath the timbers of the Owl Creek bridge.

❊   ❊   ❊

CHICKAMAUGA

One sunny autumn afternoon a child strayed away from its rude home in a small field and entered a forest unobserved. It was happy in a new sense of freedom from control, happy in the opportunity of exploration and adventure; for this child's spirit, in bodies of its ancestors, had for thousands of years been trained to memorable feats of discovery and conquest—victories in battles whose critical moments were centuries, whose victors' camps were cities of hewn stone. From the cradle of its race it had conquered its way through two continents and passing a great sea had penetrated a third, there to be born to war and dominion as a heritage.

The child was a boy aged about six years, the son of a poor planter. In his younger manhood the father had been a soldier, had fought against naked savages and followed the flag of his country into the capital of a civilized race to the far South. In the peaceful life of a planter the warrior-fire survived; once kindled, it is never extinguished. The man loved military books and pictures and the boy had understood enough to make himself a wooden sword, though even the eye of his father would hardly have known it for what it was. This weapon he now bore bravely, as became the son of an heroic race, and pausing now and again in the sunny space of the forest assumed, with some exaggeration, the postures of aggression and defense that he had been taught by the engraver's art. Made reckless by the ease with which he overcame invisible foes attempting to stay his advance, he committed the common enough military error of pushing the pursuit to a dangerous extreme, until he found himself upon the margin of a wide but shallow brook, whose rapid waters barred his direct advance against the flying foe that had crossed with illogical ease. But the intrepid victor was not to be baffled; the spirit of the race which had passed the great sea burned unconquerable in that small breast and would not be denied. Finding a place where some bowlders in the bed of the stream lay but a step or a leap apart, he made his way across and fell again upon the rear-guard of his imaginary foe, putting all to the sword.

Now that the battle had been won, prudence required that he withdraw to his base of operations. Alas; like many a mightier conqueror, and like one, the mightiest, he could not

> curb the lust for war,
> Nor learn that tempted Fate will leave the loftiest star.

Advancing from the bank of the creek he suddenly found himself confronted with a new and more formidable enemy: in the path that he was following, sat, bolt upright, with ears erect and paws suspended before it, a rabbit! With a startled cry the child turned and fled, he knew not in what direction, calling with inarticulate cries for his mother, weeping, stumbling, his tender skin cruelly torn by brambles, his little heart beating hard with terror—breathless, blind with tears—lost in the forest! Then, for more than an hour, he wandered with erring feet through the tangled undergrowth, till at last, overcome by fatigue, he lay down in a narrow space between two rocks, within a few yards of the stream and still grasping his toy sword, no longer a weapon but a companion, sobbed himself to sleep. The wood birds sang merrily above his head; the squirrels, whisking their bravery of tail, ran barking from tree to tree, unconscious of the pity of it, and somewhere far away was a strange, muffled thunder, as if the partridges were drumming in celebration of nature's victory over the son of her immemorial enslavers. And back at the little plantation, where white men and black were hastily searching the fields and hedges in alarm, a mother's heart was breaking for her missing child.

Hours passed, and then the little sleeper rose to his feet. The chill of the evening was in his limbs, the fear of the gloom in his heart. But he had rested, and he no longer wept. With some blind instinct which impelled to action he struggled through the undergrowth about him and came to a more open ground—on his right the brook, to the left a gentle acclivity studded with infrequent trees; over all, the gathering gloom of twilight. A thin, ghostly mist rose along the water. It frightened and repelled him; instead of recrossing, in the direction whence he had come, he turned his back upon it, and went forward toward the dark inclosing wood. Suddenly he saw before him a strange moving object which he took to be some large animal—a dog, a pig—he could not name it; perhaps it was a bear. He had seen pictures of bears, but knew of nothing to their discredit and had vaguely wished to meet one. But something in form or movement of this object—something in the awkwardness of its approach—told him that it was not a bear, and curiosity was stayed by fear. He stood still and as it came slowly on gained courage every moment, for he saw that at least it had not the long, menacing ears of the rabbit. Possibly his impressionable mind was half conscious of something familiar in its shambling, awkward gait. Before it had approached near enough to resolve his doubts he saw that it was followed by another and another. To right and to left were many more; the whole open space about him was alive with them—all moving toward the brook.

They were men. They crept upon their hands and knees. They used their hands only, dragging their legs. They used their knees only, their arms hanging idle at their sides. They strove to rise to their feet, but fell prone in the attempt. They did nothing naturally, and nothing alike, save only to advance foot by foot in the same direction. Singly, in pairs and in little groups, they came on through the gloom, some halting now and again while others crept slowly past them, then resuming their movement. They came by dozens and by hundreds; as far on either hand as one could see in the deepening gloom they extended and the black wood behind them appeared to be inexhaustible. The very ground seemed in motion toward the creek. Occasionally one who had paused did not again go on, but lay motionless. He was dead. Some, pausing, made strange gestures with their hands, erected their arms and lowered them again, clasped their heads; spread their palms upward, as men are sometimes seen to do in public prayer.

Not all of this did the child note; it is what would have been noted by an elder observer; he saw little but that these were men, yet crept like babes. Being men, they were not terrible, though unfamiliarly clad. He moved among them freely, going from one to another and peering into their faces with childish curiosity. All their faces were singularly white and many were streaked and gouted with red. Something in this—something too, perhaps, in their grotesque attitudes and movements—reminded him of the painted clown whom he had seen last summer in the circus, and he laughed as he watched them. But on and ever on they crept, these maimed and bleeding men, as heedless as he of the dramatic contrast between his laughter and their own ghastly gravity. To him it was a merry spectacle. He had seen his father's negroes creep upon their hands and knees for his amusement—had ridden them so, "making believe" they were his horses. He now approached one of these crawling figures from behind and with an agile movement mounted it astride. The man sank upon his breast, recovered, flung the small boy fiercely to the ground as an unbroken colt might have done, then turned upon him a face that lacked a lower jaw—from the upper teeth to the throat was a great red gap fringed with hanging shreds of flesh and splinters of bone. The unnatural prominence of nose, the absence of chin, the fierce eyes, gave this man the appearance of a great bird of prey crimsoned in throat and breast by the blood of its quarry. The man rose to his knees, the child to his feet. The man shook his fist at the child; the child, terrified at last, ran to a tree near by, got upon the farther side of it and took a more serious view of the situation. And so the clumsy multitude dragged itself slowly and painfully along in hideous pantomime—moved forward down the slope like a swarm of great black beetles, with never a sound of going—in silence profound, absolute.

Instead of darkening, the haunted landscape began to brighten. Through the belt of trees beyond the brook shone a strange red light, the trunks and branches of the trees making a black lacework against it. It struck the creeping figures and gave them monstrous shadows, which caricatured their movements on the lit grass. It fell upon their faces, touching their whiteness with a ruddy tinge, accentuating the stains with which so many of them were freaked and maculated. It sparkled on buttons and bits of metal in their clothing. Instinctively the child turned toward the growing splendor and moved down the slope with his horrible companions; in a few moments had passed the foremost of the throng—not much of a feat, considering his advantages. He placed himself in the lead, his wooden sword still in hand, and solemnly directed the march, conforming his pace to theirs and occasionally turning as if to see that his forces did not straggle. Surely such a leader never before had such a following.

Scattered about upon the ground now slowly narrowing by the

encroachment of this awful march to water, were certain articles to which, in the leader's mind, were coupled no significant associations: an occasional blanket, tightly rolled lengthwise, doubled and the ends bound together with a string; a heavy knapsack here, and there a broken rifle—such things, in short, as are found in the rear of retreating troops, the "spoor" of men flying from their hunters. Everywhere near the creek, which here had a margin of lowland, the earth was trodden into mud by the feet of men and horses. An observer of better experience in the use of his eyes would have noticed that these footprints pointed in both directions; the ground had been twice passed over—in advance and in retreat. A few hours before, these desperate, stricken men, with their more fortunate and now distant comrades, had penetrated the forest in thousands. Their successive battalions, breaking into swarms and re-forming in lines, had passed the child on every side—had almost trodden on him as he slept. The rustle and murmur of their march had not awakened him. Almost within a stone's throw of where he lay they had fought a battle; but all unheard by him were the roar of the musketry, the shock of the cannon, "the thunder of the captains and the shouting." He had slept through it all, grasping his little wooden sword with perhaps a tighter clutch in unconscious sympathy with his martial environment, but as heedless of the grandeur of the struggle as the dead who had died to make the glory.

The fire beyond the belt of woods on the farther side of the creek, reflected to earth from the canopy of its own smoke, was now suffusing the whole landscape. It transformed the sinuous line of mist to the vapor of gold. The water gleamed with dashes of red, and red, too, were many of the stones protruding above the surface. But that was blood; the less desperately wounded had stained them in crossing. On them, too, the child now crossed with eager steps; he was going to the fire. As he stood upon the farther bank he turned about to look at the companions of his march. The advance was arriving at the creek. The stronger had already drawn themselves to the brink and plunged their faces into the flood. Three or four who lay without motion appeared to have no heads. At this the child's eyes expanded with wonder; even his hospitable understanding could not accept a phenomenon implying such vitality as that. After slaking their thirst these men had not had the strength to back away from the water, nor to keep their heads above it. They were drowned. In rear of these, the open spaces of the forest showed the leader as many formless figures of his grim command as at first; but not nearly so many were in motion. He waved his cap for their en couragement and smilingly pointed with his weapon in the direction of the guiding light—a pillar of fire to this strange exodus.

Confident of the fidelity of his forces, he now entered the belt of woods, passed through it easily in the red illumination, climbed a fence, ran across a field, turning now and again to coquet with his responsive shadow, and so approached the blazing ruin of a dwelling. Desolation everywhere! In all the wide glare not a living thing was visible. He cared nothing for that; the spectacle pleased, and he danced with glee in imitation of the wavering flames. He ran about, collecting fuel, but every object that he found was too heavy for him to cast in from the distance to which the heat limited his approach. In despair he flung in his sword—a surrender to the superior forces of nature. His military career was at an end.

Shifting his position, his eyes fell upon some outbuildings which had an oddly familiar appearance, as if he had dreamed of them. He stood considering them with wonder, when suddenly the entire plantation, with its inclosing forest, seemed to turn as if upon a pivot. His little world swung half around; the points of the compass were reversed. He recognized the blazing building as his own home!

For a moment he stood stupefied by the power of the revelation, then ran with stumbling feet, making a half-circuit of the ruin. There, conspicuous in the light of the conflagration, lay the dead body of a woman—the white face turned upward, the hands thrown out and clutched full of grass, the clothing deranged, the long dark hair in tangles and full of clotted blood. The greater part of the forehead was torn away, and from the jagged hole the brain protruded, overflowing the temple, a frothy mass of gray, crowned with clusters of crimson bubbles—the work of a shell.

The child moved his little hands, making wild, uncertain gestures. He uttered a series of inarticulate and indescribable cries—something between the chattering of an ape and the gobbling of a turkey—a startling, soulless, unholy sound, the language of a devil. The child was a deaf mute.

Then he stood motionless, with quivering lips, looking down upon the wreck.

THE COUP DE GRÂCE

The fighting had been hard and continuous; that was attested by all
the senses. The very taste of battle was in the air. All was now over;
it remained only to succor the wounded and bury the dead—to "tidy
up a bit," as the humorist of a burial squad put it. A good deal of
"tidying up" was required. As far as one could see through the forests, among the splintered trees, lay wrecks of men and horses. Among
them moved the stretcher-bearers, gathering and carrying away the
few who showed signs of life. Most of the wounded had died of
neglect while the right to minister to their wants was in dispute. It
is an army regulation that the wounded must wait; the best way to
care for them is to win the battle. It must be confessed that victory
is a distinct advantage to a man requiring attention, but many do not
live to avail themselves of it.

The dead were collected in groups of a dozen or a score and laid
side by side in rows while the trenches were dug to receive them.
Some, found at too great a distance from these rallying points, were
buried where they lay. There was little attempt at identification,
though in most cases, the burial parties being detailed to glean the
same ground which they had assisted to reap, the names of the victorious dead were known and listed. The enemy's fallen had to be content with counting. But of that they got enough: many of them were
counted several times, and the total, as given afterward in the official
report of the victorious commander, denoted rather a hope than a
result.

At some little distance from the spot where one of the burial
parties had established its "bivouac of the dead," a man in the uniform of a Federal officer stood leaning against a tree. From his feet
upward to his neck his attitude was that of weariness reposing; but
he turned his head uneasily from side to side; his mind was apparently not at rest. He was perhaps uncertain in which direction to
go; he was not likely to remain long where he was, for already the
level rays of the setting sun straggled redly through the open spaces
of the wood and the weary soldiers were quitting their task for the
day. He would hardly make a night of it alone there among
the dead. Nine men in ten whom you meet after a battle inquire the
way to some fraction of the army—as if any one could know. Doubt-

less this officer was lost. After resting himself a moment he would presumably follow one of the retiring burial squads.

When all were gone he walked straight away into the forest toward the red west, its light staining his face like blood. The air of confidence with which he now strode along showed that he was on familiar ground; he had recovered his bearings. The dead on his right and on his left were unregarded as he passed. An occasional low moan from some sorely-stricken wretch whom the relief-parties had not reached, and who would have to pass a comfortless night beneath the stars with his thirst to keep him company, was equally unheeded. What, indeed, could the officer have done, being no surgeon and having no water?

At the head of a shallow ravine, a mere depression of the ground, lay a small group of bodies. He saw, and swerving suddenly from his course walked rapidly toward them. Scanning each one sharply as he passed, he stopped at last above one which lay at a slight remove from the others, near a clump of small trees. He looked at it narrowly. It seemed to stir. He stooped and laid his hand upon its face. It screamed.

The officer was Captain Downing Madwell, of a Massachusetts regiment of infantry, a daring and intelligent soldier, an honorable man.

In the regiment were two brothers named Halcrow—Caffal and Creede Halcrow. Caffal Halcrow was a sergeant in Captain Madwell's company, and these two men, the sergeant and the captain, were devoted friends. In so far as disparity of rank, difference in duties and considerations of military discipline would permit they were commonly together. They had, indeed, grown up together from childhood. A habit of the heart is not easily broken off. Caffal Halcrow had nothing military in his taste nor disposition, but the thought of separation from his friend was disagreeable; he enlisted in the company in which Madwell was second-lieutenant. Each had taken two steps upward in rank, but between the highest non-commissioned and the lowest commissioned officer the gulf is deep and wide and the old relation was maintained with difficulty and a difference.

Creede Halcrow, the brother of Caffal, was the major of the regiment—a cynical, saturnine man, between whom and Captain Madwell there was a natural antipathy which circumstances had nourished and strengthened to an active animosity. But for the restraining influence of their mutual relation to Caffal these two patriots would doubtless have endeavored to deprive their country of each other's services.

At the opening of the battle that morning the regiment was performing outpost duty a mile away from the main army. It was attacked and nearly surrounded in the forest, but stubbornly held its ground. During a lull in the fighting, Major Halcrow came to Captain Madwell. The two exchanged formal salutes, and the major said: "Captain, the colonel directs that you push your company to the head of this ravine and hold your place there until recalled. I need hardly apprise you of the dangerous character of the movement, but if you wish, you can, I suppose, turn over the command to your first-lieutenant. I was not, however, directed to authorize the substitution; it is merely a suggestion of my own, unofficially made."

To this deadly insult Captain Madwell coolly replied:

"Sir, I invite you to accompany the movement. A mounted officer would be a conspicuous mark, and I have long held the opinion that it would be better if you were dead."

The art of repartee was cultivated in military circles as early as 1862.

A half-hour later Captain Madwell's company was driven from its position at the head of the ravine, with a loss of one-third its number. Among the fallen was Sergeant Halcrow. The regiment was soon afterward forced back to the main line, and at the close of the battle was miles away. The captain was now standing at the side of the subordinate and friend.

Sergeant Halcrow was mortally hurt. His clothing was deranged; it seemed to have been violently torn apart, exposing the abdomen. Some of the buttons of his jacket had been pulled off and lay on the ground beside him and fragments of his other garments were strewn about. His leather belt was parted and had apparently been dragged from beneath him as he lay. There had been no great effusion of blood. The only visible wound was a wide, ragged opening in the abdomen. It was defiled with earth and dead leaves. Protruding from it was a loop of small intestine. In all his experience Captain Madwell had not seen a wound like this. He could neither conjecture how it was made nor explain the attendant circumstances —the strangely torn clothing, the parted belt, the besmirching of the white skin. He knelt and made a closer examination. When he rose to his feet, he turned his eyes in different directions as if looking for an enemy. Fifty yards away, on the crest of a low, thinly wooded hill, he saw several dark objects moving about among the fallen men—a herd of swine. One stood with its back to him, its shoulders sharply elevated. Its forefeet were upon a human body, its head was depressed and invisible. The bristly ridge of its chine showed black against the red west. Captain Madwell drew away his eyes and fixed them again upon the thing which had been his friend.

The man who had suffered these monstrous mutilations was alive. At intervals he moved his limbs; he moaned at every breath. He stared blankly into the face of his friend and if touched screamed. In his giant agony he had torn up the ground on which he lay; his clenched hands were full of leaves and twigs and earth. Articulate speech was beyond his power; it was impossible to know if he were sensible to anything but pain. The expression of his face was an appeal; his eyes were full of prayer. For what?

There was no misreading that look; the captain had too frequently seen it in eyes of those whose lips had still the power to formulate it by an entreaty for death. Consciously or unconsciously, this writhing fragment of humanity, this type and example of acute sensation, this handiwork of man and beast, this humble unheroic Prometheus, was imploring everything, all, the whole non-ego, for the boon of oblivion. To the earth and the sky alike, to the trees, to the man, to whatever took form in sense or consciousness, this incarnate suffering addressed that silent plea.

For what, indeed? For that which we accord to even the meanest creature without sense to demand it, denying it only to the wretched of our own race: for the blessed release, the rite of uttermost compassion, the *coup de grâce.*

Captain Madwell spoke the name of his friend. He repeated it over and over without effect until emotion choked his utterance. His tears splashed upon the livid face beneath his own and blinded himself. He saw nothing but a blurred and moving object, but the moans were more distinct than ever, interrupted at briefer intervals by sharper shrieks. He turned away, struck his hand upon his forehead, and strode from the spot. The swine, catching sight of him, threw up their crimson muzzles, regarding him suspiciously a second, and then with a gruff, concerted grunt, raced away out of sight. A horse, its foreleg splintered by a cannon-shot, lifted its head sidewise from the ground and neighed piteously. Madwell stepped forward, drew his revolver and shot the poor beast between the eyes, narrowly observing its death-struggle, which, contrary to his expectation, was violent and long; but at last it lay still. The tense muscles of its lips, which had uncovered the teeth in a horrible grin, relaxed; the sharp, clean-cut profile took on a look of profound peace and rest.

Along the distant, thinly wooded crest to westward the fringe of sunset fire had now nearly burned itself out. The light upon the trunks of the trees had faded to a tender gray; shadows were in their tops, like great dark birds aperch. Night was coming and there were miles of haunted forest between Captain Madwell and camp. Yet he stood there at the side of the dead animal, apparently lost to all sense of his surroundings. His eyes were bent upon the earth at his feet; his left hand hung loosely at his side, his right still held the pistol. Presently he lifted his face, turned it toward his dying friend and walked rapidly back to his side. He knelt upon one knee, cocked the weapon, placed the muzzle against the man's forehead, and turning away his eyes pulled the trigger. There was no report. He had used his last cartridge for the horse.

The sufferer moaned and his lips moved convulsively. The froth that ran from them had a tinge of blood.

Captain Madwell rose to his feet and drew his sword from the scabbard. He passed the fingers of his left hand along the edge from hilt to point. He held it out straight before him, as if to test his nerves. There was no visible tremor of the blade; the ray of bleak skylight that it reflected was steady and true. He stooped and with his left hand tore away the dying man's shirt, rose and placed the point of the sword just over the heart. This time he did not withdraw his eyes. Grasping the hilt with both hands, he thrust downward with all his strength and weight. The blade sank into the man's body—through his body into the earth; Captain Madwell came near falling forward, upon his work. The dying man drew up his knees and at the same time threw his right arm across his breast and grasped the steel so tightly that the knuckles of the hand visibly whitened. By a violent but vain effort to withdraw the blade the wound was enlarged; a rill of blood escaped, running sinuously down into the deranged clothing. At that moment three men stepped silently forward from behind the clump of young trees which had concealed their approach. Two were hospital attendants and carried a stretcher.

The third was Major Creede Halcrow.

ONE OFFICER, ONE MAN

Captain Graffenreid stood at the head of his company. The regiment was not engaged. It formed a part of the front line-of-battle, which stretched away to the right with a visible length of nearly two miles through the open ground. The left flank was veiled by woods; to the right also the line was lost to sight, but it extended many miles. A hundred yards in rear was a second line; behind this, the reserve brigades and divisions in column. Batteries of artillery occupied the spaces between and crowned the low hills. Groups of horsemen—generals with their staffs and escorts, and field officers of regiments behind the colors—broke the regularity of the lines and columns. Numbers of these figures of interest had field-glasses at their eyes and sat motionless, stolidly scanning the country in front; others came and went at a slow canter, bearing orders. There were squads of stretcher-bearers, ambulances, wagon-trains with ammunition, and officers' servants in rear of all—of all that was visible—for still in rear of these, along the roads, extended for many miles all that vast multitude of non-combatants who with their various *impedimenta* are assigned to the inglorious but important duty of supplying the fighters' many needs.

An army in line-of-battle awaiting attack, or prepared to deliver it, presents strange contrasts. At the front are precision, formality, fixity, and silence. Toward the rear these characteristics are less and less conspicuous, and finally, in point of space, are lost altogether in confusion, motion and noise. The homogeneous becomes heterogeneous. Definition is lacking; repose is replaced by an apparently purposeless activity; harmony vanishes in hubbub, form in disorder. Commotion everywhere and ceaseless unrest. The men who do not fight are never ready.

From his position at the right of his company in the front rank, Captain Graffenreid had an unobstructed outlook toward the enemy. A half-mile of open and nearly level ground lay before him, and beyond it an irregular wood, covering a slight acclivity; not a human being anywhere visible. He could imagine nothing more peaceful than the appearance of that pleasant landscape with its long stretches of brown fields over which the atmosphere was beginning to quiver in the heat of the morning sun. Not a sound came from forest or field—not even the barking of a dog or the crowing of a cock at the half-seen plantation house on the crest among the trees. Yet every man in those miles of men knew that he and death were face to face.

Captain Graffenreid had never in his life seen an armed enemy, and the war in which his regiment was one of the first to take the field was two years old. He had had the rare advantage of a military education, and when his comrades had marched to the front he had been detached for administrative service at the capital of his State, where it was thought that he could be most useful. Like a bad soldier he protested, and like a good one obeyed. In close official and personal relations with the governor of his State, and enjoying his confidence and favor, he had firmly refused promotion and seen his juniors elevated above him. Death had been busy in his distant regiment; vacancies among the field officers had occurred again and again; but from a chivalrous feeling that war's rewards belonged of right to those who bore the storm and stress of battle he had held his humble rank and generously advanced the fortunes of others. His silent devotion to principle had conquered at last: he had been relieved of his hateful duties and ordered to the front, and now, untried by fire, stood in the van of battle in command of a company of hardy veterans, to whom he had been only a name, and that name a by-word. By none—not even by those of his brother officers in whose favor he had waived his rights—was his devotion to duty understood. They were too busy to be just; he was looked upon as one who had shirked his duty, until forced unwillingly into the field. Too proud to explain, yet not too insensible to feel, he could only endure and hope.

Of all the Federal Army on that summer morning none had accepted battle more joyously than Anderton Graffenreid. His spirit was buoyant, his faculties were riotous. He was in a state of mental exaltation and scarcely could endure the enemy's tardiness in advancing to the attack. To him this was opportunity—for the result he cared nothing. Victory or defeat, as God might will; in one or in the other he should prove himself a soldier and a hero; he should vindicate his right to the respect of his men and the companionship of his brother officers—to the consideration of his superiors. How his heart leaped in his breast as the bugle sounded the stirring notes of the "assembly"! With what a light tread, scarcely conscious of the earth beneath his feet, he strode forward at the head of his company, and how exultingly he noted the tactical dispositions which placed his regiment in the front line! And if perchance some memory came to him of a pair of dark eyes that might take on a tenderer light in reading the account of that day's doings, who shall blame him for the unmartial thought or count it a debasement of soldierly ardor?

Suddenly, from the forest a half-mile in front—apparently from among the upper branches of the trees, but really from the ridge beyond—rose a tall column of white smoke. A moment later came a deep, jarring explosion, followed—almost attended—by a hideous rushing sound that semed to leap forward across the intervening space with inconceivable rapidity, rising from whisper to roar with too quick a gradation for attention to note the successive stages of its horrible progression! A visible tremor ran along the lines of men; all were startled into motion. Captain Graffenreid dodged and threw up his hands to one side of his head, palms outward. As he did so he heard a keen, ringing report, and saw on a hillside behind the line a fierce roll of smoke and dust—the shell's explosion. It had passed a hundred feet to his left! He heard, or fancied he heard, a low, mocking laugh and turning in the direction whence it came saw the eyes of his first lieutenant fixed upon him with an unmistakable look of amusement. He looked along the line of faces in the front ranks. The men were laughing. At him? The thought restored the color to his bloodless face—restored too much of it. His cheeks burned with a fever of shame.

The enemy's shot was not answered: the officer in command at that exposed part of the line had evidently no desire to provoke a cannonade. For the forbearance Captain Graffenreid was conscious of a sense of gratitude. He had not known that the flight of a projectile was a phenomenon of so appalling character. His conception of war had already undergone a profound change, and he was conscious that his new feeling was manifesting itself in visible perturbation. His blood was boiling in his veins; he had a choking sensation and felt that if he had a command to give it would be inaudible, or at least unintelligible. The hand in which he held his sword trembled; the other moved automatically, clutching at various parts of his clothing. He found a difficulty in standing still and fancied that his men observed it. Was it fear? He feared it was.

From somewhere away to the right came, as the wind served, a low, intermittent murmur like that of ocean in a storm—like that of a distant railway train—like that of wind among the pines—three sounds so nearly alike that the ear, unaided by the judgment, cannot distinguish them one from another. The eyes of the troops were drawn in that direction; the mounted officers turned their field-glasses that way. Mingled with the sound was an irregular throbbing. He thought it, at first, the beating of his fevered blood in his ears; next, the distant tapping of a bass drum.

"The ball is opened on the right flank," said an officer.

Captain Granffenreid understood: the sounds were musketry and artillery. He nodded and tried to smile. There was apparently nothing infectious in the smile.

Presently a light line of blue smoke-puffs broke out along the edge of the wood in front, succeeded by a crackle of rifles. There were keen, sharp hissings in the air, terminating abruptly with a thump near by. The man at Captain Graffenreid's side dropped his rifle; his knees gave way and he pitched awkwardly forward, falling upon his face. Somebody shouted "Lie down!" and the dead man was hardly distinguishable from the living. It looked as if those few rifle-shots had slain ten thousand men. Only the field officers remained erect; their concession to the emergency consisted in dismounting and sending their horses to the shelter of the low hills immediately in rear.

Captain Graffenreid lay alongside the dead man, from beneath whose breast flowed a little rill of blood. It had a faint, sweetish odor that sickened him. The face was crushed into the earth and flattened. It looked yellow already, and was repulsive. Nothing suggested the glory of a soldier's death nor mitigated the loathsomeness of the incident. He could not turn his back upon the body without facing away from his company.

He fixed his eyes upon the forest, where all again was silent. He tried to imagine what was going on there—the lines of troops forming to attack, the guns being pushed forward by hand to the edge of the open. He fancied he could see their black muzzles protruding from the undergrowth, ready to deliver their storm of missiles—such missiles as the one whose shriek had so unsettled his nerves. The distension of his eyes became painful; a mist seemed to gather before them; he could no longer see across the field, yet would not withdraw his gaze lest he see the dead man at his side.

The fire of battle was not now burning very brightly in this warrior's soul. From inaction had come introspection. He sought rather to analyze his feelings than distinguish himself by courage and devotion. The result was profoundly disappointing. He covered his face with his hands and groaned aloud.

The hoarse murmur of battle grew more and more distinct upon the right; the murmur had, indeed, become a roar, the throbbing, a thunder. The sounds had worked round obliquely to the front; evidently the enemy's left was being driven back, and the propitious moment to move against the salient angle of his line would soon arrive. The silence and mystery in front were ominous; all felt that they boded evil to the assailants.

Behind the prostrate lines sounded the hoofbeats of galloping horses; the men turned to look. A dozen staff officers were riding to the various brigade and regimental commanders, who had remounted. A moment more and there was a chorus of voices, all uttering out of time the same words—"Attention, battalion!" The men sprang to their feet and were aligned by the company commanders. They awaited the word "Forward"—awaited, too, with beating hearts and set teeth the gusts of lead and iron that were to smite them at their first movement in obedience to that word. The word was not given; the tempest did not break out. The delay was hideous, maddening! It unnerved like a respite at the guillotine.

Captain Graffenreid stood at the head of his company, the dead man at his feet. He heard the battle on the right—rattle and crash of musketry, ceaseless thunder of cannon, desultory cheers of invisible combatants. He marked ascending clouds of smoke from distant forests. He noted the sinister silence of the forest in front. These contrasting extremes affected the whole range of his sensibilities. The strain upon his nervous organization was insupportable. He grew hot and cold by turns. He panted like a dog, and then forgot to breathe until reminded by vertigo.

Suddenly he grew calm. Glancing downward, his eyes had fallen upon his naked sword, as he held it, point to earth. Foreshortened to his view, it resembled somewhat, he thought, the short heavy blade of the ancient Roman. The fancy was full of suggestion, malign, fateful, heroic!

The sergeant in the rear rank, immediately behind Captain Graffenreid, now observed a strange sight. His attention drawn by an uncommon movement made by the captain—a sudden reaching forward of the hands and their energetic withdrawal, throwing the elbows out, as in pulling an oar—he saw spring from between the officer's shoulders a bright point of metal which prolonged itself outward, nearly a half-arm's length—a blade! It was faintly streaked with crimson, and its point approached so near to the sergeant's breast, and with so quick a movement, that he shrank backward in alarm. That moment Captain Graffenreid pitched heavily forward upon the dead man and died.

A week later the major-general commanding the left corps of the Federal Army submitted the following official report:

"Sir: I have the honor to report, with regard to the action of the

19th inst., that owing to the enemy's withdrawal from my front to reinforce his beaten left, my command was not seriously engaged. My loss was as follows: Killed, one officer, one man."

❈   ❈   ❈

THE STORY OF A CONSCIENCE

I

Captain Parrol Hartroy stood at the advanced post of his picket-guard, talking in low tones with the sentinel. This post was on a turnpike which bisected the captain's camp, a half-mile in rear, though the camp was not in sight from that point. The officer was apparently giving the soldier certain instructions—was perhaps merely inquiring if all were quiet in front. As the two stood talking a man approached them from the direction of the camp, carelessly whistling, and was promptly halted by the soldier. He was evidently a civilian—a tall person, coarsely clad in the home-made stuff of yellow gray, called "butternut," which was men's only wear in the latter days of the Confederacy. On his head was a slouch felt hat, once white, from beneath which hung masses of uneven hair, seemingly unacquainted with either scissors or comb. The man's face was rather striking; a broad forehead, high nose, and thin cheeks, the mouth invisible in the full dark beard, which seemed as neglected as the hair. The eyes were large and had that steadiness and fixity of attention which so frequently mark a considering intelligence and a will not easily turned from its purpose—so say those physiognomists who have that kind of eyes. On the whole, this was a man whom one would be likely to observe and be observed by. He carried a walking-stick freshly cut from the forest and his ailing cowskin boots were white with dust.

"Show your pass," said the Federal soldier, a trifle more imperiously perhaps than he would have thought necessary if he had not been under the eye of his commander, who with folded arms looked on from the roadside.

"'Lowed you'd rec'lect me, Gineral," said the wayfarer tranquilly, while producing the paper from the pocket of his coat. There was something in his tone—perhaps a faint suggestion of irony—which

made his elevation of his obstructor to exalted rank less agreeable
to that worthy warrior than promotion is commonly found to be.
"You-all have to be purty pertickler, I reckon," he added, in a more
conciliatory tone, as if in half-apology for being halted.

Having read the pass, with his rifle resting on the ground, the
soldier handed the document back without a word, shouldered his
weapon, and returned to his commander. The civilian passed on in
the middle of the road, and when he had penetrated the circumja-
cent Confederacy a few yards resumed his whistling and was soon
out of sight beyond an angle in the road, which at that point entered
a thin forest. Suddenly the officer undid his arms from his breast,
drew a revolver from his belt and sprang forward at a run in the
same direction, leaving his sentinel in gaping astonishment at his
post. After making to the various visible forms of nature a solemn
promise to be damned, that gentleman resumed the air of stolidity
which is supposed to be appropriate to a state of alert military attention.

II

Captain Hartroy held an independent command. His force consisted of a company of infantry, a squadron of cavalry, and a section
of artillery, detached from the army to which they belonged, to
defend an important defile in the Cumberland Mountains in Tennessee. It was a field officer's command held by a line officer promoted from the ranks, where he had quietly served until "discovered."
His post was one of exceptional peril; its defense entailed a heavy
responsibility and he had wisely been given corresponding discre-
tionary powers, all the more necessary because of his distance from
the main army, the precarious nature of his communications and
the lawless character of the enemy's irregular troops infesting that
region. He had strongly fortified his little camp, which embraced
a village of a half-dozen dwellings and a country store, and had
collected a considerable quantity of supplies. To a few resident
civilians of known loyalty, with whom it was desirable to trade, and
of whose services in various ways he sometimes availed himself, he
had given written passes admitting them within his lines. It is easy
to understand that an abuse of this privilege in the interest of the
enemy might entail serious consequences. Captain Hartroy had made
an order to the effect that any one so abusing it would be summarily
shot.

While the sentinel had been examining the civilian's pass the captain had eyed the latter narrowly. He thought his appearance familiar and had at first no doubt of having given him the pass which had satisfied the sentinel. It was not until the man had got out of sight and hearing that his identity was disclosed by a revealing light from memory. With soldierly promptness of decision the officer had acted on the revelation.

III

To any but a singularly self-possessed man the apparition of an officer of the military forces, formidably clad, bearing in one hand a sheathed sword and in the other a cocked revolver, and rushing in furious pursuit, is no doubt disquieting to a high degree; upon the man to whom the pursuit was in this instance directed it appeared to have no other effect than somewhat to intensify his tranquillity. He might easily enough have escaped into the forest to the right or the left, but chose another course of action—turned and quietly faced the captain, saying as he came up: "I reckon ye must have something to say to me, which ye disremembered. What mout it be, neighbor?"

But the "neighbor" did not answer, being engaged in the unneighborly act of covering him with a cocked pistol.

"Surrender," said the captain as calmly as a slight breathlessness from exertion would permit, "or you die."

There was no menace in the manner of this demand; that was all in the matter and in the means of enforcing it. There was, too, something not altogether reassuring in the cold gray eyes that glanced along the barrel of the weapon. For a moment the two men stood looking at each other in silence; then the civilian, with no appearance of fear—with as great apparent unconcern as when complying with the less austere demand of the sentinel—slowly pulled from his pocket the paper which had satisfied that humble functionary and held it out, saying:

"I reckon this 'ere parss from Mister Hartroy is——"

"The pass is a forgery," the officer said, interrupting. "I am Captain Hartroy—and you are Dramer Brune."

It would have required a sharp eye to observe the slight pallor of the civilian's face at these words, and the only other manifestation attesting their significance was a voluntary relaxation of the thumb and fingers holding the dishonored paper, which, falling to the road, unheeded, was rolled by a gentle wind and then lay still, with a coating of dust, as in humiliation for the lie that it bore. A moment later the civilian, still looking unmoved into the barrel of the pistol, said:

"Yes, I am Dramer Brune, a Confederate spy, and your prisoner. I have on my person, as you will soon discover, a plan of your fort and its armament, a statement of the distribution of your men and their number, a map of the approaches, showing the positions of all your outposts. My life is fairly yours, but if you wish it taken in a more formal way than by your own hand, and if you are willing to spare me the indignity of marching into camp at the muzzle of your pistol, I promise you that I will neither resist, escape, nor remonstrate, but will submit to whatever penalty may be imposed."

The officer lowered his pistol, uncocked it, and thrust it into its place in his belt. Brune advanced a step, extending his right hand.

"It is the hand of a traitor and a spy," said the officer coldly, and did not take it. The other bowed.

"Come," said the captain, "let us go to camp; you shall not die until to-morrow morning."

He turned his back upon his prisoner, and these two enigmatical men retraced their steps and soon passed the sentinel, who expressed his general sense of things by a needless and exaggerated salute to his commander.

IV

Early on the morning after these events the two men, captor and captive, sat in the tent of the former. A table was between them on which lay, among a number of letters, official and private, which the captain had written during the night, the incriminating papers found upon the spy. That gentleman had slept through the night in an adjoining tent, unguarded. Both, having breakfasted, were now smoking.

"Mr. Brune," said Captain Hartroy, "you probably do not understand why I recognized you in your disguise, nor how I was aware of your name."

"I have not sought to learn, Captain," the prisoner said with quiet dignity.

"Nevertheless I should like you to know—if the story will not offend. You will perceive that my knowledge of you goes back to the autumn of 1861. At that time you were a private in an Ohio regiment—a brave and trusted soldier. To the surprise and grief of your officers and comrades you deserted and went over to the enemy. Soon afterward you were captured in a skirmish, recognized, tried by court-martial and sentenced to be shot. Awaiting the execution of the sentence you were confined, unfettered, in a freight car standing on a side track of a railway."

"At Grafton, Virginia," said Brune, pushing the ashes from his cigar with the little finger of the hand holding it, and without looking up.

"At Grafton, Virginia," the captain repeated. "One dark and stormy night a soldier who had just returned from a long, fatiguing march was put on guard over you. He sat on a cracker box inside the car, near the door, his rifle loaded and the bayonet fixed. You sat in a corner and his orders were to kill you if you attempted to rise."

"But if I *asked* to rise he might call the corporal of the guard."

"Yes. As the long silent hours wore away the soldier yielded to the demands of nature: he himself incurred the death penalty by sleeping at his post of duty."

"You did."

"What! you recognize me? you have known me all along?"

The captain had risen and was walking the floor of his tent, visibly excited. His face was flushed, the gray eyes had lost the cold, pitiless look which they had shown when Brune had seen them over the pistol barrel; they had softened wonderfully.

"I knew you," said the spy, with his customary tranquillity, "the moment you faced me, demanding my surrender. In the circumstances it would have been hardly becoming in me to recall these matters. I am perhaps a traitor, certainly a spy; but I should not wish to seem a suppliant."

The captain had paused in his walk and was facing his prisoner. There was a singular huskiness in his voice as he spoke again.

"Mr. Brune, whatever your conscience may permit you to be, you saved my life at what you must have believed the cost of your own. Until I saw you yesterday when halted by my sentinel I believed you dead—thought that you had suffered the fate which through my own crime you might easily have escaped. You had only to step from the car and leave me to take your place before the firing-squad. You had a divine compassion. You pitied my fatigue. You let me sleep, watched over me, and as the time drew near for the relief-guard to come and detect me in my crime, you gently waked me. Ah, Brune, Brune, that was well done—that was great—that——"

The captain's voice failed him; the tears were running down his face and sparkled upon his beard and his breast. Resuming his seat at the table, he buried his face in his arms and sobbed. All else was silence.

Suddenly the clear warble of a bugle was heard sounding the

"assembly." The captain started and raised his wet face from his arms; it had turned ghastly pale. Outside, in the sunlight, were heard the stir of the men falling into line; the voices of the sergeants calling the roll; the tapping of the drummers as they braced their drums. The captain spoke again:

"I ought to have confessed my fault in order to relate the story of your magnanimity; it might have procured you a pardon. A hundred times I resolved to do so, but shame prevented. Besides, your sentence was just and righteous. Well, Heaven forgive me! I said nothing, and my regiment was soon afterward ordered to Tennessee and I never heard about you."

"It was all right, sir," said Brune, without visible emotion; "I escaped and returned to my colors—the Confederate colors. I should like to add that before deserting from the Federal service I had earnestly asked a discharge, on the ground of altered convictions. I was answered by punishment."

"Ah, but if I had suffered the penalty of my crime—if you had not generously given me the life that I accepted without gratitude you would not be again in the shadow and imminence of death."

The prisoner started slightly and a look of anxiety came into his face. One would have said, too, that he was surprised. At that moment a lieutenant, the adjutant, appeared at the opening of the tent and saluted. "Captain," he said, "the battalion is formed."

Captain Hartroy had recovered his composure. He turned to the officer and said: "Lieutenant, go to Captain Graham and say that I direct him to assume command of the battalion and parade it outside the parapet. This gentleman is a deserter and a spy; he is to be shot to death in the presence of the troops. He will accompany you, unbound and unguarded."

While the adjutant waited at the door the two men inside the tent rose and exchanged ceremonious bows, Brune immediately retiring.

Half an hour later an old negro cook, the only person left in camp except the commander, was so startled by the sound of a volley of musketry that he dropped the kettle that he was lifting from a fire. But for his consternation and the hissing which the contents of the kettle made among the embers, he might also have heard, nearer at hand, the single pistol shot with which Captain Hartroy renounced the life which in conscience he could no longer keep.

In compliance with the terms of a note that he left for the officer who succeeded him in command, he was buried, like the deserter and spy, without military honors; and in the solemn shadow of the mountain which knows no more of war the two sleep well in long-forgotten graves.

※ ※ ※

PARKER ADDERSON,
PHILOSOPHER

"Prisoner, what is your name?"

"As I am to lose it at daylight tomorrow morning it is hardly worth while concealing it. Parker Adderson."

"Your rank?"

"A somewhat humble one; commissioned officers are too precious to be risked in the perilous business of a spy. I am a sergeant."

"Of what regiment?"

"You must excuse me; my answer might, for anything I know, give you an idea of whose forces are in your front. Such knowledge as that is what I came into your lines to obtain, not to impart."

"You are not without wit."

"If you have the patience to wait you will find me dull enough to-morrow."

"How do you know that you are to die to-morrow morning?"

"Among spies captured by night that is the custom. It is one of the nice observances of the profession."

The general so far laid aside the dignity appropriate to a Confederate officer of high rank and wide renown as to smile. But no one in his power and out of his favor would have drawn any happy augury from that outward and visible sign of approval. It was neither genial nor infectious; it did not communicate itself to the other persons exposed to it—the caught spy who had provoked it and the armed guard who had brought him into the tent and now stood a little apart, watching his prisoner in the yellow candle-light. It was no part of that warrior's duty to smile; he had been detailed for another purpose. The conversation was resumed; it was in character a trial for a capital offense.

"You admit, then, that you are a spy—that you came into my camp, disguised as you are in the uniform of a Confederate soldier, to obtain information secretly regarding the numbers and disposition of my troops."

"Regarding, particularly, their numbers. Their disposition I already knew. It is morose."

The general brightened again; the guard, with a severer sense of his responsibility, accentuated the austerity of his expression and stood a trifle more erect than before. Twirling his gray slouch hat round and round upon his forefinger, the spy took a leisurely survey of his surroundings. They were simple enough. The tent was a common "wall tent," about eight feet by ten in dimensions, lighted by a single tallow candle stuck into the haft of a bayonet, which was itself stuck into a pine table at which the general sat, now busily writing and apparently forgetful of his unwilling guest. An old rag carpet covered the earthen floor; an older leather trunk, a second chair and a roll of blankets were about all else that the tent contained; in General Clavering's command Confederate simplicity and penury of "pomp and circumstance" had attained their highest development. On a large nail driven into the tent pole at the entrance was suspended a sword-belt supporting a long sabre, a pistol in its holster and, absurdly enough, a bowie-knife. Of that most unmilitary weapon it was the general's habit to explain that it was a souvenir of the peaceful days when he was a civilian.

It was a stormy night. The rain cascaded upon the canvas in torrents, with the dull, drum-like sound familiar to dwellers in tents. As the whooping blasts charged upon it the frail structure shook and swayed and strained at its confining stakes and ropes.

The general finished writing, folded the half-sheet of paper and spoke to the soldier guarding Adderson: "Here, Tassman, take that to the adjutant-general; then return."

"And the prisoner, General?" said the soldier, saluting, with an inquiring glance in the direction of that unfortunate.

"Do as I said," replied the officer, curtly.

The soldier took the note and ducked himself out of the tent. General Clavering turned his handsome face toward the Federal spy, looked him in the eyes, not unkindly, and said: "It is a bad night, my man."

"For me, yes."

"Do you guess what I have written?"

"Something worth reading, I dare say. And—perhaps it is my vanity—I venture to suppose that I am mentioned in it."

"Yes; it is a memorandum for an order to be read to the troops at *reveille* concerning your execution. Also some notes for the guidance of the provost-marshal in arranging the details of that event."

"I hope, General, the spectacle will be intelligently arranged, for I shall attend it myself."

"Have you any arrangements of your own that you wish to make? Do you wish to see a chaplain, for example?"

"I could hardly secure a longer rest for myself by depriving him of some of his."

"Good God, man! do you mean to go to your death with nothing but jokes upon your lips? Do you know that this is a serious matter?"

"How can I know that? I have never been dead in all my life. I have heard that death is a serious matter, but never from any of those who have experienced it."

The general was silent for a moment; the man interested, perhaps amused him—a type not previously encountered.

"Death," he said, "is at least a loss—a loss of such happiness as we have, and of opportunities for more."

"A loss of which we shall never be conscious can be borne with composure and therefore expected without apprehension. You must have observed, General, that of all the dead men with whom it is your soldierly pleasure to strew your path none shows signs of regret."

"If the being dead is not a regrettable condition, yet the becoming so—the act of dying—appears to be distinctly disagreeable to one who has not lost the power to feel."

"Pain is disagreeable, no doubt. I never suffer it without more or less discomfort. But he who lives longest is most exposed to it. What you call dying is simply the last pain—there is really no such thing as dying. Suppose, for illustration, that I attempt to escape. You lift the revolver that you are courteously concealing in your lap, and——"

The general blushed like a girl, then laughed softly, disclosing his brilliant teeth, made a slight inclination of his handsome head and said nothing. The spy continued: "You fire, and I have in my stomach what I did not swallow. I fall, but am not dead. After a half-hour of agony I am dead. But at any given instant of that half-hour I was either alive or dead. There is no transition period.

"When I am hanged to-morrow morning it will be quite the same; while conscious I shall be living; when dead, unconscious. Nature appears to have ordered the matter quite in my interest—the way that I should have ordered it myself. It is so simple," he added with a smile, "that it seems hardly worth while to be hanged at all."

At the finish of his remarks there was a long silence. The general sat impassive, looking into the man's face, but apparently not attentive to what had been said. It was as if his eyes had mounted guard over the prisoner while his mind concerned itself with other matters. Presently he drew a long, deep breath, shuddered, as one awakened from a dreadful dream, and exclaimed almost inaudibly: "Death is horrible!"—this man of death.

"It was horrible to our savage ancestors," said the spy, gravely, "because they had not enough intelligence to dissociate the idea of consciousness from the idea of the physical forms in which it is manifested—as an even lower order of intelligence, that of the monkey, for example, may be unable to imagine a house without inhabitants, and seeing a ruined hut fancies a suffering occupant. To us it is horrible because we have inherited the tendency to think it so, accounting for the notion by wild and fanciful theories of another world—as names of places give rise to legends explaining them and reasonless conduct to philosophies in justification. You can hang me, General, but there your power of evil ends; you cannot condemn me to heaven."

The general appeared not to have heard; the spy's talk had merely turned his thoughts into an unfamiliar channel, but there they pursued their will independently to conclusions of their own. The storm had ceased, and something of the solemn spirit of the night had imparted itself to his reflections, giving them the sombre tinge of a supernatural dread. Perhaps there was an element of prescience in it. "I should not like to die," he said—"not to-night."

He was interrupted—if, indeed, he had intended to speak further—by the entrance of an officer of his staff, Captain Hasterlick, the provost-marshal. This recalled him to himself; the absent look passed away from his face.

"Captain," he said, acknowledging the officer's salute, "this man is a Yankee spy captured inside our lines with incriminating papers on him. He has confessed. How is the weather?"

"The storm is over, sir, and the moon shining."

"Good; take a file of men, conduct him at once to the parade ground, and shoot him."

A sharp cry broke from the spy's lips. He threw himself forward, thrust out his neck, expanded his eyes, clenched his hands.

"Good God!" he cried hoarsely, almost inarticulately; "you do not mean that! You forget—I am not to die until morning."

"I have said nothing of morning," replied the general, coldly; "that was an assumption of your own. You die now."

"But, General, I beg—I implore you to remember; I am to hang! It will take some time to erect the gallows—two hours—an hour. Spies are hanged; I have rights under military law. For Heaven's sake, General, consider how short——"

"Captain, observe my directions."

The officer drew his sword and fixing his eyes upon the prisoner pointed silently to the opening of the tent. The prisoner hesitated;

the officer grasped him by the collar and pushed him gently forward. As he approached the tent pole the frantic man sprang to it and with cat-like agility seized the handle of the bowie-knife, plucked the weapon from the scabbard and thrusting the captain aside leaped upon the general with the fury of a madman, hurling him to the ground and falling headlong upon him as he lay. The table was overturned, the candle extinguished and they fought blindly in the darkness. The provost-marshal sprang to the assistance of his superior officer and was himself prostrated upon the struggling forms. Curses and inarticulate cries of rage and pain came from the welter of limbs and bodies; the tent came down upon them and beneath its hampering and enveloping folds the struggle went on. Private Tassman, returning from his errand and dimly conjecturing the situation, threw down his rifle and laying hold of the flouncing canvas at random vainly tried to drag it off the men under it; and the sentinel who paced up and down in front, not daring to leave his beat though the skies should fall, discharged his rifle. The report alarmed the camp; drums beat the long roll and bugles sounded the assembly, bringing swarms of half-clad men into the moonlight, dressing as they ran, and falling into line at the sharp commands of their officers. This was well; being in line the men were under control; they stood at arms while the general's staff and the men of his escort brought order out of confusion by lifting off the fallen tent and pulling apart the breathless and bleeding actors in that strange contention.

Breathless, indeed, was one: the captain was dead; the handle of the bowie-knife, protruding from his throat, was pressed back beneath his chin until the end had caught in the angle of the jaw and the hand that delivered the blow had been unable to remove the weapon. In the dead man's hand was his sword, clenched with a grip that defied the strength of the living. Its blade was streaked with red to the hilt.

Lifted to his feet, the general sank back to the earth with a moan and fainted. Besides his bruises he had two sword-thrusts—one through the thigh, the other through the shoulder.

The spy had suffered the least damage. Apart from a broken right arm, his wounds were such only as might have been incurred in an ordinary combat with nature's weapons. But he was dazed and seemed hardly to know what had occurred. He shrank away from those attending him, cowered upon the ground and uttered unintelligible remonstrances. His face, swollen by blows and stained with gouts of blood, nevertheless showed white beneath his disheveled hair—as white as that of a corpse.

"The man is not insane," said the surgeon, preparing bandages and replying to a question; "he is suffering from fright. Who and what is he?"

Private Tassman began to explain. It was the opportunity of his life; he omitted nothing that could in any way accentuate the importance of his own relation to the night's events. When he had finished his story and was ready to begin it again nobody gave him any attention.

The general had now recovered consciousness. He raised himself upon his elbow, looked about him, and, seeing the spy crouching by a camp-fire, guarded, said simply:

"Take that man to the parade ground and shoot him."

"The general's mind wanders," said an officer standing near.

"His mind does *not* wander," the adjutant-general said. "I have a memorandum from him about this business; he had given that same order to Hasterlick"—with a motion of the hand toward the dead provost-marshal—"and, by God! it shall be executed."

Ten minutes later Sergeant Parker Adderson, of the Federal army, philosopher and wit, kneeling in the moonlight and begging incoherently for his life, was shot to death by twenty men. As the volley rang out upon the keen air of the midnight, General Clavering, lying white and still in the red glow of the camp-fire, opened his big blue eyes, looked pleasantly upon those about him and said: "How silent it all is!"

The surgeon looked at the adjutant-general, gravely and significantly. The patient's eyes slowly closed, and thus he lay for a few moments; then, his face suffused with a smile of ineffable sweetness, he said, faintly: "I suppose this must be death," and so passed away.

❊   ❊   ❊

AN AFFAIR OF OUTPOSTS

I

CONCERNING THE WISH TO BE DEAD

Two men sat in conversation. One was the Governor of the State. The year was 1861; the war was on and the Governor already famous for the intelligence and zeal with which he directed all the powers and resources of his State to the service of the Union.

"What! *you?*" the Governor was saying in evident surprise—"you too want a military commission? Really, the fifing and drumming must have effected a profound alteration in your convictions. In my character of recruiting sergeant I suppose I ought not to be fastidious, but"—there was a touch of irony in his manner—"well, have you forgotten that an oath of allegiance is required?"

"I have altered neither my convictions nor my sympathies," said the other, tranquilly. "While my sympathies are with the South, as you do me the honor to recollect, I have never doubted that the North was in the right. I am a Southerner in fact and in feeling, but it is my habit in matters of importance to act as I think, not as I feel."

The Governor was absently tapping his desk with a pencil; he did not immediately reply. After a while he said: "I have heard that there are all kinds of men in the world, so I suppose there are some like that, and doubtless you think yourself one. I've known you a long time and—pardon me—I don't think so."

"Then I am to understand that my application is denied?"

"Unless you can remove my belief that your Southern sympathies are in some degree a disqualification, yes. I do not doubt your good faith, and I know you to be abundantly fitted by intelligence and special training for the duties of an officer. Your convictions, you say, favor the Union cause, but I prefer a man with his heart in it. The heart is what men fight with."

"Look here, Governor," said the younger man, with a smile that had more light than warmth: "I have something up my sleeve—a qualification which I had hoped it would not be necessary to mention. A great military authority has given a simple recipe for being a good soldier: 'Try always to get yourself killed.' It is with that purpose that I wish to enter the service. I am not, perhaps, much of a patriot, but I wish to be dead."

The Governor looked at him rather sharply, then a little coldly. "There is a simpler and franker way," he said.

"In my family, sir," was the reply, "we do not do that—no Armisted has ever done that."

A long silence ensued and neither man looked at the other. Presently the Governor lifted his eyes from the pencil, which had resumed its tapping, and said:

"Who is she?"

"My wife."

The Governor tossed the pencil into the desk, rose and walked two or three times across the room. Then he turned to Armisted, who also had risen, looked at him more coldly than before and said: "But the man—would it not be better that he—could not the country spare him better than it can spare you? Or are the Armisteds opposed to 'the unwritten law'?"

The Armisteds, apparently, could feel an insult: the face of the younger man flushed, then paled, but he subdued himself to the service of his purpose.

"The man's identity is unknown to me," he said, calmly enough.

"Pardon me," said the Governor, with even less of visible contrition than commonly underlies those words. After a moment's reflection he added: "I shall send you to-morrow a captain's commission in the Tenth Infantry, now at Nashville, Tennessee. Good night."

"Good night, sir. I thank you."

Left alone, the Governor remained for a time motionless, leaning against his desk. Presently he shrugged his shoulders as if throwing off a burden. "This is a bad business," he said.

Seating himself at a reading-table before the fire, he took up the book nearest his hand, absently opening it. His eyes fell upon this sentence:

"When God made it necessary for an unfaithful wife to lie about her husband in justification of her own sins He had the tenderness to endow men with the folly to believe her."

He looked at the title of the book; it was, *His Excellency the Fool*.

He flung the volume into the fire.

II

HOW TO SAY WHAT IS WORTH HEARING

The enemy, defeated in two days of battle at Pittsburg Landing, had sullenly retired to Corinth, whence he had come. For manifest incompetence Grant, whose beaten army had been saved from destruction and capture by Buell's soldierly activity and skill, had been relieved of his command, which nevertheless had not been given to Buell, but to Halleck, a man of unproved powers, a theorist, sluggish, irresolute. Foot by foot his troops, always deployed in line-of-battle to resist the enemy's bickering skirmishers, always entrenching against the columns that never came, advanced across the thirty miles of forest and swamp toward an antagonist prepared to vanish at contact, like a ghost at cock-crow. It was a campaign of "excursions and alarums," of reconnoissances and countermarches, of cross-purposes and countermanded orders. For weeks the solemn farce held attention, luring distinguished civilians from fields of political ambition to see what they safely could of the horrors of war. Among these was our friend the Governor. At the headquarters of the army and in the camps of the troops from his State he was a familiar figure, attended by the several members of his personal staff, showily horsed, faultlessly betailored and bravely silk-hatted. Things of charm they were, rich in suggestions of peaceful lands beyond a sea of strife. The bedraggled soldier looked up from his trench as they passed, leaned upon his spade and audibly damned them to signify his sense of their ornamental irrelevance to the austerities of his trade.

"I think, Governor," said General Masterson one day, going into informal session atop of his horse and throwing one leg across the pommel of his saddle, his favorite posture—"I think I would not ride any farther in that direction if I were you. We've nothing out there but a line of skirmishers. That, I presume, is why I was directed to put these siege guns here: if the skirmishers are driven in the enemy will die of dejection at being unable to haul them away—they're a trifle heavy."

There is reason to fear that the unstrained quality of this military humor dropped not as the gentle rain from heaven upon the place beneath the civilian's silk hat. Anyhow he abated none of his dignity in recognition.

"I understand," he said, gravely, "that some of my men are out there—a company of the Tenth, commanded by Captain Armisted. I should like to meet him if you do not mind."

"He is worth meeting. But there's a bad bit of jungle out there, and I should advise that you leave your horse and"—with a look at the Governor's retinue—"your other impedimenta."

The Governor went forward alone and on foot. In a half-hour he had pushed through a tangled undergrowth covering a boggy soil and entered upon firm and more open ground. Here he found a half-company of infantry lounging behind a line of stacked rifles. The men wore their accoutrements—their belts, cartridge-boxes, haversacks and canteens. Some lying at full length on the dry leaves were fast asleep: others in small groups gossiped idly of this and that; a few played at cards; none was far from the line of stacked arms. To the civilian's eye the scene was one of carelessness, confusion, indifference; a soldier would have observed expectancy and readiness.

At a little distance apart an officer in fatigue uniform, armed, sat on a fallen tree noting the approach of the visitor, to whom a sergeant, rising from one of the groups, now came forward.

"I wish to see Captain Armisted," said the Governor.

The sergeant eyed him narrowly, saying nothing, pointed to the officer, and taking a rifle from one of the stacks, accompanied him.

"This man wants to see you, sir," said the sergeant, saluting. The officer rose.

It would have been a sharp eye that would have recognized him. His hair, which but a few months before had been brown, was streaked with gray. His face, tanned by exposure, was seamed as with age. A long livid scar across the forehead marked the stroke of a sabre; one cheek was drawn and puckered by the work of a bullet. Only a woman of the loyal North would have thought the man handsome.

"Armisted—Captain," said the Governor, extending his hand, "do you not know me?"

"I know you, sir, and I salute you—as the Governor of my State."

Lifting his right hand to the level of his eyes he threw it outward and downward. In the code of military etiquette there is no provision for shaking hands. That of the civilian was withdrawn. If he felt either surprise or chagrin his face did not betray it.

"It is the hand that signed your commission," he said.

"And it is the hand——"

The sentence remains unfinished. The sharp report of a rifle came from the front, followed by another and another. A bullet hissed through the forest and struck a tree near by. The men sprang from the ground and even before the captain's high, clear voice was done intoning the command "At-ten-tion!" had fallen into line in rear of the stacked arms. Again—and now through the din of a crackling fusillade—sounded the strong, deliberate sing-song of authority: "Take . . . arms!" followed by the rattle of unlocking bayonets.

Bullets from the unseen enemy were now flying thick and fast, though mostly well spent and emitting the humming sound which signified interference by twigs and rotation in the plane of flight. Two or three of the men in the line were already struck and down. A few wounded men came limping awkwardly out of the undergrowth from the skirmish line in front; most of them did not pause, but held their way with white faces and set teeth to the rear.

Suddenly there was a deep, jarring report in front, followed by the startling rush of a shell, which passing overhead exploded in the edge of a thicket, setting afire the fallen leaves. Penetrating the din—seeming to float above it like the melody of a soaring bird—rang the slow, aspirated monotones of the captain's several commands, without emphasis, without accent, musical and restful as an even-song under the harvest moon. Familiar with this tranquilizing chant in moments of imminent peril, these raw soldiers of less than a year's training yielded themselves to the spell, executing its mandates with the composure and precision of veterans. Even the distinguished civilian behind his tree, hesitating between pride and terror, was accessible to its charm and suasion. He was conscious of a fortified resolution and ran away only when the skirmishers, under orders to rally on the reserve, came out of the woods like hunted hares and formed on the left of the stiff little line, breathing hard and thankful for the boon of breath.

III

THE FIGHTING OF ONE WHOSE HEART WAS NOT IN THE QUARREL

Guided in his retreat by that of the fugitive wounded, the Governor struggled bravely to the rear through the "bad bit of jungle." He was well winded and a trifle confused. Excepting a single rifle-shot now and again, there was no sound of strife behind him; the enemy was pulling himself together for a new onset against an antagonist of whose numbers and tactical disposition he was in doubt. The fugitive felt that he would probably be spared to his country, and only commended the arrangements of Providence to that end, but in leaping a small brook in more open ground one of the arrangements incurred the mischance of a disabling sprain at the ankle. He was unable to continue his flight, for he was too fat to hop, and after several vain attempts, causing intolerable pain, seated himself on the earth to nurse his ignoble disability and deprecate the military situation.

A brisk renewal of the firing broke out and stray bullets came flitting and droning by. Then came the crash of two clean, definite volleys, followed by a continuous rattle, through which he heard the yells and cheers of the combatants, punctuated by thunderclaps of cannon. All this told him that Armisted's little command was bitterly beset and fighting at close quarters. The wounded men whom he had distanced began to straggle by on either hand, their numbers visibly augmented by new levies from the line. Singly and by twos and threes, some supporting comrades more desperately hurt than themselves, but all deaf to his appeals for assistance, they sifted through the underbrush and disappeared. The firing was increasingly louder and more distinct, and presently the ailing fugitives were succeeded by men who strode with a firmer tread, occasionally facing about and discharging their pieces, then doggedly resuming their retreat, reloading as they walked. Two or three fell as he looked, and lay motionless. One had enough of life left in him to make a pitiful attempt to drag himself to cover. A passing comrade paused beside him long enough to fire, appraised the poor devil's disability with a look and moved sullenly on, inserting a cartridge in his weapon.

In all this was none of the pomp of war—no hint of glory. Even in his distress and peril the helpless civilian could not forbear to contrast it with the gorgeous parades and reviews held in honor of himself—with the brilliant uniforms, the music, the banners, and the marching. It was an ugly and sickening business: to all that was artistic in his nature, revolting, brutal, in bad taste.

"Ugh!" he grunted, shuddering—"this is beastly! Where is the charm of it all? Where are the elevated sentiments, the devotion, the heroism, the——"

From a point somewhere near, in the direction of the pursuing enemy, rose the clear, deliberate sing-song of Captain Armisted.

"Stead-y, men—stead-y. Halt! Commence fir-ing."

The rattle of fewer than a score of rifles could be distinguished through the general uproar, and again that penetrating falsetto:

"Cease fir-ing. In re-treat . . . . maaarch!"

In a few moments this remnant had drifted slowly past the Governor, all to the right of him as they faced in retiring, the men deployed at intervals of a half-dozen paces. At the extreme left and a few yards behind came the captain. The civilian called out his name, but he did not hear. A swarm of men in gray now broke out of cover in pursuit, making directly for the spot where the Governor lay—some accident of the ground had caused them to converge upon that point: their line had become a crowd. In a last struggle for life and liberty the Governor attempted to rise, and looking back the captain saw him. Promptly, but with the same slow precision as before, he sang his commands:

"Skirm-ish-ers, halt!" The men stopped and according to rule turned to face the enemy.

"Ral-ly on the right!"—and they came in at a run, fixing bayonets and forming loosely on the man at that end of the line.

"Forward . . . to save the Gov-ern-or of your State . . . doub-le quick . . . maaarch!"

Only one man disobeyed this astonishing command! He was dead. With a cheer they sprang forward over the twenty or thirty paces between them and their task. The captain having a shorter distance to go arrived first—simultaneously with the enemy. A half-dozen hasty shots were fired at him, and the foremost man—a fellow of heroic stature, hatless and bare-breasted—made a vicious sweep at his head with a clubbed rifle. The officer parried the blow at the cost of a broken arm and drove his sword to the hilt into the giant's breast. As the body fell the weapon was wrenched from his hand and before he could pluck his revolver from the scabbard at his belt another man leaped upon him like a tiger, fastening both hands upon his throat and bearing him backward upon the prostrate Governor, still struggling to rise. This man was promptly spitted upon the bayonet of a Federal sergeant and his death-gripe on the captain's throat loosened by a kick upon each wrist. When the captain had risen he was at the rear of his men, who had all passed over and around him and were thrusting fiercely at their more numerous but less coherent antagonists. Nearly all the rifles on both sides were empty and in the crush there was neither time nor room to reload. The Confederates were at a disadvantage in that most of them lacked bayonets; they fought by bludgeoning—and a clubbed rifle is a formidable arm. The sound of the conflict was a clatter like that of the interlocking horns of battling bulls—now and then the pash of a crushed skull, an oath, or a grunt caused by the impact of a rifle's muzzle against the abdomen transfixed by its bayonet. Through an opening made by the fall of one of his men Captain Armisted sprang, with his dangling left arm; in his right hand a full-charged revolver, which he fired with rapidity and terrible effect into the thick of the gray crowd: but across the bodies of the slain the survivors in the front were pushed forward by their comrades in the rear till again they breasted the tireless bayonets. There were fewer bayonets now to breast—a beggarly half-dozen, all told. A few minutes more of this rough work—a little fighting back to back—and all would be over.

Suddenly a lively firing was heard on the right and the left: a fresh line of Federal skirmishers came forward at a run, driving before them those parts of the Confederate line that had been separated by staying the advance of the centre. And behind these new and noisy combatants, at a distance of two or three hundred yards, could be seen, indistinct among the trees a line-of-battle!

Instinctively before retiring, the crowd in gray made a tremendous rush upon its handful of antagonists, overwhelming them by mere momentum and, unable to use weapons in the crush, trampled them, stamped savagely on their limbs, their bodies, their necks, their faces; then retiring with bloody feet across its own dead it joined the general rout and the incident was at an end.

IV
THE GREAT HONOR THE GREAT

The Governor, who had been unconscious, opened his eyes and stared about him, slowly recalling the day's events. A man in the uniform of a major was kneeling beside him; he was a surgeon. Grouped about were the civilian members of the Governor's staff, their faces expressing a natural solicitude regarding their offices. A little apart stood General Masterson addressing another officer and gesticulating with a cigar. He was saying: "It was the beautifulest fight ever made—by God, sir, it was great!"

The beauty and greatness were attested by a row of dead, trimly disposed, and another of wounded, less formally placed, restless, half-naked, but bravely bebandaged.

"How do you feel, sir?" said the surgeon. "I find no wound."

"I think I am all right," the patient replied, sitting up. "It is that ankle."

The surgeon transferred his attention to the ankle, cutting away the boot. All eyes followed the knife.

In moving the leg a folded paper was uncovered. The patient picked it up and carelessly opened it. It was a letter three months old, signed "Julia." Catching sight of his name in it he read it. It was nothing very remarkable—merely a weak woman's confession of unprofitable sin—the penitence of a faithless wife deserted by her betrayer. The letter had fallen from the pocket of Captain Armisted; the reader quietly transferred it to his own.

An aide-de-camp rode up and dismounted. Advancing to the Governor he saluted.

"Sir," he said, "I am sorry to find you wounded—the Commanding General has not been informed. He presents his compliments and I am directed to say that he has ordered for to-morrow a grand review of the reserve corps in your honor. I venture to add that the General's carriage is at your service if you are able to attend."

"Be pleased to say to the Commanding General that I am deeply touched by his kindness. If you have the patience to wait a few moments you shall convey a more definite reply."

He smiled brightly and glancing at the surgeon and his assistants added: "At present—if you will permit an allusion to the horrors of peace—I am 'in the hands of my friends.'"

The humor of the great is infectious; all laughed who heard.

"Where is Captain Armisted?" the Governor asked, not altogether carelessly.

The surgeon looked up from his work, pointing silently to the nearest body in the row of dead, the features discreetly covered with a handkerchief. It was so near that the great man could have laid his hand upon it, but he did not. He may have feared it would bleed.

※   ※   ※

JUPITER DOKE, BRIGADIER-GENERAL

From the Secretary of War to the Hon. Jupiter Doke, Hardpan Crossroads, Posey County, Illinois.

WASHINGTON, November 3, 1861.

Having faith in your patriotism and ability, the President has been pleased to appoint you a brigadier-general of volunteers. Do you accept?

From the Hon. Jupiter Doke to the Secretary of War.

HARDPAN, ILLINOIS, November 9, 1861.

It is the proudest moment of my life. The office is one which should be neither sought nor declined. In times that try men's souls the patriot knows no North, no South, no East, no West. His motto should be: "My country, my whole country and nothing but my country." I accept the great trust confided in me by a free and intelligent people, and with a firm reliance on the principles of constitutional liberty, and invoking the guidance of an all-wise Providence, Ruler of Nations, shall labor so to discharge it as to leave no blot upon my political escutcheon. Say to his Excellency, the successor of the immortal Washington in the Seat of Power, that the patronage of my office will be bestowed with an eye single to securing the greatest good to the greatest number, the stability of republican institutions and the triumph of the party in all elections; and to this I pledge my life, my fortune and my sacred honor. I shall at once prepare an appropriate response to the speech of the chairman of the committee deputed to inform me of my appointment, and I trust the sentiments therein expressed will strike a sympathetic chord in the public heart, as well as command the Executive approval.

From the Secretary of War to Major-General Blount Wardorg, Commanding the Military Department of Eastern Kentucky.

WASHINGTON, November 14, 1861.

I have assigned to your department Brigadier-General Jupiter Doke, who will soon proceed to Distilleryville, on the Little Buttermilk River, and take command of the Illinois Brigade at that point, reporting to you by letter for orders. Is the route from Covington by way of Bluegrass, Opossum Corners and Horsecave still infested with bushwackers, as reported in your last dispatch? I have a plan for cleaning them out.

From Major-General Blount Wardorg to the Secretary of War.

LOUISVILLE, KENTUCKY,
November 20, 1861.

The name and services of Brigadier-General Doke are unfamiliar to me, but I shall be pleased to have the advantage of his skill. The route from Covington to Distilleryville *via* Opossum Corners and Horsecave I have been compelled to abandon to the enemy, whose guerilla warfare made it possible to keep it open without detaching too many troops from the front. The brigade at Distilleryville is supplied by steamboats up the Little Buttermilk.

From the Secretary of War to Brigadier-General Jupiter Doke, Hardpan, Illinois.

WASHINGTON, November 26, 1861.

I deeply regret that your commission had been forwarded by mail before the receipt of your letter of acceptance; so we must dispense with the formality of official notification to you by a committee. The President is highly gratified by the noble and patriotic sentiments of your letter, and directs that you proceed at once to your command at Distilleryville, Kentucky, and there report by letter to Major-General Wardorg at Louisville, for orders. It is important that the strictest secrecy be observed regarding your movements until you have passed Covington, as it is desired to hold the enemy in front of Distilleryville until you are within three days of him. Then if your approach is known it will operate as a demonstration against his right and cause him to strengthen it with his left now at Memphis, Tennessee, which it is desirable to capture first. Go by way of Bluegrass, Opossum Corners and Horsecave. All officers are expected to be in full uniform when *en route* to the front.

From Brigadier-General Jupiter Doke to the Secretary of War.

COVINGTON, KENTUCKY, December 7, 1861.

I arrived yesterday at this point, and have given my proxy to Joel Briller, Esq., my wife's cousin, and a staunch Republican, who will worthily represent Posey County in field and forum. He points with pride to a stainless record in the halls of legislation, which have often echoed to his soul-stirring eloquence on questions which lie at the very foundation of popular government. He has been called the Patrick Henry of Hardpan, where he has done yeoman's service in the cause of civil and religious liberty. Mr. Briller left for Distilleryville last evening, and the standard bearer of the Democratic host confronting that stronghold of freedom will find him a lion in his path. I have been asked to remain here and deliver some addresses to the people in a local contest involving issues of paramount importance. That duty being performed, I shall in person enter the arena of armed debate and move in the direction of the heaviest firing, burning my ships behind me. I forward by this mail to his Excellency the President a request for the appointment of my son, Jabez Leonidas Doke, as postmaster at Hardpan. I would take it, sir, as a great favor if you would give the application a strong oral indorsement, as the appointment is in the line of reform. Be kind enough to inform me what are the emoluments of the office I hold in the military arm, and if they are by salary or fees. Are there any perquisites? My mileage account will be transmitted monthly.

From Brigadier-General Jupiter Doke to Major General Blount Wardorg.

DISTILLERYVILLE, KENTUCKY,
January 12, 1862.

I arrived on the tented field yesterday by steamboat, the recent storms having inundated the landscape, covering, I understand, the greater part of a congressional district. I am pained to find that Joel Briller, Esq., a prominent citizen of Posey County, Illinois, and a far-seeing statesman who held my proxy, and who a month ago should have been thundering at the gates of Disunion, has not been heard from, and has doubtless been sacrificed upon the altar of his country. In him the American people lose a bulwark of freedom. I would respectfully move that you designate a committee to draw up resolutions of respect to his memory, and that the office holders and men under your command wear the usual badge of mourning for thirty days. I shall at once place myself at the head of affairs here, and am now ready to entertain any suggestions which you may make, looking to the better enforcement of the laws in this commonwealth. The militant Democrats on the other side of the river appear to be contemplating extreme measures. They have two large cannons facing this way, and yesterday morning, I am told, some of them came down to the water's edge and remained in session for some time, making infamous allegations.

From the Diary of Brigadier-General Jupiter Doke, at Distilleryville, Kentucky.

January 12, 1862.—On my arrival yesterday at the Henry Clay Hotel (named in honor of the late far-seeing statesman) I was waited on by a delegation consisting of the three colonels intrusted with the command of the regiments of my brigade. It was an occasion that will be memorable in the political annals of America. Forwarded copies of the speeches to the Posey *Maverick,* to be spread upon the record of the ages. The gentlemen composing the delegation unanimously reaffirmed their devotion to the principles of national unity and the Republican party. Was gratified to recognize in them men of political prominence and untarnished escutcheons. At the subsequent banquet, sentiments of lofty patriotism were expressed. Wrote to Mr. Wardorg at Louisville for instructions.

January 13, 1862.—Leased a prominent residence (the former incumbent being absent in arms against his country) for the term of one year, and wrote at once for Mrs. Brigadier-General Doke and the vital issues—excepting Jabez Leonidas. In the camp of treason opposite here there are supposed to be three thousand misguided men laying the ax at the root of the tree of liberty. They have a clear majority, many of our men having returned without leave to their constituents. We could probably not poll more than two thousand votes. Have advised my heads of regiments to make a canvass of those remaining, all bolters to be read out of the phalanx.

January 14, 1862.—Wrote to the President, asking for the contract to supply this command with firearms and regalia through my brother-in-law, prominently identified with the manufacturing interests of the country. Club of cannon soldiers arrived at Jayhawk, three miles back from here, on their way to join us in battle array. Marched my whole brigade to Jayhawk to escort them into town, but their chairman, mistaking us for the opposing party, opened fire on the head of the procession and by the extraordinary noise of the cannon balls (I had no conception of it!) so frightened my horse that I was unseated without a contest. The meeting adjourned in disorder and returning to camp I found that a deputation of the enemy had crossed the river in our absence and made a division of the loaves and fishes. Wrote to the President, applying for the Gubernatorial Chair of the Territory of Idaho.

From Editorial Article in the Posey, Illinois, "Maverick," January 20, 1862.

Brigadier-General Doke's thrilling account, in another column, of the Battle of Distilleryville will make the heart of every loyal Illinoisian leap with exultation. The brilliant exploit marks an era in military history, and as General Doke says, "lays broad and deep the foundations of American prowess in arms." As none of the troops engaged, except the gallant author-chieftain (a host in himself) hails from Posey County, he justly considered that a list of the fallen would only occupy our valuable space to the exclusion of more important matter, but his account of the strategic ruse by which he apparently abandoned his camp and so inveigled a perfidious enemy into it for the purpose of murdering the sick, the unfortunate *countertempus* at Jayhawk, the subsequent dash upon a trapped enemy flushed with a supposed success, driving their terrified legions across an impassable river which precluded pursuit—all these "moving accidents by flood and field" are related with a pen of fire and have all the terrible interest of romance.

Verily, truth is stranger than fiction and the pen is mightier than the sword. When by the graphic power of the art preservative of all arts we are brought face to face with such glorious events as these, the *Maverick's* enterprise in securing for its thousands of readers the services of so distinguished a contributor as the Great Captain who made the history as well as wrote it seems a matter of almost secondary importance. For President in 1864 (subject to the decision of the Republican National Convention) Brigadier-General Jupiter Doke, of Illinois!

From Major-General Blount Wardorg to Brigadier-General Jupiter Doke.

LOUISVILLE, January 22, 1862.

Your letter apprising me of your arrival at Distilleryville was delayed in transmission, having only just been received (open) through the courtesy of the Confederate department commander under a flag of truce. He begs me to assure you that he would consider it an act of cruelty to trouble you, and I think it would be. Maintain, however a threatening attitude, but at the least pressure retire. Your position is simply an outpost which it is not intended to hold.

From Major-General Blount Wardorg to the Secretary of War.

LOUISVILLE, January 23, 1862.

I have certain information that the enemy has concentrated twenty thousand troops of all arms on the Little Buttermilk. According to your assignment, General Doke is in command of the small brigade of raw troops opposing them. It is no part of my plan to contest the enemy's advance at that point, but I cannot hold myself responsible for any reverses to the brigade mentioned, under its present commander. I think him a fool.

From the Secretary of War to Major-General Blount Wardorg.

WASHINGTON, February 1, 1862.

The President has great faith in General Doke. If your estimate of him is correct, however, he would seem to be singularly well placed where he now is, as your plans appear to contemplate a considerable sacrifice for whatever advantages you expect to gain.

From Brigadier-General Jupiter Doke to Major-General Blount Wardorg.

DISTILLERYVILLE, February 1, 1862.

To-morrow I shall remove my headquarters to Jayhawk in order to point the way whenever my brigade retires from Distilleryville, as foreshadowed by your letter of the 22d ult. I have appointed a Committee on Retreat, the minutes of whose first meeting I transmit to you. You will perceive that the committee having been duly organized by the election of a chairman and secretary, a resolution (prepared by myself) was adopted, to the effect that in case treason again raises her hideous head on this side of the river every man of the brigade is to mount a mule, the procession to move promptly in the direction of Louisville and the loyal North. In preparation for such an emergency I have for some time been collecting mules from the resident Democracy, and have on hand 2300 in a field at Jayhawk. Eternal vigilance is the price of liberty!

From Major-General Gibeon J. Buxter, C. S. A., to the Confederate Secretary of War.

BUNG STATION, KENTUCKY,
February 4, 1862.

On the night of the 2d inst., our entire force, consisting of 25,000 men and thirty-two field pieces, under command of Major-General Simmons B. Flood, crossed by a ford to the north side of Little Buttermilk River at a point three miles from Distilleryville and moved obliquely down and away from the stream, to strike the Covington turnpike at Jayhawk; the object being, as you know, to capture Covington, destroy Cincinnati and occupy the Ohio Valley. For some months there had been in our front only a small brigade of undisciplined troops, apparently without a commander, who were useful to us, for by not disturbing them we could create an impression of our weakness. But the movement on Jayhawk having isolated them, I was about to detach an Alabama regiment to bring them in, my division being the leading one, when an earth-shaking rumble was felt and heard, and suddenly the head-of-column was struck by one of the terrible tornadoes for which this region is famous, and utterly annihilated. The tornado, I believe, passed along the entire length of the road back to the ford, dispersing or destroying our entire army; but of this I cannot be sure, for I was lifted from the earth insensible and blown back to the south side of the river. Continuous firing all night on the north side and the reports of such of our men as have recrossed at the ford convince me that the Yankee brigade has exterminated the disabled survivors. Our loss has been uncommonly heavy. Of my own division of 15,000 infantry, the casualties —killed, wounded, captured, and missing—are 14,994. Of General Dolliver Billow's division, 11,200 strong, I can find but two officers and a nigger cook. Of the artillery, 800 men, none has reported on this side of the river. General Flood is dead. I have assumed command of the expeditionary force, but owing to the heavy losses have deemed it advisable to contract my line of supplies as rapidly as possible. I shall push southward to-morrow morning early. The purposes of the campaign have been as yet but partly accomplished.

From Major-General Dolliver Billows, C. S. A., to the Confederate Secretary of War.

BUHAC, KENTUCKY, February 5, 1862.

. . . But during the 2d they had, unknown to us, been reinforced by fifty thousand cavalry, and being apprised of our movement by a spy, this vast body was drawn up in the darkness at Jayhawk, and as the head of our column reached that point at about 11 P.M., fell upon it with astonishing fury, destroying the division of General Buxter in an instant. General Baumschank's brigade of artillery, which was in the rear, may have escaped—I did not wait to see, but withdrew my division to the river at a point several miles above the ford, and at daylight ferried it across on two fence rails lashed together with a suspender. Its losses, from an effective strength of 11,200, are 11,199. General Buxter is dead. I am changing my base to Mobile, Alabama.

From Brigadier-General Schneddeker Baumschank, C. S. A., to the Confederate Secretary of War.

IODINE, KENTUCKY, February 6, 1862.

. . . Yoost den somdings occur, I know nod vot it vos—somdings mackneefcent, but it vas nod vor—und I finds meinselluf, afder leedle viles, in dis blace, midout a hors und mit no men und goons. Sheneral Peelows is deadt. You will blease be so goot as to resign me—I vights no more in a dam gontry vere I gets vipped und knows nod how it vos done.

Resolutions of Congress, February 15, 1862.

Resolved, That the thanks of Congress are due, and hereby tendered, to Brigadier-General Jupiter Doke and the gallant men under his command for their unparalleled feat of attacking—themselves only 2000 strong—an army of 25,000 men and utterly overthrowing it, killing 5327, making prisoners of 19,003, of whom more than half were wounded, taking 32 guns, 20,000 stand of small arms and, in short, the enemy's entire equipment.

Resolved, That for this unexampled victory the President be requested to designate a day of thanksgiving and public celebration of religious rites in the various churches.

Resolved, That he be requested, in further commemoration of the great event, and in reward of the gallant spirits whose deeds have added such imperishable lustre to the American arms, to appoint, with the advice and consent of the Senate, the following officer:

One major-general.

Statement of Mr. Hannibal Alcazar Peyton, of Jayhawk, Kentucky.

Dat wus a almighty dark night, sho', and dese yere ole eyes aint wuf shuks, but I's got a year like a sque'l, an' w'en I cotch de mummer o' v'ices I knowed dat gang b'long on de far side o' de ribber. So I jes' runs in de house an' wakes Marse Doke an' tells him: "Skin outer dis fo' yo' life!" An' de Lo'd bress my soul! ef dat man didn' go right fru de winder in his shir' tail an' break for to cross de mule patch! An' dem twenty-free hunerd mules dey jes' t'nk it is de debble hese'f wid de brandin' iron, an' dey bu'st outen dat patch like a yarthquake, an' pile inter de upper ford road, an' flash down it five deep, an' it full o' Confed'rates from en' to en'! . . .

❄ ❄ ❄

A HORSEMAN IN THE SKY

I

One sunny afternoon in the autumn of the year 1861 a soldier lay in a clump of laurel by the side of a road in western Virginia. He lay at full length upon his stomach, his feet resting upon the toes, his head upon the left forearm. His extended right hand loosely grasped his rifle. But for the somewhat methodical disposition of his limbs and a slight rhythmic movement of the cartridge-box at the back of his belt he might have been thought to be dead. He was asleep at his post of duty. But if detected he would be dead shortly afterward, death being the just and legal penalty of his crime.

The clump of laurel in which the criminal lay was in the angle of a road which after ascending southward a steep acclivity to that point turned sharply to the west, running along the summit for perhaps one hundred yards. There it turned southward again and went zigzagging downward through the forest. At the salient of that second angle was a large flat rock, jutting out northward, overlooking the deep valley from which the road ascended. The rock capped a high cliff; a stone dropped from its outer edge would have fallen sheer downward one thousand feet to the tops of the pines. The angle where the soldier lay was on another spur of the same cliff. Had he been awake he would have commanded a view, not only of the short arm of the road and the jutting rock, but of the entire profile of the cliff below it. It might well have made him giddy to look.

The country was wooded everywhere except at the bottom of the valley to the northward, where there was a small natural meadow, through which flowed a stream scarcely visible from the valley's rim. This open ground looked hardly larger than an ordinary door-yard, but was really several acres in extent. Its green was more vivid than that of the inclosing forest. Away beyond it rose a line of giant cliffs similar to those upon which we are supposed to stand in our survey of the savage scene, and through which the road had somehow made its climb to the summit. The configuration of the valley, indeed, was such that from this point of observation it seemed entirely shut in, and one could but have wondered how the road which found a way out of it had found a way into it, and whence came and whither went the waters of the stream that parted the meadow more than a thousand feet below.

No country is so wild and difficult but men will make it a theatre of war; concealed in the forest at the bottom of that military rat-trap, in which half a hundred men in possession of the exits might have starved an army to submission, lay five regiments of Federal infantry. They had marched all the previous day and night and were resting. At nightfall they would take to the road again, climb to the place where their unfaithful sentinel now slept, and descending the other slope of the ridge fall upon a camp of the enemy at about midnight. Their hope was to surprise it, for the road led to the rear of it. In case of failure, their position would be perilous in the extreme; and fail they surely would should accident or vigilance apprise the enemy of the movement.

II

The sleeping sentinel in the clump of laurel was a young Virginian named Carter Druse. He was the son of wealthy parents, an only child, and had known such ease and cultivation and high living as wealth and taste were able to command in the mountain country of western Virginia. His home was but a few miles from where he now lay. One morning he had risen from the breakfast-table and said, quietly but gravely: "Father, a Union regiment has arrived at Grafton. I am going to join it."

The father lifted his leonine head, looked at the son a moment in silence, and replied: "Well, go, sir, and whatever may occur do what you conceive to be your duty. Virginia, to which you are a traitor, must get on without you. Should we both live to the end of the war, we will speak further of the matter. Your mother, as the physician has informed you, is in a most critical condition; at the best she cannot be with us longer than a few weeks, but that time is precious. It would be better not to disturb her."

So Carter Druse, bowing reverently to his father, who returned the salute with a stately courtesy that masked a breaking heart, left the home of his childhood to go soldiering. By conscience and courage, by deeds of devotion and daring, he soon commended himself to his fellows and his officers; and it was to these qualities and to some knowledge of the country that he owed his selection for his present perilous duty at the extreme outpost. Nevertheless, fatigue had been stronger than resolution and he had fallen asleep. What good or bad angel came in a dream to rouse him from his state of crime, who shall say? Without a movement, without a sound, in the profound silence and the languor of the late afternoon, some invisible messenger of fate touched with unsealing finger the eyes of his consciousness—whispered into the ear of his spirit the mysterious awakening word which no human lips ever have spoken, no human memory ever has recalled. He quietly raised his forehead from his arm and looked between the masking stems of the laurels, instinctively closing his right hand about the stock of his rifle.

His first feeling was a keen artistic delight. On a colossal pedestal, the cliff,—motionless at the extreme edge of the capping rock and sharply outlined against the sky,—was an equestrian statue of impressive dignity. The figure of the man sat the figure of the horse, straight and soldierly, but with the repose of a Grecian god carved in the marble which limits the suggestion of activity. The gray costume harmonized with its aërial background; the metal of accoutrement and caparison was softened and subdued by the shadow; the animal's skin had no points of high light. A carbine strikingly foreshortened lay across the pommel of the saddle, kept in place by the right hand grasping it at the "grip"; the left hand, holding the bridle rein, was invisible. In silhouette against the sky the profile of the horse was cut with the sharpness of a cameo; it looked across the heights of air to the confronting cliffs beyond. The face of the rider, turned slightly away, showed only an outline of temple and beard; he was looking downward to the bottom of the valley. Magnified by its lift against the sky and by the soldier's testifying sense of the formidableness of a near enemy the group appeared of heroic, almost colossal, size.

For an instant Druse had a strange, half-defined feeling that he had slept to the end of the war and was looking upon a noble work of art reared upon that eminence to commemorate the deeds of an heroic past of which he had been an inglorious part. The feeling was dispelled by a slight movement of the group: the horse, without moving its feet, had drawn its body slightly backward from the verge; the man remained immobile as before. Broad awake and keenly alive to the significance of the situation, Druse now brought the butt of his rifle against his cheek by cautiously pushing the barrel forward through the bushes, cocked the piece, and glancing through the sights covered a vital spot of the horseman's breast. A touch upon the trigger and all would have been well with Carter Druse. At that instant the horseman turned his head and looked in the direction of his concealed foeman—seemed to look into his very face, into his eyes, into his brave, compassionate heart.

Is it then so terrible to kill an enemy in war—an enemy who has surprised a secret vital to the safety of one's self and comrades—an enemy more formidable for his knowledge than all his army for its numbers? Carter Druse grew pale; he shook in every limb, turned faint, and saw the statuesque group before him as black figures, rising, falling, moving unsteadily in arcs of circles in a fiery sky. His hand fell away from his weapon, his head slowly dropped until his face rested on the leaves in which he lay. This courageous gentleman and hardy soldier was near swooning from intensity of emotion.

It was not for long; in another moment his face was raised from earth, his hands resumed their places on the rifle, his forefinger sought the trigger; mind, heart, and eyes were clear, conscience and reason sound. He could not hope to capture that enemy; to alarm him would but send him dashing to his camp with his fatal news. The duty of the soldier was plain: the man must be shot dead from ambush—without warning, without a moment's spiritual preparation, with never so much as an unspoken prayer, he must be sent to his account. But no—there is a hope; he may have discovered nothing—perhaps he is but admiring the sublimity of the landscape. If permitted, he may turn and ride carelessly away in the direction whence he came. Surely it will be possible to judge at the instant of his withdrawing whether he knows. It may well be that his fixity of attention —Druse turned his head and looked through the deeps of air downward, as from the surface to the bottom of a translucent sea. He saw creeping across the green meadow a sinuous line of figures of men and horses—some foolish commander was permitting the soldiers of his escort to water their beasts in the open, in plain view from a dozen summits!

Druse withdrew his eyes from the valley and fixed them again upon the group of man and horse in the sky, and again it was through the sights of his rifle. But this time his aim was at the horse. In his memory, as if they were a divine mandate, rang the words of his father at their parting: "Whatever may occur, do what you conceive to be your duty." He was calm now. His teeth were firmly but not rigidly closed; his nerves were as tranquil as a sleeping babe's— not a tremor affected any muscle of his body; his breathing, until suspended in the act of taking aim, was regular and slow. Duty had conquered; the spirit had said to the body: "Peace, be still." He fired.

III

An officer of the Federal force, who in a spirit of adventure or in quest of knowledge had left the hidden *bivouac* in the valley, and with aimless feet had made his way to the lower edge of a small open space near the foot of the cliff, was considering what he had to gain by pushing his exploration further. At a distance of a quarter-mile before him, but apparently at a stone's throw, rose from its fringe of pines the gigantic face of rock, towering to so great a height above him that it made him giddy to look up to where its edge cut a sharp, rugged line against the sky. It presented a clean, vertical profile against a background of blue sky to a point half the way down, and of distant hills, hardly less blue, thence to the tops of the trees at its base. Lifting his eyes to the dizzy altitude of its summit the officer saw an astonishing sight—a man on horseback riding down into the valley through the air!

Straight upright sat the rider, in military fashion, with a firm seat in the saddle, a strong clutch upon the rein to hold his charger from too impetuous a plunge. From his bare head his long hair streamed upward, waving like a plume. His hands were concealed in the cloud of the horse's lifted mane. The animal's body was as level as if every hoof-stroke encountered the resistant earth. Its motions were those of a wild gallop, but even as the officer looked they ceased, with all the legs thrown sharply forward as in the act of alighting from a leap. But this was a flight!

Filled with amazement and terror by this apparition of a horseman in the sky—half believing himself the chosen scribe of some new Apocalypse, the officer was overcome by the intensity of his emotions; his legs failed him and he fell. Almost at the same instant he heard a crashing sound in the trees—a sound that died without an echo—and all was still.

The officer rose to his feet, trembling. The familiar sensation of an abraded shin recalled his dazed faculties. Pulling himself together he ran rapidly obliquely away from the cliff to a point distant from its foot; there-about he expected to find his man; and there-about he naturally failed. In the fleeting instant of his vision his imagination had been so wrought upon by the apparent grace and ease and intention of the marvelous performance that it did not occur to him that the line of march of aërial cavalry is directly downward, and that he could find the objects of his search at the very foot of the cliff. A half-hour later he returned to camp.

This officer was a wise man; he knew better than to tell an incredible truth. He said nothing of what he had seen. But when the commander asked him if in his scout he had learned anything of advantage to the expedition he answered:

"Yes, sir; there is no road leading down into this valley from the southward."

The commander, knowing better, smiled.

IV

After firing his shot, Private Carter Druse reloaded his rifle and resumed his watch. Ten minutes had hardly passed when a Federal sergeant crept cautiously to him on hands and knees. Druse neither turned his head nor looked at him, but lay without motion or sign of recognition.

"Did you fire?" the sergeant whispered.

"Yes."

"At what?"

"A horse. It was standing on yonder rock—pretty far out. You see it is no longer there. It went over the cliff."

The man's face was white, but he showed no other sign of emotion. Having answered, he turned away his eyes and said no more. The sergeant did not understand.

"See here, Druse," he said, after a moment's silence, "it's no use making a mystery. I order you to report. Was there anybody on the horse?"

"Yes."

"Well?"

"My father."

The sergeant rose to his feet and walked away. "Good God!" he said.

❄   ❄   ❄

THE MOCKING-BIRD

The time, a pleasant Sunday afternoon in the early autumn of 1861. The place, a forest's heart in the mountain region of southwestern Virginia. Private Grayrock of the Federal Army is discovered seated comfortably at the root of a great pine tree, against which he leans, his legs extended straight along the ground, his rifle lying across his thighs, his hands (clasped in order that they may not fall away to his sides) resting upon the barrel of the weapon. The contact of the back of his head with the tree has pushed his cap downward over his eyes, almost concealing them; one seeing him would say that he slept.

Private Grayrock did not sleep; to have done so would have imperiled the interests of the United States, for he was a long way outside the lines and subject to capture or death at the hands of the enemy. Moreover, he was in a frame of mind unfavorable to repose. The cause of his perturbation of spirit was this: during the previous night he had served on the picket-guard, and had been posted as a sentinel in this very forest. The night was clear, though moonless, but in the gloom of the wood the darkness was deep. Grayrock's post was at a considerable distance from those to right and left, for the pickets had been thrown out a needless distance from the camp, making the line too long for the force detailed to occupy it. The war

was young, and military camps entertained the error that while sleeping they were better protected by thin lines a long way out toward
the enemy than by thicker ones close in. And surely they needed as
long notice as possible of an enemy's approach, for they were at that
time addicted to the practice of undressing—than which nothing
could be more unsoldierly. On the morning of the memorable 6th of
April, at Shiloh, many of Grant's men when spitted on Confederate
bayonets were as naked as civilians; but it should be allowed that this
was not because of any defect in their picket line. Their error was of
another sort: they had no pickets. This is perhaps a vain digression.
I should not care to undertake to interest the reader in the fate of an
army; what we have here to consider is that of Private Grayrock.

For two hours after he had been left at his lonely post that Saturday night he stood stock-still, leaning against the trunk of a large
tree, staring into the darkness in his front and trying to recognize
known objects; for he had been posted at the same spot during the
day. But all was now different; he saw nothing in detail, but only
groups of things, whose shapes, not observed when there was something more of them to observe, were now unfamiliar. They seemed
not to have been there before. A landscape that is all trees and undergrowth, moreover, lacks definition, is confused and without accentuated points upon which attention can gain a foothold. Add the
gloom of a moonless night, and something more than great natural
intelligence and a city education is required to preserve one's knowledge of direction. And that is how it occurred that Private Grayrock,
after vigilantly watching the spaces in his front and then impru-
dently executing a circumspection of his whole dimly visible environment (silently walking around his tree to accomplish it) lost his
bearings and seriously impaired his usefulness as a sentinel. Lost at
his post—unable to say in which direction to look for an enemy's approach, and in which lay the sleeping camp for whose security he
was accountable with his life—conscious, too, of many another awkward feature of the situation and of considerations affecting his own
safety, Private Grayrock was profoundly disquieted. Nor was he
given time to recover his tranquillity, for almost at the moment that
he realized his awkward predicament he heard a stir of leaves and a
snap of fallen twigs, and turning with a stilled heart in the direction
whence it came, saw in the gloom the indistinct outlines of a human
figure.

"Halt!" shouted Private Grayrock, peremptorily as in duty bound,
backing up the command with the sharp metallic snap of his cocking
rifle—"who goes there?"

There was no answer; at least there was an instant's hesitation, and the answer, if it came, was lost in the report of the sentinel's rifle. In the silence of the night and the forest the sound was deafening, and hardly had it died away when it was repeated by the pieces of the pickets to right and left, a sympathetic fusillade. For two hours every unconverted civilian of them had been evolving enemies from his imagination, and peopling the woods in his front with them, and Grayrock's shot had started the whole encroaching host into visible existence. Having fired, all retreated, breathless, to the reserves—all but Grayrock, who did not know in what direction to retreat. When, no enemy appearing, the roused camp two miles away had undressed and got itself into bed again, and the picket line was cautiously reestablished, he was discovered bravely holding his ground, and was complimented by the officer of the guard as the one soldier of that devoted band who could rightly be considered the moral equivalent of that uncommon unit of value, "a whoop in hell."

In the mean time, however, Grayrock had made a close but unavailing search for the mortal part of the intruder at whom he had fired, and whom he had a marksman's intuitive sense of having hit; for he was one of those born experts who shoot without aim by an instinctive sense of direction, and are nearly as dangerous by night as by day. During a full half of his twenty-four years he had been a terror to the targets of all the shooting-galleries in three cities. Unable now to produce his dead game he had the discretion to hold his tongue, and was glad to observe in his officer and comrades the natural assumption that not having run away he had seen nothing hostile. His "honorable mention" had been earned by not running away anyhow.

Nevertheless, Private Grayrock was far from satisfied with the night's adventure, and when the next day he made some fair enough pretext to apply for a pass to go outside the lines, and the general commanding promptly granted it in recognition of his bravery the night before, he passed out at the point where that had been displayed. Telling the sentinel then on duty there that he had lost something,—which was true enough—he renewed the search for the person whom he supposed himself to have shot, and whom if only wounded he hoped to trail by the blood. He was no more successful by daylight than he had been in the darkness, and after covering a wide area and boldly penetrating a long distance into "the Confederacy" he gave up the search, somewhat fatigued, seated himself at the root of the great pine tree, where we have seen him, and indulged his disappointment.

It is not to be inferred that Grayrock's was the chagrin of a cruel nature balked of its bloody deed. In the clear large eyes, finely wrought lips, and broad forehead of that young man one could read quite another story, and in point of fact his character was a singularly felicitous compound of boldness and sensibility, courage and conscience.

"I find myself disappointed," he said to himself, sitting there at the bottom of the golden haze submerging the forest like a subtler sea—"disappointed in failing to discover a fellow-man dead by my hand! Do I then really wish that I had taken life in the performance of a duty as well performed without? What more could I wish? If any danger threatened, my shot averted it; that is what I was there to do. No, I am glad indeed if no human life was needlessly extinguished by me. But I am in a false position. I have suffered myself to be complimented by my officers and envied by my comrades. The camp is ringing with praise of my courage. That is not just; I know myself courageous, but this praise is for specific acts which I did not perform, or performed—otherwise. It is believed that I remained at my post bravely, without firing, whereas it was I who began the fusillade, and I did not retreat in the general alarm because bewildered. What, then, shall I do? Explain that I saw an enemy and fired? They have all said that of themselves, yet none believes it. Shall I tell a truth which, discrediting my courage, will have the effect of a lie? Ugh! it is an ugly business altogether. I wish to God I could find my man!"

And so wishing, Private Grayrock, overcome at last by the languor of the afternoon and lulled by the stilly sounds of insects droning and prosing in certain fragrant shrubs, so far forgot the interests of the United States as to fall asleep and expose himself to capture. And sleeping he dreamed.

He thought himself a boy, living in a far, fair land by the border of a great river upon which the tall steamboats moved grandly up and down beneath their towering evolutions of black smoke, which announced them long before they had rounded the bends and marked their movements when miles out of sight. With him always, at his side as he watched them, was one to whom he gave his heart and soul in love—a twin brother. Together they strolled along the banks of the stream; together explored the fields lying farther away from it, and gathered pungent mints and sticks of fragrant sassafras in the hills overlooking all—beyond which lay the Realm of Conjecture, and from which, looking southward across the great river, they caught glimpses of the Enchanted Land. Hand in hand and heart in heart they two, the only children of a widowed mother, walked in paths of light through valleys of peace, seeing new things under a new sun. And through all the golden days floated one unceasing sound—the rich, thrilling melody of a mocking-bird in a cage by the cottage door. It pervaded and possessed all the spiritual intervals of the dream, like a musical benediction. The joyous bird was always in song; its infinitely various notes seemed to flow from its throat, effortless, in bubbles and rills at each heart-beat, like the waters of a pulsing spring. That fresh, clear melody seemed, indeed, the spirit of the scene, the meaning and interpretation to sense of the mysteries of life and love.

But there came a time when the days of the dream grew dark with sorrow in a rain of tears. The good mother was dead, the meadowside home by the great river was broken up, and the brothers were parted between two of their kinsmen. William (the dreamer) went to live in a populous city in the Realm of Conjecture, and John, crossing the river into the Enchanted Land, was taken to a distant region whose people in their lives and ways were said to be strange and wicked. To him, in the distribution of the dead mother's estate, had fallen all that they deemed of value—the mocking-bird. They could be divided, but it could not, so it was carried away into the strange country, and the world of William knew it no more forever. Yet still through the aftertime of his loneliness its song filled all the dream, and seemed always sounding in his ear and in his heart.

The kinsmen who had adopted the boys were enemies, holding no communication. For a time letters full of boyish bravado and boastful narratives of the new and larger experience—grotesque descriptions of their widening lives and the new worlds they had conquered—passed between them; but these gradually became less frequent, and with William's removal to another and greater city ceased altogether. But ever through it all ran the song of the mocking-bird, and when the dreamer opened his eyes and stared through the vistas of the pine forest the cessation of its music first apprised him that he was awake.

The sun was low and red in the west; the level rays projected from the trunk of each giant pine a wall of shadow traversing the golden haze to eastward until light and shade were blended in undistinguishable blue.

Private Grayrock rose to his feet, looked cautiously about him, shouldered his rifle and set off toward camp. He had gone perhaps a half-mile, and was passing a thicket of laurel, when a bird rose from the midst of it and perching on the branch of a tree above, poured from its joyous breast so inexhaustible floods of song as but one of all God's creatures can utter in His praise. There was little in that—it was only to open the bill and breathe; yet the man stopped as if struck—stopped and let fall his rifle, looked upward at the bird, covered his eyes with his hands and wept like a child! For the moment he was, indeed, a child, in spirit and in memory, welling again by the great river, over-against the Enchanted Land! Then with an effort of the will he pulled himself together, picked up his weapon and audibly damning himself for an idiot strode on. Passing an opening that reached into the heart of the little thicket he looked in, and there, supine upon the earth, its arms all abroad, its gray uniform stained with a single spot of blood upon the breast, its white face turned sharply upward and backward, lay the image of himself!—the body of John Grayrock, dead of a gunshot wound, and still warm! He had found his man.

As the unfortunate soldier knelt beside that masterwork of civil war the shrilling bird upon the bough overhead stilled her song and, flushed with sunset's crimson glory, glided silently away through the solemn spaces of the wood. At roll-call that evening in the Federal camp the name William Grayrock brought no response, nor ever again thereafter.

※ ※ ※

GEORGE THURSTON[1]

THREE INCIDENTS IN THE LIFE OF A MAN

George Thurston was a first lieutenant and aide-de-camp on the staff of Colonel Brough, commanding a Federal brigade. Colonel Brough was only temporarily in command, as senior colonel, the brigadier-general having been severely wounded and granted a leave of absence to recover. Lieutenant Thurston was, I believe, of Colonel Brough's regiment, to which, with his chief, he would naturally have been relegated had he lived till our brigade commander's recovery. The aide whose place Thurston took had been killed in battle; Thurston's advent among us was the only change in the *personnel* of our staff consequent upon the change in commanders. We did not like him; he was unsocial. This, however, was more observed by

---

[1] Bierce's first war story, published in *Wasp* magazine, September 29, 1883.

others than by me. Whether in camp or on the march, in barracks, in tents, or *en bivouac,* my duties as topographical engineer kept me working like a beaver—all day in the saddle and half the night at my drawing-table, platting my surveys. It was hazardous work; the nearer to the enemy's lines I could penetrate, the more valuable were my field notes and the resulting maps. It was a business in which the lives of men counted as nothing against the chance of defining a road or sketching a bridge. Whole squadrons of cavalry escort had sometimes to be sent thundering against a powerful infantry outpost in order that the brief time between the charge and the inevitable retreat might be utilized in sounding a ford or determining the point of intersection of two roads.

In some of the dark corners of England and Wales they have an immemorial custom of "beating the bounds" of the parish. On a certain day of the year the whole population turns out and travels in procession from one landmark to another on the boundary line. At the most important points lads are soundly beaten with rods to make them remember the place in after life. They become authorities. Our frequent engagements with the Confederate outposts, patrols, and scouting parties had, incidentally, the same educating value; they fixed in my memory a vivid and apparently imperishable picture of the locality—a picture serving instead of accurate field notes, which, indeed, it was not always convenient to take, with carbines cracking, sabers clashing, and horses plunging all about. These spirited encounters were observations entered in red.

One morning as I set out at the head of my escort on an expedition of more than the usual hazard Lieutenant Thurston rode up alongside and asked if I had any objection to his accompanying me, the colonel commanding having given him permission.

"None whatever," I replied rather gruffly; "but in what capacity will you go? You are not a topographical engineer, and Captain Burling commands my escort."

"I will go as a spectator," he said. Removing his sword-belt and taking the pistols from his holsters he handed them to his servant, who took them back to headquarters. I realized the brutality of my remark, but not clearly seeing my way to an apology, said nothing.

That afternoon we encountered a whole regiment of the enemy's cavalry in line and a field-piece that dominated a straight mile of the turnpike by which we had approached. My escort fought deployed in the woods on both sides, but Thurston remained in the center of the road, which at intervals of a few seconds was swept by gusts of grape and canister that tore the air wide open as they passed. He had dropped the rein on the neck of his horse and sat bolt upright in the saddle, with folded arms. Soon he was down, his horse torn to pieces. From the side of the road, my pencil and field book idle, my duty forgotten, I watched him slowly disengaging himself from the wreck and rising. At that instant, the cannon having ceased firing, a burly Confederate trooper on a spirited horse dashed like a thunderbolt down the road with drawn saber. Thurston saw him coming, drew himself up to his full height, and again folded his arms. He was too brave to retreat before the word, and my uncivil words had disarmed him. He was a spectator. Another moment and he would have been split like a mackerel, but a blessed bullet tumbled his assailant into the dusty road so near that the impetus sent the body rolling to Thurston's feet. That evening, while platting my hasty survey, I found time to frame an apology, which I think took the rude, primitive form of a confession that I had spoken like a malicious idiot.

A few weeks later a part of our army made an assault upon the enemy's left. The attack, which was made upon an unknown position and across unfamiliar ground, was led by our brigade. The ground was so broken and the underbrush so thick that all mounted officers and men were compelled to fight on foot—the brigade commander and his staff included. In the *mêlée* Thurston was parted from the rest of us, and we found him, horribly wounded, only when we had taken the enemy's last defense. He was some months in hospital at Nashville, Tennessee, but finally rejoined us. He said little about his misadventure, except that he had been bewildered and had strayed into the enemy's lines and been shot down; but from one of his captors, whom we in turn had captured, we learned the particulars. "He came walking right upon us as we lay in line," said this man. "A whole company of us instantly sprang up and leveled our rifles at his breast, some of them almost touching him. 'Throw down that sword and surrender, you damned Yank!' shouted some one in authority. The fellow ran his eyes along the line of rifle barrels, folded his arms across his breast, his right hand still clutching his sword, and deliberately replied, 'I will not.' If we had all fired he would have been torn to shreds. Some of us didn't. I didn't, for one; nothing could have induced me."

When one is tranquilly looking death in the eye and refusing him any concession one naturally has a good opinion of one's self. I don't know if it was this feeling that in Thurston found expression in a stiffish attitude and folded arms; at the mess table one day, in his absence, another explanation was suggested by our quartermaster, an irreclaimable stammerer when the wine was in: "It's h—is w—ay of m-m-mastering a c-c-consti-t-tu-tional t-tendency to r—un aw—ay."

"What!" I flamed out, indignantly rising; "you intimate that Thurston is a coward—and in his absence?"

"If he w—ere a cow—wow-ard h—e w—wouldn't t-try to m-m-master it; and if he w—ere p-present I w—wouldn't d-d-dare to d-d-discuss it," was the mollifying reply.

This intrepid man, George Thurston, died an ignoble death. The brigade was in camp, with headquarters in a grove of immense trees. To an upper branch of one of these a venturesome climber had attached the two ends of a long rope and made a swing with a length of not less than one hundred feet. Plunging downward from a height of fifty feet, along the arc of a circle with such a radius, soaring to an equal altitude, pausing for one breathless instant, then sweeping dizzily backward—no one who has not tried it can conceive the terrors of such sport to the novice. Thurston came out of his tent one day and asked for instruction in the mystery of propelling the swing —the art of rising and sitting, which every boy has mastered. In a few moments he had acquired the trick and was swinging higher than the most experienced of us had dared. We shuddered to look at his fearful flights.

"St-t-top him," said the quartermaster, snailing lazily along from the mess-tent, where he had been lunching; "h—e d-doesn't know that if h—e g-g-goes c-clear over h—e'll w—ind up the sw—ing."

With such energy was that strong man cannonaded himself through the air that at each extremity of his increasing arc his body, standing in the swing, was almost horizontal. Should he once pass above the level of the rope's attachment he would be lost; the rope would slacken and he would fall vertically to a point as far below as he had gone above, and then the sudden tension of the rope would wrest it from his hands. All saw the peril—all cried out to him to desist, and gesticulated at him as, indistinct and with a noise like the rush of a cannon shot in flight, he swept past us through the lower reaches of his hideous oscillation. A woman standing at a little distance away fainted and fell unobserved. Men from the camp of a regiment near by ran in crowds to see, all shouting. Suddenly, as Thurston was on his upward curve, the shouts all ceased.

Thurston and the swing had parted—that is all that can be known; both hands at once had released the rope. The impetus of the light swing exhausted, it was falling back; the man's momentum was carrying him, almost erect, upward and forward, no longer in his arc, but with an outward curve. It could have been but an instant, yet it seemed an age. I cried out, or thought I cried out: "My God! will he never stop going up?" He passed close to the branch of a tree. I remember a feeling of delight as I thought he would clutch it and save himself. I speculated on the possibility of it sustaining his weight. He passed above it, and from my point of view was sharply outlined against the blue. At this distance of many years I can distinctly recall that image of a man in the sky, its head erect, its feet close together, its hands—I do not see its hands. All at once, with astonishing suddenness and rapidity, it turns clear over and pitches downward. There is another cry from the crowd, which has rushed instinctively forward. The man has become merely a whirling object, mostly legs. Then there is an indescribable sound—the sound of an impact that shakes the earth, and these men, familiar with death in its most awful aspects, turn sick. Many walk unsteadily away from the spot; others support themselves against the trunks of trees or sit at the roots. Death has taken an unfair advantage; he has struck with an unfamiliar weapon; he has executed a new and disquieting stratagem. We did not know that he had so ghastly resources, possibilities of terror so dismal.

Thurston's body lay on its back. One leg, bent beneath, was broken above the knee and the bone driven into the earth. The abdomen had burst; the bowels protruded. The neck was broken.

The arms were folded tightly across the breast.

✻   ✻   ✻

KILLED AT RESACA

The best soldier of our staff was Lieutenant Herman Brayle, one of the two aides-de-camp. I don't remember where the general picked him up; from some Ohio regiment, I think; none of us had previously known him, and it would have been strange if we had, for no two of us came from the same State, nor even from adjoining States. The general seemed to think that a position on his staff was a distinction that should be so judiciously conferred as not to beget any sectional jealousies and imperil the integrity of that part of the country which was still an integer. He would not even choose officers from his own command, but by some jugglery at department headquarters obtained them from other brigades. Under such circumstances, a man's services had to be very distinguished indeed to be heard of by his family and the friends of his youth; and "the speaking trump of fame" was a trifle hoarse from loquacity, anyhow.

Lieutenant Brayle was more than six feet in height and of splendid proportions, with the light hair and gray-blue eyes which men so gifted usually find associated with a high order of courage. As he was commonly in full uniform, especially in action, when most officers are content to be less flamboyantly attired, he was a very striking and conspicuous figure. As to the rest, he had a gentleman's manners, a scholar's head, and a lion's heart. His age was about thirty.

We all soon came to like Brayle as much as we admired him, and it was with sincere concern that in the engagement at Stone's River —our first action after he joined us—we observed that he had one most objectionable and unsoldierly quality: he was vain of his courage. During all the vicissitudes and mutations of that hideous encounter, whether our troops were fighting in the open cotton fields, in the cedar thickets, or behind the railway embankment, he did not once take cover, except when sternly commanded to do so by the general, who usually had other things to think of than the lives of his staff officers—or those of his men, for that matter.

In every later engagement while Brayle was with us it was the same way. He would sit his horse like an equestrian statue, in a storm of bullets and grape, in the most exposed places—wherever, in fact, duty, requiring him to go, permitted him to remain—when, without trouble and with distinct advantage to his reputation for common sense, he might have been in such security as is possible on a battlefield in the brief intervals of personal inaction.

On foot, from necessity or in deference to his dismounted commander or associates, his conduct was the same. He would stand like a rock in the open when officers and men alike had taken to cover; while men older in service and years, higher in rank and of unquestionable intrepidity, were loyally preserving behind the crest of a hill lives infinitely precious to their country, this fellow would stand, equally idle, on the ridge, facing in the direction of the sharpest fire.

When battles are going on in open ground it frequently occurs that the opposing lines, confronting each other within a stone's throw for hours, hug the earth as closely as if they loved it. The line officers in their proper places flatten themselves no less, and the field officers, their horses all killed or sent to the rear, crouch beneath the infernal canopy of hissing lead and screaming iron without a thought of personal dignity.

In such circumstances the life of a staff officer of a brigade is distinctly "not a happy one," mainly because of its precarious tenure and the unnerving alternations of emotion to which he is exposed. From a position of that comparative security from which a civilian

would ascribe his escape to a "miracle," he may be despatched with
an order to some commander of a prone regiment in the front line—
a person for the moment inconspicuous and not always easy to find
without a deal of search among men somewhat preoccupied, and in a
din in which question and answer alike must be imparted in the
sign language. It is customary in such cases to duck the head and
scuttle away on a keen run, an object of lively interest to some thousands of admiring marksmen. In returning—well, it is not customary
to return.

Brayle's practice was different. He would consign his horse to the
care of an orderly,—he loved his horse,—and walk quietly away on his
perilous errand with never a stoop of the back, his splendid figure,
accentuated by his uniform, holding the eye with a strange fascination. We watched him with suspended breath, our hearts in our
mouths. On one occasion of this kind, indeed, one of our number,
an impetuous stammerer, was so possessed by his emotion that he
shouted at me:

"I'll b-b-bet you t-two d-d-dollars they d-drop him b-b-before he
g-gets to that d-d-ditch!"

I did not accept the brutal wager; I thought they would.

Let me do justice to a brave man's memory; in all these needless ex-
posures of life there was no visible bravado nor subsequent narration.
In the few instances when some of us had ventured to remonstrate,
Brayle had smiled pleasantly and made some light reply, which, however, had not encouraged a further pursuit of the subject. Once he
said:

"Captain, if ever I come to grief by forgetting your advice, I hope
my last moments will be cheered by the sound of your beloved voice
breathing into my ear the blessed words, 'I told you so.'"

We laughed at the captain—just why we could probably not have
explained—and that afternoon when he was shot to rags from an
ambuscade Brayle remained by the body for some time, adjusting the
limbs with needless care—there in the middle of a road swept by
gusts of grape and canister! It is easy to condemn this kind of thing,
and not very difficult to refrain from imitation, but it is impossible
not to respect, and Brayle was liked none the less for the weakness
which had so heroic an expression. We wished he were not a fool,
but he went on that way to the end, sometimes hard hit, but always
returning to duty about as good as new.

Of course, it came at last; he who ignores the law of probabilities
challenges an adversary that is seldom beaten. It was at Resaca, in
Georgia, during the movement that resulted in the taking of Atlanta.
In front of our brigade the enemy's line of earthworks ran through

open fields along a slight crest. At each end of this open ground we were close up to him in the woods, but the clear ground we could not hope to occupy until night, when darkness would enable us to burrow like moles and throw up earth. At this point our line was a quarter-mile away in the edge of a wood. Roughly, we formed a semicircle, the enemy's fortified line being the chord of the arc.

"Lieutenant, go tell Colonel Ward to work up as close as he can get cover, and not to waste much ammunition in unnecessary firing. You may leave your horse."

When the general gave this direction we were in the fringe of the forest, near the right extremity of the arc. Colonel Ward was at the left. The suggestion to leave the horse obviously enough meant that Brayle was to take the longer line, through the woods and among the men. Indeed, the suggestion was needless; to go by the short route meant absolutely certain failure to deliver the message. Before any-body could interpose, Brayle had cantered lightly into the field and the enemy's works were in crackling conflagration.

"Stop that damned fool!" shouted the general.

A private of the escort, with more ambition than brains, spurred forward to obey, and within ten yards left himself and his horse dead on the field of honor.

Brayle was beyond recall, galloping easily along, parallel to the enemy and less than two hundred yards distant. He was a picture to see! His hat had been blown or shot from his head, and his long, blond hair rose and fell with the motion of his horse. He sat erect in the saddle, holding the reins lightly in his left hand, his right hang-ing carelessly at his side. An occasional glimpse of his handsome profile as he turned his head one way or the other proved that the interest which he took in what was going on was natural and without affectation.

The picture was intensely dramatic, but in no degree theatrical. Successive scores of rifles spat at him viciously as he came within range, and our own line in the edge of the timber broke out in visible and audible defense. No longer regardful of themselves or their orders, our fellows sprang to their feet, and swarming into the open sent broad sheets of bullets against the blazing crest of the offending works, which poured an answering fire into their unprotected groups with deadly effect. The artillery on both sides joined the battle, punctuating the rattle and roar with deep, earth-shaking explosions and tearing the air with storms of screaming grape, which from the enemy's side splintered the trees and spattered them with blood, and from ours defiled the smoke of his arms with banks and clouds of dust from his parapet.

My attention had been for a moment drawn to the general combat, but now, glancing down the unobscured avenue between these two thunderclouds, I saw Brayle, the cause of the carnage. Invisible now from either side, and equally doomed by friend and foe, he stood in the shot-swept space, motionless, his face toward the enemy. At some little distance lay his horse. I instantly saw what had stopped him.

As topographical engineer I had, early in the day, made a hasty examination of the ground, and now remembered that at that point was a deep and sinuous gully, crossing half the field from the enemy's line, its general course at right angles to it. From where we now were it was invisible, and Brayle had evidently not known about it. Clearly, it was impassable. Its salient angles would have afforded him absolute security if he had chosen to be satisfied with the miracle already wrought in his favor and leapt into it. He could not go forward, he would not turn back; he stood awaiting death. It did not keep him long waiting.

By some mysterious coincidence, almost instantaneously as he fell, the firing ceased, a few desultory shots at long intervals serving rather to accentuate than break the silence. It was as if both sides had suddenly repented of their profitless crime. Four stretcher-bearers of ours, following a sergeant with a white flag, soon afterward moved unmolested into the field, and made straight for Brayle's body. Several Confederate officers and men came out to meet them, and with uncovered heads assisted them to take up their sacred burden. As it was borne toward us we heard beyond the hostile works fifes and a muffled drum—a dirge. A generous enemy honored the fallen brave.

Amongst the dead man's effects was a soiled Russia-leather pocket-book. In the distribution of mementoes of our friend, which the general, as administrator, decreed, this fell to me.

A year after the close of the war, on my way to California, I opened and idly inspected it. Out of an overlooked compartment fell a letter without envelope or address. It was in a woman's handwriting, and began with words of endearment, but no name.

It had the following date line: "San Francisco, Cal., July 9, 1862." The signature was "Darling," in marks of quotation. Incidentally, in the body of the text, the writer's full name was given—Marian Mendenhall.

The letter showed evidence of cultivation and good breeding, but it was an ordinary love letter, if a love letter can be ordinary. There was not much in it, but there was something. It was this:

"Mr. Winters, whom I shall always hate for it, has been telling that at some battle in Virginia, where he got his hurt, you were seen crouching behind a tree. I think he wants to injure you in my regard, which he knows the story would do if I believed it. I could bear to hear of my soldier lover's death, but not of his cowardice."

These were the words which on that sunny afternoon, in a distant region, had slain a hundred men. Is woman weak?

One evening I called on Miss Mendenhall to return the letter to her. I intended, also, to tell her what she had done—but not that she did it. I found her in a handsome dwelling on Rincon Hill. She was beautiful, well bred—in a word, charming.

"You knew Lieutenant Herman Brayle," I said, rather abruptly. "You know, doubtless, that he fell in battle. Among his effects was found this letter from you. My errand here is to place it in your hands."

She mechanically took the letter, glanced through it with deepening color, and then, looking at me with a smile, said:

"It is very good of you, though I am sure it was hardly worth while." She started suddenly and changed color. "This stain," she said, "is it—surely it is not——"

"Madam," I said, "pardon me, but that is the blood of the truest and bravest heart that ever beat."

She hastily flung the letter on the blazing coals. "Uh! I cannot bear the sight of blood!" she said. "How did he die?"

I had involuntarily risen to rescue that scrap of paper, sacred even to me, and now stood partly behind her. As she asked the question she turned her face about and slightly upward. The light of the burning letter was reflected in her eyes and touched her cheek with a tinge of crimson like the stain upon its page. I had never seen anything so beautiful as this detestable creature.

"He was bitten by a snake," I replied.

❈   ❈   ❈

THREE AND ONE ARE ONE

In the year 1861 Barr Lassiter, a young man of twenty-two, lived with his parents and an elder sister near Carthage, Tennessee. The family were in somewhat humble circumstances, subsisting by cultivation of a small and not very fertile plantation. Owning no slaves, they were not rated among "the best people" of their neighborhood; but they were honest persons of good education, fairly well mannered and as respectable as any family could be if uncredentialed by personal dominion over the sons and daughters of Ham. The elder Lassiter had that severity of manner that so frequently affirms an uncompromising devotion to duty, and conceals a warm and affectionate disposition. He was of the iron of which martyrs are made, but in the heart of the matrix had lurked a nobler metal, fusible at a milder heat, yet never coloring nor softening the hard exterior. By both heredity and environment something of the man's inflexible character had touched the other members of the family; the Lassiter home, though not devoid of domestic affection, was a veritable citadel of duty, and duty—ah, duty is as cruel as death!

When the war came on it found in the family, as in so many others in that State, a divided sentiment; the young man was loyal to the Union, the others savagely hostile. This unhappy division begot an insupportable domestic bitterness, and when the offending son and brother left home with the avowed purpose of joining the Federal army not a hand was laid in his, not a word of farewell was spoken, not a good wish followed him out into the world whither he went to meet with such spirit as he might whatever fate awaited him.

Making his way to Nashville, already occupied by the Army of General Buell, he enlisted in the first organization that he found, a Kentucky regiment of cavalry, and in due time passed through all the stages of military evolution from raw recruit to experienced trooper. A right good trooper he was, too, although in his oral narrative from which this tale is made there was no mention of that; the fact was learned from his surviving comrades. For Barr Lassiter has answered "Here" to the sergeant whose name is Death.

Two years after he had joined it his regiment passed through the region whence he had come. The country thereabout had suffered severely from the ravages of war, having been occupied alternately (and simultaneously) by the belligerent forces, and a sanguinary struggle had occurred in the immediate vicinity of the Lassiter homestead. But of this the young trooper was not aware.

Finding himself in camp near his home, he felt a natural longing to see his parents and sister, hoping that in them, as in him, the unnatural animosities of the period had been softened by time and separation. Obtaining a leave of absence, he set foot in the late summer afternoon, and soon after the rising of the full moon was walking up the gravel path leading to the dwelling in which he had been born.

Soldiers in war age rapidly, and in youth two years are a long time. Barr Lassiter felt himself an old man, and had almost expected to find the place a ruin and a desolation. Nothing, apparently, was changed. At the sight of each dear and familiar object he was profoundly affected. His heart beat audibly, his emotion nearly suffocated him; an ache was in his throat. Unconsciously he quickened his pace until he almost ran, his long shadow making grotesque efforts to keep its place beside him.

The house was unlighted, the door open. As he approached and paused to recover control of himself his father came out and stood bare-headed in the moonlight.

"Father!" cried the young man, springing forward with outstretched hand—"Father!"

The elder man looked him sternly in the face, stood a moment motionless and without a word withdrew into the house. Bitterly disappointed, humiliated, inexpressibly hurt and altogether unnerved, the soldier dropped upon a rustic seat in deep dejection, supporting his head upon his trembling hand. But he would not have it so: he was too good a soldier to accept repulse as defeat. He rose and entered the house, passing directly to the "sitting-room."

It was dimly lighted by an uncurtained east window. On a low stool by the hearthside, the only article of furniture in the place, sat his mother, staring into a fireplace strewn with blackened embers and cold ashes. He spoke to her—tenderly, interrogatively, and with hesitation, but she neither answered, nor moved, nor seemed in any way surprised. True, there had been time for her husband to apprise her of their guilty son's return. He moved nearer and was about to lay his hand upon her arm, when his sister entered from an adjoining room, looked him full in the face, passed him without a sign of recognition and left the room by a door that was partly behind him. He had turned his head to watch her, but when she was gone his eyes again sought his mother. She too had left the place.

Barr Lassiter strode to the door by which he had entered. The moonlight on the lawn was tremulous, as if the sward were a rippling sea. The trees and their black shadows shook as in a breeze. Blended with its borders, the gravel walk seemed unsteady and insecure to step on. This young soldier knew the optical illusions produced by tears. He felt them on his cheek, and saw them sparkle on the breast of his trooper's jacket. He left the house and made his way back to camp.

The next day, with no very definite intention, with no dominant feeling that he could rightly have named, he again sought the spot.

Within a half-mile of it he met Bushrod Albro, a former playfellow and schoolmate, who greeted him warmly.

"I am going to visit my home," said the soldier.

The other looked at him rather sharply, but said nothing.

"I know," continued Lassiter, "that my folks have not changed, but——"

"There have been changes," Albro interrupted—"everything changes. I'll go with you if you don't mind. We can talk as we go."

But Albro did not talk.

Instead of a house they found only fire-blackened foundations of stone, enclosing an area of compact ashes pitted by rains.

Lassiter's astonishment was extreme.

"I could not find the right way to tell you," said Albro. "In the fight a year ago your house was burned by a Federal shell."

"And my family—where are they?"

"In Heaven, I hope. All were killed by the shell."

❈   ❈   ❈

TWO MILITARY EXECUTIONS

In the spring of the year 1862 General Buell's big army lay in camp, licking itself into shape for the campaign which resulted in the victory at Shiloh. It was a raw, untrained army, although some of its fractions had seen hard enough service, with a good deal of fighting, in the mountains of Western Virginia, and in Kentucky. The war was young and soldiering a new industry, imperfectly understood by the young American of the period, who found some features of it not altogether to his liking. Chief among these was that essential part of discipline, subordination. To one imbued from infancy with the fascinating fallacy that all men are born equal, unquestioning submission to authority is not easily mastered, and the American volunteer soldier in his "green and salad days" is among the worst known. That is how it happened that one of Buell's men, Private Bennett Story Greene, committed the indiscretion of striking his officer. Later in the war he would not have done that; like Sir Andrew Aguecheek, he would have "seen him damned" first. But time for reformation of his military manners was denied him: he was promptly arrested on complaint of the officer, tried by court-martial and sentenced to be shot.

"You might have thrashed me and let it go at that," said the condemned man to the complaining witness; "that is what you used to do at school, when you were plain Will Dudley and I was as good as you. Nobody saw me strike you; discipline would not have suffered much."

"Ben Greene, I guess you are right about that," said the lieutenant. "Will you forgive me? That is what I came to see you about."

There was no reply, and an officer putting his head in at the door of the guard-tent where the conversation had occurred, explained that the time allowed for the interview had expired. The next morning, when in the presence of the whole brigade Private Greene was shot to death by a squad of his comrades, Lieutenant Dudley turned his back upon the sorry performance and muttered a prayer for mercy, in which himself was included.

A few weeks afterward, as Buell's leading division was being ferried over the Tennessee River to assist in succoring Grant's beaten army, night was coming on, black and stormy. Through the wreck of battle the division moved, inch by inch, in the direction of the enemy, who had withdrawn a little to reform his lines. But for the lightning the darkness was absolute. Never for a moment did it cease, and ever when the thunder did not crack and roar were heard the moans of the wounded among whom the men felt their way with their feet, and upon whom they stumbled in the gloom. The dead were there, too—there were dead a-plenty.

In the first faint gray of the morning, when the swarming advance had paused to resume something of definition as a line of battle, and skirmishers had been thrown forward, word was passed along to call the roll. The first sergeant of Lieutenant Dudley's company stepped to the front and began to name the men in alphabetical order. He had no written roll, but a good memory. The men answered to their names as he ran down the alphabet to G.

"Gorham."

"Here!"

"Grayrock."

"Here!"

The sergeant's good memory was affected by habit:

"Greene."

"Here!"

The response was clear, distinct, unmistakable!

A sudden movement, an agitation of the entire company front, as from an electric shock, attested the startling character of the incident. The sergeant paled and paused. The captain strode quickly to his side and said sharply:

"Call that name again."

Apparently the Society for Psychical Research is not first in the field of curiosity concerning the Unknown.

"Bennett Greene."

"Here!"

All faces turned in the direction of the familiar voice; the two men between whom in the order of stature Greene had commonly stood in line turned and squarely confronted each other.

"Once more," commanded the inexorable investigator, and once more came—a trifle tremulously—the name of the dead man:

"Bennett Story Greene."

"Here!"

At that instant a single rifle-shot was heard, away to the front, beyond the skirmish-line, followed, almost attended, by the savage hiss of an approaching bullet which, passing through the line, struck audibly, punctuating as with a full stop the captain's exclamation, "What the devid does it mean?"

Lieutenant Dudley pushed through the ranks from his place in the rear.

"It means this," he said, throwing open his coat and displaying a visibly broadening stain of crimson on his breast. His knees gave way; he fell awkwardly and lay dead.

A little later the regiment was ordered out of line to relieve the congested front, and through some misplay in the game of battle was not again under fire. Nor did Bennett Greene, expert in military executions, ever again signify his presence at one.

❅   ❅   ❅

THE MAJOR'S TALE

In the days of the Civil War practical joking had not, I think, fallen into that disrepute which characterizes it now. That, doubtless, was owing to our extreme youth—men were much younger than now, and evermore your very young man has a boisterous spirit, running easily to horse-play. You cannot think how young the men were in the early sixties! Why, the average age of the entire Federal Army was not more than twenty-five; I doubt if it was more than twenty-three, but not having the statistics on that point (if there are any) I want to be moderate: we will say twenty-five. It is true a man of twenty-five was in that heroic time a good deal more of a man than one of that age is now; you could see that by looking at him. His face had nothing of that unripeness so conspicuous in his successor. I never see a young fellow now without observing how disagreeably young he really is; but during the war we did not think of a man's age at all unless he happened to be pretty well along in life. In that case one could not help it, for the unloveliness of age assailed the human countenance then much earlier than now; the result, I suppose, of hard service—perhaps, to some extent, of hard drink, for, bless my soul! we did shed the blood of the grape and the grain abundantly during the war. I remember thinking General Grant, who could not have been more than forty, a pretty well preserved old chap, considering his habits. As to men of middle age—say from fifty to sixty—why, they all looked fit to personate the Last of the Hittites, or the Madagascarene Methuselah, in a museum. Depend upon it, my friends, men of that time were greatly younger than men are to-day, but looked much older. The change is quite remarkable.

I said that practical joking had not then gone out of fashion. It had not, at least, in the army; though possibly in the more serious life of the civilian it had no place except in the form of tarring and feathering an occasional "copperhead." You all know, I suppose, what a "copperhead" was, so I will go directly at my story without introductory remark, as is my way.

It was a few days before the battle of Nashville. The enemy had driven us up out of northern Georgia and Alabama. At Nashville we had turned at bay and fortified, while old Pap Thomas, our commander, hurried down reinforcements and supplies from Louisville. Meantime Hood, the Confederate commander, had partly invested us and lay close enough to have tossed shells into the heart of the town. As a rule he abstained—he was afraid of killing the families of his own soldiers, I suppose, a great many of whom had lived there. I sometimes wondered what were the feelings of those fellows, gazing over our heads at their own dwellings, where their wives and children or their aged parents were perhaps suffering for the necessaries of life, and certainly (so their reasoning would run) cowering under the tyranny and power of the barbarous Yankees.

To begin, then, at the beginning. I was serving at that time on the staff of a division commander whose name I shall not disclose, for I am relating facts, and the person upon whom they bear hardest may have surviving relatives who would not care to have him traced. Our headquarters were in a large dwelling which stood just behind our line of works. This had been hastily abandoned by the civilian occupants, who had left everything pretty much as it was—had no place to store it, probably, and trusted that Heaven would preserve it from Federal cupidity and Confederate artillery. With regard to the latter we were as solicitous as they.

Rummaging about in some of the chambers and closets one evening, some of us found an abundant supply of lady-gear—gowns, shawls, bonnets, hats, petticoats and the Lord knows what; I could not at that time have named the half of it. The sight of all this pretty plunder inspired one of us with what he was pleased to call an "idea," which, when submitted to the other scamps and scapegraces of the staff, met with instant and enthusiastic approval. We proceeded at once to act upon it for the undoing of one of our comrades.

Our selected victim was an aide, Lieutenant Haberton, so to call him. He was a good soldier—as gallant a chap as ever wore spurs; but he had an intolerable weakness: he was a lady-killer, and like most of his class, even in those days, eager that all should know it. He never tired of relating his amatory exploits, and I need not say how dismal that kind of narrative is to all but the narrator. It would be dismal even if sprightly and vivacious, for all men are rivals in woman's favor, and to relate your successes to another man is to rouse in him a dumb resentment, tempered by disbelief. You will not convince him that you tell the tale for his entertainment; he will hear nothing in it but an expression of your own vanity. Moreover, as most men, whether rakes or not, are willing to be thought rakes, he is very likely to resent a stupid and unjust inference which he suspects you to have drawn from his reticence in the matter of his own adventures—namely, that he has had none. If, on the other hand, he has had no scruple in the matter and his reticence is due to lack of opportunity to talk, or of nimbleness in taking advantage of it, why, then he will be surly because you "have the floor" when he wants it himself. There are, in short, no circumstances under which a man, even from the best of motives, or no motive at all, can relate his feats of love without distinctly lowering himself in the esteem of his male auditor; and herein lies a just punishment for such as kiss and tell. In my younger days I was myself not entirely out of favor with the ladies, and have a memory stored with much concerning them which doubtless I might put into acceptable narrative had I not undertaken another tale, and if it were not my practice to relate one thing at a time, going straight away to the end, without digression.

Lieutenant Haberton was, it must be confessed, a singularly handsome man with engaging manners. He was, I suppose, judging from the imperfect view-point of my sex, what women call "fascinating." Now, the qualities which make a man attractive to ladies entail a double disadvantage. First, they are of a sort readily discerned by other men, and by none more readily than by those who lack them. Their possessor, being feared by all these, is habitually slandered by them in self-defense. To all the ladies in whose welfare they deem themselves entitled to a voice and interest they hint at the vices and general unworth of the "ladies' man" in no uncertain terms, and to their wives relate without shame the most monstrous falsehoods about him. Nor are they restrained by the consideration that he is their friend; the qualities which have engaged their own admiration make it necessary to warn away those to whom the allurement would be a peril. So the man of charming personality, while loved by all the ladies who know him well, yet not too well, must endure with such fortitude as he may the consciousness that those others who know him only "by reputation" consider him a shameless reprobate, a vicious and unworthy man—a type and example of moral depravity. To name the second disadvantage entailed by his charms: he commonly is.

In order to get forward with our busy story (and in my judgment a story once begun should not suffer impedition) it is necessary to explain that a young fellow attached to our headquarters as an orderly was notably effeminate in face and figure. He was not more than seventeen and had a perfectly smooth face and large lustrous eyes, which must have been the envy of many a beautiful woman in those days. And how beautiful the women of those days were! and how gracious! Those of the South showed in their demeanor toward us Yankees something of *hauteur*, but, for my part, I found it less insupportable than the studious indifference with which one's attentions are received by the ladies of this new generation, whom I certainly think destitute of sentiment and sensibility.

This young orderly, whose name was Arman, we persuaded—by what arguments I am not bound to say—to clothe himself in female attire and personate a lady. When we had him arrayed to our satisfaction—and a charming girl he looked—he was conducted to a sofa in the office of the adjutant-general. That officer was in the secret, as indeed were all excepting Haberton and the general; within the awful dignity hedging the latter lay possibilities of disapproval which we were unwilling to confront.

When all was ready I went to Haberton and said: "Lieutenant, there is a young woman in the adjutant-general's office. She is the daughter of the insurgent gentleman who owns this house, and has, I think, called to see about its present occupancy. We none of us know just how to talk to her, but we think perhaps you would say about the right thing—at least you will say things in the right way. Would you mind coming down?"

The lieutenant would not mind; he made a hasty toilet and joined me. As we were going along a passage toward the Presence we encountered a formidable obstacle—the general.

"I say, Broadwood," he said, addressing me in the familiar manner which meant that he was in excellent humor, "there's a lady in Lawson's office. Looks like a devilish fine girl—came on some errand of mercy or justice, no doubt. Have the goodness to conduct her to my quarters. I won't saddle you youngsters with *all* the business of this division," he added facetiously.

This was awkward; something had to be done.

"General," I said, "I did not think the lady's business of sufficient importance to bother you with it. She is one of the Sanitary Commission's nurses, and merely wants to see about some supplies for the smallpox hospital where she is on duty. I'll send her in at once."

"You need not mind," said the general, moving on; "I dare say Lawson will attend to the matter."

Ah, the gallant general! how little I thought, as I looked after his retreating figure and laughed at the success of my ruse, that within the week he would be "dead on the field of honor!" Nor was he the only one of our little military household above whom gloomed the shadow of the death angel, and who might almost have heard "the beating of his wings." On that bleak December morning a few days later, when from an hour before dawn until ten o'clock we sat on horseback on those icy hills, waiting for General Smith to open the battle miles away to the right, there were eight of us. At the close of the fighting there were three. There is now one. Bear with him yet a little while, oh, thrifty generation; he is but one of the horrors of war strayed from his era into yours. He is only the harmless skeleton at your feast and peace-dance, responding to your laughter and your footing it featly, with rattling fingers and bobbing skull— albeit upon suitable occasion, with a partner of his choosing, he might do his little dance with the best of you.

As we entered the adjutant-general's office we observed that the entire staff was there. The adjutant-general himself was exceedingly busy at his desk. The commissary of subsistence played cards with the surgeon in a bay window. The rest were in several parts of the room, reading or conversing in low tones. On a sofa in a half lighted nook of the room, at some distance from any of the groups, sat the "lady," closely veiled, her eyes modestly fixed upon her toes.

"Madam," I said, advancing with Haberton, "this officer will be pleased to serve you if it is in his power. I trust that it is."

With a bow I retired to the farther corner of the room and took part in a conversation going on there, though I had not the faintest notion what it was about, and my remarks had no relevancy to anything under the heavens. A close observer would have noticed that we were all intently watching Haberton and only "making believe" to do anything else.

He was worth watching, too; the fellow was simply an *édition de luxe* of "Turveydrop on Deportment." As the "lady" slowly unfolded her tale of grievances against our lawless soldiery and mentioned certain instances of wanton disregard of property rights—among them, as to the imminent peril of bursting our sides we partly overheard, the looting of her own wardrobe—the look of sympathetic agony in Haberton's handsome face was the very flower and fruit of histrionic art. His deferential and assenting nods at her several statements were so exquisitely performed that one could not help regretting their unsubstantial nature and the impossibility of preserving them under glass for instruction and delight of posterity. And all the time the wretch was drawing his chair nearer and nearer. Once or twice he looked about to see if we were observing, but we were in appearance blankly oblivious to all but one another and our several diversions. The low hum of our conversation, the gentle tap-tap of the cards as they fell in play and the furious scratching of the adjutant-general's pen as he turned off countless pages of words without sense were the only sounds heard. No—there was another: at long intervals the distant boom of a heavy gun, followed by the approaching rush of the shot. The enemy was amusing himself.

On these occasions the lady was perhaps not the only member of that company who was startled, but she was startled more than the others, sometimes rising from the sofa and standing with clasped hands, the authentic portrait of terror and irresolution. It was no more than natural that Haberton should at these times reseat her with infinite tenderness, assuring her of her safety and regretting her peril in the same breath. It was perhaps right that he should finally possess himself of her gloved hand and a seat beside her on the sofa; but it certainly was highly improper for him to be in the very act of possessing himself of *both* hands when—boom, *whiz*, BANG!

We all sprang to our feet. A shell had crashed into the house and exploded in the room above us. Bushels of plaster fell among us. That modest and murmurous young lady sprang erect.

"Jumping Jee-rusalem!" she cried.

Haberton, who had also risen, stood as one petrified—as a statue of himself erected on the site of his assassination. He neither spoke, nor moved, nor once took his eyes off the face of Orderly Arman, who was now flinging his girl-gear right and left, exposing his charms in the most shameless way; while out upon the night and away over the lighted camps into the black spaces between the hostile lines rolled the billows of our inexhaustible laughter! Ah, what a merry life it was in the old heroic days when men had not forgotten how to laugh!

Haberton slowly came to himself. He looked about the room less blankly; then by degrees fashioned his visage into the sickliest grin that ever libeled all smiling. He shook his head and looked knowing.

"You can't fool *me!*" he said.

❀   ❀   ❀

A RESUMED IDENTITY

I

THE REVIEW AS A FORM OF WELCOME

One summer night a man stood on a low hill overlooking a wide expanse of forest and field. By the full moon hanging low in the west he knew what he might not have known otherwise: that it was near the hour of dawn. A light mist lay along the earth, partly veiling the lower features of the landscape, but above it the taller trees showed in well-defined masses against a clear sky. Two or three farmhouses were visible through the haze, but in none of them, naturally, was a light. Nowhere, indeed, was any sign or suggestion of life except the barking of a distant dog, which, repeated with mechanical iteration, served rather to accentuate than dispel the loneliness of the scene.

The man looked curiously about him on all sides, as one who among familiar surroundings is unable to determine his exact place and part in the scheme of things. It is so, perhaps, that we shall act when, risen from the dead, we await the call to judgment.

A hundred yards away was a straight road, showing white in the moonlight. Endeavoring to orient himself, as a surveyor or navigator might say, the man moved his eyes slowly along its visible length and at a distance of a quarter-mile to the south of his station saw, dim and gray in the haze, a group of horsemen riding to the north. Behind them were men afoot, marching in column, with dimly gleaming rifles aslant above their shoulders. They moved slowly and in silence. Another group of horsemen, another regiment of infantry, another and another—all in unceasing motion toward the man's point of view, past it, and beyond. A battery of artillery followed, the cannoneers riding with folded arms on limber and caisson. And still the interminable procession came out of the obscurity to south and passed into the obscurity to north, with never a sound of voice, nor hoof, nor wheel.

The man could not rightly understand: he thought himself deaf; said so, and heard his own voice, although it had an unfamiliar quality that almost alarmed him; it disappointed his ear's expectancy in the matter of *timbre* and resonance. But he was not deaf, and that for the moment sufficed.

Then he remembered that there are natural phenomena to which some one has given the name "acoustic shadows." If you stand in an acoustic shadow there is one direction from which you will hear nothing. At the battle of Gaines's Mill, one of the fiercest conflicts of the Civil War, with a hundred guns in play, spectators a mile and a half away on the opposite side of the Chickahominy valley heard nothing of what they clearly saw. The bombardment of Port Royal, heard and felt at St. Augustine, a hundred and fifty miles to the south, was inaudible two miles to the north in a still atmosphere. A few days before the surrender at Appomattox a thunderous engagement between the commands of Sheridan and Pickett was unknown to the latter commander, a mile in the rear of his own line.

These instances were not known to the man of whom we write, but less striking ones of the same character had not escaped his observation. He was profoundly disquieted, but for another reason than the uncanny silence of that moonlight march.

"Good Lord!" he said to himself—and again it was as if another had spoken his thought—"if those people are what I take them to be we have lost the battle and they are moving on Nashville!"

Then came a thought of self—an apprehension—a strong sense of personal peril, such as in another we call fear. He stepped quickly into the shadow of a tree. And still the silent battalions moved slowly forward in the haze.

The chill of a sudden breeze upon the back of his neck drew his attention to the quarter whence it came, and turning to the east he saw a faint gray light along the horizon—the first sign of returning day. This increased his apprehension.

"I must get away from here," he thought, "or I shall be discovered and taken."

He moved out of the shadow, walking rapidly toward the graying east. From the safer seclusion of a clump of cedars he looked back. The entire column had passed out of sight: the straight white road lay bare and desolate in the moonlight!

Puzzled before, he was now inexpressibly astonished. So swift a passing of so slow an army!—he could not comprehend it. Minute after minute passed unnoted; he had lost his sense of time. He sought with a terrible earnestness a solution of the mystery, but sought in vain. When at last he roused himself from his abstraction the sun's rim was visible above the hills, but in the new conditions he found no other light than that of day; his understanding was involved as darkly in doubt as before.

On every side lay cultivated fields showing no sign of war and war's ravages. From the chimneys of the farmhouses thin ascensions of blue smoke signaled preparations for a day's peaceful toil. Having stilled its immemorial allocution to the moon, the watch-dog was assisting a negro who, prefixing a team of mules to the plow, was flatting and sharping contentedly at his task. The hero of this tale stared stupidly at the pastoral picture as if he had never seen such a thing in all his life; then he put his hand to his head, passed it through his hair and, withdrawing it, attentively considered the palm—a singular thing to do. Apparently reassured by the act, he walked confidently toward the road.

II
WHEN YOU HAVE LOST YOUR LIFE CONSULT A PHYSICIAN

Dr. Stilling Malson, of Murfreesboro, having visited a patient six or seven miles away, on the Nashville road, had remained with him all night. At daybreak he set out for home on horseback, as was the custom of doctors of the time and region. He had passed into the neighborhood of Stone's River battlefield when a man approached him from the roadside and saluted in the military fashion, with a movement of the right hand to the hat-brim. But the hat was not a military hat, the man was not in uniform and had not a martial bearing. The doctor nodded civilly, half thinking that the stranger's uncommon greeting was perhaps in deference to the historic surroundings. As the stranger evidently desired speech with him he courteously reined in his horse and waited.

"Sir," said the stranger, "although a civilian, you are perhaps an enemy."

"I am a physician," was the non-committal reply.

"Thank you," said the other. "I am a lieutenant, of the staff of General Hazen." He paused a moment and looked sharply at the person whom he was addressing, then added, "Of the Federal army."

The physician merely nodded.

"Kindly tell me," continued the other, "what has happened here. Where are the armies? Which has won the battle?"

The physician regarded his questioner curiously with half-shut eyes. After a professional scrutiny, prolonged to the limit of politeness, "Pardon me," he said; "one asking information should be willing to impart it. Are you wounded?" he added, smiling.

"Not seriously—it seems."

The man removed the unmilitary hat, put his hand to his head, passed it through his hair and, withdrawing it, attentively considered the palm.

"I was struck by a bullet and have been unconscious. It must have been a light, glancing blow: I find no blood and feel no pain. I will not trouble you for treatment, but will you kindly direct me to my command—to any part of the Federal army—if you know?"

Again the doctor did not immediately reply: he was recalling much that is recorded in the books of his profession—something about lost identity and the effect of familiar scenes in restoring it. At length he looked the man in the face, smiled, and said:

"Lieutenant, you are not wearing the uniform of your rank and service."

At this the man glanced down at his civilian attire, lifted his eyes, and said with hesitation:

"That is true. I—I don't quite understand."

Still regarding him sharply but not unsympathetically the man of science bluntly inquired:

"How old are you?"

"Twenty-three—if that has anything to do with it."

"You don't look it; I should hardly have guessed you to be just that."

The man was growing impatient. "We need not discuss that," he said; "I want to know about the army. Not two hours ago I saw a column of troops moving northward on this road. You must have met them. Be good enough to tell me the color of their clothing, which I was unable to make out, and I'll trouble you no more."

"You are quite sure that you saw them?"

"Sure? My God, sir, I could have counted them!"

"Why, really," said the physician, with an amusing consciousness of his own resemblance to the loquacious barber of the Arabian Nights, "this is very interesting. I met no troops."

The man looked at him coldly, as if he had himself observed the likeness to the barber. "It is plain," he said, "that you do not care to assist me. Sir, you may go to the devil!"

He turned and strode away, very much at random, across the dewy fields, his half-penitent tormentor quietly watching him from his point of vantage in the saddle till he disappeared beyond an array of trees.

III

THE DANGER OF LOOKING INTO A POOL OF
WATER

After leaving the road the man slackened his pace, and now went forward, rather deviously, with a distinct feeling of fatigue. He could not account for this, though truly the interminable loquacity of that country doctor offered itself in explanation. Seating himself upon a rock, he laid one hand upon his knee, back upward, and casually looked at it. It was lean and withered. He lifted both hands to his face. It was seamed and furrowed; he could trace the lines with the tips of his fingers. How strange!—a mere bullet-stroke and a brief unconsciousness should not make one a physical wreck.

"I must have been a long time in hospital," he said aloud. "Why, what a fool I am! The battle was in December, and it is now summer!" He laughed. "No wonder that fellow thought me an escaped lunatic. He was wrong: I am only an escaped patient."

At a little distance a small plot of ground enclosed by a stone wall caught his attention. With no very definite intent he rose and went to it. In the center was a square, solid monument of hewn stone. It was brown with age, weather-worn at the angles, spotted with moss and lichen. Between the massive blocks were strips of grass the leverage of whose roots had pushed them apart. In answer to the challenge of this ambitious structure Time had laid his destroying hand upon it, and it would soon be "one with Nineveh and Tyre." In an inscription on one side his eye caught a familiar name. Shaking with excitement, he craned his body across the wall and read:

HAZEN'S BRIGADE
to
The Memory of Its Soldiers
who fell at
Stone River, Dec. 31, 1862.

The man fell back from the wall, faint and sick. Almost within an arm's length was a little depression in the earth; it had been filled by a recent rain—a pool of clear water. He crept to it to revive himself, lifted the upper part of his body on his trembling arms, thrust forward his head and saw the reflection of his face, as in a mirror. He uttered a terrible cry. His arms gave way; he fell, face downward, into the pool and yielded up the life that had spanned another life.

❅   ❅   ❅

A MAN WITH TWO LIVES

Here is the queer story of David William Duck, related by himself. Duck is an old man living in Aurora, Illinois, where he is universally respected. He is commonly known, however, as "Dead Duck."

"In the autumn of 1866 I was a private soldier of the Eighteenth Infantry. My company was one of those stationed at Fort Phil Kearney, commanded by Colonel Carrington. The country is more or less familiar with the history of that garrison, particularly with the slaughter by the Sioux of a detachment of eighty-one men and officers—not one escaping—through disobedience of orders by its commander, the brave but reckless Captain Fetterman. When that occurred, I was trying to make my way with important dispatches to Fort C. F. Smith, on the Big Horn. As the country swarmed with hostile Indians, I traveled by night and concealed myself as best I could before daybreak. The better to do so, I went afoot, armed with a Henry rifle and carrying three days' rations in my haversack.

"For my second place of concealment I chose what seemed in the darkness a narrow cañon leading through a range of rocky hills. It contained many large bowlders, detached from the slopes of the hills. Behind one of these, in a clump of sage-brush, I made my bed for the day, and soon fell asleep. It seemed as if I had hardly closed my eyes, though in fact it was near midday, when I was awakened by the report of a rifle, the bullet striking the bowlder just above my body. A band of Indians had trailed me and had me nearly surrounded; the shot had been fired with an execrable aim by a fellow who had caught sight of me from the hillside above. The smoke of his rifle betrayed him, and I was no sooner on my feet than he was off his and rolling down the declivity. Then I ran in a stooping posture, dodging among the clumps of sage-brush in a storm of bullets from invisible enemies. The rascals did not rise and pursue, which I thought rather queer, for they must have known by my trail that they had to deal with only one man. The reason for their inaction was soon made clear. I had not gone a hundred yards before I reached the limit of my run—the head of the gulch which I had mistaken for a cañon. It terminated in a concave breast of rock, nearly vertical and destitute of vegetation. In that cul-de-sac I was caught like a bear in a pen. Pursuit was needless; they had only to wait.

"They waited. For two days and nights, crouching behind a rock topped with a growth of mesquite, and with the cliff at my back, suffering agonies of thirst and absolutely hopeless of deliverance, I fought the fellows at long range, firing occasionally at the smoke of their rifles, as they did at that of mine. Of course, I did not dare to close my eyes at night, and lack of sleep was a keen torture.

"I remember the morning of the third day, which I knew was to be my last. I remember, rather indistinctly, that in my desperation and delirium I sprang out into the open and began firing my repeating rifle without seeing anybody to fire at. And I remember no more of that fight.

"The next thing that I recollect was my pulling myself out of a river just at nightfall. I had not a rag of clothing and knew nothing of my whereabouts, but all that night I traveled, cold and footsore, toward the north. At daybreak I found myself at Fort C. F. Smith, my destination, but without my dispatches. The first man that I met was a sergeant named William Briscoe, whom I knew very well. You can fancy his astonishment at seeing me in that condition, and my own at his asking who the devil I was.

" 'Dave Duck,' I answered; 'who should I be?'

He stared like an owl.

" 'You do look it,' he said, and I observed that he drew a little away from me. 'What's up?' he added.

"I told him what had happened to me the day before. He heard me through, still staring; then he said:

" 'My dear fellow, if you are Dave Duck I ought to inform you that I buried you two months ago. I was out with a small scouting party and found your body, full of bullet-holes and newly scalped—somewhat mutilated otherwise, too, I am sorry to say—right where you say you made your fight. Come to my tent and I'll show you your clothing and some letters that I took from your person; the commandant has your dispatches.'

"He performed that promise. He showed me the clothing, which I resolutely put on; the letters, which I put into my pocket. He made no objection, then took me to the commandant, who heard my story and coldly ordered Briscoe to take me to the guardhouse. On the way I said:

" 'Bill Briscoe, did you really and truly bury the dead body that you found in these togs?'

" 'Sure,' he answered—'just as I told you. It was Dave Duck, all right; most of us knew him. And now, you damned impostor, you'd better tell me who you are.'

" 'I'd give something to know,' I said.

"A week later, I escaped from the guardhouse and got out of the country as fast as I could. Twice I have been back, seeking for that fateful spot in the hills, but unable to find it."

❊   ❊   ❊

THE OTHER LODGERS

"In order to take that train," said Colonel Levering, sitting in the Waldorf-Astoria hotel, "you will have to remain nearly all night in Atlanta. That is a fine city, but I advise you not to put up at the Breathitt House, one of the principal hotels. It is an old wooden building in urgent need of repairs. There are breaches in the walls that you could throw a cat through. The bedrooms have no locks on the doors, no furniture but a single chair in each, and a bedstead without bedding—just a mattress. Even these meager accommodations you cannot be sure that you will have in monopoly; you must take your chance of being stowed in with a lot of others. Sir, it is a most abominable hotel.

"The night that I passed in it was an uncomfortable night. I got in late and was shown to my room on the ground floor by an apologetic night-clerk with a tallow candle, which he considerately left with me. I was worn out by two days and a night of hard railway travel and had not entirely recovered from a gunshot wound in the head, received in an altercation. Rather than look for better quarters I lay down on the mattress without removing my clothing and fell asleep.

"Along toward morning I awoke. The moon had risen and was shining in at the uncurtained window, illuminating the room with a soft, bluish light which seemed, somehow, a bit spooky, though I dare say it had no uncommon quality; all moonlight is that way if you will observe it. Imagine my surprise and indignation when I saw the floor occupied by at least a dozen other lodgers! I sat up, earnestly damning the management of that unthinkable hotel, and was about to spring from the bed to go and make trouble for the night-clerk—him of the apologetic manner and the tallow candle— when something in the situation affected me with a strange indisposition to move. I suppose I was what a story-writer might call 'frozen with terror.' For those men were obviously all dead!

"They lay on their backs, disposed orderly along three sides of the room, their feet to the walls—against the other wall, farthest from the door, stood my bed and the chair. All the faces were covered, but under their white cloths the features of the two bodies that lay in the square patch of moonlight near the window showed in sharp profile as to nose and chin.

"I thought this is a bad dream and tried to cry out, as one does in a nightmare, but could make no sound. At last, with a desperate effort I threw my feet to the floor and passing between the two rows of clouted faces and the two bodies that lay nearest the door, I escaped from the infernal place and ran to the office. The night-clerk was there, behind the desk, sitting in the dim light of another tallow candle—just sitting and staring. He did not rise: my abrupt entrance produced no effect upon him, though I must have looked a veritable corpse myself. It occurred to me then that I had not before really observed the fellow. He was a little chap, with a colorless face and the whitest, blankest eyes I ever saw. He had no more expression than the back of my hand. His clothing was a dirty gray.

" 'Damn you!' I said; 'what do you mean?'

"Just the same, I was shaking like a leaf in the wind and did not recognize my own voice.

"The night-clerk rose, bowed (apologetically) and—well, he was no longer there, and at that moment I felt a hand laid upon my shoulder from behind. Just fancy that if you can! Unspeakably frightened, I turned and saw a portly, kind-faced gentleman, who asked:

" 'What is the matter, my friend?'

"I was not long in telling him, but before I made an end of it he went pale himself. 'See here,' he said, 'are you telling the truth?'

"I had now got myself in hand and terror had given place to indignation. 'If you dare to doubt it,' I said, 'I'll hammer the life out of you!'

" 'No,' he replied, 'don't do that; just sit down till I tell you. This is not a hotel. It used to be; afterward it was a hospital. Now it is unoccupied, awaiting a tenant. The room that you mention was the dead-room—there were always plenty of dead. The fellow that you call the night-clerk used to be that, but later he booked the patients as they were brought in. I don't understand his being here. He has been dead a few weeks.'

" 'And who are you?' I blurted out.

" 'Oh, I look after the premises. I happened to be passing just now, and seeing a light in here came in to investigate. Let us have a look into that room,' he added, lifting the sputtering candle from the desk.

" 'I'll see you at the devil first!' said I, bolting out of the door into the street.

"Sir, that Breathitt House, in Atlanta, is a beastly place! Don't you stop there."

"God forbid! Your account of it certainly does not suggest comfort. By the way, Colonel, when did all that occur?"

"In September, 1864—shortly after the seige."

❄   ❄   ❄

A BIVOUAC OF THE DEAD

Away up in the heart of the Allegheny mountains, in Pocahontas county, West Virginia, is a beautiful little valley through which flows the east fork of the Greenbrier river. At a point where the valley road intersects the old Staunton and Parkersburg turnpike, a famous thoroughfare in its day, is a post office in a farm house. The name of the place is Travelers' Repose, for it was once a tavern. Crowning some low hills within a stone's throw of the house are long lines of old Confederate fortifications, skilfully designed and so well "preserved" that an hour's work by a brigade would put them into serviceable shape for the next civil war. This place had its battle —what was called a battle in the "green and salad days" of the great rebellion. A brigade of Federal troops, the writer's regiment among them, came over Cheat mountain, fifteen miles to the westward, and, stringing its lines across the little valley, felt the enemy all day; and the enemy did a little feeling, too. There was a great cannonading, which killed about a dozen on each side; then, finding the place too strong for assault, the Federals called the affair a reconnaissance in force, and burying their dead withdrew to the more comfortable place whence they had come. Those dead now lie in a beautiful national cemetery at Grafton, duly registered, so far as identified, and companioned by other Federal dead gathered from the several camps and battlefields of West Virginia. The fallen soldier (the word "hero" appears to be a later invention) has such humble honors as it is possible to give.

> His part in all the pomp that fills
> The circuit of the Summer hills
> Is that his grave is green.

True, more than a half of the green graves in the Grafton cemetery are marked "Unknown," and sometimes it occurs that one thinks of the contradiction involved in "honoring the memory" of him of whom no memory remains to honor; but the attempt seems to do no great harm to the living, even to the logical.

A few hundred yards to the rear of the old Confederate earthworks is a wooded hill. Years ago it was not wooded. Here, among the trees and in the undergrowth, are rows of shallow depressions, discoverable by removing the accumulated forest leaves. From some of them may be taken (and reverently replaced) small thin slabs of the split stone of the country, with rude and reticent inscriptions by comrades. I found only one with a date, only one with full names of man and regiment. The entire number found was eight.

In these forgotten graves rest the Confederate dead—between eighty and one hundred, as nearly as can be made out. Some fell in the "battle;" the majority died of disease. Two, only two, have apparently been disinterred for reburial at their homes. So neglected and obscure in this *campo santo* that only he upon whose farm it is —the aged postmaster of Travelers' Repose—appears to know about it. Men living within a mile have never heard of it. Yet other men must be still living who assisted to lay these Southern soldiers where they are, and could identify some of the graves. Is there a man, North or South, who would begrudge the expense of giving to these fallen brothers the tribute of green graves? One would rather not think so. True, there are several hundreds of such places still discoverable in the track of the great war. All the stronger is the dumb demand—the silent plea of these fallen brothers to what is "likest God within the soul."

They were honest and courageous foemen, having little in common with the political madmen who persuaded them to their doom and the literary bearers of false witness in the aftertime. They did not live through the period of honorable strife into the period of vilification—did not pass from the iron age to the brazen—from the era of the sword to that of the tongue and pen. Among them is no member of the Southern Historical Society. Their valor was not the fury of the non-combatant; they have no voice in the thunder of the civilians and the shouting. Not by them are impaired the dignity and infinite pathos of the Lost Cause. Give them, these blameless gentlemen, their rightful part in all the pomp that fills the circuit of the summer hills.

1903.

III

THE WORLD OF

Tall Tales

FOREWORD

To a Westerner no explanation should be needed for the fact that Ambrose Bierce wrote twenty-three "tall tales," since this was the one form of literature that the pioneers had brought across the plains, and it probably had its origin in the frontier farm country long before that. The essence of the "tall tale" was high exaggeration presented in the deadpan manner as truthful fact; it was a hoax aimed at the listener who might be sucker enough to take the wild tale seriously, and the moment he betrayed that belief, as by a harmless question, the works blew up. Bierce isn't known to have heard tall tales in their natural habitat, the cow-camp or mining camp, but he could easily have heard them in San Francisco barrooms or at the Bohemian Club. One of the best of all "tall tales," "Plain Language from Truthful James," was offered to Bierce by Bret Harte and was refused by Bierce as being too good for the "Town Crier"—whereupon Harte published it in his *Overland Monthly* and became famous by consequence.

Bierce published at least three of his "tall tales" in his *Wasp* days, before the Hearst period. The others were written at later intervals when he had nothing else on his mind. In these "negligible" stories, as he called them, he poked satirical fun at the parental relationship, American business, education, murder, journalism, babies, and life on the sea. And the suckers indeed fell for hoaxes—solemn Eastern critics regarded these stories as out of taste and were shocked, especially, at "Oil of Dog"; psychologists claimed the "parenticide" group showed that Bierce had a suppressed desire, dating from childhood, to murder his parents. In the West, these critics and psychologists would have had to buy the drinks. What these tales did represent in practice was a hardworking satirist writing when he was relaxed.

—E. J. H.

AN IMPERFECT CONFLAGRATION

Early one June morning in 1872 I murdered my father—an act which made a deep impression on me at the time. This was before my marriage, while I was living with my parents in Wisconsin. My father and I were in the library of our home, dividing the proceeds of a burglary which we had committed that night. These consisted of household goods mostly, and the task of equitable division was difficult. We got on very well with the napkins, towels and such things, and the silverware was parted pretty nearly equally, but you can see for yourself that when you try to divide a single music-box by two without a remainder you will have trouble. It was that music-box which brought disaster and disgrace upon our family. If we had left it my poor father might now be alive.

It was a most exquisite and beautiful piece of workmanship—inlaid with costly woods and carven very curiously. It would not only play a great variety of tunes, but would whistle like a quail, bark like a dog, crow every morning at daylight whether it was wound up or not, and break the Ten Commandments. It was this last mentioned accomplishment that won my father's heart and caused him to commit the only dishonorable act of his life, though possibly he would have committed more if he had been spared: he tried to conceal that music-box from me, and declared upon his honor that he had not taken it, though I knew very well that, so far as he was concerned, the burglary had been undertaken chiefly for the purpose of obtaining it.

My father had the music-box hidden under his cloak; we had

worn cloaks by way of disguise. He had solemnly assured me that he did not take it. I knew that he did, and knew something of which he was evidently ignorant; namely, that the box would crow at daylight and betray him if I could prolong the division of profits till that time. All occurred as I wished: as the gaslight began to pale in the library and the shape of the windows was seen dimly behind the curtains, a long cock-a-doodle-doo came from beneath the old gentleman's cloak, followed by a few bars of an aria from *Tannhauser*, ending with a loud click. A small hand-axe, which we had used to break into the unlucky house, lay between us on the table; I picked it up. The old man seeing that further concealment was useless took the box from under his cloak and set it on the table. "Cut it in two if you prefer that plan," said he; "I tried to save it from destruction."

He was a passionate lover of music and could himself play the concertina with expression and feeling.

I said: "I do not question the purity of your motive: it would be presumptuous in me to sit in judgment on my father. But business is business, and with this axe I am going to effect a dissolution of our partnership unless you will consent in all future burglaries to wear a bell-punch."

"No," he said, after some reflection, "no, I could not do that; it would look like a confession of dishonesty. People would say that you distrusted me."

I could not help admiring his spirit and sensitiveness; for a moment I was proud of him and disposed to overlook his fault, but a glance at the richly jeweled music-box decided me, and, as I said, I removed the old man from this vale of tears. Having done so, I was a trifle uneasy. Not only was he my father—the author of my being —but the body would be certainly discovered. It was now broad daylight and my mother was likely to enter the library at any moment. Under the circumstances, I thought it expedient to remove her also, which I did. Then I paid off all the servants and discharged them.

That afternoon I went to the chief of police, told him what I had done and asked his advice. It would be very painful to me if the facts became publicly known. My conduct would be generally condemned; the newspapers would bring it up against me if ever I should run for office. The chief saw the force of these considerations; he was himself an assassin of wide experience. After consulting with the presiding judge of the Court of Variable Jurisdiction he advised me to conceal the bodies in one of the book-cases, get a heavy insurance on the house and burn it down. This I proceeded to do.

In the library was a book-case which my father had recently purchased of some cranky inventor and had not filled. It was in shape and size something like the old-fashioned "wardrobes" which one sees in bed-rooms without closets, but opened all the way down, like a woman's night-dress. It had glass doors. I had recently laid out my parents and they were now rigid enough to stand erect; so I stood them in this book-case, from which I had removed the shelves. I locked them in and tacked some curtains over the glass doors. The inspector from the insurance office passed a half-dozen times before the case without suspicion.

That night, after getting my policy, I set fire to the house and started through the woods to town, two miles away, where I managed to be found about the time the excitement was at its height. With cries of apprehension for the fate of my parents, I joined the rush and arrived at the fire some two hours after I had kindled it. The whole town was there as I dashed up. The house was entirely consumed, but in one end of the level bed of glowing embers, bolt upright and uninjured, was that book-case! The curtains had burned away, exposing the glass doors, through which the fierce, red light illuminated the interior. There stood my dear father "in his habit as he lived," and at his side the partner of his joys and sorrows. Not a hair of them was singed, their clothing was intact. On their heads and throats the injuries which in the accomplishment of my designs I had been compelled to inflict were conspicuous. As in the presence of a miracle, the people were silent; awe and terror had stilled every tongue. I was myself greatly affected.

Some three years later, when the events herein related had nearly faded from my memory, I went to New York to assist in passing some counterfeit United States bonds. Carelessly looking into a furniture store one day, I saw the exact counterpart of that book-case. "I bought it for a trifle from a reformed inventor," the dealer explained. "He said it was fireproof, the pores of the wood being filled with alum under hydraulic pressure and the glass made of asbestos. I don't suppose it is really fireproof—you can have it at the price of an ordinary book-case."

"No," I said, "if you cannot warrant it fireproof I won't take it"— and I bade him good morning.

I would not have had it at any price: it revived memories that were exceedingly disagreeable.

A BOTTOMLESS GRAVE

My name is John Brenwalter. My father, a drunkard, had a patent for an invention for making coffee-berries out of clay; but he was an honest man and would not himself engage in the manufacture. He was, therefore, only moderately wealthy, his royalties from his really valuable invention bringing him hardly enough to pay his expenses of litigation with rogues guilty of infringement. So I lacked many advantages enjoyed by the children of unscrupulous and dishonorable parents, and had it not been for a noble and devoted mother, who neglected all my brothers and sisters and personally supervised my education, should have grown up in ignorance and been compelled to teach school. To be the favorite child of a good woman is better than gold.

When I was nineteen years of age my father had the misfortune to die. He had always had perfect health, and his death, which occurred at the dinner table without a moment's warning, surprised no one more than himself. He had that very morning been notified that a patent had been granted him for a device to burst open safes by hydraulic pressure, without noise. The Commissioner of Patents had pronounced it the most ingenious, effective and generally meritorious invention that had ever been submitted to him, and my father had naturally looked forward to an old age of prosperity and honor. His sudden death was, therefore, a deep disappointment to him; but my mother, whose piety and resignation to the will of Heaven were conspicuous virtues of her character, was apparently less affected. At the close of the meal, when my poor father's body had been removed from the floor, she called us all into an adjoining room and addressed us as follows:

"My children, the uncommon occurrence that you have just witnessed is one of the most disagreeable incidents in a good man's life, and one in which I take little pleasure, I assure you. I beg you to believe that I had no hand in bringing it about. Of course," she added, after a pause, during which her eyes were cast down in deep thought, "of course it is better that he is dead."

She uttered this with so evident a sense of its obviousness as a self-evident truth that none of us had the courage to brave her surprise by asking an explanation. My mother's air of surprise when any of us went wrong in any way was very terrible to us. One day, when in a fit of peevish temper, I had taken the liberty to cut off the baby's ear, her simple words, "John, you surprise me!" appeared to me so sharp a reproof that after a sleepless night I went to her in tears, and throwing myself at her feet, exclaimed: "Mother, forgive me for surprising you." So now we all—including the one-eared baby —felt that it would keep matters smoother to accept without question the statement that it was better, somehow, for our dear father to be dead. My mother continued:

"I must tell you, my children, that in a case of sudden and mysterious death the law requires the Coroner to come and cut the body into pieces and submit them to a number of men who, having inspected them, pronounce the person dead. For this the Coroner gets a large sum of money. I wish to avoid that painful formality in this instance; it is one which never had the approval of—of the remains. John"—here my mother turned her angel face to me—"you are an educated lad, and very discreet. You have now an opportunity to show your gratitude for all the sacrifices that your education has entailed upon the rest of us. John, go and remove the Coroner."

Inexpressibly delighted by this proof of my mother's confidence, and by the chance to distinguish myself by an act that squared with my natural disposition, I knelt before her, carried her hand to my lips and bathed it with tears of sensibility. Before five o'clock that afternoon I had removed the Coroner.

I was immediately arrested and thrown into jail, where I passed a most uncomfortable night, being unable to sleep because of the profanity of my fellow-prisoners, two clergymen, whose theological training had given them a fertility of impious ideas and a command of blasphemous language altogether unparalleled. But along toward morning the jailer, who, sleeping in an adjoining room, had been equally disturbed, entered the cell and with a fearful oath warned the reverend gentlemen that if he heard any more swearing their sacred calling would not prevent him from turning them into the street. After that they moderated their objectionable conversation, substituting an accordion, and I slept the peaceful and refreshing sleep of youth and innocence.

The next morning I was taken before the Superior Judge, sitting as a committing magistrate, and put upon my preliminary examination. I pleaded not guilty, adding that the man whom I had murdered was a notorious Democrat. (My good mother was a Republican, and from early childhood I had been carefully instructed by her in the principles of honest government and the necessity of

suppressing factional opposition.) The Judge, elected by a Republican ballot-box with a sliding bottom, was visibly impressed by the
cogency of my plea and offered me a cigarette.

"May it please your Honor," began the District Attorney, "I do
not deem it necessary to submit any evidence in this case. Under
the law of the land you sit here as a committing magistrate. It is
therefore your duty to commit. Testimony and argument alike would
imply a doubt that your Honor means to perform your sworn duty.
That is my case."

My counsel, a brother of the deceased Coroner, rose and said:
"May it please the Court, my learned friend on the other side has
so well and eloquently stated the law governing in this case that it
only remains for me to inquire to what extent it has been already
complied with. It is true, your Honor is a committing magistrate, and
as such it is your duty to commit—what? That is a matter which the
law has wisely and justly left to your own discretion, and wisely
you have discharged already every obligation that the law imposes.
Since I have known your Honor you have done nothing but commit. You have committed embracery, theft, arson, perjury, adultery,
murder—every crime in the calendar and every excess known to the
sensual and depraved, including my learned friend, the District Attorney. You have done your whole duty as a committing magistrate,
and as there is no evidence against this worthy young man, my client,
I move that he be discharged."

An impressive silence ensued. The Judge arose, put on the black
cap and in a voice trembling with emotion sentenced me to life and
liberty. Then turning to my counsel he said, coldly but significantly:

"I will see you later."

The next morning the lawyer who had so conscientiously defended
me against a charge of murdering his own brother—with whom he
had a quarrel about some land—had disappeared and his fate is to
this day unknown.

In the meantime my poor father's body had been secretly buried
at midnight in the back yard of his late residence, with his late boots
on and the contents of his late stomach unanalyzed. "He was opposed
to display," said my dear mother, as she finished tamping down the
earth above him and assisted the children to litter the place with
straw; "his instincts were all domestic and he loved a quiet life."

My mother's application for letters of administration stated that
she had good reason to believe that the deceased was dead, for he
had not come home to his meals for several days; but the Judge of

the Crowbait Court—as she ever afterward contemptuously called it—decided that the proof of death was insufficient, and put the estate into the hands of the Public Administrator, who was his son-in-law. It was found that the liabilities were exactly balanced by the assets; there was left only the patent for the device for bursting open safes without noise, by hydraulic pressure and this had passed into the ownership of the Probate Judge and the Public Adminis-traitor—as my dear mother preferred to spell it. Thus, within a few brief months a worthy and respectable family was reduced from prosperity to crime; necessity compelled us to go to work.

In the selection of occupations we were governed by a variety of considerations, such as personal fitness, inclination, and so forth. My mother opened a select private school for instruction in the art of changing the spots upon leopard-skin rugs; my eldest brother, George Henry, who had a turn for music, became a bugler in a neighboring asylum for deaf mutes; my sister, Mary Maria, took orders for Pro-fessor Pumpernickel's Essence of Latchkeys for flavoring mineral springs, and I set up as an adjuster and gilder of crossbeams for gibbets. The other children, too young for labor, continued to steal small articles exposed in front of shops, as they had been taught.

In our intervals of leisure we decoyed travelers into our house and buried the bodies in a cellar.

In one part of this cellar we kept wines, liquors and provisions. From the rapidity of their disappearance we acquired the supersti-tious belief that the spirits of the persons buried there came at dead of night and held a festival. It was at least certain that frequently of a morning we would discover fragments of pickled meats, canned goods and such débris, littering the place, although it had been securely locked and barred against human intrusion. It was proposed to remove the provisions and store them elsewhere, but our dear mother, always generous and hospitable, said it was better to endure the loss than risk exposure: if the ghosts were denied this trifling gratification they might set on foot an investigation, which would overthrow our scheme of the division of labor, by diverting the energies of the whole family into the single industry pursued by me—we might all decorate the crossbeams of gibbets. We accepted her decision with filial submission, due to our reverence for her worldly wisdom and the purity of her character.

One night while we were all in the cellar—none dared to enter it alone—engaged in bestowing upon the Mayor of an adjoining town the solemn offices of Christian burial, my mother and the younger children, holding a candle each, while George Henry and

I labored with a spade and pick, my sister Mary Maria uttered a shriek and covered her eyes with her hands. We were all dreadfully startled and the Mayor's obsequies were instantly suspended, while with pale faces and in trembling tones we begged her to say what had alarmed her. The younger children were so agitated that they held their candles unsteadily, and the waving shadows of our figures danced with uncouth and grotesque movements on the walls and flung themselves into the most uncanny attitudes. The face of the dead man, now gleaming ghastly in the light, and now extinguished by some floating shadow, appeared at each emergence to have taken on a new and more forbidding expression, a maligner menace. Frightened even more than ourselves by the girl's scream, rats raced in multitudes about the place, squeaking shrilly, or starred the black opacity of some distant corner with steadfast eyes, mere points of green light, matching the faint phosphorescence of decay that filled the half-dug grave and seemed the visible manifestation of that faint odor of mortality which tainted the unwholesome air. The children now sobbed and clung about the limbs of their elders, dropping their candles, and we were near being left in total darkness, except for that sinister light, which slowly welled upward from the disturbed earth and overflowed the edges of the grave like a fountain.

Meanwhile my sister, crouching in the earth that had been thrown out of the excavation, had removed her hands from her face and was staring with expanded eyes into an obscure space between two wine casks.

"There it is!—there it is!" she shrieked, pointing; "God in heaven! can't you see it?"

And there indeed it was!—a human figure, dimly discernible in the gloom—a figure that wavered from side to side as if about to fall, clutching at the wine-casks for support, had stepped unsteadily forward and for one moment stood revealed in the light of our remaining candles; then it surged heavily and fell prone upon the earth. In that moment we had all recognized the figure, the face and bearing of our father—dead these ten months and buried by our own hands! —our father indubitably risen and ghastly drunk!

On the incidents of our precipitate flight from that horrible place —on the extinction of all human sentiment in that tumultuous, mad scramble up the damp and mouldy stairs—slipping, falling, pulling one another down and clambering over one another's back—the lights extinguished, babes trampled beneath the feet of their strong brothers and hurled backward to death by a mother's arm!—on all this I do not dare to dwell. My mother, my eldest brother and sister and I escaped; the others remained below, to perish of their wounds, or of their terror—some, perhaps, by flame. For within an hour we four, hastily gathering together what money and jewels we had and what clothing we could carry, fired the dwelling and fled by its light into the hills. We did not even pause to collect the insurance, and my dear mother said on her death-bed, years afterward in a distant land, that this was the only sin of omission that lay upon her conscience. Her confessor, a holy man, assured her that under the circumstances Heaven would pardon the neglect.

About ten years after our removal from the scenes of my childhood I, then a prosperous forger, returned in disguise to the spot with a view to obtaining, if possible, some treasure belonging to us, which had been buried in the cellar. I may say that I was unsuccessful: the discovery of many human bones in the ruins had set the authorities digging for more. They had found the treasure and had kept it for their honesty. The house had not been rebuilt; the whole suburb was, in fact, a desolation. So many unearthly sights and sounds had been reported thereabout that nobody would live there. As there was none to question nor molest, I resolved to gratify my filial piety by gazing once more upon the face of my beloved father, if indeed our eyes had deceived us and he was still in his grave. I remembered, too, that he had always worn an enormous diamond ring, and never having seen it nor heard of it since his death, I had reason to think he might have been buried in it. Procuring a spade, I soon located the grave in what had been the backyard and began digging. When I had got down about four feet the whole bottom fell out of the grave and I was precipitated into a large drain, falling through a long hole in its crumbling arch. There was no body, nor any vestige of one.

Unable to get out of the excavation, I crept through the drain, and having with some difficulty removed a mass of charred rubbish and blackened masonry that choked it, emerged into what had been that fateful cellar.

All was clear. My father, whatever had caused him to be "taken bad" at his meal (and I think my sainted mother could have thrown some light upon that matter) had indubitably been buried alive. The grave having been accidentally dug above the forgotten drain, and down almost to the crown of its arch, and no coffin having been used, his struggles on reviving had broken the rotten masonry and he had fallen through, escaping finally into the cellar. Feeling that he was not welcome in his own house, yet having no other, he had lived in subterranean seclusion, a witness to our thrift and a pensioner on our food; it was he who had eaten our food; it was he who had drunk our wine—he was no better than a thief! In a moment of intoxication, and feeling, no doubt, that need of companionship which is the one sympathetic link between a drunken man and his race, he had left his place of concealment at a strangely inopportune time, entailing the most deplorable consequences upon those nearest and dearest to him—a blunder that had almost the dignity of crime.

❊   ❊   ❊

THE CITY OF THE GONE AWAY

I was born of poor because honest parents, and until I was twenty-three years old never knew the possibilities of happiness latent in another person's coin. At that time Providence threw me into a deep sleep and revealed to me in a dream the folly of labor. "Behold," said a vision of a holy hermit, "the poverty and squalor of your lot and listen to the teachings of nature. You rise in the morning from your pallet of straw and go forth to your daily labor in the fields. The flowers nod their heads in friendly salutation as you pass. The lark greets you with a burst of song. The early sun sheds his temperate beams upon you, and from the dewy grass you inhale an atmosphere cool and grateful to your lungs. All nature seems to salute you with the joy of a generous servant welcoming a faithful master. You are in harmony with her gentlest mood and your soul sings within you. You begin your daily task at the plow, hopeful that the noonday will fulfill the promise of the morn, maturing the charms of the landscape and confirming its benediction upon your spirit. You follow the plow until fatigue invokes repose, and seating yourself upon the earth at the end of your furrow you expect to enjoy in fulness the delights of which you did but taste.

"Alas! the sun has climbed into a brazen sky and his beams are become a torrent. The flowers have closed their petals, confining their perfume and denying their colors to the eye. Coolness no longer exhales from the grass: the dew has vanished and the dry surface of the fields repeats the fierce heat of the sky. No longer the birds of heaven salute you with melody, but the jay harshly upbraids you from the edge of the copse. Unhappy man! all the gentle and healing ministrations of nature are denied you in punishment of your sin.

You have broken the First Commandment of the Natural Decalogue: you have labored!"

Awakening from my dream, I collected my few belongings, bade adieu to my erring parents and departed out of that land, pausing at the grave of my grandfather, who had been a priest, to take an oath that never again, Heaven helping me, would I earn an honest penny.

How long I traveled I know not, but I came at last to a great city by the sea, where I set up as a physician. The name of that place I do not now remember, for such were my activity and renown in my new profession that the Aldermen, moved by pressure of public opinion, altered it, and thenceforth the place was known as the City of the Gone Away. It is needless to say that I had no knowledge of medicine, but by securing the service of an eminent forger I obtained a diploma purporting to have been granted by the Royal Quackery of Charlatanic Empiricism at Hoodos, which, framed in immortelles and suspended by a bit of *crêpe* to a willow in front of my office, attracted the ailing in great numbers. In connection with my dispensary I conducted one of the largest undertaking establishments ever known, and as soon as my means permitted, purchased a wide tract of land and made it into a cemetery. I owned also some very profitable marble works on one side of the gateway to the cemetery, and on the other an extensive flower garden. My Mourner's Emporium was patronized by the beauty, fashion and sorrow of the city. In short, I was in a very prosperous way of business, and within a year was able to send for my parents and establish my old father very comfortably as a receiver of stolen goods—an act which I confess was saved from the reproach of filial gratitude only by my exaction of all the profits.

But the vicissitudes of fortune are avoidable only by practice of the sternest indigence: human foresight cannot provide against the envy of the gods and the tireless machinations of Fate. The widening circle of prosperity grows weaker as it spreads until the antagonistic forces which it has pushed back are made powerful by compression to resist and finally overwhelm. So great grew the renown of my skill in medicine that patients were brought to me from all the four quarters of the globe. Burdensome invalids whose tardiness in dying was a perpetual grief to their friends; wealthy testators whose legatees were desirous to come by their own; superfluous children of penitent parents and dependent parents of frugal children; wives of husbands ambitious to remarry and husbands of wives without standing in the courts of divorce—these and all conceivable classes of the surplus population were conducted to my dispensary in the City of the Gone Away. They came in incalculable multitudes.

Government agents brought me caravans of orphans, paupers, lunatics and all who had become a public charge. My skill in curing orphanism and pauperism was particularly acknowledged by a grateful parliament.

Naturally, all this promoted the public prosperity, for although I got the greater part of the money that strangers expended in the city, the rest went into the channels of trade, and I was myself a liberal investor, purchaser and employer, and a patron of the arts and sciences. The City of the Gone Away grew so rapidly that in a few years it had inclosed my cemetery, despite its own constant growth. In that fact lay the lion that rent me.

The Aldermen declared my cemetery a public evil and decided to take it from me, remove the bodies to another place and make a park of it. I was to be paid for it and could easily bribe the appraisers to fix a high price, but for a reason which will appear the decision gave me little joy. It was in vain that I protested against the sacrilege of disturbing the holy dead, although this was a powerful appeal, for in that land the dead are held in religious veneration. Temples are built in their honor and a separate priesthood maintained at the public expense, whose only duty is performance of memorial services of the most solemn and touching kind. On four days in the year there is a Festival of the Good, as it is called, when all the people lay by their work or business and, headed by the priests, march in procession through the cemeteries, adorning the graves and praying in the temples. However bad a man's life may be, it is believed that when dead he enters into a state of eternal and inexpressible happiness. To signify a doubt of this is an offense punishable by death. To deny burial to the dead, or to exhume a buried body, except under sanction of law by special dispensation and with solemn ceremony, is a crime having no stated penalty because no one has ever had the hardihood to commit it.

All these considerations were in my favor, yet so well assured were the people and their civic officers that my cemetery was injurious to the public health that it was condemned and appraised, and with terror in my heart I received three times its value and began to settle up my affairs with all speed.

A week later was the day appointed for the formal inauguration of the ceremony of removing the bodies. The day was fine and the entire population of the city and surrounding country was present at the imposing religious rites. These were directed by the mortuary priesthood in full canonicals. There was propitiatory sacrifice in the Temples of the Once, followed by a processional pageant of great splendor, ending at the cemetery. The Great Mayor in his robe of state led the procession. He was armed with a golden spade and followed by one hundred male and female singers, clad all in white and chanting the Hymn to the Gone Away. Behind these came the minor priesthood of the temples, all the civic authorities, habited in their official apparel, each carrying a living pig as an offering to the gods of the dead. Of the many divisions of the line, the last was formed by the populace, with uncovered heads, sifting dust into their hair in token of humility. In front of the mortuary chapel in the midst of the necropolis, the Supreme Priest stood in gorgeous vestments, supported on each hand by a line of bishops and other high dignitaries of his prelacy, all frowning with the utmost austerity. As the Great Mayor paused in the Presence, the minor clergy, the civic authorities, the choir and populace closed in and encompassed the spot. The Great Mayor, laying his golden spade at the feet of the Supreme Priest, knelt in silence.

"Why comest thou here, presumptuous mortal?" said the Supreme Priest in clear, deliberate tones. "Is it thy unhallowed purpose with this implement to uncover the mysteries of death and break the repose of the Good?"

The Great Mayor, still kneeling, drew from his robe a document with portentous seals: "Behold, O ineffable, thy servant, having warrant of his people, entreateth at thy holy hands the custody of the Good, to the end and purpose that they lie in fitter earth, by consecration duly prepared against their coming."

With that he placed in the sacerdotal hands the order of the Council of Aldermen decreeing the removal. Merely touching the parchment, the Supreme Priest passed it to the Head Necropolitan at his side, and raising his hands relaxed the severity of his countenance and exclaimed: "The gods comply."

Down the line of prelates on either side, his gesture, look and words were successively repeated. The Great Mayor rose to his feet, the choir began a solemn chant and, opportunely, a funeral car drawn by ten white horses with black plumes rolled in at the gate and made its way through the parting crowd to the grave selected for the occasion—that of a high official whom I had treated for chronic incumbency. The Great Mayor touched the grave with his golden spade (which he then presented to the Supreme Priest) and two stalwart diggers with iron ones set vigorously to work.

At that moment I was observed to leave the cemetery and the coun-

try; for a report of the rest of the proceedings I am indebted to my
sainted father, who related it in a letter to me, written in jail the
night before he had the irreparable misfortune to take the kink out
of a rope.

As the workmen proceeded with their excavation, four bishops
stationed themselves at the corners of the grave and in the profound
silence of the multitude, broken otherwise only by the harsh grinding
sound of spades, repeated continuously, one after another, the
solemn invocations and responses from the Ritual of the Disturbed, imploring the blessed brother to forgive. But the blessed
brother was not there. Full fathom two they mined for him in vain,
then gave it up. The priests were visibly disconcerted, the populace
was aghast, for that grave was indubitably vacant.

After a brief consultation with the Supreme Priest, the Great
Mayor ordered the workmen to open another grave. The ritual was
omitted this time until the coffin should be uncovered. There was no
coffin, no body.

The cemetery was now a scene of the wildest confusion and dis-
may. The people shouted and ran hither and thither, gesticulating,
clamoring, all talking at once, none listening. Some ran for spades,
fire-shovels, hoes, sticks, anything. Some brought carpenters' adzes,
even chisels from the marble works, and with these inadequate aids
set to work upon the first graves they came to. Others fell upon the
mounds with their bare hands, scraping away the earth as eagerly as
dogs digging for marmots. Before nightfall the surface of the
greater part of the cemetery had been upturned; every grave had
been explored to the bottom and thousands of men were tearing
away at the interspaces with as furious a frenzy as exhaustion would
permit. As night came on torches were lighted, and in the sinister
glare these frantic mortals, looking like a legion of fiends performing some unholy rite, pursued their disappointing work until they
had devastated the entire area. But not a body did they find—not
even a coffin.

The explanation is exceedingly simple. An important part of my
income had been derived from the sale of *cadavres* to medical col-
leges, which never before had been so well supplied, and which, in
added recognition of my services to science, had all bestowed upon
me diplomas, degrees and fellowships without number. But their demand for *cadavres* was unequal to my supply: by even the most
prodigal extravagances they could not consume the one-half of the
products of my skill as a physician. As to the rest, I had owned and
operated the most extensive and thoroughly appointed soapworks in

all the country. The excellence of my "Toilet Homoline" was attested by certificates from scores of the saintliest theologians, and I had one in autograph from Badelina Fatti the most famous living soaprano.

❊   ❊   ❊

CURRIED COW

My Aunt Patience, who tilled a small farm in the state of Michigan, had a favorite cow. This creature was not a good cow, nor a profitable one, for instead of devoting a part of her leisure to secretion of milk and production of veal she concentrated all her faculties on the study of kicking. She would kick all day and get up in the middle of the night to kick. She would kick at anything—hens, pigs, posts, loose stones, birds in the air and fish leaping out of the water; to this impartial and catholic-minded beef, all were equal—all similarly undeserving. Like old Timotheus, who "raised a mortal to the skies," was my Aunt Patience's cow; though, in the words of a later poet than Dryden, she did it "more harder and more frequently." It was pleasing to see her open a passage for herself through a populous barnyard. She would flash out, right and left, first with one hindleg and then with the other, and would sometimes, under favoring conditions, have a considerable number of domestic animals in the air at once.

Her kicks, too, were as admirable in quality as inexhaustible in quantity. They were incomparably superior to those of the untutored kine that had not made the art a life study—mere amateurs that kicked "by ear," as they say in music. I saw her once standing in the road, professedly fast asleep, and mechanically munching her cud with a sort of Sunday morning lassitude, as one munches one's cud in a dream. Snouting about at her side, blissfully unconscious of impending danger and wrapped up in thoughts of his sweetheart, was a gigantic black hog—a hog of about the size and general appearance of a yearling rhinoceros. Suddenly, while I looked—without a visible movement on the part of the cow—with never a perceptible tremor of her frame, nor a lapse in the placid regularity of her chewing—that hog had gone away from there—had utterly taken his leave. But away toward the pale horizon a minute black speck was traversing the empyrean with the speed of a meteor, and in a moment had disappeared, without audible report, beyond the distant hills. It may have been that hog.

Currying cows is not, I think, a common practice, even in Michigan; but as this one had never needed milking, of course she had to be subjected to some equivalent form of persecution; and irritating her skin with a currycomb was thought as disagreeable an attention as a thoughtful affection could devise. At least she thought it so; though I suspect her mistress really meant it for the good creature's temporal advantage. Anyhow my aunt always made it a condition to the employment of a farm-servant that he should curry the cow every morning; but after just enough trials to convince himself that it was not a sudden spasm, nor a mere local disturbance, the man would always give notice of an intention to quit, by pounding the beast half-dead with some foreign body and then limping home to his couch. I don't know how many men the creature removed from my aunt's employ in this way, but judging from the number of lame persons in that part of the country, I should say a good many; though some of the lameness may have been taken at second-hand from the original sufferers by their descendants, and some may have come by contagion.

I think my aunt's was a faulty system of agriculture. It is true her farm labor cost her nothing, for the laborers all left her service before any salary had accrued; but as the cow's fame spread abroad through the several States and Territories, it became increasingly difficult to obtain hands; and, after all, the favorite was imperfectly curried. It was currently remarked that the cow had kicked the farm to pieces— a rude metaphor, implying that the land was not properly cultivated, nor the buildings and fences kept in adequate repair.

It was useless to remonstrate with my aunt: she would concede everything, amending nothing. Her late husband had attempted to reform the abuse in this manner, and had had the argument all his own way until he had remonstrated himself into an early grave; and the funeral was delayed all day, until a fresh undertaker could be procured, the one originally engaged having confidingly undertaken to curry the cow at the request of the widow.

Since that time my Aunt Patience had not been in the matrimonial market; the love of that cow had usurped in her heart the place of a more natural and profitable affection. But when she saw her seeds unsown, her harvests ungarnered, her fences overtopped with rank brambles and her meadows gorgeous with the towering Canada thistle she thought it best to take a partner.

When it transpired that my Aunt Patience intended wedlock there was intense popular excitement. Every adult single male became at once a marrying man. The criminal statistics of Badger county show that in that single year more marriages occurred than in any decade before or since. But none of them was my aunt's. Men married their cooks, their laundresses, their deceased wives' mothers, their enemies' sisters—married whomsoever would wed; and any man who, by fair means or courtship, could not obtain a wife went before a justice of the peace and made an affidavit that he had some wives in Indiana. Such was the fear of being married alive by my Aunt Patience.

Now, where my aunt's affection was concerned she was, as the reader will have already surmised, a rather determined woman; and the extraordinary marrying epidemic having left but one eligible male in all that county, she had set her heart upon that one eligible male; then she went and carted him to her home. He turned out to be a long Methodist parson, named Huggins.

Aside from his unconscionable length, the Rev. Berosus Huggins was not so bad a fellow, and was nobody's fool. He was, I suppose, the most ill-favored mortal, however, in the whole northern half of America—thin, angular, cadaverous of visage and solemn out of all reason. He commonly wore a low-crowned black hat, set so far down upon his head as partly to eclipse his eyes and wholly obscure the ample glory of his ears. The only other visible article of his attire (except a brace of wrinkled cowskin boots, by which the word "polish" would have been considered the meaningless fragment of a lost language) was a tight-fitting black frock-coat, preternaturally long in the waist, the skirts of which fell about his heels, sopping up the dew. This he always wore snugly buttoned from the throat downward. In this attire he cut a tolerably spectral figure. His aspect was so conspicuously unnatural and inhuman that whenever he went into a cornfield, the predatory crows would temporarily forsake their business to settle upon him in swarms, fighting for the best seats upon his person, by way of testifying their contempt for the weak inventions of the husbandman.

The day after the wedding my Aunt Patience summoned the Rev. Berosus to the council chamber, and uttered her mind to the following intent:

"Now, Huggy, dear, I'll tell you what there is to do about the place. First, you must repair all the fences, clearing out the weeds and repressing the brambles with a strong hand. Then you will have to exterminate the Canadian thistles, mend the wagon, rig up a plow or two, and get things into ship-shape generally. This will keep you out of mischief for the better part of two years; of course you will have to give up preaching, for the present. As soon as you have—O! I forgot poor Phœbe. She"——

"Mrs. Huggins," interrupted her solemn spouse, "I shall hope to be the means, under Providence, of effecting all needful reforms in the husbandry of this farm. But the sister you mention (I trust she is not of the world's people)—have I the pleasure of knowing her? The name, indeed, sounds familiar, but"——

"Not know Phœbe!" cried my aunt, with unfeigned astonishment; "I thought everybody in Badger knew Phœbe. Why, you will have to scratch her legs, every blessed morning of your natural life!"

"I assure you, madam," rejoined the Rev. Berosus, with dignity, "it would yield me a hallowed pleasure to minister to the spiritual needs of sister Phœbe, to the extent of my feeble and unworthy ability; but, really, I fear the merely secular ministration of which you speak must be entrusted to abler and, I would respectfully suggest, female hands."

"Whyyy, youuu ooold, foooool!" replied my aunt, spreading her eyes with unbounded amazement, "Phœbe is a *cow!*"

"In that case," said the husband, with unruffled composure, "it will, of course, devolve upon me to see that her carnal welfare is properly attended to; and I shall be happy to bestow upon her legs such time as I may, without sin, snatch from my strife with Satan and the Canadian thistles."

With that the Rev. Mr. Huggins crowded his hat upon his shoulders, pronounced a brief benediction upon his bride, and betook himself to the barn-yard.

Now, it is necessary to explain that he had known from the first who Phœbe was, and was familiar, from hearsay, with all her sinful traits. Moreover, he had already done himself the honor of making her a visit, remaining in the vicinity of her person, just out of range, for more than an hour and permitting her to survey him at her leisure from every point of the compass. In short, he and Phœbe had mutually reconnoitered and prepared for action.

Amongst the articles of comfort and luxury which went to make up the good parson's *dot,* and which his wife had already caused to be conveyed to his new home, was a patent cast-iron pump, about seven feet high. This had been deposited near the barn-yard, preparatory to being set up on the planks above the barn-yard well. Mr. Huggins now sought out this invention and conveying it to its destination put it into position, screwing it firmly to the planks. He next divested himself of his long gaberdine and his hat, buttoning the former loosely about the pump, which it almost concealed, and hanging the latter upon the summit of the structure. The handle of the pump, when depressed, curved outwardly between the coat-skirts, singularly like a tail, but with this inconspicuous exception, any unprejudiced observer would have pronounced the thing Mr. Huggins, looking uncommonly well.

The preliminaries completed, the good man carefully closed the gate of the barnyard, knowing that as soon as Phœbe, who was campaigning in the kitchen garden, should note the precaution she would come and jump in to frustrate it, which eventually she did. Her master, meanwhile, had laid himself, coatless and hatless, along the outside of the close board fence, where he put in the time pleasantly, catching his death of cold and peering through a knot-hole.

At first, and for some time, the animal pretended not to see the figure on the platform. Indeed she had turned her back upon it directly she arrived, affecting a light sleep. Finding that this stratagem did not achieve the success that she had expected, she abandoned it and stood for several minutes irresolute, munching her cud in a half-hearted way, but obviously thinking very hard. Then she began nosing along the ground as if wholly absorbed in a search for something that she had lost, tacking about hither and thither, but all the time drawing nearer to the object of her wicked intention. Arrived within speaking distance, she stood for a little while confronting the fraudful figure, then put out her nose toward it, as if to be caressed, trying to create the impression that fondling and dalliance were more to her than wealth, power and the plaudits of the populace—that she had been accustomed to them all her sweet young life and could not get on without them. Then she approached a little nearer, as if to shake hands, all the while maintaining the most amiable expression of countenance and executing all manner of seductive nods and winks and smiles. Suddenly she wheeled about and with the rapidity of lightning dealt out a terrible kick—a kick of inconceivable force and fury, comparable to nothing in nature but a stroke of paralysis out of a clear sky!

The effect was magical! Cows kick, not backward but sidewise. The impact which was intended to project the counterfeit theologian into the middle of the succeeding conference week reacted upon the animal herself, and it and the pain together set her spinning like a top. Such was the velocity of her revolution that she looked like a dim, circular cow, surrounded by a continuous ring like that of the planet Saturn—the white tuft at the extremity of her sweeping tail! Presently, as the sustaining centrifugal force lessened and failed, she began to sway and wabble from side to side, and finally, toppling over on her side, rolled convulsively on her back and lay motionless with all her feet in the air, honestly believing that the world had somehow got atop of her and she was supporting it at a great sacrifice of personal comfort. Then she fainted.

How long she lay unconscious she knew not, but at last she un-closed her eyes, and catching sight of the open door of her stall, "more sweet than all the landscape smiling near," she struggled up, stood wavering upon three legs, rubbed her eyes, and was visibly bewildered as to the points of the compass. Observing the iron clergy-man standing fast by its faith, she threw it a look of grieved reproach and hobbled heart-broken into her humble habitation, a subjugated cow.

For several weeks Phœbe's right hind leg was swollen to a mon-strous growth, but by a season of judicious nursing she was "brought round all right," as her sympathetic and puzzled mistress phrased it, or "made whole," as the reticent man of God preferred to say. She was now as tractable and inoffensive "in her daily walk and conver-sation" (Huggins) as a little child. Her new master used to take her ailing leg trustfully into his lap, and for that matter, might have taken it into his mouth if he had so desired. Her entire character appeared to be radically changed—so altered that one day my Aunt Patience, who, fondly as she loved her, had never before so much as ventured to touch the hem of her garment, as it were, went con-fidently up to her to soothe her with a pan of turnips. Gad! how thinly she spread out that good old lady upon the face of an adja-cent stone wall! You could not have done it so evenly with a trowel.

❈   ❈   ❈

A REVOLT OF THE GODS

My father was a deodorizer of dead dogs, my mother kept the only shop for the sale of cats'-meat in my native city. They did not live happily; the difference in social rank was a chasm which could not be bridged by the vows of marriage. It was indeed an ill-assorted and most unlucky alliance; and as might have been foreseen it ended in disaster. One morning after the customary squabbles at breakfast, my father rose from the table, quivering and pale with wrath, and proceeding to the parsonage thrashed the clergyman who had performed the marriage ceremony. The act was generally condemned and public feeling ran so high against the offender that people would permit dead dogs to lie on their property until the fragrance was deafening rather than employ him; and the municipal authorities suffered one bloated old mastiff to utter itself from a public square in so clamorous an exhalation that passing strangers supposed themselves to be in the vicinity of a saw-mill. My father was indeed unpopular. During these dark days the family's sole dependence was on my mother's emporium for cats'-meat.

The business was profitable. In that city, which was the oldest in the world, the cat was an object of veneration. Its worship was the religion of the country. The multiplication and addition of cats were a perpetual instruction in arithmetic. Naturally, any inattention to the wants of a cat was punished with great severity in this world and the next; so my good mother numbered her patrons by the hundred. Still, with an unproductive husband and seventeen children she had some difficulty in making both ends cats'-meat; and at last the necessity of increasing the discrepancy between the cost price and the selling price of her carnal wares drove her to an expedient which proved eminently disastrous: she conceived the unlucky notion of retaliating by refusing to sell cats'-meat until the boycott was taken off her husband.

On the day when she put this resolution into practice the shop was thronged with excited customers, and others extended in turbulent and restless masses up four streets, out of sight. Inside there was nothing but cursing, crowding, shouting and menace. Intimidation was freely resorted to—several of my younger brothers and sisters being threatened with cutting up for the cats—but my mother was as firm as a rock, and the day was a black one for Sardasa, the ancient and sacred city that was the scene of these events. The lock-out was vigorously maintained, and seven hundred and fifty thousand cats went to bed hungry!

The next morning the city was found to have been placarded during the night with a proclamation of the Federated Union of Old Maids. This ancient and powerful order averred through its Supreme Executive Head that the boycotting of my father and the retaliatory lock-out of my mother were seriously imperiling the interests of religion. The proclamation went on to state that if arbitration were not adopted by noon that day all the old maids of the federation would strike—and strike they did.

The next act of this unhappy drama was an insurrection of cats.

These sacred animals, seeing themselves doomed to starvation, held a mass-meeting and marched in procession through the streets, swearing and spitting like fiends. This revolt of the gods produced such consternation that many pious persons died of fright and all business was suspended to bury them and pass terrifying resolutions.

Matters were now about as bad as it seemed possible for them to be. Meetings among representatives of the hostile interests were held, but no understanding was arrived at that would hold. Every agreement was broken as soon as made, and each element of the discord was frantically appealing to the people. A new horror was in store.

It will be remembered that my father was a deodorizer of dead dogs, but was unable to practice his useful and humble profession because no one would employ him. The dead dogs in consequence reeked rascally. Then they struck! From every vacant lot and public dumping ground, from every hedge and ditch and gutter and cistern, every crystal rill and the clabbered waters of all the canals and estuaries—from all the places, in short, which from time immemorial have been preëmpted by dead dogs and consecrated to the uses of them and their heirs and successors forever—they trooped innumerous, a ghastly crew! Their procession was a mile in length. Midway of the town it met the procession of cats in full song. The cats instantly exalted their backs and magnified their tails; the dead dogs uncovered their teeth as in life, and erected such of their bristles as still adhered to the skin.

The carnage that ensued was too awful for relation! The light of the sun was obscured by flying fur, and the battle was waged in the darkness, blindly and regardless. The swearing of the cats was audible miles away, while the fragrance of the dead dogs desolated seven provinces.

How the battle might have resulted it is impossible to say, but when it was at its fiercest the Federated Union of Old Maids came running down a side street and sprang into the thickest of the fray. A moment later my mother herself bore down upon the warring hosts, brandishing a cleaver, and laid about her with great freedom and impartiality. My father joined the fight, the municipal authorities engaged, and the general public, converging on the battle-field from all points of the compass, consumed itself in the center as it pressed in from the circumference. Last of all, the dead held a meeting in the cemetery and resolving on a general strike, began to destroy vaults, tombs, monuments, headstones, willows, angels and young sheep in marble—everything they could lay their hands on. By nightfall the living and the dead were alike exterminated, and where the ancient and sacred city of Sardasa had stood nothing remained but an excavation filled with dead bodies and building materials, shreds of cat and blue patches of decayed dog. The place is now a vast pool of stagnant water in the center of a desert.

The stirring events of those few days constituted my industrial education, and so well have I improved my advantages that I am now Chief of Misrule to the Dukes of Disorder, an organization numbering thirteen million American workingmen.

❊   ❊   ❊

OIL OF DOG

My name is Boffer Bings. I was born of honest parents in one of the humbler walks of life, my father being a manufacturer of dog-oil and my mother having a small studio in the shadow of the village church, where she disposed of unwelcome babes. In my boyhood I was trained to habits of industry; I not only assisted my father in procuring dogs for his vats, but was frequently employed by my mother to carry away the debris of her work in the studio. In performance of this duty I sometimes had need of all my natural intelligence for all the law officers of the vicinity were opposed to my mother's business. They were not elected on an opposition ticket, and the matter had never been made a political issue; it just happened so. My father's business of making dog-oil was, naturally, less unpopular, though the owners of missing dogs sometimes regarded him with suspicion, which was reflected, to some extent, upon me. My father had, as silent partners, all the physicians of the town, who seldom wrote a prescription which did not contain what they were pleased to designate as *Ol. can.* It is really the most valuable medicine ever discovered. But most persons are unwilling to make personal sacrifices for the afflicted, and it was evident that many of the fattest dogs in town had been forbidden to play with me—a fact which pained my young sensibilities, and at one time came near driving me to become a pirate.

Looking back upon those days, I cannot but regret, at times, that by indirectly bringing my beloved parents to their death I was the author of misfortunes profoundly affecting my future.

One evening while passing my father's oil factory with the body of a foundling from my mother's studio I saw a constable who seemed to be closely watching my movements. Young as I was, I had learned that a constable's acts, of whatever apparent character, are prompted by the most reprehensible motives, and I avoided him by dodging into the oilery by a side door which happened to stand ajar. I locked it at once and was alone with my dead. My father had retired for the night. The only light in the place came from the furnace, which glowed a deep, rich crimson under one of the vats, casting ruddy reflections on the walls. Within the cauldron the oil still rolled in indolent ebullition, occasionally pushing to the surface a piece of dog. Seating myself to wait for the constable to go away, I held the naked body of the foundling in my lap and tenderly stroked its short, silken hair. Ah, how beautiful it was! Even at that early age I was passionately fond of children, and as I looked upon this cherub I could almost find it in my heart to wish that the small, red wound upon its breast—the work of my dear mother—had not been mortal.

It had been my custom to throw the babes into the river which nature had thoughtfully provided for the purpose, but that night I did not dare to leave the oilery for fear of the constable. "After all," I said to myself, "it cannot greatly matter if I put it into this cauldron. My father will never know the bones from those of a puppy, and the few deaths which may result from administering another kind of oil for the incomparable *ol. can.* are not important in a population which increases so rapidly." In short, I took the first step in crime and brought myself untold sorrow by casting the babe into the cauldron.

The next day, somewhat to my surprise, my father, rubbing his hands with satisfaction, informed me and my mother that he had obtained the finest quality of oil that was ever seen; that the physicians to whom he had shown samples had so pronounced it. He added that he had no knowledge as to how the result was obtained; the dogs had been treated in all respects as usual, and were of an ordinary breed. I deemed it my duty to explain—which I did, though palsied would have been my tongue if I could have foreseen the consequences. Bewailing their previous ignorance of the advantages of combining their industries, my parents at once took measures to repair the error. My mother removed her studio to a wing of the factory building and my duties in connection with the business ceased; I was no longer required to dispose of the bodies of the small superfluous, and there was no need of alluring dogs to their doom, for my father discarded them altogether, though they still had an honorable place in the name of the oil. So suddenly thrown into idleness, I might naturally have been expected to become vicious and dissolute, but I did not. The holy influence of my dear mother was ever about me to protect me from the temptations which beset youth, and my father was a deacon in a church. Alas, that through my fault these estimable persons should have come to so bad an end!

Finding a double profit in her business, my mother now devoted herself to it with a new assiduity. She removed not only superfluous and unwelcome babes to order, but went out into the highways and byways, gathering in children of a larger growth, and even such adults as she could entice to the oilery. My father, too, enamored of the superior quality of oil produced, purveyed for his vats with diligence and zeal. The conversion of their neighbors into dog-oil became, in short, the one passion of their lives—an absorbing and overwhelming greed took possession of their souls and served them in place of a hope in Heaven—by which, also, they were inspired.

So enterprising had they now become that a public meeting was held and resolutions passed severely censuring them. It was intimated by the chairman that any further raids upon the population would be met in a spirit of hostility. My poor parents left the meeting broken-hearted, desperate and, I believe, not altogether sane. Anyhow, I deemed it prudent not to enter the oilery with them that night, but slept outside in a stable.

At about midnight some mysterious impulse caused me to rise and peer through a window into the furnace-room, where I knew my father now slept. The fires were burning as brightly as if the following day's harvest had been expected to be abundant. One of the large cauldrons was slowly "walloping" with a mysterious appearance of self-restraint, as if it bided its time to put forth its full energy. My father was not in bed; he had risen in his nightclothes and was preparing a noose in a strong cord. From the looks which he cast at the door of my mother's bedroom I knew too well the purpose that he had in mind. Speechless and motionless with terror, I could do nothing in prevention or warning. Suddenly the door of my mother's apartment was opened, noiselessly, and the two confronted each other, both apparently surprised. The lady, also, was in her nightclothes, and she held in her right hand the tool of her trade, a long, narrow-bladed dagger.

She, too, had been unable to deny herself the last profit which the unfriendly action of the citizens and my absence had left her. For one instant they looked into each other's blazing eyes and then sprang together with indescribable fury. Round and round the room they struggled, the man cursing, the woman shrieking, both fighting like demons—she to strike him with the dagger, he to strangle her with his great bare hands. I know not how long I had the unhappiness to observe this disagreeable instance of domestic infelicity, but at last, after a more than usually vigorous struggle, the combatants suddenly moved apart.

My father's breast and my mother's weapon showed evidences of contact. For another instant they glared at each other in the most unamiable way; then my poor, wounded father, feeling the hand of death upon him, leaped forward, unmindful of resistance, grasped my dear mother in his arms, dragged her to the side of the boiling cauldron, collected all his failing energies, and sprang in with her! In a moment, both had disappeared and were adding their oil to that of the committee of citizens who had called the day before with an invitation to the public meeting.

Convinced that these unhappy events closed to me every avenue to an honorable career in that town, I removed to the famous city of Otumwee, where these memoirs are written with a heart full of remorse for a heedless act entailing so dismal a commercial disaster.

✤   ✤   ✤

THE WIDOWER TURMORE

The circumstances under which Joram Turmore became a widower have never been popularly understood. I know them, naturally, for I am Joram Turmore; and my wife, the late Elizabeth Mary Turmore, is by no means ignorant of them; but although she doubtless relates them, yet they remain a secret, for not a soul has ever believed her.

When I married Elizabeth Mary Johnin she was very wealthy, otherwise I could hardly have afforded to marry, for I had not a cent, and Heaven had not put into my heart any intention to earn one. I held the Professorship of Cats in the University of Graymaulkin, and scholastic pursuits had unfitted me for the heat and burden of business or labor. Moreover, I could not forget that I was a Turmore—a member of a family whose motto from the time of William of Normandy has been *Laborare est errare*. The only known infraction of the sacred family tradition occurred when Sir Aldebaran Turmore de Peters-Turmore, an illustrious master burglar of the

seventeenth century, personally assisted at a difficult operation undertaken by some of his workmen. That blot upon our escutcheon cannot
be contemplated without the most poignant mortification.

My incumbency of the Chair of Cats in the Graymaulkin University had not, of course, been marked by any instance of mean
industry. There had never, at any one time, been more than two
students of the Noble Science, and by merely repeating the manuscript lectures of my predecessor, which I had found among his
effects (he died at sea on his way to Malta) I could sufficiently sate
their famine for knowledge without really earning even the distinction which served in place of salary.

Naturally, under the straitened circumstances, I regarded Elizabeth
Mary as a kind of special Providence. She unwisely refused to share
her fortune with me, but for that I cared nothing; for, although by
the laws of that country (as is well known) a wife has control of
her separate property during her life, it passes to the husband at her
death; nor can she dispose of it otherwise by will. The mortality
among wives is considerable, but not excessive.

Having married Elizabeth Mary and, as it were, ennobled her by
making her a Turmore, I felt that the manner of her death ought,
in some sense, to match her social distinction. If I should remove
her by any of the ordinary marital methods I should incur a just
reproach, as one destitute of a proper family pride. Yet I could not
hit upon a suitable plan.

In this emergency I decided to consult the Turmore archives, a
priceless collection of documents, comprising the records of the
family from the time of its founder in the seventh century of our
era. I knew that among these sacred muniments I should find detailed accounts of all the principal murders committed by my sainted
ancestors for forty generations. From that mass of papers I could
hardly fail to derive the most valuable suggestions.

The collection contained also most interesting relics. There were
patents of nobility granted to my forefathers for daring and ingenious
removals of pretenders to thrones, or occupants of them; stars, crosses
and other decorations attesting services of the most secret and unmentionable character; miscellaneous gifts from the world's greatest
conspirators, representing an intrinsic money value beyond compu-
tation. There were robes, jewels, swords of honor, and every kind of
"testimonials of esteem"; a king's skull fashioned into a wine cup;
the title deeds to vast estates, long alienated by confiscation, sale, or
abandonment; an illuminated breviary that had belonged to Sir Aldebaran Turmore de Peters-Turmore of accursed memory; embalmed

ears of several of the family's most renowned enemies; the small intestine of a certain unworthy Italian statesman inimical to Turmores, which, twisted into a jumping rope, had served the youth of six kindred generations—mementoes and souvenirs precious beyond the appraisals of imagination, but by the sacred mandates of tradition and sentiment forever inalienable by sale or gift.

As the head of the family, I was custodian of all these priceless heirlooms, and for their safe keeping had constructed in the basement of my dwelling a strong-room of massive masonry, whose solid stone walls and single iron door could defy alike the earthquake's shock, the tireless assaults of Time, and Cupidity's unholy hand.

To this thesaurus of the soul, redolent of sentiment and tenderness, and rich in suggestions of crime, I now repaired for hints upon assassination. To my unspeakable astonishment and grief I found it empty! Every shelf, every chest, every coffer had been rifled. Of that unique and incomparable collection not a vestige remained! Yet I proved that until I had myself unlocked the massive metal door, not a bolt nor bar had been disturbed; the seals upon the lock had been intact.

I passed the night in alternate lamentation and research, equally fruitless; the mystery was impenetrable to conjecture, the pain invincible to balm. But never once throughout that dreadful night did my firm spirit relinquish its high design against Elizabeth Mary, and daybreak found me more resolute than before to harvest the fruits of my marriage. My great loss seemed but to bring me into nearer spiritual relations with my dead ancestors, and to lay upon me a new and more inevitable obedience to the suasion that spoke in every globule of my blood.

My plan of action was soon formed, and procuring a stout cord I entered my wife's bedroom, finding her, as I expected, in a sound sleep. Before she was awake, I had her bound fast, hand and foot. She was greatly surprised and pained, but heedless of her remonstrances, delivered in a high key, I carried her into the now rifled strong-room, which I had never suffered her to enter, and of whose treasures I had not apprised her. Seating her, still bound, in an angle of the wall, I passed the next two days and nights in conveying bricks and mortar to the spot, and on the morning of the third day had her securely walled in, from floor to ceiling. All this time I gave no further heed to her pleas for mercy than (on her assurance of non-resistance, which I am bound to say she honorably observed) to grant her the freedom of her limbs. The space allowed her was about four feet by six. As I inserted the last bricks of the top course,

in contact with the ceiling of the strong-room, she bade me farewell
with what I deemed the composure of despair, and I rested from
my work, feeling that I had faithfully observed the traditions of an
ancient and illustrious family. My only bitter reflection, so far as
my own conduct was concerned, came of the consciousness that in
the performance of my design I had labored; but this no living soul
would ever know.

After a night's rest I went to the Judge of the Court of Successions
and Inheritances and made a true and sworn relation of all that I
had done—except that I ascribed to a servant the manual labor of
building the wall. His honor appointed a court commissioner, who
made a careful examination of the work, and upon his report Elizabeth Mary Turmore was, at the end of a week, formally pronounced
dead. By due process of law I was put into possession of her estate,
and although this was not by hundreds of thousands of dollars as
valuable as my lost treasures, it raised me from poverty to affluence
and brought me the respect of the great and good.

Some six months after these events strange rumors reached me
that the ghost of my deceased wife had been seen in several places
about the country, but always at a considerable distance from Graymaulkin. These rumors, which I was unable to trace to any authentic
source, differed widely in many particulars, but were alike in as-
cribing to the apparition a certain high degree of apparent worldly
prosperity combined with an audacity most uncommon in ghosts.
Not only was the spirit attired in most costly raiment, but it walked
at noonday, and even drove! I was inexpressibly annoyed by these
reports, and thinking there might be something more than superstition in the popular belief that only the spirits of the unburied dead
still walk the earth, I took some workmen equipped with picks and
crowbars into the now long unentered strong-room, and ordered them
to demolish the brick wall that I had built about the partner of my
joys. I was resolved to give the body of Elizabeth Mary such burial
as I thought her immortal part might be willing to accept as an
equivalent to the privilege of ranging at will among the haunts of
the living.

In a few minutes we had broken down the wall and, thrusting a
lamp through the breach, I looked in. Nothing! Not a bone, not
a lock of hair, not a shred of clothing—the narrow space which,
upon my affidavit, had been legally declared to hold all that was
mortal of the late Mrs. Turmore was absolutely empty! This amazing
disclosure, coming upon a mind already overwrought with too much
of mystery and excitement, was more than I could bear. I shrieked

aloud and fell in a fit. For months afterward I lay between life and
death, fevered and delirious; nor did I recover until my physician had
had the providence to take a case of valuable jewels from my safe
and leave the country.

The next summer I had occasion to visit my wine cellar, in one
corner of which I had built the now long disused strong-room. In
moving a cask of Madeira I struck it with considerable force against
the partition wall, and was surprised to observe that it displaced two
large square stones forming a part of the wall.

Applying my hands to these, I easily pushed them out entirely,
and looking through saw that they had fallen into the niche in which
I had immured my lamented wife; facing the opening which their
fall left, and at a distance of four feet, was the brickwork which my
own hands had made for that unfortunate gentlewoman's restraint.
At this significant revelation I began a search of the wine cellar.
Behind a row of casks I found four historically interesting but in-
trinsically valueless objects:

First, the mildewed remains of a ducal robe of state (Florentine)
of the eleventh century; second, an illuminated vellum breviary with
the name of Sir Aldebaran Turmore de Peters-Turmore inscribed
in colors on the title page; third, a human skull fashioned into a
drinking cup and deeply stained with wine; fourth, the iron cross
of a Knight Commander of the Imperial Austrian Order of Assassins
by Poison.

That was all—not an object having commercial value, no papers—
nothing. But this was enough to clear up the mystery of the strong-
room. My wife had early divined the existence and purpose of that
apartment, and with the skill amounting to genius had effected an
entrance by loosening the two stones in the wall.

Through that opening she had at several times abstracted the
entire collection, which doubtless she had succeeded in converting
into coin of the realm. When with an unconscious justice which
deprives me of all satisfaction in the memory I decided to build her
into the wall, by some malign fatality I selected that part of it in
which were these movable stones, and doubtless before I had fairly
finished my bricklaying she had removed them and, slipping through
into the wine cellar, replaced them as they were originally laid. From
the cellar she had easily escaped unobserved, to enjoy her infamous
gains in distant parts. I have endeavored to procure a warrant, but
the Lord High Baron of the Court of Indictment and Conviction
reminds me that she is legally dead, and says my only course is to go
before the Master in Cadavery and move for a writ of disinterment

and constructive revival. So it looks as if I must suffer without redress this great wrong at the hands of a woman devoid alike of principle and shame.

❊ ❊ ❊

THE BAPTISM OF DOBSHO

It was a wicked thing to do, certainly. I have often regretted it since, and if the opportunity of doing so again were presented I should hesitate a long time before embracing it. But I was young then, and cherished a species of humor which I have since abjured. Still, when I remember the character of the people who were burlesquing and bringing into disrepute the letter and spirit of our holy religion I feel a certain satisfaction in having contributed one feeble effort toward making them ridiculous. In consideration of the little good I may have done in that way, I beg the reader to judge my conceded error as leniently as possible. This is the story.

Some years ago the town of Harding, in Illinois, experienced "a revival of religion," as the people called it. It would have been more accurate and less profane to term it a revival of Rampageanism, for the craze originated in, and was disseminated by, the sect which I will call the Rampagean communion; and most of the leaping and howling was done in that interest. Amongst those who yielded to the influence was my friend Thomas Dobsho. Tom had been a pretty bad sinner in a small way, but he went into this new thing heart and soul. At one of the meetings he made a public confession of more sins than he ever was, or ever could have been guilty of; stopping just short of statutory crimes, and even hinting, significantly, that he could tell a good deal more if he were pressed. He wanted to join the absurd communion the very evening of his conversion. He wanted to join two or three communions. In fact, he was so carried away with his zeal that some of the brethren gave me a hint to take him home; he and I occupied adjoining apartments in the Elephant Hotel.

Tom's fervor, as it happened, came near defeating its own purpose; instead of taking him at once into the fold without reference or "character," which was their usual way, the brethren remembered against him his awful confessions and put him on probation. But

after a few weeks, during which he conducted himself like a decent
lunatic, it was decided to baptise him along with a dozen other
pretty hard cases who had been converted more recently. This sacrilegious ceremony I persuaded myself it was my duty to prevent,
though I think now I erred as to the means adopted. It was to take
place on a Sunday, and on the preceding Saturday I called on the
head revivalist, the Rev. Mr. Swin, and craved an interview.

"I come," said I, with simulated reluctance and embarrassment,
"in behalf of my friend, Brother Dobsho, to make a very delicate
and unusual request. You are, I think, going to baptise him to-
morrow, and I trust it will be to him the beginning of a new and
better life. But I don't know if you are aware that his family are all
Plungers, and that he is himself tainted with the wicked heresy of
that sect. So it is. He is, as one might say in secular metaphor, 'on
the fence' between their grievous error and the pure faith of your
church. It would be most melancholy if he should get down on the
wrong side. Although I confess with shame I have not myself embraced the truth, I hope I am not too blind to see where it lies."

"The calamity that you apprehend," said the reverend lout, after
solemn reflection, "would indeed seriously affect our friend's interest
and endanger his soul. I had not expected Brother Dobsho so soon
to give up the good fight."

"I think sir," I replied reflectively, "there is no fear of that if the
matter is skilfully managed. He is heartily with you—might I venture to say with *us?*—on every point but one. He favors immersion!
He has been so vile a sinner that he foolishly fears the more simple
rite of your church will not make him wet enough. Would you believe it? his uninstructed scruples on the point are so gross and ma-
terialistic that he actually suggested soaping himself as a preparatory
ceremony! I believe, however, if instead of sprinkling my friend, you
would pour a generous basinful of water on his head—but now that
I think of it in your enlightening presence I see that such a proceeding is quite out of the question. I fear we must let matters take
the usual course, trusting to our later efforts to prevent the backslid-
ing which may result."

The parson rose and paced the floor a moment, then suggested
that he'd better see Brother Dobsho, and labor to remove his error.
I told him I thought not; I was sure it would not be best. Argument
would only confirm him in his prejudices. So it was settled that the
subject should not be broached in that quarter. It would have been
bad for me if it had been.

When I reflect now upon the guile of that conversation, the falsehood of my representations and the wickedness of my motive I am almost ashamed to proceed with my narrative. Had the minister been other than an arrant humbug, I hope I should never have suffered myself to make him the dupe of a scheme so sacrilegious in itself, and prosecuted with so sinful a disregard of honor.

The memorable Sabbath dawned bright and beautiful. About nine o'clock the cracked old bell, rigged up on struts before the "meeting-house," began to clamor its call to service, and nearly the whole population of Harding took its way to the performance. I had taken the precaution to set my watch fifteen minutes fast. Tom was nervously preparing himself for the ordeal. He fidgeted himself into his best suit an hour before the time, carried his hat about the room in the most aimless and demented way and consulted his watch a hundred times. I was to accompany him to church, and I spent the time fussing about the room, doing the most extraordinary things in the most exasperating manner—in short, keeping up Tom's feverish excitement by every wicked device I could think of. Within a half hour of the real time for service I suddenly yelled out—

"O, I say, Tom; pardon me, but that head of yours is just frightful! Please *do* let me brush it up a bit!"

Seizing him by the shoulders I thrust him into a chair with his face to the wall, laid hold of his comb and brush, got behind him and went to work. He was trembling like a child, and knew no more what I was doing than if he had been brained. Now, Tom's head was a curiosity. His hair, which was remarkably thick, was like wire. Being cut rather short it stood out all over his scalp like the spines on a porcupine. It had been a favorite complaint of Tom's that he never could do anything to that head. I found no difficulty— I did something to it, though I blush to think what it was. I did something which I feared he might discover if he looked in the mirror, so I carelessly pulled out my watch, sprung it open, gave a start and shouted—

"By Jove! Thomas—pardon the oath—but we're late. Your watch is all wrong; look at mine! Here's your hat, old fellow; come along. There's not a moment to lose!"

Clapping his hat on his head, I pulled him out of the house, with actual violence. In five minutes more we were in the meeting-house with ever so much time to spare.

The services that day, I am told, were specially interesting and impressive, but I had a good deal else on my mind—was preoccupied, absent, inattentive. They might have varied from the usual profane exhibition in any respect and to any extent, and I should not have observed it. The first thing I clearly perceived was a rank of "converts" kneeling before the "altar," Tom at the left of the line. Then the Rev. Mr. Swin approached him, thoughtfully dipping his fingers into a small earthern bowl of water as if he had just finished dining. I was much affected: I could see nothing distinctly for my tears. My handkerchief was at my face—most of it inside. I was observed to sob spasmodically, and I am abashed to think how many sincere persons mistakenly followed my example.

With some solemn words, the purport of which I did not quite make out, except that they sounded like swearing, the minister stood before Thomas, gave me a glance of intelligence and then with an innocent expression of face, the recollection of which to this day fills me with remorse, spilled, as if by accident, the entire contents of the bowl on the head of my poor friend—that head into the hair of which I had sifted a prodigal profusion of Seidlitz-powders!

I confess it, the effect was magical—anyone who was present would tell you that. Tom's pow simmered—it seethed—it foamed yeastily, and slavered like a mad dog! It steamed and hissed, with angry spurts and flashes! In a second it had grown bigger than a small snowbank, and whiter. It surged, and boiled, and walloped, and overflowed, and sputtered—sent off feathery flakes like down from a shot swan! The froth poured creaming over his face, and got into his eyes. It was the most sinful shampooing of the season!

I cannot relate the commotion this produced, nor would I if I could. As to Tom, he sprang to his feet and staggered out of the house, groping his way between the pews, sputtering strangled profanity and gasping like a stranded fish. The other candidates for baptism rose also, shaking their pates as if to say, "No you don't, my hearty," and left the house in a body. Amidst unbroken silence the minister reascended the pulpit with the empty bowl in his hand, and was first to speak:

"Brethren and sisters," said he with calm, deliberate evenness of tone, "I have held forth in this tabernacle for many more years than I have got fingers and toes, and during that time I have known not guile, nor anger, nor any uncharitableness. As to Henry Barber, who put up this job on me, I judge him not lest I be judged. Let him take *that* and sin no more!"—and he flung the earthern bowl with so true an aim that it was shattered against my skull. The rebuke was not undeserved, I confess, and I trust I have profited by it.

THE RACE AT LEFT BOWER

"It's all very well fer you Britishers to go assin' about the country tryin' to strike the trail o' the mines you've salted down yer loose carpital in," said Colonel Jackhigh, setting his empty glass on the counter and wiping his lips with his coat sleeve; "but w'en it comes to hoss racin', w'y this pisen little beast o' mine'll take the bit in her teeth and show 'em the way to the horizon like she was takin' her mornin' stroll and they was tryin' to keep an eye on her to see she didn't do herself an injury—that's w'at she would! And she haint never run a race with anything spryer'n an Injun in all her life; she's a green amatoor, *she* is!"

"Oh, very well," said the Englishman with a quiet smile; "it is easy enough to settle the matter. My animal is in tolerably good condition, and if yours is in town we can have the race tomorrow for any stake you like, up to a hundred dollars."

"That's jest the figger," said the colonel; "dot it down, barkeep. But it's like slarterin' the innocents," he added, half-remorsefully, as he turned to leave; "it's bettin' on a dead sure thing—that's what it is! If my cayuse knew wa't I was about she'd go and break a laig to make the race a fair one."

So it was arranged that the race was to come off at three o'clock the next day, on the *mesa,* some distance from town. As soon as the news got abroad, the whole population of Left Bower and vicinity knocked off work and assembled in the various bars to discuss it. The Englishman and his horse were general favorites, and aside from the unpopularity of the colonel, nobody had ever seen his "cayuse." Still the element of patriotism came in, making the betting very nearly even.

A race-course was marked off on the *mesa* and at the appointed hour every one was there except the colonel. It was arranged that each man should ride his own horse, and the Englishman, who had acquired something of the free-and-easy bearing that distinguishes the "mining sharp," was already atop of his magnificent animal, with one leg thrown carelessly across the pommel of his Mexican saddle, as he puffed his cigar with calm confidence in the result of the race. He was conscious, too, that he possessed the secret sympathy of all, even of those who had felt it their duty to bet against him. The judge, watch in hand, was growing impatient, when the colonel appeared about a half-mile away, and bore down upon the crowd. Everyone was eager to inspect his mount; and such a mount as it proved to be was never before seen, even in Left Bower!

You have seen "perfect skeletons" of horses often enough, no doubt, but this animal was not even a perfect skeleton; there were bones missing here and there which you would not have believed the beast could have spared. "Little" the colonel called her! She was not an inch less than eighteen hands high, and long out of all reasonable proportion. She was so hollow in the back that she seemed to have been bent in a machine. She had neither tail nor mane, and her neck, as long as a man, stuck straight up into the air, supporting a head without ears. Her eyes had an expression in them of downright insanity, and the muscles of her face were afflicted with periodical convulsions that drew back the corners of her mouth and wrinkled the upper lip so as to produce a ghastly grin every two or three seconds. In color she was "claybank," with great blotches of white, as if she had been pelted with small bags of flour. The crookedness of her legs was beyond all comparison, and as to her gait it was that of a blind camel walking diagonally across innumerable deep ditches. Altogether she looked like the crude result of Nature's first experiment in equifaction.

As this libel on all horses shambled up to the starting post there was a general shout; the sympathies of the crowd changed in the twinkling of an eye! Everyone wanted to bet on her, and the Englishman himself was only restrained from doing so by a sense of honor. It was growing late, however, and the judge insisted on starting them. They got off very well together, and seeing the mare was unconscionably slow the Englishman soon pulled his animal in and permitted the ugly thing to pass him, so as to enjoy a back view of her. That sealed his fate. The course had been marked off in a circle of two miles in circumference and some twenty feet wide, the limits plainly defined by little furrows. Before the animals had gone a half mile both had been permitted to settle down into a comfortable walk, in which they continued three-fourths of the way around the ring. Then the Englishman thought it time to whip up and canter in.

But he didn't. As he came up alongside the "Lightning Express," as the crowd had begun to call her, that creature turned her head diagonally backward and let fall a smile. The encroaching beast stopped as if he had been shot! His rider plied whip, and forced him again forward upon the track of the equine hag, but with the same result.

The Englishman was now alarmed; he struggled manfully with rein and whip and shout, amidst the tremendous cheering and inextinguishable laughter of the crowd, to force his animal past, now on this side, now on that, but it would not do. Prompted by the fiend in the concavity of her back, the unthinkable quadruped dropped her grins right and left with such seasonable accuracy that again and again the competing beast was struck "all of a heap" just at the moment of seeming success. And, finally, when by a tremendous spurt his rider endeavored to thrust him by, within half a dozen lengths of the winning post, the incarnate nightmare turned squarely about and fixed upon him a portentous stare—delivering at the same time a grimace of such prodigious ghastliness that the poor thoroughbred, with an almost human scream of terror, wheeled about, and tore away to the rear with the speed of the wind, leaving the colonel an easy winner in twenty minutes and ten seconds.

❊   ❊   ❊

THE FAILURE OF HOPE & WANDEL

From Mr. Jabez Hope, in Chicago, to Mr. Pike Wandel, of New Orleans, December 2, 1877.

I will not bore you, my dear fellow, with a narrative of my journey from New Orleans to this polar region. It is cold in Chicago, believe me, and the Southron who comes here, as I did, without a relay of noses and ears will have reason to regret his mistaken economy in arranging his outfit.

To business. Lake Michigan is frozen stiff. Fancy, O child of a torrid clime, a sheet of anybody's ice, three hundred miles long, forty broad, and six feet thick! It sounds like a lie, Pikey dear, but your partner in the firm of Hope & Wandel, Wholesale Boots and Shoes, New Orleans, is never known to fib. My plan is to collar that ice. Wind up the present business and send on the money at once. I'll put up a warehouse as big as the Capitol at Washington, store it full and ship to your orders as the Southern market may require. I can send it in planks for skating floors, in statuettes for the mantel, in shavings for juleps, or in solution for ice cream and general purposes. It is a big thing!

I inclose a thin slip as a sample. Did you ever see such charming ice?

From Mr. Pike Wandel, of New Orleans, to Mr. Jabez Hope, in Chicago, December 24, 1877.

Your letter was so abominably defaced by blotting and blurring that it was entirely illegible. It must have come all the way by water. By the aid of chemicals and photography, however, I have made it out. But you forgot to inclose the sample of ice.

I have sold off everything (at an alarming sacrifice, I am sorry to say) and inclose draft for net amount. Shall begin to spar for orders at once. I trust everything to you—but, I say, has anybody tried to grow ice in *this* vicinity? There is Lake Ponchartrain, you know.

From Mr. Jabez Hope, in Chicago, to Mr. Pike Wandel, of New Orleans, February 27, 1878.

Wannie dear, it would do you good to see our new warehouse for the ice. Though made of boards, and run up rather hastily, it is as pretty as a picture, and cost a deal of money, though I pay no ground rent. It is about as big as the Capitol at Washington. Do you think it ought to have a steeple? I have it nearly filled—fifty men cutting and storing, day and night—awful cold work! By the way, the ice, which when I wrote you last was ten feet thick, is now thinner. But don't you worry; there is plenty.

Our warehouse is eight or ten miles out of town, so I am not much bothered by visitors, which is a relief. Such a giggling, sniggering lot you never saw!

It seems almost too absurdly incredible, Wannie, but do you know I believe this ice of ours gains in coldness as the warm weather comes on! I do, indeed, and you may mention the fact in the advertisements.

From Mr. Pike Wandel, of New Orleans, to Mr. Jabez Hope, in Chicago, March 7, 1878.

All goes well. I get hundreds of orders. We shall do a roaring trade as "The New Orleans and Chicago Semperfrigid Ice Company." But you have not told me whether the ice is fresh or salt. If it is fresh it won't do for cooking, and if it is salt it will spoil the mint juleps.

Is it as cold in the middle as the outside cuts are?

From Mr. Jabez Hope, from Chicago, to Mr. Pike Wandel, of New Orleans, April 3, 1878.

Navigation on the Lakes is now open, and ships are thick as ducks. I'm afloat, *en route* for Buffalo, with the assets of the New Orleans and Chicago Semperfrigid Ice Company in my vest pocket. We are busted out, my poor Pikey—we are to fortune and to fame unknown. Arrange a meeting of the creditors and don't attend.

Last night a schooner from Milwaukee was smashed into matchwood on an enormous mass of floating ice—the first berg ever seen in these waters. It is described by the survivors as being about as big as the Capitol at Washington. One-half of that iceberg belongs to you, Pikey.

The melancholy fact is, I built our warehouse on an unfavorable site, about a mile out from the shore (on the ice, you understand), and when the thaw came—O my God, Wannie, it was the saddest thing you ever saw in all your life! You will be *so* glad to know I was not in it at the time.

What a ridiculous question you ask me. My poor partner, you don't seem to know very much about the ice business.

❆   ❆   ❆

A PROVIDENTIAL INTIMATION

Mr. Algernon Jarvis, of San Francisco, got up cross. The world of Mr. Jarvis had gone wrong with him overnight, as one's world is likely to do when one sits up till morning with jovial friends, to watch it, and he was prone to resentment. No sooner, therefore, had he got himself into a neat, fashionable suit of clothing than he selected his morning walking-stick and sallied out upon the town with a vague general determination to attack something. His first victim would naturally have been his breakfast; but singularly enough, he fell upon this with so feeble an energy that he was himself beaten—to the grieved astonishment of the worthy *rôtisseur,* who had to record his hitherto puissant patron's maiden defeat. Three or four cups of *café noir* were the only captives that graced Mr. Jarvis' gastric chariot-wheels that morning.

He lit a long cigar and sauntered moodily down the street, so occupied with schemes of universal retaliation that his feet had it all their own way; in consequence of which, their owner soon found himself in the billiard-room of the Occidental Hotel. Nobody was there, but Mr. Jarvis was a privileged person; so, going to the marker's desk, he took out a little box of ivory balls, spilled them carelessly over a table and languidly assailed them with a long stick.

Presently, by the merest chance, he executed a marvelous stroke. Waiting till the astonished balls had resumed their composure, he gathered them up, replacing them in their former position. He tried the stroke again, and, naturally, did not make it. Again he placed the balls, and again he badly failed. With a vexed and humiliated air he once more put the indocile globes into position, leaned over the table and was upon the point of striking, when there sounded a solemn voice from behind:

"Bet you two bits you don't make it!"

Mr. Jarvis erected himself; he turned about and looked at the speaker, whom he found to be a stranger—one that most persons would prefer should remain a stranger. Mr. Jarvis made no reply. In the first place, he was a man of aristocratic taste, to whom a wager of "two bits" was simply vulgar. Secondly, the man who had proffered it evidently had not the money. Still it is annoying to have one's skill questioned by one's social inferiors, particularly when one has doubts of it oneself, and is otherwise ill-tempered. So Mr. Jarvis stood his cue against the table, laid off his fashionable morning-coat, resumed his stick, spread his fine figure upon the table with his back to the ceiling and took deliberate aim.

At this point Mr. Jarvis drops out of this history, and is seen no more forever. Persons of the class to which he adds lustre are sacred from the pen of the humorist; they are ridiculous but not amusing. So now we will dismiss this uninteresting young aristocrat, retaining merely his outer shell, the fashionable morning-coat, which Mr. Stenner, the gentleman, who had offered the wager, has quietly thrown across his arm and is conveying away for his own advantage.

An hour later Mr. Stenner sat in his humble lodgings at North Beach, with the pilfered garment upon his knees. He had already taken the opinion of an eminent pawnbroker on its value, and it only remained to search the pockets. Mr. Stenner's notions concerning gentlemen's coats were not so clear as they might have been. Broadly stated, they were that these garments abounded in secret pockets crowded with a wealth of bank notes interspersed with gold coins. He was therefore disappointed when his careful quest was rewarded with only a delicately perfumed handkerchief, upon which he could not hope to obtain a loan of more than ten cents; a pair of gloves too small for use and a bit of paper that was not a cheque. A second look at this, however, inspired hope. It was about the size of a flounder, ruled in wide lines, and bore in conspicuous characters the words, "Western Union Telegraph Company." Immediately below this interesting legend was much other printed matter, the purport of which was that the company did not hold itself responsible for the verbal accuracy of "the following message," and did not consider itself either morally or legally bound to forward or deliver it, nor, in short, to render any kind of service for the money paid by the sender.

Unfamiliar with telegraphy, Mr. Stenner naturally supposed that a message subject to these hard conditions must be one of not only grave importance, but questionable character. So he determined to decipher it at that time and place. In the course of the day he succeeded in so doing. It ran as follows, omitting the date and the names of persons and places, which were, of course, quite illegible:

"Buy Sally Meeker!"

Had the full force of this remarkable adjuration burst upon Mr. Stenner all at once it might have carried him away, which would not have been so bad a thing for San Francisco; but as the meaning had to percolate slowly through a dense dyke of ignorance, it produced no other immediate effect than the exclamation, "Well, I'll be bust!"

In the mouths of some persons this form of expression means a great deal. On the Stenner tongue it signified the hopeless nature of the Stenner mental confusion.

It must be confessed—by persons outside a certain limited and sordid circle—that the message lacks amplification and elaboration; in its terse, bald diction there is a ghastly suggestion of traffic in human flesh, for which in California there is no market since the abolition of slavery and the importation of thoroughbred beeves. If woman suffrage had been established all would have been clear; Mr. Stenner would at once have understood the kind of purchase advised; for in political transactions he had very often changed hands himself. But it was all a muddle, and resolving to dismiss the matter from his thoughts, he went to bed thinking of nothing else; for many hours his excited imagination would do nothing but purchase slightly damaged Sally Meekers by the bale, and retail them to itself at an enormous profit.

Next day, it flashed upon his memory who Sally Meeker was—a racing mare! At this entirely obvious solution of the problem he was overcome with amazement at his own sagacity. Rushing into the street he purchased, not Sally Meeker, but a sporting paper—and in it found the notice of a race which was to come off the following week; and, sure enough, there it was:

"Budd Doble enters g. g. Clipper; Bob Scotty enters b. g. Lightnin'; Staley Tupper enters s. s. Upandust; Sim Salper enters b. m. Sally Meeker."

It was clear now; the sender of the dispatch was "in the know." Sally Meeker was to win, and her owner, who did not know it, had offered her for sale. At that supreme moment Mr. Stenner would willingly have been a rich man! In fact he resolved to be. He at once betook him to Vallejo, where he had lived until invited away by some influential citizens of the place. There he immediately sought out an industrious friend who had an amiable weakness for draw poker, and in whom Mr. Stenner regularly encouraged that passion by going up against him every payday and despoiling him of his hard earnings. He did so this time, to the sum of one hundred dollars.

No sooner had he raked in his last pool and refused his friend's appeal for a trifling loan wherewith to pay for breakfast than he bought a check on the Bank of California, enclosed it in a letter containing merely the words "Bi Saly Meker," and dispatched it by mail to the only clergyman in San Francisco whose name he knew. Mr. Stenner had a vague notion that all kinds of business requiring strict honesty and fidelity might be profitably intrusted to the clergy; otherwise what was the use of religion? I hope I shall not be accused of disrespect to the cloth in thus bluntly setting forth Mr. Stenner's estimate of the parsons, inasmuch as I do not share it.

This business off his mind, Mr. Stenner unbent in a week's revelry; at the end of which he worked his passage down to San Francisco to secure his winnings on the race, and take charge of his peerless mare. It will be observed that his notions concerning races were somewhat confused; his experience of them had hitherto been confined to that branch of the business requiring, not technical knowledge but manual dexterity. In short, he had done no more than pick the pockets of the spectators. Arrived at San Francisco he was hastening to the dwelling of his clerical agent, when he met an acquaintance, to whom he put the triumphant question, "How about Sally Meeker?"

"Sally Meeker? Sally Meeker?" was the reply. "Oh, you mean the hoss? Why she's gone up the flume. Broke her neck the first heat. But ole Sim Salper is never a-goin' to fret hisself to a shadder about it. He struck it pizen in the mine she was named a'ter and the stock's gone up from nothin' out o' sight. You couldn't tech that stock with a ten-foot pole!"

Which was a blow to Mr. Stenner. He saw his error; the message in the coat had evidently been sent to a broker, and referred to the stock of the "Sally Meeker" mine. And he, Stenner, was a ruined man!

Suddenly a great, monstrous, misbegotten and unmentionable oath rolled from Mr. Stenner's tongue like a cannon shot hurled along an uneven floor! Might it not be that the Rev. Mr. Boltright had also misunderstood the message, and had bought, not the mare, but the stock? The thought was electrical: Mr. Stenner ran—he flew! He tarried not at walls and the smaller sort of houses, but went through or over them! In five minutes he stood before the good clergyman—and in one more had asked, in a hoarse whisper, if he had bought any "Sally Meeker."

"My good friend," was the bland reply—"my fellow traveler to the bar of God, it would better comport with your spiritual needs to inquire what you should do to be saved. But since you ask me, I will confess that having received what I am compelled to regard as a Providential intimation, accompanied with the secular means of obedience, I did put up a small margin and purchase largely of the stock you mention. The venture, I am constrained to state, was not wholly unprofitable."

Unprofitable? The good man had made a square twenty-five thousand dollars on that small margin! To conclude—he has it yet.

❊   ❊   ❊

MR. SWIDDLER'S FLIP-FLAP

Jerome Bowles (said the gentleman called Swiddler) was to be hanged on Friday, the ninth of November, at five o'clock in the afternoon. This was to occur at the town of Flatbroke, where he was then in prison. Jerome was my friend, and naturally I differed with the jury that had convicted him as to the degree of guilt implied by the conceded fact that he had shot an Indian without direct provocation. Ever since his trial I had been endeavoring to influence the Governor of the State to grant a pardon; but public sentiment was against me, a fact which I attributed partly to the innate pigheadedness of the people, and partly to the recent establishment of churches and schools which had corrupted the primitive notions of a frontier community. But I labored hard and unremittingly by all manner of direct and indirect means during the whole period in which Jerome lay under sentence of death; and on the very morning of the day set for the execution, the Governor sent for me, and saying "he did not purpose being worried by my importunities all winter," handed me the document which he had so often refused.

Armed with the precious paper, I flew to the telegraph office to send a dispatch to the Sheriff at Flatbroke. I found the operator locking the door of the office and putting up the shutters. I pleaded in vain; he said he was going to see the hanging, and really had no time to send my message. I must explain that Flatbroke was fifteen miles away; I was then at Swan Creek, the State capital.

The operator being inexorable, I ran to the railroad station to see how soon there would be a train for Flatbroke. The station man, with cool and polite malice, informed me that all the employees of the road had been given a holiday to see Jerome Bowles hanged, and had already gone by an early train; that there would be no other train till the next day.

I was now furious, but the station man quietly turned me out, locking the gates. Dashing to the nearest livery stable, I ordered a horse. Why prolong the record of my disappointment? Not a horse could I get in that town; all had been engaged weeks before to take people to the hanging. So everybody said, at least, though I now know there was a rascally conspiracy to defeat the ends of mercy, for the story of the pardon had got abroad.

It was now ten o'clock. I had only seven hours in which to do my fifteen miles afoot; but I was an excellent walker and thoroughly angry; there was no doubt of my ability to make the distance, with an hour to spare. The railway offered the best chance; it ran straight as a string across a level, treeless prairie, whereas the highway made a wide detour by way of another town.

I took to the track like a Modoc on the war path. Before I had gone a half-mile I was overtaken by "That Jim Peasley," as he was called in

Swan Creek, an incurable practical joker, loved and shunned by all who knew him. He asked me as he came up if I were "going to the show." Thinking it was best to dissemble, I told him I was, but said nothing of my intention to stop the performance; I thought it would be a lesson to That Jim to let him walk fifteen miles for nothing, for it was clear that he was going, too. Still, I wished he would go on ahead or drop behind. But he could not very well do the former, and would not do the latter; so we trudged on together.

It was a cloudy day and very sultry for that time of the year. The railway stretched away before us, between its double row of telegraph poles, in rigid sameness, terminating in a point at the horizon. On either hand the disheartening monotony of the prairie was unbroken.

I thought little of these things, however, for my mental exaltation was proof against the depressing influence of the scene. I was about to save the life of my friend—to restore a crack shot to society. Indeed I scarcely thought of That Jim, whose heels were grinding the hard gravel close behind me, except when he saw fit occasionally to propound the sententious, and I thought derisive, query, "Tired?" Of course I was, but I would have died rather than confess it.

We had gone in this way, about half the distance, probably, in much less than half the seven hours, and I was getting my second wind, when That Jim again broke the silence.

"Used to bounce in a circus, didn't you?"

This was quite true! in a season of pecuniary depression I had once put my legs into my stomach—had turned my athletic accomplishments to financial advantage. It was not a pleasant topic, and I said nothing. That Jim persisted.

"Wouldn't like to do a feller a somersault now, eh?"

The mocking tongue of this jeer was intolerable; the fellow evidently considered me "done up," so taking a short run I clapped my hands to my thighs and executed as pretty a flip-flap as ever was made without a springboard! At the moment I came erect with my head still spinning, I felt That Jim crowd past me, giving me a twirl that almost sent me off the track. A moment later he had dashed ahead at a tremendous pace, laughing derisively over his shoulder as if he had done a remarkably clever thing to gain the lead.

I was on the heels of him in less than ten minutes, though I must confess the fellow could walk amazingly. In half an hour I had run past him, and at the end of the hour, such was my slashing gait, he was a mere black dot in my rear, and appeared to be sitting on one of the rails, thoroughly used up.

Relieved of Mr. Peasley, I naturally began thinking of my poor friend in the Flatbroke jail, and it occurred to me that something might happen to hasten the execution. I knew the feeling of the country against him, and that many would be there from a distance who would naturally wish to get home before nightfall. Nor could I help admitting to myself that five o'clock was an unreasonably late hour for a hanging. Tortured with these fears, I unconsciously increased my pace with every step, until it was almost a run. I stripped off my coat and flung it away, opened my collar, and unbuttoned my waistcoat. And at last, puffing and steaming like a locomotive engine, I burst into a thin crowd of idlers on the outskirts of the town, and flourished the pardon crazily above my head, yelling, "Cut him down! —cut him down!"

Then, as every one stared in blank amazement and nobody said anything, I found time to look about me, marveling at the oddly familiar appearance of the town. As I looked, the houses, streets, and everything seemed to undergo a sudden and mysterious transposition with reference to the points of the compass, as if swinging round on a pivot; and like one awakened from a dream I found myself among accustomed scenes. To be plain about it, I was back again in Swan Creek, as right as a trivet!

It was all the work of That Jim Peasley. The designing rascal had provoked me to throw a confusing somersault, then bumped against me, turning me half round, and started on the back track, thereby inciting me to hook it in the same direction. The cloudy day, the two lines of telegraph poles, one on each side of the track, the entire sameness of the landscape to the right and left—these had all conspired to prevent my observing that I had put about.

When the excursion train returned from Flatbroke that evening the passengers were told a little story at my expense. It was just what they needed to cheer them up a bit after what they had seen; for that flip-flap of mine had broken the neck of Jerome Bowles seven miles away!

❈   ❈   ❈

THE LITTLE STORY

DRAMATIS PERSONÆ—*A Supernumerary Editor. A Probationary Contributor.*

Scene—*"The Expounder" Office.*

Probationary Contributor—Editor in?

Supernumerary Editor—Dead.

P. C.—The gods favor me. (*Produces roll of manuscript.*) Here is a little story, which I will read to you.

S. E.—O, O!

P. C.—(*Reads.*) "It was the last night of the year—a naughty, noxious, offensive night. In the principal street of San Francisco"——

S. E.—Confound San Francisco!

P. C.—It had to be somewhere. (*Reads.*)

"In the principal street of San Francisco stood a small female orphan, marking time like a volunteer. Her little bare feet imprinted cold kisses on the paving-stones as she put them down and drew them up alternately. The chilling rain was having a good time with her scalp, and toyed soppily with her hair—her own hair. The night-wind shrewdly searched her tattered garments, as if it had suspected her of smuggling. She saw crowds of determined-looking persons grimly ruining themselves in toys and confectionery for the dear ones at home, and she wished she was in a position to ruin a little—just a little. Then, as the happy throng sped by her with loads of things to make the children sick, she leaned against an iron lamp-post in front of a bake-shop and turned on the wicked envy. She thought, poor thing, she would like to be a cake—for this little girl was very hungry indeed. Then she tried again, and thought she would like to be a tart with smashed fruit inside; then she would be warmed over every day and nobody would eat her. For the child was cold as well as hungry. Finally, she tried quite hard, and thought she could be very well content as an oven; for then she would be kept always hot, and bakers would put all manner of good things into her with a long shovel."

S. E.—I've read that somewhere.

P. C.—Very likely. This little story has never been rejected by any paper to which I have offered it. It gets better, too, every time I write it. When it first appeared in *Veracity* the editor said it cost him a hundred subscribers. Just mark the improvement! (*Reads.*)

"The hours glided by—except a few that froze to the pavement—until midnight. The streets were now deserted, and the almanac having predicted a new moon about this time, the lamps had been conscientiously extinguished. Suddenly a great globe of sound fell from an adjacent church-tower, and exploded on the night with a deep metallic boom. Then all the clocks and bells began ringing-in the New Year—pounding and banging and yelling and finishing off all the nervous invalids left over from the preceding Sunday. The little orphan started from her dream, leaving a small patch of skin on the frosted lamp-post, clasped her thin blue hands and looked upward, 'with mad disquietude,'"—

S. E.—In *The Monitor* it was "with covetous eyes."

P. C.—I know it; hadn't read Byron then. Clever dog, Byron. (*Reads.*)

"Presently a cranberry tart dropped at her feet, apparently from the clouds."

S. E.—How about those angels?

P. C.—The editor of *Good Will* cut 'em out. He said San Francisco was no place for them; and I don't believe——

S. E.—There, there! Never mind. Go on with the little story.

P. C.—(*Reads.*) "As she stooped to take up the tart a veal sandwich came whizzing down, and cuffed one of her ears. Next a wheaten loaf made her dodge nimbly, and then a broad ham fell flat-footed at her toes. A sack of flour burst in the middle of the street; a side of bacon impaled itself on an iron hitching-post. Pretty soon a chain of sausages fell in a circle around her, flattening out as if a road-roller had passed over them. Then there was a lull—nothing came down but dried fish, cold puddings and flannel under-clothing; but presently her wishes began to take effect again, and a quarter of beef descended with terrific momentum upon the top of the little orphan's head."

S. E.—How did the editor of *The Reasonable Virtues* like that quarter of beef?

P. C.—Oh, he swallowed it like a little man, and stuck in a few dressed pigs of his own. I've left them out, because I don't want outsiders altering the Little Story. (*Reads.*)

"One would have thought that ought to suffice; but not so. Bedding, shoes, firkins of butter, mighty cheeses, ropes of onions, quantities of loose jam, kegs of oysters, titanic fowls, crates of crockery and glassware, assorted house-keeping things, cooking ranges, and tons of coal poured down in broad cataracts from a bounteous heaven, piling themselves above that infant to a depth of twenty feet. The weather was more than two hours in clearing up; and as late as half-past three a ponderous hogshead of sugar struck at the corner of Clay and Kearney Streets, with an impact that shook the peninsula like an earthquake and stopped every clock in town.

"At daybreak the good merchants arrived upon the scene with

shovels and wheelbarrows, and before the sun of the new year was an hour old, they had provided for all of these provisions—had stowed them away in their cellars, and nicely arranged them on their shelves, ready for sale to the deserving poor."

S. E.—And the little girl—what became of *her?*

P. C.—You mustn't get ahead of the Little Story. (*Reads.*)

"When they had got down to the wicked little orphan who had not been content with her lot some one brought a broom, and she was carefully swept and smoothed out. Then they lifted her tenderly, and carried her to the coroner. That functionary was standing in the door of his office, and with a deprecatory wave of his hand, he said to the man who was bearing her:

"'There, go away, my good fellow; there was a man here three times yesterday trying to sell me just such a map.'"

❉   ❉   ❉

MY FAVORITE MURDER

Having murdered my mother under circumstances of singular atrocity, I was arrested and put upon my trial, which lasted seven years. In charging the jury, the judge of the Court of Acquittal remarked that it was one of the most ghastly crimes that he had ever been called upon to explain away.

At this, my attorney rose and said:

"May it please your Honor, crimes are ghastly or agreeable only by comparison. If you were familiar with the details of my client's previous murder of his uncle you would discern in his later offense (if offense it may be called) something in the nature of tender forbearance and filial consideration for the feelings of the victim. The appalling ferocity of the former assassination was indeed inconsistent with any hypothesis but that of guilt; and had it not been for the fact that the honorable judge before whom he was tried was the president of a life insurance company that took risks on hanging, and in which my client held a policy, it is hard to see how he could decently have been acquitted. If your Honor would like to hear about it for instruction and guidance of your Honor's mind, this unfortunate man, my client, will consent to give himself the pain of relating it under oath."

The district attorney said: "Your Honor, I object. Such a state-ment would be in the nature of evidence, and the testimony in this case is closed. The prisoner's statement should have been introduced three years ago, in the spring of 1881."

"In a statutory sense," said the judge, "you are right, and in the Court of Objections and Technicalities you would get a ruling in your favor. But not in a Court of Acquittal. The objection is over-ruled."

"I except," said the district attorney.

"You cannot do that," the judge said. "I must remind you that in order to take an exception you must first get this case transferred for a time to the Court of Exceptions on a formal motion duly supported by affidavits. A motion to that effect by your predecessor in office was denied by me during the first year of this trial. Mr. Clerk, swear the prisoner."

The customary oath having been administered, I made the follow-ing statement, which impressed the judge with so strong a sense of the comparative triviality of the offense for which I was on trial that he made no further search for mitigating circumstances, but simply instructed the jury to acquit, and I left the court, without a stain upon my reputation:

"I was born in 1856 in Kalamakee, Mich., of honest and reputable parents, one of whom Heaven has mercifully spared to comfort me in my later years. In 1867 the family came to California and settled near Nigger Head, where my father opened a road agency and prospered beyond the dreams of avarice. He was a reticent, saturnine man then, though his increasing years have now somewhat relaxed the austerity of his disposition, and I believe that nothing but his memory of the sad event for which I am now on trial prevents him from manifesting a genuine hilarity.

"Four years after we had set up the road agency an itinerant preacher came along, and having no other way to pay for the night's lodging that we gave him, favored us with an exhortation of such power that, praise God, we were all converted to religion. My father at once sent for his brother, the Hon. William Ridley of Stockton, and on his arrival turned over the agency to him, charging him noth-ing for the franchise nor plant—the latter consisting of a Winchester rifle, a sawed-off shotgun, and an assortment of masks made out of flour sacks. The family then moved to Ghost Rock and opened a dance house. It was called 'The Saints' Rest Hurdy-Gurdy,' and the proceedings each night began with prayer. It was there that my now sainted mother, by her grace in the dance, acquired the *sobriquet* of 'The Bucking Walrus.'

"In the fall of '75 I had occasion to visit Coyote, on the road to Mahala, and took the stage at Ghost Rock. There were four other passengers. About three miles beyond Nigger Head, persons whom I identified as my Uncle William and his two sons held up the stage. Finding nothing in the express box, they went through the passengers. I acted a most honorable part in the affair, placing myself in line with the others, holding up my hands and permitting myself to be deprived of forty dollars and a gold watch. From my behavior no one could have suspected that I knew the gentlemen who gave the entertainment. A few days later, when I went to Nigger Head and asked for the return of my money and watch my uncle and cousins swore they knew nothing of the matter, and they affected a belief that my father and I had done the job ourselves in dishonest violation of commercial good faith. Uncle William even threatened to retaliate by starting an opposition dance house at Ghost Rock. As 'The Saints' Rest' had become rather unpopular, I saw that this would assuredly ruin it and prove a paying enterprise, so I told my uncle that I was willing to overlook the past if he would take me into the scheme and keep the partnership a secret from my father. This fair offer he rejected, and I then perceived that it would be better and more satisfactory if he were dead.

"My plans to that end were soon perfected, and communicating them to my dear parents I had the gratification of receiving their approval. My father said he was proud of me, and my mother promised that although her religion forbade her to assist in taking human life I should have the advantage of her prayers for my success. As a preliminary measure looking to my security in case of detection I made an application for membership in that powerful order, the Knights of Murder, and in due course was received as a member of the Ghost Rock commandery. On the day that my probation ended I was for the first time permitted to inspect the records of the order and learn who belonged to it—all the rites of initiation having been conducted in masks. Fancy my delight when, in looking over the roll of membership, I found the third name to be that of my uncle, who indeed was junior vice-chancellor of the order! Here was an opportunity exceeding my wildest dreams—to murder I could add insubordination and treachery. It was what my good mother would have called 'a special Providence.'

"At about this time something occurred which caused my cup of joy, already full, to overflow on all sides, a circular cataract of bliss.

Three men, strangers in that locality, were arrested for the stage robbery in which I had lost my money and watch. They were brought to trial and, despite my efforts to clear them and fasten the guilt upon three of the most respectable and worthy citizens of Ghost Rock, convicted on the clearest proof. The murder would now be as wanton and reasonless as I could wish.

"One morning I shouldered my Winchester rifle, and going over to my uncle's house, near Nigger Head, asked my Aunt Mary, his wife, if he were at home, adding that I had come to kill him. My aunt replied with her peculiar smile that so many gentlemen called on that errand and were afterward carried away without having performed it that I must excuse her for doubting my good faith in the matter. She said I did not look as if I would kill anybody, so as a proof of good faith I leveled my rifle and wounded a Chinaman who happened to be passing the house. She said she knew whole families that could do a thing of that kind, but Bill Ridley was a horse of another color. She said, however, that I would find him over on the other side of the creek in the sheep lot; and she added that she hoped the best man would win.

"My Aunt Mary was one of the most fair-minded women that I have ever met.

"I found my uncle down on his knees engaged in skinning a sheep. Seeing that he had neither gun nor pistol handy I had not the heart to shoot him, so I approached him, greeted him pleasantly and struck him a powerful blow on the head with the butt of my rifle. I have a very good delivery and Uncle William lay down on his side, then rolled over on his back, spread out his fingers and shivered. Before he could recover the use of his limbs I seized the knife that he had been using and cut his hamstrings. You know, doubtless, that when you sever the *tendo Achillis* the patient has no further use of his leg; it is just the same as if he had no leg. Well, I parted them both, and when he revived he was at my service. As soon as he comprehended the situation, he said:

" 'Samuel, you have got the drop on me and can afford to be generous. I have only one thing to ask of you, and that is that you carry me to the house and finish me in the bosom of my family.'

"I told him I thought that a pretty reasonable request and I would do so if he would let me put him into a wheat sack; he would be easier to carry that way and if we were seen by the neighbors *en route* it would cause less remark. He agreed to that, and going to the barn I got a sack. This, however, did not fit him; it was too short and much wider than he; so I bent his legs, forced his knees up against his breast and got him into it that way, tying the sack above his head. He was a heavy man and I had all that I could do to get him on my back, but I staggered along for some distance until I came to a swing that some of the children had suspended to the branch of an oak. Here I laid him down and sat upon him to rest, and the sight of the rope gave me a happy inspiration. In twenty minutes my uncle, still in the sack, swung free to the sport of the wind.

"I had taken down the rope, tied one end tightly about the mouth of the bag, thrown the other across the limb and hauled him up about five feet from the ground. Fastening the other end of the rope also about the mouth of the sack, I had the satisfaction to see my uncle converted into a large, fine pendulum. I must add that he was not himself entirely aware of the nature of the change that he had undergone in his relation to the exterior world, though in justice to a good man's memory I ought to say that I do not think he would in any case have wasted much of my time in vain remonstrance.

"Uncle William had a ram that was famous in all that region as a fighter. It was in a state of chronic constitutional indignation. Some deep disappointment in early life had soured its disposition and it had declared war upon the whole world. To say that it would butt anything accessible is but faintly to express the nature and scope of its military activity: the universe was its antagonist; its methods that of a projectile. It fought like the angels and devils, in mid-air, cleaving the atmosphere like a bird, describing a parabolic curve and descending upon its victim at just the exact angle of incidence to make the most of its velocity and weight. Its momentum, calculated in foot-tons, was something incredible. It had been seen to destroy a four year old bull by a single impact upon that animal's gnarly forehead. No stone wall had ever been known to resist its downward swoop; there were no trees tough enough to stay it; it would splinter them into matchwood and defile their leafy honors in the dust. This irascible and implacable brute—this incarnate thunderbolt—this monster of the upper deep, I had seen reposing in the shade of an adjacent tree, dreaming dreams of conquest and glory. It was with a view to summoning it forth to the field of honor that I suspended its master in the manner described.

"Having completed my preparations, I imparted to the avuncular pendulum a gentle oscillation, and retiring to cover behind a contiguous rock, lifted up my voice in a long rasping cry whose diminishing final note was drowned in a noise like that of a swearing cat, which emanated from the sack. Instantly that formidable sheep was upon its feet and had taken in the military situation at a glance. In a few moments it had approached, stamping, to within fifty yards of the swinging foeman, who, now retreating and anon advancing, seemed to invite the fray. Suddenly I saw the beast's head drop earthward as if depressed by the weight of its enormous horns; then a dim, white, wavy streak of sheep prolonged itself from that spot in a generally horizontal direction to within about four yards of a point immediately beneath the enemy. There it struck sharply upward, and before it had faded from my gaze at the place whence it had set out I heard a horrid thump and a piercing scream, and my poor uncle shot forward, with a slack rope higher than the limb to which he was attached. Here the rope tautened with a jerk, arresting his flight, and back he swung in a breathless curve to the other end of his arc. The ram had fallen, a heap of indistinguishable legs, wool and horns, but pulling itself together and dodging as its antagonist swept downward it retired at random, alternately shaking its head and stamping its fore-feet. When it had backed about the same distance as that from which it had delivered the assault it paused again, bowed its head as if in prayer for victory and again shot forward, dimly visible as before—a prolonging white streak with monstrous undulations, ending with a sharp ascension. Its course this time was at a right angle to its former one, and its impatience so great that it struck the enemy before he had nearly reached the lowest point of his arc. In consequence he went flying round and round in a horizontal circle whose radius was about equal to half the length of the rope, which I forgot to say was nearly twenty feet long. His shrieks, *crescendo* in approach and *diminuendo* in recession, made the rapidity of his revolution more obvious to the ear than to the eye. He had evidently not yet been struck in a vital spot. His posture in the sack and the distance from the ground at which he hung compelled the ram to operate upon his lower extremities and the end of his back. Like a plant that has struck its root into some poisonous mineral, my poor uncle was dying slowly upward.

"After delivering its second blow the ram had not again retired. The fever of battle burned hot in its heart; its brain was intoxicated with the wine of strife. Like a pugilist who in his rage forgets his skill and fights ineffectively at half-arm's length, the angry beast endeavored to reach its fleeting foe by awkward vertical leaps as he passed overhead, sometimes, indeed, succeeding in striking him feebly, but more frequently overthrown by its own misguided eagerness. But as the impetus was exhausted and the man's circles narrowed in scope and diminished in speed, bringing him nearer to the ground, these tactics produced better results, eliciting a superior quality of screams, which I greatly enjoyed.

"Suddenly, as if the bugles had sung truce, the ram suspended hostilities and walked away, thoughtfully wrinkling and smoothing its great aquiline nose, and occasionally cropping a bunch of grass and slowly munching it. It seemed to have tired of war's alarms and resolved to beat the sword into a plowshare and cultivate the arts of peace. Steadily it held its course away from the field of fame until it had gained a distance of nearly a quarter of a mile. There it stopped and stood with its rear to the foe, chewing its cud and apparently half asleep. I observed, however, an occasional slight turn of its head, as if its apathy were more affected than real.

"Meantime Uncle William's shrieks had abated with his motion, and nothing was heard from him but long, low moans, and at long intervals my name, uttered in pleading tones exceedingly grateful to my ear. Evidently the man had not the faintest notion of what was being done to him, and was inexpressibly terrified. When Death comes cloaked in mystery he is terrible indeed. Little by little my uncle's oscillations diminished, and finally he hung motionless. I went to him and was about to give him the *coup de grâce,* when I heard and felt a succession of smart shocks which shook the ground like a series of light earthquakes, and turning in the direction of the ram, saw a long cloud of dust approaching me with inconceivable rapidity and alarming effect! At a distance of some thirty yards away it stopped short, and from the near end of it rose into the air what I at first thought a great white bird. Its ascent was so smooth and easy and regular that I could not realize its extraordinary celerity, and was lost in admiration of its grace. To this day the impression remains that it was a slow, deliberate movement, the ram—for it was that animal—being upborne by some power other than its own impetus, and supported through the successive stages of its flight with infinite tenderness and care. My eyes followed its progress through the air with unspeakable pleasure, all the greater by contrast with my former terror of its approach by land. Onward and upward the noble animal sailed, its head bent down almost between its knees, its fore-feet thrown back, its hinder legs trailing to rear like the legs of a soaring heron.

"At a height of forty or fifty feet, as fond recollection presents it to view, it attained its zenith and appeared to remain an instant stationary; then, tilting suddenly forward without altering the relative position of its parts, it shot downward on a steeper and steeper course with augmenting velocity, passed immediately above me with a noise like the rush of a cannon shot and struck my poor uncle almost squarely on the top of the head! So frightful was the impact that not only the man's neck was broken, but the rope too; and the body of the deceased, forced against the earth, was crushed to pulp beneath the awful front of that meteoric sheep! The concussion stopped all the clocks between Lone Hand and Dutch Dan's, and Professor Davidson, a distinguished authority in matters seismic, who happened to be in the vicinity, promptly explained that the vibrations were from north to southwest.

"Altogether, I cannot help thinking that in point of artistic atrocity my murder of Uncle William has seldom been excelled."

❅   ❅   ❅

THE HYPNOTIST

By those of my friends who happen to know that I sometimes amuse myself with hypnotism, mind reading and kindred phenomena, I am frequently asked if I have a clear conception of the nature of whatever principle underlies them. To this question I always reply that I neither have nor desire to have. I am no investigator with an ear at the key-hole of Nature's workshop, trying with vulgar curiosity to steal the secrets of her trade. The interests of science are as little to me as mine seem to have been to science.

Doubtless the phenomena in question are simple enough, and in no way transcend our powers of comprehension if only we could find the clew; but for my part I prefer not to find it, for I am of a singularly romantic disposition, deriving more gratification from mystery than from knowledge. It was commonly remarked of me when I was a child that my big blue eyes appeared to have been made rather to look into than look out of—such was their dreamful beauty, and in my frequent periods of abstraction, their indifference to what was going on. In those peculiarities they resembled, I venture to think, the soul which lies behind them, always more intent upon some lovely conception which it has created in its own image than concerned about the laws of nature and the material frame of things. All this, irrelevant and egotistic as it may seem, is related by way of accounting for the meagreness of the light that I am able to throw upon a subject that has engaged so much of my attention, and concerning which there is so keen and general a curiosity. With my powers and opportunities, another person might doubtless have an explanation for much of what I present simply as narrative.

My first knowledge that I possessed unusual powers came to me in my fourteenth year, when at school. Happening one day to have forgotten to bring my noon-day luncheon, I gazed longingly at that of a small girl who was preparing to eat hers. Looking up, her eyes met mine and she seemed unable to withdraw them. After a moment of hesitancy she came forward in an absent kind of way and without a word surrendered her little basket with its tempting contents and walked away. Inexpressibly pleased, I relieved my hunger and destroyed the basket. After that I had not the trouble to bring a luncheon for myself: that little girl was my daily purveyor; and not infrequently in satisfying my simple need from her frugal store I combined pleasure and profit by constraining her attendance at the feast and making misleading proffer of the viands, which eventually I consumed to the last fragment. The girl was always persuaded that she had eaten all herself; and later in the day her tearful complaints of hunger surprised the teacher, entertained the pupils, earned for her the sobriquet of Greedy-Gut and filled me with a peace past understanding.

A disagreeable feature of this otherwise satisfactory condition of things was the necessary secrecy: the transfer of the luncheon, for example, had to be made at some distance from the madding crowd, in a wood; and I blush to think of the many other unworthy subterfuges entailed by the situation. As I was (and am) naturally of a frank and open disposition, these became more and more irksome, and but for the reluctance of my parents to renounce the obvious advantages of the new *régime* I would gladly have reverted to the old. The plan that I finally adopted to free myself from the consequences of my own powers excited a wide and keen interest at the time, and that part of it which consisted in the death of the girl was severely condemned, but it is hardly pertinent to the scope of this narrative.

For some years afterward I had little opportunity to practice hypnotism; such small essays as I made at it were commonly barren of other recognition than solitary confinement on a bread-and-water diet; sometimes, indeed, they elicited nothing better than the cat-o'-nine-tails. It was when I was about to leave the scene of these small disappointments that my one really important feat was performed.

I had been called into the warden's office and given a suit of civilian's clothing, a trifling sum of money and a great deal of advice, which I am bound to confess was of a much better quality than the clothing. As I was passing out of the gate into the light of freedom I suddenly turned and looking the warden gravely in the eye, soon had him in control.

"You are an ostrich," I said.

At the post-mortem examination the stomach was found to contain a great quantity of indigestible articles mostly of wood or metal. Stuck fast in the œsophagus and constituting, according to the Coroner's jury, the immediate cause of death, one door-knob.

I was by nature a good and affectionate son, but as I took my way into the great world from which I had been so long secluded I could not help remembering that all my misfortunes had flowed like a stream from the niggard economy of my parents in the matter of school luncheons; and I knew of no reason to think they had reformed.

On the road between Succotash Hill and South Asphyxia is a little open field which once contained a shanty known as Pete Gilstrap's Place, where that gentleman used to murder travelers for a living. The death of Mr. Gilstrap and the diversion of nearly all the travel to another road occurred so nearly at the same time that no one has ever been able to say which was cause and which effect. Anyhow, the field was now a desolation and the Place had long been burned. It was while going afoot to South Asphyxia, the home of my childhood, that I found both my parents on their way to the Hill. They had hitched their team and were eating luncheon under an oak tree in the center of the field. The sight of the luncheon called up painful memories of my school days and roused the sleeping lion in my breast. Approaching the guilty couple, who at once recognized me, I ventured to suggest that I share their hospitality.

"Of this cheer, my son," said the author of my being, with characteristic pomposity, which age had not withered, "there is sufficient for but two. I am not, I hope, insensible to the hunger-light in your eyes, but—"

My father has never completed that sentence; what he mistook for hunger-light was simply the earnest gaze of the hypnotist. In a few seconds he was at my service. A few more sufficed for the lady, and the dictates of a just resentment could be carried into effect. "My former father," I said, "I presume that it is known to you that you and this lady are no longer what you were?"

"I have observed a certain subtle change," was the rather dubious reply of the old gentleman; "it is perhaps attributable to age."

"It is more than that," I explained; "it goes to character—to species. You and the lady here are, in truth, two *broncos*—wild stallions both, and unfriendly."

"Why, John," exclaimed my dear mother, "you don't mean to say that I am—"

"Madam," I replied, solemnly, fixing my eyes again upon hers, "you are."

Scarcely had the words fallen from my lips when she dropped upon her hands and knees, and backing up to the old man squealed like a demon and delivered a vicious kick upon his shin! An instant later he was himself down on all-fours, headed away from her and flinging his feet at her simultaneously and successively. With equal earnestness but inferior agility, because of her hampering body-gear, she plied her own. Their flying legs crossed and mingled in the most bewildering way; their feet sometimes meeting squarely in mid-air, their bodies thrust forward, falling flat upon the ground and for a moment helpless. On recovering themselves they would resume the combat, uttering their frenzy in the nameless sounds of the furious brutes which they believed themselves to be—the whole region rang with their clamor! Round and round they wheeled, the blows of their feet falling "like lightnings from the mountain cloud." They plunged and reared backward upon their knees, struck savagely at each other with awkward descending blows of both fists at once, and dropped again upon their hands as if unable to maintain the upright position of the body. Grass and pebbles were torn from the soil by hands and feet; clothing, hair, faces inexpressibly defiled with dust and blood. Wild, inarticulate screams of rage attested the delivery of the blows; groans, grunts and gasps their receipt. Nothing more truly military was ever seen at Gettysburg or Waterloo: the valor of my dear parents in the hour of danger can never cease to be to me a source of pride and gratification. At the end of it all two battered, tattered, bloody and fragmentary vestiges of mortality attested the solemn fact that the author of the strife was an orphan.

Arrested for provoking a breach of the peace, I was, and have ever since been, tried in the Court of Technicalities and Continuances whence, after fifteen years of proceedings, my attorney is moving heaven and earth to get the case taken to the Court of Remandment for New Trials.

Such are a few of my principal experiments in the mysterious force or agency known as hypnotic suggestion. Whether or not it could be employed by a bad man for an unworthy purpose I am unable to say.

MR. MASTHEAD, JOURNALIST

While I was in Kansas I purchased a weekly newspaper—the *Claybank Thundergust of Reform*. This paper had never paid its expenses; it had ruined four consecutive publishers; but my brother-in-law, Mr. Jefferson Scandril, of Weedhaven, was going to run for the Legislature, and I naturally desired his defeat; so it became necessary to have an organ in Claybank to assist in his political extinction. When the establishment came into my hands, the editor was a fellow who had "opinions," and him I at once discharged with an admonition. I had some difficulty in procuring a successor; every man in the county applied for the place. I could not appoint one without having to fight a majority of the others, and was eventually compelled to write to a friend at Warm Springs, in the adjoining State of Missouri, to send me an editor from abroad whose instalment at the helm of manifest destiny could have no local significance.

The man he sent me was a frowsy, seedy fellow, named Masthead—not larger, apparently, than a boy of sixteen years, though it was difficult to say from the outside how much of him was editor and how much cast-off clothing; for in the matter of apparel he had acted upon his favorite professional maxim, and "sunk the individual;" his attire—eminently eclectic, and in a sense international—quite overcame him at all points. However, as my friend had assured me he was "a graduate of one of the largest institutions in his native State," I took him in and bought a pen for him. My instructions to him were brief and simple.

"Mr. Masthead," said I, "it is the policy of the *Thundergust* first, last, and all the time, in this world and the next, to resent the intrusion of Mr. Jefferson Scandril into politics."

The first thing the little rascal did was to write a withering leader denouncing Mr. Scandril as a "demagogue, the degradation of whose political opinions was only equaled by the disgustfulness of the family connections of which those opinions were the spawn!"

I hastened to point out to Mr. Masthead that it had never been the policy of the *Thundergust* to attack the family relations of an offensive candidate, although this was not strictly true.

"I am very sorry," he replied, running his head up out of his clothes till it towered as much as six inches above the table at which he sat; "no offense, I hope."

"Oh, none in the world," said I, as carelessly as I could manage it; "only I don't think it a legitimate—that is, an effective, method of attack."

"Mr. Johnson," said he—I was passing as Johnson at that time, I remember—"Mr. Johnson, I think it *is* an effective method. Personally I might perhaps prefer another line of argument in this particular case, and personally perhaps you might; but in our profession personal considerations must be blown to the winds of the horizon; we must sink the individual. In opposing the election of your relative, sir, you have set the seal of your heavy displeasure upon the sin of nepotism, and for this I respect you; nepotism must be got under! But in the display of Roman virtues, sir, we must go the whole hog. When in the interest of public morality"—Mr. Masthead was now gesticulating earnestly with the sleeves of his coat—"Virginius stabbed his daughter, was he influenced by personal considerations? When Curtius leaped into the yawning gulf, did he not sink the individual?"

I admitted that he did, but feeling in a contentious mood, prolonged the discussion by leisurely loading and capping a revolver; but, prescient of my argument, Mr. Masthead avoided refutation by hastily adjourning the debate. I sent him a note that evening, filling-in a few of the details of the policy that I had before sketched in outline. Amongst other things I submitted that it would be better for us to exalt Mr. Scandril's opponent than to degrade himself. To this Mr. Masthead reluctantly assented—"sinking the individual," he reproachfully explained, "in the dependent employee—the powerless bondsman!" The next issue of the *Thundergust* contained, under the heading, "Invigorating Zephyrs," the following editorial article:

"Last week we declared our unalterable opposition to the candidacy of Mr. Jefferson Scandril, and gave reasons for the faith that is in us. For the first time in its history this paper made a clear, thoughtful, and adequate avowal and exposition of eternal principle! Abandoning for the present the stand we then took, let us trace the antecedents of Mr. Scandril's opponent up to their source. It has been urged against Mr. Broskin that he spent some years of his life in the lunatic asylum at Warm Springs, in the adjoining commonwealth of Missouri. This cuckoo cry—raised though it is by dogs of political darkness—we shall not stoop to controvert, for it is accidentally true; but next week we shall show, as by the stroke of an enchanter's wand, that this great statesman's detractors would probably not derive any benefits from a residence in the same institution, their mental aberration being rottenly incurable!"

I thought this rather strong and not quite to the point; but Masthead said it was a fact that our candidate, who was very little known in Claybank, had "served a term" in the Warm Springs asylum, and the issue must be boldly met—that evasion and denial were but forms of prostration beneath the iron wheels of Truth! As he said this he seemed to inflate and expand so as almost to fill his clothes, and the fire of his eye somehow burned into me an impression— since effaced—that a just cause is not imperiled by a trifling concession to fact. So, leaving the matter quite in my editor's hands I went away to keep some important engagements, the paragraph having involved me in several duels with the friends of Mr. Broskin. I thought it rather hard that I should have to defend my new editor's policy against the supporters of my own candidate, particularly as I was clearly in the right and they knew nothing whatever about the matter in dispute, not one of them having ever before so much as heard of the now famous Warm Springs asylum. But I would not shirk even the humblest journalistic duty; I fought these fellows and acquitted myself as became a man of letters and a politician. The hurts I got were some time healing, and in the interval every prominent member of my party who came to Claybank to speak to the people regarded it as a simple duty to call first at my house, make a tender inquiry as to the progress of my recovery and leave a challenge. My physician forbade me to read a line of anything; the consequence was that Masthead had it all his own way with the paper. In looking over the old files now, I find that he devoted his entire talent and all the space of the paper, including what had been the advertising columns, to confessing that our candidate had been an inmate of a lunatic asylum, and contemptuously asking the opposing party what they were going to do about it.

All this time Mr. Broskin made no sign; but when the challenges became intolerable I indignantly instructed Mr. Masthead to whip round to the other side and support my brother-in-law. Masthead "sank the individual," and duly announced, with his accustomed frankness, our change of policy. Then Mr. Broskin came down to Claybank—to thank me! He was a fine, respectable-looking gentleman, and impressed me very favorably. But Masthead was in when he called, and the effect upon *him* was different. He shrank into a mere heap of old clothes, turned white, and chattered his teeth. Noting this extraordinary behavior, I at once sought an explanation.

"Mr. Broskin," said I, with a meaning glance at the trembling editor, "from certain indications I am led to fear that owing to some mistake we may have been doing you an injustice. May I ask you if you were really ever in the Lunatic asylum at Warm Springs, Missouri?"

"For three years," he replied, quietly, "I was the physician in charge of that institution. Your son"—turning to Masthead, who was flying all sorts of colors—"was, if I mistake not, one of my patients. I learn that a few weeks ago a friend of yours, named Norton, secured the young man's release upon your promise to take care of him yourself in future. I hope that home associations have improved the poor fellow. It's very sad!"

It was indeed. Norton was the name of the man to whom I had written for an editor, and who had sent me one! Norton was ever an obliging fellow.

❊ ❊ ❊

WHY I AM NOT EDITING "THE STINGER"

J. Munniglut, Proprietor, to Peter Pitchin, Editor.

"Stinger" Office, Monday, 9 a.m.
A man has called to ask "who wrote that article about Mr. Muskler." I told him to find out, and he says that is what he means to do. He has consented to amuse himself with the exchanges while I ask you. I don't approve the article.

Peter Pitchin, Editor, to J. Munniglut, Proprietor.

13 Lofer Street, Monday, 10 a.m.
Do you happen to remember how Dacier translates *Difficile est proprie communia dicere?* I've made a note of it somewhere, but can't find it. If you remember please leave a memorandum of it on your table, and I'll get it when I come down this afternoon.

P.S.—Tell the man to go away; we can't be bothered about that fellow Muskler.

J. Munniglut, Proprietor, to Peter Pitchin, Editor.

"STINGER" OFFICE, Monday, 11:30 A.M.

I can't be impolite to a stranger, you know; I must tell him *some-body* wrote it. He has finished the exchanges, and is drumming on the floor with the end of his stick; I fear the people in the shop below won't like it. Besides, the foreman says it disturbs the compositors in the next room. Suppose you come down.

Peter Pitchin, Editor, to J. Munniglut, Proprietor.

13 LOFER STREET, Monday, 1 P.M.

I have found the note I made of that translation, but it is in French and I can't make it out. Try the man with the dictionary and the "Books of Dates." They ought to last him till it's time to close the office. I shall be down early to-morrow morning.

P.S.—How big is he? Suggest a civil suit for libel.

J. Munniglut, Proprietor, to Peter Pitchin, Editor.

"STINGER" OFFICE, Monday, 3 P.M.

He looks larger than he was when he came in. I've offered him the dictionary; he says he has read it before. He is sitting on my table. Come at once!

Peter Pitchin, Editor, to J. Munniglut, Proprietor.

13 LOFER STREET, Monday, 5 P.M.

I don't think I shall. I am doing an article for this week on "The Present Aspect of the Political Horizon." Expect me *very* early to-morrow. You had better turn the man out and shut up the office.

Henry Inxling, Bookkeeper, to Peter Pitchin, Editor.

"STINGER" OFFICE, Tuesday, 8 A.M.

Mr. Munniglut has not arrived, but his friend, the large gentleman who was with him all day yesterday, is here again. He seems very desirous of seeing you, and says he will wait. Perhaps he is your cousin. I thought I would tell you he was here, so that you might hasten down.

Ought I to allow dogs in the office? The gentleman has a bull-dog.

Peter Pitchin, Editor, to Henry Inxling, Bookkeeper.

13 Lofer Street, Tuesday, 9:30 a.m.

Certainly *not;* dogs have fleas. The man is an impostor. Oblige me by turning him out. I shall come down this afternoon—*early*.

P.S.—Don't listen to the rascal's entreaties; out with him!

Henry Inxling, Bookkeeper, to Peter Pitchin, Editor.

"Stinger" Office, Tuesday, 12 m.

The gentleman carries a revolver. Would you mind coming down and reasoning with him? I have a wife and five children depending on me, and when I lose my temper I am likely to go too far. I would prefer that you should turn him out.

Peter Pitchin, Editor, to Henry Inxling, Bookkeeper.

13 Lofer Street, Tuesday, 2 p.m.

Do you suppose I can leave my private correspondence to preserve you from the intrusion and importunities of beggars? Put the scoundrel out at once—neck and heels! I know him; he's Muskler—don't you remember? Muskler, the coward, who assaulted an old man; you'll find the whole circumstances related in last Saturday's issue. Out with him—the unmanly sneak!

Henry Inxling, Bookkeeper, to Peter Pitchin, Editor.

"Stinger" Office, Tuesday Evening.

I have told him to go, and he laughed. So did the bull-dog. But he is going. He is now making a bed for the pup in one corner of your room, with some rugs and old newspapers, and appears to be about to go to dinner. I have given him your address. The foreman wants some copy to go on with. I beg you will come at once if I am to be left alone with that dog.

Peter Pitchin, Editor, to Henry Inxling, Bookkeeper.

40 Duntioner's Alley, Wednesday, 10 a.m.

I should have come down to the office last evening, but you see I have been moving. My landlady was too filthy dirty for anything! I stood it as long as I could; then I left. I'm coming directly I get your answer to this; but I want to know, first, if my blotter has been changed and my ink-well refilled. This house is a good way out, but the boy can take the car at the corner of Cobble and Slush streets.

O!—about that *man*? Of course you have not seen him since.

William Quoin, Foreman, to Peter Pitchin, Editor.

"STINGER" OFFICE, Wednesday 12 M.

I've got your note to Inxling; he ain't come down this morning. I haven't a line of copy on the hooks; the boys are all throwing in dead ads. There's a man and a dog in the proprietor's office; I don't believe they ought to be there, all alone, but they were here all Monday and yesterday, and may be connected with the business management of the paper; so I don't like to order them out. Perhaps you will come down and speak to them. We shall have to go away if you don't send copy.

Peter Pitchin, Editor, to William Quoin, Foreman.

40 DUNTIONER'S ALLEY, Wednesday, 3 P.M.

Your note astonishes me. The man you describe is a notorious thief. Get the compositors all together, and make a rush at him. Don't try to keep him, but hustle him out of town, and I'll be down as soon as I can get a button sewn on my collar.

P.S.—Give it him good!—don't mention my address and he can't complain to me how you treat him. Bust his bugle!

J. Munniglut, Proprietor, to Peter Pitchin, Editor.

"STINGER" OFFICE, Friday, 2 P.M.

Business has detained me from the office until now, and what do I find? Not a soul about the place, no copy, not a stickful of live matter on the galleys! There can be no paper this week. What you have all done with yourselves I am sure I don't know; one would suppose there had been smallpox about the place. You will please come down and explain this Hegira at once—at once, if *you* please!

P.S.—That troublesome Muskler—you may remember he dropped in on Monday to inquire about something or other—has taken a sort of shop exactly opposite here, and seems, at this distance, to be doing something to a shotgun. I presume he is a gunsmith. So we are precious well rid of *him*.

Peter Pitchin, Editor, to J. Munniglut, Proprietor.

Pier No. 3, Friday Evening.

Just a line or two to say I am suddenly called away to bury my sick mother. When that is off my mind I'll write you what I know about the Hegira, the Flight into Egypt, the Retreat of the Ten Thousand, and whatever else you would like to learn. There is nothing mean about *me!* I don't think there has been any wilful desertion. You may engage an editor for, say, fifty years, with the privilege of keeping him regularly, if, at the end of that time, I should break my neck hastening back.

P.S.—I hope that poor fellow Muskler will make a fair profit in the gunsmithing line. Jump him for an ad!

❈   ❈   ❈

CORRUPTING THE PRESS

When Joel Bird was up for Governor of Missouri, Sam Henly was editing the Berrywood *Bugle;* and no sooner was the nomination made by the State Convention than he came out hot against the party. He was an able writer, was Sam, and the lies he invented about our candidate were shocking! That, however, we endured very well, but presently Sam turned squarely about and began telling the truth. *This* was a little too much; the County Committee held a hasty meeting, and decided that it must be stopped; so I, Henry Barber, was sent for to make arrangements to that end. I knew something of Sam: had purchased him several times, and I estimated his present value at about one thousand dollars. This seemed to the committee a reasonable figure, and on my mentioning it to Sam he said "he thought that about the fair thing; it should never be said that the *Bugle* was a hard paper to deal with." There was, however, some delay in raising the money; the candidates for the local offices had not disposed of their autumn hogs yet, and were in financial straits. Some of them contributed a pig each, one gave twenty bushels of corn, another a flock of chickens; and the man who aspired to the distinction of County Judge paid his assessment with a wagon. These things had to be converted into cash at a

ruinous sacrifice, and in the meantime Sam kept pouring an incessant stream of hot shot into our political camp. Nothing I could
say would make him stay his hand; he invariably replied that it
was no bargain until he had the money. The committeemen were
furious; it required all my eloquence to prevent their declaring the
contract null and void; but at last a new, clean one thousand-dollar
note was passed over to me, which in hot haste I transferred to Sam
at his residence.

That evening there was a meeting of the committee: all seemed in
high spirits again, except Hooker of Jayhawk. This old wretch sat
back and shook his head during the entire session, and just before
adjournment said, as he took his hat to go, that p'r'aps 'twas orl right
and on the squar'; maybe thar war'n't any shenannigan, but *he* war
dubersome—yes, he war dubersome. The old curmudgeon repeated
this until I was exasperated beyond restraint.

"Mr. Hooker," said I, "I've known Sam Henly ever since he was
so high, and there isn't an honester man in old Missouri. Sam
Henly's word is as good as his note! What's more, if any gentleman
thinks he would enjoy a first-class funeral, and if he will supply the
sable accessories, I'll supply the corpse. And he can take it home
with him from this meeting."

At this point Mr. Hooker was troubled with leaving.

Having got this business off my conscience I slept late next day.
When I stepped into the street I saw at once that something was
"up." There were knots of people gathered at the corners, some reading eagerly that morning's issue of the *Bugle,* some gesticulating,
and others stalking moodily about muttering curses, not loud but
deep. Suddenly I heard an excited clamor—a confused roar of many
lungs, and the trampling of innumerable feet. In this babel of noises
I could distinguish the words "Kill him!" "Wa'm his hide!" and so
forth; and, looking up the street, I saw what seemed to be the whole
male population racing down it. I am very excitable, and, though
I did not know whose hide was to be warmed, nor why anyone was
to be killed, I shot off in front of the howling masses, shouting "Kill
him!" and "Warm his hide!" as loudly as the loudest, all the time
looking out for the victim. Down the street we flew like a storm;
then I turned a corner, thinking the scoundrel must have gone up
that street; then bolted through a public square; over a bridge; under
an arch; finally back into the main street; yelling like a panther,
and resolved to slaughter the first human being I should overtake.
The crowd followed my lead, turning as I turned, shrieking as I

shrieked, and—all at once it came to me that *I* was the man whose hide was to be warmed!

It is needless to dwell upon the sensation this discovery gave me; happily I was within a few yards of the committee rooms, and into these I dashed, closing and bolting the doors behind me, and mounting the stairs like a flash. The committee was in solemn session, sitting in a nice, even row on the front benches, each man with his elbows on his knees, and his chin resting in the palms of his hands —thinking. At each man's feet lay a neglected copy of the *Bugle*. Every member fixed his eyes on me, but no one stirred, none uttered a sound. There was something awful in this preternatural silence, made more impressive by the hoarse murmur of the crowd outside, breaking down the door. I could endure it no longer, but strode forward and snatched up the paper lying at the feet of the chairman. At the head of the editorial columns, in letters half an inch long, were the following amazing head-lines:

"Dastardly Outrage! Corruption Rampant in Our Midst! The Vampires Foiled! Henry Barber at his Old Game! The Rat Gnaws a File! The Democratic Hordes Attempt to Ride Roughshod Over a Free People! Base Endeavor to Bribe the Editor of this Paper with *a Twenty-Dollar Note!* The Money Given to the Orphan Asylum."

I read no farther, but stood stockstill in the center of the floor, and fell into a reverie. Twenty dollars! Somehow it seemed a mere trifle. Nine hundred and eighty dollars! I did not know there was so much money in the world. Twenty—no, eighty—one thousand dollars! There were big, black figures floating all over the floor. Incessant cataracts of them poured down the walls, stopped, and shied off as I looked at them, and began to go it again when I lowered my eyes. Occasionally the figures 20 would take shape somewhere about the floor, and then the figures 980 would slide up and overlay them. Then, like the lean kine of Pharoah's dream, they would all march away and devour the fat naughts of the number 1,000. And dancing like gnats in the air were myriads of little caduceus-like phantoms, thus—$$$$$. I could not at all make it out, but began to comprehend my position. Directly Old Hooker, without moving from his seat, began to drown the noise of countless feet on the stairs by elevating his thin falsetto:

"P'r'aps, Mr. Cheerman, it's orl on the squar'. We know Mr. Henly can't tell a lie; but I'm powerful dubersome that thar's a balyance dyue this yer committee from the gent who hez the flo'—if he ain't done gone laid it yout fo' sable ac—ac—fo' fyirst-class funerals."

I felt at that moment as if I should like to play the leading character in a first-class funeral myself. I felt that every man in my position ought to have a nice, comfortable coffin, with a silver door-plate, a foot-warmer, and bay-windows for his ears. How do you suppose you would have felt?

My leap from the window of that committee room, my speed in streaking it for the adjacent forest, my self-denial in ever afterward resisting the impulse to return to Berrywood and look after my political and material interests there—these I have always considered things to be justly proud of, and I hope I am proud of them.

❊   ❊   ❊

"THE BUBBLE REPUTATION"

HOW ANOTHER MAN'S WAS SOUGHT AND PRICKED

It was a stormy night in the autumn of 1930. The hour was about eleven. San Francisco lay in darkness, for the laborers at the gas works had struck and destroyed the company's property because a newspaper to which a cousin of the manager was a subscriber had censured the course of a potato merchant related by marriage to a member of the Knights of Leisure. Electric lights had not at that period been reinvented. The sky was filled with great masses of black cloud which, driven rapidly across the star-fields by winds unfelt on the earth and momentarily altering their fantastic forms, seemed instinct with a life and activity of their own and endowed with awful powers of evil, to the exercise of which they might at any time set their malignant will.

An observer standing, at this time, at the corner of Paradise avenue and Great White Throne walk in Sorrel Hill cemetery would have seen a human figure moving among the graves toward the Superintendent's residence. Dimly and fitfully visible in the intervals of thinner gloom, this figure had a most uncanny and disquieting aspect. A long black cloak shrouded it from neck to heel. Upon its head was a slouch hat, pulled down across the forehead and almost concealing the face, which was further hidden by a half-mask, only the beard being occasionally visible as the head was lifted partly above the collar of the cloak. The man wore upon his feet jack-boots whose wide, funnel-shaped legs had settled down in many a fold and crease about his ankles, as could be seen whenever accident parted the bottom of the cloak. His arms were concealed, but sometimes he stretched out the right to steady himself by a headstone as he crept stealthily but blindly over the uneven ground. At such times a close scrutiny of the hand would have disclosed in the palm the hilt of a poniard, the blade of which lay along the wrist, hidden in the sleeve. In short, the man's garb, his movements, the hour—everything proclaimed him a reporter.

But what did he there?

On the morning of that day the editor of the *Daily Malefactor* had touched the button of a bell numbered 216 and in response to the summons Mr. Longbo Spittleworth, reporter, had been shot into the room out of an inclined tube.

"I understand," said the editor, "that you are 216—am I right?"

"That," said the reporter, catching his breath and adjusting his clothing, both somewhat disordered by the celerity of his flight through the tube,—"that is my number."

"Information has reached us," continued the editor, "that the Superintendent of the Sorrel Hill cemetery—one Inhumio, whose very name suggests inhumanity—is guilty of the grossest outrages in the administration of the great trust confided to his hands by the sovereign people."

"The cemetery is private property," faintly suggested 216.

"It is alleged," continued the great man, disdaining to notice the interruption, "that in violation of popular rights he refuses to permit his accounts to be inspected by representatives of the press."

"Under the law, you know, he is responsible to the directors of the cemetery company," the reporter ventured to interject.

"They say," pursued the editor, heedless, "that the inmates are in many cases badly lodged and insufficiently clad, and that in consequence they are usually cold. It is asserted that they are never fed—except to the worms. Statements have been made to the effect that males and females are permitted to occupy the same quarters, to the incalculable detriment of public morality. Many clandestine villainies are alleged of this fiend in human shape, and it is desirable that his underground methods be unearthed in the *Malefactor*. If he resists we will drag his family skeleton from the privacy of his domestic closet. There is money in it for the paper, fame for you—are you ambitious, 216?"

"I am—bitious."

"Go, then," cried the editor, rising and waving his hand imperiously—"go and 'seek the bubble reputation'."

"The bubble shall be sought," the young man replied, and leaping into a man-hole in the floor, disappeared. A moment later the editor, who after dismissing his subordinate, had stood motionless, as if lost in thought, sprang suddenly to the man-hole and shouted down it: "Hello, 216?"

"Aye, aye, sir," came up a faint and far reply.

"About that 'bubble reputation'—you understand, I suppose, that the reputation which you are to seek is that of the other man."

In the execution of his duty, in the hope of his employer's approval, in the costume of his profession, Mr. Longbo Spittleworth, otherwise known as 216, has already occupied a place in the mind's eye of the intelligent reader. Alas for poor Mr. Inhumio!

A few days after these events that fearless, independent and enterprising guardian and guide of the public, the San Francisco *Daily Malefactor,* contained a whole-page article whose headlines are here presented with some necessary typographical mitigation:

"Hell Upon Earth! Corruption Rampant in the Management of the Sorrel Hill Cemetery. The Sacred City of the Dead in the Leprous Clutches of a Demon in Human Form. Fiendish Atrocities Committed in 'God's Acre.' The Holy Dead Thrown around Loose. Fragments of Mothers. Segregation of a Beautiful Young Lady Who in Life Was the Light of a Happy Household. A Superintendent Who Is an Ex-Convict. How He Murdered His Neighbor to Start the Cemetery. He Buries His Own Dead Elsewhere. Extraordinary Insolence to a Representative of the Public Press. Little Eliza's Last Words: 'Mamma, Feed Me to the Pigs.' A Moonshiner Who Runs an Illicit Bone-Button Factory in One Corner of the Grounds. Buried Head Downward. Revolting Mausoleistic Orgies. Dancing on the Dead. Devilish Mutilation—a Pile of Late Lamented Noses and Sainted Ears. No Separation of the Sexes; Petitions for Chaperons Unheeded. 'Veal' as Supplied to the Superintendent's Employees. A Miscreant's Record from His Birth. Disgusting Subserviency of Our Contemporaries and Strong Indications of Collusion. Nameless Abnormalities. 'Doubled Up Like a Nut-Cracker.' 'Wasn't Planted White.' Horribly Significant Reduction in the Price of Lard. The Question of the Hour: Whom Do You Fry Your Doughnuts In?"

A SHIPWRECKOLLECTION

As I left the house she said I was a cruel old thing, and not a bit nice, and she hoped I never, never *would* come back. So I shipped as mate on the *Mudlark,* bound from London to wherever the captain might think it expedient to sail. It had not been thought advisable to hamper Captain Abersouth with orders, for when he could not have his own way, it had been observed, he would contrive in some ingenious way to make the voyage unprofitable. The owners of the *Mudlark* had grown wise in their generation, and now let him do pretty much as he pleased, carrying such cargoes as he fancied to ports where the nicest women were. On the voyage of which I write he had taken no cargo at all; he said it would only make the *Mudlark* heavy and slow. To hear this mariner talk one would have supposed he did not know very much about commerce.

We had a few passengers—not nearly so many as we had laid in basins and stewards for; for before coming off to the ship most of those who had bought tickets would inquire whither she was bound, and when not informed would go back to their hotels and send a bandit on board to remove their baggage. But there were enough left to be rather troublesome. They cultivated the rolling gait peculiar to sailors when drunk, and the upper deck was hardly wide enough for them to go from the forecastle to the binnacle to set their watches by the ship's compass. They were always petitioning Captain Abersouth to let the big anchor go, just to hear it plunge in the water, threatening in case of refusal to write to the newspapers. A favorite amusement with them was to sit in the lee of the bulwarks, relating their experiences in former voyages—voyages distinguished in every instance by two remarkable features, the frequency of unprecedented hurricanes and the entire immunity of the narrator from seasickness. It was very interesting to see them sitting in a row telling these things, each man with a basin between his legs.

One day there arose a great storm. The sea walked over the ship as if it had never seen a ship before and meant to enjoy it all it could. The *Mudlark* labored very much—far more, indeed, than the crew did; for these innocents had discovered in possession of one of their number a pair of leather-seated trousers, and would do nothing but sit and play cards for them; in a month from leaving port each sailor had owned them a dozen times. They were so worn by being pushed over to the winner that there was little but the seat remaining, and that immortal part the captain finally kicked overboard—not maliciously, nor in an unfriendly spirit, but because he had a habit of kicking the seats of trousers.

The storm increased in violence until it succeeded in so straining the *Mudlark* that she took in water like a teetotaler; then it appeared to get relief directly. This may be said in justice to a storm at sea: when it has broken off your masts, pulled out your rudder, carried away your boats and made a nice hole in some inaccessible part of your hull it will often go away in search of a fresh ship, leaving you to take such measures for your comfort as you may think fit. In our case the captain thought fit to sit on the taffrail reading a three-volume novel.

Seeing he had got about half way through the second volume, at which point the lovers would naturally be involved in the most hopeless and heart-rending difficulties, I thought he would be in a particularly cheerful humor, so I approached him and informed him the ship was going down.

"Well," said he, closing the book, but keeping his forefinger between the pages to mark his place, "she never would be good for much after such a shaking-up as this. But, I say—I wish you would just send the bo'sm for'd there to break up that prayer-meeting. The *Mudlark* isn't a seamen's chapel, I suppose."

"But," I replied, impatiently, "can't something be done to lighten the ship?"

"Well," he drawled, reflectively, "seeing she hasn't any masts left to cut away, nor any cargo to—stay, you might throw over some of the heaviest of the passengers if you think it would do any good."

It was a happy thought—the intuition of genius. Walking rapidly forward to the foc's'le, which, being highest out of water, was crowded with passengers, I seized a stout old gentleman by the nape of the neck, pushed him up to the rail, and chucked him over. He did not touch the water: he fell on the apex of a cone of sharks which sprang up from the sea to meet him, their noses gathered to a point, their tails just clearing the surface. I think it unlikely that the old gentleman knew what disposition had been made of him. Next, I hurled over a woman and flung a fat baby to the wild winds. The former was sharked out of sight, the same as the old man; the latter divided amongst the gulls.

I am relating these things exactly as they occurred. It would be very easy to make a fine story out of all this material—to tell how that, while I was engaged in lightening the ship, I was touched by the self-sacrificing spirit of a beautiful young woman, who, to save the life of her lover, pushed her aged mother forward to where I was operating, imploring me to take the old lady, but spare, O, spare her dear Henry. I might go on to set forth how that I not only did take the old lady, as requested, but immediately seized dear Henry, and sent him flying as far as I could to leeward, having first broken his back across the rail and pulled a double-fistful of his curly hair out. I might proceed to state that, feeling appeased, I then stole the long boat and taking the beautiful maiden pulled away from the ill-fated ship to the church of St. Massaker, Fiji, where we were united by a knot which I afterward untied with my teeth by eating her. But, in truth, nothing of all this occurred, and I can not afford to be the first writer to tell a lie just to interest the reader. What really did occur is this: as I stood on the quarter-deck, heaving over the passengers, one after another, Captain Abersouth, having finished his novel, walked aft and quietly hove *me* over.

The sensations of a drowning man have been so often related that I shall only briefly explain that memory at once displayed her treasures: all the scenes of my eventful life crowded, though without confusion or fighting, into my mind. I saw my whole career spread out before me, like a map of Central Africa since the discovery of the gorilla. There were the cradle in which I had lain, as a child, stupefied with soothing syrups; the perambulator, seated in which and propelled from behind, I overthrew the schoolmaster, and in which my infantile spine received its curvature; the nursery-maid, surrendering her lips alternately to me and the gardener; the old home of my youth, with the ivy and the mortgage on it; my eldest brother, who by will succeeded to the family debts; my sister, who ran away with the Count von Pretzel, coachman to a most respectable New York family; my mother, standing in the attitude of a saint, pressing with both hands her prayer-book against the patent palpitators from Madame Fahertini's; my venerable father, sitting in his chimney corner, his silvered head bowed upon his breast, his withered hands crossed patiently in his lap, waiting with Christian resignation for death, and drunk as a lord—all this, and much more, came before my mind's eye, and there was no charge for admission to the show. Then there was a ringing sound in my ears, my senses swam better than I could, and as I sank down, down, through fathomless depths, the amber light falling through the water above my head failed and darkened into blackness. Suddenly my feet struck something firm—it was the bottom. Thank heaven, I was saved!

THE CAPTAIN OF THE "CAMEL"

This ship was named the *Camel.* In some ways she was an extraordinary vessel. She measured six hundred tons; but when she had taken in enough ballast to keep her from upsetting like a shot duck, and was provisioned for a three months' voyage, it was necessary to be mighty fastidious in the choice of freight and passengers. For illustration, as she was about to leave port a boat came alongside with two passengers, a man and his wife. They had booked the day before, but had remained ashore to get one more decent meal before committing themselves to the "briny cheap," as the man called the ship's fare. The woman came aboard, and the man was preparing to follow, when the captain leaned over the side and saw him.

"Well," said the captain, "what do *you* want?"

"What do *I* want?" said the man, laying hold of the ladder. "I'm a-going to embark in this here ship—that's what I want."

"Not with all that fat on you," roared the captain. "You don't weigh an ounce less than eighteen stone, and I've got to have in my anchor yet. You wouldn't have me leave the anchor, I suppose?"

The man said he did not care about the anchor—he was just as God had made him (he looked as if his cook had had something to do with it) and, sink or swim, he purposed embarking in that ship. A good deal of wrangling ensued, but one of the sailors finally threw the man a cork life-preserver, and the captain said that would lighten him and he might come abroad.

This was Captain Abersouth, formerly of the *Mudlark*—as good a seaman as ever sat on the taffrail reading a three volume novel. Nothing could equal this man's passion for literature. For every voyage he laid in so many bales of novels that there was no stowage for the cargo. There were novels in the hold, and novels between-decks, and novels in the saloon, and in the passengers' beds.

The *Camel* had been designed and built by her owner, an architect in the City, and she looked about as much like a ship as Noah's Ark did. She had bay windows and a veranda; a cornice and doors at the waterline. These doors had knockers and servant's bells. There had been a futile attempt at an area. The passenger saloon was on the upper deck, and had a tile roof. To this humplike structure the ship owed her name. Her designer had erected several churches—

that of St. Ignotus is still used as a brewery in Hotbath Meadows—and, possessed of the ecclesiastic idea, had give the *Camel* a transept; but, finding this impeded her passage through the water, he had it removed. This weakened the vessel amidships. The mainmast was something like a steeple. It had a weathercock. From this spire the eye commanded one of the finest views in England.

Such was the *Camel* when I joined her in 1864 for a voyage of discovery to the South Pole. The expedition was under the "auspices" of the Royal Society for the Promotion of Fair Play. At a meeting of this excellent association, it had been "resolved" that the partiality of science for the North Pole was an invidious distinction between two objects equally meritorious; that Nature had marked her disapproval of it in the case of Sir John Franklin and many of his imitators; that it served them very well right; that this enterprise should be undertaken as a protest against the spirit of undue bias; and, finally, that no part of the responsibility or expense should devolve upon the society in its corporate character, but any individual member might contribute to the fund if he were fool enough. It is only common justice to say that none of them was. The *Camel* merely parted her cable one day while I happened to be on board—drifted out of the harbor southward, followed by the execrations of all who knew her, and could not get back. In two months she had crossed the equator, and the heat began to grow insupportable.

Suddenly we were becalmed. There had been a fine breeze up to three o'clock in the afternoon and the ship had made as much as two knots an hour when without a word of warning the sails began to belly the wrong way, owing to the impetus that the ship had acquired; and then, as this expired, they hung as limp and lifeless as the skirts of a claw-hammer coat. The *Camel* not only stood stock still but moved a little backward toward England. Old Ben the boatswain said that he'd never knowed but one deader calm, and that, he explained, was when Preacher Jack, the reformed sailor, had got excited in a sermon in a seaman's chapel and shouted that the Archangel Michael would chuck the Dragon into the brig and give him a taste of the rope's-end, damn his eyes!

We lay in this woful state for the better part of a year, when, growing impatient, the crew deputed me to look up the captain and see if something could not be done about it. I found him in a remote cobwebby corner between-decks, with a book in his hand. On one side of him, the cords newly cut, were three bales of "Ouida"; on the other a mountain of Miss M. E. Braddon towered above his head.

He had finished "Ouida" and was tackling Miss Braddon. He was greatly changed.

"Captain Abersouth," said I, rising on tiptoe so as to overlook the lower slopes of Miss Braddon, "will you be good enough to tell me how long this thing is going on?"

"Can't say, I'm sure," he replied without pulling his eyes off the page. "They'll probably make up about the middle of the book. In the meantime old Pondronummus will foul his top-hamper and take out his papers for Looney Haven, and young Monshure de Boojower will come in for a million. Then if the proud and fair Angelica doesn't luff and come into his wake after pizening that sea lawyer, Thundermuzzle, I don't know nothing about the deeps and shallers of the human heart."

I could not take so hopeful a view of the situation, and went on deck, feeling very much discouraged. I had no sooner got my head out than I observed that the ship was moving at a high rate of speed!

We had on board a bullock and a Dutchman. The bullock was chained by the neck to the foremast, but the Dutchman was allowed a good deal of liberty, being shut up at night only. There was bad blood between the two—a feud of long standing, having its origin in the Dutchman's appetite for milk and the bullock's sense of personal dignity; the particular cause of offense it would be tedious to relate. Taking advantage of his enemy's afternoon *siesta,* the Dutchman had now managed to sneak by him, and had gone out on the bowsprit to fish. When the animal waked and saw the other creature enjoying himself he straddled his chain, leveled his horns, got his hind feet against the mast and laid a course for the offender. The chain was strong, the mast firm, and the ship, as Byron says, "walked the water like a thing of course."

After that we kept the Dutchman right where he was, night and day, the old *Camel* making better speed than she had ever done in the most favorable gale. We held due south.

We had now been a long time without sufficient food, particularly meat. We could spare neither the bullock nor the Dutchman; and the ship's carpenter, that traditional first aid to the famished, was a mere bag of bones. The fish would neither bite nor be bitten. Most of the running-tackle of the ship had been used for macaroni soup; all the leather work, our shoes included, had been devoured in omelettes; with oakum and tar we had made fairly supportable salad. After a brief experimental career as tripe the sails had departed this life forever. Only two courses remained from which to choose; we could eat one another, as is the etiquette of the sea, or partake of Captain

Abersouth's novels. Dreadful alternative!—but a choice. And it is seldom, I think, that starving sailormen are offered a shipload of the best popular authors ready-roasted by the critics.

We ate that fiction. The works that the captain had thrown aside lasted six months, for most of them were by the best-selling authors and were pretty tough. After they were gone—of course some had to be given to the bullock and the Dutchman—we stood by the captain, taking the other books from his hands as he finished them. Sometimes, when we were apparently at our last gasp, he would skip a whole page of moralizing, or a bit of description; and always, as soon as he clearly foresaw the *dénoûement*—which he generally did at about the middle of the second volume—the work was handed over to us without a word of repining.

The effect of this diet was not unpleasant but remarkable. Physically, it sustained us: mentally, it exalted us; morally, it made us but a trifle worse than we were. We talked as no human beings ever talked before. Our wit was polished but without point. As in a stage broadsword combat, every cut has its parry, so in our conversation every remark suggested the reply, and this necessitated a certain rejoinder. The sequence once interrupted, the whole was bosh; when the thread was broken the beads were seen to be waxen and hollow.

We made love to one another, and plotted darkly in the deepest obscurity of the hold. Each set of conspirators had its proper listener at the hatch. These, leaning too far over would bump their heads together and fight. Occasionally there was confusion amongst them: two or more would assert a right to overhear the same plot. I remember at one time the cook, the carpenter, the second assistant-surgeon, and an able seaman contended with handspikes for the honor of betraying my confidence. Once there were three masked murderers of the second watch bending at the same instant over the sleeping form of a cabin-boy, who had been heard to mutter, a week previously, that he had "Gold! gold!" the accumulation of eighty—yes, eighty—years' piracy on the high seas, while sitting as M.P. for the borough of Zaccheus-cum-Down, and attending church regularly. I saw the captain of the foretop surrounded by suitors for his hand, while he was himself fingering the edge of a packing-case, and singing an amorous ditty to a lady-love shaving at a mirror.

Our diction consisted, in about equal parts, of classical allusion, quotation from the stable, simper from the scullery, cant from the clubs, and the technical slang of heraldry. We boasted much of ancestry, and admired the whiteness of our hands whenever the skin was visible through a fault in the grease and tar. Next to love, the vegetable kingdom, murder, arson, adultery and ritual, we talked most of art. The wooden figure-head of the *Camel*, representing a Guinea nigger detecting a bad smell, and the monochrome picture of two back-broken dolphins on the stern, acquired a new importance. The Dutchman had destroyed the nose of the one by kicking his toes against it, and the other was nearly obliterated by the slops of the cook; but each had its daily pilgrimage, and each constantly developed occult beauties of design and subtle excellences of execution. On the whole we were greatly altered; and if the supply of contemporary fiction had been equal to the demand, the *Camel*, I fear, would not have been strong enough to contain the moral and æsthetic forces fired by the maceration of the brains of authors in the gastric juices of sailors.

Having now got the ship's literature off his mind into ours, the captain went on deck for the first time since leaving port. We were still steering the same course, and taking his first observation of the sun, the captain discovered that we were in latitude 83° south. The heat was insufferable; the air was like the breath of a furnace within a furnace. The sea steamed like a boiling cauldron, and in the vapor our bodies were temptingly parboiled—our ultimate meal was preparing. Warped by the sun, the ship held both ends high out of the water; the deck of the forecastle was an inclined plane, on which the bullock labored at a disadvantage; but the bowsprit was now vertical and the Dutchman's tenure precarious. A thermometer hung against the mainmast, and we grouped ourselves about it as the captain went up to examine the register.

"One hundred and ninety degrees Fahrenheit!" he muttered in evident astonishment. "Impossible!" Turning sharply about, he ran his eyes over us, and inquired in a peremptory tone, "who's been in command while I was runnin' my eye over that book?"

"Well, captain," I replied, as respectfully as I knew how, "the fourth day out I had the unhappiness to be drawn into a dispute about a game of cards with your first and second officers. In the absence of those excellent seamen, sir, I thought it my duty to assume control of the ship."

"Killed 'em, hey?"

"Sir, they committed suicide by questioning the efficacy of four kings and an ace."

"Well, you lubber, what have you to say in defense of this extraordinary weather?"

"Sir, it is no fault of mine. We are far—very far south, and it is now the middle of July. The weather is uncomfortable, I admit; but considering the latitude and season, it is not, I protest, unseasonable."

"Latitude and season!" he shrieked, livid with rage—"latitude and season! Why, you junk-rigged, flat-bottomed, meadow lugger, don't you know any better than that? Didn't yer little baby brother ever tell ye that southern latitudes is colder than northern, and that July is the middle o' winter here? Go below, you son of a scullion, or I'll break your bones!"

"Oh! very well," I replied; "I'm not going to stay on deck and listen to such low language as that, I warn you. Have it your own way."

The words had no sooner left my lips, than a piercing cold wind caused me to cast my eye upon the thermometer. In the new régime of science the mercury was descending rapidly; but in a moment the instrument was obscured by a blinding fall of snow. Towering icebergs rose from the water on every side, hanging their jagged masses hundreds of feet above the masthead, and shutting us completely in. The ship twisted and writhed; her decks bulged upward, and every timber groaned and cracked like the report of a pistol. The *Camel* was frozen fast. The jerk of her sudden stopping snapped the bullock's chain, and sent both that animal and the Dutchman over the bows, to accomplish their warfare on the ice.

Elbowing my way forward to go below, as I had threatened, I saw the crew tumble to the deck on either hand like ten-pins. They were frozen stiff. Passing the captain, I asked him sneeringly how he liked the weather under the new régime. He replied with a vacant stare. The chill had penetrated to the brain, and affected his mind. He murmured:

"In this delightful spot, happy in the world's esteem, and surrounded by all that makes existence dear, they passed the remainder of their lives. The End."

His jaw dropped. The captain of the *Camel* was dead.

❄   ❄   ❄

THE MAN OVERBOARD

I

The good ship *Nupple-duck* was drifting rapidly upon a sunken coral reef, which seemed to extend a reasonless number of leagues to the right and left without a break, and I was reading Macaulay's

"Naseby Fight" to the man at the wheel. Everything was, in fact, going on as nicely as heart could wish, when Captain Abersouth, standing on the companion-stair, poked his head above deck and asked where we were. Pausing in my reading, I informed him that we had got as far as the disastrous repulse of Prince Rupert's cavalry, adding that if he would have the goodness to hold his jaw we should be making it awkward for the wounded in about three minutes, and he might bear a hand at the pockets of the slain. Just then the ship struck heavily, and went down!

Calling another ship, I stepped aboard, and gave directions to be taken to No. 900 Tottenham Court Road, where I had an aunt; then, walking aft to the man at the wheel, asked him if he would like to hear me read "Naseby Fight." He thought he would: he would like to hear that, and then I might pass on to something else—Kinglake's "Crimean War," the proceedings at the trial of Warren Hastings, or some such trifle, just to wile away the time till eight bells.

All this time heavy clouds had been gathering along the horizon directly in front of the ship, and a deputation of passengers now came to the man at the wheel to demand that she be put about, or she would run into them, which the spokesman explained would be unusual. I thought at the time that it certainly was not the regular thing to do, but, as I was myself only a passenger, did not deem it expedient to take a part in the heated discussion that ensued; and, after all, it did not seem likely that the weather in those clouds would be much worse than that in Tottenham Court Road, where I had an aunt.

It was finally decided to refer the matter to arbitration, and after many names had been submitted and rejected by both sides, it was agreed that the captain of the ship should act as arbitrator if his consent could be obtained, and I was delegated to conduct the negotiations to that end. With considerable difficulty, I persuaded him to accept the responsibility.

He was a feeble-minded sort of fellow named Troutbeck, who was always in a funk lest he should make enemies; never reflecting that most men would a little rather be his enemies than not. He had once been the ship's cook, but had cooked so poisonously ill that he had been forcibly transferred from galley to quarter-deck by the dyspeptic survivors of his culinary career.

The little captain went aft with me to listen to arguments of the dissatisfied passengers and the obstinate steersman, as to whether we should take our chances in the clouds, or tail off and run for the opposite horizon; but on approaching the wheel, we found both helmsman and passengers in a condition of profound astonishment, rolling their eyes about towards every point of the compass, and shaking their heads in hopeless perplexity. It was rather remarkable, certainly: the bank of cloud which had worried the landsmen was now directly astern, and the ship was cutting along lively in her own wake, toward the point from which she had come, and straight away from Tottenham Court Road! Everybody declared it was a miracle; the chaplain was piped up for prayers, and the man at the wheel was as truly penitent as if he had been detected robbing an empty poor-box.

The explanation was simple enough, and dawned upon me the moment I saw how matters stood. During the dispute between the helmsman and the deputation, the former had renounced his wheel to gesticulate, and I, thinking no harm, had amused myself, during a rather tedious debate, by revolving the thing this way and that, and had unconsciously put the ship about. By a coincidence not unusual in low latitudes, the wind had effected a corresponding transposition at the same time, and was now bowling us as merrily back toward the place where I had embarked, as it had previously wafted us in the direction of Tottenham Court Road, where I had an aunt. I must here so far anticipate, as to explain that some years later these various incidents—particularly the reading of "Naseby Fight"—led to the adoption, in our mercantile marine, of a rule which I believe is still extant, to the effect that one must not speak to the man at the wheel unless the man at the wheel speaks first.

II

It is only by inadvertence that I have omitted the information that the vessel in which I was now a pervading influence was the *Bonnyclabber* (Troutbeck, master), of Malvern Heights.

The *Bonnyclabber's* reactionary course had now brought her to the spot at which I had taken passage. Passengers and crew, fatigued by their somewhat awkward attempts to manifest their gratitude for our miraculous deliverance from the cloud-bank, were snoring peacefully in unconsidered attitudes about the deck, when the lookout man, perched on the supreme extremity of the mainmast, consuming a cold sausage, began an apparently preconcerted series of extraordinary and unimaginable noises. He coughed, sneezed, and barked simultaneously—bleated in one breath, and cackled in the next—sputteringly shrieked, and chatteringly squealed, with a bass of suffocated roars. There were desolutory vocal explosions, tapering off in long wails, half smothered in unintelligible small-talk. He whistled, wheezed, and trumpeted; began to sharp, thought better of it and flatted; neighed like a horse, and then thundered like a drum! Through it all he continued making incomprehensible signals with one hand while clutching his throat with the other. Presently he gave it up, and silently descended to the deck.

By this time we were all attention; and no sooner had he set foot amongst us, than he was assailed with a tempest of questions which, had they been visible, would have resembled a flight of pigeons. He made no reply—not even by a look, but passed through our enclosing mass with a grim, defiant step, a face deathly white, and a set of the jaw as of one repressing an ambitious dinner, or ignoring a venomous toothache. For the poor man was choking!

Passing down the companion-way, the patient sought the surgeon's cabin, with the ship's company at his heels. The surgeon was fast asleep, the lark-like performance at the masthead having been inaudible in that lower region. While some of us were holding a whisky-bottle to the medical nose, in order to apprise the medical intelligence of the demand upon it, the patient seated himself in statuesque silence. By this time his pallor, which was but the mark of a determined mind, had given place to a fervent crimson, which visibly deepened into a pronounced purple, and was ultimately superseded by a clouded blue, shot through with opalescent gleams, and smitten with variable streaks of black. The face was swollen and shapeless, the neck puffy. The eyes protruded like pegs of a hat-stand.

Pretty soon the doctor was got awake, and after making a careful examination of his patient, remarking that it was a lovely case of *stopupagus æsophagi,* took a tool and set to work, producing with no difficulty a cold sausage of the size, figure, and general bearing of a somewhat self-important banana. The operation had been performed amid breathless silence, but the moment it was concluded the patient, whose neck and head had visibly collapsed, sprang to his feet and shouted:

"Man overboard!"

That is what he had been trying to say.

There was a confused rush to the upper deck, and everybody flung something over the ship's side—a life-belt, a chicken-coop, a coil of rope, a spar, an old sail, a pocket handkerchief, an iron crowbar— any movable article which it was thought might be useful to a drowning man who had followed the vessel during the hour that had elapsed since the initial alarm at the mast-head. In a few moments the ship was pretty nearly dismantled of everything that could be easily renounced, and some excitable passenger having cut away the boats there was nothing more that we could do, though the chaplain explained that if the ill-fated gentleman in the wet did not turn up after a while it was his intention to stand at the stern and read the burial service of the Church of England.

Presently it occurred to some ingenious person to inquire who had gone overboard, and all hands being mustered and the roll called, to our great chagrin every man answered to his name, passengers and all! Captain Troutbeck, however, held that in a matter of so great importance a simple roll-call was insufficient, and with an assertion of authority that was encouraging insisted that every person on board be separately sworn. The result was the same; nobody was missing and the captain, begging pardon for having doubted our veracity, retired to his cabin to avoid further responsibility, but expressed a hope that for the purpose of having everything properly recorded in the log-book we would apprise him of any further action that we might think it advisable to take. I smiled as I remembered that in the interest of the unknown gentleman whose peril we had overestimated I had flung the log-book over the ship's side.

Soon afterward I felt suddenly inspired with one of those great ideas that come to most men only once or twice in a lifetime, and to the ordinary story teller never. Hastily reconvening the ship's company I mounted the capstan and thus addressed them:

"Shipmates, there has been a mistake. In the fervor of an ill-considered compassion we have made pretty free with certain movable property of an eminent firm of shipowners of Malvern Heights. For this we shall undoubtedly be called to account if we are ever so fortunate as to drop anchor in Tottenham Court Road, where I have an aunt. It would add strength to our defence if we could show to the satisfaction of a jury of our peers that in heeding the sacred promptings of humanity we had acted with some small degree of common sense. If, for example, we could make it appear that there really was a man overboard, who might have been comforted and sustained by the material consolation that we so lavishly dispensed in the form of buoyant articles belonging to others, the British heart would find in that fact a mitigating circumstance pleading eloquently in our favor. Gentlemen and ship's officers, I venture to propose that we do now throw a man overboard."

The effect was electrical: the motion was carried by acclamation and there was a unanimous rush for the now wretched mariner whose false alarm at the masthead was the cause of our embarrassment, but on second thoughts it was decided to substitute Captain Troutbeck, as less generally useful and more undeviatingly in error. The sailor had made one mistake of considerable magnitude, but the captain's entire existence was a mistake altogether. He was fetched up from his cabin and chucked over.

At 900 Tottenham Road Court lived an aunt of mine—a good old lady who had brought me up by hand and taught me many wholesome lessons in morality, which in my later life have proved of extreme value. Foremost among these I may mention her solemn and oft-repeated injunction never to tell a lie without a definite and specific reason for doing so. Many years' experience in the violation of this principle enables me to speak with authority as to its general soundness. I have, therefore, much pleasure in making a slight correction in the preceding chapter of this tolerably true history. It was there affirmed that I threw the *Bonnyclabber's* log-book into the sea. The statement is entirely false, and I can discover no reason for having made it that will for a moment weigh against those I now have for the preservation of that log-book.

The progress of the story has developed new necessities, and I now find it convenient to quote from that book passages which it could not have contained if cast into the sea at the time stated; for if thrown upon the resources of my imagination I might find the temptation to exaggerate too strong to be resisted.

It is needless to worry the reader with those entries in the book referring to events already related. Our record will begin on the day of the captain's consignment to the deep, after which era I made the entries myself.

"June 22nd.—Not much doing in the way of gales, but heavy swells left over from some previous blow. Latitude and longitude not notably different from last observation. Ship laboring a trifle, owing to lack of top-hamper, everything of that kind having been cut away in consequence of Captain Troutbeck having accidently fallen overboard while fishing from the bowsprit. Also threw over cargo and everything that we could spare. Miss our sails rather, but if they save our dear captain, we shall be content. Weather flagrant.

"23d.—Nothing from Captain Troutbeck. Dead calm—also dead whale. The passengers having become preposterous in various ways, Mr. Martin, the chief officer, had three of the ringleaders tied up and rope's-ended. He thought it advisable also to flog an equal number of the crew, by way of being impartial. Weather ludicrous.

"24th.—Captain still prefers to stop away, and does not telegraph. The 'captain of the foretop'—there isn't any foretop now—

was put in irons to-day by Mr. Martin for eating cold sausage while on look-out. Mr. Martin has flogged the steward, who had neglected to holy-stone the binnacle and paint the deadlights. The steward is a good fellow all the same. Weather iniquitous.

"25th.—Can't think whatever has become of Captain Troutbeck. He must be getting hungry by this time; for although he has his fishing-tackle with him, he has no bait. Mr. Martin inspected the entries in this book to-day. He is a most excellent and humane officer. Weather inexcusable.

"26th.—All hope of hearing from the Captain has been abandoned. We have sacrificed everything to save him; but now, if we could procure the loan of a mast and some sails, we should proceed on our voyage. Mr. Martin has knocked the coxswain overboard for sneezing. He is an experienced seaman, a capable officer, and a Christian gentleman—damn his eyes! Weather tormenting.

"27th.—Another inspection of this book by Mr. Martin. Farewell, vain world! Break it gently to my aunt in Tottenham Court Road."

In the concluding sentences of this record, as it now lies before me, the handwriting is not very legible: they were penned under circumstances singularly unfavorable. Mr. Martin stood behind me with his eyes fixed on the page; and in order to secure a better view, had twisted the machinery of the engine he called his hand into the hair of my head, depressing that globe to such an extent that my nose was flattened against the surface of the table, and I had no small difficulty in discerning the lines through my eyebrows. I was not accustomed to writing in that position: it had not been taught in the only school that I ever attended. I therefore felt justified in bringing the record to a somewhat abrupt close, and immediately went on deck with Mr. Martin, he preceding me up the companion-stairs on foot, I following, not on horseback, but on my own, the connection between us being maintained without important alteration.

Arriving on deck, I thought it advisable, in the interest of peace and quietness, to pursue him in the same manner to the side of the ship, where I parted from him forever with many expressions of regret, which might have been heard at a considerable distance.

Of the subsequent fate of the *Bonnyclabber,* I can only say that the log-book from which I have quoted was found some years later in the stomach of a whale, along with some shreds of clothing, a few buttons and several decayed life-belts. It contained only one new entry, in a straggling handwriting, as if it had been penned in the dark:

"july2th foundered svivors rescude by wale wether stuffy no nues from capting trowtbeck Sammle martin cheef Ofcer."

Let us now take a retrospective glance at the situation. The ship *Nupple-duck,* (Abersouth, master) had, it will be remembered, gone down with all on board except me. I had escaped on the ship *Bonny-clabber* (Troutbeck) which I had quitted owing to a misunderstanding with the chief officer, and was now unattached. That is how matters stood when, rising on an unusually high wave, and casting my eye in the direction of Tottenham Court Road—that is, backward along the course pursued by the *Bonnyclabber* and toward the spot at which the *Nupple-duck* had been swallowed up—I saw a quantity of what appeared to be wreckage. It turned out to be some of the stuff that we had thrown overboard under a misapprehension. The several articles had been compiled and, so to speak, carefully edited. They were, in fact, lashed together, forming a raft. On a stool in the center of it—not, apparently navigating it, but rather with the subdued and dignified bearing of a passenger, sat Captain Abersouth, of the *Nupple-duck,* reading a novel.

Our meeting was not cordial. He remembered me as a man of literary taste superior to his own and harbored resentment, and although he made no opposition to my taking passage with him I could see that his acquiescence was due rather to his muscular inferiority than to the circumstance that I was damp and taking cold. Merely acknowledging his presence with a nod as I climbed abroad, I seated myself and inquired if he would care to hear the concluding stanzas of "Naseby Fight."

"No," he replied, looking up from his novel, "no, Claude Reginald Gump, writer of sea stories, I've done with you. When you sank the *Nupple-duck* some days ago you probably thought that you had made an end of me. That was clever of you, but I came to the surface and followed the other ship—the one on which you escaped. It was I that the sailor saw from the masthead. I saw him see me. It was for me that all that stuff was hove overboard. Good—I made it into this raft. It was, I think, the next day that I passed the floating body of a man whom I recognized as my old friend Billy Troutbeck —he used to be a cook on a man-o'-war. It gives me pleasure to be the means of saving your life, but I eschew you. The moment that we reach port our paths part. You remember that in the very first sentence of this story you began to drive my ship, the *Nupple-duck,* on to a reef of coral."

I was compelled to confess that this was true, and he continued his inhospitable reproaches:

"Before you had written half a column you sent her to the bottom, with me and the crew. But *you*—you escaped."

"That is true," I replied; "I cannot deny that the facts are correctly stated."

"And in a story before that, you took me and my mates of the ship *Camel* into the heart of the South Polar Sea and left us frozen dead in the ice, like flies in amber. But you did not leave yourself there—you escaped."

"Really, Captain," I said, "your memory is singularly accurate, considering the many hardships that you have had to undergo; many a man would have gone mad."

"And a long time before that," Captain Abersouth resumed, after a pause, more, apparently, to con his memory than to enjoy my good opinion of it, "you lost me at sea—look here; I didn't read anything but George Eliot at that time, but I'm *told* that you lost me at sea in the *Mudlark*. Have I been misinformed?"

I could not say he had been misinformed.

"You yourself escaped on that occasion, I think."

It was true. Being usually the hero of my own stories, I commonly do manage to live through one, in order to figure to advantage in the next. It is from artistic necessity: no reader would take much interest in a hero who was dead before the beginning of the tale. I endeavored to explain this to Captain Abersouth. He shook his head.

"No," said he, "it's cowardly, that's the way I look at it."

Suddenly an effulgent idea began to dawn upon me, and I let it have its way until my mind was perfectly luminous. Then I rose from my seat, and frowning down into the upturned face of my accuser, spoke in severe and rasping accents thus:

"Captain Abersouth, in the various perils you and I have encountered together in the classical literature of the period, if I have always escaped and you have always perished; if I lost you at sea in the *Mudlark*, froze you into the ice at the South Pole in the *Camel* and drowned you in the *Nupple-duck*, pray be good enough to tell me whom I have the honor to address."

It was a blow to the poor man: no one was ever so disconcerted. Flinging aside his novel, he put up his hands and began to scratch his head and think. It was beautiful to see him think, but it seemed to distress him and pointing significantly over the side of the raft I suggested as delicately as possible that it was time to act. He rose to his feet and fixing upon me a look of reproach which I shall remember as long as I can, cast himself into the deep. As to me—I escaped.

A CARGO OF CAT

On the 16th day of June, 1874, the ship *Mary Jane* sailed from Malta, heavily laden with cat. This cargo gave us a good deal of trouble. It was not in bales, but had been dumped into the hold loose. Captain Doble, who had once commanded a ship that carried coals, said he had found that plan the best. When the hold was full of cat the hatch was battened down and we felt good. Unfortunately the mate, thinking the cats would be thirsty, introduced a hose into one of the hatches and pumped in a considerable quantity of water, and the cats of the lower levels were all drowned.

You have seen a dead cat in a pond: you remember its circumference at the waist. Water multiplies the magnitude of a dead cat by ten. On the first day out, it was observed that the ship was much strained. She was three feet wider than usual and as much as ten feet shorter. The convexity of her deck was visibly augmented fore and aft, but she turned up at both ends. Her rudder was clean out of water and she would answer the helm only when running directly against a strong breeze: the rudder, when perverted to one side, would rub against the wind and slew her around; and then she wouldn't steer any more. Owing to the curvature of the keel, the masts came together at the top, and a sailor who had gone up the foremast got bewildered, came down the mizzenmast, looked out over the stern at the receding shores of Malta and shouted: "Land, ho!" The ship's fastenings were all giving way; the water on each side was lashed into foam by the tempest of flying bolts that she shed at every pulsation of the cargo. She was quietly wrecking herself without assistance from wind or wave, by the sheer internal energy of feline expansion.

I went to the skipper about it. He was in his favorite position, sitting on the deck, supporting his back against the binnacle, making a V of his legs, and smoking.

"Captain Doble," I said, respectfully touching my hat, which was really not worthy of respect, "this floating palace is afflicted with curvature of the spine and is likewise greatly swollen."

Without raising his eyes he courteously acknowledged my presence by knocking the ashes from his pipe.

"Permit me, Captain," I said, with simple dignity, "to repeat that this ship is much swollen."

"If that is true," said the gallant mariner, reaching for his tobacco pouch, "I think it would be as well to swab her down with liniment. There's a bottle of it in my cabin. Better suggest it to the mate."

"But, Captain, there is no time for empirical treatment; some of the planks at the water line have started."

The skipper rose and looked out over the stern, toward the land; he fixed his eyes on the foaming wake; he gazed into the water to starboard and to port. Then he said:

"My friend, the whole darned thing has started."

Sadly and silently I turned from that obdurate man and walked forward. Suddenly "there was a burst of thunder sound!" The hatch that had held down the cargo was flung whirling into space and sailed in the air like a blown leaf. Pushing upward through the hatchway was a smooth, square column of cat. Grandly and impressively it grew—slowly, serenely, majestically it rose toward the welkin, the relaxing keel parting the mastheads to give it a fair chance. I have stood at Naples and seen Vesuvius painting the town red—from Catania have marked afar, upon the flanks of Ætna, the lava's awful pursuit of the astonished rooster and the despairing pig. The fiery flow from Kilauea's crater, thrusting itself into the forests and licking the entire country clean, is as familiar to me as my mother-tongue. I have seen glaciers, a thousand years old and quite bald, heading for a valley full of tourists at the rate of an inch a month. I have seen a saturated solution of mining camp going down a mountain river, to make a sociable call on the valley farmers. I have stood behind a tree on the battle-field and seen a compact square mile of armed men moving with irresistible momentum to the rear. Whenever anything grand in magnitude or motion is billed to appear I commonly manage to beat my way into the show, and in reporting it I am a man of unscrupulous veracity; but I have seldom observed anything like that solid gray column of Maltese cat!

It is unnecessary to explain, I suppose, that each individual grimalkin in the outfit, with that readiness of resource which distinguishes the species, had grappled with tooth and nail as many others as it could hook on to. This preserved the formation. It made the column so stiff that when the ship rolled (and the *Mary Jane* was a devil to roll) it swayed from side to side like a mast, and the Mate said if it grew much taller he would have to order it cut away or it would capsize us.

Some of the sailors went to work at the pumps, but these discharged nothing but fur. Captain Doble raised his eyes from his toes and shouted: "Let go the anchor!" but being assured that nobody was touching it, apologized and resumed his revery. The chaplain said if there were no objections he would like to offer up a prayer, and a gambler from Chicago, producing a pack of cards, proposed to throw round for the first jack. The parson's plan was adopted, and as he uttered the final "amen," the cats struck up a hymn.

All the living ones were now above deck, and every mother's son of them sang. Each had a pretty fair voice, but no ear. Nearly all their notes in the upper register were more or less cracked and disobedient. The remarkable thing about the voices was their range. In that crowd were cats of seventeen octaves, and the average could not have been less than twelve.

Number of cats, as per invoice	127,000
Estimated number dead swellers	6,000
Total songsters	121,000
Average number octaves per cat	12
Total octaves	1,452,000

It was a great concert. It lasted three days and nights, or, counting each night as seven days, twenty-four days altogether, and we could not go below for provisions. At the end of that time the cook came for'd shaking up some beans in a hat, and holding a large knife.

"Shipmates," said he, "we have done all that mortals can do. Let us now draw lots."

We were blindfolded in turn, and drew, but just as the cook was forcing the fatal black bean upon the fattest man, the concert closed with a suddenness that waked the man on the lookout. A moment later every grimalkin relaxed his hold on his neighbors, the column lost its cohesion and, with 121,000 dull, sickening thuds that beat as one, the whole business fell to the deck. Then with a wild farewell wail that feline host sprang spitting into the sea and struck out southward for the African shore!

The southern extension of Italy, as every schoolboy knows, resembles in shape an enormous boot. We had drifted within sight of it. The cats in the fabric had spied it, and their alert imaginations were instantly affected with a lively sense of the size, weight and probable momentum of its flung boot-jack.